A Book of
American Martyrs

NOVELS BY JOYCE CAROL OATES

With Shuddering Fall (1964)

A Garden of Earthly Delights (1967)

Expensive People (1968)

them (1969)

Wonderland (1971)

Do with Me What You Will (1973)

The Assassins (1975)

Childwold (1976)

Son of the Morning (1978)

Unholy Loves (1979)

Bellefleur (1980)

Angel of Light (1981)

A Bloodsmoor Romance (1982)

Mysteries of Winterthurn (1984)

Solstice (1985)

Marya: A Life (1986)

You Must Remember This (1987)

American Appetites (1989)

Because It Is Bitter, and Because It Is My Heart (1990)

Black Water (1992)

Foxfire: Confessions of a Girl Gang (1993)

A Book of American Martyrs

Joyce Carol Oates

HARPER LUXE

An Imprint of HarperCollins*Publishers*

HarperCollins
PUBLISHERS
Since 1817

A BOOK OF AMERICAN MARTYRS. Copyright © 2017 by The Ontario Review, Inc. All rights reserved. Printed in the United States of America. No part of this book may be used or reproduced in any manner whatsoever without written permission except in the case of brief quotations embodied in critical articles and reviews. For information address HarperCollins Publishers, 195 Broadway, New York, NY 10007.

HarperCollins books may be purchased for educational, business, or sales promotional use. For information please e-mail the Special Markets Department at SPsales@harpercollins.com.

FIRST HARPERLUXE EDITION

ISBN: 978-0-06-264442-8

HarperLuxe™ is a trademark of HarperCollins Publishers.

Library of Congress Cataloging-in-Publication Data is available upon request.

17 18 19 20 21   ID/LSC   10 9 8 7 6 5 4 3 2 1

For Chase Twichell
and Russell Banks,
and
for my husband
and first reader,
Charlie Gross

Contents

THE LIFE AND DEATH OF GUS VOORHEES: AN ARCHIVE

THE CONSOLATION OF GRIEF: SEPTEMBER 2011–FEBRUARY 2012

Soldier of God:

Luther Amos Dunphy

November 2, 1999

Muskegee Falls, Ohio

Only say the word and my soul shall be healed.

The Lord commanded me. In all that befell, it was His hand that did not waver.

Cries rang out—"Stand back!"

It was Voorhees at whom the shotgun was first aimed. The abortion doctor in a hoarse voice sternly saying, "Stand back! Put down that gun!"

And others crying, "No! No!"

So swiftly the Lord executed my movements, there was not time in the eyes of the enemy to register fear or alarm. There was no terror but only raw surprise. As I strode into the driveway in the wake of the abortion providers' Dodge minivan with the shotgun to my shoulder and barrels uplifted there were many who stared at me in astonishment and awe for protesters had been forbidden by law to assemble in the driveway as for several years we had been forbidden to assemble with our picket signs or even in prayer in the grassless yard in front of the Broome County Women's Center and yet here was one of these, of the Army of God, who some of them knew to be Luther Dunphy, disobeying this law boldly striding past the barrier and following the abortion providers' minivan up the driveway faster than you would expect a man of his size to move, and without hesitation.

God guide my hand! God do not allow me to fail.

The one of the enemy known as Augustus Voorhees had just climbed out of the van. It was 7:26 A.M. The Women's Center did not open to admit the clientele (that is, pregnant girls and women who believed they did not wish to become *mothers*) until 8:00 A.M. The abortion doctor (of my height almost exactly which is six foot one inch and his disheveled graying hair resembling my own) had thought to arrive early to avoid protesters and to enter at the rear of the Center but in his shrewdness there was folly, for the Muskegee Falls police security did not usually arrive until 7:30 A.M. (and sometimes later) and by the time police were summoned on this morning, his life would bleed away like the life of a gut-shot hog. Nor had Voorhees seen me less than six feet close behind him and rapidly overtaking him until a look in his companion's face roused him to turn with an expression of utter surprise and shock.

"No! Stand back! Don't—"

Already in this instant the trigger was being pulled, the barrels aimed at the abortion doctor at above the level of his chest, and the blast of the first barrel knocked Augustus Voorhees backward and tore into his lower jaw and throat in a way terrible to behold as if the Lord had dealt His wrath with a single smote of a great claw; for shrewdly I had aimed high, not knowing if the abortion murderer was wearing a bulletproof vest. (Later it was revealed that Voorhees was not so protected—in defiance of the fate that would befall him.) Yet even so, in the midst of this deafening explosion, the Lord steadied my hands as calmly I turned the barrels onto the accomplice "escort" close by now screaming, "No! No! Don't shoot!" in clumsy desperation trying to back away and with arms and hands feebly shielding his body but these words came belated, and were no more heeded than the cries of the black-feathered birds flocking in the winter sky overhead as the second shot blasted away the face and much of the throat of the accomplice propelling the now-lifeless body backward as the lifeless body of Voorhees had been propelled, and these bodies crumpled together on the asphalt driveway in front of the van freely gushing blood—within seconds, as the Lord had willed.

In the ecstasy of the Lord coursing through my arms and hands like electricity I scarcely felt the recoil of the blast as it struck my shoulder like the kick of a mule, only the numbness that came after, and an ache deep in the bone.

"God have mercy! God forgive you. . . ."

These words, I had prepared to murmur as I crouched above the fallen sinner (for I believed that Voorhees would die unrepentant) but at the time of utterance it may have been that I spoke too softly to be heard above the scattered cries and screams behind me.

Few had witnessed the execution. For it was early in the day, and less than a dozen protesters had gathered in front of the Center.

So slowly, these seconds were passing. For it was as if Luther Dunphy stood a little to the side, observing. What he saw and what he heard came *mutedly* to him from that distance.

Calmly too, for all this the Lord had set out before me like a geological map, that has not the confusion of place-names of an ordinary map but only the sculpted contours of the land, I laid the Mossberg twelve-gauge double-barrel shotgun carefully on the driveway on a little rise of asphalt with cracks perpendicular to each other, that suggested to the eye—(to my eye)—the Cross.

Some twelve feet from the fallen men, and from the weapon (laid against the Cross), and at a perpendicular to the weapon, I knelt.

Between the fallen men and the weapon, and between the weapon and Luther Dunphy, and between Luther Dunphy and the fallen men, in a line might be drawn establishing a triangle of (uneven) sides and at its peak the Cross of Crucifixion you would want to say was *accidental* in the asphalt and would never have been detected by any human eye, except for the intervention of the Lord guiding my hand.

I am a big man and I am (no longer) a limber man. My knee joints often ache, it is said with the onset of arthritis. The bones of my hips and the muscles of my lower back often ache but in defiance of such pain I never complain to my employer nor to my fellow roofers nor do I suggest any sensation of pain on the job or at home (except if my dear wife notices, and it is not possible to dissemble to her who knows me so well through sixteen years of marriage) and in the aftermath now of the assassination of the abortion provider and his accomplice I took care to kneel with my arms uplifted (though now heavy-seeming, tremulous and numb) to await the arrival of the Muskegee police.

Dear God I commend my soul to You. If it is Your will, I will be joined with you in Heaven this very hour.

Bowed my head with shut eyes, and eyes rimmed with tears. For I understood that my (mortal) life as Luther Dunphy had ended, in the asphalt driveway of the Women's Center on this second day of November 1999. My life as a loving Christian husband and father and a private citizen of Muskegee Falls, Ohio. That I was born in Sandusky, Ohio, on March 6, 1960, and would die now, in this place, seemed to me clear for I had "read" this inscription on a grave marker but the night before. *The Lord giveth, and the Lord taketh away.*

In deep prayer they would find me with my arms upraised in the posture of surrender and my hands visible, holding no weapon. Deep-immersed in prayer "as if entranced" but "cooperative" (as it would be reported) as Broome County police officers approached with drawn weapons.

And in my heart I pleaded with the Lord to give me sanctuary with Him in this hour. Pleaded with the Lord, let me make an end of this now. For I will be their captive, and I will be tried in their socialist atheist court of law, that has forsaken You. And I will be jeered at and ridiculed and in the end, in their atheist court I will be sentenced to death. But it will be their way of death which will not be speedy. Truly I understand it will be protracted and shameful and it may be, I will not be strong enough to withstand despair. For a sentence of Death Row will wear away at my soul, in the way that a great abyss is worn out of rock. Pleaded with the Lord in His mercy to allow me to make some threatening gesture to the police upon their arrival, that they would shoot me down where I knelt. That they would execute me in a barrage of bullets that there would be three of us laid lifeless on the asphalt driveway on that morning as a sign to all the world, the abortion butchery must stop.

But the Lord did not give this permission to me, in His inscrutable wisdom. Though the Lord had been close to me as the heart beating in my rib cage now the Lord had withdrawn from me to His mountain, to observe His servant and His soldier in the aftermath of His mission.

And so, I did not die that morning. Instead, the Lord caused a numbness to pass into me, of utter submission. I was handcuffed and taken into the custody of the State of Ohio from which, in my lifetime, I will never be released.

Turns

A life is a matter of *turns*. As I call them.
A *turn* is a sudden surprise. As if your shoulders
are gripped from behind and you are forcibly *turned* to
see something hidden to you, until that moment.

A *turn*, and you are never the same again. "The
scales fell from my eyes." Though all who know you
will swear that it is but you whom (they believe) they
know.

Ten days before the execution of Voorhees it was
"pure chance" that I'd arrived at the Women's Center
several minutes earlier than my usual time of arrival,
which is approximately between 7:45 A.M. and 8:00
A.M. But this day, there was less traffic on the highway than usual, it seemed, and so when I arrived and
parked in the street, there was but one other protester

in front of the Center, who was a familiar face to me, a man of about ten years older than me (I was soon to become thirty-nine), but I did not know his full name only "Stockard"—which might have been his first name, or his surname. There was a look about this man of dignity and determination that made you think he was a *man of God* but (maybe) a Catholic priest not wearing his priest clothes. Or, as it happens sometimes, a *former priest*. As I am, not a *former minister* but a *former lay minister* in the St. Paul Missionary Church of Jesus. And we greeted each other like friends, but cautious friends, for I am not one to shake hands and am wary of the "glad-handed" (as they are called), and we fell to talking quietly (as others were arriving, singly and in pairs—we stood a little apart) and he told me that the abortion doctor Voorhees was already inside the Center. Voorhees had arrived before 7:30 A.M. being driven in a van by the "escort" (to his shame, this volunteer at the Broome County Women's Center was retired U.S. Army Major Timothy Barron, fifty-eight years old) and taken to the rear of the building to park out of sight of the street. The staff (all of them women of whom several are "registered nurses") employed or volunteering at the Center will arrive before 8:00 A.M. and it is at 8:00 A.M. when the first of the mothers begin to arrive and by then, the police security have arrived, usually between 7:30 A.M. and 7:45 A.M. But this day, the police security (which consists of two Muskegee Falls officers who remain in or near their vehicle unless there is cause for them to approach the Center) did not arrive until 7:51 A.M.

Carefully I asked of my comrade, "Did he mean that the abortion doctor will arrive here sometimes so many minutes before the police guards?"—and Stockard said yes, he believed that was more so lately than it had been.

He said, "Voorhees gets here early so that he can be safe inside before the doors open."

There was a quiet sort of fury in his uttering of *Voorhees*.

Voorhees was the (new) director of the Center who had come here in July 1999 from his work as an abortion provider in Michigan. We knew of him that he had long been associated with Planned Parenthood and that he was a medical doctor whose specialty was obstetrics and gynecology. He had come to Muskegee Falls following the resignation of the previous (female) director who had headed the Center for just seven months.

For a brief while, it had seemed possible that the Broome County Women's Center would be closed down. Our campaign was to discourage and discredit all who were associated with the Center. Some had suggested burning down the Center—(but I was not one of these, at the time). But there came "Augustus Voorhees" whose reputation was such, his name was prominent on the WANTED: BABY KILLERS AMONG US list posted in newsletters including the ARMY OF GOD Sentinel.

At this time in October 1999, Voorhees was number three on the list. Until the assassination of the abortion provider Paul Erich, in Livingston, Kentucky, by Shaun Harris, six weeks before, Voorhees had been number four.

As murderers are removed from the list, others move up.

Currently there are nineteen names on the WANTED list of which all are (male) medical doctors who have betrayed their mission to *do no harm.*

There has been much agitation in the (socialist, atheist) media to "censor" the ARMY OF GOD website. Demands that the WANTED: BABY KILLERS AMONG US list be taken down. But it is our First Amendment right under the U.S. Constitution—freedom of speech.

As it is our right as U.S. citizens to bear arms.

The Army of God understands that each abortion murderer who is assassinated means the saving of infants' lives. If Voorhees could be struck down, the babies that were to be murdered by his hand and by other abortion doctors in emulation of him would have another chance at life.

For each day there were between fifteen and twenty infants slain in the Muskegee Center alone by the abortionist's instruments (by our estimate). These terrible numbers you could multiply by the many abortion providers through the United States—on some days, there are hundreds of deaths!

It is sickening that a single infant should die in such a way, and indeed, if there were but *one single death*, any Christian would be compelled to rise up in protest.

In the way that my comrade uttered the name *Voorhees*, all this disgust and outrage was communicated.

That morning, I did not inquire further about the arrival time of the abortion doctor Voorhees. I did not betray to my comrade any special interest or concern. I am not a man for whom speech comes readily and my instinct is to protect another, it is my habit as a husband and father. In the event that I acted upon the information that Stockard provided, I did not want this innocent man to be arrested by police as an accessory to any action of my own, for it is well known, as our leaders have warned us, not to involve others in our actions in any way for the police will cast a wide net to accuse, vilify, and punish the innocent, beginning with our families and extending to other protesters. Instead, I took up my picket sign as if this were any other morning in my life though there was a powerful buzzing in my head, for very joy I could not think clearly.

God had sent me a personal message, which it was not possible to ignore or misinterpret—*The murderer is not protected! He is vulnerable.*

To my shame, I had not (yet) the strength to confront this *turn*. By the end of the morning, when I left the vigil at the Women's Center, to drive to my workplace, the sensation of joy had vanished and I was left agitated, and "jumpy"—I was trying not to think of *that*.

For some days, it was *that*. Like something floating in my eye, that was not "real" and yet distracting. So that, when you stare at something, it is the miniature floating rod that you are trying not to see, yet cannot not-see.

That. The possibility that the Lord God, Who has spoken to others and has shown the way in which His will might be fulfilled in the world of humankind, might have spoken at last to *me*—this was terrifying to me, for it could not be shared with anyone, even my dear wife.

Yet whenever I was alone, or drifted away in my

thoughts from others (including even my younger children pulling at my sleeves or nudging their heads against me, in their way of pleading *Dad-dee look!* that tore at my heart) it was of *that* I was made aware.

Lately he's been arriving early. Before the police guard.

How many minutes?—could be ten minutes, twelve . . .

He is a murderer, and also a coward. Hiding himself inside among women whom he victimizes—butchers.

Voorhees. One of those on the List.

Had Stockard uttered these words to me? Or had Stockard communicated these words, without speaking?

His eyes shone with feeling behind rimless glasses, octagonal in shape. He had no need to say—*The murderer must be stopped! One of us must stop him.*

At work, laying shingles for the roof of a house overlooking a ravine in a residential neighborhood of Muskegee Falls (a new "colonial" of a size that could contain two houses of the size of my own as the lot itself was three acres, six times the size of my property), as I hammered nails each blow of the hammer was a strike to the heart—*A baby is being hammered to death, a baby is being sucked out of its mother's womb, a baby is denied birth, a baby will die.* And a woman's or a girl's body has been violated by the abortionist's instrument as her soul has been violated. For those who are meant by the Lord to be mothers are often *brainwashed,* and have no idea to what they are consenting.

A woman does not know her own mind. Especially a woman who has become pregnant, whose mental state has been thrown into disruption by what are called "hormones."

All of the women of my acquaintance, my mother, my sister, and my dear wife Edna Mae, have acknowledged this. And troubled women whom it was my task to comfort, when I was a lay minister in our church. Often a woman will say, she did not mean what she'd said when she was angry or upset, a kind of madness had come over her. It is *that time of month.* Or it is *hot flashes.* As Satan speaks through the female mouth that becomes ugly and contorted. And there is a feeling of Satan in her thoughts. The weakness of a woman or a girl in "giving in" to a man is not the worst sin, but one to be forgiven as Jesus forgave Mary Magdalene. But it is a fact—*A woman must be protected from the most terrible mistake of her life.*

The thought that our own precious children might have died by the abortionist's hand, if circumstances had been different. For there is a blindness to fate, that cannot be comprehended.

A child is *yourself.* And yet, of course a child is *not yourself, and unknowable.*

We are here on earth to protect and love one another and it is to the least of these, the children and infants, we are most responsible.

On the roofs of strangers' houses such thoughts came to me often. All my worklife it has been such, beginning at age fourteen in Sandusky where my father was a carpenter and roofer and first brought me to work-sites with him. My father was not a man easy in his speech and it was rare for him to touch me (or any of my brothers or sisters) except at such a time when he might grab my hand to secure me as I stepped onto a roof—*Got you!*

Like a blessing it seemed, Dad gripping my hand tight.

It is distressing to me, there is not so much roofing and carpentry work now available to a boy so young. It is not likely that I can bring Luke to a work-site with me and expect Fischer Construction to take him on.

Nor is it clear that Luke wants to work as I do. Or that he would be so capable with his hands as I was at that age.

When you climb onto the roof of any building, you are elevated above your natural state. There are thoughts that come to you only on the roofs of such buildings because the first fact is, when you straighten your back, and lift your eyes, the sky will open above you in a way that is different from when you are on the ground. Trees are not above you, some trees are beneath you or you are on a level with them. At fourteen such climbs onto the roofs of houses were exciting to me, it was thrilling to take up a hammer and to work beside my father and to know that my father was *damn proud* of me as he would say (if not to me, to others), and to see the envy in the eyes of the other men, that my father had such a son as Luther, and such a good worker, and never complaining or bored like other boys. I was not yet prepared for the wisdom of the Lord (for there was coarseness in my soul at that age) yet from the start the "opening" of the sky made a strong impression on me. It is hard to explain what this was except I knew myself filled with the unease of knowing that no act of mine would be unobserved and unjudged.

This is the first fact, the "openness" of the sky, and the second is, the (usual) roof will be *at a slant* beneath your feet and so this is different from your standing on the ground flat-footed. You do not take any roof for granted, for it is likely to be *at a slant* and you must be alert at all times. This is not true for standing on the ground. Even a drunken man will take for granted, the evenness of the ground. For the roof, you require work-boots with grip-soles. You require a cap to shade your eyes from the sun. You require gloves. In a bad dream you are on a (steep-slanted) roof exposed, and you do not have a hat or gloves or sturdy work-boots and when you search for the ladder you see that the ladder has been removed and there is no way down.

Sweat breaks out everywhere on your body, when you see that the ladder has been removed.

If you jump from the roof you may break both legs. You may break your back, your neck. You make your way around the roof, weak-kneed, squatting on your heels, searching for the ladder that is not there; and it is strange, no one is around. Never in actual life are you alone on a roof with a hammer in your hand, not once in memory since the age of fourteen, yet in the dream, the ladder has been taken away, and the other men are gone including the foreman, and the sky overhead is— "open."

In the early years the excitement was, each morning, what new thoughts would come to me that day!— for always there are new thoughts, that press from the sky.

It was then, the Lord often spoke to me. Jesus spoke to me, to console me in a time of trouble but also, to rejoice with me in a time of happiness.

For you do not always know that *you are happy*, unless it is revealed to you.

That *you are blessed*, as with children and a loving and devoted Christian wife, and a (mostly) steady job even in times of "recession"—this, you may need to be informed by one whose knowledge is greater than your own.

Except since Daphne, the thoughts are not new. Like flypaper, where the flies are caught and buzzing. And no fly that is caught on the sticky paper will ever be free of it though more flies will appear, trapped and buzzing.

These are *buzzing thoughts.*

In the hot months especially this was so. The stink of tar paper softening in the sun, that is a smell like mice, mice-carcasses, in a cellar. From a distance I could hear the others talking together. And there was the noise of hammering. But the *buzzing thoughts* intervened.

My heels dug into the (slanted) planks, and my breath came thick and with effort. Sweat trickling down my sides. The stink of my body oozing sweat like tears.

But since Stockard had spoken to me, and an understanding had passed between us, it was a new time. The sky was pearl-colored, and bright. You could not see the sun but still, the air was bright. There were clouds of such astonishing forms, it was a temptation to stare at them for long minutes. It was a temptation to observe the clouds passing. And now the summer was gone, it had come to be late October and a white light seemed to reflect upward from the tar paper.

The light of Heaven. Your eyes are open now.

My hammer-blows were forceful, precise. Driving three-inch nails into the shingles, securing them in descending rows. With each blow of my hammer came the questions—who would be next? Who would be the next to step forward? To strike against the enemy? As my comrades have bravely stepped forward in Florida, in Kentucky, in Michigan, in New York, and in Ohio.

Defending the unborn. Justifiable homicide.

It had tugged at my conscience, that a comrade in the Army of God, James Kopp, known to me only by name, had assassinated the abortion doctor Barnett Slepian in Buffalo, New York, nearly one year ago, on Veterans Day (November 11) 1998, and was now sentenced to life in prison without the possibility of parole. Many of us are praying for him, that he will not sink into despair. Some years earlier, the martyr Michael Griffin had stepped forward to assassinate the notorious abortion doctor David Gunn at a women's clinic in Pensacola, Florida, and had traded his life for his. And there was

Terence Mitchell in Traverse City, Michigan—whom we prayed for last year—found guilty of homicide and sentenced to life in prison.

In Livingston, Kentucky, there was Shaun Harris who'd shot down the abortionist Paul Erich, and had not yet come to trial . . .

Now the Lord had turned His eye upon Luther Dunphy and I could not hide. On the roof of the house overlooking the ravine, the rich man's house, in the eye of the sun pounding on my head through the cloth cap, into my brain. As if it were a problem in geometry in my son Luke's textbook I was made to realize that there is a *next person to act* and that this person would be—*me*.

"Only say the word. My soul shall be healed."

There had been other sharp *turns* in my life. These *turns* that had altered the course of my life, usually without my realizing at the time, but only later. But never a *turn* so clear as the Lord's mission for me.

For the remainder of that day I worked harder than anyone else in our crew. Harder than the younger men who spend too much time talking and laughing together, uttering profanities, telling dirty jokes. As if your own lips are not polluted, in the telling of dirty jokes. And such laughter, over-loud, like hyenas braying, wears away the soul.

You, Luther Dunphy. You are the chosen one.

You, to bring down the abortion murderer Voorhees that your Christian brethren may rejoice.

There is an agitation in hammering nails but it is a controlled agitation. All carpentry is a controlled action, to a purpose. One nail, and another nail. A sequence of nails, in the construction of a house. How many nails, how many blows of the hammer!—*the Lord God looks upon Luther Dunphy in wonder, in whom He is well pleased.*

"Luther? Hey—"

Voices from below lifting in my direction which I heard (of course I heard) but at a distance, through the distraction of the more urgent voice whispering in my ears.

The foreman Ed Fischer was calling to me. And another, calling my name. But in the shock of realizing that Luther Dunphy had been singled out by the Lord, and that Luther Dunphy was *me*, I could not seem to reply but stared down at them dumbly.

Sure Luther Dunphy *was an excellent roofer. Luther was a super employee in every way. Responsible, reliable, never hurried, never did a careless or half-assed job, never drank on the job, never got into a fight with anybody, worked with us for eleven years and only* took time off, maybe six weeks, recovering from an accident that almost killed him. And even then, he came back as soon as he could, and you could see the pain in his face sometimes but he never complained.

It was rare for Luther to lose his temper unlike most of these guys we work with. Nor did he use profanities or obscenities unlike these guys who it's fuck this, fuck that, every fucking thing, that's all they can say . . . It wasn't such a surprise to learn in the news, he'd studied to be a minister in some Bible school in Toledo, before he moved here.

Except, it was obvious Luther took care what he said. He wouldn't talk behind anybody's back, for sure. He never got angry—that you could see.

With this recession we're not building as much as we used to. Some guys I had to lay off, but I tried to use Luther Dunphy as much as I could. He had the experience, and the skill, and this family with young kids, so sure, there was worry there, he'd have a worried look in his face if I told him his workhours were cut back. But he never got angry.

Sometimes, Luther would "go off"—he would look at you, if you spoke to him, but he wouldn't see you—in his eyes there was a kind of blank, like in eyes that are open when a person is asleep . . .

This terrible accident he had last year out on the

highway—one of his young children was killed, and Luther was driving. Nobody ever talked to him about that—how the hell would you know what to say . . .

We knew that Luther was a member of that evangelical church—what's it called—St. Paul Missionary Church of Jesus. We knew that he was active in the anti-abortion picketing at the Women's Center, that they call a "vigil." But nobody would've guessed it would go so far—that Luther Dunphy of all people would shoot down two individuals in cold blood, even if they were baby-murderers themselves, Jesus nobody could have foreseen that.

The Miracle of the
Little Hand

The first time I knew of the *Little Hand* was stunning to me.

It was a time when Edna Mae had newly come into my life. And the St. Paul Missionary Church of Jesus had come into my life. It was a time of great happiness but a time when often I would feel a choking sensation in my throat, that made it very difficult to breathe, and I could not speak, and tears brimmed in my eyes, of the kind of tears that come into your eyes in dry heat, and not in sorrow; for I *was not* sorrowful or backward-looking, but joyous, that I would soon be married, and my dear Edna Mae and I would begin our family.

At the church there were pamphlets for us to take, and to pass to friends and neighbors, and to leave in selected places, and one of these had on its cover a picture of a *little hand* you could see had to be the hand of an infant so small it had only just been born; or had not yet been born.

The Miracle of the Little Hand

In the midst of an abortion as the abortion doctor was about to forcibly remove with his bloody instruments the (living) infant from its mother's womb suddenly the doctor saw a movement at the mouth of the womb, and felt a touch—as he stared in astonishment the little hand of the infant closed about the finger of the doctor and squeezed as if to cry

I am alive! I am alive!
Don't kill me, I am alive!

And so it came to pass, the abortion was halted. For neither the doctor nor the nurse in attendance (who had witnessed the Little Hand) could proceed. From that hour onward, the doctor did not perform another abortion but came to be a defender of the unborn, organizing other doctors in the crusade against abortion. The nurse did not ever assist with any abortion again, and helped to organize other medical workers in the crusade against abortion. The young mother too experienced a change of heart and chose to keep the baby, who came to full term and was born after a normal delivery at a healthy weight of — pounds.

So it is, the Little Hand clutches at the hearts of all.

Edna Mae had given me the pamphlet to read. Quietly then Edna Mae approached me, and touched my arm with her hand, and saw that my face was ashen, and that the love and the terror of the Lord were in my heart, and silently she embraced me.

Defending the Defenseless

There are two victims in every abortion: a dead baby, and a dead conscience."

These were the words of Mother Teresa. A Roman Catholic saint she was, of whom we had not heard. Her words uttered in the voice of Professor Willard Wohlman.

The question was, What is your own conscience? What is God telling *you?*

How do you know when you have been chosen by God to behave in a way of *disobedience to the state?*

How do you know when it is God's wish that you should *take the life of another, by your own hand?*

In June 1998 we drove two hundred miles from Muskegee Falls which is on the Muskegee River (forty miles north of Marion, Ohio) across the width of the state to

Huntington, West Virginia, to hear the renowned Professor Willard Wohlman speak on "Christian pro-life" issues. The title of the evening was *Defending the Defenseless: Life Advocacy in the Age of Abortion.*

Soon after Daphne this had been, in the fifth month of grieving, and so Edna Mae had accompanied me, for my dear wife had difficulty remaining alone in the house without me, with just the children and not their father, for a reason so strange to me I cannot speak of it here for it is of the renowned Professor I wish to speak.

Edna Mae saying to me *You have to watch me, Luther. You have to be in the next room at least. It is not enough just to think of me and to pray for me, that is not enough, Luther.*

At home, the older children would look after the younger. And there was Edna Mae's sister Noreen to come by each day to oversee.

He is Professor Willard Wohlman of a distinguished New England university. He has written many scholarly books and has served as an adviser to the President on issues of morality and ethics. He has appeared on television. He has debated abortion, contraception, "planned parenthood" and "same-sex" marriage. His most renowned book is *The Sacred Vision in the Secular World* which was a best seller for many months. Of his essays it is "One Man, One Woman: Christian

Marriage" and "The Conscience of a Christian" that Edna Mae and I have read and discussed together.

Sometimes now I think it is Professor Wohlman's voice which I hear in my head in the way that the words of the Lord are communicated to me, and the two come together in a single voice like rolling thunder.

A dead baby. A dead conscience.

What is God telling you?

At St. Joseph's Catholic Church in Huntington, in a hall beside the church Professor Wohlman spoke. The event was sponsored by the American Coalition of Life Activists. Some eighteen of us, from our church in Muskegee Falls, who belonged to the Army of God of Broome County, and some others (like our pastor who did not wish to officially "ally" himself with the Army) drove to Huntington in several vehicles to attend this meeting.

The Coalition is made up of Protestant and Catholic organizations that have united in common opposition to the Supreme Court decision *Roe v. Wade* of 1973. There is a distrust of the (atheist/socialist) state and federal governments interfering with individuals. It is a fact, *abortion is murder*—this belief is shared by all of us.

It does not matter if a woman's pregnancy was caused by rape or incest or any mitigating factor. For how could it matter, to the infant in the womb, or to God who is the father of all? Of course, it could not.

Our wives do not argue in these matters. But they listen closely to us, and it is rare for them to disagree.

Edna Mae does not "know" that her husband is a member of the Army of God and has made certain vows. There is no need to speak of this as there is no need to speak of such things aloud, that are never questioned.

Many times in our church our young pastor Reverend Dennis had spoken of Williard Wohlman. It had been Reverend Dennis's idea that we drive from Muskegee Falls to Huntington, West Virginia, in a little caravan.

There was excitement in this! Reverend Dennis said how like pilgrims we were, in making this journey. I had not felt such a flurry of hope and expectation since years ago when I had first driven to Toledo, to begin studies at the Toledo School of Ministry when I was a young man still.

I had discovered online that Willard Wohlman had studied in a Jesuit seminary in Chicago as a young man but left without taking his vows to become a priest. He had been a "staunch Democrat" for all of his life until the Democrat party threw its support behind abortion on request, at which point he broke from the party to take an independent position as he called it.

"Oh! So many . . ."

Edna Mae gripped my hand tight meaning to murmur *So many people* but her voice faltered as we entered the church hall in Huntington. It was not common in Edna Mae's life now to enter any place where faces were unfamiliar, and so many faces!—she did not attend any church services except our services at our church where everyone is known to everyone else and is like a family, where you do not need even to look at another person to register his identity.

It was painful for me to see my dear wife's face at this time for her youthful features had aged with the ravages of grief, and the spirit of the Lord that had shone so bright in her eyes since she'd been a girl seemed to have vanished like a lighted wick that has been turned so low, the flame has died out.

There was a slackness to her skin, and a puffiness beneath her eyes, that had to do with the medications she was prescribed. I did not like my dear wife to take these medications, but the doctor assured us, they were necessary for Edna Mae at this time.

Edna Mae pulled at me, as a child might tug at an adult's hand. There was an unusual eagerness about her conjoined with dread, that showed itself in her curious posture, in which her shoulders hunched forward like the shoulders of one bracing herself against a strong wind. It made me uneasy, Edna Mae was wearing a badly rumpled raincoat of a dark purple material thin as vinyl and on her feet flimsy shoes like house slippers that exposed much of her white feet that appeared to be bare as her legs were bare and very white.

I did not want to think what Edna Mae might be wearing beneath the raincoat which hurriedly she had taken from a closet. It was a fear of mine, my dear wife would not be properly dressed beneath the coat, in a public place, yet I had not thought to inspect her, in our hurry at leaving at the prepared time.

"Luther! Hurry. *Here.*"

I am not so bold, as to wish to sit in the very first row of any gathering. I am a tall man, with a wide frame, and it is very easy for me to become exposed, as the eyes of strangers move upon me without sympathy or recognition; my cheeks grow ruddy with the slightest provocation and especially a birthmark shaped like a spade, of a coarse red sandpaper skin-texture, on my left cheek. And Edna Mae too, until recently, had been a shy person, but no longer, for a wild sort of sorrow gripped her like an invisible creature that had her in its coils causing her sometimes to laugh shrilly for no evident reason.

From our seats at the very front of the hall, but far to one side, Edna Mae craned her neck to stare up at the stage. Her thin white hands she clasped before her at the level of her chest in a prayerful way that would seem show-offy to one who did not know my dear unhappy wife.

It is a new thing for some of us, to be at ease in the presence of Roman Catholics. It has long been known that the Roman Catholic Church considers itself the only true Christian church, which is unacceptable and historically inaccurate, but the Coalition (which was formed in the late 1970s) is based upon opposition to our common enemy and takes precedence over the divisions between us. Protestants and Catholics alike are drawn together in the service of the unborn who are threatened by the abortion providers, for nothing is more important than defending the unborn who cannot defend themselves.

There is a disapproval of birth control as well—the ugly word is contraceptives—to support and encourage a promiscuous lifestyle to which teenagers are particularly susceptible, influenced by TV, crude popular music, movies and "sex education" classes in the public schools.

Edna Mae and I had never talked of such things before our loss of Daphne. For the babies born to us had seemed to come from the Lord God with ease, with only His blessing. (At least, Edna Mae did not ever complain of physical discomfort in pregnancy or childbirth or child rearing or being "flooded" in her mind as she did now.) But lately it seemed Edna Mae wished to speak of certain things that were embarrassing to me, having to do not only with Daphne but also with the other children, and with "female troubles," as she would speak of them within the hearing of the children as well, as if she did not quite comprehend what she was saying; and this was deeply embarrassing to our eleven-year-old Dawn especially, who was becoming disrespectful to her mother. There were some other issues, not known to me, between Edna Mae and her family—her mother, her sisters. And it was becoming obvious, Edna Mae would neglect her housekeeping to watch Christian TV during the day, that left her excited and restless and quick to weep, by the time I returned home.

I would prepare the meal, if needed. The older daughters and me.

Operation Rescue had been much publicized on Christian TV and radio, and in churches and community centers through Ohio. At our church our minister had been speaking of it for months. It was thrilling to see so many people entering the hall and to know that these strangers were our allies. By my estimate— (my mind will add numbers and multiply of its own volition, as in this case twenty-two seats in a row, and thirty rows of seats)—there were 660 persons in the hall by ten minutes after seven o'clock when the program began.

The pastor of St. Joseph's Church greeted us. Then, the head of the Coalition, who is a minister in the Gallipolis Baptist Church (Ohio), came out onto the platform to introduce Professor Willard Wohlman.

By this time there was much excitement in the hall. There was no mistaking—*The spirit of the Lord is with us.*

Professor Willard Wohlman was not an imposing man. Very like a professor—or a teacher—he looked, in his fifties, or slightly older, of only medium height, with a slight stoop, thinning gray hair brushed back from his high forehead and a narrow waxy-seeming nose. He wore a dark brown suit that looked to be of good quality, and a white dress shirt and tie. But his eyes!—these were alight with feeling behind rimless glasses that seemed to catch fire as he spoke. And a voice of velvety softness like a radio voice that could turn sharp suddenly.

In this voice that was fascinating to hear, for you had to *listen to each word*, Professor Wohlman would speak for sixty-five minutes. He did not speak like the preachers to whom we were accustomed but in a quieter voice like one who is addressing *you*. He spoke of the "moral rot" of the "secular state"—the "barbaric brutality" of *Roe v. Wade* which he made us smile sadly to hear as "*Woe v. Wade.*"—"That has sanctioned the State to murder the innocents."

Then, the Professor began to speak more forcefully of the "need for a Christian army" to counter the "abortion forces." From his lips I heard a word I had never heard before—"feticide"—that was terrible to comprehend for it meant, as Professor Wohlman explained, *the murder of a fetus.*

At this point, Edna Mae began to weep. Almost silently my dear wife pressed a tissue against her eyes with bowed head and her shoulders quivering, as if she might shrink from anyone who tried to comfort her. And so I did not touch her, sitting with my face warm, and my blood beating hard, scarcely hearing the Professor's words though I did not turn my eyes away from his face as he stood at the podium above me, speaking with the calmness of rectitude.

Much of what the Professor said was difficult to follow. In our church, it is not in the nature of our ministers to reason in such ways. And so it was clear, the difference between the Roman Catholic professor and the others of us lay in such reasoning, that you could follow, to an extent, as the Professor spoke; but you could never recall what he said afterward, still less repeat it to another person. For the Professor took up "natural law" as a way of refuting those who argued for abortion—"It is their error to claim that the fetus, which is formed of the female egg and the male sperm conjoined, and is thus an entirely *new entity*, is not a human being, in embryonic form; and then, when this claim is answered, they argue that, yes, a fetus *is a human being*, but *it is not yet a person in a legal sense.*"

Professor Wohlman paused, to allow his audience to register the outrage of such a statement; then he continued, "Such an argument would allow society to dispose of human beings who are not deemed fully 'persons'—children born with physical and mental disabilities, adults who have suffered strokes and other impairments, the elderly who can no longer fend for themselves but must depend upon others. Once you argue that one class of human beings has the right to pass judgment upon all other human beings, to declare which are, and which are not, 'persons,' you have opened the door to the Nazi Holocaust—to genocide—to the power of the State to determine our lives. *This must not be allowed to happen. The butchery of each innocent infant must not go unacknowledged—unmourned.*"

Trying to follow the Professor was like making

your way through a marshy area where suddenly your foot might sink. For it seemed, the Professor quoted Latin—(or so it seemed, these foreign-sounding words had to be Latin); he spoke of a "Church father"—(a name pronounced as "Au-*gus*-tin")—and to a Catholic theologian of the medieval era—("Thomas A-*qui*-nus"). Both of these were, the Professor said, *saints.*

Saints! In the New Testament, all Christians are *saints.*

This is a strange idea to us, that some human beings are claimed to be *saints* in a way not taken from the New Testament. For in the New Testament it is clear, there is only one way to God, and that is Jesus Christ who is our Savior, but who is not a *saint.*

It was a new thought to me, that the approach to God might not be so easy as we had been taught. Even in the ministry school in Toledo, you would take your subject from the Bible, that would be the center of your sermon so that you would read these familiar verses to the congregation, and talk about the story in the verses, and even that had been a challenge to me for I did not have any original ideas about any sermons, but could only imitate sermons that I had heard, or that were given to me to study as good examples of sermons, and sometimes even then I would not know what to say, my tongue seemed to swell inside my mouth and my mind would be blank. But Professor Wohlman did not read a single verse from the Bible!

Professor Wohlman did not have a Bible with him at the podium, it appeared. How strange this was, I did not have time to consider at the time.

Across the aisle from Edna Mae and me, in the first row of seats, sat an older woman whom I had reason to believe was Professor Wohlman's wife. Mrs. Wohlman was a heavyset woman with a white skin that looked glazed, as with tiny wrinkles. She was stern-faced, somber. Her thin lips were pursed tight as she gazed upward at her husband standing at the podium, bathed in light. I wondered—was Mrs. Wohlman proud of the Professor? Could *she* understand him?

In the Coalition newsletter I'd learned that the Wohlmans had been married for forty-six years. They had had seven children of whom two had died prematurely—one, of childhood leukemia; the other, in a transportation accident involving fellow American soldiers, in Vietnam.

I wondered if the Professor had a way of reasoning, with his special insight, that might better explain the death of a young person, than the ways in which a Protestant might reason.

In the Coalition newsletter I had learned that Willard Wohlman was the "preeminent" Christian conservative philosopher of our time. At an "Ivy League university" (as it was called) the Professor taught courses in moral philosophy, political theory, and jurisprudence— (which I had to suppose dealt with juries and the law). One of his former Jesuit instructors at Loyola of Chicago had said of Willard Wohlman that he was "the most brilliant student" he'd ever encountered.

In an interview, Wohlman was asked why he had left the seminary without becoming a priest. His reply was a humble one—"I was made to realize that God had another plan for my life."

The Order of Jesus was the most exacting of all Catholic orders, Wohlman had said. Poverty, chastity, obedience—he had wished to pledge himself to these. Yet, he had been given to know, by an intervention of God, that his life outside the Order would be more challenging.

Professor Wohlman shifted tone now to speak of persons well known to us—*Michael Griffin. Lionel Greene. Terence Mitchell.* Pictures of these men were projected onto a screen behind the Professor and caused much surprise and comment in the audience. For the men were acclaimed soldiers of (the secret organization) Operation Rescue who had shot abortion providers and who had been imprisoned by the government as a consequence.

Michael Griffin and Lionel Greene had been tried, convicted, and sentenced to life in prison in Pensacola, Florida, and in Waynesboro, Indiana, in 1994 and 1995 respectively. Terence Mitchell had been arrested in March 1998 for slaying an abortion provider in Traverse City, Michigan, and was awaiting trial at this time.

Professor Wohlman spoke of how these men had "dared to step forward" to "take extreme action"; in defense of the unborn, they had committed "justifiable homicide."

Terence Mitchell, who was twenty-nine, a former U.S. Marine and a member of the Catholic right-to-life organization The Lambs of Christ, had spent many hours in prayer before driving to the abortion clinic in Traverse City with a double-barreled shotgun; after the shooting of the abortion doctor he made no attempt to escape from police but surrendered his weapon and made a full confession to authorities. "And what did Terence Mitchell say?—'I had no choice. If I had not stopped the abortion doctor, he would have killed more babies that day.'"

Professor Wohlman gazed up at the projected pictures of Griffin, Greene, Mitchell. These faces were familiar to us for we had seen them many times online. Yet, they were powerful to behold at this time.

I felt a clutch in my heart, Terence Mitchell looked

very *young*. Even with his beard he was young enough to be my son it almost seemed.

The young ex-Marine's troubled eyes, fixed upon us. We were made to feel shame for our safe and selfish lives, that Jesus would look upon with scorn if he were not our Savior who loves us and does not judge harshly.

In a grave voice Professor Wohlman continued: "In some quarters these courageous men are considered 'criminals'—'murderers.' But we know better. I have argued that such acts are 'morally justifiable homicide.' There is no 'homicide' in a war, for instance—a soldier is not a criminal or a murderer for engaging with the enemy. It is the same situation here. Any act of civil disobedience, in opposition to state-sanctioned murder, is 'justified.' For consider, would you have any choice except to interfere, if a child were being assaulted and murdered before your eyes? If, here, on this platform, at this very moment, a young child were being violently stabbed to death, hacked to death with a butcher knife, screaming in terror and in pain . . . If you could stop the pervert-murderer from killing the child, of course you would. If such a horrible sight happened before your eyes, not one of you could stand by helplessly and do nothing. *You could not*."

The Professor spoke quietly but his voice quavered with feeling. His fingers clenched and unclenched.

Light flashed in his eyeglasses. I saw that he wore black-polished shoes, leather dress shoes, with flat thin soles, that would not grip a surface at a slant, and would be dangerous on any slippery surface.

There was quiet in the hall—the hush of indrawn breaths. Only beside me Edna Mae continued to sob.

I was blinking back tears of rage, not sorrow. My hands, that were bigger than the Professor's, were also clenching and unclenching. Like one who steps backward carelessly at the edge of a roof I felt the danger of a sudden plunge.

That sickening sensation of *losing balance.*

For some seconds as if in prayer the Professor stood in silence, his head bowed, as we in the audience gazed at him, in the shared horror of an innocent child murdered before our eyes.

I was not unfamiliar with photographs of aborted babies. These piteous and gruesome pictures on picket signs we are supplied by the Coalition, to bear aloft in front of the abortion clinic and sometimes in the roadway, to force individuals to *see* what it is, they are not wishing to *see.* And there is the *Little Hand,* you will see everywhere. Such pictures always tear at my insides, as they are meant to do. But Professor Wohlman was able to make us "see" a living child on the platform, murdered before our eyes.

"And always, and forever, unless we stop them, the abortion murderers will be destroying and dismembering babies in their mothers' wombs, with the consent of the godless government. Unless we stop them."

Through the hall there were murmurs of assent. My hands were clenched in fists now, pressing on my knees.

Next, Professor Wohlman told us that he was drawing up a "revolutionary" petition that would be available to us from our church leaders, or from the Coalition newsletter, and he hoped we would take it into our hearts, and tell others about it. He hoped that we would sign this petition and mail copies to a list of individuals which would be posted online and which included our elected officials, our congressmen, and the President of the United States.

"Here is what the petition will say:

"'We, the undersigned, declare a State of War in the struggle to defend innocent human life.

"'We declare our allegiance to the Word of Jesus, and not the Law of Man.

"'We declare that we will not shrink from *taking all earthly action required to defend innocent human life*—including the use of force.

"'We declare that whatever force is necessary to defend the life of a born child is legitimate to defend the life of an unborn child.

"'We declare that the martyrs Michael Griffin, Lionel Greene, Terence Mitchell, though they may have broken the law of the state, have not broken the law of God; though they have shot abortion providers who were about to commit the terrible act of feticide, they are not guilty of murder but of intervening in premeditated murder. That is to say, these courageous men committed acts of defense against murderers not to save their own lives but the lives of unborn children. Therefore, their use of lethal force was justified. We will pray that the court will comprehend this in the case of Terence Mitchell, and acquit him of the charges brought against him by the State of Michigan.'"

Professor Wohlman gazed out into the audience as if he were gazing into our hearts. His eyes searched us out row upon row. His eyes moved upon *me*.

To me, Luther Dunphy, the Professor seemed now to speak with special earnestness as he concluded his speech:

"Know you this, my sisters and brothers in Christ: there are martyrs for every cause that speaks to the heart of mankind. It may be that Terence Mitchell will be acquitted—(and will live out his days knowing that he had been forced to shed blood)—or it may be that Terence Mitchell will not be acquitted, like his comrades, and will be incarcerated by the state. Like Michael Griffin and Lionel Greene, he may be sentenced to life in prison. These fates, no one can predict. Yet God observes, and God will reward. There have been martyrs for our cause, and there will be martyrs to come. Pray for our brave martyrs, and pray for ourselves, that we have the strength to act as we must, when we must."

In the crowded hall there were many cries and murmurs—"Amen."

And mine among them—"Amen."

After the talk, I remained sitting in my seat. For I could not rouse myself to rise just yet, and depart. Some others also remained in the seats about us while others stood in the aisles speaking to one another in lowered voices.

Edna Mae tugged at my arm, but I could not seem to move. How had it happened, the Professor had addressed *me*.

"What is this, Luther? Where are we? Why are we here?"—Edna Mae spoke with a vague sort of anxiety, yet smiling, or trying to smile, hesitantly touching my arm.

It was disturbing to me, to see how my dear wife, though (I was sure) she'd been listening intently to the Professor for the past hour, had now the air of one who has been wakened from a dream and has no clear idea where she is.

Gently I explained to Edna Mae where we were, and why we had come to Huntington, West Virginia, that evening with friends from our church. A faint recollection came into her worried eyes.

I had no doubt that Edna Mae would soon realize where we were, especially when she saw familiar faces. As often when she has taken her medication, as prescribed by our doctor, she requires a few minutes to orient herself if she is in an unfamiliar place, once I have explained to her where we are.

"And where are the children, Luther?—outside in the car?"

"No, dear. We didn't bring them, remember? They are back home safely."

This was a strange way to speak—*back home safely.* As if the children had been away, and had returned home. As often it happened when I spoke, because I am not so easy with speaking as others, and if someone is looking at my mouth, I would say words that came to my lips without understanding what I said.

"We're in Huntington, West Virginia, dear. But now we're headed home."

"Of course—'West Virginia.' I knew this." Edna

Mae smiled, a childish-sly smile, to hide her confusion. "—I was testing *you*, Luther."

Edna Mae had not noticed that her wadded tear-dampened tissue had fallen to the floor and so quickly I stooped to pick it up and hide it away in my pocket. Trying not to think that the Edna Mae of a few months ago would have been stricken with embarrassment, at such personal carelessness for which she'd often scolded the children. As she'd have been at the sight of herself in the rumpled raincoat with matted hair brushed behind her ears, a smear of lipstick on her mouth and what might have been spots of "rouge" on her sallow cheeks.

On the walk outside the hall several members of the congregation were waiting for us, for we would drive home together in a kind of caravan, into the night.

Reverend Dennis and the others were speaking excitedly of the meeting. I was sorry to seem abrupt with them for I could not trust myself to speak in a normal way, after Professor Wohlman's words that had entered my heart. Also it was painful to me, to observe others speaking with my dear wife, and Edna Mae attempting to answer them, for I did not like the way their eyes moved over her, the women's eyes especially, with the greed of birds pecking in the dirt.

It was not like me to avoid speaking with Reverend Dennis whom I revered as a true Christian minister, nor was it like me to be rude to the minister's wife. All I recall is that quickly we walked away to our car that was parked close by—that is, with my hand gripping Edna Mae's arm I urged her to walk as quickly as she could. If Edna Mae was surprised to see these familiar faces, in this unfamiliar setting, there was no time for her to exclaim. Behind us was the murmur which I am not sure if I heard—*Poor Edna Mae!*

In our car, Edna Mae lapsed almost at once into sleep, beside me. Where once my dear wife would have been alert and anxious about my driving at night on the interstate, where trailer-trucks come roaring up behind you flashing lights to blind you in the rearview mirror, and to pass dangerously close at eighty miles an hour, now Edna Mae took no mind at all of the situation like a creature that cares only to curl up to sleep.

It seemed to me that Edna Mae had drawn up her bare legs beneath her as a child might, to sleep. Yet each time I glanced at her, I saw that this was not so and that she was slumped sitting-up in the seat, her head flung back and her mouth open.

Soon her breathing was damp-sounding, a kind of hoarse pant. Since Daphne, Edna Mae either did not sleep at all, or slept too much—a heavy, sodden sleep from which she could hardly be wakened. (It was disagreeable to hear the children shouting at their mother to wake her where she might have fallen asleep on a sofa perhaps, even at times on the living room or kitchen floor. Especially Dawn's exasperated voice—"Maw*maw*! Wake up!")

In this heavy sleep Edna Mae was breathing strangely, as she'd begun to do in recent months. For several seconds she would seem to cease breathing as I listened, though trying not to listen, and counting seconds when she had ceased to breathe—one, two, three . . . six, eight, ten—before there came a catch in her throat like the clicking-open of a wet lock, and a sudden snorting noise of such loudness she was awakened, drawing in breaths like a drowning person . . . But soon then she lapsed back into sleep again, and after a few minutes cease to breathe. Ever more often this would happen, and I would nudge my dear wife, and say her name to urge her to breathe, for this strangeness did not happen when she was awake but only when she was sleeping very deeply, so that it was a matter of Edna Mae *remembering to breathe*, as others of us, for some reason, do not need to remember.

What would happen to Edna Mae, if I did not wake her, to rouse her to breathe? Was there an understanding in this, sent by God, that I was to interpret?—badly it worried me, like picking off tiny thorn-seeds from my trouser cuffs, that you can never come to the end of picking-off, for I did not understand.

Though knowing that Operation Rescue was to be a *turn* in my heart. This, I seemed to know even before we'd made our plans to drive to West Virginia.

Thinking calmly how the Professor had looked into my heart, he had seen *me*.

Pray for our brave martyrs. And pray for ourselves . . .

For weeks I had been planning to attend *Defending the Defenseless*. But I had not thought that Edna Mae would accompany me on such a long drive, for she has been unwell. It was surprising to me, she'd suddenly said *Take me with you, Luther—I am afraid to be alone in the house without you. You have to watch over me.*

At first I could not comprehend what this might mean. For often Edna Mae is alone in the house when the children are at school, and I am at work through the day. But then, as Edna Mae spoke further, in a wandering manner, with interruptions of breathless laughter, it seemed to develop that my dear wife was afraid of being alone in the house without her husband to watch over her *in the night*.

This could only mean—(so I thought)—that Edna

Mae was afraid that she might injure herself in my absence.

By accident, she might take an overdose of her medication. Or, less by accident, she might "injure" herself with a sharp knife, or in some other terrible way.

Of course—*Edna Mae did not mean this. It is a way of saying how sad she is, how unhappy. How badly she needs her husband to protect her.*

Thought of this responsibility filled my heart with a husband's love. And for my dear children, the love of a Christian father.

That night, after we returned past midnight to Muskegee Falls, and to the (darkened) house, Edna Mae was scarcely able to keep her eyes open as I helped her from the car, and into the house; she had difficulty keeping her balance as I half-carried her upstairs to our bedroom. As we ascended the stairs two things seemed to occur simultaneously: the sound of a door shutting in the upstairs hall, and the appearance, at the top of the stairs, of our thirteen-year-old Luke in pajamas, and barefoot, staring down at us with worried eyes. Though I was not quick-witted enough to comprehend this at the time, it is likely that one of our daughters, probably Dawn, was responsible for shutting the door, quickly entering the room she shared with her sister Anita before we could see her; while

Luke, the child most like me, a boy with young-old eyes, remained to greet us, and to ask what was wrong with his mother?—and I said, trying for a jovial tone, "Not a thing is wrong, son, except that your mother is *up past her bedtime.*"

Still the boy stared at us, unconvinced. It is rare that one sees a child's forehead so visibly furrowed, as Luke's; and it is upsetting to observe how the boy gnaws at his lower lip, as if to draw blood. Often it seems to me that I see a small mottled-red birthmark on the boy's left cheek—in fact there is none. (Yet I can't stop myself from looking—many times in a single day.) I felt as though a vise had seized my heart, for our first-born will surely grow to be as tall and as big-framed as his father, and there is a helplessness in such, for it will be your responsibility to protect others who are smaller and weaker than you; and it is very easy to *lose balance* in such a frame, and you are always exposed—the sky is always "open" above you. In a lowered voice I said, "Go back to bed, son. You have school tomorrow."

Yet worriedly the boy persisted—"Is Mawmaw OK?"

"Mawmaw is *tired.* And I am *tired,* son. Don't tempt me!"—still in a jovial voice though the boy understood the look in my eyes, of warning, of love laced with warning, or warning laced with love; and quickly he drew away, and returned to the room he shared with his younger brother, barefoot and silent as if indeed my hand had been raised against him which it had not.

It is a terrible responsibility to be the progenitor of new life. In a dream it came to me years ago after the first of them was born—*Increase and multiply* is the curse of humankind.

But this was not the (recognizable) voice of the Lord, or of Jesus. It was a (possible) voice of mockery, to test Luther Dunphy who had aspired to be a minister in the St. Paul Missionary Church of Jesus and was on trial at that time.

In our bedroom removing Edna Mae's clothing with clumsy fingers. Beneath the raincoat my dear wife had not been naked (as I had feared) but wore a soiled flannel shirt that might've belonged to one of the older children, and a soiled corduroy skirt that looked as if it had been retrieved from the dirty-clothes basket, no stockings or socks and her undergarments (which I would not remove) were grayish from many launderings and loosely fitted her shrunken frame.

Since Daphne, my poor dear wife has lost fifteen pounds at least. While I have gained weight in my torso, a fatty tumor like a fist encasing my heart.

Clumsily too I pulled Edna Mae's cotton nightgown down over her head and for a moment the nightgown was caught, and Edna Mae struggled weakly against me, her face hidden. Too late seeing that the nightgown was inside-out. But already Edna Mae had slumped back on the bed and into a light doze, openmouthed. A string of saliva on her chin. I would help her into the bed and draw the bedclothes up upon her and pray that we would get through this night for these were nights that seemed dangerous to me, in the nights, weeks, months after Daphne when there was yet indecision as when a jury is deliberating a verdict regarding you but which you do not fully comprehend.

The bedroom was dim-lit. On my knees I prayed beside the bed. It is my habit at such times—the oldest prayer of my childhood which I had been taught to repeat in echo of my father's voice *Our Father Who art in heaven, hallowed be Thy name. Thy kingdom come . . .* —for such words are a consolation as whiskey had once been a consolation.

In the dark for some time I lay awake beside my dear wife. I was very exhausted and yet could not seem to sleep for my body felt large and clumsy to me, and I needed to shower, for my body smelled of sweat, yet there was no time now, the hour was nearing 2:00 A.M. My (right) foot on the gas pedal ached from the pressure and became a foot-cramp—(for I suffer from foot- and leg-cramps often in the night). The interstate highway was rushing at me but dimly illuminated in the headlights of my vehicle and it was not clear—(in my anxiety, I did not wish to experiment by turning the wheel)—if my hands gripping the steering wheel possessed any power to "steer" the vehicle or whether the wheel was a false wheel provided for me to (falsely) placate me. As when it was said of the lifeless child *She is with the angels now.*

And yet, it was the father who said these words, was it?—for it was my task to bring the news to the other children.

"Your sister is with the angels now. There is no need for tears."

Like fingernails scraped on a blackboard, the sound of tears. Such a sound is not bearable.

There had come Edna Mae's muffled voice to the children somewhere upstairs that they must not cry, they must not cry for crying would displease their father, if they had to cry they must hide away to cry or wait until their father was not within earshot did they understand?

The muffled aggrieved yet practical-minded female voice, of which I was not (altogether) certain, that I had heard it or imagined it, nor the children's voices in reply, I did not seem to hear.

So tired! It is that state when tiny stars and the faces of strangers seem to rush at us behind our closed eyes.

Yet it was not comfortable in our bed where the bed-clothes had come to smell of our bodies and the ooze of grief. And the ooze of anger. And disgust. For it had fallen to me lately, to change the bedclothes, when my poor dear wife could not remember if she had changed the bedclothes or not, when obviously she had not, nor had my poor dear wife remembered to bathe herself as once she had been so fastidious, she had laughed at herself. And now, days passed and (it seemed to me) Edna Mae did not change her undergarments, and she did not wash or even, at times, brush her hair.

Explaining to the children that their mother was very tired. Their mother was *prescribed medication* which made her tired and so they must take care of Mawmaw, at this sad time in our lives.

Our bed was "queen size." Yet my feet pushed against the end of the bed, and were always tugging out the sheets there. I would lie on my side facing away from Edna Mae, and my eyes shut tight. In this posi-tion I felt like something that has toppled over in the cemetery, that had fallen from one of the larger grave-stones, heavily into the grasses and could not be righted again. And Edna Mae beside me, not on her side facing out but on her back, which was not a good position, for on her back Edna Mae would breathe irregularly, and wetly, beneath the white-wool quilt Edna Mae's mother had knitted for us for a wedding present, that she had explained was a *diamond stitch*, and that had once been so beautiful, it seemed amazing to me that my mother-in-law had knitted it and I had known myself blessed, that Edna Mae's family would accept me as their son though (it was clear to me if not to them) Luther Dunphy *was not worthy*.

And now it seemed to me again, as the Professor's gaze had lighted upon mine, that I was not a true protector of the weak and helpless, but a coward who had no right to call himself a Christian.

A Christian is one who will sacrifice his life, in martyrdom. I have long known this, but did not want to acknowledge it for it is far easier to hide within the family, to claim that the love and protection of your own family is your sole responsibility.

How long it was, how many minutes, lying awake and trying to sleep despite these condemning thoughts and trying not to listen to the labored breathing of the woman beside me. Until at last—as I knew it would—her breath seemed to stop—and then, after some desperate seconds, during which it sounded as if she was being strangled, I would nudge her awake begging—"Edna Mae. *Breathe.*"

And then, my poor dear wife would emit a startled snort, and for a confused moment she would seem to be awake; then lapsed back into sleep, close beside me.

She is with Daphne now. The child has her.

Almost I could see our daughter's small arms tight around Edna Mae's neck, pulling her down into blackness like black muck.

Yet there was no sound from the child. It is rare that you will encounter a child who makes no sound.

She is happiest with Daphne. They are with the angels. It will be the kindest thing, to send the mother there, to be with the child to comfort her.

This night was not the first night that I had pondered my responsibility to my poor dear wife. Yet this was the first time that I dared to raise myself on my elbow, beside her, and removed my pillow from its place and considered how, to put the grieving mother out of her misery, it would be a mercy; and the words *misery, mercy* echoed in my mind as sometimes a popular song will seem to catch itself in your mind and resist expulsion like something sinewy caught between the teeth. *Misery, mercy.* Jesus seemed to be urging me, to this contemplation. For this could not be an accident—could it? The very sounds of the words, like music.

For of all beings Jesus is most kind, and does not wish us to suffer as He suffered in our place. Tentatively I lifted the pillow to ease down against Edna Mae's face, that would grow contorted as her breathing began again to slow, and a choking sensation seemed to grip her causing her mouth to twitch and grimace in a grin like a Hallowe'en pumpkin that is not like any expression on the face of my poor dear wife, that I have ever seen, and that filled me with dismay.

She will not struggle long. For you are strong, and know what must be done.

It is true, I am far stronger than Edna Mae. And yet, the strength of a smaller being, a child for instance, or a cat, can be considerable, and a surprise. And if the creature rakes your hands with her claws, your strength will be daunted.

Still, if I pressed the pillow hard against her face, and pinioned her head against the other pillow, and that against the mattress, and if I did not weaken, Edna Mae would not struggle long. And it would be a *mercy*, to put the poor woman out of her *misery*.

Edna Mae would not then grieve for our lost child, who is with the angels and with Jesus. It is wrong of Edna Mae to so mourn Daphne, if God has taken her to dwell with Jesus. In this she is a poor model for the children.

It is not always clear what our duties are. I am the father, and I am responsible. If I were to put Edna Mae out of her misery, I would not be blamed. That is, I would not be blamed by God.

Her eyes cast on me would not then blame me. She would not caution the children not to cry within their father's hearing.

In the morning Edna Mae will (probably) not recall where we were tonight. If I recollect for her, and repeat some of the remarks of Willard Wohlman, she will quickly say yes, she remembers. And indeed, she will remember something.

The difference between true and false memories is not always clear.

I had begun to press the pillow harder upon Edna Mae's face. The entire face must be hidden (from my eyes) though it is only the mouth and nose that must be covered. Close in the darkness Jesus stood by to observe.

If she resists, then you must take away the pillow at once. It will be her choice, Luther. Not yours.

Yet the pressure of the pillow on the face was not extreme. It was as Jesus advised, the choice must be Edna Mae's and not mine.

The thought came to me also, with the force of a hammerstroke—"If I smother my wife it will be a clear sign that God does not favor me. God does not have a plan for me."

Similar thoughts, I had sometimes spoken aloud. On rooftops, where the hammering of nails into fresh lumber would disguise my words and no one would hear.

When it had become clear to me that I would not be a minister in the St. Paul Missionary Church, despite the strong wish in my heart to be such, but only a *lay minister*, for there was doubt among the elders as to my ability to "capture the attention" of a congregation, and doubt regarding other aspects of the minister's life. At first it was wounding to me, to realize this, but then, as it was explained to me by persons whom I admired, it was God's decision and not theirs—*It is the will of God, we have only to accept it.*

And then, when this explained to me, by an elderly minister whom I respected above all others, suddenly the scales fell from my eyes, and I understood.

The will of God, we have only to accept.

There are many ways to serve God, Luther. There is not only the way of ministry.

This is the great wisdom of our lives. You do not struggle against God's plan for you. Nor do you attempt to appropriate a plan for yourself, in pretense that it is God's plan.

The pillow was pressed a little harder against Edna Mae's face, and now she began to move her head, and to struggle. And still, I pressed the pillow harder, and at this Edna Mae began to writhe as a cat might writhe, in a sudden eruption of panic, not clawing at my hands (as I'd feared) but gripping my wrists, to shove them away; and through the pillow I could hear muffled cries—*No! No no . . .*

At once, I lifted the pillow from the contorted white face. Now spittle covered the lips and the eyes were blinking frantically.

"Edna Mae, dear you are having a nightmare . . . You have been choking in your sleep."

It was true, Edna Mae had been making strangulated noises in her sleep. Her breath came in quick spurts as if she'd been running. Now she was sitting up in bed frightened and confused like one who has no idea where she is.

As Edna Mae was panting, and half-sobbing, gently I gripped her thin shoulders and shook her, to steady her.

"Edna Mae! Stop! It was only a bad dream—you're safe now."

I groped for the bedside lamp, that seemed to have become overturned as if in a struggle. Carefully I set it upright and switched on the light. In the dim light Edna Mae stared at my face as if trying to identify me.

The pupils of her eyes were dilated and appeared all black. On the little table beside Edna Mae's side of the bed was Edna Mae's well-worn Bible (which she had had since she'd been a girl) and one of Daphne's small stuffed toys, that looked like the fuzzy cinnamon-colored bear I had disposed of weeks ago.

"You were sleeping on your stomach, Edna Mae, with your face in the pillow. You panicked when you couldn't breathe. See, the pillow is wet from your mouth . . ."

With something of her former fastidious distaste Edna Mae shuddered. It is embarrassing to her to be reminded of such behavior, or any kind of personal slovenliness. I would not reproach her.

My way with the family and with any young person is to speak gently and kindly and without any harsh judgment for that was a key insight from my training as a (lay) minister.

A Christian is one who makes others feel good about themselves, and hopeful. Not ashamed, or sad, or anxious.

Edna Mae stared now at the bedside clock. The numerals were 2:11 A.M. which she did not seem to comprehend, for the hour was so late for us it did not seem real. Both windows of the room showed only darkness outside pressed flat against the glass like a face so close you cannot see its features.

"Oh, Luther! I'm sorry. I've been keeping you awake . . ."

I told my dear wife not to be silly, she had not been keeping me awake.

With a murmur of apology Edna Mae pushed herself from the bed.

Through the cotton nightgown the vertebrae of her spine were outlined, the poor woman had grown so thin. When I offered to help her she pushed away my hand with a little laugh of chagrin. For it seemed now that she was fully awake. With some effort she made her way unsteadily out into the hall and into the bathroom just outside the door.

So softly she moved, barefoot, I could not hear her footfall. I hoped that she would not collapse, and I would run to her, and the children would be wakened and hurry from their rooms . . . By this time I was sweating profusely, and wiped my face on an edge of the sheet.

A sensation of sickness deepened in my bowels, I could not believe what I had contemplated doing to my dear wife—*smothering Edna Mae? Putting her out of her misery?*

"But that is not allowed. I know, that is not allowed."

These words I spoke aloud in a kind of childlike wonder. If Jesus was a witness I wanted him to hear.

From the bathroom I could hear a toilet flush, and I could hear the faucet. The pipes are old in this house and should be replaced, soon. I could hear the *click!* of the medicine cabinet when it was opened, and I could hear the shaking of pills out of a small container, onto the palm of my wife's hand.

Almost, I could see my dear wife's hand shaking.

And yet, so tired had I become, and how heavy-lidded my eyes, I understood that I could not really see Edna Mae shaking her white pills into the palm of her hand, through the wall.

Then, there was another sound. Pills slipped through Edna Mae's fingers onto the floor. There came a sharp little intake of her breath—"Oh! Oh God"—as she stooped to grope for the small white pills and to pick them up one by one from the linoleum floor, that was not a clean floor.

Again now there came a running of water, and a moaning sound of pipes. And the *click!* this time of a glass being set upon the porcelain sink just a little too hard.

When Edna Mae returned to our bed she was yet more unsteady on her feet. Her face was papery-white but mottled a rough red in the cheeks as with hives. Her eyes were puffy and bloodshot and yet (I saw) there was something sly in those eyes, the stubbornness of secrecy. Her hair was matted and sticking up in tufts like the feathers of a scrawny chicken.

My beloved Edna Mae! My heart was suffused with love for her, not as she was now but as she had been, when I had first seen her in the church at Mad River, at the age of seventeen in another lifetime it seemed, before she'd lifted her shy eyes to see *me*.

So young, both of us! By then, I had dropped out of high school. I had decided to make my own way and not to work with my father as my father had wished and instead to spend the summer with my uncle and aunt in Mad River thirty miles south of Muskegee Falls working on their dairy farm.

If I had not gone to stay in Mad River that summer.

If I had not gone to that church service, that Sunday morning.

But it was decreed by the Lord, this would happen. It was decreed that Edna Mae Reiser and Luther Amos Dunphy would meet in that place and at that time in June 1977, that our children would be born each in time. For in no other way could our lives have progressed, that these children would be born as they were, and baptized in Jesus.

The Edna Mae that *is*, and the Edna Mae that *was*. Hardly would you think that the woman of thirty-six or -seven (I was not absolutely certain of Edna Mae's age as I am not ever certain of the children's exact ages for they are changing all the time, and so the family laughs at their *Dad-dee* who is always being corrected and scolded) could even be the mother of the seventeen-year-old Edna Mae Kaiser with her round face and shy eyes.

Not of the same type, you would think. Not the same blood.

In my memory, Edna Mae is wearing a white dress in the church. (For she was a nurse's aide, I would discover.) Yet, Edna Mae has always laughed at me, saying no, she had not been wearing any *white dress* that day!—she had certainly not been wearing a uniform to church. What she'd been wearing was a pink flower-print dress, and white ballerina slippers.)

Now Edna Mae was complaining of something I could not fully comprehend, how tired it made her, to drive at night. How selfish it was, that I should make her drive, when she hated to drive at night, and was afraid to drive at night, on the interstate especially, and now she had a headache, and needed to take some medication and get back to sleep right away.

This was a surprise! For Edna Mae had not driven any vehicle since the shock of January of this year. I was sure of this. Luke or Dawn would have told me. Never would I have asked my dear wife to drive on the interstate at night even when she'd been in good health. But I did not refute her now which would only make matters worse.

"Have you taken more of those damn pills, Edna Mae? When you have to get up in a few hours?"

It was like a slap, to utter *damn* to Edna Mae. But it was a light sort of slap, to get her attention, and not to insult her as a harsher word would have done.

The shock of hearing our daughter Dawn mutter the *f*-word a few weeks ago, in the kitchen slamming drawers talking to herself when she'd thought no one was within hearing. *F—k you, f—kface just f—k you, got it?*—laughing in contempt imagining an exchange with one of her school classmates.

The shock of it had been such, I backed away into the garage. And reentered the house dazed a few minutes later, to avoid a confrontation with the child.

Of course, I knew that Edna Mae had taken one or more pills in the bathroom. I knew that Edna Mae would not be able to get up in the morning before the children left for school, and I left for work. The older children would help the younger as they had been doing since January and it would not be surprising to them, to return home from school in the afternoon to discover their mother groggy and slurred of speech still in her nightgown.

I know, these are said to be "addictive" pills the doctor has prescribed for my dear wife. I know that there is a problem of "dependency." But the doctor has insisted, Edna Mae would be "severely depressed" without them.

It is a sin against Jesus, to be *depressed*. If you are *in despair*, it is an insult to Jesus who died for your sins, as if Jesus is not adequate for you, but I do not want to tell Edna Mae this fact for fear of making things worse for her.

In a woman, the weaknesses of a man are doubled, or trebled. Their will to withstand the temptation of despair is like the muscles of their shoulders and upper arms, lacking in development.

Quickly I rose from the bed, that badly needed changing. (I did not want to see if, in her moment of panic, when it seemed that she might be suffocating, my poor dear wife had wetted herself and the bedclothes.) I helped Edna Mae back into bed, and adjusted her pillow beneath her head, and sat for a while with her, caressing her hand that was strangely hot and dry.

"Which time is this, Luther?"

"Which *time*?"

"I know where we are but—when . . . ?"

Our minister has said, there is a time beyond time. You will have no words to speak of it. This is a thought that has come to me too, when I stand up, lifting my head, seeing quickly the arrangement of clouds in the sky, and the types of clouds—their particular shapes, colors, thicknesses.

In silent reply to her question I gripped Edna Mae's hand tight.

We have faith, that meaning will come to us from above. Like a light-falling warm rain that blesses.

It was a blessing now, soon then Edna Mae lapsed back into sleep. I was confident that she would not recall any of her nightmare of choking, in the morning.

That is a blessing of bad dreams, they are quickly forgotten.

While Edna Mae slept in our bed, with opened mouth, and damp hoarse breath, but less agitation than before, I felt my own agitation gradually subside; and a feeling of gratitude filled my heart. For it seemed to be decided, I was not meant to put my dear wife out of *misery.* And it was not so clear, that God did not have a special destiny for Luther Dunphy.

Quietly I switched off the light and slid beneath the covers beside the female body.

"Thank you, God. You have shown me the way as I have prayed You would."

Soon after this, without informing my dear wife I became a member of Operation Rescue, which I discovered through the Army of God newsletter. In all, I would attend only three meetings and at these, I would not speak. But, with the others, I would vow to *lay my life on the line for Jesus.*

The Lost Daughter

In January 1998 it happened. Though I saw the other vehicle turning out onto the highway I could not brake my vehicle in time.

In a lightly falling snow it happened. And the highway beginning to glaze over with a thin glittering film of ice.

This too was a *turn* in my soul. Jesus, forgive me!

Some distance ahead saw the pickup continuing out onto the highway through the stop sign. At the County Line Road this was, just outside town. Where I would drive sometimes, to the county landfill. It is not a much-used road and so there is no traffic light only just a stop sign. In a lightly falling snow the pickup was not so visible as it would have been in bright sunshine for the chassis was of no-color like stone worn smooth.

When you are driving on the state highway north of Muskegee Falls the speed limit is fifty-five miles an hour. There are few traffic lights.

So suddenly this happened, the pickup in the farthest-right lane.

Always there is a refusal to see what your eyes are seeing, when it is a terrible sight. When another has dared to behave so willfully and in violation of the law. For this was what's called a *rolling stop* and it is in violation of the law.

Returning home from a morning of Saturday chores, and less than a mile from home. And in my distracted state—(for there is much to think about when your workhours have been cut back by one-third and in a family of five children of whom one has been diagnosed with a *neurological condition*)—seeming to hesitate for just a moment, a fraction of a moment, thinking—*No. You are not going to push out onto the highway. Not in front of me.*

It is not like me, to think in such a way. Except sometimes behind the wheel of my vehicle when others seek to cut me off or take advantage. And even then, when turning at a light, a left-turn for instance, it is (usually) my custom to allow the driver in the opposite lane to turn first, out of friendliness; for a young minister who was much admired, in Toledo, had behaved in such a way, in imitation of Jesus, and had made an impression upon me. Also it is rare for me to speed on any road, for "anger management" has taught me to master such aggressiveness, as it is called, on the road as elsewhere.

Turning the other cheek as Jesus bade us is just good sound advice, we were told. The person who is hurt by anger, is *you.*

But it seemed, the pickup at County Line Road had scarcely slowed its speed before continuing out into the busy highway. Whoever was at the wheel of the vehicle could see how traffic in the farthest-right lane was speeding toward him and could gauge (it is to be supposed) that there was (probably) not sufficient time for him to turn onto the highway and increase his speed to prevent a collision, yet boldly he proceeded just the same.

He would be a young man, I guessed. A teenager.

Possibly a man of my age. But not a woman, and not an elderly man.

From somewhere close by came a terrible sound of a horn, or horns. And even as my foot leapt to the brake, to press down hard, it was too late to avoid a collision with the vehicle directly in front of me, that was traveling at a speed more or less identical to my own, but now was being braked by its driver, to avoid hitting the pickup in the lane ahead; and without thinking, for there was no time to think, I turned the wheel of my vehicle sharply to the left, and pressed down the brake pedal even as the tires were skidding on the ice-film. Within seconds there was a three-vehicle collision even as—(as we would afterward learn)—the pickup continued on the highway, in the right lane, speeding away without (it seemed) a backward glance; and the guilty driver never apprehended.

In a soft-falling snow this happened. Out of a sky of banked clouds like soiled snow. And my voice raised in disbelief, and in fury—*No! God damn you NO.*

But there came at once the impact, the front of my vehicle slamming against the rear of the vehicle in front of me, at some speed below fifty miles an hour, but not much below; and the two vehicles skidding, spinning like bumper cars at a carnival; and almost immediately a third vehicle, unseen by me until then, a station wagon driven by a young woman with her elderly mother in the passenger's seat was struck by our skidding vehicles, and swerved also onto the median, and came to a thunderous crash against the guardrail.

No time to think—*I am in a crash. I will die.*

No time to pray—*Jesus help me! God help me!*

So swiftly this happened, my vehicle had skidded into the others, and the vehicle like the others would be *totaled*, metal crumpled like an accordion; and there came the terrible impact, and then—silence like the silence after a thunderclap, that has rent the sky.

Then, cries of surprise, fear, pain . . .

In the confusion it seemed that my vehicle had exploded, this was the air bag striking my chest and upper arms, and releasing too some sort of acid, that would badly burn my face. And it seemed at this point that I lost consciousness, for my head had been whipped forward, as if it might be flung off my neck, and a sour taste arose in my mouth, of bile. And then, I was no longer behind the wheel but had been flung outside onto the pavement. It would be told to me that I had unbuckled the seat belt but I would not recall this. I would recall crawling on hands and knees on the freezing pavement, and trying to crawl in broken glass, or in something shattered like Plexiglas, and my mouth was filled with blood, and a pressure on my chest would not allow me to breathe.

Out of the confusion came cries and shouts, and footsteps near my head, and soon then a deafening siren, and I knew myself being lifted but had no idea where I would be taken. I could not *see* and yet, a jangle of blinding lights flooded my eyes, and I could not *breathe*, and yet my lungs were being made to breathe a freezing-cold air that pierced my chest.

In a speeding vehicle, I was being transported to a hospital in Springfield which is eighteen miles away. At the time, I did not know this. Nor did I understand that it was a *crash* that had occurred. I did not know that other vehicles were taking other crash victims to the hospital—I did not know the word for *ambulance*, or for *hospital*. What was strange was, and would seem wonderful to me, I did not feel fear. I did not feel panic. I did not even feel regret except a mild disappointment, that I would not now be going home as I had planned; I would not see my dear family again nor any human face again, it was given to me to know. And a beam of light descended before me, that was a kind of highway, for it had taken the place of the highway, and would lift me into it, and still I did not feel terror for—(though I could not see Him)—I felt the presence of Jesus within me.

It would seem to me—(though I did not ever see Him with my actual eyes)—that my life was "saved" by Jesus; at the same time, it was given to me to know that my life *was in Jesus*, and that there was no distinction between *Jesus* and *Luther Dunphy*.

And so, there was no fear. It was like slipping into water that is warm, and tranquil—you cannot tell where your skin leaves off, and where the water begins.

And the water buoys you aloft, as if you were an infant with no need for an agitation of your arms and legs or for any kind of fear.

For how long I remained in this state of tranquility and calm, I do not know. It would be told to me later that I had arrived in the ER unconscious and with low blood pressure, in a *state of shock*. It would be told to me later, the terrible news that others had died in the crash, though there was another survivor like myself, in the same hospital; and that I was on *life support* for forty-eight hours.

It is very strange to "awaken"—as if you have chosen to "awaken"—when this is not the case: you do not have any choice. The surprise of opening my eyes in a room of white walls, beeping machines, and air like the interior of a refrigerator, and seeing the faces of strangers, that kept slipping from me like a film that is dissolving, for I could not maintain the attention required to remain awake for more than a few seconds. And still later, there came my dear wife Edna Mae (though somewhat confused with my mother when she'd been Edna Mae's age) to touch my hand, and to weep over me, and to pray for me; and others whom I knew, whose faces were familiar to me. And so I knew, that Jesus had sent me back to these people for it was *not yet my time to join Him.*

My skull, it was said, had been *fractured* in a thin crack along the crown. Injuries to the vertebrae of my lower back, and both arms badly sprained, and my right shoulder dislocated, and broken ribs, and overall *trauma* as they called it. And many facial lacerations and bruises and the acid-burns. And two black eyes! Yet the pain was a floating sensation, that I could climb upon as you could climb upon an air mattress in a swimming pool; and if I maintained diligence I did not sink into the pain, and did not feel the worst of the pain, that seemed to be happening in a distant place inside my own body, like an ugly noise that is heard in a distant room, throbbing and pulsing. Though afterward it would be evident to me that this sensation was the consequence of morphine being made to drip into my vein, and was not good for me, and so as soon as I could make my wishes known to the medical staff I told them *No more morphine!*

In St. Paul Missionary Church we do not believe in drugs (except prescription, when unavoidable), marijuana, alcoholic beverages, tobacco. We believe that at all moments of your life your soul is in communication with Jesus and that this communication must not be defiled, as you would not defile a newly washed window.

And later they would tell me, what sorrow it is, your poor darling little girl was taken from you. And Edna

Mae had to be kept from me in the hospital, for she wept and sobbed so badly. But I did not recall that any child of mine had been in the vehicle with me. I was sure that this was so.

When I could speak calmly I said *No. She was not with me. There was no one with me.*

And they said, *Luther, she was! Your daughter Daphne was with you, in the baby-seat in the back, for you were bringing her home from her grandmother's, and she has died of her injuries in the crash.*

(Was it the baby of whom they spoke? My little girl who was but three years old? But I was certain, no child of mine had been anywhere near the crash.)

Later it would be revealed, the identities of the others who had suffered in the crash, of whom two had died; and yet the identity of the driver who had fled the scene, who had not been apprehended, having committed *vehicular manslaughter*, would not be ever known.

How many times I protested—*I did not bring Daphne with me! I did not.*

God has seen fit to punish my wickedness in many ways but not in that way for the child was innocent, and God would protect her.

When I returned home from the hospital it was some time before I could walk without assistance, and then without a cane. And it was a long time before I could return to work, and then with much slowness and caution (of pain, in my lower back in particular). But with the help of God, I did return. *I did not once complain, for I was grateful of my life; and I understood that, when my life is taken from me, by God, it will be a time not of sorrow but of rejoicing.*

It happened that, my dear wife would not speak of Daphne as the others did. Edna Mae did not try to convince me that our three-year-old daughter had been in the vehicle with me for Edna Mae would not speak of the little girl at all. And others in the family told me, there was no need to think of it.

It is over now. God has taken her to His side, she is with the angels now.

After some time, it was possible for Edna Mae to embrace me, and for me to embrace Edna Mae, and not to speak of our loss. It seemed clear that Edna Mae forgave me, for my error in taking the vehicle out onto the highway at that time, in the falling snow where visibility was poor, and a fine film of ice was forming on the pavement.

The fury in my heart at the driver of the pickup truck, that may have displeased God, I did not mention to Edna Mae, or to anyone.

I do not think that my vehicle was speeding at the time of the crash. There was never any accusation of that. Nor that I had failed to respond quickly enough, to jam my foot against the brake pedal, and to turn the steering wheel to avoid the crash though turning the wheel was to no avail, it seemed.

Though it is true, my thoughts were distracting to me. Like gnats in a cloud about my head such thoughts made me vexed and impatient and filled my heart with belligerence, that the sight of the pickup failing to stop for the stop sign and instead venturing out onto the highway did not make me fearful (as it should have) but of a mind to punish.

No! I will not slow down for you.

God damn you.

A jubilance of rage filled my heart like the cry of a trumpet—but almost at once, my foot was on the brake. Except too late.

Though it would be told to us, who'd survived the crash, that there was nothing we could have done to save ourselves.

Whatever happened to our Daphne, she was gone from our lives. For as long as I was injured, I understood that this was my punishment for what had happened, though it would be told to me that it was not my fault. Skull fracture, brain swelling—dislocated shoulder, lower back—though I did not take "painkillers" (as they are called) yet my memory was poor, and for a long time my eyesight was splotched as when you have gazed too directly into the sun. If you said to me "Luther, we are going out at noon," ten minutes later I could not remember that you had said anything at all; and at work, once I was able to return, Ed Fischer had to instruct me carefully what to do more than once.

Sometimes I would remember that something important had been told to me, but I would not remember what it was. And other times I would not remember that something had been told to me at all.

You are not to blame. *Jesus has taken her to dwell with him.*

This was explained to me by our pastor, as by others in our church who prayed for my recovery and also the recovery of Edna Mae who seemed to fall ill, even as I grew stronger.

It was a discipline of mine, when I was at home, and later when I was returned to work, to study the accident from every angle. Plainly I could see that *there was no three-year-old in the vehicle, in the child's seat in the rear.*

How many times in my lifetime as a father have I buckled a small child into the rear seat, sometimes children into two child-seats beside each other, and I did not do this, I am sure, on that day. What had flashed through my mind in the crash was the thought—*If I die, at least no one else will die with me.*

Somewhere behind my eyes I would see it begin. A sick sensation in my gut for there was no way to stop it. The pickup truck on County Line Road—hardly slowing at the stop sign—pushing out into the right lane about two hundred feet ahead—(the driver, invisible to me, making a quick decision that he can accelerate fast enough to avoid being struck by the first vehicle speeding toward him)—(yes it is a chance a driver might take—it is a chance I had probably taken in my own lifetime more than once, but never when anyone was in the vehicle with me)—for there is the expectation that, though you don't have the right-of-way, you can rely upon traffic to (probably) slow down for you.

And so, the driver in front of me braked his vehicle, before I could begin to brake mine. So my vehicle slammed into the rear of his, amid the sound of brakes shrieking—and then, the crash like an avalanche that seemed to go on, and *on.*

You are shaken like a rag doll. You are lost to yourself.

Once a crash has happened, it cannot be undone. But before the crash happens, there is a strange sensation almost of *slowness* when (you think) you have enough time to make a decision, you believe you have time, turning your wheel in another direction (for instance) that will avoid the collision, or begin braking sooner, or later—and the crash might be averted, or would happen differently.

In slow motion I would see the accident. Waking from sleep I would realize, I was seeing the accident. Speaking with another person I would see the accident. As in a film in which everything is clear at first, and then begins to break up, and to melt. And I would hear the brakes, that were the brakes of my own vehicle, and I would hear the sickening sound of skidding, swerving, crashing. And I would hear the screams. *I did not hear a child cry.*

My vehicle (which was a 1993 Dodge sedan I had taken for inspection only a few weeks before, and which was deemed in good condition despite ninety thousand miles on the odometer) struck and recoiled from the vehicle in front of me, and was thrown against the median guardrail. After the stunned first moments of the crash I could feel the air quiver, I could feel vibrations in the air like vibrations in water, there was a shuddering of metal, and smashed glass in shapes like frost, the dented squeezed-together hood that looked as if a giant had lowered his foot upon it, and his weight.

There was a hissing as of steam. And the shouts, calls for help.

The crash was one of the *turns* of my life, I would realize later. At the time I was not able to comprehend its meaning. For a long time afterward my head often pounded with pain, and my neck, and back—my legs, knees—even my feet—which was distracting for I am not a man who cares to show pain to others, or any kind of distress to signify self-pity. And so I could not work out if the accident had been the fault of Luther Dunphy in a way no one (else) would know; or whether the accident had been just partly my fault; or whether it was entirely the fault of the driver of the pickup, and my involvement in it like the others' involvement was *accidental*.

Yet, I understood that my relationship with God was almost certainly closer than the relationship of anyone else involved in the crash with God, and my relationship with Jesus.

Our minister all but told me this, in counseling me after the crash. There are Christians whose ties to God are more intimate, and of whom God expects more than He expects of other Christians, that is just a fact—Scripture is filled with such individuals. Our minister has said, as in Biblical times, so it would be now.

Many times I tried to appeal to God, but God only granted me to know that it was all that I could ask, to be allowed to live after my injuries.

In the ER in Springfield, I had (possibly) died. I believe that my heart had been "restarted." The cardiologist had told me something like this. I did not want to know details but I understood that the prayers of my family had persuaded God to have mercy on me.

Yet it seemed wrong to me, and a bitter thing—(I mean, in secret; I would not have defied God)—that God had taken my little girl's life, and not mine. For when I returned home, Daphne was not there any longer.

Though my darling little girl had not died in the crash, she had passed away at this time, and was now *gone.*

Many times I imagined how, if God had given me a chance, I would have said unhesitating to Him, "Take my life, and spare hers"—and I would have laughed in saying so, a bright flame lighting up my face, and my voice loud in jubilance as (a long time ago) it had sometimes been, when I had been drinking in my days of ignorant and blind bachelorhood.

That poor child! *She was a little Down's child, they are called—Daphne. The sweetest girl, we loved her so much.*

Edna Mae and Luther loved her, and all of the family—her brothers and sisters including even that

*mouthy girl with the weasel face what's-her-name—
Dawn. Her grandmother Marlene Dunphy (who lives
next-door to us) was always begging Edna Mae to let
Daphne visit with her because Daphne was so happy
all the time, you could see her little round face light
up at just the sight of you and she'd make these excited little giggles and wave her hands. She liked to be
held, and hugged, and kissed—she liked to cuddle and
never shrank away like another child would do, who
gets restless being hugged too tight and if it goes on a
little too long.*

*There was something wrong with Daphne's mouth.
They said her mouth was wrongly shaped, too narrow
for her tongue. And sometimes, you would see her
tongue like a dog's tongue panting. But you got used
to it. You couldn't always make sense of what she
was saying because of this oversized tongue and also
her voice was high-pitched like a chattering bird but
usually you could guess it was something like I love
Grandma—she'd been taught to say.*

*It's as people say, the Down's babies are special to
God. Daphne was not the only one of these in Muskegee Falls. And there are the "retarded"—"mildly retarded." They are certainly special compared to other
children—so-called normal.*

There has never been a "brattish" Down's child. On

some online Down's site Marlene Dunphy showed me, this was stated as a fact of medical history.

Marlene had some online connection with parents and grandparents of Down's children, she spent time on. But Edna Mae and Luther had no interest in this. You could not even raise the subject to them, Edna Mae would be upset and Luther would be furious.

The Dunphys' little girl Daphne was the youngest of the children and the last baby (it was supposed) Edna Mae would have. What Edna Mae herself thought no one actually knew. Before she was married she'd been trained as a nurse or maybe a nurse's aide and used to talk of returning to work when the children were older not just because they needed the money—(it was pretty obvious they needed the money, all those children and the way the house needed fixing up, the old battered car Luther had to drive, and somebody always sick)—but because she liked to work, loved to work in a hospital or nursing home setting (she said), because helping people made her happy, it was why we are on earth (she said). Definitely Edna Mae Dunphy was happiest with a small baby in the house. Nursing a baby at the breast, that made her happy. Taking care of a sick child, that made her happy. There are women like that—I am not one of them, but I know two or three of them—(right in my family)—this is a state of mind pathetic because eventually the babies will grow up, and there's a time when they don't want you even to look at them let alone touch and hug them, and you will be yearning for these big hulking kids to be small again and there is nothing to take their place.

Except, a Down's child will not grow up. A Down's child will not ever push you away or sneer at you. Or move out of the house.

Daphne was so special because she was happy-seeming all the time. Even when (it was revealed) she wasn't all that well. She would cough and choke like (possibly) she was allergic to something like pollen or cat hairs and she could be restless, if she had to sit in something that confined her like a stroller. Singing was exciting to her, songs she'd hear on the radio she would sing with the radio voices as if they were actual people in the room with her.

As an infant Daphne had been baptized in the St. Paul Missionary Church. She was taken with the family to services most Sundays and Wednesday evenings and if she got too excitable and chattered too loud Edna Mae would take her outside to wait in the car.

Everybody in the congregation loved little Daphne Dunphy. The minister blessed her, as one of Jesus's own.

They say that Down's children are strange-looking

with those sort of flat, moon faces like a Mongol face but Daphne did not look so much like this she looked more like a doll with pretty painted-on features. Her hair was pale brown and wavy and her eyes were beautiful though small and slanted in her face and just slightly crossed so you could never tell which eye was looking at you. Her grandmother had told us, she'd been born with weak lungs and a weak heart—the Dunphys were considering whether to get heart surgery for her as doctors were suggesting, or to put their trust in the Lord.

This was a surprise to hear. You would think the heart surgery (in Columbus at the medical school) would be very expensive but Luther was saying, a "pediatric cardiologist" would operate on Daphne for no fee or for some fee that a third party would pay but Luther worried that this was some kind of welfare or federal government program he did not believe in. Whether it was his church beliefs, or Luther Dunphy himself, he would become upset over the issue of "federal subsidies" and "welfare"—the "Socialist state" which was a "godless atheistical state."

Daphne was hard of hearing in both ears, but she'd got to the point she could read lips, almost. She would stare at your face as if she was holding her breath. No other children cared so much about any adult! The Dunphys began to worry that something was wrong when Daphne didn't learn to crawl until she was a year old—and finally was able to walk when she was about two, if somebody had hold of her hand. She could not eat food like other children, there was some problem with chewing and swallowing. And there was low thyroid, that had to be corrected with medication (which the Dunphys did not like to give her). You could see that Daphne had "developmental" problems just by the look of her. It was sad when she got old enough to see what other children her age could do, that she could not do; this was frustrating to her, and made her cry. But she was happy just to be with her mother, and didn't need to play with anyone else. She could recognize herself in the mirror unlike a dog or a cat can do, and liked to wave her hands and laugh at herself like a little monkey.

There was nothing unusual about the Dunphy family. A normal family (more or less) until Daphne was born. And even that—some kind of learning disability, or handicap, isn't so unusual in a family. Luther Dunphy worked for Fischer Construction, roofing and carpentry. He and Edna Mae belonged to that evangelical church on Cross Creek Road where Luther had done a lot of the carpentry and roof work and painting and was always donating his time doing repairs. Even after he'd had that terrible accident and almost died, and was in the hospital for six weeks, soon as he got back to work he was over at the church, helping out. There were two boys and two girls older than Daphne. The older boy Luke was a worrier, his grandma said, like Luther, but a good reliable boy like his dad. The older girl Dawn had some trouble in school getting along with the other children but the younger girl was a pretty little girl quiet and well liked.

Edna Mae's sister Noreen was telling us how Edna Mae had had some bleeding in the pregnancy, which was her sixth or seventh pregnancy because she'd had a miscarriage or two over the years. And people were saying Luther should be protective of his wife, and not make her pregnant all the time. Her own family was saying Edna Mae was too old, and should have known better. But how is it the woman's fault! It is more the man's fault. And if you looked at Luther Dunphy, and at Edna Mae, you'd see right away whose fault it was— had to be Luther, pushing himself on the woman like some big rutting stallion. You'd see sometimes, a look in Luther's face, in his eyes, like a struck match hurriedly shook out—just the remains of it. For sure, Luther had strong feelings no matter how he hid them.

And Edna Mae always giving in to anyone, that smile like a rubber band stretched tight to bursting. Her hair was falling out, you could see the scalp beneath, and around her left thumbnail scabs where she'd bitten it. That kind of good Christian woman who wouldn't lift a hand to protect herself, if somebody came at her with a baseball bat. If she was drowning.

The doctor in Muskegee Falls had sent Edna Mae to have prenatal screening at the hospital in Springfield, because she'd been having pains and bleeding, and she hadn't wanted to go, she was afraid of the hospital "doing something" to her when she was being examined. It was very hard for Edna Mae to consent to a pelvic exam, even when it was explained carefully to her and there was a nurse right beside her. And Luther didn't trust any hospital, either. About all they trusted was their church—not just any Christian church but only their own church. (Which taught their followers to be suspicious of other Christian churches.) But Edna Mae finally went to have the test when she was four months pregnant, am-ny-o-syn-tho-sis, and so they were informed that the baby would be born with deficits as it is called, including respiratory and neurological, and cardiac—they can see all that in an X-ray these days, in the mother's womb. Of course, they can see if it's a boy or a girl—but they won't tell you if you don't want to know. (The Dunphys did not want to know.) And so, the doctor told Edna Mae and Luther there's a strong probability of Down's syndrome and explained what it was. He told Edna Mae and Luther to think hard whether they would like the pregnancy "terminated"—which he could do at the hospital, as a regular surgical procedure.

Of course, both Edna Mae and Luther were very upset about this. They left the hospital right away, and drove home.

Edna Mae flat-out did not believe this diagnosis. She refused to discuss any "termination" with any doctor. The baby was alive to her, she could feel the baby alive inside her! She said that Jesus would take care of her and her baby, she had had only healthy babies in the past and Jesus would look after her now. They would all pray for a healthy baby. Luther was even more emphatic than Edna Mae, he did not say much to anyone but definitely, he would never agree to "termination" which was what they did in Nazi and Communist countries—like "sterilization." They would all pray specially hard for a healthy baby and that would be enough.

(Some of us are not so sure what we believe. In our church which is not evangelical like the Dunphys' church there are no hard-fast beliefs. In fact it is not a good idea to talk about such things, like politics, the ones that revere the President and the ones that hate him, or how people feel about the Gulf War, or any war. Luther Dunphy was not one to speak much still less to argue. The deeper a man's feelings are, the quieter he is. Which can be deceiving, as Luther's actions have proven. You could see the stubbornness in the man's face for as long as we have known him. The set of his jaw like the set of a horse's jaw when the horse has made its mind up and nothing can change it.)

Some folks I know argue that if God sends you a child, God is sending you that child with the understanding that you can bear it. God is not going to send you a child you can't love, or take care of as required—I believe this. At the same time there are Christians who would "terminate" a pregnancy like Edna Mae's as it was prescribed and would be performed in a hospital and not at an abortion clinic.

It is not anything to be ashamed of. That is my opinion. Edna Mae and Luther felt differently of course. To them, it would be like murder. But I think if the mother is married, and there is a father—and the doctor suggests it—it is nothing like abortion which is plain murder and should be outlawed.

So, they returned home, and never went back to Springfield. And Edna Mae took care of herself by trying not to work too hard and brought the baby to full term. They did a lot of praying, all of the family. And at the church people prayed for them. And the *baby was born on schedule, and did not appear to be so badly afflicted. By the time I was invited to see Daphne at Marlene's house, she was a few weeks old and not so strange-looking though very small and wrinkled with a round face and small slanted eyes and her funny cute little tongue poking out. She was noted to be very sweet and observant, for an infant. And when she cried, she did not sound angry so you wanted to press your hands over your ears and run out of the room.*

After a while like a year or so people began to say that the Dunphys' new baby was "not right"—and it was said by some, this was a retarded baby or a Down's baby. But there were many beautiful things about Daphne you could see instead, if you took time. And you could see why Edna Mae was always holding her, and fussing over her.

When we heard that this little angel had been killed in the car crash out on the highway we all just burst into tears. It was such a shock! Three years old, and she hadn't even seemed that old. It was so sad. Because you would think, the poor little girl had not ever had an actual life, and now the life that had been granted to her had been taken from her.

The ways of God are mysterious, that is a fact. That cannot be stressed too strongly.

And you would feel so sorry for Edna Mae, who had loved the little girl so much. And for Luther, who had loved her too, and had been driving the car.

That, Luther Dunphy would never get over. That he'd been driving that car.

Sin

At age twelve, and for years to come, I dwelt in filth and shame.

All of my friends were like myself. All the boys I knew. It is vile even to recall. Especially, my mother shrank from me. She would see the sheets on my bed, and my underwear, that was filth-stained. But if I tried to wash these myself she would know this, too.

It was awkward between us, when we were alone together in a room. There was not much to say, I did not blame my mother for detesting me, as I would not blame anyone. Yet sometimes, in eating with the family and in clearing the table afterward, I would intentionally drop a fork, a plate, a glass, that my mother would react, if only in surprise; and my brothers would laugh at me, for they sided with one another, against me as the youngest; and my father would command me to clean up the mess I'd made which I would do, sulky and silent.

Women saw me staring at them, at their breasts, bellies and legs. My face went slack, my eyes felt hooded like a snake's eyes, yet helpless to look away. And between my legs, my "thing" like a snake, that moved of its own volition and grew hard, and could not be stopped. At school, the teachers were all women, in eighth grade. In all my classes I was positioned at the back of the room with other boys whom the teachers did not like or perhaps feared. The back of my desk could be made to press against the wall to grate away the paint and leave a mark. With my knees I could lift my desk and let it fall, to make a noise. The startled look in the teacher's face meant that she would like to chide me, and send me from the room, but did not dare.

In Upper Sandusky Middle School Felice Sipper was coarsely talked-of. In a higher grade was Beverly Sipper, who would have to drop out of school in tenth grade because she was pregnant, and in a lower grade, in the elementary school Irene Sipper and her brother with the shaved head (shaved to prevent lice) Ronald Sipper. It was said of the Sippers who lived in a trailer by the railroad yard that they were *poor white trash*.

In eighth grade crude, cruel things were said of

Felice Sipper. Even the nice girls scorned her, and all the boys. Her name was scrawled on walls. On a concrete overpass in red spray paint was scrawled FELICE SIPER SUCKS COCK.

Boys who were my friends had scrawled these things. From an empty classroom I had taken chalk-stubs, we could use for brick walls though the chalked words washed off in the rain. There were others whose names were scrawled in public derision, both girls and boys, but it was Felice Sipper who drew the most excited attention. Our teachers would not look at her, for the sight of the pimply-faced girl in her cheap nylon sweaters and oversized skirts, that skidded about her thin waist so that the side-zipper was not in its proper place, was offensive to their eyes.

I felt sorry for Felice Sipper. I tried to rub away some of the nasty words with my wetted fist, if no one was observing.

I saw the hurt and weakness in the girl's face, as she stood at her locker in the eighth grade corridor trying to ignore stares and whispers, and a lust came over me like a lust to kill.

Alone, I would follow Felice Sipper after school. She saw me, and looked frightened. If she started to run, I would not run after her. I would whistle loudly, and laugh to myself. I would turn in another direction but I would not hurry, for I did not want Felice to think that I had been following her, and was now not-following her.

Felice had entered the dripping underpass at Union Street. I had waited until some older girls ascended the steps and were gone and then I entered, from the other side. Felice was walking slowly with eyes downcast as if she was not aware of me even as I stood before her.

"You are a dirty girl. You will go to hell when you die."

Felice tried to move past me. I blocked her way.

Felice was much smaller than I was. Her head barely came to my shoulder. Her hair was matted and odd-colored like straw. She had a sallow blemished dark-toned skin, she was not "white" like the rest of us. Yet her hair was not Negro hair and her lips were not Negro lips.

When she tried to turn, to run from me, I grabbed her arm that was skinny as a stick.

"Don't you care, you're a dirty slut who will go to hell?"

"Leave me alone! *You're* a dirty slut—*you can go to hell.*"

It was shocking to me, and thrilling, Felice Sipper's eyes flashed at me in sudden hatred and defiance as a cornered animal's might flash, in the instant before it sinks its teeth into your throat.

When I saw this, I relented and let her go. It was rare—it had never happened—that a smaller child, girl or boy, had confronted me in this way, or any friend of mine. For we never approached anyone who was of our sizes, or our ages, who might so defy us.

And Felice ran, and in running called back over her shoulder what sounded like, "Fuck you, asshole! I hate you—hope you *die*."

Felice's voice was high-pitched like a bird's shriek. Her words were so surprising to me, I did not follow after her but watched her run away where I stood in the dripping smelly underpass.

I did not tell my friends about this encounter. I did not tell anyone and yet it seemed to be known, Luther Dunphy had a claim of some kind on Felice Sipper, other boys dared not interfere.

By the store at the depot I would see her, and if she was alone I would approach her. Of the girls Felice had a way of standing like a doe about to leap and run, one of her feet at an angle, toeing the pavement.

And I would stand a few feet away, as if not altogether aware of her. Or, I might go into the store and buy a bottle of Coke and return, and there was Felice

Sipper sneering in my direction, wiping her nose on the edge of her hand. "*You!* What the hell do *you* want."

If I held out the Coke for Felice to drink, Felice would shake her head *No!* with a look of contempt but if I offered another time or two, she might relent, and take the bottle from me, and drink from the bottle where my mouth had been, and seeing this—that Felice Sipper was putting her mouth to the very place where I had put my mouth—made me dizzy with excitement.

"What d'you say, F'lice?"—I would say; and Felice would say, curling her lip, "Thank you." And I would say, "'Thank you, what" (meaning that Felice should say *Thank you Luther*), but Felice would say, sneering, "Thank you, asshole."

Out back of the depot, in a part of the railroad yard where old freight cars were kept rusting amid tall grasses, Felice Sipper would allow the older boys to touch her, and to do things to her. They shared cigarettes, beer. They might give Felice loose change, taken from their mothers' wallets. It was different for me, that I was never with other boys, but always alone, for there was the special understanding between Felice Sipper and me.

Sometimes, Felice did not want to do the things I wanted to do, but she could not say *No!* for fear of angering me. Her reaction of disgust was a high laughing shriek like a bird that has been outraged but unlike a bird, she did not take flight. She did not ever scream or fight, that I could recall.

Sometimes I "disciplined" her, as my parents used to "discipline" me when I was younger—my mother with the flat of her bare hand, my father with his belt looped and coiled like a snake. This would make the sensation stronger. I was excited by her tears, her running nose and smeared mouth. My hand on the nape of Felice's neck shoved her head down, like a dog's head down, in obedience to her master.

There was a sharp taste to Felice Sipper, like salt. I liked it that her fingernails were edged with dirt like my own, though they were smaller fingernails, and her hands were small with bones light as a sparrow's that I could have crushed in my hand at any time, but did not, and Felice would know this, and (I thought) would like me for this. Her older sister Beverly would paint Felice's nails, bright red, dark purple, which was exciting to me, even when the polish began to chip. There was a dark green plastic-looking cross Felice wore sometimes, she said was "jade," and had belonged to her grandmother, but Felice and her family did not go to church, she said nobody in the family believed in God except if things went wrong it was *God's will.*

I asked Felice weren't they afraid, not to go to

church, maybe God would be angry with them and punish them, and Felice said shrugging her shoulders that that had already happened.

Once, it would be the last time, though I did not know this at the time, we were in one of the old freight cars, where I knelt on dried leaves and debris, and Felice Sipper cursed me kicking at me with her bare legs. The flash of her bare, white belly was exciting to me, and the thin fuzz between her legs. When I was finished I could not move but lay panting on my back amid the leaves and litter stunned as if an electric current had run through me leaving me paralyzed.

It was not clear to me why, why at that time, and not at another, earlier time, that Felice Sipper became disgusted and angry with me, and after she was dressed again, and her face wiped and her eyes glaring, out of some pocket she took a jackknife, I saw just the flash of the blade in her hands before it sank into my leg at the thigh, and the pain of it was such that I could not comprehend what was happening, and was scrambling to escape when the blade came again, this time in my side, between my ribs, and Felice was crying at me what sounded like *Hate hate hate you pig* and then she was gone, jumped out of the freight car and ran away.

From four stab-wounds I was bleeding. The pain

was like a loud, deafening noise, I could not comprehend it but tried to sit up whimpering, staunching the blood flow. The wounds had come swift but shallow, and had not severed any vein or artery (so it seemed). I was panting hard. My hands were shaking. It took some time to soak up the blood. By pressing against the wounds, I could stop the worst of the bleeding.

When I crawled out of the freight car it was dusk. I would be late for supper and would enter the house by the rear, in a way to avoid my family in the kitchen, and upstairs in the bathroom I would wash the wounds, and try to put bandages over them, and hide away the bloodied clothing where I could throw it out at another time. When I came downstairs my mother said, "Luther! Are you ill?—your face is so white." My father saw that I was ill, and did not chastise me. My brothers Norman and Jonathan would have laughed but saw that something had happened to me. While trying to eat I felt a wave of nausea and dizziness come over me, and became very light-headed and would have fallen onto the floor if one of my brothers had not caught me.

My mother believed that I had the flu. Often in Sandusky when you did not feel well, when you felt sick-to-death and wanted to die, it would be said *You have a touch of the flu.*

I did not hate Felice Sipper but was eager to see her

again. Yet I would not ever see her again for the news was, the Sippers had had to move away from Sandusky, their relatives in the tar paper house had evicted them. And only much later, I would realize that the stab of Felice Sipper's blade into my (sinful) flesh had been a warning of Jesus, that I had gone too far, and if I did not desist, a worse punishment would follow.

There were boys we chased, and knocked to the ground, and kicked, and rubbed their faces in the dirt. A boy (from the special class at school) we chased along the creek, into a patch of mud, pulled down his pants, rubbed mud and little stones and grit onto his groin, his penis, until he screamed and wept for us to stop.

Another time, after a boy had reported one of my friends to the school principal for stealing out of lockers we chased him into the railroad yard and "hog-tied" him—wrists tied behind his back and his ankles tied and connected to his wrists and a noose looped around his neck so if he tried to free himself he'd be strangled.

Didn't we care that he might die, somebody might ask.

After we left, and the guys went home, I doubled back to the railroad yard to untie Albert Metzer and remove the filthy rag we'd stuffed in his mouth. I said for him not to tell anybody or he would be killed and Albert could scarcely speak, but whispered *Yes*.

So grateful for me saving him, he almost kissed my hands.

But then the next evening police officers came to my house, and were met by my father, who called me downstairs, and they asked me questions about Albert Metzer and I said no, I didn't know anything about it, whatever had been done to him, I had no idea. But I was stammering so they could hardly understand me and it was obvious that I was lying.

Still, the police went away. Out by their patrol car my father stood talking with them and whatever he said to them, or they said to him, they did not arrest me but drove away.

In the doorway of the room I shared with Jonathan my father stood regarding me with eyes of disgust. He asked me what I knew about the boy who'd been "almost strangled" and "had had to be taken to a hospital" and I repeated that I didn't know anything, I had had nothing to do with it.

I was stammering so badly now, tears started from my eyes.

My father was holding something in his hand, at about the level of his thigh. I did not want to look at it too closely but it appeared to be of the size of a hammer, and wrapped in a towel or cloth. When I tried to slip past my father, to run down the stairs, he struck me with this object, on my back, on my buttocks, and as I fell, on the side of my head. I fell heavily, and a thought comforted me—*Now it is over. I can die.*

In the place where I had fallen Jesus awaited me. I saw that Jesus was displeased with me but he would not speak harshly to me, as my father did, to reprimand me.

My father did not ever explain to my mother (who heard us from downstairs) why he had "disciplined" me in this way and why for a long time afterward he would not look at me, and did not wish that I would enter any room in which he was; why I had to eat my meals alone in the kitchen after the rest of the family had finished. It was not the behavior against Albert Metzer that infuriated him so much as the fact that I would try to lie to *him.*

Even when I accompanied my father to work, and worked beside him at a construction site, he did not speak to me except when necessary. Though he was a Christian my father did not easily forgive, and he did not easily forget. Eventually his fury and disgust at me diminished with time like a slow wearing-out in the way that a new-polished linoleum floor loses its shine and becomes dull with grime and you cease to notice it.

I was sick to think that my father did not love me—

now. He had loved me (maybe) as a father would love his son but now, since I had disappointed him, and had no way to stammer an apology nor even an explanation or excuse, for having dared to lie to him, he could not look upon me with love or even patience. And once I had seen in my mother's face, when by accident I turned clumsily in the kitchen, in a small space, and came near to colliding with her, a look of fright—*She thinks that I would hit her. She thinks that I am an animal.*

One by one my older brothers had disappointed my father, in their own ways. But they would mature, and move away from home, and marry, and have children; and he would look upon them as men like himself, and forgive them. Or rather, he would forget his anger at them, when they were ignorant boys and lived in the house with them, taking up so much room; and so in that way he would forgive them, also.

It was at that time that I came to realize how Jesus *does not reprimand us.* The way of the world is to accuse and punish but it is Jesus within us that will speak to us when the time is ripe, in our own voices. For of course we know all there is to know of the teachings of Jesus. *For God sent not his Son into the world to condemn the world; but that the world through him might be saved.*

These things we know, that Jesus has died *for us.*

Though in the blindness and fever of rutting sin we are ignorant of it, and pretend not to know.

Still, with girls I continued to behave badly. If a girl was aloof to me I hated her as *stuck-up* and if she was friendly to me I hated her as *sluttish.* I am ashamed to say, when I first met Edna Mae Reiser, it was sexthoughts that came to me in a rush and not a wish to "love." Though I understood this girl to be a good, Christian girl, and respected her. It was impressive to me too, that Edna Mae was training as a nurse's aide and worked part-time at a nursing home in Muskegee Falls.

After we first met, we did not meet again for some months. For I was seeing another girl then. I would see adult women, one of them a divorcée with small children.

By then I had dropped out of high school. My grades were C's and D's except in vocational arts (shop) where my grades were B's and where our teacher Mr. Bidenmann often asked me to help out the other students who were unskilled and clumsy using their hands.

When I met Edna Mae Reiser another time I was not so shy. Though I knew that Edna Mae was a virgin, and very innocent of men, yet I coerced her into certain acts against her wishes, and made her cry. I felt sorry for her but also impatient with her, for it was a dirty thing I had made her do, touching me with her bare hand, and letting me touch her. And other things that passed between us, that I made Edna Mae comply with, that would have provoked Felice Sipper to stab me in the gut. And then later, it was around Christmas-time, when we were alone together in her parents' house that smelled of fresh-cut evergreens, I saw a look in Edna Mae's face that was stiff and pleading and I heard myself say, You have shamed yourself. I don't want to see you again.

It was for the thrill of saying such words that I said them. I had not ever said such words before in my life but now I went away disgusted, or pretending to be disgusted. I did not call Edna Mae for twelve days but returned to seeing another, older girl from high school who did not expect so much of me. In the parking lot of the nursing home I waited in my car to observe Edna Mae walking into the rear of the building, in her white nurse's aide uniform, and with thin white stockings and white crepe-soled shoes, sometimes with other girls in white uniforms, and sometimes alone.

In my thoughts I loved her, if she would love me. Yet the sex-act had come between us. Though I had forced this act upon Edna Mae, yet it seemed to me that she had behaved weakly in not stopping me. I disliked her for this weakness in giving in to me. Like a rutting hog I could not stop myself. The slime of my semen on the girl's thighs was so vivid to me that if I recalled it later, I was excited at once, and my penis hard as a rod.

The sex-heat was everywhere in me. My blood beat hard and fast from my groin up into my belly and chest. My tongue felt engorged in my mouth, like a penis. My body had become a great Thing, engorged and upright, barely able to stagger. If I did not seize and stroke myself, I could not endure it. And yet if I gave in, I was overcome with disgust. I had not attended Bible school for years and did not regularly attend church but recalled Jesus's words *If thine eye offend thee pluck it out and cast it from thee; it is better for thee to enter into life with one eye, rather than having two eyes to be cast into hell fire.*

In the old barn behind our house in Sandusky at my father's workbench (which my brothers and I were forbidden to touch) there came to be a screwdriver in my shaking hand. It was one of the larger screwdrivers in my father's toolbox. For a long shaking moment gripping the tool in both hands bringing its (dull) point slowly to my face thinking *Pluck it out! Pluck it out, pig!*—but in the end, I had not the courage.

Yet Jesus did not judge me. This was a great relief to me at the time and would prepare me for later in my life, when Jesus would come into my heart of His choice to save *me*.

My friends (who had also quit school to work during the day) and I went drinking until we were sick to our stomachs. We pissed, and we vomited. We were happy only in the company of one another for we did not judge one another (as our families judged us) and yet, when we were not drinking we shrank from the sight of one another. Often we fought. We had no idea why, we hated each other like brothers who have had to share a room and a smelly bed for too long. In a filthy lavatory in a tavern on Overhill Road when I entered I saw one of them at a urinal, his face was flushed and coarse, there was a red pimple or pustule on his cheek that drew my eye, and a drunken rage came over me, and I seized him around the neck and tried to throw him down, I beat him with my fists and kicked him where he had fallen, I shoved him so that he struck his head on the urinal, and I did not help him up but hurriedly left the tavern; and had only the mildest worry that my friend might die of a skull fracture or a broken neck.

My knuckles were swollen and bleeding from the attack. Even my feet ached, where I had kicked the unresisting body. There were lacerations in my face, there was a shortness to my breath, the old wound between my ribs ached where Felice Sipper had sank the three-inch jackknife blade.

I did not see my friends for weeks. I had no news of my friend who'd been beaten and his skull cracked against the urinal but I did not think he had died or was hospitalized for there was nothing about this in the newspaper or on local TV. I made calls to Edna Mae Reiser who did not return them. But I persevered, and left messages with her mother and came to know Mrs. Reiser, through these conversations; and felt that Mrs. Reiser, who did not know Luther Dunphy, yet liked me. Then, at another time, I saw my friends again, as one of them had enlisted in the U.S. Army and would be leaving soon for boot camp, at this exciting time (for it was made to seem exciting on TV) when the Soviet army had invaded a remote Asian country called Afghanistan, in defiance of U.S. warnings, and there was a promise of a new war now between the United States and Soviet Russia; and the subject of the beating in the men's lavatory came up, and my friends were embarrassed looking at me. *Luther, you never found out who did that to you? Never saw his face? Fucker should be killed.*

When I was baptized for the second time, at age twenty-two, by the pastor of the St. Paul Missionary

Church, Jesus rejoiced in my heart. Jesus did not need to say—*I knew that you would come to me, Luther. All those years I was waiting, I knew.*

Very quickly it had happened. Edna Mae had brought me with her to a new church, in Muskegee Falls, about which her friends had told her. At once stepping into this church (that was not fully finished and smelled of new lumber) I felt a turmoil in my soul as if I had come home, and would be recognized here.

The pastor was much younger than our pastor in the Sandusky church, who had never seemed to like me, and had always confused me with my brothers. This pastor greeted me with a smile and welcomed me as a friend. He was my height, and my approximate weight, but with wavy sand-colored hair, and pale gray eyes of unusual frankness and warmth. He might have been thirty-five years old. Warmly he asked me to call him "Dennis"—not "Reverend Dennis." As soon as Reverend Dennis mentioned the work needing to be done on the church, insulation and shingle-laying, I told him that I would like to help him; and when he said, he was not sure that the church could afford a professional roofer, I told him I did not expect to be paid, it was for the sake of the church and for the sake of Jesus.

These words came from me without preparation. At once I felt my heart suffused with joy, and the look in Edna Mae's face was one of astonishment and adoration.

When we were alone together Edna Mae wept with me, in sheer happiness. She said how she loved me, and had forgiven me the hurt I had done her, and would not give it another thought. By then, without either of us knowing, she was six weeks pregnant with our first son, Luke.

Soon then, within a few weeks, both Edna Mae and I were baptized in the St. Paul Missionary Church of Jesus. And soon after that, we were married.

The Calling

You must follow your heart, Luther. If you are absolutely certain that this is what you want."

It was a curious mannerism of our pastor that, when he smiled, his face seemed to contract for just an instant, as if in pain; and when he laughed, his laughter was silent, and seemed to wrack his body with a kind of pain also.

Stiffly I said, "It is not what I want, Reverend Dennis, but what the Lord has called me to."

"Has He! Well."

I had hoped that Reverend Dennis would clasp my hand in a brotherly gesture as often he did, with Edna Mae and me, and other members of the congregation, in greeting us at the church door, and saying good-bye to us, at the end of services. But he did not seem so friendly now. The childish eagerness I had brought to him was like a warm patch of sunshine with no place to fall upon. It was not like our beloved pastor, to seem so awkward with a fellow Christian who had come to him with a joyous expectation.

I had been excited to reveal to Reverend Dennis the news of my hopes for a career in the church, which I had been discussing with Edna Mae for months, and about which we had prayed together for guidance; but Reverend Dennis did not greet this revelation as I had anticipated. Instead, after I spoke for some minutes, telling him of my plan to become a minister in the Missionary Church, like him, as I was inspired by his sermons and by his example, Reverend Dennis deflected the subject by asking me about my family, and my work, and where we were living in Muskegee Falls, in a voice that did not indicate enthusiasm but with only a common sort of friendly inquiry, as if he had hardly been listening to my words at all.

For some perplexing minutes Reverend Dennis even inquired after my parents, who lived in Sandusky, whom he had met only once, at my wedding three years before.

It was hard for me to reply. I could not think of the right words. My parents were not happy with me, for converting to the St. Paul Missionary Church, though my mother was eager to see her grandchildren, and deeply hurt, that Edna Mae and I did not seem to have time to visit Sandusky as my mother wished, and that we did not invite them to visit us often. (This was not Edna Mae's wish of course. For Edna Mae declared that she "loved" my parents—all of my family. But I did not care to visit with my father, as my father did not care to visit with us. In this way, there was a stalemate as it is called, I think—for neither my father nor I would give in. As I was a husband and a father now, embarked upon my own life, *I did not intend to give in to the old man.*)

"You might begin with missionary work, Luther. You don't need to be an ordained minister to 'minister' to our brethren in Africa."

Missionary! I had not expected this.

Reverend Dennis went on to tell me, much of what I already knew from his sermons, that he had been a missionary in West Africa for six years, in his early twenties; he was fond of saying, with one of his quick, pained smiles, that some of the "most joyous" days of his life were spent there, despite many difficulties including illness (malaria, dengue fever).

"The challenges of a Christian in such a place are— well, almost overwhelming! Africans don't seem so impressed with a 'savior' as you would think, considering how they live—how poor, and uneducated. They didn't seem to take Hell seriously—they'd smile, and shake their heads. Heaven was very hard to explain to them as a *spiritual place*. They seemed confused about Jesus, if He was a man or a 'god,' and it was clear that they had no concept of 'immortality.' Half the time I didn't know how much they understood of our teachings, and how much they were just pretending to understand, as children will do. We'd established a little school there, teaching English and arithmetic as well as instruction in the Gospels. We had many converts, or at least it had seemed so . . . as I say, it was difficult to tell how serious they were when they welcomed Jesus into their hearts, and how deep our teachings went. They were very somber sometimes, and then at other times they laughed uproariously—we never knew why! Our mission ended tragically when a civil war broke out and we had to flee. Eventually, half the population was slaughtered by the other half."

Reverend Dennis's lips twitched in a smile. A shiver of mirth passed through his body.

For the first time, as I was seated facing our pastor, I could see his face close up, and marveled at the pale, stony hue of his eyes; and saw a thin, jagged line, seemingly a scar, across his throat, that made me shudder with the thought that it had been inflicted in Africa, by one of his savage "converts." Reverend Dennis did not look so young and handsome as he appeared in the pulpit when his face was transformed with the joy of the Lord.

What did I care about the *African mission!* How could Reverend Dennis who had seemed so friendly to me, like a true brother, and not like my own brothers who were indifferent to me, imagine that I would willingly leave my home, my young family, my work and responsibilities to live with African natives, to convert them to Christianity? Nor did I feel comfortable around Negroes here in the United States, much of the time.

"They are 'children of God,' too, you know, Luther— the Africans."

Reverend Dennis spoke in a slight chiding way, as if reading my mind.

I could not think of a reply. It seemed that Reverend Dennis was staring at my mouth, that began to tremble.

"If you have come to think that you have a 'calling' . . ."

A calling. The word that had seemed sacred to me, and to Edna Mae, was sounding now faintly preposterous. I was reminded of Mrs. S—— whose sly intonations and jarring laughter were so confusing to us in Sunday school.

". . . you are interested, Luther, in enrolling in a

ministry school? When would this be practical for you, d'you think?"

I was trying not to betray my disappointment, that the pastor whom I so admired was speaking to me in so doubtful and discouraging a tone as if he did not seem to think that I had a "calling"—as obviously, he'd had himself at my age. I knew that Reverend Dennis had studied and been ordained at the Toledo School of Ministry, and had hoped that he would recommend me there.

Soon after our marriage Edna Mae and I moved to Muskegee Falls, to be closer to the St. Paul Missionary Church. This was a small town of about the size of Sandusky where there were opportunities for me to find work that did not depend upon the intervention of my father. For I was a proud young husband and father, and did not like to be known as Nathaniel Dunphy's *youngest son*. And if I found work as a roofer or carpenter, I did not like to be working for the same construction company as my father, as I had been doing since the age of fourteen.

In this new place, in a rented clapboard house on Front Street that I had repainted outside and in, I was very happy with my life. There were commonplace worries about supporting my family, and a fear that a child might be taken ill, or that Edna Mae might lapse into melancholy (as she had following the birth of our second child, for several months), but these were of little consequence set beside the certitude that the St. Paul Missionary Church of Jesus was the "true" church, and that I was meant, like Reverend Dennis, to be a minister in this church.

(I had not ever been able to call our pastor "Dennis" as he requested. For I did not feel as if we were [yet] equals.)

From the first sermon of Reverend Dennis which I'd heard, when Edna Mae had first brought me to the church, I had felt such awe and admiration for the young pastor, and such excitement in his presence, it came to seem that God had led me to him for a purpose; as God had led me to Edna Mae Reiser at a time in my life when I was hardly more than a brute creature, undeserving of spiritual happiness.

That had been a time of mortal danger, as well. The beating in the tavern lavatory, that might have ended in a man's death, had made a powerful impression upon me.

God has spared you this time, Luther. But you are warned.

From that time onward I avoided my old friends. I had not invited them to my wedding for (as Edna Mae said) there would be no alcoholic drinks served at the reception, and my friends would not be happy if they could not drink.

After that we did not see one another again; and when the news came to me that our friend who had enlisted in the army had been killed in a helicopter accident while stationed in the Middle East, I felt a stab of horror and pity for him, and fell to my knees to pray for him. But I did not make any effort to contact his family, or our mutual friends.

For that had been my life of *depravity and sin.* My life was very different now. I did not drink more than two or three beers a week, and sometimes none at all. For Edna Mae did not drink, as most members of the St. Paul Missionary Church did not drink even carbonated beverages; and while my dear wife never expressed any evident disapproval of my drinking, I could sense that she felt unease at my behavior, and would keep the children away from me as if she feared I might injure them at such a time.

If I stooped to brush my lips against her cheek, Edna Mae might turn away, just slightly; as, in bed, if there was beer on my breath, Edna Mae would murmur sleepily *Good night!* and turn away from me.

If I were to touch her, to caress her soft, dense body, that had become softer and denser with pregnancies, Edna Mae would lie very still and unresisting; for a wife would never resist a husband, as Edna Mae knew. But she would not turn to me, in bed; she would not slip her arms around my neck in a girlish gesture of love, if there was but a trace of beer on my breath. That I respected my wife prevented me from turning her forcibly to me, which I would never do except if I was drunk, and I was never drunk any longer, at that time in our marriage.

The St. Paul Missionary Church of Jesus teaches the spiritual life which is a life of purity. You do not pollute your being with alcohol, carbonated beverages, cigarettes or any kind of tobacco, chewing gum, refined sugar, sugar substitutes, or foods known to be artificially colored. Gambling of any kind was forbidden including even such card games as gin rummy and the board game *Monopoly*. Church members were advised not to own television sets, to prevent their children from being corrupted. Christian radio stations were recommended. Most movies were not recommended. No form of contraception was recommended except *abstinence.*

(When I had first heard this word, I had not known its meaning! A very strange notion it seemed to me, if a man and a woman had become married, how or why should they practice *abstinence?* Abstaining from intercourse with a wife, with whom you slept in a bed each night, did not seem possible for a man with a man's normal appetites.)

(At this time, I am not sure that I even knew the uglier word *abortion*.)

"And what about finances, Luther? Can you afford to stop working, to become a full-time student?"

"I was hoping there might be a scholarship . . . I was thinking of the Toledo School of Ministry."

Reverend Dennis frowned at this remark. I had hoped that he might smile in recognition. But instead he spoke slowly, not meeting my eye, "Wel-ll, there are not many scholarships at Toledo, I'm afraid. Just a few, and they are usually given to younger men, just out of high school."

I expected Reverend Dennis to say *I was one of these, of course. Just out of high school. Scholarship.*

As I had rehearsed, I said humbly that I had not really planned to be a full-time student. I would not be comfortable with *not-working*, as I had worked, in one way or another, since fourteen.

"Edna Mae and I have calculated that I can continue with my work in Muskegee Falls, about thirty hours a week, which would leave me time to commute to Toledo for my classes on two days, and would bring in enough income for us—for a while. And we have been trying to save, also."

"But, Luther—what a grueling schedule! Most of the students at Toledo will be full-time, and they will live closer to the school. A few will have families, like you, but they probably won't be working and commuting."

"We have worked it out, Edna Mae and me. She is as hopeful that I can become a minister of the St. Paul Missionary Church as I am. And there is Jesus—I feel that He will help me, too." Stubbornly I spoke, and would not give in.

"Well, Luther! I see that you are very serious. But you should know that the life of a pastor is not so easy, and it does not pay well. Probably less well, my friend, than your wages as a carpenter."

This had not occurred to me. I had not thought about *being paid* to be a pastor like Reverend Dennis.

Seeing the look of confusion in my face Reverend Dennis said, "Come back and see me another time, Luther, after you have thought this through a little more. And give more thought to the practicality of your situation, with your young family . . ."

"Thank you, Reverend Dennis. I will."

Though my conversation with Reverend Dennis was not what I had anticipated, I did not allow myself to become discouraged, but continued to pray, and to read all that I could about ministry schools in Ohio and close by; especially, I focused upon the Toledo

School of Ministry, and began a correspondence with the dean there, sending the man carefully written letters, composed with Edna Mae's help. And after several weeks, during which time I frequently spoke with Reverend Dennis after church services, and at other times, our pastor acknowledged finally, with a lifting of his hands (as in a blessing) that it looked as if I had a *calling* after all—"You are very resolute, Luther! God be with you."

Very kindly, Reverend Dennis agreed to recommend me to the Toledo School of Ministry where my application was accepted, and where I was invited to begin my course of enrollment in the fall of 1986. He even offered to recommend me for a scholarship— (though I would not count upon this, for I could not feel that Reverend Dennis's recommendation would be enthusiastic). For most students the program of instruction could be completed in a single term, but as I could only attend school part-time, and would be commuting from Muskegee Falls to Toledo to take two courses each term, instead of four, I would be lucky to complete my degree in a year.

"But will they guarantee you a church, Luther? When you graduate?"—Edna Mae would ask, worriedly.

So many times Edna Mae asked this question, I fell

into the habit of replying with a shrug—"Ask Reverend Dennis. *He* made the promise."

"Jesus, thank you for your help! I want only to spread Your word."

Many times alone in my vehicle, driving to Toledo, returning to Muskegee Falls, I uttered these words aloud, for solace.

There began then a difficult time in my life, that became ever more burdensome and fretful in the winter months of 1986 to 1987, when the drive from Muskegee Falls to Toledo, a distance of approximately eighty miles, was often buffeted by strong winds and driving snow; and once or twice, midway between, I was forced to turn back, as the highway had become impassable.

Even on clear days the commuting was very tiring, as I soon discovered. On the mornings I drove to Toledo, which were Mondays and Wednesdays, I would wake before dawn out of nervousness and excitement, and hurriedly eat breakfast in the kitchen alone, and leave before 6:00 A.M. for my first class ("The Minister's Bible") was at 9:00 A.M. and I did not want to be delayed by my family. My second class ("The Craft and Art of Preaching") was at 2:00 P.M. Following this,

I would try to work on my assignments in the school library, before starting off for home at about 5:00 P.M. On my workdays, which were Tuesdays/ Thursdays/ Fridays, my foreman insisted that I work longer hours than I had been doing, and so I often began work at seven o'clock in the morning, and worked through the day until seven at night, with but a half-hour break for lunch. (Of course, I was very grateful for this work. I understood that my foreman was sympathetic with me, as one who is studying to become a minister, and at the same time supporting a wife and young children.) Reeling with exhaustion I would drive home, and eat a meal saved in the oven for me, as Edna Mae bathed the children and put them to bed. Often on these nights I was too tired to exchange more than a few words with Edna Mae before falling into bed myself. I understood that my schedule was very hard on her, for she had no one to help her with the household, and two young children to care for, and her health was not always so good. (Edna Mae had a respiratory weakness, as it was called. If she caught a bad cold it would likely turn into bronchitis if not pneumonia. Often too, it seemed that Edna Mae might be pregnant again, which excited and upset her, and when this turned out to be a "false alarm," was a relief to her, and yet saddening.) Still I was fired with hope, at the prospect of becoming a minister. *I will be like Christ, a carpenter. I will build my own church with my own hands and be revered like no other minister in the St. Paul Missionary Church.*

Except, I did not find the Toledo School of Ministry to be what I had anticipated. There were costs beyond tuition, which were called "fees"—also, my textbooks were more expensive than I had known books could be. Most of my fellow students were younger than I was, and seemed hardly more than high school boys; yet they were aloof to me, as they were (perhaps) intimidated by my size, like the smaller boys in the Sandusky schools who had been fearful of me and yet believed themselves superior to me, because their grades were higher. *Little bastards I could break you with one hand. Fuckers.*

A strange anger rose in me, like heat bubbling through tar. I was not aware of this anger until suddenly it emerged leaving me breathless.

There were a very few students at the ministry school older than I was—men in their forties and fifties who had decided to "make a career change" and become ministers. Two had been schoolteachers, and one an accountant. Another had been a "lay minister" in a church in Michigan, for thirty-two years! I felt for these individuals a sympathy tinged with pity, if not scorn, of the kind Reverend Dennis had seemed to feel for me, for I saw how unlikely it would be, that these middle-aged men would ever be chosen for a "pastor-ship" at any church.

It was a *young pastor* who would be favored, suf-fused with the joy and strength of Jesus, whom the congregation would love as a son or a brother. Not an older man who had failed at a secular life and was turn-ing now to the church as a convalescent might enter a hospital.

Nor was I finding my courses so interesting. In the years since leaving school I had fallen out of the habit of reading books—any kind of protracted reading, that required concentration, made my eyes ache. Studying the Old and New Testaments for "The Minister's Bible" mostly involved reading Bible verses, many of which I had already memorized as a boy. Though I could not have recited the verses aloud yet, when I tried to read them silently, my mind knew the words beforehand, as a monkey might, and so I had trouble comprehending almost anything I was assigned to read in the Bible, out of restlessness and boredom.

In the school library where I spent time between classes, and tried to work on my assignments, often I felt very sleepy, and yet restless. It was difficult for me to take notes on my assignments for I kept read-ing and rereading the same passages, as they did not seem so very different from other passages, on other pages and in other books. Sometimes I found myself sitting slumped at a table with my head lowered, my face against the tabletop as if I had fallen asleep and had been there a long time and could not remember where I was.

Luth-er!

Our instructors were retired ministers from St. Paul Missionary churches in the Midwest. Once, like Reverend Dennis, they had been missionaries in Africa, as well as in China and Central America, but now they were elderly and slow-speaking, and often seemed not to know how to answer questions put to them by students. (Not by me: I had no questions for my teachers and was surprised by the questions my classmates thought up, for instance where had Satan been, before God had created the Garden of Eden? Had there been dinosaurs in the Garden of Eden, or flying reptiles? And had God created lice, ticks, parasites, and germs as well, and were all of these species to be herded onto Noah's Ark, and saved? But why?) Not one faculty member at the Toledo school was half so engaging and exciting as Reverend Dennis, even those who were middle-aged and not elderly.

It was something of a shock to me (as it should not have been) that the course titled "The Craft and Art of

Preaching" would involve actual preaching on my part. Though I imagined myself preaching like Reverend Dennis in the pulpit one day, to a rapt audience of believers, I could not imagine preparing an actual sermon for that day. I believed that I could speak as well as, or better than, most of my fellow students, but when I began to speak I often stammered and lost my way, and broke out into a sweat. I could not bear the others staring at me, and taking note of the birthmark on my cheek.

Sign of the beast. Luther Dunphy.

My instructor Reverend Lundquist was patient with me, and tried to praise me, but I did not seem to know how to "compose" a sermon except by recalling what other preachers had said. The sample sermons in our textbook *How to Prepare Sermons* by Williams Evans—("Jesus Is Your Closest Friend," "The Joy of the Resurrection," "Satan's Bid for Your Soul," "Meet the Holy Spirit," "False Gods in America," "The True Meaning of Christmas," "The Second Coming: Will You Be Prepared?")—were very familiar, for everyone used them as models, and were not inspiring. When I could, I attended church services at the church attached to the school, but the preachers there lacked the fire and joy of Reverend Dennis, and as I was very tired much of the time, I would nod off to sleep in the midst of their preaching. It was utterly baffling to me, how a minister might "think up" a subject about which he could preach, without another minister to imitate.

Sermons were meant to be on diverse subjects, and for special occasions—Christmas, Easter, weddings, baptisms, funerals. On the subject of baptism, for instance, I did not know what to say that had not already been said many times, and would be familiar to any congregation; I had no knowledge of this subject apart from what my instructors had told us, which were mostly quotations from the Gospels. (The favorite being *John 3:5. Jesus answered, Truly, truly, I say unto you, Except a man be born of water and of the Spirit, he cannot enter into the kingdom of God.*) But if I tried to repeat what others had said, the words were flat and unconvincing, taken out of my spiral notebook, and my "sermon" was very short.

Even the subject of abortion, which was in the newspapers often since President Reagan had vowed to make abortion illegal again in the United States, and which roused such passion in others, did not seem to inspire me. When I tried to imitate the words of Reverend Dennis, who preached against abortion as it was *a slaughter of innocents*, my words did not sound convincing though I knew them to be absolutely true.

It was told to us that the St. Paul Missionary Church like other evangelical churches through the United

States was united in opposing what was called *abortion on demand*, as they were united in opposing *socialism, communism, atheism,* and *homosexuality.* There were legislators friendly to our cause in all the states, and many groups organized to take cases to the Supreme Court of the United States, to determine that abortion might be declared illegal once again, as it had been before 1973, and abortion clinics shut down. When I heard Reverend Dennis preach on this subject I felt my heart pound dangerously hard for the words *slaughter of the innocents* were terrible to contemplate; but still, when it was my turn to stand at a pulpit at the front of the room and "preach" on this subject in our class in Toledo, my voice quavered, and my knees, and I spoke so softly and so rapidly, Reverend Lundquist had to interrupt—"Luth-er! Slow down, son. Please."

My face reddened. I dared not glance up to see the other students exchange smirking glances.

In this class my grade would be B- at the end of the term. I did not want to think that this was the lowest grade in the class of twelve students for it would make me envy and hate my classmates, and (kindly, white-haired) Reverend Lundquist (who spent much of the class hour reminiscing to us of his early days as a minister in the Methodist church, in Barnstead, Oklahoma), and this was upsetting to me as a Christian.

The old man will never recommend you for a pastorship. Even if you earn your degree. You may as well give up, right now.

Save on tuition, fool. Save on gas.

Luth-er!

In "The Minister's Bible," in reading *Genesis*, our instructor Reverend Dilts told us that the story of the Garden of Eden had taken place approximately ten thousand years ago; but one of the younger students questioned whether it was a greater time than that, like fifty thousand years—(so he seemed to have been told by some revered authority). Also, there were claims by "atheistic scientists" that human beings had not been created by God but were descended from apes and monkeys. Reverend Dilts told us heatedly that these were ridiculous ideas with no basis in Scripture.

In my notebook I took down these facts—*10,000 yrs./50,000 yrs.* Carefully I underlined *10,000 yrs.* for this was Reverend Dilts's figure, that would likely be on our final exam.

It seemed to be upsetting to others in the class, as to Reverend Dilts, that many Americans were coming to believe atheistic and socialist ideas as a result of public school teaching and science courses in the schools, more upsetting yet "sex education," but I was too tired or distracted to feel strongly about these issues, and often woke startled from a light doze, embarrassed to think that Reverend Dilts might have noticed. (I am sure that Reverend Dilts did notice!) At such times I felt shame, and anxiety, that I was wasting my earnings on tuition at the school, and that Edna Mae would be crushed if I did not graduate with a diploma. My teeth chattered with a strange sort of cold, as if I was frightened, and once Reverend Dilts turned to me, with a quizzical look as if I had spoken aloud—"Luke? Excuse me—Luther? What do *you* think?"

What did I *think*? I had not been following the discussion closely. It was a week when we were fearful of Edna Mae being pregnant—again—and a week when both the children had infected ears—and a week when a customer had complained to our employer that some stairway carpentry work done by another man and myself was *not what he had asked for*, that might have to be torn out and done again. All that I could think was that the discussion in class had to do with atheism in the public schools, and a ban on prayer that was the fault of the Supreme Court (?) in Washington, D.C., that was the result of socialist influence on the judges (?). It came to me to say, "It is the will of Satan."

These words leapt to my lips. I could not think of another syllable more.

Reverend Dilts spoke slowly: "'The will of Satan.' Yes. I think you are right, Luther. Just in my lifetime, since the presidency of Franklin Delano Roosevelt, the legion of Satan is gathering strength in the United States."

A shiver ran through the class. It was possible, for I was light-headed from fatigue, to imagine the shadowy face of Satan at one of the windows of the classroom, grinning at the back of Reverend Dilts's head, without the elderly man taking note.

One of the younger, bright students in the class, whom I had come to hate for his brightness, and the obvious favoritism Reverend Dilts felt for him, asked, "Will we go to war one day, Reverend?"—and Reverend Dilts said, with satisfaction, "We are already at war with the atheist-enemy, son. It has only just begun *and we will bury them.*"

War? What did they mean? I would have thought they meant war like in Vietnam, or in Korea . . . It would be some time before I realized that they meant a war within the United States, Christians against atheists for the soul of America.

But I say unto you, *That whosoever looketh on a woman to lust after her hath committed adultery with her already in his heart.*

It is painful to confess that I did not remain faithful to my dear wife for more than three years; and that my betrayal of my marriage and my family came at a shameful time, when I was a student at the Toledo School of Ministry and (you would have thought) I had dedicated to myself to Jesus with all the more fervor, to prepare to serve Him for the remainder of my life.

Even before that time, I will confess that I lusted after women in my heart. In all places, even in church. Even with Edna Mae and my children beside me and a warm child's hand clasped in mine.

Sometimes the women were strangers to me glimpsed in a store, on the street. Sometimes they were acquaintances, even wives of homeowners for whom I was working.

Sometimes they were not women but girls. Driving along Front Street at Second Avenue, at the high school . . . Suddenly there was Felice Sipper at the curb waiting for the light, toeing the sidewalk in her way that drew my eye to her, helpless. She did not seem aware of me as I stared at her through the windshield of my car hazy with oak tree pollen.

Of course, it was not Felice. I was twenty-eight years old, it would not ever be Felice Sipper again.

Those days in early spring (1987) when the air began to warm at midday and a terrible restlessness overcame me and I could not bear to remain in the over-heated ministry school any longer but dared to cut my afternoon class—this term, the afternoon course was "Pastoring." It was a short drive to the old, inner city of Toledo along the Maumee River where there were many taverns within a few blocks, and in none of these were likely to be individuals who knew me, or had ever heard of Luther Dunphy, or the St. Paul Mission-ary Church of Jesus. What happiness I felt in stepping inside one of these!—the relief and satisfaction of one who has come to the right place at last, that has been awaiting him.

The particular smells of a tavern, even the smells of a filthy lavatory, urinals, puddled floors, bluish smoke of cigarettes and cigars—tears sprang to my eyes, these were so wonderful. On the mirror behind the bar, a light film of dust. High above the bar a tele-vision set perched at an angle and its screen bright with color as a child's coloring book and even the ad-vertisements were thrilling to me, as they were mys-terious and forbidden.

H'lo friend. What'll you have?

Anything on tap. Ale?

At the bar I would sit on a stool with a worn cushion, that seemed to fit my buttocks. I would sit and lean forward onto my elbows and observe the flickering TV and see in the facing mirror the grinning Satan-face friendly to me and no judging.

Live around here?

Muskegee Falls.

Where's that?

North of Springfield.

What brings you to Toledo?

The call of Jesus.

Eh? Call of—?

Jesus.

In time it happened that the bartender and certain of the other patrons came to know who I was—a student at the *min'stry school* whom they called *Rev'rend*. This made me smile for it was flattering, though I knew they were joking, yet their joking carried with it an awareness of the seriousness of my mission and some respect for me, I think.

Sometimes without intending it I would fall into a conversation with a woman. For always there was at least one woman in the bar, it did not matter which of the several bars for always in the bar there was a woman who might recognize me, and call me *Rev'rend*. She would buy me a drink, or I would buy her a drink. She would lay her hand lightly on my arm and if it was dusk, on overcast days as early as 6:00 P.M., she would ask if I would like to come home with her for a meal. And I would thank her and explain that I had to drive to Muskegee Falls very soon, to eat supper with my family.

How far is that, to your home?

Eighty miles.

Eighty miles! Isn't it already too late for supper, Rev'rend?

But then, as time passed so quickly, it was no longer dusk but dark, and somehow it happened, I would find myself with the woman, in her house, or an upstairs half of a house, and a terrible weakness would overcome me in all my limbs, and a roaring in my ears, that I could not resist the woman offering me another beer, or ale; at last, touching me in a way to greatly arouse me, as I would touch her; inviting me into her bedroom, and into her bed that was unmade, and smelled of the woman's body. And so it came about, not once but several times, more times than I wish to recall, in the spring of 1987 when the shame of my behavior was like an oily rag rubbing across a clean mirror-surface, to cloud it.

Though I was married and rejoiced in my marriage, as in my beloved young children, and though I was determined that I would become a minister of the St. Paul

Missionary Church, yet I was with whores often in the city of Toledo, when the weakness came upon me. With just a hurried call to Edna Mae with an excuse that my car had broken down, or had a tire needing to be repaired, I would stay overnight in one of these places; often, I would make the call from the woman's phone as she stood behind me stroking my back with her warm hands. In my dear wife's voice a fear of me, and in the background a child's cry—*Dad-dee? Where is Dad-dee?*

A woman will believe you, for a woman will want to believe you.

This is the wisdom of Satan. Yet it is true wisdom, though it is of Satan.

Soon, in the spring of 1987, though it was rare that Edna Mae and I were together *in that way*, Edna Mae found herself pregnant again. But in the agitation of those months, when often I stayed away overnight in Toledo, and missed work the next morning in Muskegee Falls, with no convincing excuse to my employer, and Edna Mae understood that I was not telling the truth to her, yet would not accuse me—she became stricken with cramps one day, when I was not with her, and lost the baby after three months of pregnancy.

In the bedroom of our house this was. So terrible an experience, and so much blood lost, the mattress and box springs would have to be replaced. So awful, Edna Mae would not be well for some time.

And such fear instilled in our young children, seeing their mother swathed in blood, and blood-clots on the bathroom floor, and their mother screaming in agony and despair and their father nowhere near as a husband and father should have been.

The women in Toledo were cast from me in disgust, after I had made use of them. That they did give themselves to me so readily and yet expressed surprise and even hurt when I recoiled from them—this was surprising to me.

On my knees I prayed in secret.

I am ashamed, Jesus. I have used whores, and I have betrayed my dear wife and children.

And Jesus would say, so quietly I could almost not hear—*The women are not whores, Luther. They are your sisters in my name. But it is true you have used them, and you have betrayed your dear wife and children.*

At the ministry school they seemed to know, how Luther Dunphy had become a troubled man. For my grades in the second term were lower than in the first term, for often I did not hand in my assignments at all. Reading was ever harder for me, and caused darting pains behind my eyes. If I slipped away to a tavern at noon, and returned for my afternoon class, a smell of ale emanated from me, and my appearance might have been flushed and disheveled and all in the classroom knew what a sinner I was, what a failure. There was a satisfaction in this, in the eyes of the others. For even a Christian does not know himself *blessed* unless he knows how another is *not-blessed.*

The dean called me to his office to say how disappointed he was, and how disappointed Reverend Dennis was, that I was doing so poorly in my classes, after "allowances" had been made for me to enroll as a special student.

(*Allowances*? I was not aware of these, I was sure. The requirement of graduation from high school had been waived, but this was all that I had been informed.)

In a vexed voice the dean asked if I would like to withdraw from my classes? He could return to me some of the tuition and fees, if so; for he knew how I and my wife had sacrificed to allow for my enrollment at the school.

In an instant I was sober. I told him *No!* I would never give up.

"I would sooner die, than give up my calling to spread the word of Jesus."

The St. Paul Missionary Church *of Jesus does not condone violence against individuals or property. The Church has always decried all acts in violation of state and federal law and is not associated in any way with radical organizations like Operation Rescue.*

The Toledo School of Ministry declines to release the academic transcripts of Luther Amos Dunphy to the media. It is a matter of public record that Mr. Dunphy graduated with a diploma in Ministry Science in May 1987.

It is not corroborated by any official spokesman for the St. Paul Missionary Church or the Toledo School of Ministry that Luther Amos Dunphy joined the militant anti-abortion movements Army of God and Operation Rescue because he had been unable to secure a position as a minister. It is a matter of public record that Mr. Dunphy was a lay minister attached to the St. Paul Missionary Church of Muskegee Falls, Ohio, in the years 1988–1999.

A lay minister is a member of the congregation who involves himself in the activities of the church, assisting the minister in numerous ways as needed— counseling, visiting the sick, teaching Bible classes, helping with the upkeep of the church property. As Mr. Dunphy was a skilled roofer and carpenter, he is said to have provided such services for the church intermittently.

A lay minister does not normally receive a salary.

Reverend Dennis Kuhn, of the Muskegee Falls church, has cooperated fully with local and state law enforcement and Broome County prosecutors in their investigation into the shooting deaths allegedly committed by Mr. Dunphy at the Broome County Women's Center on November 2, 1999. Reverend Kuhn has acknowledged that he is a member of the American Coalition of Life Activists and the Pro-Life Action League, which are anti-abortion organizations, but he is not a member of the Army of God and Operation Rescue.

Reverend Kuhn has issued a statement to the media:

"It was with grave concern and absolute shock that I learned that Luther Dunphy, a longtime member of our congregation, is the (alleged) shooter in the deaths of two individuals associated with the Broome County Women's Center. Neither I nor anyone else in our congregation of whom I am aware had any knowledge of Luther Dunphy's active involvement in Operation Rescue. Neither I nor anyone else in our congregation of whom I am aware had any knowledge of Luther Dunphy's (alleged) intention to 'assassinate' the abortion providers. Though our church is staunchly pro-life— and opposed to abortion in any way, shape, or form, as a legally sanctioned slaughter of the innocents in the United States of the present time—we do not, and we have not ever, condoned violence against the practitioners of abortion and those associated with them. We do not condone violations of state and federal law and we do not excuse those who commit such violations despite our sympathy for their moral convictions.

"It is a profound step from believing that abortion is state-sanctified murder to believing that an individual has the right to 'assassinate' an abortion murderer. The St. Paul Missionary Church of Jesus is adamantly opposed to such an act and is in no way associated with the practitioner of such an act.

"Though I remain in contact with Luther Dunphy, currently incarcerated at Chillicothe Correctional Facility, Chillicothe, Ohio, I am not in a position to provide any sort of information about him, or to convey remarks made by him, to any third party or to the media. It is true, I am involved in the Luther Dunphy Defense Fund, which welcomes donations to aid in Luther's appeal to the Ohio State Supreme Court—checks, money orders, cash. As little as a few dollars, as much as several hundred—or thousand . . . All are welcome, and greatly appreciated in the name of Jesus."

A Soldier of Christ

Whoever sheds the blood of man, by man shall his blood be shed, for God made man in his own image.

Through the long night these words sounded in my ears. Several times I started from sleep, believing that I had heard these words of *Genesis* in our bedroom, in our bed in a hoarse and grave voice not recognizable to me. And that Edna Mae who slept her fitful sweating sedated sleep beside me would be wakened too, having heard.

For at last it was the early morning of November 2 which by certain signs of God had been decreed to be *the day of execution.*

"Lord, I will do Your bidding. If this is Your wish."

Whoever sheds the blood of man . . . The abortionist-murderer has shed the blood not of men but of unborn babies. His just punishment will be that another will shed his blood in a public place, that all the world will gaze upon him fallen and defeated.

I had no doubt this was God's wish. But it was a slow matter for me to accept that this was God's wish for Luther Dunphy to enact.

In the ministry school in Toledo, in the library I had read, or tried to read, *A Book of Martyrs* by the Englishman John Foxe. It was a very old book of the 1500s (so long ago a time, I could not imagine what sorts of people lived then) that had been "updated" for the modern reader. The book was not easy reading, even so. These depictions of the torture-deaths and martyrdoms of Protestant Christians in opposition to the "Roman papacy" were difficult for me to read for more than a few minutes at a time. I was left feeling weak and anxious not knowing why at that time.

Yet now, it was clear that God had been guiding me then. Like one who is blindfolded, led by another's hand in utter trust and faithfulness.

I would feel a thrill of pride, I thought, that one day the distinguished Professor Wohlman would project a photograph of Luther Dunphy up on a screen, and speak admiringly of me to a large audience as a *martyr in the cause.*

I had not the slightest doubt that I would be arrested, and tried for murder, if I was successful in my mission. As others before me had done, most recently Terence Mitchell who'd been tried and found guilty, sentenced to prison in northern Wisconsin without the possibility of parole.

Pray for our brave martyrs, and pray for ourselves, that we have the strength to act as we must, when we must.

I was not a brave or courageous soldier for the cause. At meetings of Operation Rescue, I sat silent and down-looking while others spoke with passion. At all times since Stockard had confided in me I was very frightened and could not cease hoping that the Lord would change His plans for me and release me back into my ordinary life.

Your own daughter, the murderer would strike in her mother's womb if he had been able.

Sometimes it seemed, when my mind was tired and confused, in the worst hours of the night, that our beloved Daphne had been struck down on the highway by the abortionist-murderers and not by an unknown driver of a pickup truck. (And in my mind it had come to seem that the pickup truck had struck my car, or that my car had slammed into the pickup.) And so it seemed, executing the abortionist-murderer Voorhees was intended by God as a way of exacting justice for our daughter.

Another time it seemed to me, I felt the touch of the Little Hand on my arm; and when I opened my eyes to see—(for I was half-asleep with tiredness)—it was but a memory of Daphne as a little girl, clutching at my arm—*Dad-dee!*

Many days had passed as in a trance. Since Stockard had confided in me that the abortion doctor had now the custom of arriving early at the Center, before the police guards. For there seemed no refutation of that—why otherwise would God have sent me such information? Other signs had been sent to me, I could not equally deny. Three nights ago on *The Tom McCarthy Hour* which Edna Mae and I sometimes watch together there was a fierce discussion of "the shame and outrage" of abortion and pictures of "abortionist-murderers" were displayed on the screen—six faces and names known to me from the WANTED: BABY KILLERS AMONG US list, and among these Augustus Voorhees.

It was a surprise to see this. On the TV screen Voorhees looked like any other man. It was shocking to me, you would not pick him out in the street to be an emissary of Satan.

In the set of his features Voorhees reminded me of one of the roofers in our crew who was always cheerful, or tried to give that impression. Always he called to me—*Luth! How's it going, man?*—as if he did not expect an answer beyond a smile and a shrug, that was enough for him. Voorhees was somewhat older than Sam, at age forty-six. In the picture Voorhees was frowning, and serious, and had a look (it seemed to me) of sadness, and guilt.

I felt a stir of excitement, and terrible unease. Recalling my reluctance as a boy to pull the trigger, sighting a deer in the scope of my rifle, while my uncle and others chided me for my slowness.

On TV Tom McCarthy was furious. His uplifted voice seemed to be aimed at me. *Baby killers* he was saying. *Outrage, slaughter of innocents. Abortion-mill clinics, Planned Parenthood spreading promiscuity . . .* It was not surprising, he said, that Christians were beginning to rise up to strike at the enemy, not just to picket and protest outside the abortion clinics but to take more *courageous means.*

Carefully, Tom McCarthy did not utter the words *assassination, execution.* He did not utter the words *soldier, Army of God, Operation Rescue.*

With mock mourning Tom McCarthy spoke of an abortion provider who'd been shot down in Kentucky six weeks before, by a man named Shaun Harris—

"Think of it this way: the doctor wasn't killed, only just terminated in the third trimester."

Now a picture of Shaun Harris appeared on the screen. He was a solid-bodied man of about forty with a rifle gripped in his right hand, the stock resting on his thigh and the barrel aimed upward.

Then, in quick succession photographs of Michael Griffin, Lionel Greene, and Terence Mitchell.

Each of the photographs had been taken outdoors. The men were unsmiling, grim, squinting into the sun. Griffin was bare-headed, the others wore work hats. Tom McCarthy reported that all were serving life sentences in maximum security prisons.

He went on to speak of Harris, Griffin, Greene, and Mitchell as *soldiers in an undeclared war.* While he did not openly condone their *civil disobedience* (he said) yet it was clear that he admired them, very much.

"It's a pathetic, cowardly pseudo-socialist country in which the heroic men who take the moral law into their own hands are 'murderers' while cold-blooded 'murderers' are—your friendly local 'abortion-providers.'"

Tom McCarthy spoke with a sneer. I felt a thrill of hope, that McCarthy might one day approve of *me.*

But now there came onto the screen a picture of a rose-colored gravestone that had been purchased by the Pro-Life Action League of Simcoe, Illinois, and placed in a cemetery there, to commemorate the deaths of more than seven hundred babies "made to perish" by abortion in a single year—

HOLY INNOCENTS
PREBORN CHILDREN OF GOD
Jan. 1–Dec. 31, 1997

When the TV shifted to an advertisement I felt great relief. Edna Mae had been staring at the screen, and at the gravestone, with a quivering intensity.

I knew she was thinking of our daughter's gravestone in the little cemetery behind our church, that was not much more than an open field, with few graves there at this time, as the St. Paul Missionary Church of Muskegee Falls had only been founded in 1983. And our congregation, as Reverend Dennis likes to boast, is a *young and vigorous congregation brimming with health.*

"What do you think of those men, who have 'taken the moral law into their own hands' and shot the abortion doctors?"—for suddenly it seemed crucial to me, I must ask Edna Mae this question.

The word *abortion* sounded strange on my lips. I had not ever uttered this ugly word aloud, and certainly would not have uttered such an ugly word to my dear wife, except under these circumstances.

For I understood that my time was rapidly running out.

For I recalled now a remark made by my grandfather on his eighty-eighth birthday that was not self-pitying, but kindly, and smiling—*Well. Guess the old man's time is running out, eh?*

Edna Mae turned her eyes to me, blinking slowly. I saw that her eyes were damp and slightly bloodshot and at the corners of her mouth was a chalky substance. She had not changed from her soiled flannel bathrobe that day. The older children and I had prepared our evening meal, which Edna Mae had barely eaten.

I had to think, after I was gone Edna Mae would shake herself awake, and stop taking those pills that were eating away at her soul. For I could not plead with her any more than I had done, and I could not force her to stop. But if I departed, and was not always here in the house to oversee the children, and to buy groceries, Edna Mae would revert to her former self, I believed. For Jesus would guide her.

No doubt, it was surprising to my dear wife that I would ask such a question of her since it was not like me to ask such questions of anyone. In a slow voice she said:

"I think—I think of how terrible it is—for their wives and mothers and their children if they have children . . . I think that there are many lives that are ended when a man is a soldier for Christ—not just the abortion-doctors' lives."

It was surprising to me too, that my wife should speak in this way, seriously, as if she had given the question some thought.

Adding then, "It is not for us to judge. We are to anoint the feet of the martyr, that is all."

Lay your life on the line *for Jesus.*

Through the long night lying with eyes open to the faint light from a window in darkness and heart beating quickly in dread of what I must do. My fingertips caressed the rough scar on my side, between my ribs where Felice Sipper had sunk her little jackknife blade, as often I caressed that scar, and another on my thigh, to give a kind of comfort in the night. Many times swallowing, or trying to swallow—my mouth was very dry.

So shivering and restless through the night, though I was badly sweating also, I had to creep from the room to use the bathroom several times. For there was something pinching my bladder causing me to urinate in hot, frothing spurts and the smell of my urine sharp and metallic.

I feared that my bowels would turn to water, scalding. No shame like the shame of losing control of his bowels, when a soldier has embarked upon a sacred mission.

Finally at 5:20 A.M. rising from bed as quietly as I could.

"This will be the final time. My final night in this bed."

A kind of wonder came upon me, at this realization. And yet I did not touch my lips to my dear wife's forehead for fear of waking her and disturbing her.

It was a strange remark that Edna Mae had made the other evening. There was this side to my wife, that surprised me. As when I would learn that she had sometimes visited the grave of our little girl, without telling me and without having asked me to come with her.

But Edna Mae had no suspicion of my plans. If she'd had, she would certainly have tried to stop me.

Slow then like a man in a dream closing the door to that room.

Slow then in the hall. Saying good-bye to the children: in the boys' room Luke and Noah asleep in their bed, in the girls' room Dawn and Anita. And there was one other—so it seemed to me, for a moment.

Thank you God, for these children. I have been blessed.

Such love I felt for them! Such regret, I would not ever be their *Dad-dee* again but instead a man who had chosen another life and would become a stranger to them, in the service of the Lord.

Descending silently two flights of stairs into the basement to prepare.

No more dreaded hour than the hour to come.

I had laid out my clothes the night before, in the basement. Recalling the previous summer at J.C. Penney where I'd bought the children sneakers and for myself, for some reason I could not then have named, a khaki-colored long-sleeved T-shirt that had seemed to me a soldier's shirt, and khaki trousers with deep pockets on both legs in which I could carry ammunition if required.

"Would you like to try those on?"—so the saleswoman asked of me, in a friendly way. But I told her that was not necessary, the trousers were in my size according to the label.

Edna Mae had used to laugh at me, that my clothes were sometimes of sizes too large for me. Since childhood, this had been so, for my mother had not wanted to be all the time buying me new clothes, and so purchased clothing large enough for me to "grow into"— which seemed very reasonable to me.

Later, when I lived by myself, I kept the same habits. For it has never seemed to me to feel right, if clothes are a "fit."

I smiled to recall that afternoon with the children. It was rare for us to be alone together in such a way. The saleswoman asked their names and proudly I told them—"Luke—and Dawn—and Noah—and Anita . . ." And another time, it seemed to me that there was someone missing, that took my breath away so that the saleswoman waited for me to continue to speak and the children were made uncomfortable.

But they'd been well behaved at the mall. Not like those children who run wild, screaming and colliding with shoppers.

They would wear their new sneakers home, and I would take the old sneakers home in boxes. The sneakers were bright-colored.

Thanks, Daddy! These're cool.

Then, I took them for ice cream. It was almost 5:00 P.M. Edna Mae was not to know. It is a precious sly thing, to have a secret from the children's mother.

I realized then, I had seen in a dream-vision my own grave marker, the night before. It was confused in my memory with the grave of the *Holy Innocents Preborn Children of God* in the cemetery in Illinois but I had seen it clearly—*Luther Amos Dunphy 1960*—but then, I had not seen the date of my death. Instead of a numeral engraved in the stone there was a blur.

And so I had known, God would not relent. God would direct me to the execution. It would be done, there was no turning back.

The Mossberg shotgun, that my grandfather had left to me years ago, I had also prepared the night before. This heavy gun I had not fired in twelve years I had cleaned, but I had not yet loaded. For even so recently I had thought, God might relent. Also, you must never keep a loaded weapon in a household with children.

Hands so shaky, fingers so numb I could hardly fit the shells inside.

Such moisture in my eyes, I could not see clearly. A moment's panic at the thought that, at the crucial instant, I would not be able to see my target clearly.

Recalling how when I had hunted with my father, uncles, and cousins in the woods outside Sandusky, and had been so eager to keep up with the men, and so fearful of their scorn, I had more than once misfired this very shotgun and sent buckshot into an open field missing the target—in that case, a pheasant.

Other times, I had hoped to bring down a deer with a rifle shot. But I had only (once) wounded the animal, and had been badly shaken by the sight. Mostly, I had not fired at all.

To aim at, to shoot at, a human being standing only a few yards away—*God, help me! God give me strength.*

By this time I was trembling so badly, I could barely maneuver the zipper of my black nylon jacket.

At last ascending the stairs to the kitchen, and switching on the overhead light. This too for the last time! On the refrigerator were crayon drawings by the younger children, I had not really seen before—giraffe, elephant, tiger. (Whose were these? Anita's? Why these animals? Suddenly, I wanted so badly to know.) And there the linoleum floor worn thin at the sink and at the table, I had promised Edna Mae I would replace, but had not.

Hurriedly drinking from a quart milk container. I could not risk any food, even cereal, for fear that I would become nauseated.

My black nylon windbreaker, that fell to the knees, and would hide the shotgun. Or, would hide the shotgun as much as required. For I would not be closely observed by many, until it was too late.

A work-cap pulled down low onto my forehead. It is a habit I have, the rim leaves a red mark in my skin Edna Mae had once rubbed with her fingers, to smooth away.

On the kitchen phone, that is an apricot-colored plastic wall phone, quickly I called Ed Fischer at his business number which I knew he would not answer, at this early hour. Telling Ed that I would not be able to come to work that day for a reason I would explain later.

Not wanting to think how Ed would react, when he heard. How the others on the crew, my friends I had known for many years since moving here, would react when they heard.

A sensation of hope came to me, that I often felt at such times, stepping outside and breathing in the air of early morning. Today it was a cold sharp air. There is a pleasure too in turning the ignition and hearing the motor come to life, and thinking of how, in a car, you could drive for thousands of miles along highways—to California, and Alaska . . .

The summer I'd spent with relatives in Mad River, working on their dairy farm, I had first wanted to drive with my high school friend to Alaska and work on the salmon fishing boats there. But our plans hadn't worked out.

In that, the hand of God had guided me. I had not known at the time.

Driving to the Broome County Women's Center along the familiar route. Two point six miles. And this too, for the last time. My heart clutched to see at an intersection ahead, a pickup truck braking to a stop at a stop sign.

As I was arriving earlier than usual at the Women's Center, there were more places to park closer to the Center.

Since the vandalism committed against the Center this past summer, no parking was allowed on the street near the Center. The Center's windows had been shuttered. There had been red spray paint on the walls, that had been power-washed away, or painted-over. *Baby killers. Burn in Hell.* I had not been involved in these acts committed by certain members of the Army of God whose names were to be kept from Reverend Dennis, for the Reverend's good.

At this hour, 7:20 A.M. there were few protesters. But there was Stockard standing on the sidewalk at the front, in conversation with five or six protesters, who had come to the site in a minivan, from Springfield. I did not know their names but knew their faces and knew them to be Catholics. In the way that Stockard spoke with them, and their deference to him, I felt again that Stockard had been a priest, and was not now a priest, and I wondered at this, but it was too late for me to inquire.

I felt such anguish!—I had wanted to be a minister

of the St. Paul Missionary Church of Jesus, and speak of the word of Jesus to all who would listen. But the church would not have me, and God too had rejected me as one who would spread His word.

The law had been passed in Ohio some years ago, that protesters had to keep no less than seven feet from the abortion providers and staff, and were forbidden to congregate on the front walk or to block passage to the front door of the Center; but often, this law was overlooked.

The Center would not unlock its doors until 8:00 A.M. and no mothers would arrive before then; when they did arrive some would hesitate to leave their vehicles until a volunteer escort approached, to help them past the protesters now crying at them—*No! No! Don't do it!*

And the familiar chant that echoed so often in my brain like an angry pulse beating—

Free choice is a lie,

Nobody's baby chooses to die.

At this hour there were no mothers arriving. But Voorhees would be arriving shortly. This, I knew with certainty.

God guide my hand. God do not allow me to fail.

It was decreed. It would not be altered. Those babies scheduled to be murdered this morning, would not be murdered if I could but act as decreed. And those babies whom the abortionist was to murder in days to come, might yet be spared.

Waiting in my vehicle with the motor turned off. I had been sweating inside my clothes but now, I was becoming calm. At last, at about 7:25 A.M., the dark blue Dodge minivan arrived and pulled into the Center driveway. At first I could not see which of the men in the front of the van was Voorhees for there were two men, then I saw that Voorhees was the passenger, beside him sat his "escort" who was his bodyguard, one of the Center volunteers whom we saw often and who was particularly aggressive and defiant to us.

In an instant, I was out of my vehicle.

In the driveway behind the minivan, moving swiftly. Already Voorhees had stepped out of the vehicle. I had no difficulty identifying the man for I knew his face well. And I had no difficulty seeing my target for my vision had strangely narrowed, it was wonderful how God had narrowed my vision like a tunnel, or a telescope, so that I saw only the target, and no other distractions.

Already my shotgun was lifted to my shoulder, I was aiming and firing even as the abortionist tried to dissuade me with hoarse shouted words—"Stand back! Put down that gun!"

In the foolishness of utter surprise the doomed man raised his arm, his hand with extended fingers—as if to appeal to me, or to shield his face from the blast.

And afterward over the fallen and bleeding man I crouched and my lips moved numbly.

"God have mercy! God forgive you."

Soon then, it was over. On my knees I awaited the police.

If I shut my eyes I can shut out voices as well. Crude and ignorant voices of those that *know not what they do.*

Since that time it is God I am addressing and not humankind.

Not those who love me, no more than those who hate me.

If God does not answer me, it does not mean that God does not hear me and bless me as His soldier.

Only say the word and my soul shall be healed.

The Life and Death of

Gus Voorhees:

An Archive

Abortionist's Daughter

You must be grateful, he didn't kill *you*."

Memory, Undated

Why can't we live with Daddy?"

Because it's dangerous to live with Daddy.

"Don't you love Daddy? Are you mad at Daddy?"

Yes. I am mad at Daddy. But yes, I love Daddy.

Memory, Undated: Flying Glass

Her mouth was so dry, it felt like her tongue was all stitches!

Black-thread stitches, she'd seen on her daddy's forearm when the gauze bandage was removed, and the sight of it was so terrible, she shrank away and could not even scream.

Oh what has happened to Daddy what has happened

They'd said flying glass. Something had been thrown through a window, and there had come—*flying glass.*

Sixty-six stitches in Daddy's left arm, that was covered in wiry dark hairs.

Sixty-six black-thread stitches so ugly, the sight of them penetrated her brain like shrapnel.

Sixty-six black-thread stitches but Daddy laughed saying he was grateful for at the ER they'd told him it had been sheer luck that one of the three-inch glass slivers hadn't severed a major artery in his arm.

Shut her eyes tight. Had not wanted to see. Her brother Darren stared and stared.

My brother memorized everything, I think.

Of that life in Michigan, that is lost to me.

I don't remember anything clearly. Like shattered glass. You see how it has fallen to the floor, but you can't imagine what it was like before it was shattered not the shape of it, not even the size.

I don't remember but if I write down a few words, other words will (sometimes) follow unexpectedly.

"Her mouth was so dry, it felt like her tongue was all stitches!"

"Rot In Hell"

After Daddy died our mother received letters in the mail or jammed into her mailbox or shoved inside the screen door of her house or (a few times) shoved beneath the windshield wiper of the car she was driving.

It was a mistake to open such letters, she knew. And yet.

So awful, she might fall to her knees on the (hard-wood) floor clutching such a letter in her hand.

Her face was a face crushed in a vise of pain. Her face was a face you dared not look at, the fear was you might burst into laughter like a silly child scared to death.

Now you know what its like you athiest bitch. You & yours will rot in Hell.
BABY KILLERS

Interview(s)

What do you remember most about your father Dr. Augustus—"Gus"—Voorhees?

What do you remember most about your family life in Michigan?

And where specifically did you live in Michigan?— Ann Arbor, Grand Rapids, Saginaw, Bay City and— one or two residences in Detroit?

Did you always live with both your parents, or did your father sometimes live elsewhere? And if so, did Dr. Voorhees try to get home often?

Did you ever visit him?

How were his absences explained by your mother— (if they were explained)? Did you and your siblings miss not having a father you saw more often?

How did you and your family feel, having to move so frequently?

Did it interfere with your schooling? Your social life?

(Did you have a "social life"?)

Were your teachers aware of who your father was? Your classmates, friends? Your neighbors? How did that impact upon your relationships?

Were you proud of your father?

Did you (sometimes) resent your father?

Did you love your father?

It was said—by your father—that your mother Jenna Matheson was the "ideal wife/companion" for him— did it seem to you, and to your brother and sister, as far as you can speak for them, that your parents' marriage was "ideal"?

Did your mother ever express regret, or disappointment, or frustration that she'd had to set her law career aside, to help further your father's work?—to be a full-time mother and assistant for Dr. Voorhees, for many years?

Was your mother a "full-time" mother—or is that an exaggeration?

Was it known to you and your siblings that your father was a "tireless crusader" for women's reproductive rights in the Midwest and in Michigan especially?

Was it known to you that your father was a "crusader" for abortion rights?

Did you know, as children, what "abortion rights" meant?

Did you know that your father performed abortions?

Did you know that your father had many enemies?

Did you know that your father was considered "difficult"—even by those who were his allies?

Have you read your father's published writings? His (famous, controversial) address to the National Women's Leadership Conference in 1987, in Washington, D.C.—are you familiar with that?

"There cannot be a free democracy in which one sex is shackled to 'biological destiny'"—are you familiar with this much-reiterated remark of Dr. Gus Voorhees?

Do you or have you ever felt, as a girl, that you are "shackled to 'biological destiny'"—or did you inherit a strong feminist identity from your parents?

Is there anything you regret, from your childhood in Michigan? Anything you wish might have been otherwise?—(excluding of course the tragic ending to your father's life).

Were your parents happy?

What was it like to be a child of Gus Voorhees?

And for your mother—what do you think it was like for Jenna Matheson to be Gus Voorhees's wife?

Were you aware as children of the many threats against your father's life?

Were you aware of acts of vandalism, death threats, bomb threats directed against the women's centers with which your father was associated? And how did your mother react to these, so far as you know?

In the Free Choice movement Gus Voorhees has been called a "great man"—"a brave martyr for the cause"; but in the Pro-Life movement Gus Voorhees has been called, for example, by the conservative Catholic philosopher Willard Wolhman, a "thoroughly evil, amoral man"—a "mass murderer as evil as a Nazi war criminal." How do you and your family feel about such extreme reactions to Dr. Voorhees?

How was the news broken to you and your siblings, that your father had been killed on November 2, 1999, at the Broome County, Ohio, Women's Center in Muskegee Falls, Ohio?

Were you informed, at the time, that Dr. Voorhees had been assassinated by a lone gunman associated with the right-wing Christian organizations Army of God and Operation Rescue?—or did you learn these details at a later date, when you were older?

Were you allowed—in time—to read about your father's death, or to watch TV news or documentaries? Did you attend any of the several memorials for Dr. Voorhees in Ann Arbor, Lansing, Detroit?

Was your father's death a terrible shock to you, your brother Darren, and your sister Melissa? Did your loss draw you closer together—or did your loss have the opposite effect?

Your mother Jenna Matheson has refused all requests for interviews following your father's death—is this for reasons of privacy, for reasons of (mental) health, or is your mother preparing a memoir of her life with Gus Voorhees and is not inclined to share personal memories with the media?

Where does your mother live at the present time? (Are you aware that mail sent to Jenna Matheson at any former address is returned to the sender as "undeliverable"?)

Are you "close" to your mother at the present time?

Do you (and your family) feel that a sentence of death is appropriate for the assassin of your father? Will such a sentence bring "closure" to you (and your family)?

Dr. Voorhees was an adamant and outspoken opponent of the death penalty—are you?

Revenge

G od help me to be strong.
Help me to be cruel like the world.

We were children made mean by grief. We were children with wizened little crabapple hearts and death's-head grins. You would do well, if you were a nice child, to stay out of our way.

I said, Why should they have a father and a mother? I hate them.

Sometimes I said, Why should they be happy? I hate them.

We conspired to kidnap their little wiry-haired dog who barked too much. We fantasized hiding their

Airedale they called Mutt, in someplace where they wouldn't think to look, and we would feed Mutt, and Mutt would come to love *us.* And Darren said if Mutt doesn't cooperate we kill him.

Cooperate how?—(I had to ask.)

By obeying us.

Obeying us—how? (I had to ask. I needed to hear my brother articulate what we would do, to feel the thrill of knowing we might do it.)

By doing what we command him, stupid. By wagging his tail and loving *us.*

It was exciting and alarming, to think (seriously?) of kidnapping our neighbors' dog. For these were neighbors who'd befriended us—who'd taken pity on us, and admired our mother. At times my heart would stop, and beat hard and start again, when Darren stooped over me saying in his whisper-voice—*What'll we do? We kill him.*

Kill him—how? (Had to ask.)

Same way I'm gonna *kill you,* asshole!

And Darren would pummel me, and slap my face once, twice, three times, not really hard slaps (of which my brother was more than capable) but swift stinging slaps of humiliation, that left my cheeks burning and made tears spring from my eyes but I did not cry.

It was crucial, *I did not cry.*

Of course, nothing came of our plot to kidnap Mutt. Nothing came of our wish for revenge. We were too old to be children, in fact. You would need special eyes to see how grief was rotting us from the inside-out, stunted children, ugly troll-children it would have been a mercy to shoot with a sniper's rifle—*one, two.*

"Evil"—"Heaven"

G ood news, kids! There is no evil."
      This was the way he talked. Sometimes.

Went on to assure us there's no *Devil*, no *Satan*, no *Hell.*

There is—(maybe)—*Heaven* but it isn't anywhere far away or anything special.

And we demanded to know, why isn't *Heaven* anything special?

(You always hear of *Heaven* being so special.)

And Daddy said, because *Heaven* is just two things: human love, and human patience.

And all love is, is patience. Taking time. Focusing, and taking time. That's love.

This was disappointing to us! This was not anything

we wanted to hear. We were too young to have a clue how special *human love* and *human patience* were, how rare and fleeting, and if Daddy might be laughing at us, you could never tell if Daddy was serious or laughing or serious-laughing, both at once.

The last time at Katechay Island.

No premonition. Not a clue.

At the shore at Katechay Island, on Wild Fowl Bay (an inlet of Saginaw Bay/Lake Huron). Not the sandy beach where people swam in warm weather but the farther beach which was coarse and pebbly and the sand dunes were hard-packed and cold even in the sun. The beach there was littered with kelp, rotted pieces of wood, long-rotted little fish and bodies of birds, scattered bones. It was a blinding-bright day to be near the water, a cold day, and a windy day, so that the water was like something shaken, sharp as tinfoil, and there was nowhere for your eye to remain, always the water was changing, and if you looked too hard, the sight of it was hurtful.

It was a hike along the shore, that last hike that no one knew was *last.* A two-point-five-mile hike, Daddy said.

On our hikes Daddy would announce the distance, going and returning. For some of us were not such strong hikers as others. Some of us had to be assured,

Daddy would pick us up in his arms and carry us back, if our legs grew tired, if our knees buckled.

For Daddy always assured with a wink: Nobody's going to be abandoned.

Gus Voorhees was a doctor, he favored precision. Blood tests, scans of internal organs, X-rays and MRIs. Not-knowing is not a virtue, you may pay for not-knowing with your life.

Kids, always remember: Ignorance is *not bliss.*

If he asked you a question, you must give a precise answer. You must not mumble vaguely, and you must meet his eye.

Hey. Look up. Look *here.*

Daddy was naturally a smiler. So when Daddy did not smile, you knew it.

Out of breath trying to keep up with Daddy! Sand-dune hills and little ravines, that disintegrated when we stepped near them, and pulled at our feet. Wind rushing against our faces, sucking away our breaths and making our eyes water foolishly as if we were crying.

Yet, we would keep up with Daddy. Naomi and Melissa, the little girls, determined to keep up in the wake of their longer-legged brother Darren, and Darren in the wake of Daddy who'd become distracted, forget where he was, stride on ahead.

Oh Daddy!—wait.

Wait for us. Daddy!

This day, this hiking-day at the shore at Wild Fowl Bay had not seemed like a special day. It had not seemed like a day to be remembered and so, much of it has been lost. Like tattered flags flying at the lighthouse lunch place, at Bay Point. What the flags were meant to be, you couldn't tell because they were so faded. Daddy had driven us in the station wagon from our (rented) house near Bay City, an hour and twenty minutes drive to Katechay Island where there was a cabin we could use, belonging to friends of Daddy's and Mommy's who had given them the key. Except it was the end of summer, already it was late September, and the air was getting cold, even in the sun. And if the sun was obscured by clouds dark like crayon scribbles, you were made to shiver.

It was confusing to us, where Daddy had been in the weeks before this. For sometimes it was more than one place, and we could not remember the names which (perhaps) we resented, and did not want to remember. On this day, Daddy had returned early that morning from wherever he'd been, somewhere in northern Michigan where (as Daddy said) he was desperately needed as a consultant.

Desperately!—Mommy laughed. *Is it ever anything less than desperate?*

Adding, *And what of us—are we* not desperate?

So Daddy was saying, not to Mommy (who hadn't come hiking with us but had stayed back at the picnic table with her typewriter) but to us, that there was no *evil*, but there was *Heaven*, if you kept in mind that *Heaven* wasn't anything special or surprising; it might be just a hike along the shore, on a windy day, in late September; in itself not memorable, but the point is, if you can remember that we did this, we were here together, we stopped for lunch at Bay Point, even if it wasn't a great lunch we were together, the five of us, no matter what happens afterward—this is *Heaven*. Got it, kids?

OK, Daddy, we said. It embarrassed us when Daddy spoke to us as to another adult, too *seriously*.

Y'know what, kids?—promise me you will scatter my ashes here after I die.

After I die. It is possible, none of us heard this.

A child does not hear *die* on a parent's lips. No.

Of course we'd have said yes. Anything Daddy wanted us to say, we'd say, and anything Daddy wanted us to believe, we'd believe. Even if we had not a clue what Daddy was talking about this time as other times.

Special Surgery

Something to do with *babies*. What did that mean? We knew where babies came from. We thought we knew, for our parents had told us. Animal babies, and human babies. (But birds were different, and reptiles. Their babies came out of eggs.) (*Why* did some babies come out of their mother's bellies and other babies came out of eggs, like chicken eggs you could eat? That was never made clear.) We were embarrassed and excited to consider the place where *we had come from*, which was supposed to be Mommy's belly.

(We did not believe this really. It was so funny! Like one of Daddy's silly jokes that made you laugh so hard you wetted yourself. But we had to pretend we believed it. *Out of Mommy's belly, when it was time to be born.*)

(Anxiously Naomi said to Darren, Mommy's belly isn't big enough. We could never be that little, to fit inside. Naomi swallowed hard at the thought of it, such a terrible thought that made her eyelids flutter and a sick, choking sensation arise in her throat, for what if—somehow—it was made to be, Naomi would have to fit inside Mommy's belly again though she was too big. This thought made her queasy and shivery for it could not even be articulated, it was so awful like the illustrations in her favorite storybook where poor Alice had unwisely nibbled at a mushroom and grew too big to fit in a normal-sized room but had to shove her arm up a chimney and another arm outside a window and her head crushed against the ceiling . . . Though she was terrified at the thought Darren just laughed at her and gave her a little shove that signaled a kind of forgiveness even as it signaled how silly she was, and how much younger and weaker than he.)

(Of the children Naomi was the *worrywart* as Daddy called her. *How's my little worrywart?* Naomi was not sure if a *worrywart* was an actual *wart* which was a kind of hard ugly pimple on the back of an older person's hand, or on a face, terrible-ugly to look at so it wasn't nice to be called a *worrywart* though it seemed clear that Daddy was just teasing and you were expected to laugh when Daddy teased.)

We were not told exactly what our father did, that made living with him *dangerous*.

We knew that our father was a doctor—*Dr. Voorhees*. But we were not sure what kind of doctor he was.

Something to do with *babies*. We thought.

When it was explained to us that there are women and girls who require a special surgery, that only doctors trained like our father could provide. These are women and girls who have found that they are *pregnant*, and the pregnancy is *unwanted*.

A pregnancy is *unwanted* for many reasons and one of them might be, it is a threat to the life of the mother.

Another is, it has come at the wrong time in the mother's life.

And another, it is a result of something forced upon the mother, that the mother *did not want and should not have to bear*.

It was related to us that there were doctors like our father who provided this surgery not only because it was badly needed but also because it was a surgery that some others opposed, on religious grounds, or "moral" grounds, a doctor like our father had to be very careful that he was not attacked by these individuals who opposed it.

We did not know what this meant—*attacked.*

Like in a movie? On TV? *Attacked* with knives, guns? *Attacked* with a bomb?

Darren was the one to ask questions. Naomi sucked her fingers and smiled foolishly. (Melissa was too young to be told anything that would frighten her.)

Of the Voorhees children Darren was the oldest. Naomi was three years younger than Darren and Melissa was two years younger than Naomi. It gave Darren immense satisfaction to know that *he would always be older than his sisters. He would always be taller, bigger, smarter and stronger.*

That meant that Darren could protect his sisters if they required protection. Or, he could discipline his sisters if they required discipline in the absence of our parents.

We were not exactly sure what *preg-nan-cy* meant. We were told but somehow, we did not quite comprehend. At least, Naomi did not comprehend. *Preg-nan-cy* was a scary word like *cancer* you would not say aloud so that an adult might overhear.

Preg-nan-cy was a matter of *free choice*, we were told.

A woman must have control over her body, that is a fundamental human right.

Darren who was always having to argue to show how smart he was, how more astute than his young sisters, smarty-Darren said, A man, too?—and Daddy and Mommy said *Yes of course. A man, too.*

"Would Daddy Hurt Me?"

Melissa was *adopted*. Melissa had been *chosen*. Unlike Darren and Naomi who had come into the family *by chance*.

Yet one day Melissa said to Mommy in her whispery little mouse-voice, "If you and Daddy didn't want me, would Daddy hurt *me*?"—and quickly Mommy said, "Oh but your Mommy and Daddy want *you*. All of *you*."

By *all of you* Mommy meant Darren and Naomi also.

By *all of you* Mommy wanted Melissa to know that she was not any sort of outsider, but *one of us: brother, sister, sister*.

(And was Naomi there, a witness to this exchange? She would surmise that she'd had to be in the kitchen with Mommy and Melissa, to hear these words. She could not have been elsewhere in the house. She would not have been eavesdropping. She was with Mommy and Melissa in the kitchen in the shingle-board house on Drummond Street in Grand Rapids where Melissa and Naomi went to the Montessori school but Darren went to the middle school and where Daddy was a physician/surgeon attached to the Grand Rapids University Medical Center and Mommy was a *stay-at-home mom* who was a legal consultant for the local Planned Parenthood office.)

(The little girls loved to help Mommy in the kitchen. Preparing meals, cleaning up after meals. It was pleasant for Naomi because she was two years older than Melissa and more capable than Melissa, and Mommy would know this. Mommy encouraged Naomi to instruct Melissa, and this made Naomi feel good. Each girl had her own colored sponge to rinse dishes—Naomi's was pink, and Melissa's was green. These colors could not vary. Carefully the girls set the rinsed dishes neatly in the dishwasher for it made them happy when Mommy praised them—*Thank you, girls! You did a perfect job.*)

But today in that soft little mouse-voice Melissa said, "Nobody wanted *me*. My real Mommy gave me away."

"But—but"—Mommy stammered not seeming to know what to say—"but she didn't *mean it*, Melissa."

Didn't mean it! These words of my mother's were so weak and unconvincing, Naomi would pretend that she had not heard.

"Adopted"

Why'd they want *her*. Why aren't we enough . . ."
This question all children ask of their parents, when a new baby is brought into the household. The most reasonable of questions, but no answer will satisfy.

Darren was outraged, resentful. Naomi was deeply wounded.

Why aren't we enough. Oh!

Years later Naomi would recall observing their parents with the *new baby*, from a staircase. And Darren on the step below her, fretting.

Friends were dropping by to see the *new baby*. This was in the (rented) house on Seventh Street, Ann Arbor. In the living room where the baby had been brought, shimmering halos of light. Squeals of delight, uplifted voices both female and male. Giddy happiness of adults that makes children uneasy.

Of course, Darren and Naomi had been prepared by their parents for the *new baby*, the *adoption*. Still it was a shock. It was certainly a surprise!

Already at six Darren was concerned with the (hidden? secret?) motives behind the actions of others, which he distrusted. He had not liked it when the other *new baby* had come into the household several years before, who'd turned out to be his sister Naomi he'd grown to tolerate.

But the *new baby* was particularly unwelcome. For now there were two small girls in the household where before there'd been but one and there was a particular softness to girls that aroused, in adults, emotions of a kind Darren knew he could not arouse.

At three Naomi was a very young child and yet concerned that somehow, in some way she could not anticipate, the *new baby* would involve her in a way that was beyond her.

Twenty years later the question has still the power to wound her in her weakest moments.

Why weren't we enough . . .

Pretty doll-like Melissa with her thick dark eyelashes and small perfect features was a little Chinese girl-orphan whom Mommy and Daddy had adopted through "contacts" in Shanghai. Darren claimed to remember that they'd flown to Shanghai to bring Melissa back with them!—but Naomi was not so sure about this.

Darren would claim that he'd been at the airport to see the plane "fly away"—and he'd been at the airport when the plane had "landed." (None of this was true, evidently. But Darren had insisted it was so.)

Naomi, who had no memory of when the *new baby* had been brought home, only when the *new baby* seemed to have been home for a while, was told that she'd been "very excited" about her new little sister and had wanted to hold her "all the time"—but none of these memories remained with her.

Much that has been related to me I must accept on faith. The memories of others confused with my own which have vanished.

Shut my eyes and see the shotgun blast striking my father's face and all that was Daddy was destroyed in that instant including his children's memories of him and so what point is there in trying to excavate them, if they are lost?—yet if Naomi examined her mother's photograph albums that were brimming with loose snapshots and Polaroids she would discover many pictures from childhood, many of the mid- and late 1990s after Melissa had come into the Voorhees household.

She would spread these photographs on a table for all to contemplate.

Evidence: the (visual) record of a *happy family.*

It would leave her teary-eyed and shaky to examine these pictures too closely. Little Melissa and Naomi cuddling with Mommy in a porch swing, little Melissa and Naomi lifted into Daddy's muscled arms . . .

Sometimes Daddy had a beard. Other times, Daddy did not have a beard. Daddy's beard was not the color of his hair (which was a gingery-toast color), Daddy's beard was wiry and white, and threaded with dark crinkly hairs. Daddy's beard was *scratchy-funny.*

In Grand Rapids there were not many Chinese people. It was rare to see any except at the Chinese restaurants which were Mommy's and Daddy's favorite restaurants in Grand Rapids. In Naomi's school there were no Chinese children.

At first you saw that Melissa was different-looking from other children but soon, you did not see that at all. You did not "see" anything unusual about Melissa except that her hair was very black and very silky and shiny and that her eyes were different-shaped than other people's eyes and she was very pretty like a doll. And there was a stillness and watchfulness about her which you would not see in other children.

Which was why sometimes at school or in some

public place (like the Grand Rapids mall) it was surprising that others stared at her so openly, seeing her
with her family; or that older children dared to say
stupid mean things revealing their own ignorance.

Little Chinee girl?

Hey little Chink-Chink.

Where'd you come from, Chink-Chink?

Melissa did not seem to hear these taunts. Mommy
walked us quickly away. We did not look back.

Comm-un-NISTS!

It was rare that Daddy was with us on excursions to
the mall or to the grocery store. And so, if Daddy was
with us, no one would make such crude remarks, that
we could hear.

It had been explained to Darren and Naomi what
"adoption" meant. The subject had been brought up
as if casually and set aside for another time and then
brought up again, the second time in more detail.
And the third time in greater detail. This was the
way our parents approached such matters: methodically. So we were made to understand that we would
have a new little sister in the family who was *adopted*.
Carefully this was presented by both Mommy and
Daddy who read us Chinese storybooks for children,
showed us Chinese picture books and played videos

on our TV of Chinese people, Chinese art, Chinese history.

It was related to us: "Melissa" was just a little girl but she came from a great, ancient civilization that had cultivated the arts, and science, and agriculture, and had built waterways and roadways and the Great Wall when (as Daddy said) his ancestors were still swinging from trees.

For a long while, in one of my dreamy states I would see human figures swinging from trees like monkeys. I would feel unease and worry and yet, I would find myself smiling.

His being has suffused mine. I would try to escape but I do not want to escape. His being is everywhere. It is his eyes through which I look, at sights he never saw, yet he interprets them for me.

Before the adoption, Mommy and Daddy were showing us pictures of Melissa. Already this felt to us like a betrayal, the way the pictures were brought out to us, the way we were summoned, to sit together on the sofa, in a way that felt unnatural, even posed; we understood that our parents must have had these pictures for a while, and must have discussed them together, in the privacy of their bedroom from which at certain times we were barred; yet they were behaving now as if the pictures were new, and expected us to react to them as they did.

"Well—what do you think?"

Instead, Darren said nothing. Naomi said nothing.

"Your new little sister is beautiful—isn't she?"

Warily, Darren shrugged. Naomi frowned, sucking at her fingers.

Despite even the evidence of the pictures the affronted brother and sister did not entirely believe that they would have a new, little sister from China or from anywhere else. Darren did not believe it really, and Naomi did not think about it *at all.*

But then, one day a seven-month-old baby with feathery tufts of thin black hair was brought into the house in Grand Rapids, in Mommy's arms, and with Daddy close beside, and from that time onward Melissa was their *little sister.*

It was shocking, the baby was *real.* The children had not been able to comprehend even the idea of the baby, and now the baby was *real.*

You could run away to hide. You could gape and blink into the bassinet. You could act very silly chattering and laughing like a monkey, or you could be very quiet, clenching your jaws so your back teeth ached. It made no difference really, Mommy and Daddy would scarcely notice.

Darren glowered with resentment and jealousy, Naomi knew he'd have liked to strangle the new little sister. For a long time he could not utter the name "Melissa"—as Naomi did.

Meanly they whispered together. Wished their parents would send Melissa back to China! Nobody needed her.

Too young to consider that obviously there was something lacking in the family, our parents had felt the need for a third child when our father was in his late forties and our mother at about the age when bearing a child was beginning to be "problematic"—and at a time when our father's work was becoming increasingly dangerous.

But Melissa was *so little*, it was hard for Darren and Naomi to hate her for long.

Such a nice feeling when Melissa began to recognize them and to smile at them, within weeks of her arrival. Such a nice feeling when Melissa closed her tiny fist around your finger! And Melissa shook both her hands at Darren excitedly as if she had a particular message for him. The kitten-squeaks she made were not intelligible but Darren pretended he could understand.

"How much can the baby understand of what we say?"—Naomi was anxious to know.

"The baby understands *feelingly.*"

(This was a Shakespearean line, Naomi would recall years later. At the time it was uttered by Daddy as if it were his own and very likely, from Gus Voorhees's perspective, it was his own.)

Not until a few years later, when Melissa was old enough to understand, or to understand partly, did Mommy and Daddy explain to her that she'd been *adopted.*

They told Melissa she'd been *chosen.* Unlike most children who are born to their parents—like Darren and Naomi, for instance—who'd come into the world as surprises— ("but very special surprises")—Melissa had been *freely and deliberately chosen.*

In his serious-Daddy voice Daddy said:

"An adopted child is a chosen child. An adopted child is a very much-wanted child. An adopted child has two sets of parents, and is in the world doubly. There are the biological parents—whom she may someday discover, if she wishes—at least, the biological mother. And there are the adoptive parents—who have chosen her out of multitudes."

The strange word was *multitudes.* We did not know what to make of it. There was something terrible in the thought—a vast sea of little babies, and Melissa among them, but hardly distinguishable from any of them. No wonder that she cast her eyes down, and waited for the ordeal to end.

The White Box

H ey Nao-miii! Something for you."

It was a white box. But not a clean white box. One of those boxes for doughnuts, with grease stains.

This was not the Grand Rapids Montessori school now. We had moved to Saginaw, Michigan. With each school there were fewer names I would care to know and I did not know the names of these girls grinning at Melissa and me.

Afterward I would surmise that they were not the ones who'd prepared the box for us. Whoever had imagined this "gift" had to be older. In middle school or even in high school.

"Hey Naomi. You c'n take it, for your sister and you."

(I did not want to think that the actual words were nasal-mumbled *for your chink sister and you*.)

They were excited. Their eyes darted and glittered.

Yet I seemed to think—*Do they like me? Really?*

My hands were shaking with excitement, or with dread.

"Go on, open it Nao-miii. It's for *you*."

My heart leapt with hope. Lifted like leaves sucked by a sudden wind. For I was so lonely here wherever (most recently) *here* was.

As I unfastened the string crudely tied around the box, squatting over it, and Melissa staring silently at the box, I tried not to see how there were others, older children, boys as well as girls, standing at a little distance by the corner of the school wall, watching.

I opened the box. A nasty smell lifted.

I blinked, and stared. Melissa gave a little cry.

I kicked the box from me, and grabbed Melissa's hand, and pulled her blindly with me, back into the school.

Hot clumps of bile rose into my mouth, I was stooped, gagging.

Vomit on the floor, and on my sneakers. And poor Melissa terrified asking what was it? what had it been?—for she hadn't seen what was in the box, not clearly as I had.

That night Melissa woke screaming in the bed next to mine.

After Mommy had switched off our bedside light in the shape of a fuzzy sheep I had lain with my eyes shut tight trying not to see the box, and what was mangled and bleeding inside the box, and I had not been able to sleep.

"It was just a dream, honey. A bad dream."

Mommy hugged Melissa who was whimpering and shivering.

Mommy asked me if I had any idea what it was that had so frightened my little sister—the "bad dream."

No idea.

In Mommy's arms Melissa quieted, after a while. I felt such jealousy seeing them, my mother who was so beautiful (I thought) and my little sister who was so pretty, huddled together. The white woolly sheep that was our bedside lamp cast a warm light outward but caused sharp shadows, shadows like knife-blades, in the folds of the bedclothes of both beds, and in the space beneath the beds where something might be hiding.

"It's this place—Saginaw. We're not wanted here. We don't want to be here."

Mommy spoke in a hoarse whisper. Mommy was

hugging Melissa who clung to her panting. There was an air of reproach in Mommy's voice that meant *Your father is to blame. Not me!*

"You're sure that something hasn't happened, Naomi? To Melissa? To you? At school?"

I shook my head *no*. I was not happy at being wakened even if, in fact, I had not been asleep.

And what could I have told my mother? There were no adequate words.

When I asked Darren, Does Daddy kill babies?—my brother grimaced and said loftily that wasn't what they called them.

I did not understand this. What was *them*? Who was *they*?

Darren said, *Feet-usses.* They call them *feet-usses*, stupid.

"So Clumsy"

Another time on the stairs to the gym at Saginaw Elementary South the big Biedenk girl pushed me from behind, caused me to fall and turn my ankle. Trying not to cry, the pain came so hard.

See how you like it bitch! Your old man's a damn fuckin baby killer.

It had been an accident on the stairs. I would explain to adults.

I was in a hurry, I hadn't looked down. I missed a step. I fell.

My own fault I am so clumsy.

"A Baby Killer Lives in Your Neighborhood"

When these (mustard-yellow) flyers first appeared, stuffed into neighbors' mailboxes and beneath the windshield wipers of neighbors' vehicles, shoved inside screen doors, nailed to telephone posts on our block—torn, tattered, wind-blown—flattened against chain-link fences including (even) our own—floating facedown in puddles like mute dead things—we did not know for our excuse was *We are children, we are not required to know.*

And what little we knew we did not acknowledge for to know a thing is not the same as acknowledging that you know a thing, especially to your parents; and if you do not acknowledge that you know a thing, you are not obliged to know it nor are you obliged to remember it.

Darren knew, but Naomi did not. Melissa did not.

Not for a long time not for years Melissa did not.

And yet: Melissa we'd seen stooping to pick up one of the ugly mustard-yellow flyers from the rain-slick sidewalk near our house, staring at it, smoothing it with her small hands and staring at it, perplexed? curious?—seemingly not alarmed or frightened; folding it and slipping it into her backpack as if for safe-keeping.

Also: small white wooden crosses pounded into the ground, in the night, in front of the clinic headed by Gus Voorhees that had to be hurriedly removed by staffers when they arrived in the morning *which we had not seen with our own eyes and consequently would not remember.*

As we did not hear the chanted *Our Father, Hail Mary!*

As we did not hear the singsong verse like a lullaby gone wrong:

Free choice is a lie,
Nobody's baby chooses to die.

Application,
University of Michigan
School of Arts and Sciences*

*T*ell us about your background. Where you were born, where you grew up, your childhood and family memories. Why you want to attend the University of Michigan and what you hope to discover here.

Because it was a story related to us many times. We were a family in Ann Arbor.

Because I was born in the university hospital in Ann Arbor, April 7, 1987.

---

* This application was never completed, and never sent.

Because we were happy then.

Because there are special facilities at U-M for students with *disabilities*.

Because my father Dr. Gus Voorhees graduated summa cum laude with a B.A. from the School of Arts and Sciences in 1974 and from the U-M medical school with a specialization in obstetrical surgery and public health. Because my father had expressed a wish that all of his children would attend the University of Michigan and it is my hope to attend in honor of him.

Because my father did not abandon me but loved me.

Because my family is broken now. Because I am broken.

Because by attending the University of Michigan at Ann Arbor, I will be living in the place my parents lived.

Because it has been related to me that my young mother pushed me in a stroller on Ann Arbor streets, on walkways and across the university campus when I was a baby. Because my young father carried me in a backpack when we hiked in the arboretum.

Because it has been related to me that we lived in a rented "duplex" on Third Street and later in an apartment building on State Street. Because it has been related to me that my parents' favorite restaurant was Szechuan Kitchen on State Street where there were tables outside in a courtyard, in warm weather, and there, I would be seated in a high chair.

Because it has been related to me *We were so happy then!*

Because it was the time before Daddy was gone away from us so much.

Because it was a time when, when Daddy was away, there was not a fear that Daddy would not return.

Because I remember none of this time clearly and what I do remember is the kind of memory you would have of a film you had seen only once long ago.

Because it is the kind of memory you would have of a film you had not believed to be important at the time while what was important to you was if you were hungry, and if you had to go to the bathroom—the urgency of needing to be taken quickly to a bathroom by your mother before there was an accident.

Such petty anguish, the (physical) being of a child. These are our first memories and we do not cherish them.

And so I am hoping that, if I am admitted to the University of Michigan at Ann Arbor, I will remember some of the happiness of my lost life.

―――――

Because the university of Michigan at Ann Arbor is one of the great public universities in the United States.

Because my parents believed in public education and not in private education because my parents had faith in "democracy" which is not so popular today.

Because they had hope for their children. Because I am one of their children.

Because I am trying to understand—the responsibility of the "bloodline."

Because my father did not believe in questioning *what you know instinctively to be your duty.*

Because my father Gus Voorhees enrolled as a freshman at the University of Michigan at Ann Arbor when he was eighteen years old and it is my quest to discover how he became the person he was subsequently—if it is possible to know such a thing.

Because in a few months I will be eighteen years old.

Because they met in that place—Ann Arbor, Michigan. Without that place, and that time, they would not have met.

My brother Darren would not be alive. I would not be alive.

Our sister Melissa would be alive but living in Shanghai (?). Or perhaps, Melissa would not be alive.

On a trip to China in the 1980s traveling by boat on the Yangtze River he'd seen corpses of infants swirling in the mud-colored water.

Girl babies we were told.

Because he'd seen, and had not forgotten.

Because there is so little we can do. Yet it is our duty, to do it.

Because he had not lost faith and because I am hoping to learn what faith is.

Because when my father was murdered on November 2, 1999, all his memory of our family was obliterated in the instant of a shotgun's explosion.

Because we are that family, we have been obliterated in that instant.

Because what is lost can be retrieved only with effort.

Because if I am admitted to U-M at Ann Arbor I will continue the archive of my father Gus Voorhees's life (and death). Because I will use the university library to research thoroughly and methodically as I have not (yet) attempted.

Because years were lost when I could not begin.

Because randomly and haphazardly I began the archive after my father's death not knowing what I was doing as a rat will save items woven into a nest and now that I am older, and am less *disabled*, I will continue the archive more deliberately. Because my mother was angry with me when she discovered what I had been doing that I had not been doing deliberately but (it seemed to her) secretly because I did not want her to see it and so it was hidden away in an inadequate place where there was dampness, and much of the material has been torn, rotted, and ruined. Because my mother presumed that what I was doing was deliberate and secret because it appeared that way to her who had no idea what I was doing because I did not know myself what I was doing because my thoughts were scattered and it was not clear to me, that "Naomi" was the same person from one day to the next and that this person was to be trusted.

Because if I am admitted as a freshman to the University I will behave then like a freshman at the University. Because I will mimic the behavior of other students that is visible and from this I think that I can successfully deduce behavior that is not visible.

Because my mother said *I am sorry, I can't be your mother any longer.*

Because my mother said *You must make your own way. I am sorry.*

Because after my father died there was a sickness in my soul.

Because as a girl I hated those who had both parents living.

Because there was a terrible rage in me even as I smiled at them thinking *Some day you will know. Some day they will be dead.*

Because it has been years, the murderer is still alive in the Ohio prison.

Because we are waiting for his death—his *execution.*

Because it is a sick hateful thing, to be waiting for another's *execution.*

Because if I am admitted to the University I will use every facility in the library to research the life and death of Gus Voorhees. What has been done haphazardly and childishly will be done with care, I vow.

Because there is microfilm in the library, I will learn to examine. I will use computers.

I will search for letters, snapshots, manuscripts— every sort of documentation. I will search.

I will interview people in Ann Arbor and Ypsilanti

who knew my father. People who knew my parents. Doctors and staff at the hospital, women's health center. Friends, neighbors. I will go to them and I will say *Do you remember me, I am Gus Voorhees's daughter Naomi.*

"False Alarm": June 1997

Were your parents happy?

What was it like to be a child of Gus Voorhees?

And for your mother—what do you think it was like for Jenna Matheson to be Gus Voorhees's wife for sixteen years?

"Because I say it's not."

My weird brother Darren had it fixed in his brain, the way something stringy might fix itself between your teeth, and slowly drive you crazy if you couldn't remove it, that our mother's decision, or rather our mother's sudden change-of-plans, was not a good idea.

I persisted—"Why not? What's the difference?"

"It's not good to change plans impulsively."

"You're being ridiculous."

"*You're* ridiculous."

Exasperated my brother glared at me. Deliberately my eye sought out the patches of acne on his forehead and cheeks, that kept Darren from being a strikingly attractive boy.

He said, with the righteous stubbornness with which he practiced his braying trumpet outside in the garage where my mother had banished him with a plea of *Darren, please! Some of us are trying to retain our sanity*: "She should call first."

"How do you know she hasn't called?"

"Because I *asked her.* And she said 'That isn't necessary.'"

Darren had caught the haughty calm of our mother's voice but not the quaver beneath. Such mockery, if that's what it was, made me uneasy for the obvious and abiding truth was, I loved our mother much more than I loved my difficult brother.

"Why don't you call Dad yourself, then? If you think it's so crucial."

"Why should I call Dad! *She's* his damn wife."

In Darren's lips *she* was a hateful hissing word meant to shock.

He added: "She's got some agenda, she doesn't want us to know about."

"'Agenda'—what's that?"

"Some *idea*. Some *reason*. God damn *motive*."

Lanky, loose-limbed Darren. At thirteen he was nearly as tall as our mother and he loomed over me when he wished as if to threaten me with his very being. Out of a strange sibling shyness he seemed to avoid Melissa whom he did not wish to bully but with whom he found it difficult to speak.

Essentially, Darren was protective of his younger sisters. If it came to that. For such protectiveness is a responsible brother's *duty*.

"Oh, hell. Who *cares*."

Darren spoke in sudden exasperation, disgust.

We were upstairs in the narrow low-ceilinged hall that buzzed faintly at times with flies you could not always see. Rudely my brother pushed past me as if my questions had annoyed him. Might've avoided bumping into me if he'd tried but he didn't try, breathing loudly through his mouth like an animal hot-panting, eager to get away before he committed worse damage to his sister.

In a family of more than two siblings there is the inevitable oldest sibling, could be a girl, in this case a boy, burdened with a precocious knowledge of family politics that excludes the other siblings who remain therefore young, oblivious. Such responsibility is thankless,

Darren seemed to know beforehand, as it is unavoidable.

One day I would be asked if my brother had been an angry child, or an unusually emotional child, before our father's death, and I would say protectively *My brother was a normal boy for his age, his class, and his time. We were a normal family and we were happy except when we were confused about whether we were happy or not because we were made to think about it, and to wonder.*

And did we love one another?—yes. We did.

"You kids! c'mon! We're late."

From downstairs Mom called us. That voice!

A bright voice, a happy-seeming voice, a voice of motherly no-nonsense. The TV-Mom voice at the (playful) edge of patience lifting up the stairs—"Get down here, *mes amis,* or we're leaving without you!"

Here was a festive voice. You might almost think.

Not the voice we'd (over)hear on the phone pleading begging *Gus please return this call. Gus I am so worried about you where are you darling.*

Melissa was already downstairs—or already outside, buckled into her seat in the station wagon—for (adopted, ontologically insecure) Melissa was *never late.*

Indeed, if Mom had wanted us to leave the house promptly at noon it was now several minutes after noon and it was proper for her to betray exasperation.

Quickly we descended the stairs. In the lead Darren was heavy-footed as often he was in the (rented) house on the Salt Hill Road which he resented, as if he'd hoped to break the wooden steps.

Close behind him Naomi did not—quite—dare to be too close for fear of treading on her brother's heels which would provoke Darren to turn furiously upon her, striking her with the flat of his hand as you'd discipline a too-eager dog.

Sometimes (it might be confessed) Naomi trod upon her brother's heels out of younger-sister mischief, or sibling-spite; such small assaults were deliberate enough, yet easily confused with accidental assaults for which it was unjust to be blamed.

"Watch *out*."

"I didn't do it *on purpose*."

Almost in tandem we ran from the house. For always there was the half-pleasurable touch of child-panic—

Wait!—wait for me.

A bright warm day in mid-June in Huron County, Michigan: school had been out just one week.

An incandescent light shimmered from the sky

that was bleached of color, reflecting the rough water of Lake Huron five miles to the north, and not visible from the Salt Hill Road.

In a blur of pale lilac—linen slacks, matching jacket—our mother slid into the driver's seat of the Chevy station wagon. Her glossy dark hair was plaited into a single thick braid that fell between her shoulder blades. Her eyes, that tended to water in bright air, were shielded behind sunglasses, and her mouth, described by our father (embarrassingly) as *eminently kissable*, was a dark plum color.

Beside our mother was our little sister Melissa pert and darkly pretty. So small, and so unobtrusive, you might almost miss that she was there.

But always, Melissa *was*.

We did not like to consider—(Darren and Naomi did not like to consider)—how frequently Melissa sat in front with our mother or, less frequently, our father. Overnight it had happened, seemingly irrevocably, that as soon as Melissa was old enough not to be strapped into the demeaning child-seat in the rear, she sat in the passenger's seat beside the driver.

We did not complain, *we took not the slightest notice*.

But having so often to be together in the backseat of a vehicle, the two of us older siblings, thrown into each other's company and forced to stare steely-eyed out the side windows pointedly ignoring each other—that wasn't so great.

Now, we were (almost) late. Hurriedly Mom backed the Chevy station wagon down the rutted and puddled driveway at an angle, cursing beneath her breath—"Damn!"

Our (rented) house three miles west of the small town of St. Croix, Michigan, was a clapboard house dingy-white as a gull's soiled feathers. It was a forget-table house, a house you could not "see" if you were not standing before it; not a house to nourish memories though it was, or would become, a house to nourish regret like the toadstools that emerged out of wet soil around its base.

Seven miles in the opposite direction from St. Croix (population 11,400) was the smaller town of Bad Axe (population 3,040). Our mother had said, when we'd moved to rural Huron County from Saginaw, at least we're not living in a place called *Bad Axe*. No one would believe me!

The clapboard farmhouse had been built atop an uneven knoll, an upstairs lump of land like a thumb. In the stone foundation was a faint numeral—1939.

The unpaved driveway veered and careened downhill to Salt Hill Road where the aluminum mailbox stood atilt and scarified from numerous collisions.

There had been another house in St. Croix which our parents had rented, or had intended to rent, several months before. This was a ranch-style house on a residential street (only just three blocks from St. Croix Elementary, which Melissa would attend) into which we'd been partly moved when something had gone wrong, a misunderstanding about the terms of the lease, or a disagreement between the landlord and my father, or a "dispute"—and the boxes we'd unpacked had had to be hastily and humbly repacked, and the rental trailer reloaded, so that within a single harried day we moved another time, to the very farmhouse on Salt Hill Road which my parents had seen, and had rejected, my mother with particular vigor, weeks before.

It was a vague promise of our father's that we would find another, more suitable house in St. Croix soon.

To spare us the rural school buses, which had not been very pleasant for any of us, in the first week or so of school, our mother usually drove us to and from school.

(Our parents had asked us not to speak of the school buses. Not to complain. Bullying, harassment, sexual threats—"rough behavior"—we would be spared the rural-America school bus experience but were not to think that we were in any way *superior to* the boys who were the sons of our Huron County neighbors.)

(For our parents were adamant, idealistic, [usually] unyielding liberals. They did not believe in anything other than public schooling and hoped to convince each other that their children's sojourn in the Huron County public school system would not sabotage our educations or our opportunity to attend first-rank universities.)

In the station wagon Darren was restless, fretting.

"Mom, did you call Dad? Does he know we're coming to meet him first?"—Darren couldn't resist asking.

"Darren, no. I have to drop the car off at the garage to get it inspected. *You* know that."

"But—"

"We'll get to the Center before your father leaves. Please don't catastrophize!"

That was our father's most earnest admonition to his family—*Please don't catastrophize.* This was an entirely made-up word, we would one day discover. And it did not—ever—apply to our father himself.

Dad operated within so tightly wound and so intricately structured a schedule, nearly always running late, fleeing phone calls, searching for mislaid car keys, wallet, sometimes even his shoes, he could not bear the anxieties of others in addition to his own.

It was sharp-eyed Darren who'd discovered just that

morning that the inspection sticker on the Chevy station wagon was outdated by five months. With grim-gleeful reproach he'd run to tell our mother that she was in danger of getting a ticket, possibly getting arrested, driving without a valid 1997 sticker issued by the Michigan Department of Motor Vehicles—"You or Dad better take the car to get inspected, fast!"

Dad had his own, newer car, that is his *pre-owned* 1993 Volvo, and Mom had inherited the 1991 Chevy station wagon for her full-time use. Thus responsibility for the station wagon had fallen between the two adults like a ball indifferently dropped, rolling heedlessly about at their feet, unacknowledged.

The original plan for the day had been to meet Dad for lunch at one o'clock at a lakeshore restaurant called The Cove, which was our parents' new favorite restaurant, overlooking Lake Huron five miles north of our house; Dad would be driving to The Cove from the center of St. Croix, a distance of two miles. That morning, however, without consulting him, Mom had conceived of a "brilliant—and pragmatic" new idea: we would drive to St. Croix and drop the station wagon off at a garage, and we would walk the short distance to the women's center where Gus Voorhees was physician-in-chief, and surprise him—"You kids never see your father at work. You deserve that." Then, Mom reasoned, our father would drive us all to The Cove, and by the time we returned from lunch, in the early afternoon, the station wagon would be ready to be picked up at the garage.

Of course, prissy Darren objected to this plan on two grounds: it was a *change of plans*, which seemed to nettle him on principle; and, what if our father left for The Cove before we got to the women's center, how would we get to the restaurant?

"Don't be ridiculous, Darren. We'll get to the Center by twelve-thirty. Your father won't leave for the restaurant until at least quarter to one. Gus Voorhees has never been early for anything, and he isn't likely to start today."

"I think you'd better call Dad anyway."

"Your father doesn't like nuisance calls at work. We'll just surprise him."

"It isn't a *nuisance call*. It's us!"

"Your father doesn't like *unnecessary calls*. He's a busy man."

"But—what if he leaves early for the Cove?"

Brainless as a parrot my brother was repeating himself. And so grim was he presenting these superficial objections, our mother laughed at him. How could that possibly happen! Why was he being so silly! There was something edgy and provocative in our mother's laughter like the scratching of fingernails on a blackboard.

"But—but—what if the station wagon isn't ready to be picked up when we're back from lunch? How'll we get home?"—this was Darren's fumbling *coup de grâce*.

"'How will we *get home*?'—Darren, we live three miles away. There will always be a way to *get home*."

In the rearview mirror our mother's eyes flashed at us in warning yet still she was smiling. Her mood was cheery, ebullient.

How beautiful she seemed, to us! Before the ravaging.

Mom said that if the station wagon wasn't ready when we returned from lunch, we could wait in the public library—"I want to go there anyway, to pick up a book. It may not be Ann Arbor but the library isn't bad."

So frequently our mother would preface a wistful remark with *It may not be Ann Arbor but . . .*

We'd lived in Ann Arbor long ago. To me, a lifetime ago.

Darren scornfully refuted most of my memories of Ann Arbor as mistaken, fraudulent. Especially I was eager to recall a place and a time where (we all knew, she hardly disguised her feelings) my mother had been

happier. I had been born—(that is, I'd been *told so*)—
at the University of Michigan Medical School Hospital
where at the time Gus Voorhees was a physician on the
staff; soon afterward, he shifted his interests to another kind of medical care, public health, community-
oriented, female-centered, and we moved away. Of
Ann Arbor I could remember little clearly except a
vast, hilly park of hiking trails to which I'd been taken
as a small child in a backpack on my father's back—
the excitement of those hikes, a pleasurable jolting like
being rocked in a cradle, seeing the park spread out astonishingly before my eyes even as, so strangely, I was
being carried backward . . .

Mom had hiked with us of course in this beautiful
place they called the *arboretum*. And Darren too—I
had to assume. Only vaguely did I remember *him*.

On the drive into St. Croix through open fields, past
farmhouses and small clapboard houses dingy-white
and *cruddy* (Darren's most frequently used word) as
our own, Darren shifted his shoulders and lanky-long
legs in the seat beside me, and continued to fret, in an
undertone meant for our mother to hear. At last she
said, peering at him in the rearview mirror:

"Look, Darren—it's my birthday, practically. I should
get to do what I want to do on my damned birthday."

"Your birthday isn't until next week!"

Our mother's blatant misstatements of fact seemed to particularly aggrieve Darren. At thirteen he'd become increasingly literal-minded, fussy and judgmental—not about himself but about the rest of us. Especially, our parents' attempts at humor offended him, as if, in his ears, such humor was meant to obscure a harsher and more profound reality hovering like mist beyond the ragged foliage surrounding our house.

Our mother was saying, pleading: "Look. I'm sure that's why your father wanted to have an 'excursion' today. He'll be gone next week—to Washington, D.C. And he was away last weekend. Please just try to relax, Darren. You seem so—angry . . ."

Darren muttered what sounded like *angry! Jesus* and squirmed in his seat, kicking the back of the driver's seat.

In our family there had come to be the tradition of the *family excursion*. These were sudden adventures planned by our father—usually impromptu, when a *window of opportunity* opened in his crowded schedule—involving a few hours *snatched from oblivion* as he liked to say. The *family excursion* had the air of the unexpected and the surprise; it could not ever involve any other persons, only the Voorhees family (two adults, three children); invariably it involved driving somewhere, as far as possible given restraints of time and common sense—once, to Houghton Lake; another time, to Saginaw Bay at Katechay Point. Rare that Gus Voorhees could take a few days off in succession—(more precisely, rare that Gus Voorhees would want to take a few days off in succession)—but when he could, and we didn't have school, he drove "my brood" to Mackinac Island in northern Michigan where we stayed in a ramshackle cabin that belonged to relatives.

These were our happiest times. You would surmise.

It wasn't often that our mother was so ebullient and funny, as she was on this day; not often that she smiled so much, and with such *dazzle*.

Except possibly, too much *dazzle*.

Our mother had made an effort to dress for this excursion. Not her usual flannel shirts, T-shirts, torn jeans, grimy Nike running shoes or, more often, at least indoors, no shoes at all; but rather the stylish lilac-colored linen suit purchased at a consignment shop in the Detroit suburb of Birmingham—(for Mom purchased most of her clothes at consignment shops, on principle: she was morally outraged by the prices of most clothes). She'd brushed and braided her almost waist-length hair, she'd "made up" her face. *She has prepared herself to be beautiful for Gus Voorhees though she is (she knows: she accepts) not a beautiful woman but rather an ardent and intense woman who*

can (sometimes) convince a man (that man) that she is
beautiful or, if she is not beautiful, that beauty does not
matter: ardor and intensity matter.

Often there were times—days, weeks—when our
mother did not smile much. When a smile from her felt
like a rubber band being stretched tight—tighter. On
the worst days of the interminable Michigan winter
now behind us. (You did not ever want to think: yes,
and before us, too.) On those evenings when our father
didn't come home for an evening meal because he was
elsewhere, at another meal; or he was away altogether,
in another part of the state, or in another state; he was
"dining with" wealthy contributors (in Birmingham,
Bloomfield Hills, Grosse Pointe) to women's organizations, who happened to be (older, lonely) wealthy
women for whom time spent in the company of Gus
Voorhees was a thrill.

He'd become something of a male-feminist hero
in Michigan, in some quarters, having made an im-
passioned presentation before the Michigan state
legislature in 1981 that convinced enough of the (pre-
dominantly conservative) legislators to vote into law
the establishment of a special commission on women's
reproductive medical rights, on which Gus Voorhees
had served. The legislature also approved a budget
increase for women's community medical services, a

controversial subject in Michigan as elsewhere in the
United States: should public funds be used to provide
abortions? And which kinds of abortion?—therapeutic,
following rape or incest, elective? Should public funds
be used to provide contraception? Social welfare issues
that had seemed to have been decided definitively years
before were revealed as not decided at all, rather they
were continually under attack, and increasingly vulnerable since the Presidential election of Ronald Reagan in
1980. No issues aroused more passion in both political parties, and with each elected legislature, and each
new campaign to maintain, increase, or decrease the
budget, Gus Voorhees was involved as a public-health
physician-spokesman.

Our father had long been "under attack" from his
enemies—(we would learn after his death). We'd been
allowed to see some of the friendlier responses in the
media—articles in newspapers in Ann Arbor and
Detroit, cover stories in the *University of Michigan
Alumni Bulletin, Michigan Public Health* and *Michigan Life,* a profile on Gus Voorhees—"Crusader for
Women's Rights"—in the *New York Times Magazine.*

By the age of forty he'd virtually surrendered a private life. So our mother would say wistfully yet with an
air (we thought) of pride.

Famous? Infamous.

Can't separate the two.

Winter afternoons shading into dusk when we would find our mother lying on the sagging brass bed upstairs in her and Dad's bedroom, a cheerless room with fraying wallpaper like wet tissue, with a damp towel over her face—(for she suffered every two or three weeks from what she called *idiopathic migraine*); or, on better days, we would find our mother upstairs in the low-ceilinged room she called her office, at a table facing a dormer window, working on her IBM personal computer squarely before her, frowning and intense and often excited. As Jenna Matheson (who was qualified to practice law in Michigan) she sent and received countless emails; she made and received countless calls; she could immerse herself as deeply in her work as our father did in his, or nearly. She was a legal consultant for women's rights organizations in Ann Arbor, Grand Rapids, and Saginaw, as well as Michigan Planned Parenthood, with which she was most associated; she was an editor for *Women and the Law: An American Review,* which was published by a coalition of women's legal associations, at the University of Chicago Law School. She was always writing book reviews, essays—for years she'd been revising her one-hundred-page Master's thesis (English, University of Wisconsin) titled *The*

Battered Woman: Portraits of the Female Self in Literature, in the hope of getting it published.

Sometimes as we approached our mother's office we would hear her on the phone; we would hear her speak sharply and incisively; we might hear her laugh in a way we did not often hear her laugh, in our presence. We might hear her muttering to herself, sighing. And again, laughing. If we knocked on the (usually ajar) door our mother would turn to us with a quick vague squinting-guilty smile—"Oh Christ! Is it that late? Time to *eat?*"

At Dante's auto repair Mom gave the station wagon keys to the mechanic: "It isn't a new vehicle, obviously. It may need some fixing-up. There's been a rattle in the engine, or somewhere beneath the hood, for a while. The left rear tire seems a little *flat.* Please change the oil, or—whatever you usually do. Thank you!" In a little procession we walked to the Huron County Women's Center three blocks away on South Main Street. Now the sky had cleared, to a degree: the pale incandescent light seemed to fall directly from above, sunshine filtered through gaseous clouds. The sidewalks of St. Croix were not much populated as in a painting by Edward Hopper and so we did not imagine—*We are being observed. Family of Dr. Gus Voorhees baby killer.*

We'd heard much from our parents about the women's center in St. Croix, for which our father had first been a consulting physician and, more recently, head of the staff, but we had not visited it until now—that is, Darren, Naomi, and Melissa had not visited the Center; we were not sure if our mother had, since her remarks about the Center were cryptic and ambiguous.

That place! That place that has swallowed your father's life.

It will be a relief when we can leave here. This is "interim"—not "permanent."

The Huron County Women's Center turned out to be a nondescript cement-block building at the far end of South Main, in a neighborhood of warehouses, discount furniture and carpet stores, rubble-strewn vacant lots. The building might have been a small factory, not a medical center; it did not seem to be a medical center "newly opened"; a single-story building set back in a grassless lot, with oddly shuttered windows like great blind eyes. You could see—we could see—that there'd been graffiti on the sand-colored walls that had been crudely repainted and had dried in uneven patches like mange. Beside the building an asphalt parking lot was crowded with vehicles of the general type and quality of our 1991 Chevy station wagon: vehicles that would have drawn from Darren the adjective *cruddy.*

Much of South Main looked derelict and abandoned. What a disappointment! It did not seem possible that our father Gus Voorhees whom we'd been led to think was *a very special person* worked here.

Then we saw, on the sidewalk in front of the Center, a dozen or more people (men, women) standing oddly still, with picket signs resting on their shoulders. We could not see the words on the picket signs, or the pictures—(for some picket signs bore pictures). Several of the picketers also held what appeared to be bead necklaces in their hands, which one day I would know to be *rosaries.* These individuals seemed to come alive, seeing us. Quickly our mother said, "Ignore them! Please. *Do not look at them.*"

Hurriedly we crossed the lot slantwise toward the front door of the Center, to avoid passing too near these strangers. Even so, Darren stared insolently at them. His boy's face, subtly blemished as if wind- or sun-burnt, was taut with a kind of mortified and indignant shock; his eyes gave no sign of *seeing.* Frightened Melissa, and frightened Naomi, willing to be commanded by their mother, hurried along pulled by her and made no attempt to *see.*

The picketers called after us—but we did not hear.

We are praying for you. God bless you!

God forgives you.

God loves you.

These were nonsensical words, truly we did not hear. Naomi resisted the powerful instinct to shove fingers into her mouth and to suck, which helped to not-hear.

Those beautiful children have been born—they are blessed of God!

Pray for all children—blessed of God!

The heavy metallic front doors of the Center were locked and were windowless also. On the much-painted cement walls beside the doors you could see shadow-shapes of words scrawled beneath the paint, but you could not read the words.

Other shapes, spidery and spiky, might've been swastikas. A small calm voice warned me—*Don't look closely, Naomi.*

Often this voice came to me, at such times when I felt like one making her way across a raised platform that is very narrow, the width of a plank. The warning is *Don't look closely, you will fall.* This voice had first slipped into my head at the time of the white box.

Is it strange, the voice addressed *Naomi?*—as if Naomi herself were not the source of the voice?

I have not asked any psychologist, therapist, or

doctor if such a voice is "normal"—or if it is a kind of low-mimetic schizophrenia. For truly I don't hear the voice, it is more as if I feel it.

Sometimes you feel vibrations in your skull, along your spine. The tingling of nerve-endings. Without such nerves, there is no pain—without pain, there is no consciousness.

And did I know, at age ten, what a *swastika* was, and what a *swastika* meant? I did not.

Though very possibly, Darren knew.

We were quiet now. Our mother had ceased her bright nervous chatter as she rang a buzzer beside the front door. How badly we wanted not to be here!

The picketers continued to call to us, as one might call to stray dogs for whom they had little hope— *Hello? Here! Listen—please. God bless.* There must have been a rule, a law, something regulated, that forbade the picketers from following us up the walk, to the front door of the Huron County Woman's Center, but our mother was uneasy, glancing over her shoulder as if she feared the picketers might rush at us. She fumbled to ring the buzzer another time. And again, when there was no response from inside, she rang the buzzer. How awful this was! Our father worked *here*.

A sensation of dread rose in my chest, I could not

bring myself to look at my brother and to see in his pinched face how he was vindicated—*We should not have come here! This is a mistake.*

At last the heavy door was opened by an agitated-looking woman in a white nurse's uniform who told us she was sorry, the Center was closed. Our mother protested, "'Closed'? You can't be closed! Your hours are nine to five. Has something happened?"

"The Center will be open again later this afternoon . . . We are seeing no new clients right now, only just people with appointments."

"I'm not a 'client'—I'm not here about a procedure. I'm Dr. Voorhees's wife, he's expecting me."

It was gratifying, it was miraculous, how the words *I'm Dr. Voorhees's wife* opened the door to us, that had been virtually shut in our faces.

In any case our mother was pushing her way inside— "And these are Dr. Voorhees's children. Excuse us!"

Another staff person, also in a white uniform, came to see what our mother wanted; to this woman, in a nervous belligerent voice, our mother identified herself another time, as well as us—"These are Dr. Voorhees's children. *He's expecting us.*"

The white-uniformed women were trying to explain to our mother that Dr. Voorhees was "very busy" right now, but they would tell him that she was here, and waiting for him. Our mother said anxiously, "But has something happened? Is anyone—hurt? Why are you closed in the middle of the day?"

"Dr. Voorhees will tell you—"

"He's all right? Is everyone—all right? What happened? Is it safe in here?"

So my mother questioned the nurses, who did not know how to answer her, and who may not have known the answers to her questions. There seemed to us *children of Dr. Voorhees* nowhere to go: forward or back.

Yet, we could not go *back*. Our mother was tugging us *forward*.

Sick with dread we followed her farther inside the building. The sleek dark thick braid between her shoulder blades, the uplifted high-held head. There was an odor here of something sharp and disinfectant like the clear-liquid ammonia with which our mother wiped our insect bites and minor injuries before putting on bandages, that made us feel like choking.

Fluorescent lights in the ceiling were over-bright, blinding. My mother's raised voice was all we could hear.

"What has happened? Why are you all standing around? Where is my husband?"

We were in a waiting room where indeed people were

standing indecisively as in the aftermath of a crisis. No one was sitting: all of the vinyl seats lining the walls were empty. We did not see our father, we did not see any man at all. There were nurses here, or nurses' aides; there were several women and girls in street clothes, presumably patients and/or their mothers—"clients." One of the girls, who might have been as young as sixteen, was visibly trembling; another young woman was being comforted by an older woman, possibly her mother. The waiting room was like any other waiting room and yet—no one was sitting down. Our mother asked one of the women in street clothes (the one who looked as if she were a mother) what had happened and was told breathlessly—"We don't know. They won't tell us. Maybe somebody has died . . ."

These words so bluntly spoken by a stranger. Only just overheard, utterly by chance. *Maybe somebody has died . . .*

It was that kind of place—was it? A smell of disinfectant, a surgery. We knew that our father was a *surgeon*.

You could not imagine what a *surgeon* did. You did not want to imagine.

If the *surgeon* is your father, particularly you do not want to imagine.

In this room, in this waiting room, no one seemed

to know what had happened, not yet. If the staff knew, the staff did not say. The staff was concerned with calming the visitors to the Center—that was the task. There must not be hysteria!

Our mother had other intentions. Our mother pulled us—literally, gripping our arms—gripping Darren's arm, and Naomi's, and so positioning the smaller Melissa that she was made to come with us, forced forward at a quick march—out of the waiting room and into a corridor, and along the corridor—blindly (it seemed)—or (possibly) our mother was being led by the older nurse, who had taken responsibility for her, and for us; for our mother had a way of demanding attention, despite her anxiety, and confusion, that made others defer to her. And now, suddenly we saw our father, who had not yet seen us: Dr. Voorhees in white cord physician's coat, and clean creased khaki pants, standing at a waist-high Formica-topped counter where a package that had been wrapped in plain brown paper lay partially opened. Our father was trying to comfort a middle-aged woman, one of the nursing staff, who looked as if she'd had a shock of some kind, who had slumped in a chair behind the counter.

The woman was ashen-faced, shaken. She was pressing a hand against her bosomy chest as if her heart pained her and she was breathing rapidly, and shallowly. In this emergency situation (it seemed) our father Dr. Voorhees was providing comfort to the stricken woman. He was speaking reasonably to her—he was calling her "Ellen." Telling "Ellen" it was *all right*.

Everything all right. No danger.

False alarm. All clear!

Whatever had happened, had happened within minutes of our arrival: now was the aftermath.

Our mother had not dared call to him. Almost shyly she hesitated, and held us back as well.

Seeing that others were glancing at us, our father turned to see us, and the expression in his face changed: surprise, and more than surprise.

"Jenna! Jesus! What are you doing here?"

"What happened? Is there—danger?

"No! Not at all. It was nothing."

"Was it—is that—a bomb?"

"No. It is not a bomb."

Yet there was the package, partly unwrapped. It was the center of attention, on the Formica-topped counter. Presumably, the woman named Ellen had opened the package. Or had almost opened it.

(Had someone stopped Ellen? Shouted at her? Shoved her away from the counter? There was an air of heightened vigilance in the room as of disaster deflected.)

The mysterious package measured approximately

twelve by eighteen inches. It appeared to be ordinary—of course. Yet its presence had badly frightened
a number of individuals.

Our father came to us, and roughly hugged us, each
in turn. He appeared dazed. He was trying to smile.
What we heard from him sounded like *You kids!
Jesus!* He gripped us very tight, and then released us.
Though his manner was meant to be casual, and not
agitated, it was clear that our father was agitated; it
was clear that he didn't realize how hard he squeezed
us, causing Melissa to whimper. We could not respond
to his embrace, for it was too tight, and then it was
too fleeting; we could not breathe for to breathe in
this place was to breathe in the sharp medicinal odor,
which was repulsive to us. Even Darren was frightened, and Naomi was terrified that she would gag
and vomit. Melissa whimpered with fear, so that our
mother had to kneel beside her, and comfort her—
"Melissa, honey! Nothing has happened, you're all
right. We are all perfectly—all right!"

Our mother laughed breathlessly as if this was a way
to convince the panicked child.

Melissa whispered in our mother's ear *Did somebody die?* and our mother replied with her startled
breathless laugh *Of course not, silly. Absolutely not.*

It was a scene of confusion. Badly Naomi wanted to be elsewhere to suck her fingers, and be *still.*

Yet our father Dr. Voorhees was in charge here. There was comfort, there was solace, in the fact of Dr. Voorhees.

Our father had positioned himself to block our view of the counter as he seemed to be trying to block a clear view of us, his distraught family, from his staff. With what startled and alert eyes, the nurses stared at our mother, and at us.

Dr. Voorhees's family. His children . . .

Always, there is curiosity about the abortionist's children.

What was inside the package, the cardboard box, obscured by wadded newspaper pages, something small, mechanical, possibly an alarm clock, ticking?—we could not see.

Irritably, nervously our father was saying: "It's nothing. It's a false alarm. Rhoda, clear the office—please take care of Ellen. Let's get back to normal, we've wasted enough time."

False alarm. Bomb? But no, not a bomb.

Nor did the package contain what the greasy white box had contained, that my classmates in Saginaw had given me.

At least, we could not see anything like that in the box on the counter. Someone had shut up the box, stuffed in the newspaper pages. Should the police be called?—Dr. Voorhees did not think so.

False alarm, no need for police. No need to call attention to the Center.

We can handle this. Return to normal. In stride.

And so within minutes, it seemed to be so: most of the staff had left the room, and the middle-aged woman named Ellen who'd been sitting down, panicked, light-headed, was dabbing at her flushed face with a tissue, joking of *hot flashes.*

"Let me see that box"—inevitably, our mother would say these words.

We had known, without knowing that we knew, that, being Jenna Matheson, our mother would say *Let me see that box.*

And we'd known that our father would say sharply—*No.*

"You don't think that you should call 911, Gus?"

And again our father curtly told her—*No.* The situation was entirely under control, and that was it.

Our father escorted us out of this room and into another, smaller room, that was his office. Clearly he wanted to speak with my mother, and he did not want his staff to overhear.

The desk in this office was heaped with papers, documents, manila folders. Aluminum bookshelves against the walls were crammed. Amid the clutter on the desk was a single family photo in a faux-leather frame—the Voorhees family of several years ago when Melissa had been a toddler, and Daddy's beard had been darker.

Strange to see us smiling so happily at the camera—including little Naomi with shy shadowed eyes.

"*That* photo! I was wondering where it had gone."

Our mother spoke with an air of pleasurable surprise. The tension between her and our father had not yet abated.

Haphazardly taped to the wall in our father's office were newspaper articles and photos. These were mostly impersonal—

Ohio Legislature Votes to Restrict Abortion Rights, Michigan State Advisory on Women's Reproductive Rights Drafts Resolution, US Supreme Court Ruling Jeopardizes Roe v. Wade?—but there was a grainy picture of our embarrassed-looking father in graduation cap, gown, hood above the caption *Controversial Abortion Rights Advocate U-M Alum Voorhees Receives Honorary Doctorate, Public Service, U-M Commencement.*

On a shelf was an upright glass rectangle commemorating an award to *Dr. Gus Voorhees* from the National

Abortion Rights Action league, in 1992; on another shelf, partly hidden by a stack of pamphlets, a brass medallion issued by the Planned Parenthood Federation of America, 1995.

Of our father's public, professional life we knew little. While he was alive we were sheltered in a kind of benign ignorance.

You could see that in the outer wall of our father's office there had been a single window at one time, now bricked over. You realized that windows would have left the interior of the Center and the individuals within vulnerable to attacks from outside.

"We'll just wait here for a few minutes. We can shut the door."

Our father spoke expansively, like one who is about to clap his hands together.

As if he wasn't angry with our mother but only just relieved that we were all safe—and that the crisis was over—he seized our mother's hand, and kissed it playfully; it was like him to squeeze our hands, our arms, run his fingers through our hair, stoop to brush his lips against our cheeks, to demonstrate that he loved us, and that we were *his*. Such gestures of fatherly affection were purely physical, instinctive.

Gus Voorhees was tall, imposing. He was thick-bodied, square-built, solid. His hair that had once been a warm gingery-brown (like the soft fuzz of Naomi's teddy bear) was mostly gray and his short, wiry beard was a lighter shade of gray as if it were the beard of another man. The corners of his eyes were deeply creased from smiling, squinting, grimacing. In his forehead were odd, vertical lines and both his cheeks were lightly pitted, roughened. He had a look of being *used, battered* like a man who isn't young, and has not the expectations of youth; a man you might trust, who would be kind to you.

Not at all accusingly, only inquisitively, with a clenched smile our father asked our mother why she'd come to the Center, instead of meeting him at the lake as they'd planned; and our mother said, just slightly on edge, "*Why* did I come here? It's a public place, isn't it? Why should I *not come here*?" and our father said, keeping his voice even, and still holding our mother's hand, that seemed about to escape from his, "Well. Sometimes things happen here that are unexpected. Like today."

"But today was unusual, I think?"—our mother asked; and our father said, "Yes. Today was unusual. That is so."

And then, after a pause: "You might have called first, Jenna."

"Yes! I might have called."

It was not clear if our mother spoke repentantly, or defiantly. She seemed about to say more, but did not.

"It's just that, this is a place where things might happen that are unexpected. Not often, in fact rarely, but—the unexpected can happen here. As it did today."

In the adult faces was a fever of excitement, as if each had caught the other in subterfuge. We children might not have been present, each of our parents was so captivated by the other, and by what the other might say.

"I wanted the children to see where you work, I think. I want them to be properly proud of you, as I am."

"Are you being sarcastic, darling?"

"No! My God, no."

Our mother laughed, uneasily. Our father was kneading her hand, the delicate bones of the back of her hand, harder than he meant to do, so that she pulled away from him, but not emphatically enough to free her hand.

There was a sexual heat between them, the strain of things not-said, and the strain of playing out a scene in front of (child) witnesses.

Speaking carefully our mother was explaining why we'd come to St. Croix instead of driving to The Cove: there'd been the "domestic crisis" of the station wagon and the five-months expired sticker. Like a TV Mom she laughed, baring her teeth. "Your sharp-eyed son discovered it—fortunately. He thinks I might have been *arrested*."

Darren protested, "I didn't say that."

"Five months expired! Christ. Good for you, Darren."

Darren shifted his shoulders uncomfortably as if he thought our father might be teasing him. Slyly I said, "You did say Mom might be arrested. I heard you."

"I *did not*."

In her subdued voice, in her chastised voice, our mother was telling our father that if he thought it was a better idea, he should remain at the Center, and not trouble to take us to lunch. "It's been upsetting here. Even a false alarm is upsetting. You might want to assure your staff . . ."

Quickly our father said of course not, he had no intention of altering his plans for the afternoon. He had set aside a block of time for lunch at Lake Huron—two hours. His Wednesday afternoons were usually kept free for nonclinical matters. He had a late-afternoon meeting and would be at the Center until around 7:00 P.M. and the next day was solidly scheduled with medical appointments and the day after that he would be flying to Washington, D.C., for a conference at the NIH—the National Institutes of Health.

"I see you so rarely, all of you together—this is a special occasion. A *family excursion.*"

"But—"

"No. It's *private life.* Only a true emergency could derail it."

Then, after a pause: "We don't let these people intimidate us."

Quickly our mother spoke, before one of us could ask who *these people* might be, "I know that, Gus. Of course."

"We never do. We don't miss a beat. We don't publicize what we do, if we can avoid it."

"You are right. I know. Yes."

"Here's the key to the Volvo, Jen. Just wait in the car and I'll be there in ten minutes. *Don't* interact with the picketers—they might know about the incident, or they might not. We don't interact with them."

"Of course, I know! I know—'we don't interact with the enemy.'"

We drove to Lake Huron that afternoon, after all. The *family excursion* had not been deflected.

In our father's Volvo and with our father at the wheel.

For here was authority, and here was comfort. Here was *the familiar,* which is *comfort.*

And at the shore of Lake Huron, beyond a beach strewn with pebbles and kelp, near-deserted on this gusty day, the incandescent sky opened dazzlingly before us.

Like the lifting of headache. A tight band around the head that is the band of pain.

Whatever might have happened, did not happen.

This is happiness. This is love.

The Cove was not so attractive as we'd recalled. Perhaps it had been battered in a recent storm. A loose sign swung and banged in the wind, annoying to our mother. Yet it was wonderful to be seated out on the deck of the restaurant, overlooking the lake—so vast a lake, the farther shore of Ontario, Canada, was not visible.

A faint horizon, hazy and ill-defined—you had to imagine a farther shore.

My father declared that this was a "surprise, celebratory" lunch—a "birthday lunch" for our mother. He had not yet purchased her present (he said) but had something very special in mind, which she would discover next week, on her proper birthday.

"Gus, thank you! I love you."

"We all love *you.*"

Below The Cove was a dock where rowboats, canoes, kayaks were for rent. But Lake Huron was rough that day, and the air was chilly for mid-June, and there were few customers.

Still, Darren wanted to take out a kayak, in defiance of our mother who would worry about him.

"Mom, Jesus! I'll be fine."

"Why don't you and Dad go in a double kayak?"

"There aren't any double kayaks here."

"Well—a canoe?"

But Darren didn't want to take out a canoe. We saw that Dad was disappointed, by the genial way in which he supported Darren, that was meant to show he was not disappointed.

I saw that my prissy brother would have his way. He *would have his way,* so that we had to worry about him.

Hiking along the beach, and along a muddy inlet, where shorebirds swarmed and shrieked, for something had died there. A briny soft-rotting odor, shell-less things, unprotected flesh about which iridescent insects buzzed antic with life.

Frantic with life.

Nobody's baby chooses to die.

Your nostrils pinched, you felt a gagging sensation and quickly turned away.

We watched Darren paddle along the shore. Rough, choppy waves. He'd become a skilled kayaker, our father had instructed him. He did not glance back at us but surely he felt our eyes on him.

Meanly I thought—*I hope he capsizes.*

I did not want my brother to drown. (I think.) But I would have smiled if Darren had capsized in the kayak.

Except they'd have run to him. Both our parents would have waded out into the surf, to "save" him.

The hard-packed sand made walking difficult. And the wind taking away our breaths like a wet mouth sucking at our mouths. We hiked behind our parents who were speaking earnestly together—my little sister and me, hand in hand—(I had taken Melissa's small hand, I loved to feel that small hand in mine and to tug my sister a little faster)—overhearing fragments of our parents' conversation.

Why did you come today, Jenna?

I—don't know.

You brought the children. It was premediated.

I don't know, Gus. I don't think so.

But you do know.

I think—it was to show them—something . . .

And did that happen? What you'd intended?

No. Or—I don't know.

And for a while they walked in silence, and I saw that my father was gripping my mother's hand and that they were walking close together, awkwardly close together so that they were thrown just slightly off balance, and yet they continued to walk in that way, ducking their heads against the wind that tore at my mother's hair in particular loosening wisps and tendrils about her forehead. And I would think then, as I would think through my life, there are connections between people, there are secret connections between people who are essentially strangers to you, you can't know, can't guess. And you can't judge.

Was it a bomb, Gus?

I've told you—no.

I mean, something amateur that didn't work—obviously. You can tell me.

I did tell you, Jenna: it was not a bomb.

But was it meant to be a bomb? Meant to kill you all?

Meant to frighten us, intimidate us. But it was a false alarm.

Have there been others?

Here? St. Croix? No.

But elsewhere?

Maybe.

Ann Arbor? Grand Rapids?

Maybe . . .

Don't you think that you've proved a point, Gus? That you could stop now?

"*Proved a point*"—? *What point? I'm a doctor. I help people who need me.*

There are other doctors. Younger doctors.

You're asking me to give up? Would you really respect me, then?

It wouldn't be giving up. It would be letting other people take over. Return to a normal clinical practice.

In Ann Arbor?

Yes! Well—anywhere.

Jenna, I will—I've promised. But not just yet.

"Savior of the desperate"... "crusader"... It's like emotional blackmail, they won't let you go.

Look, I can't brood over my work each time there's a crisis. That's not the way I am.

But you're not just yourself—"Gus Voorhees." You are our children's father, and you are my husband.

My work is my mission for now—that's it.

Today might have been the end . . .

Jenna, there are threats all the time. We are not going to be intimidated.

The children were frightened today—they will have questions for me tomorrow, I'm sure.

Children take their emotional cues from their parents. They will be looking to their mother to know what to feel.

I have to hide from them what I feel! You know that.

Just explain to them—their father is committed to his work, and there are ideological enemies . . .

"Ideological"!—they're vicious, fanatics. Army of God they call themselves.

But the law is protecting us. The law is on our side.

The law can't protect you twenty-four hours a day.

That's just to intimidate.

They've shot doctors. They've sent mail bombs . . .

Those terrorists have been apprehended. They're in prison.

You don't think there are more? Of course there are more—Soldiers of God they call themselves.

Jenna, please. This was meant to be a day off . . .

*You've seen the publications? The lists?—*WANTED: BABY KILLERS AMONG US. *And "Dr. Gus Voorhees" is high on that list.*

I told you not to look at that garbage! For Christ's sake.

Not look, and pretend they aren't there?

I don't give a damn about the lists or the threats. I don't pay any attention to them. And I'm not going to quit because I've been frightened.

Then you admit—you've been frightened?

You aren't quitting your work, Jenna. I'm not quitting mine.

My work is—theoretical! No one even knows my name. But "Dr. Gus Voorhees" is a name everyone knows.

That's a mistake. I'm sorry about that. But I've been moving around. I don't stay in one place. And when I leave a clinic, things quiet down—as in Grand Rapids.

All I can think is if that bomb had gone off today, your children wouldn't have a father.

I've told you, it wasn't a bomb—actually.

What was it then?

A clumsy threat. A mockery.

A mockery?

A Bible verse . . .

A Bible verse?

A hand-printed message taped to the alarm clock— "Whoever sheds the blood of man, by man shall his blood be shed, for God made man in his own image."

That's a threat . . .

Of course it's a threat. But I am not "threatened."

Gus, you have to report that to the St. Croix police! The Michigan State Police . . .

We've reported other threats. The police know.

What other threats?

Anywhere. Everywhere. Abortion clinics. The police know, including the state police.

But this threat, today . . .

There are hundreds—thousands—of threats against abortion clinics. We're not going to back down.

The staff at the Center—how must they feel!

I've told them I would understand if anyone wants to quit. And I'm sure that there will be some . . .

Well—other doctors quit, who've been doing what you've been doing for more than ten years. You'd promised—after Saginaw . . .

But not immediately.

A year? Two years?

Two years is too soon. That isn't realistic.

You will say—"Three years is too soon!" Your children should mean more to you than these strangers . . .

Of course they do. Don't be ridiculous, Jenna.

I'm not being ridiculous! There have been abortion doctors murdered—clinics bombed. It will happen again, such terrible things are said on television, that should be outlawed . . .

There are people who support us, too. We have many supporters. Try to see this as a mission—that will have an end, in another five years perhaps . . .

Five years! That is wholly unrealistic. The first thing Reagan said when he was inaugurated was, he intended to reverse Roe v. Wade . . .

But it didn't happen. It won't happen.

It certainly can! If the Republicans get a majority—if there's a Republican President . . .

Look, Jenna: our children will see that we have beliefs. That we don't give up.

On your grave marker, will that be the epigraph?

Darren brought the kayak safely back to the dock. Nimble as a monkey he climbed out of the shaky boat as we all applauded.

By 3:30 P.M. we'd returned to St. Croix. By then, the Chevy station wagon was ready for our mother to pick up.

On the left side of the driver's windshield was the new inspection sticker for 1997.

"No Good Deed Goes Unpunished": A Personal Testimony

August 2006*

D r. *Voorhees!—please help me.*

They came to him in desperation. They came to him after dark and sometimes they came in disguise.

It didn't matter where, really. You'd think so, but no.

As likely in Ann Arbor or Detroit as in some small town like St. Croix or Muskegee Falls, Ohio.

If the clinic was open until 6:00 P.M. they might come then. When the protesters had gone home.

---

* Leonard McMahan, recorded August 11–12, 2006, Ann Arbor, Michigan.

Sometimes one was waiting in the parking lot. Just—standing there, waiting.

His car which was usually the last vehicle in the lot. She'd be standing close by. In winter, gripping her mittened hands and her faint breath steaming.

Hello? Yes? Did you want to talk to me?—but she'd back away hurriedly. Before he could see her face she was panicked and running and gone.

In a light snowfall, her footprints just visible. Such small prints!

In the wintry dark, snow in patches on the ground. Snow in heaps. Snow glittering coldly in lights from the street.

Dr. Voorhees? Is *that who you are? Please—help me . . .*

She was young—just a girl. Could've been sixteen, fourteen.

Or, she was in her twenties. Already a mother, and fatigue in her face.

Or, she was older. Heavy face, frightened eyes. Opened mouth panting in terror of her audacity in so addressing the *abortion-doctor-murderer.*

In all of these, who approached him in such ways, the desperation of those who believed themselves damned.

What am I doing, what will come of this, what sin,

what punishment, what shame and sorrow scathing as the fires of Hell.

Gus Voorhees had been surprised, the first several times. Astonished seeing one of those whom he recognized as a protester who'd been kneeling on the sidewalk in front of the clinic for months chanting in singsong with her comrades—

Free choice is a lie,
Nobody's baby chooses to die.

Free choice is a lie,
Nobody's baby chooses to die.

Earnest and maddening in seemingly tireless repetition to infinity you could not hear (except you could imagine) through the shut windows of the Clinic.

Free choice is a lie,
Nobody's baby chooses to die.

One of those who'd brandished picket signs out on the street—magnified photos of aborted fetuses, mangled and bleeding; signs decrying the clinic staff as MURDERERS, BABY KILLERS; signs pleading DO NOT KILL YOUR BABY, GOD LOVES YOUR BABY.

Visitors to the clinic had to run the gauntlet of these ardent Christian protesters who were supposed to keep at least seven feet away from them but who often surged forward when a girl or a woman arrived, screaming at her. Girls and women seeking birth control. Girls and women seeking appointments to have abortions. Girls and women scheduled for abortions and very frightened.

Don't kill your baby! God loves your baby! God loves YOU!

The clinic provided volunteer escorts to help visitors make their way inside. Sometimes, the volunteer escorts were involved in shouting/shoving matches with the most ardent of the protesters.

Murderer! Baby killer! You will rot in Hell.

But by late afternoon the protesters began to melt away. By dusk all were gone. Their greatest vigilance was during the daylight hours.

And so, at dusk, this girl/woman waiting for Dr. Voorhees at the rear of the clinic was alone. In her apprehension and indecision and in her terror waiting to see the notorious Voorhees who was (as she knew) of the Devil. Because she was desperate now. Because it was happening to her now. Because now it wasn't someone else's desperation but her own. Summoning her strength and courage to speak with this man so reviled and hated she would find herself pleading like a child *Please—please help me* and the doctor's reply was sympathetic but regretful *You will have to come to the clinic during our hours, you will have to speak with our nurse-receptionist, I am so sorry please understand there is nothing that I can do for you tonight.*

And the protesting voice *But you could! You could, Dr. Voorhees! I know you could.*

I'm sorry. I can't.

You could! You could!—incredulous that the very Devil would not capitulate to her, in the committing of this enormous sin.

Only just the tired-sounding man who was Gus Voorhees for whom she and her Christian comrades had prayed for months even as (they supposed) he was beyond praying for saying *Would you like to give me your name? A number where you could be reached?*

No! No.

In despair hiding her face. For she could not reveal her name to him, she dared not. And she could not risk giving him a number, for a phone shared by others. Until finally Voorhees relented, in pity of the distraught girl/woman he relented saying *Come back tomorrow at this time. Someone will see you, and examine you. And then we'll proceed—maybe. After-hours. I'll be here. All right?*

These were devout Christian women and girls who did not "believe" in abortion. They'd been instructed by their elders to consider abortion a terrible sin— the "slaughter of the innocents." They would not alter their beliefs (usually) except just this single time for they knew (they prayed) that God would forgive and God would understand. Jesus would forgive and understand. Because there is nowhere else to turn in such desperation except the Devil's party Voorhees the Baby Killer.

Because I can't let anyone know that I am pregnant, Dr. Voorhees.

Because they would hate me forever. They would never forgive me for shaming them.

Because I am not able to have this baby. Because I am not well . . . I am out of breath and there is a pain in my chest, sometimes I think that I will faint. There is diabetes in our family, I am afraid to have a blood test.

I have never been to any hospital. No one in our family has.

We do not believe in blood transplants—is that what they are called?—we do not believe.

Because I am too old. I have had my babies, I can't have any more I think I will die. I am so tired.

Because I will lose my job. Because I can't commute ninety minutes a day if I am pregnant, if I have another baby I will lose my job. I can't afford to lose my job I will be evicted.

Because the father is gone. Because he is not coming back.

Because the father would kill me, if he knew.

Because the father is married.

Because the father has too many children already.

Because the father would deny it, he would say that I am lying.

Because the father would say that it was my fault, that I came to him . . .

Because my parents would be disgusted. Because my father would never speak to me again so ashamed in the eyes of the church and our neighbors.

Because I am too young. Because I want to finish school.

Because girls who had babies who had to get married did not finish school and are not happy now. I know some of these girls . . .

Because I don't know how this happened. I did not want it to happen.

Because it is the same man as with my sister. Because he is engaged to my sister. Because my sister cannot know!

Because it is a secret, he said he would strangle me if I told.

Because I tried to do it to myself, with an ice pick. But I was too afraid, I could not.

Because I hit myself with my fists in the stomach. Because I was sick to my stomach vomiting and choking but that was all.

Because there is no hope for me, if you do not help me.

Because he is so old.

Because he is too young.

Because he went away into the Army. He could not come home.

Because he lives right next-door. We would see him all the time and his family would see us.

Because they would not believe me anyway if I told his name.

Because they would believe him.

Because one other time it happened, a girl from our church said it was him but no one believed her, everyone was disgusted with her and her family and they had to move away.

Because I did not want to be with him in such a way but he made me to prove that I loved him. Because if I tell, he will never love me again.

Because if there is no baby he will not know. Then

he might love me again some other time but if this is known, he will never love me again.

Because we might become engaged. If this goes away.

Because nobody will love me again and I would not blame them.

Because everyone who knows will speak of me in scorn and disgust. Because they will say of me, she has broken her parents' hearts she is a whore.

Because God will understand. It is just this one time.

He'd saved lives. Lives of girls and women.

Girls who'd tried to abort themselves out of shame. Girls who'd allowed pregnancies to go full term seeming not to know that they were pregnant and in the very midst of labor screaming in denial. Pregnant women who'd avoided seeing a doctor though knowing, or guessing, that the fetus had died and that it was death they carried in the womb and not life. Girls who hid their pregnancies inside their clothes, tight-corseted. And their milk-fat breasts flattened against their chests. *You would think it was 1955, or 1935. You would not think such terrible things happened any longer.*

Out of ignorance? Religious intolerance?

Out of a wish to be good. And to appear good.

Some of them were Pentecostals. There'd been two or three Amish, in rural western Michigan. A scattering of Catholics in the Detroit area.

Some of the very young girls had been made pregnant by—stepfathers, or fathers? Uncles? Older brothers, cousins? They were too terrified to speak. They "did not know." They "did not remember." In the Crisis Pregnancy Center at Port Huron just before closing there came a distraught mother with her thirteen-year-old daughter who was three months pregnant showing a round hard little belly straining against her white cotton underpants. Scarcely did the mother listen as he'd tried to explain *This is statutory rape at least, your daughter is too young to consent to a sexual act* and the mother winced and blushed hearing such frank vulgar speech in the doctor's mouth and the girl stared downward at the tile floor numbed and mute, stricken paralyzed by shame, pale skin, pale eyebrows and lashes, lank white-blond hair and eyes like an albino's so he wondered if she might be legally blind, her eyes didn't seem to focus upon him even when he addressed her in his kindly gentle fatherly voice. And he thought *Is she mentally impaired?* In frustration and fury thinking *Dear God! Neither has any idea what has happened to her.*

In their religion (so far as he understood their religion) it did not matter if a pregnancy was the result of rape or incest, abortion was against God's law. Abortion was a sin and a crime and a disgrace for it was the "slaughter of innocents." You would not say the word aloud—"Abortion." The mother had not once uttered this word to Dr. Voorhees in her rapid whispered pleading for *help*.

He repeated what he'd said. And repeated what he'd said. For much of what he said to such distraught persons had to be said, repeated, numerous times. A dozen times. *Statutory rape. Too young to consent. Must report. State law. Serious crime. This child has been a victim.* And the mother cried *No! Doctor please no it will be the end of our family.*

She was begging for the pregnancy to be "fixed." She would bring the girl to the clinic in the night. She would pay what she had—320 dollars, she'd saved.

And he felt such sorrow, he had to tell her *No. Not without reporting this rape.*

And the woman was furious finally. The woman was furious at *him*.

You will suffer in Hell, Doctor! Jesus hates you.

And she took the girl away, and he never saw them again.

Another he would not forget. N—— C—— gave her age as thirty-seven and begged him *No one must know.*

Waiting for the doctor in the parking lot behind the clinic (in Saginaw) at dusk shivering and frightened telling him in a quavering voice that she was pregnant for the fifth time, she had four young children at home, she could not tell her husband who would want her to have the baby, it was the belief of their church that babies are from God, each baby is blessed by God, wept and pleaded with the doctor who was able to convince her to return to the clinic during daytime hours; and she did return, and signed in, and was interviewed, and examined by one of the young doctors, who estimated that she was seven weeks pregnant; she begged for the pregnancy to be "fixed"—and so she was given an appointment (with Dr. Voorhees: she had insisted upon him) for a surgical abortion, on a particular date, at a particular time, very elaborately the date and time had to be worked out for the woman seemed to have virtually no freedom, no time for herself; every minute of every hour of every day appeared to be prescribed; except on this particular day there might be the excuse that the woman was driving to Traverse City to visit an elderly relative in a nursing home. And so after several phone calls and two postponements (one of them within a few hours of the procedure) the surgical abortion was arranged for the latest possible hour of the day, that would allow the patient to recover from the ordeal of the procedure. And the woman came to the clinic white-faced but determined to go through with the procedure which took, including presurgical prep, hardly an hour. And afterward in the recovery room she was reported to have lain quietly enough, though praying in an undertone, and distracted when asked questions by a nurse. But she'd been all right. She had insisted she was all right. And then, after about ninety minutes, she'd gone away.

You would think, that was the end of it. But you'd be wrong.

Twelve days later a bearded middle-aged man showed up at the clinic demanding to speak with Gus Voorhees he called *the abortionist-murderer.*

He was a lawyer for the Methodist Emmanuel Church of Saginaw, he said. He had an "affidavit" from one of the church members, N—— C——, claiming that she'd been drugged and held captive by Dr. Voorhees and the medical staff at the clinic and made to submit to an "illegal operation" killing her baby. The family of N—— C—— and the Methodist Emmanuel Church of

Saginaw were demanding $15 million in "damages" or they would go to the Saginaw police. They would go to the local newspaper, TV . . .

Eventually, they settled for just $3,500.

Are you surprised? *Often, we paid. When reasonable amounts of money were involved and we couldn't take the risk of a civil trial.*

You wouldn't have known. Such settlements are kept quiet. But your mother knew, presumably. If Gus hadn't told her, someone else would have.

How many?—maybe a dozen, in all. These were spurious lawsuits initiated by plaintiffs like the Saginaw church, or individuals representing women who'd had abortions and when it was discovered, they claimed that they'd been "drugged" and "coerced." For our firm—(be sure you get the name right, it's Federman, McMahan, & Scapalini, Ann Arbor)—it was mostly pro bono—we have a longtime commitment to the sort of community medical care your father and his associates have been providing in Michigan.

We settled with the Saginaw church though it was extortion pure and simple. We advised Gus not to go to trial, you never know what a jury or even a judge might award such a plaintiff if the "bereaved" mother gave testimony weeping and praying on the witness stand. There was a strong possibility a judge would have tossed out the suit but we couldn't take that chance, given the rural judiciary in some counties in Michigan.

Not the woman N—— C——, in this case. We didn't think she was behind it. Someone else. There's always someone else. The woman isn't the one to initiate a lawsuit but someone who is using her—Follow the sperm trail.

The one who impregnates the woman is likely to be the one who uses her.

One thing we learned: a woman's religion—(even if she calls herself a Born-Again Christian)—doesn't seem to make any difference, when it comes to abortion. That is not generally known, and most people would not believe it.

Your father was not vindictive. If he could, he turned no one away. He trusted people—too much, sometimes.

He'd gone into public health medicine knowing he'd never make money. With a private practice in the Detroit suburbs, he could've been a very wealthy man. And he'd be alive now.

Wait—don't get the wrong impression, Naomi. Maybe I've been giving the wrong impression.

For an abortion-provider doctor, with so many enemies, your father was actually sued very rarely. Mal-

practice suits are not uncommon through all medical specialties.

He knew this. He didn't complain. He had a great sense of humor, like an ancient Greek stoic. One of our friends knitted a sampler for him, for his office wall in Saginaw—NO GOOD DEED GOES UNPUNISHED.

Look, I loved Gus. I loved your father. But working with him wasn't always easy. He took a great risk going to Ohio when he did, after the women's center there had almost been shut down. He knew—or he'd been told—that there was a heavily organized anti-abortion movement in that part of Ohio funded by conservative Republicans. It was a political shit-storm he stepped into, he tried to pretend wasn't there. And once he arrived in Ohio, he ignored everything except running the center.

Gus never learned to delegate authority and at times he'd become emotional. He lacked what you'd call "nuance"—"diplomacy."

It doesn't help to denounce a Michigan legislator as a "moral troglodyte"—even when it's true.

You know, speaking of Gus Voorhees at the memorials for him, writing about him, is not so difficult. There's a language for that—the elevated language of eulogy. But this you're asking me, remembering the actual work Gus did, the work we did for him, the crazy lawsuits, the extortion, blackmail, threats . . . It's like

Gus is in the room with me shaking his head, laughing. We came through a lot together.

Was Gus Voorhees a "visionary"?—I don't know, Naomi. I think he was an idealist who worked damn hard. Certainly he had greatness of spirit, magnanimity— more than any other individual I've met.

But that brings with it a kind of blindness, too.

Your father always assumed—(all evidence to the contrary!)—that his cause was so just, so sensible and so selfless, his model the social welfare states of northern Europe that provide free health coverage to all citizens and have no restrictions about abortion, that eventually everyone would understand. He seemed to think that even the "enemy" understood, fundamentally, and could be won over . . .

Consider the Biblical Jesus. Not as the son of God (as the Biblical Jesus thought of himself, which we might recognize as delusional) but as a visionary; a man so convinced of his own goodness and the justice of his mission, he can't comprehend that anyone might disagree with him let alone want to harm or kill him.

Of course I don't mean that Gus Voorhees was "delusional"—don't look at me as if I've stuck a knife in your heart. You told me to speak openly and so I have.

Your father was afflicted with the sort of blindness

that some religious visionaries are afflicted. I wouldn't call it "hubris"—he was never proud or arrogant. He was unknowing.

Your mother understood, I think. Jenna always understood. But she couldn't convince Gus—no one could.

That there was a religious war in the United States for the hearts and minds of citizens—voters. There is a war.

And in a war, innocent people die.

Jigsaw

Yes? Oh Gus! Thank God! Where are you?

Our mother on the phone. Through the floorboards we might hear her, the lift of her voice, the eager-girl relief. If there was something craven in it, something desperate, we did not hear for we felt the same relief ourselves.

Daddy! Daddy calling home.

Flint. Battle Creek. Kalamazoo.

Bay City (south of Saginaw Bay, an inlet of Lake Huron). South Haven (western Michigan, on Lake Michigan). Traverse City (south of Grand Traverse Bay, Lake Michigan).

Cheboygan in the northern part of the state, on Lake Huron.

Petoskey, on Lake Michigan.

Sault Ste. Marie at the northernmost point of Michigan, at the Canadian border; to the west, Whitefish Bay (on Lake Superior), to the east, Lake Huron.

Port Huron at Sarnia (Ontario), at the southernmost point of Lake Huron.

Lansing. East Lansing. Midland. Jackson.

Owosso. Ypsilanti. Ann Arbor.

Detroit and suburbs: Hamtramck, Livonia, Ferndale, East Detroit.

Grand Rapids. Saginaw. St. Croix.

It will help to think of a jigsaw puzzle in the ovoid shape of Michigan. Square-cut or rectangular counties—placement of cities and towns—near-symmetrical arrangement of the major lakes: Lake Michigan to the west, Lake Huron to the east, embracing the thumb-shape of Michigan, meeting at the Mackinaw Bridge in the north.

A jigsaw puzzle that was also a game board. And the piece, the single player, moved tirelessly about the game board.

Often he called us en route, from an interstate restaurant, or from the house of a friend—"Hey. It's me. Just checking in." Always he called us when he arrived at his destination, and had checked into a motel.

It is Michigan I recall. Shut my eyes and the map of the state surfaces like something glimpsed in rippling water. Though it was in Ohio that our father died.

"Like A Candle Blown Out"

S he was alone when the call came.

Alone because the children were in school. Alone in the dingy clapboard house on Salt Hill Road in Huron County, Michigan.

Alone, alone! Long she would recall the strangeness of the word, an echo aerated by melancholy vowels—*alone*.

At 9:18 A.M., November 2, 1999, when the call came she was alone because the children were at school in the small rural town of St. Croix, and because her husband was away in Ohio.

We are living separately for the time being. But we are not separated.

If you are curious, ask Gus. It was his decision.

The surprise, the shock of the call. It is a stranger's voice that will bring you the news to tear your life in two.

Like an arm torn out of its socket—first there is disbelief, then a throb of pure astonished being, then immeasurable pain and gushing blood.

That first instant, of disbelief.

The soul crying *No! No.*

She'd been alone. Always she would remember.

He had abandoned her. *He* had not been with her, to comfort and console. To hold her flailing limbs, her body like the body of a twitching frog as the scalpel cuts the beautiful delicate belly-skin toward the beating heart.

Oh Gus! Gus.

Calm and quiet of the austere old farmhouse in the morning after the children were gone.

After she'd driven them to their schools in St. Croix, and returned to the house alone.

She did not mind driving the children into town five mornings a week—not so much. Between wintry fields where frost glinted amid broken cornstalks and ravaged acres of wheat. Overhead, circling hawks they were still excited to identify—*red-tailed, marsh-hawk.* And picking the children up in the mid-afternoon, when she might have errands to do, truly she didn't mind.

It was a time to be alone with them. When Darren could not drift off distant, disengaged.

Melissa always sat in the passenger's seat, beside Jenna. Between them was a (magical, thrilling) rapport Jenna did not—(she had to admit)—feel for the older children much, any longer. Though of course she loved Naomi and Darren as much as she loved Melissa.

Why had they adopted the little Chinese-girl orphan?—a question that everyone who knew Gus and Jenna Voorhees had wanted to ask.

She could not have said. Not clearly.

For it was wrong to say—*We felt it is our duty.*

Crude and misleading to say—*It is the duty of some of us, who can afford to take into our homes a child who, otherwise . . .*

More accurate to say—*Because we wanted to love— another child.*

More accurate—*Because we could. Because it was time for another. Because another baby of our own was not practical. Because we had love to spare.*

She did not want to think that Gus's wish for another child, an adopted child, preferably Chinese, had something in it deeply irrational, unexamined.

She did not want to think that her acquiescence to her husband's wish had something in it deeply craven, insecure. Or that her fear of displeasing Gus Voorhees in virtually any way, small, large, petty, profound was a fear that was justified.

"I think it was to renew our marriage. Like renewing our 'vows.'"

These measured words she had several times said, about their adoption of Melissa.

Was this true? *Renewing our vows* sounded naively upbeat, optimistic. For you would certainly not want to say *Out of fear that our marriage was floundering, we reached out blindly for another baby. Are we so different from other couples?*

The older children were becoming mysterious to her. It was clear, they didn't need her nearly so much as Melissa needed her. At twelve Naomi was secretive and elusive; at fifteen, Darren was unpredictable in his moods. To hug Darren was to risk being shoved away with a look of acute embarrassment—*Hey Jesus, Mom.*

At times her very body ached, in memory of them; in memory of the terrible intimacy of pregnancy, childbirth, nursing that had so defined her in the early years of marriage. Now, her son and her daughter regarded her warily. Since Gus had departed, they seemed to blame her.

Though only Melissa would inquire for only Melissa loved Jenna enough to trust her.

Why can't we live with Daddy?

Don't you love Daddy? Are you mad at Daddy?
Doesn't Daddy like to live with us anymore?

When the call came at 9:18 A.M. of November 2, 1999, she did not answer it.

Thinking, it would not be Gus because Gus would never call at such a time. Through each weekday morning he was likely to be in surgery. And often in the early hours of the morning he performed those difficult surgical abortions that involved late-term impaired fetuses and mothers whose lives were endangered, which other surgeons would not perform.

His work wasn't invariably abortion-on-demand. Much of his work was therapeutic abortion. Dilation and evacuation in the second trimester of a malformed fetus, a fetus whose heartbeat has ceased. In the third trimester, the malformed fetus injected with digoxin to precipitate a miscarriage. A considerable fraction of his practice was obstetrics—he did not destroy fetuses but saved them. He treated ectopic pregnancies. He treated pregnant women with cervical, uterine, ovarian cancer. He performed caesarians. He delivered babies whose mothers had been seriously injured in accidents, or were seriously ill. He repaired (surgically) the ravages of childbirth in mothers for whom childbirth had been devastating and would have proved fatal. But his enemies did not allow such distinctions and in their defamation of Gus Voorhees, it was as *Baby Killer* he was known.

Mustard-yellow flyers—*A Baby Killer lives in your neighborhood.*

(How awful, Melissa had brought one of these home! She'd found it on the sidewalk in front of their house in Saginaw.)

The bomb threat at the Center in St. Croix. Graffiti on the shuttered windows, small white wooden crosses scattered on the walk in front of the building, picket signs, kneeling protesters, rosaries. . . The maddening chant she heard sometimes in her sleep, in that twilit region between sleep and waking.

Free-choice is a lie,
Nobody's baby chooses to die.

It was true: but you did not want to think so.

The fetus wished to live. Stubbornly, sometimes astonishingly—the fetus struggled to live. But the power of its life—or its death—had to reside with the mother. No other alternative was possible.

She tried not to think of these matters. Especially, the picket signs brandishing images of unspeakable horror—dead, mutilated, dismembered human infants any one of which (if circumstances had been altered) might have been her own beloved children. And yes, the realization that her husband was a surgeon who performed abortions, routinely. There was a kind of poison that seeped into her soul, if she allowed herself to think of such charges and of those whom Gus and his associates casually called *the enemy.*

It made her anxious, it made her resentful, that her husband so immersed himself in his work, and in the internal politics of his work, he seemed scarcely to know how the world regarded him, or to care.

Was it arrogance, or simple self-abnegation. Gus did not know what he might have known, if he'd cared more.

Look, Jenna! My work, my life stands for itself. That will have to be my defense.

She was climbing the stairs to the second floor. Steep and narrow and creaking beneath her weight. Feeling her heart suffused with happiness at the prospect of being, for a few hours at least, alone.

She'd laughed, breathless. Feeling so strangely *free.*

She would not have expected that she'd come to feel a kind of stoic comfort in the house on the Salt Hill Road, that had not been their first choice here in Huron County. At least, she did not hate it any longer.

In the numerous places they'd lived, since deciding to live together, and deciding to marry, the responsibility had been (tacitly) hers, to establish a household. No one had told her this—certainly, Gus had not told her—but she'd understood, and had been equal to the task, and had taken pride in it. When she and Gus Voorhees had met she'd been completing her final year of law school at the University of Michigan, while Gus was a second-year resident at the medical school hospital; already Gus was involved in public health and community medicine, and Jenna had been a volunteer for Legal Aid. She would pass her Michigan bar exam on the first try but she hadn't been ambitious for a private career in the law. Working to reform the economic situation of women in the state, providing legal counsel to organizations promoting women's reproductive rights, these were her missions, but they were part of her life, and not her life. *A career is not a life*—her mother had warned her.

In sixteen years of marriage she'd never ceased working except when she'd had very young children, and when they'd flown to Shanghai to adopt Melissa, which had involved nearly three weeks. But her work was executed in the interstices of her husband's more complicated schedule. The life of the household centered upon him, and upon the children; to herself, Jenna had become a sort of blur, a figure in motion.

So long as she loved Gus Voorhees, none of this mattered. Rarely had she thought of *career, life.* So long as he'd seemed to love her.

But often, Gus was away. If indeed he was living with his family he was frequently away on weekends.

In May 1997 they'd moved from Saginaw, Michigan, to Huron Township, when Gus Voorhees had taken over the administration of the floundering Huron County Women's Center. Not long after the St. Croix center had stabilized, Gus had been approached by the Ohio Board of Medicine to take over a floundering women's center in a rural township in Ohio, where anti-abortion agitators had vandalized the Center, forced out the director, and hounded out many of the staff. It was to be an emergency appointment, and a highly publicized appointment, made in the face of local opposition, given media attention in Ohio and in such national publications as *USAToday.* Jenna had been astonished when Gus hadn't declined overtures from the Board at once. How could he be serious?— moving *again*?

He explained to her: if the Broome County Women's Center closed women in the area would have to drive at least one hundred miles just for contraceptive prescriptions, still farther for abortions.

That anti-abortion opponents in Ohio were taking a particular stand against Gus Voorhees had seemed, perversely, to provoke and stimulate him.

She'd told him no! He was needed right here in Michigan.

He'd told her he was needed more in Broome County, Ohio.

This was true, she supposed. But why did it matter? How many counties in the United States might have been described as *needing Gus Voorhees*, or someone very like him.

Wasn't it dangerous in Broome County, Ohio?—Jenna had demanded; and Gus had said, as she might have known he would say, that it was dangerous everywhere, and he wasn't going to factor in his personal comfort.

"'Personal comfort'!—I hate you."

She'd wanted to scream at him. She'd wanted to push him from her. She'd wanted to harden her heart against him, that he had not the power to hurt her further.

Despite her pleas Gus had said *yes* to the Ohio offer which was to include security provisions—protection for the Center, and the staff, by armed law enforcement. Gus would also have the power of hiring a completely new medical and support staff for the Center. Several young doctors, female and male. There was money for a radiology lab. For the first three years at least, there was the promise of more money from the state of Ohio than he'd had at his disposal in Huron County.

She wasn't sure if Gus really wanted her to relocate to Ohio with him. If he really wanted to bring the children into a potentially dangerous environment. Yet, Gus asked. Gus asked repeatedly. Jenna responded adamantly *no*.

Another move! Another house! New schools for the children! It would be a nightmare.

I think you really don't mean this. You're begging us to come because you know we will not. Should you be married at all, Gus? Should you have had children?

That's ridiculous! That's a terrible accusation, Jenna.

Is it? Ask the children.

You ask the children—when they're grown up and can judge.

Any criticism of Gus as a father stung him, infuriated him—Jenna could see the rage in his eyes.

He would pit the children against her, she thought. If it came to a separation, divorce.

Even if the mother were awarded primary custody, it would be the father whom they revered, whom they knew so less intimately than they knew the mother.

You're making me hate you. And I'm afraid of you.

Ridiculous! This subject is closed.

On tiptoes Melissa stood to whisper to her mother—
"Don't make us move, Mommy! I will want to die."

This disturbing plea, Jenna pretended not to hear.
Not entirely.

"Of course we're not moving again, Melissa.
Anyway—not so soon."

Bizarre to hear the word *die* on the lips of a seven-
year-old. Even if Melissa was a precocious child.

Knowledge of *dying, death* seemed to be trickling
down to ever-younger children. Jenna and Gus had
been stunned to hear that the sixteen-year-old son of
friends in Ann Arbor had committed suicide by hanging himself in his room, on the night of the first day of
school in September—no note, no (evident) warning,
a total surprise to high school friends as to the family.
They'd known the boy since he'd been an infant and
could only say to each other numbly—*But Mikey had
always seemed so normal . . .*

Jenna communicated best with her youngest child
by hugs and kisses, she thought. Words were supple-
mental.

After an interlude of (evident) misery and resentment Darren had begun at last to make friends at
St. Croix High School. (Jenna had had glimpses of
these "friends"—she wasn't sure what she thought of

the sulky-faced boys who barely mumbled *H'lo Mz V'rhees* when Darren had no alternative but to introduce them. Involuntarily came the cruel adolescent term—*losers*.) Darren had grown lanky-limbed and evasive, with ironic eyes, prone to moods; quick to lash out to hurt (his mother, his sister Naomi) at the slightest provocation. If his grades at the St. Croix school were high, he shrugged in adolescent embarrassment; if his grades were less than high, he was stricken with adolescent shame. He'd been dismayed and angered by his father's decision to work in Ohio but he'd seemed to blame Jenna as well, which she understood: for Darren was one to *blame*.

There'd been talk of Darren going to visit Gus. But no weekend had been quite ideal for a visit, so far.

Perversely, as if to confound Jenna, Darren had said that he'd be willing for the family to move to Ohio, anytime. Saying with a smirk, "How much worse can cruddy-rural Ohio be than cruddy-rural Michigan?"— and Jenna said, "Ohio is a death-penalty state. Michigan has never executed in its history."

Darren stared at her, startled by this rejoinder.

What did that mean? Why had she told him?

But he'd understood. Ohio was a more conservative state than Michigan. As a young child Darren had learned to narrow his eyes at the sight or sound of the word "conservative."

Anti-black. Anti-women's rights. Anti-equality. Anti-liberal. Anti-abortion.

The enemy.

"Ohio has yet to repeal the death penalty. Their legislature is not persuadable by rational argument. By contrast, Wisconsin executed just one person in its history, long ago; and capital punishment was banished in Minnesota in 1911. And Michigan has the most remarkable history of any state: not one execution."

How passionately Jenna spoke! These little speeches she would make to her children from time to time, often startling them. You were made to realize (if you were a child of Jenna Matheson) that she cared deeply for things about which you knew very little, and that this suggested a Jenna Matheson who wasn't only just Mom.

Meanly Darren said, "But Daddy is leaving anyway. So, who cares?" and Jenna said, stung, "Obviously, I care. And you should, also."

If you loved me . . .

Of course I love you, darling. It isn't that simple.

But—is love simple?

Don't speak in riddles, Jenna. You know we have our work to do.

She wondered: was his departure a prelude to formal separation, divorce? Gus would not be the one to make such a suggestion but, if Jenna broached it, he might agree, with alacrity. She'd known men who had goaded their anxious wives/lovers into such rash suggestions . . . Emotional outbursts that can't be retracted.

Since Gus had departed Jenna found herself in the habit of glancing out windows in the farmhouse, toward the road. Any movement she saw on the Salt Hill Road, or thought she saw, any glimpse of a random passing vehicle, stirred a childlike sort of anticipation: would the vehicle turn into the driveway? Was it Gus, coming home unexpectedly?

Darling, I've changed my mind.

It was a crazy idea. It was sheer hubris. You were right . . .

But she wasn't right, she supposed. It was small-minded of her, it was craven and cowardly, to expect of her husband that he think of her and the children before thinking of his work that effected so many desperate women and girls.

And some of them adored him—of course. He had "saved" their lives—he had "made their lives possible."

Not just women who'd desperately needed to terminate pregnancies but nurses, nurse-practitioners, fellow doctors with whom Gus Voorhees had worked. He'd insisted—(Jenna was ashamed to think that they had ever had such a conversation)—that he loved *her*; he would always *love her*; if there were other women whom he found attractive fleetingly, if there were other women who seemed to find him attractive— "That's only natural, Jenna. But let me say again—*I love you.*"

She did believe this. She wanted to believe it. But how badly she missed him!

Driving into town was painful now that her husband was no longer at the Huron County Women's Center and there was no (evident) reason for Jenna and the children continuing to live here. When she encountered acquaintances in the grocery store, or staffers from the Center, she was struck by their seeming to assume that "Dr. Voorhees" would be returning to St. Croix, and that the move to Ohio wasn't permanent.

Vaguely Jenna said, she hoped so. Gus tended to go where he was most needed . . .

"We miss Dr. Voorhees! He always makes us laugh."

"Does he! Yes."

She went away feeling both slightly deceptive and yet cheered. Of course—Gus would return to St. Croix, in a year or two. Surely, he would return to Michigan.

Or by then, he'd have convinced Jenna and the children to join him in Ohio, after all.

Jenna thought of the poet Percy Shelley who'd boasted strangely of himself—*I always go on until I am stopped. And I never am stopped.*

Except of course, Shelley was stopped, at a young age.

And Gus Voorhees would be stopped—one day.

But now, alone. And elated to be alone. She told herself.

For the first time since Gus had moved to Ohio in the stifling heat of August she was feeling good to be alone.

Don't say that I am abandoning you and the children, Jenna! I am not, you know I am not.

Come with me? In a few months . . .

But she would not. She was determined, she *would not.*

For she felt bitterly how he loved his work, essentially. Not his wife, and not his children.

His ideal of *Gus Voorhees* whom others so admired and revered.

Oh, she was grateful that he was gone! His hands touching her hair, stroking her cheeks, her neck, her arms—his murmurous voice—his mouth grazing hers. She was sick with love for him, she could not bear the thought of him. Waking in the night in the sunken crater of a mattress feeling his weight against her, feeling his breath—she wanted to die, she could not bear such loneliness. What a poor substitute the children were, needy for *her*! But she was needy for the husband, the man. In a delirium craving what only her husband could give her, and no one else.

Yet telling herself a very different story: how grateful to be alone. If not to be alone for always, for this morning at least. Precious uninterrupted hours of work at the plain pine table in the small upstairs room she called her study with its slanted ceiling, meager view of dun-colored fields, a rattly old space heater turned high.

I lock my door upon myself—a poet had said.

I turn my key and there's—happiness.

She heard the phone ring downstairs. God damn.

She felt now a stab of guilt. Not freedom but something like a vise tightening around her chest.

She had no phone extension in this room. She did not want a phone extension in this room. Her work, so long executed in the interstices of her husband's and her children's schedules, called to her, like something that is dying of thirst. *No, no!—don't stop so soon.*

She'd just begun to work. The room was drafty and damp, she'd had to plug in a space heater. She'd warmed her hands by gripping a coffee mug tight. It was not fair, she did not want to be interrupted.

She was typing on an electronic typewriter—an old, durable office model with almost silent keys. Laboriously she was assembling material to mail to a women's organization in Detroit for which she'd become a sort of *pro bono* legal consultant. Though she hoped to be paid for her work, eventually.

If you give away your services you can't expect to be paid for your services. Isn't that logical, Jenna?—so Jenna's mother-in-law Madelena had asked, not unreasonably.

It would not be said of the mother-in-law Madelena Kein that she was a professional woman who gave away her services cheaply, or indeed at all.

(Madelena Kein headed the Institute for Independent Study at New York University, where she had a joint appointment in philosophy and linguistics. She'd been, for a few years, when Gus was very young, Madelena Kein-Voorhees, but she'd been Madelena Kein—Professor Madelena Kein—for a long time. Gus could not recall when his parents were divorced, precisely—his mother had moved away, to live and teach in New York City, sometime before the formal divorce from Gus's physician-father in Birmingham, Michigan. She had willingly surrendered all claims to joint custody of her son by moving away in defiance of a court order and yet, so far as Jenna could determine, Gus did not seem to resent his ambitious mother for having left him; if he'd been hurt by her behavior, he did not dwell upon this hurt but seemed instead proud of her—at a distance. Madelena had not come to Gus's wedding and she'd only rarely visited his family for, as she'd liked to say, as if it were a witty *bon mot*, she had but a "minimal interest in being someone's *grammuddy*.")

Gus had told Jenna not to be intimidated by his mother—"It's bad enough that I am intimidated by her. She won't bother *you*."

In fact Jenna was quite taken with the glamorous, mysterious, and absent mother who had not the slightest inclination to interfere with her son's private life. In another lifetime, they might have been friends.

In the early years of marriage Jenna had been so grateful to be Gus Voorhees's wife that she had not—ever—complained of being lonely, or left behind, or (subtly, not crudely) exploited by him. Gus Voorhees was the first man she had ever loved—emotionally, sexually. Intellectually.

It had seemed to her from the start that Gus did not (probably) love her quite so deeply as she loved him. Not because Gus's attentions were scattered, rather more that Gus had not the capacity to love so deeply as she loved. Such yearning, such need, Jenna understood to be weakness and not strength.

That Gus was not weak as she was weak, she reasoned she could not blame him.

Unless—she misunderstood her husband? That a man did not *need* love so much as another might not mean that he did not *love* as much as another.

As a young wife Jenna had taken a stoic sort of pride in not-complaining of the exigencies of her married life: so much that fell totally upon her shoulders as the wife of a very busy physician-surgeon with a commitment to women's public health issues. She had not-complained while maintaining households (one child, two children, at last three) in diverse regions of Michigan to which Gus's work had brought him. She'd helped Gus in his career that was like a locomotive rushing ever faster along a curving track—not just typing (of course—that was the minimum) but composing, assembling, researching and preparing talks and papers on women's reproductive health issues and legal rights for Dr. Voorhees who was frequently invited to give keynote speeches, to appear at fund-raisers, to consult, to collaborate. Gus Voorhees too was expected to work *pro bono*, often. It was rare that he worked fewer than one hundred hours a week.

She'd have liked to speak to Madelena Kein. Just to ask a single question.

Did you leave your family because you loved them too much? Because you understood that love and pride are a baited hook you swallow unwittingly and discover one day that it is tangled in your guts?

Alone in the house, that morning. Hearing the phone ring downstairs. Glancing at her watch—9:18 A.M.

Damn phone!—she would not be distracted.

Hearing the voice mail recording, and a muffled message. For she was too far away to hear distinctly, and so immersed in her work, which was already delayed by a day, she tried not to be distracted as another woman might have been for whom *aloneness* was a state of unease.

And the phone ringing again, soon after.

Thinking again in exasperation, or in mounting alarm: it would not ever be Gus calling at this prime time of morning nor would it be a call from the children's schools, she was sure.

She was sure!

Hearing the phone again. Nervously pushing back her chair.

Oh hell. All right. I will see what it is.

Rapidly descending the (steep, narrow, creaking)

stairway, brushing her hair out of her face, daring to think *This had better be worth it.*

Unknowing. not-yet-knowing.

For the remainder of her life my mother will recall herself in those minutes suffused in wet-glistening light from a window.

She will try to reconstruct the scene. Envisioning the woman who imagines herself Gus Voorhees's wife, annoyed with her husband, uncertain of her husband, rehearsing words with her (absent) husband while not knowing that she isn't his wife any longer but his widow, descending the stairs to the first floor of the house.

A woman who is (not yet) a widow at 9:18 A.M. of November 2, 1999, in the old clapboard house on the Salt Hill Road.

Where we'd thought we were not so happy. Where we'd complained, whined. Flies in the walls! Only imagine.

In the kitchen my mother pauses, listening. The voice mail mechanism in the telephone has been activated. A woman whose voice she doesn't recognize is addressing her urgently.

Mrs. Voorhees? If you are home please call us im-

mediately. There has been an emergency. Our number is—

It is the number of the Broome County Women's Center in Muskegee Falls, Ohio, which my mother recognizes at once.

And so quickly she picks up the receiver while the woman is speaking.

"Hello? *Hello?*"

"Mrs. Voorhees? Is that—you?"

"Yes of course. What is it?"

"Mrs. Voorhees—are you sitting down? Please?"

A nurse. Has to be. Someone with medical training.

Sharply my mother says *yes.* She is sitting down. (Though in fact, in her confusion, in mounting panic my mother is not sitting down; she is leaning onto a chair, awkwardly, one knee on the chair and her trembling body off balance.)

The voice is a distraught voice. Breathless and uncomfortably close. My mother grips the receiver tight unable to stop the hemorrhaging words.

"I'm afraid that—that—your husband has been injured—badly injured . . . Mrs. Voorhees? Are you still there?"

Through a roaring in her ears she hears herself murmur impatiently *yes.*

"—emergency situation, an attack—single assailant—shotgun—"

And then, somehow I was on the floor.

I was standing with the phone in my hand and I was listening and understanding every word but then came the word shotgun which I heard like a gun going off close beside my head—SHOTGUN. And I was on the floor, my head struck the counter by the sink as I fell. I was on the cold linoleum floor of a room I would not have been able to identify as a kitchen still less the kitchen of the rented house on Salt Hill Road in Huron County, Michigan; and the phone receiver was beside me swinging on its cord. I remember that I could hear a voice coming out of the receiver—a little voice. And then I was lifting myself dazed feeling the strain in my shoulders you feel when you are doing push-ups. And my head was throbbing and I was thinking—Did I faint? Is that what happened?—the first time in my life, such a thing had happened to me.

It was amazing. It was an astonishment. Relief swept over me like warm water—It isn't so bad. Like a candle blown out. I will never be afraid of dying again.

The Archivist Interviewed

Are you Naomi Anne Voorhees, daughter of Jenna and Gus Voorhees, born in 1987 in Ann Arbor, Michigan?

Are you undertaking this "archival research" with the blessing of your mother, or is it undertaken out of pure selfishness, and desperation, to know your slain father?

If you are Naomi, and no one else, how can you claim to appropriate your mother's voice? Her most private, fleeting thoughts?

Are you aware that your mother Jenna Matheson has refused to speak to interviewers about such private matters in the more than six years since your father's death?

Will you acknowledge that your mother has steadfastly refused to speak to you on this subject?—that she does not care to "heave her heart into her mouth" as you have done?

Will you acknowledge that you have violated your mother's privacy, as you have violated the privacy of your sister Melissa and your brother Darren, and others? Have you no shame?

How as a university dropout can you imagine you have the intellectual ability required to be a thorough and disinterested archivist of your father Gus Voorhees's complicated life?

How can you claim to know what you have not personally experienced? How do you dare?

Indeed, how can you claim at the age of nineteen to recall in such detail what you'd (allegedly) experienced as a child in a time of upheaval and distress when by the account of others you'd suffered a kind of "traumatic amnesia" following your father's death?

Do you really know even "Naomi Anne Voorhees"—or is she a desperate construct, like the others?

Law of Exponents

N aomi."

In seventh-grade math, first period. She is hunched over her desk fiercely concentrating on a pre-algebra math problem the teacher has written on the blackboard. *Clack, clack!*—the sound of chalk striking like a sharp-beaked bird against a window.

She likes math! Especially since beginning seventh grade now that math doesn't mean mere arithmetic.

But she has to grip tight. Grip the pencil tight. In a panic of falling.

For she can't seem to comprehend certain of the laws of exponents.

Has tried, but *cannot.*

If the exponent is 1, then you get just the number

(example $9^1 = 9$) but if the exponent is 0, then you get 1 (example $9^0 = 1$).

Why, she has asked, don't you get 0?

For 9 times 0 is 0—isn't it? Or, 9 multiplied 0 times is 0—obviously!

Yet, the teacher (who is not a mathematician but a seventh-grade math teacher) just smiles and says that's the *law of exponents*.

Students are expected to memorize. Don't try to understand.

But Naomi *wants to understand*.

It is maddening to her that the "law" is, if the exponent is 0 you always, invariably, get 1.

How can it be, if you multiply a number by 0, you will not get 0? Why are exponents different from multiplying when that is what exponents mean— multiplying.

Also, it is crucial to Naomi Voorhees to solve problems *fast*.

In-class math problems are a race. A frantic game. Whoever raises his/her hand and gives the correct answer first is the *winner*.

"Naomi—?"

She glances up. She squints. What is it—what does Mrs. Bregman want?

So absorbed has Naomi been in the blackboard problem—

$$11^2 - 3 =$$

—so eager to be the first to solve it, she is not aware that Mrs. Bregman has gone to open the classroom door; that the school principal Mr. Cameron is speaking earnestly with Mrs. Bregman in the corridor as everyone in class—(except Naomi Voorhees)—observes them curiously; and now, Mrs. Bregman turns back to the class and is saying in a soft voice, yet a recognizably agitated voice, "Naomi? Can you come here, please?"

What you never want to hear: your name.

In such circumstances: your name.

Mrs. Bregman is a pug-faced woman who smiles too much but Mrs. Bregman is not smiling now.

Naomi fumbles to put down her pencil. She is reluctant to surrender the game to a rival!

In the margin of her paper she has been multiplying numbers but in her haste has (probably) made a mistake. Yet, she can't risk taking time to check, for another student will rush to supply the answer before she does. (Naomi has two rivals in Mrs. Bregman's math class: John Beaver and Alice Czechi. John is as smart as Naomi usually, but he isn't quite so fast—John raises his hand just a heartbeat after Naomi. Alice isn't as smart as either Naomi or John but has the advantage of being able to be more patiently methodical than either; when Alice raises her hand, she is rarely mistaken.)

Damn! Naomi's pencil rolls across the desk and clatters onto the floor.

If she stoops to reach for it she will have to touch with her fingertips (at least) the scummy pool beneath her desk where a greenish-smelly excrement has accumulated, the sickness of her inability to comprehend a basic law of exponents, that maddens her, and makes her grind her teeth—*why is it, 9 to the 0 power is neither 9 nor 0 but 1?*

"Naomi—dear?"

Naomi is trapped in her desk—first seat, farthest row against the windows, exposed to all eyes. Her face is smarting. She can taste something like black sludge at the back of her mouth. Singled out so inanely, so stupidly, so unforgivably—*dear.* Mrs. Bregman has never called anyone in the class *dear* before! Poor Naomi Voorhees! Naked as if her clothes have been torn from her and her scrawny body exposed. A plain girl, a self-conscious girl, a girl with brown hair and slate-colored eyes; a girl with a pained smile and a girl with a sarcastic mouth; one of the tall girls in seventh grade with a tendency to slouch her shoulders to appear less-tall . . .

"Please bring your books and backpack with you, Naomi."

Even worse than hearing your name: being told to bring your things with you for you will not be returning.

In this early phase of *The Death of Gus Voorhees* the wife of Gus Voorhees is not yet *a widow* for she is behaving in a way to demonstrate to her husband how capable she is, how reliable, how he can depend upon her, how deeply she loves him. *See? I can do this. They have not stopped me.*

Not yet *a widow* but Gus Voorhees's brave and remarkable wife, Jenna.

Despite her shock she manages to telephone our schools: St. Croix Elementary, St. Croix Middle, St. Croix High. She is able to identify herself and to explain that there has been *a family emergency.* She identifies the children and does not confuse one school with another. She informs whomever she is speaking with that someone will be coming to take the Voorhees children out of school within the hour and that they should be prepared to leave at once.

Gus Voorhees's widow has been contacted by Michigan State police who have been contacted by Ohio State police. It is urgent, they are saying, that Jenna and the children be taken to a *safe house* as soon as possible.

But first, Jenna calls Ellen Farlane who was Gus's administrative assistant at the Huron County Women's Center, their closest friend in St. Croix. *Ellen! This is Jenna, Gus's wife. Something terrible has happened to Gus in Ohio, we need your help.*

She calls our father's parents—of course. She speaks with our grandfather (in Birmingham, Michigan) but she is able to leave only a voice message for our grandmother (living in New York City, long divorced from our grandfather). *Something terrible has happened to Gus, I won't be here to speak with you, I will be going to him.*

She may call other, crucial numbers. She will not remember clearly. At some point she calls her parents in Evanston, Illinois, but leaves a cryptic phone message.

Call when you can. But I won't be here. Emergency in Ohio. I will be going there soon.

Children are all right. Safe. Gus in hospital.

She calls, or tries to call, our father's oldest Ann Arbor friends. Our father's attorney-friend in Ann Arbor, Lenny McMahan, who is Darren's godfather. And other friends of Gus Voorhees scattered through Michigan. His beloved mentor, now retired from the University of

Michigan medical school—*Something has happened to Gus. I don't have details. I wanted to prepare you.*

Jenna knows that if she hangs up the phone it will ring again immediately and this will frighten her.

At this time Ellen Farlane has gone to pick up the Voorhees children at their schools which are within a few blocks of one another. She is accompanied by a young nurse from the Center. Ellen Farlane is grim-faced and wet-eyed in a dark green nylon jacket hastily thrown over a white uniform.

Naomi is dazed and suspicious. Why has she been summoned out of math class? Why doesn't Mr. Cameron tell her what the *family emergency* is?—(doesn't he know?). She will not *be seated* in the principal's outer office but is pacing about like a trapped animal as the principal's assistant tries to smile at her, to comfort her.

"Has something happened to my father? What is it?"—Naomi demands bravely. But all she is told is that her mother has called, it is a *family emergency* and someone is coming to pick her up.

Not her mother, then. Not Jenna.

It isn't her mother to whom the *emergency* has happened, obviously. And yet, it isn't her mother who is coming to pick her up.

There is a kind of vacuum, an emptiness. Naomi is

confounded by such a blank. It is like trying to comprehend how the exponent 0 must result in the number 1—she can't do it.

Her tongue has gone numb, cold. Pulses beat wildly in her head. Sometimes when she is agitated she fears that she will become insane, such pulses beating and in what she knows to be her brain, for what beats wildly is in danger of bursting, and what bursts into a brain will cause insanity—she believes. But her fear of *going insane* is normally bracketed by the calm and orderliness of the exterior world, that would judge her harshly, and lock her away from view; but now it seems to her, judging by the behavior of the adults at her school, their inability to speak clearly and even to look her in the face, there has been some catastrophe in the *exterior world*, that has nothing to do with her.

At last, Ellen Farlane arrives at the principal's office breathless—"Naomi! Come with me, dear."

Naomi is stunned. She has had no warning it would be *her*—the heavyset middle-aged woman who'd been her father's nurse-assistant at the Center—panting and flush-faced and calling her *Naomi*, daring to take her arm.

Stammering she asks if something has happened to her father but Ellen Farlane will only repeat what the principal has said—*your mother called, it is a family emergency.*

In Ellen's station wagon, in the rear seat, Naomi slips in beside her little sister Melissa—how strange to see Melissa here! Both girls are stiff with fear.

Naomi should comfort her sister, she knows. This is expected of a big girl of twelve.

All she can do is grip Melissa's small hand. She is hoping that Melissa will not cry for then there is the danger that Naomi might cry.

Ellen Farlane drives to the high school to pick up Darren. Naomi is thinking how strange it is, how offensive, how she hates it, to be captive in a stranger's vehicle, a station wagon where, on the floor at her feet, are remnants of others' lives—a torn envelope, a woman's glove, a child's plastic toy. It's as if she has already lost her own place in the world. She shuts her eyes to review the math lessons of the past several days, rapidly working out in her head problems in ascending order of difficulty—

$$7^3 = 343$$

$$(-10)^4 = 10,000$$

$$13^7 =$$

but it is very distracting to multiply thirteen exponentially to the power of seven—($13 \times 13 \times 13 \times 13 \times 13 \times 13 \times 13$)—within seconds she becomes hopelessly confused.

When she blunders in math, when she can't comprehend a formula, she feels an acute stab of pain in the gut, a thrill of something like nausea. *Stupid. Failure. Ugly. Don't deserve to live.*

At the high school Darren is waiting by the rear entrance in his unzipped fleece jacket. He is not alone: a somber-looking woman is waiting with him, probably someone from the principal's office. Like Naomi he too registers shock at the sight of their father's assistant Ellen Farlane—for a confused moment he must think, as Naomi had, that their father is still in St. Croix and not in Ohio after all, and it's at the Port Huron Women's Center that whatever has happened to Gus Voorhees has happened.

White-faced, stiff-moving, Darren grabs at the handle of the rear door and climbs inside.

It is shocking to Naomi, her brother is livid with rage. "He's dead. He's been shot. What else? *Fuck.*"

In the driveway of the rented farmhouse on Salt Hill Road there are vehicles we have never seen before. One of these is a Michigan State police cruiser.

Police! Has someone been killed—in the house?

Before we can enter the house our mother rushes at us, to hug us. It is cold, snowflakes are falling, lightly, wetly—yet there is our mother outside bare-headed and without a jacket waiting for us which we feel to be wrong, and which we do not like. We see that our mother is crying and that her face is sallow and swollen and we do not like that at all, we are offended and frightened that strangers will see her in such a state. Also, her hair is disheveled and she seems totally unaware.

Each of us in turn our mother hugs, tremulous, kissing us haphazardly, like a drunk woman, so we shrink from her, in fear. How can it be, this woman is *our mother*—we do not want this distraught woman to be *our mother*.

We do not want to be the children of such a *mother*, and we do not want to be the children of disaster.

"Something has happened to your father . . ."

We stop hearing. We do not hear.

Your father. In Ohio.

Shotgun attack. This morning.

Shot down in driveway.

Assailant in custody.

We hear some of this. We do not hear—(we are certain)—any words that resemble *Your father is dead.*

Inside the house there are two uniformed police officers. They greet us solemnly and we see in their faces unmistakably—*Your father is dead.*

Yet, this is not revealed to us. It is believed to be a good idea to take us into another room, while our mother speaks with the officers.

Soon then, it is revealed that our mother is preparing to be driven to Muskegee Falls, Ohio. She speaks evasively saying that she will be "seeing" our father there and that she will call us as soon as she can.

Is our father in the hospital?—we ask.

Evasively our mother says yes, she thinks that our father is "in the hospital"—but she isn't sure.

There are "conflicting reports." She is "waiting to hear."

A friend is driving her to Ohio, one of the (male) volunteer escorts at the Port Huron Women's Center. It is astonishing to us to learn that they are leaving as soon as the friend arrives.

We beg our mother to let us come with her. Even Darren begs but our mother says no.

Oh honey not a good idea. Not right now.

Someone will take care of you.

The phone rings. Ellen Farlane answers it and when she places the palm of her hand over the receiver and tells our mother who is calling our mother shakes her head sharply—*No.*

(Who is it? Why won't our mother speak to him? The fleeting thought comes to us, the caller might be our father and in her distraught state our mother is making a terrible mistake.)

We follow our mother upstairs into the large bedroom where she stuffs things hurriedly into a bag. It is the sort of haste for which our mother often scolds us and some of these items—wallet, car keys—fall onto the floor. We ask our mother why can't we go with her, we want to go with her, we want to see Daddy and our mother shakes her head—*No.*

Darren says, "He's dead isn't he?"—but Naomi speaks over her brother saying, "Is Daddy in the hospital? Is that where you are going?"

Evasively our mother shakes her head as if she hasn't heard us. She's unsteady on her feet and so when she descends the narrow steps to the first floor Darren follows close behind her prepared to grab her arm if she falls.

Downstairs, the phone rings again. The police officers have stepped outside, we can hear the frantic squawk of the police radio.

Ellen Farlane tries to get our mother to drink a glass of orange juice before she leaves for Ohio—a half-glass, at least—but our mother can only bring the glass to her lips, and then lower it.

Someone gives her an apple, out of a bowl on the table.

This is a bowl of Macintosh apples, which are Daddy's favorite apple. Children like Macintosh apples less, the skins are so tough, and get stuck between your teeth.

Take the apple, our mother Jenna is urged. Try to eat the apple in the car.

At another time we would be bemused, such things are being said to our mother by strangers in our kitchen.

There is something astonishing about it, the things that are said at such times.

I will call you. Someone will call.

Arrangements have to be made. I have to be there.

Don't be afraid—I will be thinking of you.

The plan seems to be that we will stay with friends in Ann Arbor named Casey. Then, in a day or two, our mother would join us.

Then, the plan is that we will be driven to Birmingham, to stay with our grandparents for a few days.

A few days! This is upsetting.

We don't want to stay with our grandparents in Birmingham if our father isn't with us. This would not seem right.

In pleading voices we ask why we can't come with our mother to Ohio and our mother says more sharply that that is not a good idea.

There are many things she has to do in Ohio, our mother says. *But maybe after that. Maybe in a day or two . . .*

Our mother's voice is hoarse, almost inaudible. The pupils of her eyes are tiny as pinpricks. Still she hugs us, or tries to—Darren edges away, shrugging her off. Melissa is eager to be held but Naomi is stiff, resistant.

Our voices ask, what has happened to Daddy? Is Daddy—hurt?

Is Daddy in the hospital in Ohio?

Is Daddy—

(The voices do not say *dead*. It will be months before the voices can say *dead*.)

Our parents' friend arrives to drive our mother to Ohio. We are kept in another room, we are not allowed to witness their meeting though we hear an uplifted (male) voice—*Jenna! My God.*

There are too many people arriving at the house on Salt Hill Road. There is not enough room for so many vehicles in the driveway and there is not enough room in the downstairs of the house for so many people. There are even more police officers!

Are we *in danger*? Is the family of Gus Voorhees *in danger?*

Our mother leaves the house. We see her walking

unsteadily in the driveway and wonder what the police officers are thinking.

We'd overheard our father remark to our mother, months ago when he'd still been working at the Port Huron Center—*The police resent us. That's pretty obvious.*

Through the daytime hours there were two officers assigned to guard the Center. There were volunteers (both male and female) who helped with security and with escorting women and girls into the building past the gauntlet of protesters. Even so, the facade of the Port Huron Center had been defaced by graffiti several times and many mornings there was evidence of vandalism—overturned trash cans, garbage scattered across the property.

"Mom?—Mom, wait!"—it's Naomi who has run after Jenna, waving frantically as the vehicle backs out of the driveway; but the driver knows better than to stop. All Naomi can see of our mother is that she has hidden her face in her hands.

She is a coward. We hate her!

Later we will learn, there were death threats made to the family of Gus Voorhees on this day and for days following.

These were calls received by several women's centers with which our father had been associated as well as by abortion providers in Michigan and Ohio who'd had no contact with our father.

Message to the wife of baby killer Voorhees how'd you like your kids murdered? Eye for an eye?

So much time has passed yet it is only eleven o'clock in the morning! Naomi stares at the clock face, the hand seems to have frozen.

She is very tired. She has been crying, for her father is dead.

Still, no one has uttered the word *dead*.

If you are a child like Naomi who is a harsh critic of herself you are likely to be astonished when—at last—the world punishes you as you'd thought you deserved.

Because I am ugly and stupid and clumsy it is not fair to punish my father. Please don't let that happen . . .

The shock of a *family emergency* is that the child learns it has nothing to do with her.

The phone rings, rings. In another room someone answers it.

Ellen Farlane is telling Naomi and Melissa that they must be brave, this is a *terrible thing*.

But they are safe. They will be safe.

Nothing will happen to *them*.

Friends of Jenna's have arrived. There is much hugging, there are tears. Naomi runs to hide in the upstairs bathroom.

The plan is, we might stay with these friends until our mother returns from Ohio or until we are summoned to Ohio. Darren is beginning to say *no*, Darren is beginning to balk, but Naomi and Melissa are not strong enough to say *no*.

The phone rings. We determine that it isn't our father who is calling. We slip away to hide.

There is a place in the cellar we can hide, except we are afraid of the cellar. The bad smell in the cellar. The smelly bad things Mom found in the cellar, so nasty they could not be named.

The plan is, someone is coming soon to drive the three of us to Ann Arbor within the hour and there we will stay with the McMahans, which is upsetting to us for we have never visited with the McMahans without our parents. Naomi begins to feel anxious, for what will she talk about with these people? She doesn't really like Mr. McMahan so much, he is a lawyer who is always disputing her father, contradicting Gus and questioning his "data" though of course Mr. McMahan and Gus are old, close friends and respect each other. (The men have told the tale many times of how they'd both "pledged" Sigma Nu as freshmen at U-M—then, soon afterward, when the nature of fraternity life was revealed to them, as well as the monthly amount in dues and fees they'd have to pay, both men had "depledged." The point of the story is, the children surmise—*Who would believe it? Gus Voorhees, Lenny McMahan— Sigma Nu fraternity?)* Still, Naomi has noticed how Mr. McMahan rarely nods in agreement when Gus speaks, as others do, as if he knows more of Gus Voorhees than the others, and isn't so easily won over.

He's dead. They *killed him.*

Who—? Who killed him?

The ones who'd said they would. Shot him down this morning.

Darren speaks flatly, bitterly. Of course, it is true. All this while we have known.

Except, Melissa has not known. It will be a long time before Melissa ceases to ask—*Where is Daddy? When is Daddy coming home?*

Why can't we go live with Daddy?

There will be a funeral for Gus Voorhees, but not in Ohio. The funeral will be in Ann Arbor where we will all be staying.

Not today, not tomorrow.

But when is today, and when is tomorrow?

Darren speaks flatly, bitterly. Darren has said he *will never forgive* our mother.

Why?—Naomi asks; and Darren says because our mother didn't want to move to Ohio to be with our father, if we'd all been living there this would not have happened.

But how do you know that? How can you say that?—Naomi asks, astonished; and Darren says *Just go to hell. You don't know shit.*

Soon after, Naomi hears a furious braying sound outside, in the old hay barn—her brother playing his trumpet like a summoning of the dead.

By the time Leonard McMahan arrives at the house at Salt Hill Road the sky has darkened. Our mother has not yet called home and Ellen Farlane has heated chicken noodle soup for us and has helped us pack our things—pajamas, toothbrushes, socks and underwear, clothing and school things.

"I hope we never come back to this fucking place."

"We have to come back. We have *school*."

Naomi has considered saying *We have fucking school* to impress her foul-mouthed brother but at the last moment she doesn't dare.

Soon, however, she will dare. *Fuck this fucking place* she will dare.

Fuck you I hate you fuck-face who the fuck do you think you are just go to hell—will you?

Seated in the Michigan State Police cruiser two police officers remain on the property, at the crest of the driveway. When Naomi listens closely she can hear the cacophonous sound of their radio.

What are the police officers talking about? Are they laughing? Are they thinking—*Well, he got what he deserved. Killing babies like he did what'd he think would happen to him someday.*

Driving to Ann Arbor in pelting icy rain. In the front seat Leonard and Chrissie McMahan sit stiffly, not knowing what to say to the Voorhees children who have lost their father—who will never see their daddy again. The McMahans' words of sympathy and comfort have trailed off into an awkward silence. So many times they have said *You will be all right. Nothing will happen to you. Your father was so proud of you and he loved you so much. Your mother is a very brave woman.*

It is all bullshit, Naomi thinks. No one wants to be *brave!* What you want is to be *alive.*

This is the beginning of a succession of displacements. Being driven from one (temporary) residence to another. Sometimes their mother is with them, and sometimes not. Sometimes the three of them are together, and sometimes not. (In time, increasingly not.) Being sympathized-with, comforted. Hearing the formula words. *Your father was a great, brave man. Your father was loved by all who knew him. Your father would be so proud of you if he knew.*

Proud is like *brave*, Naomi thinks. *Alive* is what matters.

After a while there will be fewer tears. A kind of wet ash instead of tears streaking their young faces.

It is the abrupt end of childhood. Even for Darren who is fifteen years old who might (plausibly) have thought that he wasn't a child any longer, it is the abrupt and irrevocable end.

On this trip to Ann Arbor along icy-rain-lashed roads Darren has let his head fall against the car window beside him numbed to the vibrations of the glass against his skull, he has not been listening to anything the McMahans have been saying and if he had been, he would have taken no comfort, for it isn't comfort Darren wants, it is revenge. Melissa is just a little girl, she has only a vague comprehension of *dead, death* which is like an enormous space it hurts to try to see, the *up* of it, and the *down* of it, and it's a whitely blinding space like a vast warehouse, her brain hurts seeing it; and so, Melissa has fallen asleep exhausted. Beside her Naomi has been rethinking the situation, maybe she isn't being punished, maybe she isn't important enough to be punished, or to bring about a punishment of her father; in fact, there might have been a mistake, her father is in another hospital in Ohio not the one her mother was told he was in, her father was shot by an *anti-abortion protester* but it was only a warning shot and when they arrive in Ann Arbor there will be a message waiting for them from their mother. *Good news after all! Sorry to alarm you but Daddy says hello.*

Beyond this, Naomi hasn't imagined. Not just yet.

"Remains"

Mrs. Voorhees?"

Was this a question? Did such a question imply that she had a choice?—she was, or she was not, *Mrs. Voorhees.*

"Step through here. Please."

So it wasn't a question. It was a commandment.

Her eyes were watering badly. *Dry eye* it was called.

Paradoxically, *dry eye* results in watering eyes. For the afflicted eye lacks sufficient moisture, precipitating tears and blurred vision.

Such tears are easily mistaken for the tears precipitated by emotion.

"And through here. I've got the door . . ."

She was being led somewhere. There was an elevator, that moved slowly. Descending into the earth.

She had not spoken more than a few words for approximately five hours. In the interim her throat seemed to have closed.

There had been no urgent need for speech for whatever had happened, had happened.

Are you sitting down? Please.

"Step through here, Mrs. Voorhees."

Whoever these strangers were—Broome County, Ohio, medical examiner, law enforcement officer, county prosecutor—they spoke softly to her. She'd been introduced to them upstairs, she'd even shaken their hands—(had she?)—but the memory had already faded, sucked into a kind of vacuum.

This day had begun a very long time ago as if on another planet.

Ringing telephone in an empty house. Her first instinct had been the correct one: *do not answer.*

Beyond that now. Too late.

When confused, smile.

A faint courteous questioning smile—*Yes? Excuse me?*

Like most girls she'd been trained to smile since childhood. Smile at your elders, at individuals who have authority over you. Smile if frightened. Smile if you can't quite hear what they are telling you. Smile to express yourself—*sweet, docile, cooperative, surpassingly well-mannered, "good."* Smile at men.

Like crossing a balance beam, in gymnastics. You move with exquisite caution and concentration so that you will not "lose" your balance and crash ignominiously to the hardwood gym floor.

What was expected of her. As the slain man's widow she would comport herself with dignity.

Would not dissolve into weeping, hysterics. Would not collapse into a paroxysm of self-pity.

What the widow must avoid: *self-pity*.

They left the slow-moving elevator and were making their way along a corridor of the ground floor of the Broome County Hospital. A strong odor of disinfectant made her nostrils pinch.

Again, a door was being opened for her. A heavy door.

"Please step through here, Mrs. Voorhees."

Mrs. Voorhees. So carefully enunciated, you would think this was a rare medical condition or illness.

Now she felt a flurry of something like panic. Very much, her instinct warned her not to enter this room.

Yet amid a roaring on all sides she stepped— bravely— into a large refrigerated room humming with ventilators.

Her eyes glanced upward involuntarily. The ceiling was high overhead, covered in slate-colored squares.

Frigid air flowed downward from vents in these squares like grimacing teeth.

"Mrs. Voorhees . . ."

The medical examiner was explaining something to her. He seemed less kindly than the other men but perhaps that was her imagination. He was a short square-built gnome-man with a bald head, tufted white eyebrows who dwelt here, in the netherworld below the hospital. He was a physician, of course—a pathologist.

What had Gus said about pathologists?—no malpractice insurance, their patients never complain.

Her brain was exhausted from strain and for a confused moment she worried that she was supposed to know the gnome-man, he'd been a medical associate of Gus's?

In anyplace where he lived, or spent a duration of time, Gus became acquainted with many individuals and of these, a number were invariably persons of distinction.

Fellow doctors, public health officials. Local politicians—mayor, congressman, senator. Lawyers. By now Gus would know them on a first-name basis.

"It's a formality but it's state law. You only have to look briefly, Mrs. Voorhees."

The roaring of the ventilators made hearing difficult. Or perhaps it was a roaring in her ears.

Gus had told her, many times—*It's just your heartbeat. Breathe calmly, relax. It will subside.*

She was being led—inexorably, inescapably—to a table on aluminum rollers, beneath a pitilessly bright light. On the table was what appeared to be a human body entirely covered by a white shroud.

By the dimensions of the body and the size of the (vertical, bare) feet beneath the shroud, you would surmise that this was a man's body.

Cautiously, the shroud was drawn away from the face and upper body.

"Oh."

She stepped back. A gust of cold wind pushed her.

But this terribly mutilated individual was not Gus— was he? Almost, Jenna felt a wave of relief.

For it was not Gus after all. Even the hair that looked shredded, clotted with something dark like paint, was not her husband's streaked-gray hair. There'd been some misunderstanding . . .

She was a visitor here, a guest. She did not want to make too much of such a misunderstanding. For (it was unavoidable to think) her husband's remains might indeed be in the room, elsewhere. These well-intentioned gentlemen had led her to the wrong table and they had drawn away from the lifeless body the wrong shroud.

She was feeling light-headed. What relief!

Ridiculous errors happened all the time. No one had predicted the fall of the Berlin Wall, for instance. All the brainpower of the CIA and other intelligence agencies, highly trained individuals whose entire careers had focused upon the two Germanys, and yet—no one had seemed to anticipate what would be described in retrospect as inevitable.

No, this body was not Gus Voorhees. Certainly, the (ruined, devastated) face was not his.

Not recognizably Gus Voorhees.

The remains of Gus Voorhees.

"Mrs. Voorhees?"

Her voice was very low, almost inaudible—"Yes."

"Excuse me? Did you say—'yes'?"

"Yes."

"Yes, this is—Dr. Voorhees? Is that what you are saying?"

More clearly she said now, "Yes. It is Dr. Voorhees."

"It is your husband, Dr. Voorhees."

Not a question now but a statement. No further reply was expected of her.

Carefully the shroud was drawn back over the devastated face. The body on the table was very still, not breathing. With wonder she stared at the contours of the white shroud, that did not move at all even in the area of the torso where there might (presumably) have been breathing.

For what seemed like a long time then she stood, staring at the body on the table covered by the shroud. Something was unclear to her—what to do? What to do *now*?

It was an existential predicament. Gus would have understood.

Since there is no reason for doing anything it is difficult to choose which of (pointless) possibilities you will choose to do next.

Or, you will not choose to do.

Her legs were very tired, leaden. Her hands felt oddly heavy, to lift them would require an effort.

Perversely, her head felt light. The veins and arteries were shrinking to mere pencil lines, oxygen was being shut off in her brain.

"Mrs. Voorhees, we can leave now. This way—"

Gallantly an arm was extended, to support her at the waist if required.

"Yes. Thank you."

They would treat her as if she were a convalescent. Or rather, an invalid.

A woman who has lost her husband is *invalid*, thus an invalid.

In reverse the little journey was repeated. Leaving the morgue, entering the elevator. Silence of her companions in deference to her condition of *invalidism*.

(Did they exchange glances? She did not see but perhaps she sensed.)

At the first floor the elevator stopped, the door opened. The friends who'd driven her from Michigan were waiting for her—for a fleeting instant she would wonder why they were here, in this strange place.

In her face that was taut and drained of blood and yet resolute they saw that some decision had been made in the netherworld below. A crossing-over, a point of no return.

Almost brightly she informed them yes, it was Gus. Of course. "And how surprised Gus would be, to see you here—in Ohio."

She was staggering in a surf that had not seemed so threatening until now. She was keeping her balance by an exertion of arms, legs, uplifted head. She knew she must speak to their friends. She must console them, they'd had such a shock. It was a widow's duty, at this awkward juncture.

"You know what Gus would say—exactly what Gus

would say—seeing that you're all here, let's find a good place for dinner before we start back home."

The face was not a face but a raw wound. The mouth was gone, there was nothing to kiss. The eyes were gone. I think that I had planned to lie beside him and hold him if he was cold or frightened in this strange place but that was not possible. The terrible thing that had been done to him had torn him almost in two. If I had not known that this was Gus, I could not have identified him. But it was possible to see in the devastated face something of Gus's face. He had been so handsome! In The Tibetan Book of the Dead it is said that the deceased soul remains in or near the body, in the Bardo state, for twenty days. And so, Gus might have been there, still. Though he would have laughed at me—he didn't believe in the soul outliving the body. He was a materialist, a scientist. Yet he was an idealist. He did believe that we were spiritual beings—only that our spirits did not outlive our bodies.

Then, it was a sudden concern, that with Gus gone, the children would be taken from me. Under a state law, of which we'd known nothing beforehand. And I think—then—I began to break down, and may have *begun crying, trying to explain to whoever it was, who was with me—trying to explain that the children were ours equally—their father's and mine—and that they should not be taken from me, I would be a good mother to them—"Please believe me . . ."*

Rejoice!

BABY KILLER SHOT DOWN IN OHIO

VICTORY FOR JESUS

REJOICE, THE BABY KILLER VOORHEES HAS BEEN STOPPED!

In a trance of horror and loathing he discovered such proclamations. Such revelations in luridly printed newsletters, bulletins and newspapers that made their way into the mailbox or were discovered shoved beneath a weathered welcome mat or the very windshield wiper of his mother's car.

He could not stop himself from turning the pages. He could not stop himself from reading what was, so unbelievably, there to be read. Each time extracting from himself a promise to stop, to not succumb another time. But he *could not.*

Once, he would discover a cardboard box of these publications, in the trunk of a minivan belonging to a lawyer friend of his father's. *Accumulating evidence*—it was explained.

Army of God, Christians Awake!, National Coalition of Life Activists, L.I.F.E. America, Children of Jesus, National Right to Life, US United for Life, Crusade for Life, Gospel of Light, Heritage Life Ministries, Libertarian Activists for Life, Midwest Coalition for Life, National League for Life.

In what would have seemed to the casual eye ordinary, small-town newspapers:

ABORTION-DOCTOR-MURDERER VOORHEES SHOT DOWN IN OHIO

ABORTION-DOCTOR-MURDERER PREVENTED FROM PERFORMING ANY MORE ABORTIONS!

NOTORIOUS BABY KILLER VOORHEES DIES, OHIO ABORTION CLINIC

OPERATION RESCUE CLAIMS VICTORY

REJOICE! ANOTHER ABORTION-MURDERER HAS CEASED HIS EVIL

SOLDIER OF JESUS IN POLICE CUSTODY
FOLLOWING OHIO SHOOTING

DEFENSE FUND FOR LUTHER DUNPHY
SEND CHECKS, MONEY ORDERS, CASH
C/O ARMY OF GOD AMERICA

Accompanying these lurid words were photographs of his father. The likenesses of Gus Voorhees were unsmiling and grim and not Gus Voorhees as Darren recalled him for some seemed to have been defaced, disfigured.

Yet there was one photograph, had to have been a family snapshot—(but how had his father's enemies acquired it?)—Gus Voorhees standing cross-armed in front of a white brick wall, in a khaki jacket, smiling tensely, squinting in the sun. Strangely, his father appeared older in this picture than he'd ever been in life, his hair more silver—Darren was sure.

Baby Killer Voorhees Gone to His Reward in Hell

Months ago, a year or more ago, his father had extracted from Darren a promise *never to read the anti-abortion propaganda. Not ever.*

He'd asked *Why* and his father squeezed his shoulder with a pained smile saying *Because I'm asking you, Darren. Please.*

The enemy. Anti-abortion activists. Threats. Ugly images. Just ignore.

Darren hadn't quite realized, his beloved father Gus Voorhees was a particular target in these publications. In his childish naiveté he'd imagined, or perhaps he had wished to imagine, that the hostility was ideological, political.

Their beliefs are contrary to ours, Gus had explained. The debate will have to be hammered out in the voting booths of America.

Debate! The kind of adult idealism you took for granted, without questioning. (Possibly) you rolled your eyes, it was so schoolteacherish. But a good kind of schoolteacherish.

Now Darren was discovering a looking-glass world where the murderers of abortion providers were honored as "heroes"—"martyrs." These were "soldiers of God" or "soldiers of Jesus" who had traded their lives to "defend the defenseless." These were men named Griffin, Greene, Mitchell—and now Dunphy. In the looking-glass world of the anti-abortion movement, in the glossier publications their faces were made luminous as the faces of saints.

Just ignore, Darren. There is much garbage printed, as there is much garbage in the world, which you can't change. But you can live your life without having to know.

But was this true? His father had been mistaken in such a belief.

His parents would never have allowed him to read such material, in the days before Gus had been killed. They'd feared "brain-rot" in all their children and so had not even owned a television set. Religious propaganda, anti-Socialist and anti-Communist publications, popular pornographic magazines like *Hustler*—all were equally abhorrent to them though (as Darren teased) they believed in free speech, freedom of the press and opposed censorship. It had been an innocent era, Darren would one day realize, before the Internet brought the depths of the human psyche into the household—from the infinitely precious to the unspeakably filthy, soul-withering.

For what remained of the Voorhees family it was the aftermath of life. A posthumous life. There was no one to monitor a boy as shrewd, calculating, and devious as Darren. His devastated mother had become transformed into a personage acclaimed in the world as *Gus Voorhees's widow*—the more ravaged Jenna appeared, the more of a martyr. The effort of performing as Gus Voorhees's widow required all her strength and so she had little time for such petty concerns as censoring her children's reading materials and she was not often in close proximity to her teenaged son in any case.

He was sickened by the anti-abortion propaganda but mesmerized as well. Where other boys his age were discovering pornography Darren had discovered a very special pornography just for him.

It was like touching himself—his genitals. He did not want to, such weakness disgusted him, but in his half-sleep he found himself doing so, his hand moved of its own eager volition. And in his private hiding places for reading forbidden material his fingers moved of their own perverse volition turning pages.

Like refuse bobbing in water, the celebration of his father's murder went on and on. Like excrement, among the refuse. Who could have predicted, there would be so much rejoicing?—so many strangers with strong opinions? Individuals who had (evidently) (without knowing him) detested Gus Voorhees and rejoiced in his murder.

And all of them self-identified Christians, rejoicing in the deaths of abortion doctors.

Of course, there had been other deaths—"executions" as they were called. Voorhees was only the most recent triumph.

And since Voorhees's death, and the removal of his name from WANTED: BABY KILLERS AMONG US, the abortion doctors listed below him had been moved up. At number four, where Voorhees had been, was a Dr.

Friedlander aligned with an abortion clinic in Talla-hassee.

The list was an invitation to "execute." Darren wondered if Friedlander and the others knew about it, and if they monitored the anti-abortion sites. Probably, yes. For how could they resist?

Yet, his father had insisted that he did not look at these publications. He had (surely) not allowed Jenna to look. (But Jenna would not have wished to look.)

But now, Darren was alone. No one to observe.

There was a particular fascination with the murderer—*Luther Dunphy.*

His father's murderer! His mouth went dry.

Luther Dunphy, 39. Muskegee Falls, Ohio. Lay minister, St. Paul Missionary Church of Jesus. Roofer, carpenter. Wife Edna Mae, two sons and two daughters. Formerly of Sandusky, Ohio. "Pray for me."

In these pictures Dunphy was smiling faintly, shyly. He had the guarded look of a man who does not smile often or easily. In one picture taken outdoors on a summer day he stood with his family—wife, children. The scrawny grinning wife held a baby in her arms. The elder of two daughters, thick-set, plain-faced, about ten years old, smirked at the camera. There was a thin-faced boy—in the photo, about Darren's age.

Darren felt a thrill of sheer hatred for this boy, whose father was alive and not dead.

Luther Dunphy was a tall hulking slope-shouldered man who in several photographs wore a baseball cap pulled low over his forehead. His head appeared small in proportion to his body. His upper arms were muscled. His face did not suggest the face of a murderer and was in fact a face of no distinction except that on his cheek was a discoloration like a mashed red berry.

Staring at Dunphy, Darren felt hatred like black acid rising at the back of his mouth. It filled him with rage, that his father's murderer was still alive and that, in some quarters, among avid Christians, Dunphy was revered as a kind of hero, a "soldier of Jesus" and a "martyr."

Luther Dunphy is currently incarcerated in the Muskegee Falls Men's Detention as police investigate the alleged shootings attributed to him. So far, Dunphy is said to have "cooperated" with the investigation. There have not yet been discovered any co-conspirators in the alleged shootings. Dunphy is not available for interviews and has indicated that he will refuse most requests. The Broome County Court has appointed a lawyer to represent him but Luther Dunphy is said to have declined legal counsel. Through his minister Rev-

erend Dennis Kuhn of the St. Paul Missionary Church of Jesus, Muskegee Falls, Dunphy has stated that he does not consider his alleged actions of November 2, 1999, "murder" or "homicide" but "an act of God" as he was "defending the defenseless"—he was preventing the abortion-doctor Voorhees from performing abortions "that day and all days to follow."

Luther Dunphy has further stated that he will not participate in any trial for it is only God's judgment that applies to him. But, he has stated that he will "not contest" his legal situation. He has told Reverend Kuhn that he does not wish donations to a defense fund but asks his supporters to "pray for him."

With difficulty Darren read these words. Not for the first time he read these words, and not for the last time. His eyes misted over, irritably he wiped away tears.

"'May your soul rot in Hell.' That's my prayer, fucker."

Children of the Deceased

H e'd said *There is no evil.*
We could not believe him now.

Stunned and trancelike those days pushing through a scrim of something clotted like the mucus that sticks eyelashes together and blurs vision.

Not for a long time was it believable that our father had died for there was always the possibility that the phone would ring and it would be Daddy. Or, Daddy would come home unannounced—just walk in the door.

"Hey kids! Hiya."

It was a possibility that might come to you light and magical as a hummingbird whose tiny wings vibrate so rapidly you cannot really see them even as you knew (you had been told) that he was ashes now—bits of bone, ashes.

(You had not seen the ashes. But you knew *Gus Voorhees is ashes now.*)

The paradox was: he'd always traveled so frequently. So it was logical, if Dad was gone, Dad was *elsewhere*.

As our mother complained he was *gone all the time*—and so, Daddy was traveling or was at the new place in Ohio but would certainly come home. Sometime.

With a part of our mind we understood *He is dead, he is gone. He is not coming home. He is ashes.* But this part of our mind could not always prevail.

It was a terrible thing, our mother had caused our father to be burnt to ashes. Our mother had made this decision without consulting us. She had made this decision because (as she said) Gus had always spoken positively of cremation—or rather, he'd spoken disdainfully of conventional burial.

The funeral service in Ann Arbor, we'd attended. We were dazed, uncertain. We had not seen our father's body, for by that time, our father's body had been cremated.

His ashes were in an urn approximately two feet high made of a dark earthen material. No one could seriously believe that Gus Voorhees could fit into that urn! It was fascinating to observe because you knew it could not be so which fed the idea (that thrived in the interstices of adults' attention when your mind skidded and careened like a runaway vehicle on a steep mountain road) that our father was somewhere else, our father was alive (of course) somewhere else and would return to us when he wished.

Katechay Island—this was where Daddy's ashes should be scattered.

When we told our mother she seemed scarcely to hear us. She had made plans for our father's ashes to be buried in an Ann Arbor cemetery—the suggestion had been made to her by friends for whom a specific place, a site, a *grave* for Gus Voorhees seemed crucial.

Darren protested, "Dad's ashes should be scattered on Katechay Island because that's what he wanted. He loved the island and he was happy there. Then we could come visit him anytime."

Our mother stared at Darren. Her mouth worked as if she meant to smile but could not. In the careful voice we knew to be her "headache voice" (which meant that Jenna was trying very hard to keep a mild throbbing pain from blossoming into migraine) she told him Katechay was not practical at the present time—"It's a long drive to the island. It would be a very depressing drive. I don't feel strong enough to attempt it. And no one would ever go there to 'visit.'"

Stubbornly Darren said, "I would! I would go to visit."

When our mother did not reply Darren persisted: "The point is, Dad would want his ashes scattered there. In a beautiful place. I think he would."

"He wouldn't have wanted it. He wasn't the type. He hated theatrical gestures."

Our mother spoke with a sob in her voice, not of grief (Darren thought) but of anger. Prudently, he retreated.

But next morning Darren brought up the subject again and this time our mother interrupted him to say that the matter was "settled"—our father's ashes were to be buried, in the urn, in the cemetery just two miles from the McMahans' house where we'd been staying.

"Jesus, Mom! I think—"

"Please. There is nothing more to discuss."

Our mother moved to slip past Darren but Darren blocked her way. For a tense moment he looked as if he might shove her, or shout into her face, and our mother was frightened, but did not step aside; it was Darren who turned, and ran out of the room cursing her—*God damn you, I hate you.*

Cautiously Naomi stepped back out of their mother's range of vision. She'd learned that, since their father's death, their mother did not seem to *see* quite so well as she had; it was like her to miss a step descending stairs, and to almost stumble; though her eyes were open, her attention was elsewhere. Naomi was disturbed that her brother had said such terrible things to their mother and yet a childish part of her was satisfied too.

If you had loved Daddy more, he wouldn't have left us. None of this would have happened. You are to blame, I hate you too.

"Naomi? What is it?"

"What is *what?*"

"You seem always to be—well, clearing your throat—and your voice has been hoarse for days . . ."

"I'm *sorry. I can't help it.*"

"Do you have a sore throat, or—a cold? . . ."

Furious, Naomi slammed out of the room. She could not bear it, such close scrutiny which angered her even more than its reverse—our mother's distraction.

Soon after our father's disappearance from our lives—(which she did not exactly acknowledge to be *death*)—Naomi began to feel her throat constrict at unpredictable times. It was silly, like coughing and sputtering, very annoying, embarrassing. She had difficulty swallowing and could not speak always clearly. She felt a curious sensation in her mouth like Novocain. Her tongue felt swollen, and was very tender.

If she tried to speak, her voice was hoarse and inaudible; soon she gave up trying. She saw her surroundings at a remove as if looking through the wrong end of a telescope. Often she saw people speaking to her but could not hear them. She was in dread of beginning school in this new place where no one knew her though everyone knew whose daughter she was.

The abortionist's daughter. Her father was killed.

There was something wrong inside her mouth. Contorting her face before a mirror she could see— almost—an ugly black stitching in her tongue, that rendered speech painful. How had such a thing happened!

The mutilation of her mouth was confused (somehow) with what had happened to our father in Ohio. *Shotgun blast. Point-blank. Upper chest, throat, lower face devastated.* (How did Naomi know this? Somehow, she knew. She and Darren knew far more than the naive adults surrounding them could have guessed.)

Often, Naomi approached Darren just to be near him. She assured him he didn't have to talk to her, he didn't have to acknowledge her, she would not intrude in whatever he was doing—(at his computer); she just did not want to be alone. "Play with Melissa," Darren said negligently, "she needs *you*." But Naomi did not want to be *needed*, she had not enough strength.

And how insulting to her, her grief snubbed by her brother as if *play* might be a remedy.

Naomi seemed to Darren exactly wrong in all ways. She was too old for childish behavior and yet too young to be taken seriously as a *teenager*. She had nothing of the funky-sexy chic of certain Ann Arbor schoolgirls of her age who were as likely to be Asian, Caribbean-American, Hispanic, Eastern European as Caucasian; these were the American-born children of university professors and research scientists who knew how to wear tight jeans, tight little "tops" and sparkly sneakers, how even to disguise blotched skin as poor Naomi never would. It was adolescent-boy disgust Darren preferred to feel for his sister rather than dismay: her skin was *both blotched and chalky-white*.

More seriously, there were purplish crescents beneath her eyes. She had acquired a habit of swallowing compulsively as if her mouth were very dry and often when she tried to speak her voice was hoarse, scarcely audible.

"Go away. Don't follow me around. It's God damned depressing just to see you."

"But—"

"I am *not you*. Get that!"

His grief he carried secure in his arms as you would carry an explosive device that is very delicately primed to detonate.

His grief was precious to him. His sister's grief was excruciating, unbearable.

In Ann Arbor in the snowy fields beyond the McMahans' house where he prowled by night. In secret slipping from the darkened house to run, run, run like a furious goat—a ram with curled, lethal horns—until his heart beat hard with a kind of angry jubilance.

Such secret times, Darren plotted revenge.

His brain was bright with fire. He imagined that his eyes, glimpsed from a little distance, were flame.

Eye for an eye, tooth for a tooth.

He'd have liked (he thought) to travel to Ohio, to seek out the Dunphys.

The Dunphy son who was his approximate age. He'd have liked to murder *him*.

It would not be difficult to set a house on fire, in the night. You would sprinkle kerosene around the foundation of the house, you would encircle the house completely so that no one could escape.

Then, you would strike a match. You would toss the match.

You would run, run, run until your heart burst.

He did feel better if he ran until he was exhausted. It gave him great happiness that no one knew where he was.

His lungs sucked in air. His heart scuttled inside his chest like a trapped, frantic rat. He knew, he'd disappointed the McMahans. They had opened their household to the remnants of Gus Voorhees's family but it was not working out as they'd hoped. Especially, Darren was not accessible to them though he was Leonard McMahan's godson.

What the fuck does that even mean—godson?

Some whim of his father's. The men had been old, close friends like brothers—Gus Voorhees, Lenny McMahan. But what had that to do with *him*?

Some nights, he ran for miles until his legs ached. Craned his neck staring at the night sky as if he'd never seen it before. Scattered stars, so many pinpricks of light! Once, his father had told him of a conviction he'd had as a boy peering at an anatomical text, marveling at the musculature of the human body, that the personal life was a means to bring us to the impersonal, larger life—the life of science, of an objective and shared truth; and there was tremendous solace in that, in the *impersonal.*

"The 'impersonal' is our salvation. It is where we all meet—it breaks the solitude of the self."

Darren wanted to believe this. But his skin chafed with grief, and fury at this grief; his heart was an open wound. Much of the time he was thinking—without knowing what he was thinking—that his father he'd loved had betrayed him.

Yet there was the possibility, somewhere in the night sky—*It has not happened yet, on one of those stars.*

In his favorite graphic novel titled *ZeroTimeZero* time was sliced into strips winding through the universe. There were fleets of vast space cruisers the size of the *Queen Mary* filled with individuals seeking their lost lives. Something had gone wrong, time had become fragmented and slivered and no longer linear. It was perfectly plausible in such a universe that something that was *past tense* on one planet was *future tense* on another. The same individual was *dead, alive, not-yet-born* simultaneously.

You could search through distant galaxies in one of the space cruisers, for eternity. What kept you going was the faith that whatever you sought existed, somewhere.

Voice Mail

She would not return to the rented farmhouse on Salt Hill Road for some time. She would not bring the children until it was unavoidable—of course they had to retrieve their belongings, their clothes. There were documents, legal and financial records. There were (never unpacked) boxes of books. They had to "close up" the house for which the widow of Gus Voorhees was still obliged to pay monthly rent though the thought of living in the house again was vile and repugnant to her as if her husband had died in the house and not hundreds of miles away.

Seeing the cheerless house from the road they were paralyzed with dread. Melissa began to whimper, Jenna groped for the little girl's mittened hand to comfort her. In the backseat Darren whispered what sounded like *Jesus! Fuck*. Naomi was very still.

"Wouldn't you wonder who might live in such a place? *Why* would anyone live in such a place?"

In the aftermath of our father's death it was like our mother to make such remarks as if she were thinking out loud. We understood that her questions were not true questions but Naomi ventured an answer.

"People have to live somewhere, Mom."

"Exactly! Until one day they don't."

Our mother didn't have a plan for us to begin moving from the house that day. She had failed to bring packing boxes or suitcases. She had not discussed the house with us as she had not discussed the future with us except in the most pragmatic of terms—*next week, tomorrow. Day after tomorrow.* The house on Salt Hill Road she referred to tersely as *the house in the country*. It seemed to the older children (who monitored their mother's behavior covertly) that in speaking of *the house in the country* Jenna sometimes did not recall the actual name of the township, the road.

As we would hear our mother speak of *my husband* as if she'd forgotten or mislaid our father's name or found the name too painful to speak as it was too painful to hear.

In a pleading voice, Naomi said, "We're not getting out, Mom—are we? Nothing has been plowed."

Our mother laughed. It was a sound like breaking twigs.

"Did you imagine we would drive this distance to *sit in the car*? Of course we're getting out."

With great effort we made our way through the snow, that came to our knees; even Melissa was not allowed to remain in the warm car but had to come with us, fitting her tiny booted feet in the impressions made by our larger boots. ("I can't let you stay in the car with the motor running. There's a danger of toxic fumes.")

It was a misty winter afternoon. You could not have said if you were fully awake or whether this was the continuation of a dream. All color was bleached to the hue of bone marrow except for the rust-red of a few wizened crab apples on stunted trees beside the house. Darren had gone first to help clear the way for the others and on the back steps he stamped his feet hard, and kicked at the snow. His face was tight-knotted, furious. Clumps of snow fell from the farmhouse roof onto our heads.

"Give me the key, Mom. Christ!"

Darren forced the door open, that led into the kitchen. More snow fell from above. Naomi who'd had difficulty sleeping since her father's death half-shut her eyes seeing (not for the first time but more vividly than usual) a snowy-white bird, a predator-bird, in this case an owl, beak and talons shining, swooping at her face.

Naomi had learned to cringe protectively from such (feigned) assaults without actually—literally—cringing so that others could see. It was a skill she'd newly developed, in which she took the most pathetic pride.

"Just go inside, Darren. We're right behind you."

Our mother nudged Darren forward. Naomi and Melissa followed.

The interior of the old farmhouse appeared to be considerably colder than the outside air. The rooms appeared to be smaller—(Naomi was put in mind of rooms in a dollhouse, except in this case there were not dolls but human inhabitants). The rooms were untidy as if a strong wind had blown through them. A scrim of pathos hung over all. (Naomi tried not to think— *Somebody has died here.*)

No one wanted to go upstairs. Many of his clothes remained, he had not taken them with him to Ohio. Pairs of shoes, useless and terrible to behold.

In the bottom drawer of a bureau, a jumble of heavy woolen hiking socks. An old wallet, leather worn thin and inside, a very old U-M ID card. *Augustus Voorhees U-M Medical School.*

None of the Voorhees children wished to search out

possessions, clothes, schoolbooks left behind in the hasty departure of early November.

(Our mother had withdrawn us from the St. Croix schools. We would not ever return of course. In our mother's mind it sometimes seemed that our father had died not in the driveway of the women's shelter in Ohio but in the driveway of the women's shelter in St. Croix and often the two were commingled in our minds as well.)

(We would be enrolled in Ann Arbor public schools, in January 2000. We would continue to live with the McMahans until our mother made a firm decision where we would live permanently.)

(But was anything "permanent" now? Not one of the remaining family thought so.)

Floorboards creaked beneath our boots like breaking ice. We winced as if we were in danger. Our breaths steamed faintly—this was proof of being alive!

Our mother said, musing, "It is like being ghosts, isn't it?—returning to a mausoleum where they'd come from."

Since our father had died and she'd been driven to Muskegee Falls, Ohio, to identify what are called *remains*, our mother was not the person we remembered.

The elder children were particularly conscious of this change in Jenna. Naomi reached surreptitiously into her mouth to touch the rough stitches in her tongue, taking a kind of solace in seeing yes, the stitches were there.

"Oh! Nasty flies."

Melissa shuddered. The kitchen counters and the sink were stippled with the bodies of tiny black flies. More flies lay on windowsills, and on the tile floor.

Also on the windowsills were house plants. Our mother's abandoned houseplants which no one remembered until now.

Potted geraniums that had sickened and died and strewn their shriveled petals on the sill and on the floor. Yet, several red flowers remained on one of the plants, on skeletal branches.

Melissa hurried to the sink, to run water into a glass to water the geraniums; but when she turned the faucet the pipes groaned, and only a trickle of discolored water came out.

Silly Melissa! The older children laughed, to see their beautiful little sister so eager to water the geraniums as she'd often done in their former life in this house.

"Never mind, Melissa. The plants are dead. Watering won't help now."

Yet our mother touched a forefinger to the calcified dirt in one of the pots. We were remembering now, what we'd forgotten, how in each of our rented houses our mother had set out a row of houseplants in clay pots, mostly geraniums. She had not been a serious keeper of plants but she'd liked the cheeriness of vivid-red geraniums in the wintertime.

"Look! My address book."

Jenna was surprised to find a small spiral notebook on an end of the counter.

Mixed with a hastily assembled pile of old copies of the *New Yorker, Nation, New York Review of Books,* and newspapers Naomi discovered a swath of math homework papers— problems she'd solved weeks ago, before her father's death, but that looked unfamiliar to her now.

Her brain fumbled at the problems. She'd forgotten something crucial. $-18(12^4)$—she'd lost the key . . .

A rancid-stale smell pervaded the kitchen. Darren opened the refrigerator to reveal a sight of such ordinariness—*a half-gallon container of milk, a quart container of orange juice, part of a loaf of bread, discolored celery stalks, a discolored head of lettuce, discolored grapes*—it was shocking to us, baffling.

"Oh, terrible! Everything has spoiled and smells."

Our mother pushed the refrigerator door shut.

Next, we noticed a winking red light on a small table. The telephone.

We would listen to the voice mail messages. Our mother activated the machine. There was a sequence of calls dating back to early November. In most cases as soon as a caller said *Hello* our mother deleted the message—"I've heard this." Or, when a caller identified himself, quickly she deleted the message—"I don't have to hear this."

Then suddenly we were listening to our father.

Suddenly, our father's voice lifting exactly as we recalled, yet had forgotten we recalled.

H'lo there? Anybody home?

(Pause)

Jenna? Darling? Will you pick up, please?

(Pause)

Is anyone there?

(Pause)

Well—I'll try again. If I can, tonight.

I'm sorry that—well, you know.

I think I've been distracted by—what's going on here.

(Pause)

If I sound exhausted—I am!

(Pause)

I have a new idea, Jenna—about next year. Or, rather, next summer. When the children are finished with school. I looked up the date—June eighteenth.

(Pause)

OK. Sorry to miss you.

Love you.

(Pause)

Love all of you.

(Pause)

Good-bye . . .

(Pause)

H'lo? Did I hear someone? Is someone—there?

(Pause)

OK, guys. Love you. I'll call back soon.

G'bye.

Then, silence.

The shock of it, our father's voice! We could not quite comprehend what we'd heard.

"Should I play it again?"—Darren asked eagerly.

"No! No, wait."

Our mother had to sit down on one of the kitchen chairs. Her face had gone white, her mouth was trembling.

Another message clicked on the voice mail, a stranger's voice, which Darren deleted.

"Turn it off for now, Darren. Please."

Darren switched off the machine. The little red light vanished.

In the freezing kitchen of the rented farmhouse on Salt Hill Road which we had not ever imagined we would reenter we were waiting, we had no idea what we would do next.

"New Idea"

How many times we would ask ourselves what had Gus meant by a *new idea*—what did this *new idea* have to do with the end of the school year in June?

Darren said it was obvious: Dad was planning to leave Ohio and move back to Michigan to live with us.

Naomi said, less certainly: Dad was (possibly) going to quit working in women's centers and clinics, and become another kind of doctor (that people didn't hate!).

Melissa said: Oh, Did Daddy have a surprise for us?

Overhearing, Jenna would say bitterly: Better for your father not to have called us at all than to have called and left that message, to fester in our hearts.

Laughter

They tried to tell me you were—dead! Of course I didn't believe it, we know how people exaggerate.

Often, she had this dream. She and Gus laughing together. Except it was the sound of a harsh wind rustling and not true laughter. Except when she could see clearly, it wasn't Gus.

The People of the State of Ohio v. Luther Amos Dunphy

December 2000

Greedy and self-punishing her eyes fastened upon him. It was her strategy to sit in the Broome County Courthouse where she could observe the defendant Luther Dunphy more or less continuously yet not conspicuously for she knew (of course she knew) how others observed *her*.

A widow exists in the eyes of beholders. In her own eyes she is likely to be invisible.

And so she knew how they were measuring her. *Is that her?—the doctor's wife?*

Or, less friendly—*The abortionist's wife?*

Those individuals in the crowded courtroom who were *on Gus Voorhees's side* and those who were *on the side of the enemy.*

Most days the defendant wore a sand-colored corduroy jacket that fitted his broad shoulders tightly though sometimes he wore a dark-hued jacket of a synthetic-seeming material like acrylic fiber. His trousers were dark and lacked a discernible crease. His shirt was white and appeared wrinkled. (Worn with a necktie most days but if without a tie, the shirt remained unbuttoned at the throat as if the collar was too tight for the man's muscular neck.) Dunphy's faded hair had been buzz cut like a military haircut and was sharply receding from his forehead. His negligently shaved jowls sagged. In profile she saw him. A heavy face, the face of an aged and baffled boy. Cheeks flushed and lined, dull-red blemish or birthmark in the creased skin and indentations beneath his eyes that were rigidly fixed on the judge, the witnesses, the gesticulating and quarrelsome attorneys as if he dared not glance to the side—dared not glance toward *her.*

If Jenna hadn't known that on his most recent birthday Luther Dunphy was forty years old she'd have guessed that he was ten years older. His muscled-softening body was a slow landslide. His hands were a workingman's hands, now useless. Mornings at the defense table he was able to sit reasonably straight but by mid-afternoon his shoulders began to slump, his head began to sink toward his chest. It was not possible to imagine what Dunphy was thinking as he heard, or gave the appearance of hearing, a succession of prosecution witnesses describing the shootings on the morning of November 2, 1999, and identifying him as the "lone shooter"—whether the man was righteous, defiant, indifferent, resigned. Though more than once, in the afternoon, his eyes nearly closed and a warning remark of the judge provoked Dunphy's attorney to nudge him awake.

"Not in my courtroom, sir. Witness will continue."

Jenna was keenly disappointed, Dunphy would not testify in his own defense. At least, that was what the Broome County prosecutor had told her.

He'd told her that no competent defense attorney would have allowed this (guilty) defendant to be cross-examined. In fact, very few witnesses would be called to testify on Luther Dunphy's behalf while the prosecution would present more than thirty witnesses of whom most were eyewitnesses to the homicides and would describe what they'd seen with dramatic intensity.

The prosecutor had charged Luther Dunphy with

two counts of first degree homicide and he was (he'd informed Jenna) determined not to settle for less: not a lesser degree of homicide, and not manslaughter.

Manslaughter!—Jenna was incensed. How could such a lesser charge even be considered.

"It won't be manslaughter, Mrs. Voorhees. Don't worry. The jury will vote unanimously for first degree homicide, I am certain. And if they do, they will deliberate again to decide whether to send Dunphy to prison for life without parole or to the death chamber."

Death chamber. The archaic words evoked a shiver. As if death were waiting in a chamber, and the condemned man is made to enter the chamber. Jenna felt a flush of excitement and dread—*He should die, for what he did to Gus and to that other innocent man. He does not deserve to live.*

(**Urgently she** was asking him, what did he want. Did he want the man who'd killed him to die. And Gus allowed her to know, not in words precisely, for the dream was blurred as a windshield in pelting rain, that he did not want Luther Dunphy to die of course—he did not believe in the death penalty, he did not want anyone to die at the hands of the State. And she felt a rush of fury for him, for her dear lost husband, that he should be so forgiving even now, when his enemies did not care for his forgiveness and did not regret his death.)

"Yes. I want him to die."

Or was it: "I want him sentenced to death. I want everyone to know, he has been sentenced to death. That my husband's death is a profound loss and the murderer must pay with his own life." Whether she wanted the man actually to die was another issue.

Of course, Jenna wouldn't have spoken this way to Gus. Such vindictive words in his wife's mouth would have shocked and dismayed him.

They had always disapproved of capital punishment. This was barbaric, unworthy of a civilized society. They did not know a single person among their wide circle of friends and professional associates who might have supported capital punishment; as (they liked to say, with a smile) they didn't know a single person who voted Republican.

In fact of course they did. But they did not acknowledge this possibility.

Did she want Luther Dunphy to *die.*

Or did she want Luther Dunphy to *repent.*

It was true, she felt for her husband's murderer a sick sort of fascination. She could not have said if she was incensed or if she was relieved that the self-ordained "soldier of God" seemed oblivious of her presence in the courtroom, less than twenty feet from her, as he appeared to be oblivious of others in the courtroom who yearned to make eye contact with him, to smile their support of him, to call out to him quickly before one of the bailiffs intervened.

We are praying for you, Luther.

God won't forget you, Luther! Jesus won't forget.

Such individuals were escorted out of the courtroom. Their faces shone with righteousness. They were members of the Christian prayer vigil assembled in front of the dignified old granite courthouse who knelt on the sidewalk and on the stone steps each day of the trial taking care to leave just enough space for others to pass by. These were peaceful demonstrators, for the most part—their picket signs didn't depict aborted infants but only words—RIGHT TO LIFE. NOBODY'S BABY CHOOSES TO DIE. FREE LUTHER DUNPHY.

When she saw these signs, Jenna looked quickly away. She felt that her heart would burst—her head would burst! It was unbearable, that Luther Dunphy should be so defended.

Yet, she understood. Of course.

What had Gus said—*Never engage with the enemy.*

In Muskegee Falls, entering and departing the Broome County Courthouse, Jenna was never allowed to be alone. Even going to a women's restroom, she was not allowed to be alone; another woman would accompany her. Always there was someone with her from the prosecutor's office, or from law enforcement, and there were friends, old friends from Ann Arbor and newer friends from Ohio, associated with the women's center where Gus Voorhees had worked when he'd been shot down.

Often, the women took Jenna's hand. Slipping fingers through her fingers, squeezing and gripping. One or two were widows, she'd been told. A widow will tell you, if you are a widow. For there is a sisterhood of sorts.

Don't look at them. Just look at me, we can talk together. Don't let them upset you, Jenna. Try to smile at me. Yes! Like that.

It was bizarre to her, that the anti-abortion protesters should hate her. Didn't they consider that she'd been punished enough, having lost her husband?

Even now, a year after Gus's death, Jenna continued to receive sporadic hate mail from *the enemy*, which was forwarded to her in Ann Arbor. She rarely saw such messages, for others intervened and hid them from her, or destroyed them. She dreaded her children being approached, receiving ugly threats—*You will be next following the Baby Killer Doctor. You & yours, you will not be spared.* (She had sent the children away to live with their grandparents in Birmingham, Michigan, for an indeterminate period of time; in Ann Arbor, the "Voorhees" children were too visible.)

But it wasn't opponents of abortion solely, or mentally unstable persons raging at Gus Voorhees as if he were still alive, from whom Jenna had to be protected; it was also "media people"—journalists, TV camera crews. Most of these (she believed) were sympathetic with the prosecution's case. Especially the women were staunch supporters of abortion, pro-choice. Still, Jenna declined all requests for interviews.

"Not now. Not yet! Sometime. Please understand."

She'd begun refusing such requests even from publications with which she and Gus had been associated immediately after Gus's death. She had understood the political value of addressing a shocked public after the assassination of a prominent abortion-provider—(and the assassination of an abortion center escort)—but she had been too exhausted, and too stricken with grief. She had hidden even (at times) from her oldest and most loyal friends; even from her parents, and her children. And later, when she'd been a little stronger, she had not wanted to squander her strength in such a way; she did not want to talk about her husband as if he were a political "issue."

About the trial that had been so frequently, so maddeningly delayed, she felt fierce, self-protective. The trial was all-consuming and obsessive and therefore she had nothing to say about it to an interviewer; she did not even like to speak of it with friends and prochoice associates, and when she called her children, each night, she said little of the trial, and wanted only to know how (in obsessive detail, that made the eldest children impatient) they were.

To Jenna the trial of Luther Dunphy was an endurance like swimming underwater, holding her breath for as long as she could, and then a little longer. She dared not draw breath too quickly for she would drown.

Her friends were determined to protect her. Since Gus's death they had surrounded her, shielded her. The trial of Luther Dunphy had loomed before them for more than a year.

"We will have justice, Jenna! Soon it will be over."

Soon? Over? Jenna wondered what this could possibly mean. Gus's absence from her life, and from the world, would never be over, no matter the outcome of the trial.

On the stone steps of the courthouse she took care to avoid the prayer vigil protesters. In the corner of her eye she saw how they regarded her, the widow of the man whose death they cheered. Did they hate her, as one of *the enemy*? Could they feel something more complicated for her—pity, if not sympathy? To them, she was the wife of a "baby killer"—that was her identity. She wanted to turn to them, to confront them— *You are dangerous fanatics—religious lunatics! Your wrathful God does not exist, you are brainwashed and absurd.*

But she knew it was not so simple. She knew how Gus would feel: though the protesters were mistaken, they were well-intentioned. Their religious leaders mobilized them for political reasons to undermine the "welfare state"—the "godless atheism" of a more equitably distributed economy. Like right-wing politicians who pretended to be populist to draw voters they were financed by wealthy companies and corporations who cared only for electing governments that favored business. Among gay marriage, contraception, women's reproductive rights, abortion was the singular emotional issue, the rallying cry—*No baby chooses to die.*

How manipulated these people were! How naive, politically. Yet, their emotions were sincere. Their rage was certainly sincere.

In their presence Jenna wore dark glasses on even overcast days and she wore dark, woolen clothing not because she was a widow but because the occasion of the trial was a somber one and bright colors had come to offend and hurt her eyes.

Mrs. Voorhees—?

No. She was polite, she was courteous, but she did not glance around.

Inside the courtroom Jenna took her place each morning in the row behind the prosecutors' table. The Broome County Courthouse was a very old building dating to the early 1900s but the interior had been renovated, "modernized." There were windows with sharp clear panes and a hardwood floor, slightly warped, that had been sanded and polished; twenty-two rows of seats were new but hard against the buttocks of a slender person. Jenna felt a leap of eagerness, of hunger, seeing that Luther Dunphy was being escorted into the courtroom by Broome County sheriff's deputies, his hands cuffed before him; as he was seated at the defense table with his two court-appointed attorneys, the handcuffs were removed. It was always startling to see how Dunphy loomed over the attorneys: he was well over six feet tall, he weighed over two hundred pounds. He was a strong man, if he wished to be. You could see how if he were enraged Luther Dunphy could be very dangerous.

She was waiting for him to turn to her. To seek her out. The widow of the man he had murdered.

394 · JOYCE CAROL OATES

Their eyes would lock. The murderer, and the widow of the murdered man. *Are you ashamed, are you shattered in your soul? For what you have done?*

Dunphy had denied that he'd had anything to do with the death of Timothy Barron, the fifty-eight-year-old volunteer whom he'd shot after he'd shot Gus Voorhees. He would not discuss this second death (it was said) even with his lawyer. Though witness after witness recounted the shootings, describing how he had shot both men, and forensic evidence unquestioningly identified the single shotgun used, yet Dunphy refused to acknowledge Barron's death; he could not accept that he'd killed a longtime resident of Muskegee Falls who was not an "abortion doctor."

Jenna thought it preposterous, the man had readily, even proudly confessed that he'd shot the "abortion doctor" for reasons of "self-defense" but he refused to acknowledge his second victim.

Insane! Or very cunning.

There was no defense—obviously. The defendant did not deny having killed at least one of his victims and he had been seen by numerous witnesses including even law enforcement officers.

Yet, the plea was "not guilty." The trial had been postponed several times. The defense's strategy was to postpone as long as possible—this was a typical defense

ploy, when guilt was so clear-cut. At first, Dunphy's attorney was going to argue that his client was "not guilty"
for reasons of extenuating circumstances; then, strategy
shifted, and Dunphy's attorney argued that he was "mentally unfit" to participate in his trial. Predictably, psychiatrists for the defense reported that Luther Dunphy was
"delusional"—"borderline schizophrenic"—"bipolar"
while psychiatrists for the prosecution reported that
Luther Dunphy was "of reasonably sound mind"—
"capable of understanding that he had broken the law"
and "capable of participating in his own defense." After
months of delay and prevarication the Broome County
judge had ruled that Dunphy was not delusional to the
degree that he couldn't participate in the trial, thus the
trial would proceed.

Did Jenna think that Luther Dunphy was insane?
All that she'd read about him, all that she'd been told by
prosecutors, led her to think yes, the man was insane;
he heard voices, he'd claimed; he believed he was fulfill-
ing the will of God in shooting two unarmed men. Yet,
there were many for whom this wasn't "insanity"—in
the context of religious belief, it was certainly not "insanity."

There were many more religious persons in the
United States than there were secular persons; of these,
the great majority were Christians. A serious Christian

would have to accept that, if God so willed, God might speak directly to him; it would be illogical to be a believing Christian and deny that God, or Christ, could have such a power. In this way, Luther Dunphy was not insane in his beliefs; in his actions, he had violated the law, but not as an insane person.

The defense's argument was a shrewd one: Luther Dunphy had not committed any crime in "defending" the "defenseless"—that is, unborn babies scheduled to be aborted that very morning in the Broome County Women's Center; under the law, one is allowed to commit an act of homicide in order to defend oneself or others. By presenting this act as idealistic, altruistic, and motivated by Christian charity, and in no way self-aggrandizing, the defense attorney was claiming that the defendant had acted *selflessly*. He had also suggested that his client, though seemingly "of sound mind and body" at the present time, had been "in a state of extreme mental duress" at the time of the shootings.

Which would provoke any juror to think, reasonably: had Luther Dunphy been insane? *Was* he insane, even now?

Jenna didn't want to think that Gus would have diagnosed Luther Dunphy as mentally unfit to stand trial. He'd often remarked that many of the most desperate girls and women who came to abortion clinics, the poorest ones, seemed to him mentally unstable if not actually ill. And a good many were suicidal, threatening to kill themselves if they could not terminate their pregnancies.

Jenna had begun to notice, with much interest, the family and relatives of the defendant, seated in two rows directly behind the defense table. These had been pointed out to her by the prosecutor's staff. Most fascinating to her was the murderer's wife—*the other wife*. Her name, Jenna knew from the newspapers, was Edna Mae; she'd been a nurse's aide before marrying at a young age. And there, beside Edna Mae, the murderer's children—at least, two children in their early teens who appeared to be brothers or (the younger had a plain pale face defiantly sexless) a brother and a sister, who resembled their father in the shape of their faces and about the eyes.

The *other wife* resembled a frayed cloth doll. Her unkempt fair brown hair she'd covered carelessly with a scarf that kept unknotting, slipping off her head. She wore a fleece-lined jacket, trousers, square-toed rubber boots. Her thin face was paste-colored and her eyebrows were penciled in arcs of mild surprise. Mrs. Dunphy too appeared older than her probable age as if her life had been sucked from her, from within. While court was in session her small mouth was often open, her lips moving in what Jenna supposed was silent prayer.

Silent prayer to *what, whom?*—Jenna wondered.

Did Edna Mae Dunphy truly think that her psychopath husband might be *not guilty?*

This *other wife* had not once glanced in Jenna's direction though others around her (family, relatives?) often glanced at Jenna coldly, disdainfully and disapprovingly. The sallow-skinned boy, who might have been a year or two older than Darren. The plain-faced girl (Jenna saw now, this was almost certainly a girl) who might have been Naomi's age. She wondered how the son and daughter of Luther Dunphy must feel— their father on trial for murder.

Did they love him, regardless? Did they approve of his act of violence, were they indeed *his children?*

Jenna thought it curious, and worthy of note, that Mrs. Dunphy was allowing her children to attend the trial at which their father was (almost certainly) going to be found guilty of murder. Or hadn't Mrs. Dunphy the power to bar the teenagers from the courtroom? Jenna saw how in the courtroom there appeared to be virtually no communication between the mother and the teenaged children. From time to time the girl shifted about restlessly in her seat; she did not like to hear testimony condemning her father, and she was often annoyed or embarrassed or anxious about her mother—for Edna Mae Dunphy sometimes appeared dazed or sedated as if not entirely aware of her surroundings; while the boy, more mature than his sulky sister, thus more responsible, took care to help his mother get to her feet, and to guide her, with a subtle grip of her elbow, into and out of the crowded courtroom. Jenna saw them elsewhere in the courthouse, and always the boy was overseeing the mother while the stonily impassive daughter ignored them both. How protective of his mother, this boy of fourteen! Jenna was moved, even as Jenna did not like to see; she did not want to feel any sympathy for the Dunphys, that would complicate her feeling for the father. She'd been able to banish her own young-adolescent children from the trial because they were living far from Muskegee Falls, Ohio, and she would allow them nowhere near.

Mom, please! I want to attend the trial with you.

Darren, no. That is not going to happen.

Behind the defendant's family were Dunphy relatives who attended the trial less regularly than Edna Mae and the children. These were solitary men who frowned menacingly during the testimony of prosecution witnesses; sometimes, they left the courtroom abruptly. There was a man of thickset middle age resembling Luther Dunphy, an older brother perhaps,

with a hatchet-sharp face, who stared in mute incredulous fury at officers of the court (judge, lawyers,
guards, bailiffs) as if he believed they might wish to
impinge upon his freedom of movement; he seemed, at
times, particularly disgusted with his brother's court-
appointed lawyer who (it may have seemed to him) was
not speaking vehemently enough on Luther's behalf.
But between Luther Dunphy and this individual there
never passed a glance; it seemed to Jenna quite possible that Luther didn't know the man was there.
Beside him there sometimes sat an older couple who
appeared ravaged as if with illness—the defendant's
parents. They were an elderly couple who appeared to
be in their early eighties. The man was heavyset, with
flesh-colored hearing aids prominent in both ears. The
woman was frail, anxious. Jenna felt pity for them, and
impatience. It was not their fault that their son had
become a murderer—(was it?)—but they had to be
pleading with their God to save him.

*Luther is not guilty. Luther killed those two men
but—we know—he is not guilty.*

They had to be praying with some desperation,
to save their son from a first-degree conviction, that
might bring with it a death sentence.

While court was in session Luther Dunphy did not
glance around at his family and relatives though he

must have been aware of them behind him. Like a man in a trance he appeared to be listening to the procession of witnesses—repeatedly hearing his name uttered—but he did not react. Jenna didn't want to think *He is with God. He imagines that.*

Jenna wondered if Dunphy did indeed think of himself as a soldier. One who takes orders, does another's bidding. He kills, but he is not a murderer.

He didn't really look like a murderer—he didn't look like *the enemy.* His wife Edna Mae, his children, most of the Dunphy relatives she'd seen did not look like *the enemy.* Except for two or three of the glaring men they did not look vicious, or malevolent, or evil, or psychopathic; even the girl with the smirking mouth whose eyes fixed boldly and defiantly on Jenna's face did not seem so very different from girls her age Jenna might see in Ann Arbor, high school girls, middle school girls, girls at the Ypsilanti mall, girls trailing after their families at Walmart, Target, Home Depot, girls embarrassed of their ill-kempt mothers.

A girl very different from her daughter Naomi. A girl who might (Jenna supposed) have intimidated Naomi, if they were at the same school.

Gus would recognize the Dunphys: lower-income working-class or welfare citizens of the sort who might well be his community health clients. Very easy

to imagine Edna Mae Dunphy pleading with Jenna
Matheson in the Ann Arbor Legal Aid office in which
she'd once worked, in desperate need of legal advice.

*Please help us! My husband—my children's father—
made a terrible mistake and got involved with the Army
of God—they sent him out to kill, and he killed . . .*

But Jenna did not want to think of the Dunphys
like this. She shifted in her seat, and looked away from
Edna Mae Dunphy's wan impassive face. The Dunphys were *the enemy*, she could not bear to contemplate them otherwise.

Like dirty water it swept over her. A wave of visceral
horror that left her dazed, exhausted and gagging.

As soon as she was alone. Where no one could observe *the widow.*

As soon as she could flee the Broome County Courthouse. Flee even the well-intentioned, the sympathetic who wanted only to grasp her hands and hold
her trapped in the effusion of their attention—*Please
accept our condolences, Mrs. Voorhees! We were all so
shocked, such a terrible thing, never before in Muskegee Falls which is a friendly place, the world will have
such an erroneous impression of our community . . .*
Alone in the privacy of her hotel room in which she
was staying for the duration of the trial.

In Muskegee Falls she'd insisted upon staying in a hotel, not in someone's home. Many people had graciously invited her to stay with them but Jenna had declined all invitations. She had not the energy to talk with people, even to listen to people talk to her. She had not the capacity to be *commiserated-with*, continuously; and she could not bear being told for the ten-thousandth time that her husband had been a wonderful man, a generous man, a courageous man, a selfless man, a beloved friend, colleague who was terribly missed.

I know. I know. I miss him too. What more can I say to you.

Above all she did not want people to misinterpret her bouts of panic, despair, nausea. Her life had collapsed when Gus had died as abruptly as if she'd been stricken by a virulent illness. She could summon strength when required, but she could not sustain strength for very long. Like a blown-up balloon that gradually leaks air, and has to be replenished. And when she was totally deflated, defeated, lying near-comatose on a hotel bed, teeth chattering with cold, she did not want another person to observe her, and be concerned for her; she did not want a well-intentioned friend to insist upon taking her to a doctor, still less calling an ambulance. That was all she needed, to be forcibly hospitalized in

Muskegee Falls, Ohio! Like all the doctors they knew Gus had horror stories of the quality of medical care in "outpost" hospitals. It was another fact of widow-hood (which perhaps only a widow could know) that such attacks always subsided within an hour or so. If she didn't develop tachycardia, or a migraine headache, or acute nausea, in which case she would do well to stay away from other people overnight.

You're just upset, darling. You'll be fine. Breathe deeply.

The only remedy was waiting, solitude. Feeling Gus's presence, consoling her.

Almost, if she drifted into sleep, she could grasp his hand. Or, rather—Gus would grasp her hand.

You've gotten through this in the past. You will again now. Try to sleep for a while.

She'd had to hide such weakness from the children of course. If she could not be strong for the children she did not want them to see her at all.

In the past several months the *grief-attacks* had been coming with lessening frequency but now, in Muskegee Falls, where the total focus of her attention, her concentration, was on the trial, and she was forced to hear the most devastating accounts of her husband's death, and to listen to the reports of law enforcement officers, emergency medical technicians, the county medical examiner, she was as vulnerable as she'd been a year ago.

The realization that Gus was dead, and had vanished from the earth while his murderer remained alive, untouched, in his stubborn, insular trance, that no one could enter—this swept over her at least once a day, when she returned to the hotel, and left her shattered.

She felt the need to explain to Gus: "No matter where I go, you aren't here. You are—*nowhere.*"

Or, rather—"Reduced to ashes."

She had not brought Gus's ashes to the cemetery where she'd purchased a plot. (Only just a single plot because as she reasoned her body too would be cremated, eventually; a double plot is not required when husband and wife have been reduced to ashes.) She had had too much to think about though she had not (yet) given in to Darren, that Gus's ashes should be scattered at Katechay Island.

One thing she'd have wished to keep from Gus— (though surely Gus wouldn't have been surprised)— was the fact that many individuals attending the trial, as elsewhere in the country, supported the man who had murdered him. This was painful to realize, though it should not have been surprising.

Since the arrest of Luther Dunphy there had been much publicity about the case. And now with the onset of the trial, yet more publicity.

A wealthy Midwestern manufacturer named Baer, associated with right-wing politics, had taken out TV advertisements extolling Dunphy as a "martyr" for the Right-to-Life movement. An evangelical preacher was exhorting his millions of viewers on cable TV to pray for Luther Dunphy's release. On Fox News, which was covering the trial as "breaking news," a popular commentator named Tom McCarthy whom Jenna had never seen, or wished to see, frequently praised Dunphy as a "soldier of God" and excoriated Gus Voorhees and the pro-choice movement as a "pack of atheist-socialist baby killers."

Of course, Tom McCarthy always paused to make it "abundantly clear" that he did not believe in, condone, or in any way encourage violence.

The single time that Jenna had forced herself to watch the terrifying *Tom McCarthy Hour* she'd had the impression that, as Tom McCarthy said these words, he'd all but winked at the television audience.

Violence? Noooo. Not me!

Anti-abortion organizations—or, as they called themselves, Right-to-Life organizations—had rallied to provide a defense fund to replace Dunphy's court-appointed attorney with a high-profile attorney but—unexpectedly—Dunphy had refused to accept a new attorney, and had refused to cooperate with the defense fund. He had not denied having shot the "abortion doctor" but he would not enter a plea of either *guilty* or *not guilty*; his attorney had entered the plea in his place, *not guilty*. The defendant's position seemed to be that he would submit to a trial but he would not actively defend himself for he did not accept that he had committed any crime, "in the eyes of God"—killing Voorhees was not a "crime."

Indeed, having killed Voorhees was a matter of pride for him while having killed Barron was a matter of shame.

(Timothy Barron had been a native of Muskegee Falls. From what Jenna knew of him he'd been an exceptional person. Gus had spoken of him warmly; of course, Jenna had never met him. She had supposed that, in Muskegee Falls, where she was staying at a hotel, she might have been invited to visit with the Barrons during the trial, and might have befriended them; but they had not expressed much interest in meeting Gus Voorhees's widow. She'd been introduced to them in the prosecutor's office—wife, adult daughters, adult son, a brother of the deceased man—but to her surprise they'd been stiffly polite and not at all friendly.

Jenna was made to realize that of course, they blamed
Gus for Timothy Barron's death: if not for Gus, Timothy Barron would still be alive.)

Each evening after the trial Jenna called the children. This was a high point of her day—though it was
not an easy hour or so, and left her shaken.

Always she spoke with Melissa first. For it was her
youngest child who most needed her, and missed her.

Melissa never asked about the trial for Melissa was
acutely sensitive to her mother's wishes, even over a
telephone; but Darren and Naomi wanted to know how
the trial was going, and all Jenna could tell them was,
"It seems to be going well. Each day is exhausting."
Darren had said several times that he wanted to attend
the trial and Jenna had told him without hesitation *No.*

"I should be there, if something goes wrong. If they
find that bastard not guilty."

Jenna flinched at her son's casual profanity—
bastard. It had not been like Gus to speak with casual
profanity, only if he'd been seriously annoyed or angry.
But Darren seemed more frequently angry. Or rather,
Darren seemed infrequently not-angry.

"Please don't think that way, Darren. I've been
assured the trial will turn out—as it should. There's
nothing we can do about it in any case except wait, and
hope."

"Right. It's the other side that *prays*."

Darren handed over the receiver to Naomi who spoke to her mother in a lowered voice, almost inaudibly. Almost it seemed to Jenna that her once-articulate daughter had acquired a speech impediment.

After a few frustrating minutes on the line with Naomi, Jenna felt an impulse to scream at her.

Don't! Damn you! Don't do this. We are all trying not to be crazy, don't you dare give in.

"Naomi? What did you say? I'm having trouble hearing you, this line is poor."

"Yeh. OK."

"'OK'—what?"

"'This line is poor.'" Naomi paused, and then said, with startling clarity, words Jenna had never heard from her before, "This line is *shitty*."

"Well. You could try to speak louder, then. Couldn't you?"

She was trying not to react with surprise at her daughter's vulgar expression—*shitty*.

This was new, in Naomi. Jenna would have to adjust.

The children were sixteen, thirteen. Not really children any longer. Childhood had ended.

She spoke with Naomi for a few more minutes with strained patience. Naomi's replies were muffled and might have been laughter, or coughing.

Jenna listened fiercely. Possibly, Darren was there also, beside his sister, and the two were laughing at *her*.

Because she was their mother, and she loved them? Because they had lost the essential bond between them, that had been possible only with their father? Because they now could not escape one another?

Near the end of the prosecution's presentation, in what would be the final week of the trial, Jenna realized to her horror—*It is Gus who is on trial. Not Luther Dunphy.*

She'd been slow to realize this stunning fact. She'd been reluctant.

In exacting detail the succession of prosecution witnesses had described the murders, again, again, and again—but the motive for the murders, which was very carefully questioned by the prosecutor, was always questioned by the defense attorney with the consequence that the jury was hearing, repeatedly, that Luther Dunphy had acted as he had in order to "defend the defenseless."

These were witnesses who'd seen Luther Dunphy approach Dr. Voorhees and the volunteer Barron, remove a double-barreled shotgun from inside his jacket, and begin firing with no warning. Again and again this scene was envisioned so that Jenna had become numbed by its repetition yet holding her breath, unable to breathe until the witness stepped down.

Witnesses who'd seen Luther Dunphy at the prayer vigil many times of whom some knew his name, and some did not; but all could identify him in the court-room.

Most of these were right-to-life protesters. They were yet obliged to testify against Luther Dunphy for they had sworn to tell the truth and would be guilty of contempt of court otherwise.

And do you see the man with the shotgun here in the courtroom today? Can you point him out, please?

Yes. That's him.

Perhaps the witness spoke with regret. Perhaps with sorrow. But there was no mistaking the identification.

So singled-out, Luther Dunphy shifted his shoulders uncomfortably. A faint flush came into his doughy face. He did not look up but stared at the table in front of him. His big hands clenched into fists on his knees. He was one who had lived his life at the margin of others' attention. Perhaps since boyhood he had not wished to be singled out.

Among the witnesses were medical workers at the Women's Center who'd just been arriving at the Center at the time of the shootings, who had fled to hide behind a Dumpster in terror of being shot. There were the

Broome County sheriff's deputies who'd been on guard duty at the Center that morning, whom the sudden outburst of gunfire had taken totally by surprise. There were emergency medical technicians who'd rushed to the scene of the carnage, too late to help either of the stricken men.

There was the county medical examiner, who'd drawn back the shroud from Gus Voorhees's devastated face and upper body.

You have determined—death was instantaneous for both men?

Yes. Certainly.

She had no need to listen yet she was listening. She had no need to look at photographs of the fallen men projected on a screen yet she was looking. It was required for Gus's sake, she thought. His terrible suffering should be shared, if at a distance. His terrible suffering should be revealed to as many witnesses as possible.

In the jury box the jurors listened, and the jurors looked. For the most part their expressions were impassive. They were very ordinary-seeming men and women—nine men, five women. (Twelve jurors, two alternates.) All white-skinned, and all middle-aged or older. Jenna would have liked to see younger jurors, and more women. (The ideal juror, from her perspective, would have been a young black woman.) She did not want to think of the power that resided in these strangers, to punish the guilty man as he deserved, to provide some measure of justice for the victims.

Mostly, Jenna tried not to observe the jurors for fear she might see something in their faces that might upset her. Tersely she'd said to a friend in Michigan, with whom she often spoke on the phone, that the jurors had seemed to her *rural*.

It wasn't a joke exactly. Well yes, it was a joke. But not exactly.

On the final day of the prosecution's case a former Catholic priest took the witness stand. Through a haze of headache pain Jenna listened with mounting alarm.

This was a hostile witness, the prosecutor had told Jenna. The ex-priest had not wanted to testify though he was an eyewitness to the shootings; he'd been served a subpoena by the district attorney and had had no choice but to cooperate, under penalty of being found in contempt of court.

Donald Stockard had left his church parish in Lincoln, Nebraska, in 1996, and had left the priesthood the following year. He'd been a protester at the Broome County Women's Center for several months but he had not, he insisted, known Luther Dunphy by name.

"Mr. Stockard—or, excuse me, shall I say 'Father Stockard'?"

"I am no longer a priest as I explained. 'Mr. Stockard' is fine."

"And why are you no longer a priest, Mr. Stockard?"

"For a—personal reason."

"Was it because your parish in Lincoln was unhappy with you? Complained to the bishop about your sermons? Wasn't that it?"

"It was a confluence of reasons . . ."

"'A confluence of reasons'—can you explain?"

"I did not feel—I do not feel—that the Catholic church has been sufficiently active in opposing abortions—legalized infanticide—in the United States . . ."

Stockard spoke haltingly. He was very ill at ease, with a sallow, damp-looking skin, a faint stammer. His face was long and morose and his mouth quivered with emotion.

"You were disciplined by your bishop—wasn't that it, Mr. Stockard? You were moved out of the parish and forbidden to 'recruit' anti-abortion protesters . . ."

"I elected to quit the priesthood. I was not 'fired.' My decision to quit was not made quickly but after much anguish . . . I still have strong ties to my parish in Lincoln. I have strong ties to my beliefs. I am not so alone as people think."

Jenna saw how, for the first time since the start of the trial, Luther Dunphy lifted his head, and regarded the witness with concern. He was sitting very still, his fists now on the table in front of him. Stockard, in the witness chair, stared blinking at the prosecutor as if he feared about what the prosecutor would ask next.

But the prosecutor only asked Stockard to describe what he'd seen at the Women's Center on the morning of November 2, 1999.

Stockard said that he'd just glimpsed Luther Dunphy that morning, and had not spoken with him. Dunphy had hurried past him without seeming to see him standing on the sidewalk in front of the Center, just before the attack.

He had not, Stockard said, exactly seen the attack; he'd seen Luther Dunphy following behind the mini-van that had turned into the driveway, and he'd heard the shotgun explosions a second later which were deafening, and with others he'd recoiled in panic and confusion, backing away—looking for places to take cover . . .

"You saw the fallen men? It was clear to you what had happened?"

"I—I think I saw the fallen men. It wasn't clear—immediately—what had happened. We were all—we were terrified, frankly. The first thing you think in such a situation is that your life is in danger—your instinct is to run away . . ."

"Your instinct wasn't to run to the fallen men, and see if they needed aid?"

"In these circumstances, I'm afraid—I did not . . ."

"And why was that?"

"I told you—I was in fear of my life . . ."

"Were you hiding?"

"Some of us were—we'd tried to hide . . . No one knew exactly what had happened. It was very confusing."

"But you'd recognized Luther Dunphy, with the shotgun?"

"I don't think I knew Luther's name. I—I don't think we had exchanged names. What had happened had happened so fast, I wasn't able to think clearly . . . No one knew if there might be more than one person with a gun. Or if the person with the gun was going to shoot again."

"Were there police officers at the scene?"

"Yes—two deputies. They were stationed at the Center. But they didn't seem to know what to do either, at first . . . Then other law enforcement officers arrived, and an ambulance."

"And where was Luther Dunphy all this while? Did he try to flee the scene?"

"No. He was kneeling in the driveway just waiting.

He'd put the shotgun down on the ground . . . I think he did that. Or maybe I learned that later. But he did not try to flee. It looked like he was praying."

"He was praying?"

"It looked like he was praying. That's what other people have said also."

"Did you see for yourself that Luther Dunphy was 'praying,' or was this something you'd heard from others?"

"I—don't know. It's very confused in my mind."

"But you saw the fallen men?"

"I—I did see—the fallen men . . . But I didn't recognize them, I didn't know who they were."

"Did you surmise that they were Dr. Voorhees and his driver?"

"I—might have. I did know Voorhees—we all knew Voorhees. And the driver, he was familiar to us. One of the volunteers at the Center . . . I didn't know his name."

"Major Timothy Barron. That is his name."

"Yes. I know now."

"Mr. Stockard, did you conspire with Luther Dunphy to assassinate Augustus Voorhees and Timothy Barron on the morning of November 2, 1999?"

"No. I did not."

"Did you know beforehand of the defendant's intention to assassinate Augustus Voorhees and Timothy Barron on the morning of November 2, 1999?"

"No. I did not."

"You *did not?*"

"I—I did not."

"Did you ever speak to Luther Dunphy about Dr. Voorhees? In any way?"

"I—might have. But just briefly."

"Did you ever encourage him—in any way?"

"No . . ."

"Can you recall what you talked about?"

"Not clearly . . ."

Stockard was very uneasy now. At the defense table Luther Dunphy had ceased looking at him, and was staring at his clenched hands.

"You have been observed talking together, Mr. Stockard. Several witnesses have told us. But you can't recall what you talked about?"

"I . . . I recall that Luther Dunphy happened to mention that he'd noticed that the abortion doctor and his escort sometimes arrived before the police guard, at about seven-thirty A.M., and that this was—surprising. He asked me if it was routine, that Voorhees arrived as much as twenty minutes before the police."

"And what did you tell him, Mr. Stockard?"

"I told him—I think I told him—that I had not noticed . . ."

"Was it common for you to arrive so early, when the Center doesn't open until eight A.M.?"

"It opens for the public at eight A.M. It opens for women seeking to abort their innocent babies. But the medical staff arrives earlier of course. And so, some of us arrive earlier."

"Including Luther Dunphy?"

"I am not aware of Luther Dunphy's schedule. It was my impression—though I didn't think much about it, at the time—that most of the protesters arrived at varying times, and some days, some did not come at all. There were protesters more likely to come in the morning, and protesters more likely to come in the afternoon. Sometimes, they ceased coming altogether—they never returned. If someone was missing, I would not be likely to notice—I didn't keep track in that way."

"Did Luther Dunphy often miss a vigil?"

"I think he is a carpenter, or a roofer. He has a demanding job. He may have been working part-time . . . None of this I knew at the time, but I have read in the paper since his arrest. I've tried to explain, I did not know the schedule of any of my fellow protesters."

"Did you speak often to Luther Dunphy, though you claim not to have known his name?"

"No. I did not speak often to him."

"And why did you speak with him on this particular occasion?"

"I think he spoke to *me* . . . He just fell to talking, as people do. We are bound by a common interest for which we feel strongly—'defending the defenseless.'"

"Can you elaborate, Mr. Stockard, what you told Luther Dunphy?"

"I might have told him—in reply to his question—that it did seem to be, lately, that Voorhees was arriving earlier than the police guards. I mean, I agreed with his observation. I think that was how it was . . ."

"And what else did you say?"

"What else did I *say*? I—I don't know—maybe I mentioned that Voorhees sometimes drove the van himself, and his escort took the passenger's seat. They came to the Center together most days. But I think that Voorhees didn't feel the need for an escort—a kind of bodyguard. That's what we'd heard."

"And why would anyone on the staff at the Women's Center require a 'bodyguard'?"

"They would not. It was all exaggerated, for

publicity—that right-to-life protesters were intrusive and violent and that they, the abortionists, had to be protected from them—from us."

"There is no need for bodyguards? Or law enforcement?"

"Not usually. There is not."

"But sometimes?"

"Not—often."

"Really, Mr. Stockard? Since two individuals were killed who'd turned up for work at the Center, by one of your Right-to-Life protesters, it doesn't seem to you that there is any *need*?"

"But not usually. Not often . . ."

"Will you answer a little more clearly, whether Luther Dunphy asked you specifically about the time of arrival of Dr. Voorhees, in relationship to the arrival of the police officers?"

"I don't know what you mean . . ."

"Did Luther Dunphy *ask you*, or did you *volunteer the information?*"

Stockard hesitated. His long somber face was damp with perspiration. He was blinking rapidly as if he could not bear to look at the prosecutor; and he could not bring himself to look at Luther Dunphy who was seated only a few yards away.

"I think that it was me—it was I—who asked him. And Luther Dunphy who volunteered the information."

"But why did he tell you this, if indeed he told you?"

"Why? I don't know why . . . We talked about Voorhees, and the Center, and abortions, and the need to stop legalized infanticide, an abomination . . . We talked about many things."

"But you've just said, you rarely talked."

"Except this one time . . ."

"And what did Luther Dunphy say, after he'd volunteered the information about Voorhees's arrival?"

"I—I do not recall that he said anything further."

"He did not say *anything further*?"

"He did not. Not that I recall."

"He did not say—'Voorhees is unprotected then. He could be killed then. There are a few minutes when he is vulnerable—he could be killed.' But Luther Dunphy did not say that?"

"No! Of course not."

"And you did not say that?"

"Of course not."

"And when was this exchange, Mr. Stockard?"

"When? I—I'm not sure—maybe a week, ten days before . . ."

"Before the shooting?"

Stockard sat very still and did not speak until the

prosecutor repeated his question and he said, in his halting voice, that trembled with indignation and anger, "Y-Yes. Before the shooting."

Next, the prosecutor asked Stockard if he'd noticed that following the exchange Luther Dunphy began to arrive early each morning at the Women's Center and he replied nervously that he didn't know—he had never taken "much particular notice" of his fellow protesters for there were many protesters, as he'd tried to explain; they came to the Center, they participated in the demonstrations, then they weren't seen again for a while— but then, they might show up again. He didn't know any names, or if he did, they were just first names— "Not surnames."

"Was it, on the whole, an orderly demonstration?"

"Yes! Our demonstrations are fundamentally prayer."

"But there are some disruptions, at times?"

"When there are new protesters. Sometimes a new protester is more vocal."

"Do protesters become upset?"

"Of course. When women seek to 'terminate' their pregnancies, to murder their babies in their wombs, it is certainly upsetting—it should be upsetting."

"And so, there are 'encounters' at the Center? Routinely?"

"Not routinely . . ."

"But 'encounters' are not uncommon?"

"I would have to say—yes, not uncommon."

"Protesters are forbidden by Ohio state law to approach the young women entering such clinics too closely, isn't that correct?"

"That is correct. That is state law."

"Do you abide by this 'state law,' Mr. Stockard?"

"It is a secular law . . ."

"As distinct from—?"

"A sacred law."

"There are two laws, then?"

"There is certainly a sacred law, which does not change. And there is secular law, which changes with each new election." Stockard spoke ironically.

"'Father Stockard'—isn't it true, you are sometimes—still—called 'Father'?"

"N-No . . . Not often."

"But sometimes?"

"I don't encourage it . . ."

"Why would an individual call you 'Father Stockard'?"

"Well, likely it would be a younger person . . . Or someone who'd known me in my parish years ago."

"But you don't encourage the usage?"

"No."

"And why is that?"

"Because I am no longer a priest. I am 'defrocked.'"

"Yet it was your own choice, you say? To be 'defrocked'?"

"'Defrocked' is meant to be ironic. I applied to be released from the priesthood, and this was granted to me, after some years of effort. But I remain a Catholic, and will all of my life."

"You were not 'excommunicated' from the Church."

"Of course not! That would never be."

"Are you a member of the American Coalition of Life Activists?"

"Y-Yes . . ."

"And you've signed their public statement supporting the 'justifiable homicide' of abortion providers?"

"I—I may have signed the statement . . ."

"You do believe in 'justifiable homicide' of abortion providers?"

"That would depend upon the circumstances."

"What do you mean—'circumstances'?"

"Homicide is 'justifiable' in defense of others' lives. You are allowed to defend yourself, for instance. And you are allowed to defend others."

"Homicide—murder—is 'justifiable' depending upon circumstances of your own interpretation?"

"We all believe in a higher law . . ."

"Are you a member of the secret organization Operation Rescue?"

"No."

"Do you know anything about Operation Rescue?"

"No . . ."

"Really, no?"

"I have read some things . . ."

"Were you aware that Luther Dunphy was a member of Operation Rescue?"

"No."

"You know, Mr. Stockard, the penalty for perjury can be years in prison. 'Lying under oath . . .'"

"I did not know that Luther Dunphy belonged to Operation Rescue until I read about it in the newspaper."

"You were a Catholic priest from 1974 to 1996, is this correct?"

"Yes."

"At the start of our exchange you'd said that you had voluntarily left the Church, and not because parishioners had complained of you proselytizing for the Right-to-Life movement, and not because the bishop had 'terminated' you."

"Yes . . ."

"Isn't it the case, Mr. Stockard, that you were several times arrested in anti-abortion protests in the early and mid-1990s, in Madison, Wisconsin?—in Minneapolis-

St. Paul?—in Columbus, Youngstown, and Cincinnati, as recently as spring 1999?"

"That might be. You seem to know."

"Would you describe yourself as a militant anti-abortionist, Mr. Stockard?"

"'Militant'?—no."

"No?"

"I am not a *militant.* I am an *activist* in the cause, but my commitment is to *active non-violence.*"

"Yet you've supported militancy in the anti-abortion movement?"

"Yes I have supported militancy, if it is another's genuine belief."

"Not for yourself but for another? *Militancy—violence?*"

"It is not for me to judge others in this struggle. It is a war against abortion which is the murder of the defenseless and it is a war against the forces that have inspired to support and protect abortion, and in this struggle we have differing stratagems."

"What do you think—personally—of the 'stratagem' of Luther Dunphy?"

"Luther Dunphy is a soldier of God who has put his life on the line for his beliefs. The rest of us bear witness—we but 'stand and wait.'"

"You admire Luther Dunphy, then?"

"Yes. I admire Luther Dunphy."

"You consider Luther Dunphy's act of premeditated, cold-blooded murder of two defenseless persons 'admirable'?"

"I've said—I do not in any way condone violence. And especially against Timothy Barron who was not an imminent threat to any baby or baby's mother."

"But you admire Dunphy for shooting Voorhees?"

"Voorhees was an abortion doctor. There is no question that, if he had not been stopped, he would have killed babies that day, as he'd killed hundreds of babies over the years with impunity."

"You believe that homicide is 'justifiable' under these circumstances?"

"Don't you, sir? Doesn't everyone?"

"I am asking *you*, Mr. Stockard. 'Everyone' is not involved here."

"If infants' lives are at immediate risk, the abortionist must be stopped."

"*Must be stopped.* And this includes—murder?"

"It is not murder but self-defense."

"*Self*-defense?"

The prosecutor spoke in a voice heavy with sarcasm, that made Jenna flinch. She was feeling uneasy, the mood of the courtroom was hushed with attention and (it seemed to her) respect for the ex-priest's position, as for the stammer and warmth of his words that were like raw cries from the heart.

"If—if you saw someone about to murder an infant, for instance with a knife, you would be obliged to attack him, wouldn't you, to save the infant; it is your moral duty to try to prevent the infant being killed."

"Even in violation of the law?"

"That's the secular law. The law passed by the legislature of Ohio in the wake of *Roe v. Wade* of 1973. But there is a higher law. There is always a law higher than the secular—as in Nazi Germany in the time of the death camps and experimentation on human beings, there was a higher law in defiance of the secular law."

"But the State of Ohio isn't Nazi Germany, Mr. Stockard! And the Muskegee Falls Women's Center is not the Holocaust."

"Where innocent lives are destroyed, there is a Holocaust. The abortion in the mother's womb is the Holocaust."

"Mr. Stockard, did you advise parishioners and young people to break the law when you were a priest in Lincoln?"

"No."

"Really—no?"

"Not nearly as much as I should have."

"That's a clear-cut answer, Father! Thank you."

"But I did not advise anyone to break the law. Only to follow their conscience. They will tell you."

"Yet, you claim that you have not actively conspired in murdering an abortion doctor."

"I have not . . ."

"And why have you not?"

"I am not proud of my prudence. My cowardice."

Stockard was trembling now. His voice quavered, he was barely audible.

There came a ripple of emotion through the courtroom, like a current of water. Jenna could not help but feel it herself. The former priest with his tormented face had made a strong impression on all who'd heard him speak, including even the elderly judge whose expression was usually opaque, impassive.

Belatedly, the prosecutor realized this. He sensed the jurors' sympathies, and abruptly ceased his cross-examination. But now it was the defense attorney's turn, and his questions were respectful, drawing from Stockard such protracted admiration for Luther Dunphy, and such passion for the Right-to-Life movement, as well as vilification of the Pro-Choice movement, that the prosecutor was forced to object several times. Like an attorney in a TV show he leapt to his feet. He spoke sharply. He spoke with an edge of sarcasm. This was not strategic. This was an error. In dismay Jenna could feel a shift in the atmosphere of the courtroom subtle as a heartbeat.

So many times the term *defending the defenseless* had been uttered, it hung in the air of the courtroom like a bad smell. There was no way to ignore it, and it would not be possible to forget it.

At last the ordeal was over. Stockard had been questioned for more than an hour. But he was defiant, he had triumphed. His eyes shone with tears.

And now, as he returned to his seat in the courtroom, he dared to look at Luther Dunphy who had been listening to his testimony with something like wonder, and yearning. Jenna steeled herself.

The priest will take his hand now. He will bless him!

But this didn't happen. Stockard passed close by Luther Dunphy unsteady on his feet as if exhausted.

Soon after this, the trial ended.

The defense called few witnesses, and all of these were individuals attesting to Luther Dunphy's "character"— the most persuasive was the minister of Dunphy's church who claimed that Luther Dunphy was the "most devout Christian" he knew, and that Luther Dunphy would not have "willingly" done any harm to any living thing.

How was it possible, then, the prosecutor asked him, that Luther Dunphy had shot two unarmed men, in cold blood, without warning?—and Reverend Kuhn said humbly that he did not know.

He'd visited Luther Dunphy in the detention house, he said. They prayed together but they didn't talk much about what had happened—"Mostly we just pray to God for the strength to understand. We are waiting for that strength to suffuse us."

The trial ended. The jury deliberated. She waited.

In the Muskegee Falls Inn, in her room on the fourth, top floor she waited.

Alone she waited. In terror of the jury's decision she waited.

The prosecutor had assured her, there could be no verdict other than guilty. Under the law, jurors had to convict. The argument that Luther Dunphy had committed two murders as a kind of "self-defense" was unacceptable.

On the fourth morning of waiting she wakened before dawn with the sudden wish to see where Gus had died.

She had not seen the Broome County Women's Center which was (she'd been told) a ten-minute walk from the hotel. She had not been driven past the Center. She had not requested this, and no one had offered.

Quickly she dressed, in her dark, heavy clothes, and

tied a scarf around her head, and walked out along the deserted street. Main Street, Third Street, Ferry Street, Howard Avenue . . . Her eyes blurred with moisture as she tried to read the street signs in the cold air. When she saw the Women's Center at Howard Avenue and Ventor she felt a sensation of vertigo—had her husband died for *that?*

The Broome County Women's Center was slightly larger than the Huron County Women's Center. A single-story building you would identify as a clinic or community center subsisting on public funds. Its windows had been bricked up. Graffiti had been scrawled on its walls, and inexpertly painted over. It was set back from the street in a grassless space into which litter had drifted and was partly covered by snow. She had been told that since the assassinations, and subsequent threats and vandalism at the Center resulting in a loss of staff, the Center had been "struggling" to stay open; at the front entrance was a prominent sign *CLOSED.*

Did *CLOSED* mean temporarily, or permanent? Jenna did not want to know.

She did know that Gus and the volunteer-escort Timothy Barron had been shot down in the asphalt driveway beside the Center, not at the street but nearer the parking lot at the rear.

Bravely she walked up the driveway. She was trembling badly. Her eyes were now leaking tears from the cold. The asphalt pavement was covered with a thin layer of ice and powdery snow, in some places rippled, ribbed. It was dangerous to walk here without caution. Did she dare to peer closely at the driveway, in the area where it was likely Gus had died; did she dare to pause, to stare at the ground, steeling herself to see . . .

Gus why did you come to this forlorn place? I hate you, I will never forgive you. Oh Gus.

She saw nothing beneath the ice. She wiped at her eyes, still she saw nothing. She had been imagining the figure of a man imprinted in the pavement, arms spread like the wings of an angel, a large man, Gus's size, but she saw nothing.

She'd been imagining dark stains in the pavement. But the pavement itself was dark, beneath the ice crust. Splotches of mud. Cracks in the asphalt, through which sinewy weeds had pushed, now dead. Blown against a chain-link fence nearby was a lacework of shredded paper, debris. She had been told (Gus had told her) that the Women's Center property was "well maintained" but this did not appear to be the case, if it had ever been. Other properties on the block were in disrepair, some were vacant. The largest property was a sprawling lumberyard. Had her husband really died *here?*—

and another man, *here*? A place so empty of meaning? It did not seem possible.

Awkwardly she knelt. Not to pray but to peer more closely at the pavement. The rippled, ribbed ice obscured her vision. With a gloved hand she rubbed away snow—nothing was revealed beneath.

Inside her heavy clothes she was beginning to perspire imagining the minivan turning into the driveway and proceeding to the rear—stopping, and parking, and out of the passenger's side Gus climbed— and out of the driver's side Timothy Barron climbed—and there came rushing at them a man with a double-barreled shotgun, already lifting the gun, aiming and firing at their heads . . .

It had been over within seconds. The men's lives extinguished, within seconds.

"God, don't abandon these men. They need you, too."

These pleading words leapt from her. She would have been embarrassed to recall afterward and soon she would forget entirely.

She returned to the hotel. She would postpone for another time a trip to 81 Shawnee Street which was the address of the one-bedroom apartment Gus had rented in Muskegee Falls, where there were belongings of his to be removed . . . She had no idea how to "remove" these belongings, she could not bear to think of it. Her brain went blank and dead at the prospect.

We will help you, Jenna. Please let us help you—but she was not hearing these words.

In her hotel room she was feeling very tired as if she'd climbed many flights of stairs though (in fact) she'd taken the slow crankily-moving elevator as she usually did. Her brain seemed to hurt. She was seeming to recall that yes, she had actually seen stains in the asphalt, beneath the powdery snow. Yes, she'd been warned beforehand that the Women's Center was closed. (Always the careful qualifier—"Temporarily closed.") In the musty-smelling room on the fourth, top floor of the Muskegee Falls Inn she would sit on the edge of the oddly high bed facing the window (that overlooked at a distance of a quarter mile the snowy Muskegee River) but seeing nothing for she was awaiting the call from the prosecutor that would come near noon of that day December 18, 2000, to summon her to the Broome County, Ohio, Courthouse to hear the jury's decision.

═══════

I'm sorry. I don't care to defend my ballot.

I voted not guilty for reasons of "justifiable homicide."

I don't care to defend my ballot or my religious views. I follow my conscience.

We were in the jury room deliberating for three and a half days, and we wore one another down like teeth grating and grinding but nobody wore me down.

On the third day my voice was trembling but I said to the foreman and the others at that end of the table, what the abortion doctors do to babies you are trying to do to me. And they looked at me like I was crazy or sick or had screamed at them in some language they pretended they did not know.

I was excited then. I was not afraid. I said, I am not a defenseless baby in some woman's womb. You can't silence me that easy. You can't abort me.

After that, we didn't communicate much. I was Juror Number 8. I had an ally Juror Number 2 who began to vote with me. Edith came to sit beside me. She said she'd been praying to make a correct decision. We had both brought our Bibles into the jury room, which was allowed. No newspapers—of course. No reading material except the Bible we were allowed to read if we read silently and not aloud. So I would read my Bible, my favorite books which are St. Luke and St. John and some parts of the Psalms and Revelation while there were these long discussions by just five jurors that took up so many hours. They were always asking the bailiff to run to the judge with some question to show how smart they were, the female especially who was a high school principal she allowed you to know every chance she could. But I'd made up my mind at the vou-yar deer on the first day.

You are supposed to say if you are "prejudiced" or had read about the case in the newspapers or heard of it on TV but I did not say this when I was being questioned for they would not have chosen me to be a juror, and it is my right as a citizen to be a juror. In my life I have been a juror in three trials but not ever a trial for "two counts of homicide." Right away I looked at Luther Dunphy and saw that man was a true Christian, in his heart he had only concern for the unborn to be slaughtered. There was no other motive for him to act. This was a "selfless" act as his lawyer would say. That was the instant, I believe that God had summoned me to that courthouse that day to vote as He would wish.

I knew that I would vote not guilty and nobody could change my mind. And that was how it was.

The prosecutor would try to malign that man, who had done his duty as a Christian as he saw it. They would not let him testify like the others did—"witnesses." He was made to sit silent at the little table at the front of the courtroom. He would shut his eyes and you could see *that he was praying, his mouth would move in silence. In his way of setting his shoulders and the worried cast of his eyes I was reminded of my uncle who was my father's oldest brother who had died when I was in eighth grade. My uncle had been a good man and you could see that Luther Dunphy was a good man. The more the prosecutor tried to portray him as a "murderer," the more clear it was that he was not. For Jesus was in the courtroom with us, you could feel His presence. Once, on a morning in the last week of the trial, which was the fifth week, a bird of the size of a pigeon flew against a courtroom window—you could not see the actual bird but only its shadow, and you could hear the noise it made hitting the glass—and I turned toward Edith, and a wild look passed between us—The spirit of the Lord was in our presence.*

We could not discuss the case during the trial, in the jury room. We could not say a word outside the courthouse or inside the courthouse until the trial was ended! We were brought to the courthouse by a shuttle bus to a special door at the rear of the building that was guarded by Broome County sheriff's men, and we exited by that door, and boarded the shuttle bus to avoid the picketers and protesters at the front of the courthouse who would shout and scream at us, if they saw us. For half of them wanted Luther Dunphy freed.

And the other half wanted Luther Dunphy found guilty. And they hated one another, and had to be kept apart from one another. And there were TV camera crews there also, tying up traffic in the streets.

Inside the courtroom we just had to listen to all that talk, talk, talk of the lawyers. Every damn thing the prosecutor would say if he would say it once, he would say it a dozen times. There was too much about shotgun shells or casings—whatever they call it. Identifying Luther Dunphy. So many witnesses speaking for the abortion doctor and the other one—the driver of the van—hearing what a good man Dr. Voorhees was, how "selfless" and "dedicated" to helping women and girls—and the other one who'd gotten in the way of the gunfire (so it seemed to me)—what a "good husband and father"—you just stopped hearing it after a while. I did listen to the priest from Nebraska. He spoke from the heart and knew of what he spoke, the defense of the defenseless. And the pastor of Luther Dunphy's church—there was a true man of God, you could see. The prosecutor was sarcastic hoping to make them say incriminating things against Luther Dunphy but they would not.

Once the trial was over, it was different in the jury room. Almost everybody wanted to talk. Like the tower of Babel it was, everybody talking at once. So the foreman *instructed us to speak one by one around the table and say what we believed, was Luther Dunphy guilty as charged, or not guilty. And it was shocking to me, it was sickening to me, that ten jurors out of twelve believed that this innocent man was guilty when he had acted to protect living babies. One juror had not made up her mind yet—(this was Edith)—and the other was me.*

What about the law to protect a living baby? Babies? Nobody wished to talk about that law.

So it was, after four and a half days we could not agree. The talk turned bitter and bullying but we would never give in, for Edith and I were certain in our hearts that Luther Dunphy was not guilty of any crime of God. It was like Pontius Pilate saying to the Jews, this man is not a criminal, and the Jews saying Yes, yes! He is a criminal, he is to be crucified because we want him crucified.

After a point if I tried to speak, they would cut me off. Edith did not speak at all for she knew how they would leap onto her. And so, I did nothing more than say again, and again, as many times as they would ask me, why I did not believe that Luther Dunphy was guilty of any actual crime, and why I would not vote that he was guilty for it was a "higher law"—as Luther Dunphy's lawyer argued—"the law of God"—and our country is based upon this principle of rebellion and upon the higher law and by this, Luther Dunphy is a hero and not a criminal.

So it happened, we could not agree. Each ballot it was ten against two—Edith and I would never change our minds. And so the trial was declared a "mistrial" by the judge. I could see, the judge seemed to know who I was, and who Edith was, and he hated our guts as the other jurors did. When I tell this I sound calm and easy but at that time, I was not. Each night sick to my stomach and not able to sleep but we would not give in, for Jesus had spoken. The spirit of the Lord had spoken.

When the jury was called back into the courtroom, and the judge declared the mistrial, at the table where he was sitting Luther Dunphy stared toward us for a moment without seeming to hear. And when the judge repeated his words there were outcries in the court-room, of disbelief, and happiness, but also of anger, and the judge rapped his gavel hard, and bailiffs and guards came forward to block people from pushing into the aisles and by this time Luther Dunphy was on his knees on the hardwood floor, giving thanks to the Lord and his face streaked with tears.

Later when we were leaving the courthouse I hoped that I would see Luther Dunphy one last time, it seemed to me that Luther Dunphy might come to shake my hand, and Edith's hand, for we had saved his life, for several of the jurors had expressed a wish that Luther Dunphy should be sentenced to death and not just to life in prison, but this did not happen of course.

If there was to be a second trial, I would pray that God would look after Luther Dunphy another time in his hour of need.

These five weeks were a strained time in my life but always I would look back upon the trial of Luther Dunphy that was a mistrial as the time in my life when my life had purpose.

Before that, and after, I am not always so sure. But I am sure of that time.

"Mistrial": Widow of the Deceased

Trial ends, jurors dismissed.

Cheers, cries of triumph in the courtroom, that ripple outside within seconds onto the stone steps, into the street.

Not *not guilty.* But *mistrial.*

Still, this is perceived as a (temporary) victory for the defendant—the defense.

She is so stunned, *mistrial* doesn't immediately register.

For some seconds paralyzed where she sits, staring and blinking at the judge who has now turned away, rising, with an expression of prissy disapproval, displeasure as if the jurors reporting "hopeless deadlock" have personally offended his honor.

Much of this she won't remember afterward. Rapid

vertiginous ride in a roller coaster that rushes you breathless and dazed to your point of origin. *Is this it?—this?* That Luther Dunphy did not turn toward her (as she'd fantacized through more than three weeks he might) and *lock eyes with hers* but appeared to be as stunned by the non-verdict as well.

"Mistrial": Children of the Deceased

We knew, we'd known, no one had to tell us. I mean Darren and Naomi. Twins joined at *hate*.

Someone called our grandfather with the news. Not our mother.

Someone who was with her attending the trial in Ohio.

Shithole, OHIO (credit: Darren).

Can't even remember when Mom finally called us. Or a woman friend called us, and put Mom on the phone, and all Mom could do was say *I'm sorry, I'm sorry* crying and choking so it made us want to puke, so disgusted.

So sorry, they did not convict him. The judge dismissed the jury after four days. "Mistrial." Oh God.

Hung up the fucking phone so hard, fucking plastic

receiver ricocheted and fell onto the floor. Kicked and stomped fucking plastic receiver until it was just fucking *pieces*.

"Naomi! Stop! What are you doing, Naomi! *Stop*."

Ran out of the room. Out of the house. What do you *fucking care*, you are not our real grandmother *fuck you*.

She'd sent us away. Out of Ann Arbor where too many knew *Voorhees*.

Possibly, there'd been danger. Threats against the children of Gus Voorhees. We were never (exactly) told. Even Darren, who demanded (of the McMahans) to be told what was going on, anything and everything that involved our mother and us, did not really know.

You know what people (adults) tell you. Essentially, you know what people (adults) want you to know.

Too much in the media about *Gus Voorhees, abortion provider, shot down, anti-abortion assassin*. Too much about *trial ending in a stunning upset: mistrial*.

There would be another trial. Dunphy would remain in custody. (It was said.)

Another trial was imminent, and more media. More TV, more Tom McCarthy spewing hate, more front-page headlines, photos. More *baby killer, Army of God, martyr*.

More distraction for our mother. More dread. Ever

closer to the breaking-point. (We did not want to ac-knowledge.)

Asshole at Ann Arbor High says to Darren if I was you, Voorhees, know what?—I'd change my last name.

Fuck you, you are not *me*.

Hey! Just sayin.

Just sayin *fuck you*, asshole.

(What followed from this Darren didn't say. Darren's hate stories ended in one-liners by Darren deftly uttered like TV stand-up comedy.)

(At sixteen Darren stood five feet eleven with slumped shoulders like a raptor hunched on a fence. He smiled rarely but when he did smile it was a razor-flash of pure adolescent drop-dead cynicism. His long arms were ropey-muscled and his habit of clenching and unclenching his fists did not encourage other boys to "mess" with him even when they were insulted.)

At her school where Naomi was in eighth grade the most valuable information she'd learned was to avoid restrooms between classes. These were danger zones even when no words were directed at her. Girls' eyes shifting to her face in the mirror above the sinks, sharp like ice picks. Possibly (probably) they'd been talking about her before she entered, or maybe just the sight of the "new girl" drew their rapt and pitiless attention.

That's her. Voorhees.

Oh God the one whose father—

Abortion-doctor—

—got himself killed?

Tried not to use a restroom if she could help it. No more than she could help it. Having to go (often badly) to the bathroom, waiting—miserably—for an opportunity not fraught with peril.

She's pathetic. Jesus!

Feel sorry for her . . .

Oh sure it's real sad but what'd anybody expect, killing babies for a living, someday somebody's going to kill you.

Wasn't sure if she actually heard these words. Maybe she dreamt them. Maybe she muttered them to herself.

It came to be frequent, so frequent she knew they were laughing at her, and her teachers were pitying her, how she would avoid the girls' restroom and wait until she could not bear it any longer, pressure in her bladder, terror of losing control of her bladder, in class, in class where everyone would see, and smell, and would *never ever* forget, until at least white-faced and desperate Naomi would raise her trembling hand, and the (usually sympathetic) teacher would excuse her, and she would hurry to the nearest girls' restroom in acute distress trying not to imagine (oh she could not allow herself to imagine!) how the teacher might be joking about her to the class—*Naomi is right on time today! We were all waiting.*

None of this our mother knew. Of course.

Yet we were not happy when our mother sent us to live with our father's father and his wife in Birmingham, Michigan. Just far enough from Ann Arbor (she reasoned) that the name *Voorhees* wouldn't be so potent.

For, in Birmingham, there was already a much-respected *Dr. Voorhees*—our grandfather. *Clement Voorhees, MD, Birmingham Gastrointestinal Associates, Birmingham Medical Arts Bldg., 114 Cranbrook Way, Birmingham, Michigan.*

The Voorhees grandparents wanted us badly. It was their promise, Birmingham was wholly unlike Ann Arbor where everything was *left-wing, political.*

Crime was virtually nonexistent in Birmingham. Suburban policemen were polite, courteous—to (white-skinned) residents.

Never could it have happened, our Voorhees grandfather said, that his son would have been *shot down* in broad daylight in Birmingham, Michigan!

(There was no counterpart in Birmingham to the women's care clinics with which Gus Voorhees had been associated, that provided abortions for women without money to pay for them; but there was a private clinic in West Bloomfield, and a suite in the Birming-

ham Medical Arts Building, staffed by reputable OB/
GYN doctors, where such surgical interventions were
provided.)

At one time (we were told) it had been expected that
Gus Voorhees would join his father's lucrative practice
in Birmingham. Father and son would be resident surgeons at the (top-ranked) William Beaumont Hospital
in Royal Oak. But son disappointed father by becoming radicalized at U-M in the sour aftermath of the
Vietnam War, one of a small but vocal number of pre-
med students with an activist interest in public health,
women's rights, abortion.

Gus's mother Madelena, who'd divorced the elder
Dr. Voorhees in 1967, to depart for a new-invented life
in New York City, had told her doctor-son that he was
throwing away—"almost literally"—millions of dollars in income by declining gastrointestinal medicine
in favor of OB/GY public-welfare medicine; and our
father had reputedly said, "Well, that's too bad. But
I'm not in it for the money. Obviously!"

Amazing photos of Gus Voorhees in his early and
mid-twenties. Long-wild-haired, red headband, fierce
wiry beard. A defiant young man picketing with other
young men and women his age, both whites and blacks,
marching in streets and avenues flanked by masked
and uniformed police officers in riot gear.

Oh! Oh God. Gus.

Yes, that was Gus.

We had seen these photos in family albums, many times. We'd been fascinated, and we'd laughed at Daddy's Afro hair, bristling beard, bell-bottom jeans.

Overall, we did not like Daddy's beards. Even Melissa complained of scratchy kisses.

At the memorial service for Gus Voorhees in the Unitarian Church in Ann Arbor these pictures projected onto a screen evoked shrieks of wounded laughter and tears from the gathering.

In the front row the children of the deceased hid their eyes. Hid their tears. Did not want to see. Did not want to hear. These pictures of their young father filled them with dismay, despair. How they'd have liked to have known *him*.

The more love for the father, the more his death was awful.

Really we knew little of our father's complicated relationship with his father. We did not often visit the elder Voorheeses, who rarely, perhaps never, visited us in our rented places in Michigan very different from their residence in Birmingham. Nor did we see much of our mother's parents, who lived in Evanston, Illinois. There had been some estrangement between the sets of grandparents, perhaps. Disapproval, even opposition, over the "radical" lifestyle Gus Voorhees cultivated, and was responsible for having drawn Jenna with him, and "endangering the children."

Grandfather Voorhees's wife Adele was our *step-grandmother* determined to be nice to the *step-grandchildren* as if we were orphans which, since our mother was alive, *we were not.*

Grandma Adele, she wished to be called. She had no grandchildren "of her own."

Soon, Grandma Adele would complain tearfully of Darren and Naomi to our mother: we were "withdrawn"—we were "hostile"—we were "irritable"—we did not "observe ordinary good manners."

Note to Mom: There is a difference between *living with* and (merely) *staying with.* Jenna believed that we were *living with* our grandparents in the big white brick Colonial at 19 Gascoyne Drive, Birmingham, Michigan, because that was her fantasy. But even Melissa knew that we were (merely) *staying with* them.

For how long?—it was natural for us to ask.

But if we asked Mom, her answer was evasive—"I don't know. We will see what happens."

We were waiting for Mom to establish a new *home*

for us. Though we did not quite phrase it that way, we had not the vocabulary.

We might have reasonably wondered: where was *home*, now that Daddy was gone?

The places we'd lived with Daddy, the houses that had been *homes*, though rented and temporary, were all gone.

We'd had to vacate the farmhouse on Salt Hill Road in Huron County—of course. There was nothing in that part of Michigan for Jenna. No possibilities for a life within a few miles of the St. Croix Women's Center that had once been so crucial in our father's life.

Ludicrous to have ever thought of that house as *home*.

We had taken with us only what we could fit into the station wagon that day, crushed into the rear of the vehicle: a chaotic selection of our belongings and clothing, grabbed and carried to the vehicle, flung inside. (These included several of Daddy's sport coats, sweaters, shirts and neckties which our mother could not bear to leave behind though she left behind many of her own things—"I never want to see these again.")

Before the farmhouse in Huron County we'd lived in a (rented) house in Saginaw, and before Saginaw, in a (rented) house in Grand Rapids. Before that, in a long-ago time when Darren had been a little boy, and Naomi newly born, and Melissa not-yet-born on the far side of the earth, we'd lived in Ann Arbor which was the only city our parents considered home—yet to us, Ann Arbor was never *home*.

Our parents had many friends here. Like the Mc-Mahans, many of these friends offered to open their houses to us, for "as long as you want."

Of course, Jenna could not accept such hospitality forever. Soon she would make decisions, rent a place to establish a *home*.

"When things settle down. When things are less crazy. When I see where I will be working. When the trial is over . . ."

Mom spoke to us with a smile but it was a strained and unconvincing smile. It seemed likely (to us) that our mother would be working in Ann Arbor but she postponed making decisions; we looked at several places to rent, so that we could move out of the Mc-Mahans' house, but no place was quite suitable. Where once Jenna Matheson had been capable of quick assured judgments now she seemed baffled by choices, the more choices the more baffled, and could put off for days the simplest of decisions—whether to say yes to another invitation to accept another award or honor in Gus Voorhees's name, or whether to say, in a breathy whisper "No! No more."

Once, when Naomi answered the phone, it was our

Matheson grandmother in Evanston, Illinois, demanding to speak with Jenna; told that Jenna wasn't home, grandmother Matheson complained tearfully to Naomi that her daughter never returned calls from her or from her father, had not replied to their repeated invitations to visit and to stay with them, had not even cashed checks they'd sent to her . . .

"Why won't your mother speak with us? Is she so busy, doesn't she want our help, what have we *done*?"

Astonished and embarrassed Naomi promised her distraught grandmother that she would tell her mother to call that very night.

("Oh God, is my mother bothering *you*? Don't answer the phone, don't even bother checking the ID. Just *don't answer.* I will go through the messages after they accumulate. *I promise.*")

Though Darren and Naomi had come to hate Ann Arbor they did not want to move to Birmingham. Above all they did not want to enroll in Birmingham schools—new schools! Almost every year of their lives, new schools. Our mother had destroyed our family by refusing to move to Ohio with our father but we'd moved anyway, eventually—to the McMahans in Ann Arbor.

"You and Dad care a lot for women's rights, children

on welfare, abortions—what about your own children's rights? Don't we have any?"

We'd put this question to Mom more than once. Darren's brainchild he wielded against her from time to time like a switchblade knife.

We'd never dared to ask Dad, not quite.

Mom had no reply to this rude question other than nervous laughter. It was her strategy (we supposed) to pretend that her dear clever children Darren and Naomi meant to be funny.

Later, after Dad was killed, and Darren had been reading about the killing online, as he'd been forbidden, Darren said with a smirk: "All those years, we were 'collateral damage.' We never knew."

"All we want for you children is to have normal-seeming lives. We will do what we can. We love you!"—our Voorhees grandfather welcomed us to the big old white Colonial house with a two-floor foyer and a glittering chandelier provoking the mad thought to skitter through Darren's sick brain—*Ideal for swinging like a monkey.*

Grandma Adele hugged, kissed us. Melissa may have hugged in return, stiffly.

Yes, our grandfather did say *normal-seeming.*

Grandpa Clem (as he hoped we would call him) did not say *normal*—he was not naive.

Grandma Adele was such a silly idea! Just because our grandfather had married this powdery-faced "chic" older woman with bright lipstick, hopeful eyes, and red-rinsed hair, and just because she was (we had to admit) very, very sweet, very nice, very patient, very kind, very considerate of us, her *step*-grandchildren, why would anyone expect us to be nice to *her*?

Well, of course—Melissa was nice to both our grand-parents.

Perhaps because she was adopted, and not of our Voorhees bloodline, Melissa did not hate with quite the fervor we hated; or rather, Melissa did not seem to know *hate* at all.

Within a few days of moving into the elder Voor-hees's house Melissa snuggled with Grandma Adele watching *101 Dalmatians* on the large-screen TV in the sumptuous walnut-wood-lined den while Darren and Naomi skulked in their respective rooms upstairs with doors shut.

(Eventually, Naomi went to knock softly on Darren's door. Just could not stay away from her brother though his response—*Yeh? What the fuck do you want?*—was not encouraging.)

Shocking to us, that Grandpa Clem who'd always

been such a forceful person, ready to contradict our father, genial, generous, very fit for a man of his age, seemed to have been visibly stricken by our father's death. Grandpa was shorter than we recalled—shorter than Darren. His eyelids were tremulous and there was a tremor in his left hand which he tried to disguise by grasping it with the other hand; when he saw that we'd noticed he told us that the tremor was harmless—not to be confused with the tremor of Parkinson's disease.

He'd cut back on his medical practice and no longer performed surgery. Yet he would not consider retiring as his wife wished; he could not bear a future, he said, in a retirement village in Florida.

He had followed the trial at a distance. But he had followed the trial fanatically. Our grandmother Adele chided him, when she thought we were out of earshot: "There's nothing you can do about it, Clem! Your son is gone. But your grandchildren are here, you can love *them*."

We were stricken with guilt hearing this. We had to laugh, hearing this. We thought—*Nobody would love us, if they knew us.*

It is Darren and Naomi of whom I speak. Our sweet little adopted Chinese-girl sister everyone adored was not one of *us*.

For mostly Darren and Naomi were hidden away

upstairs in their rooms immersed in lurid fantasies of revenge as other adolescents are immersed in lurid fantasies of one another.

Darren cultivated a crude, zestful, funny sort of skill for drawing comics in imitation of R. Crumb and *Zap Comix*. Naomi interspersed fantasies of setting fires to houses with a renewed interest in math/algebra in which despite the distractions of her miserable life she could excel.

Elaborate plots poisoning the Dunphys' dog. (We knew the Dunphys had to have a dog, the pictures we'd seen of the Dunphy family were of *dog people*.) Darren knew (thought he knew) how to acquire a gun in the city of Detroit (he'd take the Woodward Avenue bus south into the dangerous, depopulated, nearly-all-black city with three hundred dollars in cash hidden on his person) and with this gun someday soon he would shoot through the windows of the Luther Dunphy residence somewhere in Ohio, we had no idea where.

Naomi said, practically: We could just set some fires here. Some stupid Christian churches.

Darren said: That is such an asshole idea, I'll pretend I never heard it. We are saving our revenge for *the enemy*.

Naomi: OK. but where is *the enemy?*

Darren: Shithole, Ohio. We'll find 'em.

"Just For You"

This is painful to recall. This is not easy.

We knew that our mother was not-well and that we should not have been judging her harshly. But (maybe) we had no one else close enough to us, to wound.

Oh your mother is such a remarkable woman! She has been so strong this past year, so brave . . .

Bullshit we knew but dared not say. To reveal any emotion was an invitation to being hugged and wept over.

In the aftermath of her husband's death Jenna Matheson had become a (modestly) paid consultant for women's centers in Michigan and the Midwest, as her husband had been. In addition, Jenna provided legal counsel, assisted in litigation, settlements of lawsuits.

With several others in the Pro-Choice movement she addressed the Michigan state legislature with a plea for an increase in the budget for women's health care. She was named by the governor to the Michigan State Task Force on Women's Rights which met each month in Lansing. She was one of several lawyers representing a coalition of abortion providers suing right-to-life websites like *Army of God* which continued to post *WANTED: BABY KILLER AMONG US* lists despite the assassinations of several abortion doctors. (The lawsuit met with defeat when a federal judge ruled that such online postings, though "repellent," were protected by the First Amendment as free speech.) Pro-choice colleagues solicited contributions to establish the Augustus Voorhees Foundation which was to fund the first Augustus Voorhees Visiting Professorship in Women's Public Health at the University of Michigan; Jenna was actively involved in soliciting more funds to expand the foundation, to establish professorships at other universities. She gave talks and papers and keynote addresses, she participated in conferences, she served on panels fiercely discussing *the heavy boot of the status quo on the napes of our necks.*

Like toadstools blossoming by night in dank spongy earth there had emerged a complicated sub-career in the netherworld of her life that involved the acceptance of (posthumous) awards and honors for Dr. Gus Voorhees: rarely renumerative though (of course) the widow's travel and accommodations were paid for. Everywhere she went she was embraced and she was cherished. A highlight of the past several months— (she knew that Gus would be thrilled)—was Jenna's acceptance for him of the posthumous honor Humanist of the Year from the American Humanists' Association; this required a speech Jenna deftly culled together from numerous speeches of Gus's. In her spare time she worked tirelessly on articles and book reviews for such journals as *Women's Law Forum*, *Berkeley Journal of Gender Law and Justice*, *Women's Review of Books*, *Nation*, *New Republic*, *Harper's*, *Mother Jones*.

It wasn't clear where she was living. Or rather, where she was staying. In the Ann Arbor area, or not far away. She seemed to have no fixed address, not even a post office box. She was itinerant, a perpetual "guest"—she lived out of a suitcase, a backpack, the rear of the station wagon. Sometimes she visited us in Birmingham where her Voorhees in-laws kept a beautifully furnished guest room in perpetual readiness for her—"Jenna, please know that you are always, always welcome with us." It was strange for us to be living in a house in which our mother was an occasional guest but we understood that our mother never wanted to stay

more than a few days with us out of a fear (we surmised) of being trapped with us and unable to leave.

Also, our mother feared Gus's father and stepmother
commiserating with her. She'd grown to fear the tears
of others as a contagion that might devastate her as
salt water carelessly sprinkled will devastate expensive
leather.

Usually in these months following the "mistrial" she
was traveling. Or, she was between engagements, not
exclusively in Michigan but elsewhere in the Midwest
or in the Northeast, on the West Coast, even in Texas
(Austin), and so it wasn't practical to fly all the way
back home to Michigan—"I'm fine here. They're putting me up at the college as a guest." Or, "There's a
cottage on the property, they've been wonderful saying
I can say as long as I want and what an ideal place this
will be for me to finish that piece for *Harper's*." Or,
"It's for just a quarter. Ten weeks! All I need to do is
live in the all-women residential college with a view
of the Pacific Ocean, have meals with undergraduates
and give a few tutorials, judge an essay contest on 'New
Frontiers for Feminism,' give a public lecture . . . I
don't get paid exactly but there is an 'honorarium.'"

There was not yet a *home* for us. But (our mother
wanted us to know) she had not given up trying to
find one.

In the meantime she'd stored some things in her in-laws' house. They had pressed her, and she had given in. Her books, Gus's books, hundreds of books, were shelved in various rooms of the house including the basement, more or less haphazardly; when Jenna found a permanent place for us to live together we would arrange the books in a proper order, as our father had promised he would oversee, someday. In the guest room reserved for her, our mother had filled most of the walk-in cedar closet with our father's clothes—the frayed old camel-hair sport coat, the tweed coat with the worn leather elbow patches, the Shetland sweater now sadly riddled with moth holes, neckties Dad had never worn except under duress. The "new, fancy" charcoal gray wool three-button suit with the vest we'd teased him about for he'd looked like a banker and not—our father. Waterstained running shoes, dress shoes, sandals. Even socks, paired. Neatly organized in the closet along with her own less substantial clothing on hangers. We could enter this closet at any time if we were feeling lonely.

"Please shut the door! This is for just us."

Grandpa Clem and Grandma Adele were downstairs. Perhaps they had visitors: there were voices. Our mother was staying in her room in the house on

Gascoyne Drive, Birmingham, just overnight for she'd arrived from Chicago that afternoon and would be leaving again for a conference in Seattle in the morning. She was a very busy woman! She was breathless! She'd done something strange and radical with her hair, which was graying and had thinned badly since November 1999, cutting it short, brushing it back severely from her thin face so she looked (Naomi thought) like a scalped bird, with large blinking blind-seeming eyes.

Most radically she'd lost weight. Breasts, hips. She'd ceased to be female. In ceasing to be female very shrewdly she'd ceased to be maternal.

Seeing Mom after several weeks we'd stared at her as if trying to identify her. Then Melissa cried, "Mommy!" and ran to her to be swept into her arms and hugged even as frowning Naomi held back and especially frowning Darren hung back out of distrust.

Who are you, fuck you. Your fault Dad is dead you left him all alone and kept us with you. We don't love you.

That night, she tapped the bed beside her in the guest room reserved for her, that we might sit beside her. We saw on her thin wrist a man's wristwatch with a black strap, that fitted her loosely: Dad's watch.

"Just for us. Just for *you*. We won't tell your grandparents. Our secret."

She had a small recorder. She was not adept with mechanical things but she managed to play it for us.

Oh we had not heard since the first time. We'd forgotten.

H'lo there? Anybody home?

(Pause)

Jenna? Darling? Will you pick up, please?

(Pause)

Is anyone there?

(Pause)

Well—I'll try again. If I can, tonight.

I'm sorry that—well, you know.

I think I've been distracted by—what's going on here.

(Pause)

If I sound exhausted—I am!

(Pause)

I have a new idea, Jenna—about next year. Or, rather, next summer. When the children are finished with school. I looked up the date—June eighteenth.

(Pause)

OK. Sorry to miss you.

Love you.

(Pause)

Love all of you.

(Pause)

Good-bye . . .

(Pause)

H'lo? Did I hear someone? Is someone—there?

(Pause)

OK, guys. Love you. I'll call back soon.

G'bye.

"No More"

Early she'd wakened. Very quietly—stealthily—she was leaving us for Seattle.

A car had come for her, sleek-dark hired car like a torpedo in the twilit air before dawn waiting, motor running, headlights in the driveway below. And Naomi panicked and ran after her barefoot on the stairs for she was leaving without saying good-bye as she had arrived without (it seemed to us) saying hello. "Mom, wait! When will we see you again . . ."

But already she was at the door, with her suitcase. Already, about to step outside.

"Mom! *Mom!*"

Her thinning shale-colored hair had been brushed back severely from her face. Her thin taut body that had reverted to the neuter body of a young girl and was no longer a mother's body was hidden inside a shape-

less dark coat that fell nearly to her ankles. Her face—
that had once been a beautiful face, or nearly—was
now worn, wan, alabaster-pale—bloodless. (Darren
had said *Jesus! She looks exsanguinated* liking the
sound of words extravagant and reckless and angry in
Zap Comix style.) Her eyebrows seemed to have disappeared. Her eyelashes were brittle and broken. The
eyes were naked, raw.

"Aren't you going to say good-bye to anyone? Not
even Melissa?"

Excitedly Naomi spoke. Not accusingly but with
a sound of child-fear, that entered the marrow of the
(fleeing) mother's bones like radium.

She was shaking her head now. She was fully awake.
"Mom? Wait . . ."

In the doorway Jenna hesitated. She had not seemed
to hear Naomi's question yet she turned to Naomi her
wide damp blind-seeming eyes. And she was smiling, a
faint, terrible smile.

Shocking to Naomi, the face was a mirror-face.
Almost, her own face reflected at her. But a tired face,
an extinguished face, a baffled face. And in the eyes,
for an instant, something like the dull blank of non-
recognition.

"Naomi! I didn't want to wake you, to say good-bye.
Or—the others . . ."

Vaguely she spoke. Apologetically.

Then Jenna said, as if she'd only just now thought of it, as if this chance meeting with her elder daughter at the very moment of her departure had provoked the disclosure that would have otherwise remained unarticulated, "D'you know, it's funny, after we listened to Gus's voice last night, I was thinking—not for the first time actually, but this time more clearly— how I'd always taken for granted that we are meant to help one another here on earth—(forgive me: 'here on earth' is such a cliché! Gus would laugh at me)—to be good, to be generous, to be kind and loving and forgiving to one another. Whenever I meet another person, instinctively I smile at him—or her; I am obliged to be generous, to be kind, to be thoughtful, to think of the other, to think conscientiously of the other, and not of myself. Of course. Your father was like this, too—in his own way, a more aggressive way. Where I am fearful, Gus was fearless. He believed passionately in this response to life . . . But in the past year it has become clear to me that really, none of this matters."

Naomi wasn't sure she'd heard correctly. *None* of this matters?

None of—what?

She was the bad girl, the skeptic. Naomi, and her brother Darren. Both skeptics. Sharp-tongued kids, bratty kids, kids who roll their eyes during Pledge of Allegiance. Smart-ass kids with high I.Q.s and low tolerance for others. Kids with wizened little crab apples for hearts.

Abortionist's kids. Well, they all got what they deserved didn't they.

Naomi stood blinking at her mother wondering— was she supposed to laugh? Was this remark a joke? (Though Jenna did not appear to be joking.) (Had Jenna said anything remotely funny, amusing, ironically funny, even witty since November 1999?) Was her mother actually expecting Naomi to agree with these astonishing words?

With the air of someone who had worked out for herself a mathematical theorem that is commonly known yet no less remarkable for being commonly known Jenna continued:

"It doesn't matter if we are kind to each other, or not. If Gus was superhumanly dedicated to his work, his 'mission'—if he sometimes worked twelve hours a day—drove thousands of miles for fifteen years of his life to advance a cause of—of—whatever had seemed important to us all . . . The only fact now is, Gus is dead; Gus is not here; Gus is silent; Gus has ceased to exist and Gus is not coming back. The world will prevail without him—in a few decades no one will even remember that he'd lived. Or that he'd died as a 'martyr.' That is the only important fact about Gus Voorhees now."

Naomi was alarmed now. It was not like her mother to speak to her at such length at all—not for a long time. She tasted panic, her badly stitched-together mouth had gone dry. She wanted to nudge against her mother, wanted to cry *But, Mommy! You are my Mommy.* You would expect Jenna to (instinctively) embrace the frightened fourteen-year-old and console her for such harsh words—(Naomi expected this)—but that did not happen. In the same slow wondering voice Jenna said, "I think I've known this for a while. I have not been feeling so well for a while. I've said that I am a weak person—I mean, I am a fearful person. Fear is weak, debilitating. Fear is a kind of cancer that enters our bones. I can't be 'there' for you any longer, Naomi. You and the others. All of the others—Gus's others. I am just too tired. You will have to make your own way."

Naomi was stunned. Her stitched-together mouth would not allow her to protest.

"I can't be your 'Mommy' any longer. No more."

In the horseshoe driveway the sleek black car waited with its motor running. The driver came to take Jenna's suitcase, to place it in the trunk. "Mrs. Voorhees? Detroit airport?"—"Yes. Thank you."

Jenna turned from Naomi leaving the girl stunned and staring after her. Poor Naomi whose sarcastic mean-girl tongue was useless.

Jenna turned from Naomi walking carefully as if the steps, the front walk, were coated with ice; gripping a railing with the caution of one who is near-blind but can see gradations of light.

If only she'd fallen! Missed a step, slipped and fell, revealed how ill she was, how not-herself, not to be blamed, injured herself, broken and weeping.

It was a scene that, in a film, even in one of Darren's lurid comic books, would not end so incompletely: the mother would relent, would hurry back, would (weepingly) embrace the (weeping) girl; or, if not relent, if not hurry back, at least glance back, and smile, and wave.

Be brave, darling. Without Mommy you will have to be brave but you can do it.

But this did not occur. In the doorway in pajamas, barefoot, tasting something bitter-black in her mouth, the girl stood staring after the departing mother, scarcely seeing how the mother climbed into the waiting car, how the driver shut the door after her and went around to the driver's seat, and very calmly drove away.

The Ant

Her life would be a small life now. Not even a widow's life now. An ant making its cautious way around the rim of a plate, she smiled to think. *I can do that. What remains of my strength will allow me to do that.*

"The Hammer"

December 18, 2000—
March 4, 2006

Broome County Courthouse,
December 18, 2000

M istrial.

Was it over? Was he released? Was he—*free?*

For why was there rejoicing in the courtroom, if he had not been released? Rejoicing among those who were supporters of Luther Dunphy?—even as others who hated him and were his enemies stared in dismay and disbelief.

Jurors, you are dismissed. You may leave.

Defendant is remanded to custody. Bailiffs will clear the courtroom.

The judge's voice was flat, contemptuous. Frowning white-haired man who could not depart from the courtroom quickly enough through a (private) door at the rear.

He'd believed that Luther Dunphy was guilty! Now

it was clear and in that instant, Luther felt a stab of joy, defiance.

Shut his eyes tight to thank the Lord. He understood that the trial had failed, the jurors had not voted to convict him. In the courtroom there were uplifted voices and amid these ecstatic cries of *Luther! Luther Dunphy! God has spared you.*

Turning then, to seek out the faces of his wife and children who were seated behind him. For the days of the trial he had seemed to forget them—he had scarcely glanced at them. But there was Edna Mae on her feet, but dazedly, and her smile uncertain and confused, and her eyes so wet with tears it seemed she could not possibly see him; and Luke and Dawn his children whom scarcely he recognized, for they had grown in his absence from their household, also on their feet, and looking about smiling in confusion.

His lawyer was very excited.

Pumping Luther's hand in congratulation, and his fingers clammy-cold so Luther understood how anxious the man had been and how incredulous now. Almost, his lawyer embraced him but Luther stood stiffly apart.

"I'm—free? I can go home?"

"No, Luther. You're still in custody. You'll be returned to detention. But you were *not convicted*—that's the good news."

He'd known that. Of course, he could not be *freed*.

He had surrendered his soul to the Lord, he could not now take it back. Never could he be an ordinary man again, husband, father, son and in all these found wanting.

"Very, very good news, Luther. It will take a while—for me—for the news to sink in . . ."

Luther understood now that his own lawyer believed that he was guilty. In the courtroom there had been a game of some kind, in which the opposing lawyers contended, the prosecution with conspicuously more assistants than the defense, and so, though badly outmatched, Luther's lawyer had not lost. That to him was triumph—he had not lost.

The lawyer was a young man in his early thirties with prominent gums, a way of smiling that suggested the nervous smile of a dog, and something of a dog's craven eagerness.

"I'll file to dismiss the charges, Luther. That's the next step."

"But I can't go home? Isn't there—bail?"

"I'll apply for bail. But I wouldn't count on it, since the charge is two counts of homicide."

Two counts. Homicide. Hearing this Luther would hear nothing else clearly.

He wanted to protest as he'd protested many times: he had not shot the second man. From the first he had denied that he had shot Timothy Barron but they persisted in accusing him. It was a cover-up for the Broome County deputies who'd shot Barron by mistake—he knew. That could be the only explanation. All of the witnesses had lied including even—(he could not comprehend this and so had given up thinking about it for the wisdom of Jesus is, it is to no purpose to provoke great anguish in your heart if you are powerless to overcome it)—the ex-priest Stockard who was his friend. And even Reverend Dennis who had intervened with him, with Jesus, had not seemed to believe him, *he had not killed Barron.* This great injustice no one seemed to care about not even his lawyer who spoke now heedlessly and excitedly rejoicing in the good news of the *mistrial.*

The jurors had not thought he'd killed the men. Or rather, they had not thought that Luther Dunphy was a *killer.* That was the meaning of the "mistrial"—they had rejected the prosecution's case against him; yet, the judge had not freed him. It was confusing to him, though he did not truly wish to be free, that he was not now free.

Later it would be explained to him: two jurors had

held out against the other ten jurors who had voted *guilty.* This would seem to him the unmistakable will of the Lord, intervening in the way of grace.

"Luther! Luther!"—Edna Mae's hoarse voice was startling to him, in this place amid strangers.

He felt an instant's fear for her—that his dear wife who had been unwell, whose graying hair was disheveled and whose clothing was loose and shapeless on her as the clothing of a much larger woman, would be exposed to the eyes of mocking strangers at a time when Luther could not protect her as a husband should protect his wife.

"Luther! Thank God."

It was not allowed, or should not have been allowed—for the defendant was to be led from the courtroom by Broome County deputies, as usual; but there came Edna Mae weeping with happiness, and the uniformed men stepped aside, that Luther Dunphy might embrace the sobbing woman, who clung to him murmuring words of such joy and heartbreak, he could not absorb them; for it seemed too that Edna Mae must have thought he would be freed, and return home to them—if not at this hour, then soon.

Poor Edna Mae!—her hair felt brittle, and smelled of something like ashes. Her clothing smelled of her anxious unwashed female body.

And there came his beloved son Luke, taller than Luther recalled, whose sharp-boned boy's face too shone with tears; and his daughter Dawn, who was not crying, but rather laughing with a kind of animal joy, harsh, jubilant. Her small deep-set eyes gleamed like a lynx's eyes, in sudden light.

Luther's other children, the younger children, he did not see. For a moment he could barely recall them. A girl, a boy . . . A baby girl. *Increase and multiply* had been the commandment, he had obeyed.

Now Luther Dunphy too was weeping, awkwardly stooping to embrace wife, son, daughter until the deputies tugged at him—"Mr. Dunphy, time to go"—and led him away.

And outside in a light-falling snow at the rear of the courthouse they were awaiting him—members of the St. Paul Missionary congregation, his brothers and sisters of the Army of God bearing picket signs, supporters of Luther Dunphy barred from the courtroom cheering him now as one might cheer a soldier returning victorious from war—"Luther! Luther! God bless you, Luther!" In the street were TV camera crews, and cries of reporters—"Luther? Luther look here"—flashes from cameras borne by individuals who darted close, risking the ire of police officers shouting angrily at them to get back. "Luther! Are you surprised by the 'jury deadlock'? Is this a 'sign from Jesus'—you will be found not guilty? Luther can you *smile*?" So astonished by this attention which was like a great blinding beam of light pulsing in his face, Luther halted blinking in confusion even as the now-impatient deputies urged him forcibly into the gray van bearing on its sides in black letters the humbling words *Broome County Men's Detention*.

In truth he was relieved. Grateful for the door shutting, and the van pulling away through the crowd, that he was no longer required to acknowledge.

And inside the courthouse, his family—his dear wife, his children, his Dunphy relatives he hadn't had time to speak with—it was a relief to have escaped them, for now.

His wrists were shackled. His ankles were not shackled which was a kindness to him. There was a rough sort of comfort in this familiar place, in the windowless rear of the vehicle where he was seated on a kind of bench, hard beneath his buttocks as they made their way over a cracked and jarring roadway.

It had been a long time since Luther had *sunk* into any seat, as into a cushion or a soft mattress in anything that resembled a house. If he'd thought of it he would have felt a shiver of contempt for the *softness* of his old life.

At such interludes, in transition between the courthouse and the detention facility, he felt most at peace. His brain was awake but blank as a sky of pale drifting clouds. He was not happy, but he was not unhappy. Clutching his right wrist with his left hand and his left wrist with his right hand he'd found that (without shifting in his seat) he could exert a considerable strain in his arm and shoulder muscles and in that way strengthen these muscles. There were similar exercises he could do with his calf and thigh muscles, without moving or calling attention to himself.

Even in the courtroom, during the interminable trial, he could exercise certain muscles, in secret.

One of the guards was telling him a mistrial is a "rare occurrence"—like a "draw" in a fight—"real unpopular."

He should know, the guard confided, there would be another trial. He wasn't finished yet. The Broome County D.A. had his reputation on the line and would not give up so easily.

"But next time I predict, Luther—you'll walk out of the courthouse a free man."

Free man. Luther wondered was this in mockery.

The deputy had turned to speak to Luther through the grated Plexiglas partition as the other deputy drove. His manner was frank and confiding. How surprising it was, to learn belatedly that the deputy who was the elder of the two did not think he was guilty though the deputy wore the gray-blue uniform of the Broome County sheriff's department and had not displayed any particular warmth or solicitude for Luther Dunphy before, that Luther could recall.

Thank you, Jesus. Among even our enemies there are friends.

This was a wonderment to him. For he had several times thought, in the courtroom, a captive animal amid those others who could roam free as they wished, and when they wished, that, if he reached for the police service revolver of one of the guards, and if he could manage to extricate it from its holster, the other guard, and perhaps other armed men in the courtroom, would shoot him down dead—and make an end of it.

"Because—hey Luther?—you did what the rest of us don't have the guts to do, that's why. Killing a baby killer." The deputy paused, considering. "Yah. That took guts."

Beside him the other deputy drove in silence for several minutes. Luther saw the tension in the man's shoulders and neck and sensed opposition until at last he spoke, bitterly:

"Except he killed Tim Barron. What about that?"

"Well—Jesus! That was some kind of bad luck for Barron. That wasn't what they call premeditated."

"Look, I knew Tim Barron. He was a Vietnam vet. He was a great guy and shouldn't have been shot down like that, like he was by this asshole son of a bitch thinking he's Christ-almighty."

The first deputy was abashed and did not reply.

In the rear of the van Luther Dunphy shut his eyes, and shut his ears.

"This Day You Shall Be With Me In Paradise"

This went back a long time. For she was a big girl now.

Shocked and astonished saying she did not understand how anyone could *kill a baby*.

In her loud girl's voice she spoke like someone inside a great tin tub, calling upward aggrieved with no expectation or hope of being heard.

It was the bawling voice of her childhood that had been sabotaged when her Daddy had been taken from her. So she would come to believe.

Killing a baby! Her breath came short, she shivered at the thought.

She could not ever do such a thing.

490 · JOYCE CAROL OATES

This was before Daphne. Though confused in her memory with Daphne the little baby sister *not-quite-right.*

Her mother had been very upset. Her mother had not wished to speak of this subject which had aroused the children's curiosity since their father had joined what was called a *prayer vigil* in town in front of a building called the women's center. Though their father was reticent about the purpose of the *prayer vigil* and discouraged questions about it in his way that warned you not to persist yet Dawn demanded to know more when Daddy was not present, plucking at Mawmaw's arm, and would not cease until Mawmaw answered her.

You are in my face get the hell out of my face her brother Luke would say meanly to her for even as a young child Dawn had a way of leaning aggressively close, lifting her baffled perplexed disbelieving and indignant face into another's face which (she came to know) was a wrong thing to do, a mistake that offended others, and provoked them to shove her roughly away yet in her astonishment often Dawn could not resist for it was imperative that she know, *she must know;* and so she was most demanding of Mawmaw (who was weaker than other adults) and would always give in to her if she persisted.

For at this time, Mawmaw was a loving mother. She was a young mother, not thirty years old. With her pregnancies she had gained as much as twenty pounds filling out her hips, her breasts, her cheeks. Her face was a plain-pretty face round as a dinner plate and the faint creases at the corners of her mouth were the result of eager smiles, for as a young mother, and a young wife, and a young daughter-in-law hopeful of making a good impression on her husband's parents, Edna Mae was one aiming to *please*. Her skin was naturally rosy.

But she was a shy young girl. Even as a woman, she remained a girl. There were some things you did not speak of, not even between husband and wife, and certainly you did not speak of such things to your children, as you would not (comfortably) speak of such things to your own parents. And so now deeply embarrassed, not meeting her daughter's eye, Edna Mae told Dawn in a lowered voice that the women did not actually *kill their babies that had been born* but rather *their babies that had not yet been born.*

"How'd they do that," Dawn demanded with incredulous laughter. "Where's the baby at if it isn't *born?*"

With great awkwardness Edna Mae tried to explain to her that a baby was inside its mother's belly before it was born. (For hadn't Dawn seen Aunt Noreen's fat old momma cat Smoky who was "bulging" with kittens half the time? It was like that.) A baby was inside its mother's belly for nine months before it was born and at any time before that, it could be injured if its mother was injured or (Edna Mae could scarcely bring herself to utter such words) did something to herself, to her belly, to the baby in her belly, that caused it to *die.*

Dawn stood very still. Dawn heard these astonishing words without quite registering all of them, just yet.

Slowly as if she were groping her way in a darkened room Edna Mae said that—she believed— these mothers did not really understand that a *baby was being killed.* The women—(oh, some of them were mere girls!)— believed that they would be causing to die something that was not a baby but—(Edna Mae was unclear about this)—some little stunted thing like a kitten that does not have a soul.

This too was perplexing to Dawn. For why'd anybody want to kill a *kitten*?

Edna Mae hesitated not knowing if she should reveal that many people (including Dawn's Dunphy grandfather up in Mad River) got rid of unwanted kittens— and puppies—all the time because, well—they did not want them; but she decided not to tell her already agitated daughter this fact, Dawn would learn all too soon for herself.

Edna Mae said that the women—and girls—did not

want to be burdened with children because they did not want to give up their selfish lives and because (she thought) they did not actually understand that a baby is a living *soul from God* if nobody had explained to them.

Also, they did not want a baby for reasons of having to work, or for reasons of money; or because they were not married, and did not want to raise a child alone; or because they were not married and were ashamed to be having a child alone, without a father, or a husband . . .

"Wait," Dawn protested. "How'd they have a baby if there wasn't no *father?*"

Now Edna Mae was deeply embarrassed. She'd been glancing away from Dawn toward the kitchen doorway as if expecting that someone would step through and interrupt the exchange.

Dawn did not know exactly how mothers and fathers brought forth babies. From sly remarks made by her brother, and by other boys, she knew that there was something forbidden about it, that only grown-ups would know, and that it might be wrong to ask. But she had to ask her mother how a baby could be, if there was not a *father.* That did not make sense!

But Edna Mae was flushing crimson, and could not speak.

Dawn demanded, "Then why wouldn't Jesus stop them?"

Edna Mae glanced again wincingly toward the doorway. But no one had appeared.

Reluctantly she said, "Well—Jesus stops some of them. The bad women. Jesus punishes them. After getting rid of their babies they are never right in their minds again, can't have babies when they want to have babies, and are ninety percent more likely than other women to—to die of . . ."

"What, Mawmaw? Die of—what?"

Edna Mae could not bring herself to murmur the awful words aloud but leaned down, to whisper in the rapt child's ear what sounded to Dawn like *breath cancer*, and *cancer of the worm*.

Years later after Dawn's father had been arrested and taken from them and no one in Muskegee Falls was talking of anything else than what Luther Dunphy had done in the driveway of the Broome County Women's Center on an ordinary weekday morning Dawn would ask her mother again why Jesus let such things happen and Edna Mae would say that that was why their father had acted as he had: to stop innocent babies from being killed.

"There was no one else to act for Jesus. Only your

father." Edna Mae paused as if searching for more words then said in a breathless exhalation: "'This—this day you shall be with me in Paradise.'"

What did these words mean? Did Edna Mae even know? They had burst from her like something long pent-up.

She was not the young Mawmaw of just a few years before but a worn and anxious woman with tremors in both eyelids and in both hands. Because she could not sleep at night otherwise Dr. Hills prescribed for her a certain kind of pill—*Oxie-con-tin*—that made her sleepy much of the time and, when she was not sleepy, agitated and short-tempered. It would seem to Dawn that, when her daddy shot the two *baby killer men* in the driveway across town, he had somehow shot Mawmaw too; you would hear of such accidents when men were hunting out in the fields, how a spray of bird shot would (somehow) strike another hunter though (the shooter would claim) he had not aimed anywhere near. Accounts afterward were always vehement—such misfirings were *accidental*. No one was to blame for they were *accidental*. And now often in the midst of talking, even in the midst of eating a meal the older children had prepared, their distracted mother might cease talking and slip into a light doze, embarrassing to behold, her eyelids shutting, and her mouth easing open like a fish's mouth agape.

But at this time, when the effect of the powerful pill seemed to have worn off, and an agitation of the nerves had not yet set in, Edna Mae spoke to her older daughter with passion. Her eyes were clear and alert and focused upon Dawn's face in a way so fierce that Dawn felt pride in Mawmaw, that she had not felt in some time. And Mawmaw was smiling in a kind of triumph. Dawn had no actual idea what Mawmaw's words meant but she recognized them from the Bible, the words of Jesus on the cross crying out to His Father in heaven, or from one of Reverend Dennis's sermons, and understood that the meaning was good news, rejoicing and not lamentation.

This day you shall be with me in Paradise.

The Christian Girl

Trust Jesus. If Jesus abides in your heart, you can do no evil. And no evil will be done unto you."

This was told to her. Visiting Daddy in the detention facility and the chaplain there who was a retired Baptist minister and a former missionary in the dark continent of Africa (he said proudly) said these words which were familiar to her though she could not have recollected them herself—she had not a "way with words" as others did. But she understood the chaplain, and understood by the quiet in her daddy's face, that was a tired face, yet a calm face, a face that had passed beyond the fretfulness of ordinary people, this was the bond between them, and among all of the Dunphys, that would abide forever.

(But—was it true? When she was alone, and sad-feeling, she could not remember the consoling words of the adults. Could she trust Jesus?)

She told no one, she'd begun to be afraid. For there was doubt in her heart, that she could trust Jesus.

It was like on TV, she'd used to see at a neighbor girl's house (for Mawmaw and Daddy did not allow the small-screen TV in their house to be turned to such programs), you heard people speaking in a normal-seeming way but then came music, scary music, that the TV people did not seem to hear, that should have warned them that something was wrong, and something very bad would happen in another few minutes. So scary you could hardly bear it, but wanted to press your hands over your eyes.

For consider: Jesus had urged her daddy to shoot the *baby killers* with his shotgun but now (it seemed) Jesus had abandoned Daddy in the Broome County Men's Detention Center where they could visit him for just one hour once a week on Saturdays. And if something went wrong and the facility was "in lockdown" they could not visit Daddy even then but were turned away at the front entrance by smirking guards.

Just one visit to the ugly detention facility on a hill

above the Mad River looking like one of the old shut-down textile mills and you understood that Jesus was nowhere near such a crummy place! Only just prisoners, guards who couldn't get decent jobs elsewhere, and sad-faced visitors thrown together as in a smelly anteroom of Hell.

Crummy was a new word Luke used often in this new place where they'd had to come to live. What Luke said Dawn was likely to pick up like those little thistle thorns that catch on your clothes, then catch everywhere.

Shitty was another word. But it was a bad word.

The Dunphy children pleaded with their mother: when was Daddy going to come back to live with them?

Except not Luke. Luke who was the oldest did not plead with Edna Mae or with anyone. In silence Luke listened to whatever faltering words their distraught mother said to placate them but the expression on Luke's face of profound sadness and rage suggested that he did not believe a word poor Mawmaw said.

"Daddy will be home soon. There will be a trial—and then Daddy will come home." Edna Mae paused, lightly panting. She smiled and her damp eyes moved in their sockets with halfhearted levity. "It's a secret just now but Reverend Dennis is saying the Governor can 'commute' the sentence—if there is one. The

Governor is a strong Christian believer in Right-to-Life."

More than once over a period of months and eventually over a year following their father's arrest Edna Mae would utter these thrilled words in more or less the same way evoking the Governor of the State of Ohio; and Dawn would crease her young forehead into a deep-ribbed frown asking, "And then—what? Daddy will come home?"

"Daddy will come home."

"But what does 'commute' mean, Mawmaw?"

Commute. It was a strange word you would never hear except possibly on TV, or in a courtroom. *Commute.*

"It means what it says! The Governor has the power to bring Daddy home even if there's a trial. No matter how the trial turns out."

Edna Mae was exasperated. The subject was closed.

And yet, Edna Mae's words hovered in the air. For there was something fearful in these words which the children did not want to consider—the thought that, in this new crowded place where they'd moved to stay with Edna Mae's aunt Mary Kay Mack in her one-story shingleboard house on the outskirts of Mad River Junction, there was no room for a man of Daddy's size.

There was no room for a man at all.

"**Why do** they do that?"—it made her angry for some reason, possibly it was a joke, some stupid joke of boys, like when the boys at school waggled their tongues in their mouths in-out, in-out and burst into monkey laughter the girls did their best to ignore.

"Do what?"

"*That.*"

Angrily she pointed overhead. In Mad River Junction in her aunt's neighborhood on a stupid steep hill she stared upward at the offensive sight in the power lines: frayed old sneakers attached by their laces, flung over the power lines and dangling like disembodied feet.

First days they'd moved here, on Depot Street, one two three she'd counted them, fucking stupid sneakers, four five times she counted them, craning her neck, grinning upward and her heart racing in fury.

"Yah, it's kind of weird. Stupid."

"Who does it?"

"Who? How'd I know?"

No one could explain. Dawn was exasperated, for the sneakers drew her eyes upward repeatedly and involuntarily and appeared to be perfectly good sneakers no filthier or more frayed than her own.

Also she had reason to dislike Mad River Junction

for the air smelled of creosote from the sprawl of a train yard at the foot of their aunt's hill. And no one knew them here as they'd been known in Muskegee Falls before what had happened to their father so all that was said of them was *Those new people, you know— Luther Dunphy's family that had to move here.*

Or—*That crazy guy who killed people in Muskegee Falls with a shotgun, they put away in the nuthouse. His wife and kids.*

She was thirteen years old. And then she was fourteen.

Made to transfer from the Muskegee Falls school to the Mad River school she'd been kept back a year. She had hated the Muskegee Falls school but after Mr. Barron had been shot (it was explained to her) there was such dislike of the Dunphys in Muskegee Falls they could not continue to live in their old house even though (it was not exactly explained to Dawn but she understood) the St. Paul Missionary Church and "donors" from Army of God were helping out financially while their father was not able to provide for his family.

But Dawn had worse problems in the new town with "reading comprehension" and "writing skills" than she'd had back in Muskegee Falls. Arithmetic was now called math, a dizzying swirl of numerals that made her feel nauseated.

It will be best for your daughter to repeat eighth grade. That way she will have a solid foundation to build upon, to advance.

Luke too would've been made to take his year over, tenth grade in high school, but Luke was sixteen which was the legal age to quit school in Ohio and so shrugged and told them fuck it he was quitting, he'd had enough of *crummy shitty school.*

Dawn did not want to quit school—not yet. She did not want to displease Daddy at such a time.

And yet: fourteen years old and in eighth grade (which she'd already finished in Muskegee Falls) so she towered over the girls and was of a height with the taller boys.

She'd begged the woman in the principal's office with the prissy eyeglasses could she take the test again, thinking she would remember the answers the second time, but it did not work out that way for the second test was all different questions and her score was even lower than the first.

"Eighth grade will not be so bad. You will be a little ahead of the other students, Dawn. Look at it that way!"

She had grown inches in a single year. She stood

five feet five inches tall. She weighed 130 pounds. All that worry about Daddy—her stomach was always empty-feeling, needing to be filled. She was solid-built as a young heifer with hard-muscled shoulders, arms, thighs, legs that wanted to lower her into a crouch, for better protection. Her feet were large as her brother Luke's feet and held the grip of the earth firm as hooves.

Luke and Dawn watched TV boxing when everyone else was in bed at Aunt Mary Kay's house. In their aunt's house Edna Mae did not have such control over the TV as she'd had in Muskegee Falls where, when their crummy old set no longer worked, Edna Mae hadn't gotten it repaired for months and there was nothing of interest they were allowed to watch anyway.

TV boxing came on late on one of the cable channels—10:00 P.M. to midnight. Her and Luke's favorite boxers were Roy Jones Jr., Floyd Mayweather, Arturo Gatti, and Mike Tyson—who wasn't heavyweight champion any longer but in film clips you saw him, Ironman Mike Tyson.

They cheered the winning boxers. Sneered at the losers dripping blood onto the canvas.

"I could box as good as some of these guys," Dawn said. "I bet I could."

"Bet you *could not*."

"There's girls boxing now. I could be one of them."

"Women's boxing is such shit. People just like to see their titties jiggle and their asses. Don't kid yourself."

Dawn's face flamed. Her brother was like most of the boys she knew, he could say nasty things to shock and silence you, and to wound you deeply, without seeming to know what he did. Or, if he knew, not giving a damn.

Seemed like, now their father was gone, and their mother sick or sleeping most of the time, there was no one to hear Luke say crude nasty things right inside the house where he'd never have dared, before. And Dawn was more and more saying bad words, like her tongue was too big for her mouth and could not be controlled.

Shitty. Fuck. These words came into her head to suffuse her with shame and dismay, that Jesus would hear such nastiness.

But Jesus understood. Jesus would not *judge.*

Stubbornly she said to Luke: "Still, I bet I could. If I tried."

"Tried what?"

"Tried to be a boxer."

Luke laughed, dismissively. He said:

"A boxer uses his feet, to move around fast. A boxer uses his brains, to figure out what to do. You'd stand there like some half-ass and get hit in the face and go down in a heap—*knockout.*" Luke laughed meanly as if seeing this spectacle on TV right now.

"If I was trained, I'd know better what to do. They use their 'jab'—see?" Dawn jabbed with her left arm, fiercely.

Just holding her arm in such a way, and "jabbing"—it did feel like an effort. Just in a second or two her arm felt heavy.

Luke sneered: "Y'think Mawmaw would let you show yourself half-naked in some little T-shirt and shorts—in public? Or *him*?"

All the time now it seemed, Luke referred to their father as *him*. Since the arrest when they'd taken him away to the detention it was rare for Luke to speak of *Daddy*, or *my father.*

This was so disrespectful! It just made Dawn feel sad, when talk turned onto *him*.

"Anyway," Luke said, "it's against what Jesus teaches. 'Turn the other cheek.'"

You'd have thought that Luke was joking. But Luke never joked about Jesus. He'd told Dawn that Reverend Dennis had taken him aside, after their father was arrested, and said now that their father was away—"for a while, we don't know how long"—it was up to Luke to take his place, as best he could. It would be a time of trial for them all, not just the Dunphys but also their friends and neighbors and the church congregation, all put to the test. Terrible things would be said to them and of them but they must not weaken and lower themselves to the level of their enemies who hated Jesus.

"'Turn the other cheek is the hardest test a Christian must face'"—Luke spoke in a way strangulated with emotion and with fury, you could not have said which.

Jesus walked beside her. Climbing the Depot Street hill she would realize he was with her, with a little shock. For Jesus was so *quiet.*

Alone and feeling sorry for herself like some sniveling silly girl and there came Jesus at her left side, for always it was her left side, where there was some cloudiness in the edge of her vision; and Jesus would nudge her left arm light as a curtain stirred in the breeze and say in his gentle voice *Rejoice rejoice!* and she would say *Oh—why?* and Jesus would say *Because this day you shall be with me in paradise.* In that instant all doubt and suspicion melted away and it was like long ago before her father was taken from them and before Daphne was taken from them and they'd never seen their baby sister again.

These were words like music. These were words

she'd heard at church on Good Friday. At the time of hearing she had not fully comprehended the words for anything at church gave her trouble to comprehend, any public utterances, meant for others to hear and so floating over her head. For somehow she found it difficult to concentrate when others were around, it was like riding in a car—someone was driving, but it was not you; so you didn't pay attention to where you were going.

Luke had his license and was driving the car. Not Edna Mae, not often now. And Luke was a skilled driver, maneuvering into a parking place, backing up the car in cautious little surges as if he'd been driving all his life.

Now he'd quit school Luke had a job with the county. This meant outdoor work repairing and clearing roads, cleaning up storm debris, snow removal. If it wasn't for tax deductions he'd have made very good money. Dawn was disappointed, her brother moved out of Aunt Mary Kay's house as soon as he could.

Because this day. With me in Paradise.

Meaning that Dawn Dunphy was singled out for some special reason as Luther Dunphy had been singled out. The choice had been made and was out of her hands.

Still she had to ask if her father would come back home soon?—and Jesus whispered to her *Your father will come back home when there is a home for him. Pray.*

Our father *who art in Heaven.*

She began to pray as soon as she woke in the morning. Falling asleep at night was stepping down stairs and each step a prayer until the bottom step just— vanished!

She would not take the school bus with her young sister Anita and her young brother Noah. She preferred to walk to her school—two miles each way. Her hard hoof-feet bore her urgently forward. Her muscled thighs grew ever harder, stronger. And as she walked, she prayed. Each step—right step, left step—and each step a prayer. And each square of pavement a prayer. (But she must never step on cracks in the sidewalk, that nullified all the prayers preceding.) Approaching the new school which was Mad River Junction Middle School she dared not look up (to see who might be watching her) but had to concentrate fiercely on the pavement riddled with a network of cracks. For even the smallest crack had the power of nullification and mockery of the Lord.

Ringing bells in the corridors hurt her ears. Here too was mockery if you listened closely.

The first day at the new school she'd had to go alone. For Edna Mae had to take the younger children to the elementary school and Aunt Mary Kay had to work at Walmart—her workday began at 4:00 A.M. in the stockroom. Of course Dawn Dunphy was registered at the new school—(Aunt Mary Kay had seen to that)—so it was just a matter of returning to the school on a Monday morning. But something like a hawk's talons gripped her heart, icy-cold, soon as she pushed inside the front door of the building, so she had to turn back blindly, and flee; and the next day she got a little farther, to the doorway of the "homeroom" to which she'd been assigned, and then again she had to flee, for she could not breathe; but the third day she managed to get inside the room, staring at the floor, panting and shivering, and the homeroom teacher known to her as Miss Schine spoke gently to her—"You are—Dawn? Dawn Dunphy? Welcome!"

Their eyes like broken glass. She could feel the small shallow cuts in her skin oozing blood.

"OK if I sit here?"

"Actually no. It is not OK."

Stiffly she smiled. Felt the hot blood rush into her face and knew that her distress was visible and that they would laugh all the more at her, still she smiled for that was Jesus's way.

"There's plenty of seats over there. See?"

"OK. Thanks."

Thanks! Now the eyes laughed, for this was such a craven reply. Her face aflame she turned blindly, and went to another table where boys had sprawled amid a greasy clutter of paper bags, paper plates, glistening patches of wet. Hyena laughter and moans of strangulated hilarity. And here too eyes shifted upon her but these were not sharp cutting eyes of the girls, sly and sidelong; these were blunt, thrilled.

"Hiya. You gonna sit with us, Daw-en?"

Daw-en was Miss Schine's way of pronouncing her name. *Daw-en Dun-phy* a way of such extreme care, caution and frank unease it had become a joke.

"We ain't gonna bite, Daw-en."

They laughed. Like snarling dogs they bared and snapped their teeth.

She sat. Blindly pulled out a chair, sat. There was a roaring in her ears. She dared not approach another table. But not facing the boys, and not exactly at the table. Just a corner of the sticky Formica top where she could remove her lunch from the crinkly paper bag, unfold the waxed paper, lift out the sandwiches she had prepared for herself that morning—Kraft cheese-slices bright orange and smeared with mustard between pieces of white bread. And gingersnap cookies cracked and broken and yet delicious. She ate turned from the boys in the hope that they would not see her. Ducked her head eating as a dog might eat, rapidly, almost in stealth, in fear that its food would be snatched from it.

The boys were thrilled. The boys rubbed their hands over their bodies, chests, bellies, thighs, groins. They were ninth graders. They were big, boisterous boys whom other boys avoided. In her space at the corner of the table she ignored them. Jesus said *I will not abandon you to your enemies.*

"Hey Daw-en."

She tried to ignore them. But she dared not provoke them to anger, she knew.

"You gonna give us some of them cookies?"

No was what she wanted to say but *yes OK* was what Jesus urged her to say.

She didn't smile. Her forehead was creased. Yet she passed the gingersnaps to the boys, all of the ginger-snaps but one, which was the worst-cracked and crumbling, which she kept for herself.

Billy Beams devoured a cookie with smacking lips.

He was grinning foolishly, though he was (it seemed) just a little contrite, that Dawn Dunphy had given him a gingersnap cookie so willingly.

"Billy Beams" was the name she believed was the boy's name. She had only heard the name spoken aloud in classes, she had never seen it written.

Billy Beams was in ninth grade and old for ninth grade by a year or two. He'd been kept back and now his friends were younger boys.

"You'd be good-looking, Daw-en Dun-phy—y'know how?"

She did not want to know. She was part-turned from the boys, and preparing to escape. Hoping that they would decide to leave first for the bell for one o'clock was about to ring.

The boys were laughing loudly. Had Billy Beams said something she hadn't heard? She did not want to turn to him. She was preparing to jump to her feet, and run away; but Jesus urged her to remain just another minute, to show that she wasn't afraid.

Billy Beams had snatched up a paper bag, holding it upside-down, and pretending to lower it over Dawn's head, so the boys laughed even louder, and Dawn shrank away in embarrassment.

"—that's how, Dun-phy."

Her face aflame she jumped to her feet, clumsily

knocking the chair aside. It was all she could do, to run from the cafeteria. She did not glance back at the boys who were hooting and hollering and Billy Beams was the loudest and the crudest and where Jesus should have been, close beside her to console her, to murmur in her ear, Dawn realized there was no one.

Miss Schine was *Penelope Schine*, she'd discovered.

No idea how "Pen-el-op-e" was pronounced but it seemed to her a very beautiful name like something in a song.

Miss Schine was taller than Dawn Dunphy by maybe an inch but her waist was half Dawn Dunphy's waist (it looked like!) and her face was long and slender and her eyes warmly friendly eyes that "lit up" in laughter: Miss Schine might tease you, but it was a gentle teasing not the hurtful teasing of other teachers.

Was Miss Schine *pretty?* Dawn thought so!

Hearing others say Miss Schine was *horse-faced* and her fine, flyaway hair *real weird* but Dawn thought that Miss Schine was very pretty and her hair that was a muted shade of brown mixed with darker and lighter hairs you could see glittering in the sun when Miss Schine went to the window by the blackboard to stand—Miss Schine's hair was fascinating to Dawn. And her voice like something liquid shining with light.

"Good morning, Dawn! Beautiful day isn't it!"

What was nice about Miss Schine was, if she asked you a question, you didn't need to answer except with a quick little nod of the head to indicate *yes*. For it was like Miss Schine was talking for you, you could participate in talking with Miss Schine by just listening and nodding *yes* or murmuring *yeh, OK*. And sometimes Miss Schine sounded so smart and so happy! Just listening to Miss Schine made you feel smart and happy, too.

Soon then word came to them there was to be a second trial.

A second time *The People of the State of Ohio v. Luther Amos Dunphy*.

The children were told that this was good news. For Daddy could not return home to them, it seemed, except if there was another trial to clear his name.

This trial would be held in the Broome County Courthouse as the first trial had been held and the judge would be the same judge and the prosecutor would be the same prosecutor and the court-appointed defense attorney would be the same defense attorney and when Dawn heard this she laughed scornfully asking what was the point of a second stupid trial if everything was the same as the first?—and her aunt

Mary Kay said with smug satisfaction, for she did not like her niece's brash mouth, "Oh no, Dawn. You are wrong. Not everything will be the same. The jurors will be different—all of them."

Could not breathe. Could not sit still. In the over-heated classrooms her body oozed oily sweat and at the nape of her neck her heavy hair was damp. Her brain was awake but like a TV on mute. She saw teachers' mouths move but did not hear words.

It was soon after the news had come to them, that there would be a second trial in Muskegee Falls.

This news had been in the newspaper and on TV and there was nowhere to hide.

Photograph of *Luther Amos Dunphy*. Photograph of *Augustus Dunphy, MD*. Side by side like estranged brothers and each gazing somberly into the camera eye.

"Didja know that ladies kill their own babies?"—like accusations these remarks leapt from the lips of Dawn Dunphy in the girls' gym locker room or in the girls' lavatory where some of the older girls congregated between classes. Eagerly, with a terrible earnestness, Dawn Dunphy proffered information no one wished to hear: "They toss them out with the garbage or flush them down the toilet, then."

And, "Didja know, a baby is up inside you, like right

here"—(pushing the palm of her hand against her belly)—"until it gets big enough to breathe by itself, and it comes out? And sometimes a lady will kill it, when it comes out."

They shrank from her in disgust and in dismay. The girls with the cut-glass eyes and mouths smeared scarlet. And shyer girls, Christian girls like herself who knew little of what Dawn Dunphy knew and were frightened by her words as by the vehemence of an Old Testament prophet speaking a crude and indecipherable tongue.

As they shrank from her not meeting her eye in haste pushing out the door to escape from Dawn Dunphy a wild anger and despair rose in her: "You don't believe me? You think I am lying? You will find out, then—*it will happen to you.*"

She had no idea what she was saying. Her tongue swelled like a demon-tongue, like (she'd sometimes seen) her brother Luke's thing between his legs swelling red and rubbery-stiff like a living thing possessed by a demon. To Dawn's chagrin these strange words that leapt from her, that could not be retracted.

She was reported to the school principal Mrs. Morehead. But when the principal spoke to her Dawn was silent and abashed and stared at the floor between them slowly shaking her head as if she could not remember or rather as if there were something unwieldy inside her head which she had to shake loose, that it might resettle more comfortably.

"Are you denying that you said these things, Dawn? Is that what you are trying to tell me?"—Mrs. Morehead spoke cautiously.

You could not trust them, Mrs. Morehead was thinking. White trailer-trash.

Dawn was very still, though breathing audibly. Mrs. Morehead perceived that the girl's sparrow-colored hair had very likely not been combed or brushed in days and a shivery sensation came over her of visceral dread, that the girl's head was infested with lice; and that a single louse would leap from Dawn Dunphy's head to her, and infest *her*.

Mrs. Morehead knew whose daughter Dawn Dunphy was. All of Mad River Junction knew of Luther Dunphy who had been born and raised less than seven miles away and had brought national shame upon this part of Ohio taking instructions from the Lord.

"Dawn? Did you hear me? Please answer."

The words seemed to float upward harmless and mildly silly like the down of feathers.

The silence between Mrs. Morehead and the girl grew strained. The principal believed herself to be something of a force for enlightenment and reform in this rural county of Ohio but she could not hope to reason with a "mentally disabled" girl though she understood that it was her duty to educate the girl, or to try, at taxpayers' expense. What was crucial was to keep a discreet distance from the girl so no lice could leap onto her and scuttle up her neck to hide, nest, breed in her hair; and so with a seasoned administrator's wary but hopeful smile Mrs. Morehead said, "Well. You won't say these upsetting things again, I hope. Or—I will have to speak with your mother, Dawn."

At last Dawn glared up at the principal. Mrs. Morehead was shocked to see the flat yellow cat-eyes of derision.

"It's Mawmaw who told me these things right out of the Bible. They are true and you know it. Why'd she be surprised?"

News came that the trial had been postponed for three months! Luther's lawyer had sounded elated on the phone so Aunt Mary Kay interpreted this as good news—"As good news as we can expect."

But why was it good news? Dawn wondered. The longer the trial was put off, the longer her father would remain in the detention facility which was equivalent to *prison*. So it was like Luther Dunphy was *incarcerated* at the present time, without an actual sentence. And despite the fact that he was an innocent man.

Our father. *In Heaven. Help us.*

Sighted prowling the halls of the middle school. Possibly she'd forgotten which classroom she belonged in. Which period it was. Which bells had rung. A tall girl with thick eyebrows beginning to grow together over the bridge of her nose, wide sloping shoulders, short-armed and -legged and with large feet. At the drinking fountain which was low to the floor she had to crouch, bending her knees; she drank thirstily, with a kind of abandon, knowing herself vulnerable to enemies at such moments, the expanse of her back and the back of her head unprotected.

Penelope Schine went to look for Dawn Dunphy and discovered the girl sitting on steps at the rear of the school, midway between the first and the second floors, very still, staring at the sky through a window, dense deep dark-ribbed clouds like the hollowed-out inside of a great leviathan, that held her entranced. She'd asked to be excused from homeroom study hour to use the restroom but had not then returned out of shyness or obstinacy or forgetfulness and so Miss Schine approached her to ask gently if anything was wrong? With a shy duck of her head the girl said in a whisper that she was looking for *Our Father who art in Heaven.*

Miss Schine knew of the trial at Muskegee Falls, and of the *mistrial.* She had followed closely news of the double homicide at the women's center the previous year and she had heard that there was to be a second trial of Luther Dunphy. She felt great sympathy for the Dunphy girl. She did not like it that colleagues of hers had assigned seats at the rear of their classrooms to Dawn Dunphy because she was a big-boned girl, and a troublesome girl; they did not like to look at her too closely; they did not like to *smell her.* And so they'd relegated her to the very rear of their classrooms with the worst of the boys, and tried to forget her.

Miss Schine asked Dawn Dunphy how she was liking her new school and Dawn shifted her shoulders uncomfortably and mumbled what sounded like *It's OK.*

Miss Schine did not ask Dawn if she'd made friends yet—(she knew the answer: No)—but Miss Schine did ask her if she was having any difficulties with her classes and if she thought she might need extra help after school—"Or during study hour. Which is right now. I could help you if . . ."

When Dawn did not reply Miss Schine did not pursue

the subject. For she saw that Dawn's frizzy dun-colored hair was a mass of snarls and she wondered—did she dare to offer the girl a comb? A hairbrush? Would that be offensive, and insulting to the girl?

A powerful smell of underarms lifted from the girl for Dawn Dunphy was not in the habit of bathing frequently, it seemed; and (possibly) the Dunphy mother did not "believe" in using deodorants.

Or rather, the mother might not believe that a girl of Dawn's age might require a deodorant.

There were evangelical Christians in the Mad River school district who forbade deodorants as they forbade movies, radio and TV; most books including such classic American novels as *Huckleberry Finn* and *To Kill a Mockingbird;* soda pop that was "colored" or "carbonated"; vaccinations and inoculations. The use of Tampax was "indecent" and "sinful"—girls and women had to use sanitary cloths made of thick cotton, that could be laundered.

Penelope Schine recalled how at the start of the school year Dawn Dunphy's mother had been one of several parents in the district who had objected to their children being vaccinated—she'd refused to be convinced by the school nurse and by Mrs. Morehead that it was urgent for her children to get shots, and that the shots were "harmless." Mrs. Dunphy had said that vaccinations showed a distrust of God for if you resorted to such a measure, it was the same as declaring that you did not trust God to care for you.

These parents had the right to forbid vaccinations for their children under Ohio state law. So, the children were excused.

Fortunately, there had not (yet) been an onset of flu this year.

Miss Schine deliberated: she would buy a small plastic hairbrush for Dawn at the drugstore, and give it to the girl next day in homeroom or after school. The risk was offending the mother, but this was a risk she must take.

But purchasing a deodorant for the girl—this seemed more intrusive, somehow. Maybe not a good idea just yet.

Next, Miss Schine asked Dawn if she was "feeling sad" about anything and if so, did she want to talk about it; and Dawn said, with startling frankness, that yes, she did feel sad—"My father doesn't live with us now and we don't know when he will come home."

Miss Schine did not know how to respond to this and could think only to say, "Really! That is—that is sad . . ."

"He got arrested for something he didn't do—he didn't do in the way they are saying. Because it was something Daddy *had to do.* And they don't let him out when it's supposed to be 'innocent till proven guilty.' But that's a lie."

Miss Schine was surprised that Dawn Dunphy spoke at such length, and with such clarity. It was the first time she'd heard Dawn utter even a complete sentence.

Very likely, the girl was not mildly retarded, as her other teachers were saying. Miss Schine had looked at Dawn Dunphy's test scores and wondered if it was test-taking that was the problem. Less confident students were made anxious by tests and performed poorly, thus insuring that, next time, they would perform even more poorly.

Miss Schine was uncertain what to say. It did not surprise her that the daughter of a man who'd shot two men down in cold blood—in a public place—might yet perceive the father as somehow "innocent"; she understood blood-loyalty, family ties. Faith that is *blind*—the strongest faith.

She told Dawn that she had heard of some of this "trouble"—and thought it was a "very sad" situation. Maybe the second trial would "help clear things up . . ." Dawn should know, however, that there were several other students in the school with relatives who were *incarcerated*—the situation was not so uncommon in Farloe County.

But now Dawn glared up at Penelope Schine. She'd remained seated on the stairs, hugging her knees to her chest and gazing up at Miss Schine, and she spoke hotly now, and loudly: "People like that are *criminals*. They belong in prison. My Daddy isn't like them. My Daddy Luther Dunphy is a soldier of God."

Soon then she began to turn up after school. I would be in my homeroom preparing to leave, clearing my desk, and there she was stammering she'd forgotten something and she'd go to search through her desk seeming embarrassed and excited. She had trouble understanding some of her math homework so I would help her—she wasn't so comfortable asking the math teacher for extra help. She had trouble "organizing her thoughts" for writing so I would help her—I was her teacher for eighth grade English and she was always silent in class, just sitting kind of tense and anxious and furrowing her forehead so I wanted to go to her and smooth her forehead with my fingers—I hate to see a child frowning so hard . . . She seemed to understand when I was speaking with her and she could do problems while I watched but—for some reason—she seemed to forget what she'd learned from one time to the next. But getting help for homework was just the pretext. The girl was lonely and she wanted to talk.

This was around the time I gave her a hairbrush—just an inexpensive little pink plastic hairbrush from the drugstore. I'm sure she had one at home—there had to be at least one hairbrush in the Dunphy house!—but having this seemed to inspire her, so she began brushing her hair—(not when I was around; she'd just show up at school in the morning looking much, much better). I mulled over whether to give her one of those little stick deodorants—for girls—and finally I did this, and she was embarrassed, and muttered something like OK, and did not thank me; but I think she used this too, and she didn't seem to smell so strongly as she had, or maybe I was getting used to her, and didn't so much mind.

She brought me a dozen oatmeal cookies she said she and her aunt had baked—they were very homemade-looking cookies that crumbled easily but they were delicious!

After snow fell during one of our school days there was Dawn outside in the parking lot at my little Nissan and she'd brushed away the snow and ice from the windshield—from all the windows! It was a total surprise to me that she even knew which car in the lot was mine.

But I didn't offer her a ride home. Possibly she would have said no thank you, but if she'd said yes, and I drove her home, and the mother found out, that might have presented problems. And if I drove one of my students home just once, she might expect to be driven home again; and if others found out, or other teachers, that would definitely present problems. So I never knew where she lived but I had the idea—I don't know why—that she had a considerable distance to walk and that she wouldn't take the school bus, and I could imagine why not.

And one day suddenly when we were alone together in my homeroom she said, Miss Schine, did you know people kill babies?—and nobody cares; and I asked what did she mean, who kills babies?—and she said, looking like she was about to cry, At the 'bortion clinics. They kill them and dump the baby-bodies different places. And nobody cares.

I was shocked to hear an eighth grader say such things. I don't know what I said—something like, Oh that's terrible, Dawn . . .

She asked had I ever heard of it, and I said no, I didn't think so. (Because I could not say yes. Not to an eighth grader.) And she said, They don't have one of them here, I guess—'bortion clinic. There was one in Muskegee Falls where we lived, a "women's center" they called it . . . And I said, Did they! (Thinking, Oh my God that was where her father had shot the men, the abortion doctor and the other man, who'd been his driver. *That was what she was talking about—why she was so earnest and emotional. But I could not—I could not acknowledge this.*) She asked me did I think the babies who were cut into little pieces would go to heaven and I swallowed hard and said yes.

On Valentine's Day Dawn left a beautiful valentine for me on my desk, about ten inches high, inside a large white envelope. She'd made the valentine that was in the shape of a heart out of scraps of white satin sewn together and dozens of hearts she'd drawn with a red marker pen and inside in red ink was—

> Dear Miss Schine
> You are my Vallentine
> I LOVE YOU
>   Your Vallentine Freind

There were a few other valentines for me from students but nothing like Dawn Dunphy's which was so special. I think I still have it somewhere at home . . . Every Valentine's Day I make up cards for all my homeroom students, girls and boys both, but the cards are just commercial cards from the drugstore, so of course I had one for Dawn Dunphy but it was not a special card, nothing like hers. I think that she was happy enough to receive it but maybe she was a little hurt, it was just such an ordinary valentine compared to hers. (Oh I hate Valentine's Day! I just dread February fourteenth! It's so cruel at school especially, some of the popular girls get dozens of valentines and girls like Dawn Dunphy get none—not one. Which is why I make sure I have valentines for everyone.)

But then, the next Saturday I encountered Dawn Dunphy and a short heavyset woman at the mall, at first I thought the woman might be Mrs. Dunphy but turned out she was an aunt, and I was with my fiancé Rolly on our way to Bed, Bath, and Beyond and Dawn stared at him and seemed very distracted by him; and the following Monday at school Dawn was waiting for me by my car and asked if my brother lived in the same house with me and if we lived with our parents, and I told her that Rolly was not my brother but my fiancé and she didn't seem to hear this or possibly to understand. But after that things were not so friendly between us. I mean, on Dawn's side. She didn't smile at me so much and she didn't drop into my classroom so much and I could see that I had disappointed her. It might have been around this time that her father's second trial began, over in Broome County. It was on TV every night—not the TV camera in the court-room but outside in the street, and reports on how the trial was progressing, and many pictures of Luther Dunphy—and Dr. Voorhees—every night. So it wasn't a good time for Dawn Dunphy, I knew. And what she had to endure at school I could imagine. She'd show up in the morning for homeroom then disappear an hour later. She was missing classes, and her grades were poor. And one day she said to me with this strange look in her face, a kind of smile, but her eyes were not smiling, People say you are married, Miss Schine, and I said, Really? Who?—(because I doubted this could be true for Rolly and I had set our wedding date for June tenth and everyone who knew us knew this fact)—and Dawn said vaguely, Oh just people. That's what they are saying. And I said, But why? Why'd they say such a thing? and Dawn said, with this mean little twist to her mouth, and her eyes narrowed almost shut, Because they say you are preg-nent, Miss Schine. Because your belly is getting big and you are preg-nent, Miss Schine. That is what they are saying.

I was so shocked, I could not stammer any reply. And Dawn Dunphy just laughed and pushed past me. And that was the end of what you might have called our friendship—whatever it was . . . That was the end.

Trial

The date was set for the trial. Then, the date was postponed.

A new date was set. Then, the new date was postponed.

"God will never allow you to be judged, Luther. I think that must be it"—so the chaplain said, laying a hand on Luther's shoulder.

Wincing, Luther did not shake off the man's heavy reassuring hand.

"If the second trial ends in a deadlock also, that's it—the prosecutor won't try again."

And, "All we need is one hold-out, Luther! Out of twelve, *one.*"

With boyish excitement the court-appointed attorney consulted with his taciturn and somber-faced client whose lower face was covered now in a metallic-gray stubble and whose skin, creased and fine-wrinkled, had grown parchment-colored as if with the passage of decades. His eyes, though alert and seemingly watchful, were ringed with fatigue as if he rarely slept.

Both guards and other detainees in the detention facility admired Luther Dunphy for his *Christian faith, kindness, composure.* Most of all, *not talking bullshit like everybody else.*

Guards understood that they could trust Luther Dunphy. Doubt if he'd walk away from the facility if every door was unlocked.

Somebody tried to push him around, in the dining hall for instance, he didn't fight back though you could see a look in his eye, like a match struck, what he'd do if he was in some other place without guards to inhibit him.

The size of Luther Dunphy. Even losing weight and his face getting thinner he was still a big man at two hundred pounds (or so) and in a prison facility it is size you respect, mostly.

Excess flesh melted from him. In his cell he did push-ups, sit-ups, rapidly touching his toes, flexing his arm and shoulder muscles as if he were lifting weights, running in place. Tirelessly he ran in place. His body broke out into a sweat but he barely panted, his heart-beat was slow and measured.

Some defendants talk. Some defendants talk non-stop. But some, like Luther Dunphy, do not talk much. These are the very best defendants.

God, that man was like a sphinx—with us at least. Like he didn't really care about the trial because he be-lieved himself to be in a place where it could not touch him. First time I'd ever met a zealot—a "religious fanatic"—up close. Luther Dunphy was absolutely convinced that he'd done nothing wrong—in fact, he had done something absolutely right: he'd taken orders as a "soldier of God."

It was like he'd done what he had done. And he was not going to think about it further.

Right away he'd acknowledged that he killed the abortion doctor. He would not acknowledge that he'd killed the other man.

Yet, he was not insane. We dug up a psychologist from Toledo to argue yes, Luther Dunphy was "inca-pable mentally of participating in his own defense" but the judge didn't buy it.

(Only crazy thing about Dunphy was, he'd refused to replace me with a private lawyer. He never accepted the Army of God defense fund money—he had some principle about that.)

At the first trial we lucked out—prosecution had an absolutely airtight case but not one but two wacky Christian females held out for not guilty. Everybody wanted to strangle the old bags including the judge but that was how it went down. Being that the trial was taking place in the same county, with the same juror pool of Protestant Christians, it wasn't all that far-fetched a mistrial might happen again.

I said to Luther, Just pray to God the way you did the other time and Luther said, deadpan, Why would I pray? God has already made up His mind.

Morning of the second trial seventeen miles away in Broome County Edna Mae could not rouse herself from bed when her daughter Dawn tried to wake her.

"Mawmaw! Wake *up."*

But Edna Mae *could not wake up.*

Lethargy heavy as a leaded net lay upon all her limbs rendering her helpless.

Her eyelids too were heavy as lead.

The insolent daughter went so far as to push up one of Edna Mae's eyes with her thumb shouting *Wake up wake up WAKE UP MAWMAW* but it was not to happen.

Luther's older brother Norman was coming by the house, on the drive from Sandusky, to take his sister-in-law Edna Mae with him to Muskegee Falls; but when Norman arrived, in a car bearing three other Dunphy relatives, Edna Mae was still in bed, and not yet fully conscious.

Dawn ran out front to meet them. "Guess you'll have to go without Mawmaw."

She felt a stab of shame, seeing how her uncle Norman exchanged a glance with his younger brother Jonathan. As if it didn't surprise any of the Dunphys that Luther's wife was letting him down when he needed her.

"'Mawmaw' not feeling well again? That's it?"

There was a sneering emphasis on both *Mawmaw* and *again*. Dawn understood that her uncle was furious with Edna Mae and by extension with Dawn—with all of Luther's family.

Still she said: "Tell Daddy hello, Uncle Norman. Tell him we're praying for him! Please."

Usually, in the presence of her father's brothers, Dawn was self-conscious and mute; her wish was not to be noticed by them. But something of Miss Schine's manner had influenced her. Though Miss Schine had betrayed her and was no longer her friend often she found herself thinking—*This is how Miss Schine would speak.*

Each morning she brushed her hair with the pretty

blue plastic hairbrush Miss Schine had given her. Sometimes she dared to look into a mirror, hoping she would not be too *homely* that day.

Her uncle Norman stared at Dawn as if he'd never seen her before. Finally muttering, "Yeh. OK. Sure. I will. If they let me near him."

It had been decided that neither Dawn nor Luke would attend the new trial. Dawn could not miss school, and Luke could not take off from work. Their great-aunt Mary Kay Mack had expressed a wish to attend the trial to provide "moral support" for her niece's husband but did not dare request time out from Walmart for fear she'd be summarily fired.

Edna Mae felt so bad! She'd fully intended to come with the Dunphys to Muskegee Falls—(she had laid out her best clothes the night before)—but was so exhausted when Dawn tried to wake her that she could scarcely lift her head from the pillow, and could not keep her eyes open.

Oxycontin pills Edna Mae swallowed down with water from her scummy bathroom plastic cup the night before. Problem was she could not remember if she'd taken her daily dosage, 15 milligrams OxyContin three times a day, or if she'd miscounted, and had taken one or even two too many.

Before the trouble at the Women's Center Luther had sometimes counted out the pills for Edna Mae, leaving them on the bureau top in their bedroom each morning. He'd tried to hide the pills from Edna Mae so she couldn't take more than her daily allotment. But now, there was no one to oversee her. Mary Kay Mack was prescribed for diet pills that left her edgy and over-excited and forgetful and she could not take time to oversee Edna Mae's medications as well as her own.

Worst thing, Edna Mae's bowels were constipated. Bad stomach cramps! Dr. Hills had warned her about this "unfortunate" side effect of the OxyContin but when Edna Mae tried to cut back on the pills her nerves became tight as piano wire you could strum to make shiver and shudder up and down her spine and she'd get to crying and could not stop.

————

"Sounds like they're just presenting the same 'evidence' as the first time. Witnesses going to say how they saw Luther with a shotgun running up the driveway. How the gunshots scared the hell out of them, they'd been desperate to hide."

Norman Dunphy laughed harshly at this imagined scene funny as some stupid thing on TV.

No one else laughed. Dawn was trying not to see her daddy behaving in such a way.

If she gave it thought, she could understand—her daddy had not ever behaved in such a way but people were accusing him.

Bearing false witness. That was it.

Edna Mae was sitting in a sort of daze listening to her brother-in-law without exactly seeming to hear his actual words. Meekly now she asked how Luther was?—and Norman said, frowning, "Well. He missed *you.*"

Did he! Edna Mae blinked as if she'd been slapped.

Dawn saw the meanness in her uncle's hatchet-sharp face. That little tinge of self-righteousness in the man's mouth, knowing he'd hurt his brother's wife he had come to dislike.

All of the Dunphys had come to dislike Edna Mae. Even the elder Dunphys, Dawn's grandparents.

Among the Dunphys there was even talk that Edna Mae was to blame for what Luther had done. The St. Paul Missionary Church and all this Army of God bullshit was entirely the fault of *her.*

After the first day's session at the Broome County Courthouse Norman stopped by the house on Depot

Street in Mad River Junction on his way home to Sandusky with the others. By this time—late afternoon—
Edna Mae was fully awake and reasonably well groomed
and had even smeared red lipstick onto her thin mouth
because she knew that Norman Dunphy approved of
women who made some attempt to appear attractive to
men though he might yet be contemptuous of the attempt.

Abashed and anxious Edna Mae provided her
visitors—(all males of Luther's generation: Luther's
parents had not attended the trial)—with a fumbled-
together meal out of the refrigerator. Not an actual
supper but just a "bite to eat" until they returned home.

In an embittered and derisive manner Norman
spoke of the first day's session at the courthouse. He
disliked the judge—"Thinks he's better than anybody
else. Just the look on his damn face." And how strange
it was, Luther sitting at the same damn table as at the
first trial and wearing the same damn clothes; and the
same damn "public defender lawyer" with him saying
the same damn things, and the "prosecutor" repeating
the same things too.

"Seems like he could do more for himself. The first
trial, he didn't testify. Seems like he could try to explain what he did, like that priest did for him . . ."

It had been a shock to the Dunphy brothers that

their youngest brother Luther had done such a thing—acted so publicly. There was consternation among the Dunphy relatives, most of whom lived in Sandusky and the surrounding countryside, that Luther had done something so extreme to cast all the family in the "public spotlight."

Edna Mae listened for an opening in her brother-in-law's incensed speech to ask, in her meek abashed voice, a voice pleading not to be brushed away like an annoying gnat, if any one of them had had a chance to speak to Luther in the courthouse; and Norman said impatiently, no—"They don't like you to try that. You can't get close. They figure, somebody could pass a weapon to the 'defendant.' If you could get past the metal detector with some kind of plastic knife, maybe that's what they're figuring."

"Did he seem—well? Did he . . ."

"Did he seem *well?* What the Christ is that—*well?* The man is on trial for his life, he's been locked up for a year, you're asking does he seem *well?* What the fuck do you think, 'Edna Mae'!"

No mistaking the contempt in Norman's way of pronouncing *Edna Mae.* The word *fuck* was so utterly shocking, possibly Edna Mae had not even heard it. (Dawn hoped so.)

Quickly Jonathan said, "He's doing OK, Edna. He's

holding up. We'll go see him next Saturday—some of us. He knows it's hard for you. Try not to worry."

Try not to worry. Edna Mae blinked away tears, this was the kindest thing anyone in the Dunphy family had said to her since the trouble began.

One thing different about the trial, there were not so many Right-to-Life people in the courtroom or outside on the steps. Not so many demonstrators with picket signs. "It's like people are forgetting Luther. Some other 'soldier of God' is taking his place."

Norman spoke ironically. But it was so: an anti-abortion protester had been arrested recently for shooting up a women's medical clinic in Wichita, Kansas. Jake Rachtel too was aligned with the Army of God and Operation Rescue and spoke of himself as a "soldier of God." Just a few nights before Tom McCarthy of *The Tom McCarthy Hour* had praised the "brave martyr" who'd held more than one dozen women and girls hostage in the clinic, had wounded (but not killed) three medical workers, getting himself wounded by law enforcement with a bullet lodged near his spine.

Dawn was listening to the adults' conversation. She had not gone to school that day: rather, she had approached the school building but had been unable to force herself to enter. It was terrifying to her, her daddy was being *tried* and she could do nothing about it . . . Much of the day she'd spent wandering at the scrubby outskirts of town and in the partly abandoned train yard, at one point descending into a steep ravine littered with debris where, in overturned rusted oil drums, puddles of stagnant water had accumulated and each puddle had glittered excitedly as if both welcoming her and excluding her.

Jesus, are you here? Jesus please—help my daddy!

Badly Dawn wanted to ask her uncle Norman more about her father but she knew from past experience that her uncle would reply to her curtly without so much as glancing at her. Norman was friendly to Luke and the younger children but didn't seem to like Dawn, and did not trouble to disguise the fact.

Why, she didn't know. Because Uncle Norman thought she was homely?

Homely was a word the men used. *Homely* referred exclusively to girls and women.

It made her feel bad, to be *homely*. But after a while, it made her feel angry and wanting to hit somebody, hard.

What was unfair was that Dawn had often felt invisible in the family when Luke had been present; but now that Luke lived somewhere else, Dawn was still invisible.

"There's nobody has forgotten Daddy! Not in our church either. They talk about him and pray for him all the time."

(This was not true, maybe. Edna Mae hadn't taken Dawn and the younger children to Muskegee Falls to Reverend Dennis's church for some time for they only went if Luke or Mary Kay was willing to drive them. Edna Mae rarely drove at all now.)

Norman regarded Dawn and Edna Mae with a look of pity.

"Well. Good. But there's a problem, I think." Norman had changed the subject, and was looking shrewd now. "About money."

It had long been a troubled issue among the Dunphys, what to do about the defense fund sponsored by the Army of God. So far as Edna Mae knew there had been contributions to the fund from "all across the United States and some foreign nations as well"—as the website boasted. But Luther had been adamant that he *did not want and would not accept charity.* Repeatedly he'd refused to dismiss the lawyer appointed for him by the Broome County public defender's office and hire a private lawyer. It seemed to be Luther's belief that God would care for his family, somehow. Nobody needed to *stoop to begging.*

Unknown to Luther, Edna Mae had been accepting what were called *gifts*, or *loans*—from persons sympathetic with the family's plight, who contributed to the Army of God fund or to similar funds for Luther Dunphy. And there had been donations from the St. Paul Missionary Church, generous at first, but in recent months diminished.

The Dunphys had been helping to support Luther's family too, but grudgingly. Many times it had been pointed out to Edna Mae that Luther's elderly parents had not "money to spare"; Luther's brothers and cousins had their own needy families and had not "money to burn." Not one of the Dunphys intended to take out a second mortgage to pay for the mess Luther had got himself into.

Norman said, "Y'know what I'd like? To see how damn much money there is in that fund before they skim off the top."

"'Skim off the top'—? What do you mean?"

"This 'Army of God.' Who the hell are they? People send money for Luther that goes to *them*. All I can figure from the website is their 'headquarters' are someplace in Illinois, a post office box! Sons of bitches are using my brother to make money."

"But—they give Mawmaw money . . ."

"Sure. They give her something. But if we investigated, what'd you think we would find?"

Dawn was openmouthed. She'd never thought of such a thing!

"We'd find the bastards are stealing from *us*."

Edna Mae protested weakly. She did not believe, truly she did not believe, that anyone was stealing from Luther. She could not believe this for everyone had been so nice to her, and so sorry for what had happened.

"They do give us money, Norman. Hundreds of dollars—since last year . . . Luther would be so upset if he knew—the one thing he can't accept is 'charity.' Please don't let him know anything about this, I beg you."

Norman rose to his feet abruptly. He was ready to leave, he'd had enough of his infuriating sister-in-law.

"If my brother is so 'upset' with charity, why the hell'd he abandon his family for the rest of us to support? God damn son of a bitch thinking he is Christ-almighty, maybe Christ-almighty should support *him*."

The Dunphys left. In their wake, dirtied plates, glasses, cutlery and crumpled napkins. And that smell of masculine indignation, rage like something singed.

Edna Mae wept silently unable to move from her chair. Dawn started to clear the table, throwing things into the kitchen sink and running water hot until steam blinded her eyes. Her lips moved silently—*Jesus help us. Jesus show us the way, the truth, and the Light.*

The Great Tribulation
September 2001

. . . do not run in the halls or on the stairs. All students return to your homerooms immediately. Repeat: all students return to your homerooms immediately and quietly and do not run.

She had not been listening. But she was listening now.

Waking from her trance. Waking at once, and quickly standing as others in the classroom were standing confused and frightened, clutching their books.

. . . . in orderly fashion file out of your classrooms and in orderly fashion return to your homerooms at once. Repeat THIS IS AN EMERGENCY all students will please return to your homeroom for further instructions immediately and quietly and do not run in the halls or on the stairs.

Defiantly she'd been pressing the flaps of her ears against her ears to drown out the teacher's droning voice. Pressing the flaps of her ears against her ears to create a muffled/buzzing sound that was comforting, entrancing. It was a new habit she did in her classrooms, head lowered, shoulders hunched at her desk at the back of the room, eyes lowered or half-shut, or frankly shut, forehead furrowed as in an intensity of thought utterly detached from and in opposition to the droning effort of the teacher at the front of the room chalking numerals or words onto the blackboard which blurred and faded if she stared at them.

Some sort of moisture flooded into her eyes when she tried to see. She did not think that her eyesight was poor. She did not accept that she might need glasses. (She saw sharply outside. Outdoors! Saw what she wanted to see.) It was the nature of what she was expected to look at, and understand, there at the front of the room, she bitterly resented.

She had not been thinking of algebra but of her father seventeen miles away in the courthouse in Muskegee Falls. She had not been thinking of algebra or of her other classes on any of the days of the new school term but she had been thinking of her father in the courthouse in Muskegee Falls and feeling sick with guilt that she was not there; and sick with dread that her father was *being tried*.

It was not possible to concentrate on schoolwork as it was not possible to sleep at night while her father was *being tried*. No things were possible of normal life yet she was obliged to pretend as if they were. Not-hearing what was said to her sometimes, cruel remarks flung in her direction like carelessly flung stones that might strike their target or might not—*That's Dunphy. Her father is the crazy one with the shotgun, on trial for his life.*

On the front walk, girls from the high school suddenly approaching her, surrounding her, and one of them saying in a bemused voice—*What kind of point are you trying to make? Like, you're not FEMALE? So—what are you? Look like you belong in the Stone Age.*

She'd heard a reference to *Stone Age* in the past— had had no idea what the words meant. One of her teachers remarking to the class that there are "some people" living in the United States today who want to turn back the calendar to the Stone Age and she'd wondered uneasily if this was a remark addressed to her or about her or her family . . .

She'd felt such shame. Wanted to shrink up like one of those inchworms you step on, on the sidewalk, curl up to make themselves smaller.

No. She'd felt such rage. Flaring up inside her sudden and hot. Fingers flexing she'd have liked to make into a fist to hit the girl in her smirking face and draw blood.

And when the other girls screamed, rush at them striking with both fists the smirking faces until all were bloodied and retreating in terror from the wrath of the Hammer.

Jesus had said *I bring not peace but a sword.* In Dawn's vision the sword of Jesus was a hammer.

Sleepless nights had yielded the Hammer of Jesus. Somehow the vision had come to her fully formed. She'd wanted to speak of it to another person, to Reverend Dennis (maybe) but was unable to force out the words when she'd had the opportunity.

She knew only a little of the Great Tribulation. This would be a time of hardship, trouble, disaster, the "last days" just before Jesus returned to establish His kingdom on earth and to convert the Jews of Israel . . . None of this was clear to her. She had never listened very carefully. She had no idea when it would come—in a hundred years, in a thousand years, in a few years. She could not think that her father's *being tried* in the Broome County Courthouse was in any way related to such a massive prophecy but of course in such matters Dawn Dunphy could not know with any certainty.

Truth that passeth understanding. The way, the truth, and the Light.

It was her habit now at school to deliberately not-hear. For they had "passed" her into ninth grade, she knew—it was no secret. Other students known to be barely literate unable to read, write, do math at their grade level similarly "passed" out of eighth grade and into ninth grade were expected to quit on their six-teenth birthdays and give the school district no more trouble but Dawn Dunphy did not intend to quit but to graduate.

Her daddy had told her he would be proud of her if she graduated. Her daddy had been unhappy, that Luke had quit on the morning of his sixteenth birthday. She had said—*I will, Daddy. I will graduate. I promise.*

Seated at the back of the classroom where no one listened. The *dead zone* all coarse-mouthed boys and among them the sole girl Dawn Dunphy in shirt un-tucked over dungarees and frayed size-ten sneakers with her hair crudely shorn (scissor-cut by her aunt Mary Kay) to expose the back of her neck. Through the first week of algebra class she had tried to pay at-tention despite the boys' stupid mutterings and jokes, she had tried to make sense of what the teacher was saying, jotting numerals and equations onto the blackboard in clicking white chalk . . . But somehow then she'd given up, thinking of her father *being tried*.

The Hammer of Jesus! She'd have liked to wield such a hammer if it was a giant hammer like something coming out of a cloud to devastate the courthouse and the men's detention facility like Samson bringing down the walls of the temple.

In ninth grade she did not have Miss Schine for homeroom. She did not love Miss Schine (who had betrayed her) but she missed her very badly. But there was no excuse for wandering over into the eighth grade corridor for all who saw her (including Miss Schine) would know why she was there and would mock and laugh at her.

In Miss Schine's homeroom (which had also been her English class and study hall) Dawn Dunphy had been seated in the front row of seats. But in her new homeroom, she was seated at the very rear of the room. And in all her ninth grade classes, she was seated at the very rear of the room. Bitterly she hated this, her teachers dismissing her, expecting her to quit at sixteen like the other poorly performing students and troublemakers, "learning disabled" boys and girls for whom no one had patience.

Abruptly then on this Tuesday in September the class was interrupted. You could almost not recognize the principal's voice over the loudspeaker, it was so strangely agitated, breathless.

This is an emergency announcement. All students are to immediately leave their classrooms and return to their homerooms for further instructions . . .

Filing out of the classroom and into the corridor, that was already crowded, chaotic. You would think there was a fire at the school except the fire alarm wasn't ringing, they were accustomed to the deafening alarms ringing for fire drill once a week and now there was silence except for the loudspeaker voice repeating the emergency announcement like a robot except it was a real person, you could hear breathing and a faint stammering of words.

Like others she'd grabbed her things. Books, backpack. Her heart was thudding in her chest for she was imagining the Hammer of Jesus striking the school . . .

One minute pressing her fingers against her ears to muffle sound and to hear more clearly the BEAT BEAT BEAT of her blood and the next minute on her feet with the others trying not to push, shove, panic on the stairs and then in homeroom sinking into her desk at the back of the room, that had been shoved sideways in a scramble by other students to get to their desks, disoriented by the blank looks of the adults, blank frightened looks of adults usually composed and in control and in possession of all knowledge.

Then, when they were seated, the loudspeaker voice continued in a jagged lurching fashion:

"It has been announced that the United States has been attacked by a foreign country. There have been bombings in New York City and in Washington, D.C. It is not known if the President of the United States has been killed but it is known that thousands of people have been killed by 'terrorist' explosions and more attacks are expected. It is being advised that you remain in your homerooms until further notice when you will be allowed to return to your homes . . ."

In Dawn's homeroom the teacher Mrs. Lichtman had to sit at her desk, suddenly faint, very white in the face. Terrifying to see a teacher so frightened, and not to know what was happening and what would come next. The usually smirking boys were as quiet as the others, abashed and apprehensive. Amid them Dawn Dunphy sat entranced as if Jesus had answered her prayer in a way she had not expected and could not comprehend, just yet.

We listened for airplanes, we believed that bombs were being dropped. We were led to believe that an invasion had begun from a foreign country. Our principal Mrs. Morehead kept repeating what she'd said like that was all she knew and all she could say and she did not know how to stop. And then at last, the loudspeaker was switched onto radio news, and we were listening to radio news without knowing what any of it meant, still we were waiting for bombs to fall on our school, and for airplanes to crash into our school, and it was only after parents began to arrive at the school to take kids home that we could leave, and all of us went home to watch TV with our parents all that day September 11, 2001, when the World Trade Center was destroyed and we watched the twin towers explode and collapse and explode and collapse a thousand times in a flaming cataclysm like the wrath of God.

In Muskegee Falls at the Broome County Courthouse the trial of Luther Dunphy was interrupted. Jurors were dismissed until further notice, the courtroom and the courthouse were cleared, the defendant Dunphy was returned in handcuffs and ankle shackles to men's detention. The trial would not resume until the following Tuesday by which time it was determined by Broome County law enforcement that the likelihood of a terrorist attack in Muskegee Falls was not high.

Nationwide the United States remained in a state of high emergency.

The Broome County Courthouse would be secured

with extra Ohio State Police guards both in the court-room and outside the building. Each person who entered the courthouse and passed through the metal detector was scrupulously examined and many were questioned at length. There were (unsubstantiated) rumors of bombs set to explode inside and near the courthouse but it was never made clear whose bombs they were supposed to be—Muslim terrorists or Right-to-Life activists.

Afternoon, evening, and into the night of September 11, 2001, they watched TV news in the house on Depot Street. At first they shifted restlessly from channel to channel but settled finally on the familiar cable-news channel that broadcast *The Tom McCarthy Hour.*

Never had Edna Mae been so riveted by the TV screen. Never had she allowed the younger children to watch the kind of TV she feared would give them "bad thoughts" and "nightmares." But things seemed different now, a curious excited calm to Mawmaw observed by Dawn and by Luke (who'd come to his aunt's house to watch news of the "terrorist attacks" with his family, when his workhours were cut short) as if all that Mawmaw had feared and hoped-for had come true and there was no point in trying to shield her young children from knowledge of God's terrible wrath.

The flaming explosions of the World Trade Center twin towers were many times replayed. Footage of the chaotic streets of New York City, shocking sights you were not meant to see—human figures falling from high buildings, bodies indistinguishable from the rubble in which they lay. Fires, sirens. Though it was midday, it was twilight at Ground Zero. Long after the original explosions the air was aswirl with something like ashes, shredded paper and pulverized bone. A news commentator stunned by what he was seeing made a clumsy joke about rats, supposed to be millions of rats in New York City, what's become of the rat population?—but no one laughed. Cut to another replay of the falling of the twin towers. Overlapping and contentious voices.

The United States has been attacked by a foreign country.

Which country?

One of the Arab countries. Or maybe more than one. In the Middle East.

Why?—because Arabs are followers of Mohammed and not Jesus Christ. These are "Mohammedans" who hate our U.S. democracy and want to kill us.

They are called "Muslims . . ."

They are sometimes called "Mohammedans"—that is a term that is used.

Generally they are called "Muslims." Their religion is "Islam."

"Is-lam"—is that their name for themselves, or is it our name for them? They are worshippers of a "prophet"—Mohammed . . .

They have a hatred of Christianity and a hatred of Jews and it has been their goal since 1948 to destroy the State of Israel.

Why?—there is a hatred in the Muslim world of an open freedom-loving society that is educated like the United States.

There is a hatred of Jews because Jews are superior to their Arab neighbors as demonstrated in the Six-Day War . . .

Today's terrorist attacks are just the beginning. If they are not stopped by U.S. airpower they will destroy the "free world." They hate all Christians. They are enemies of Jews as well and it is their goal to destroy the State of Israel before the coming of Christ and the conversion of the Jews.

Another time they saw the tower burst into flames. And another time, the second tower struck by the careening airplane. And—(it was always a miracle, if but a miracle of horror)—another time, as they stared, the towers collapsed in flame and rising dust like clouds of vapor.

Edna Mae suddenly realized. This had to be the beginning of the "last days"—the start of the Great Tribulation.

She recalled to Dawn and Luke how the last time she'd taken them to visit Luther in the detention facility, they'd been surprised at how much leaner he'd become, and his hair grayer and sparser; how hard-muscled his shoulders and upper arms, as if he'd been exercising in his cell. And how quiet Luther was, a new calmness in him, seeming just to smile at them without hearing much of what they said, for Edna Mae chattered nervously at such times, and even Dawn heard herself say inane things. But then, when they'd been about to leave, Luther leaned forward to touch the opened palm of his hand on the Plexiglas barrier, in silence—"Like he was blessing us. Like Jesus would do. He didn't say a word. But—maybe—*he knew.*"

By this time Aunt Mary Kay had gone to bed. The younger children had fallen asleep on the sofa exhausted. Dawn and Luke exchanged a glance, and a shudder.

Edna Mae continued, with a vague smile: "He was thinking maybe he wouldn't see us again. In our earthly selves. But he didn't want to scare us . . ."

Luke said: "You think Dad was predicting the *future*? That's crazy."

Edna Mae protested: "You know how your father is. He worries about us and not about himself."

"Christ, Mom! That is so weird."

"It is *not weird*. What do you think is happening now, these bombs, and 'terrorists'—and your father— what happened to him . . . All at the same time."

"Jesus!"

"You watch your mouth, Luke! Taking the Lord's name in vain . . ."

"Jesus is not the 'Lord.' Jesus is the 'son.' Just so's you know, Mawmaw."

Luke did not pronounce *Mawmaw* with any of the childish tenderness with which he'd once pronounced it but rather with an air of disdain. Stricken by his rudeness Edna Mae slapped his shoulder with the flat of her hand, and Luke laughed.

"Jesus forgive *you*. I hope He will."

"I wouldn't hold my breath, Mom. Jesus has plenty of work cut out for him without giving a damn about us."

"That's a terrible thing to say."

"It's a true thing to say."

Dawn was helping the younger children to bed. First Noah, then Anita. She hoped that, in the morning, they might have forgotten much of what they'd seen on the TV; she did not think it was a good idea for Edna Mae to have let them watch.

When she came downstairs Edna Mae and Luke were still bickering. Luke was on his way out—why didn't he just *leave*? And Edna Mae was so exhausted she could barely keep her balance swaying and staggering like a drunk woman—why didn't Mawmaw just *go to bed?*

Dawn thought how strange it was, how embarrassing almost—(she wouldn't have wanted Miss Schine to know!)—at this late hour of this terrible day her mother and her brother were standing there bickering about something so profound as *the end of the world.*

Not since he'd arrived in Muskegee Falls seventeen years before as an ardent young minister had anyone in the St. Paul Missionary congregation seen Reverend Dennis so emotional in the pulpit.

It was as if the hell-fires of the World Trade Center towers were lapping at the very roof and windows of the church. Almost, you could see in Reverend Dennis's ruddy face and wet glaring eyes the gleam of these fires. He had removed his preacher's dark formal coat and he had torn open the collar of his white cotton shirt at the throat; he had rolled the sleeves to his elbows and it was fascinating to see how, when he waved his arms, the sleeves inched downward, and he had to push them up again, impatiently. His graying dark hair was damp with perspiration like gel. His voice was piercing as a horn you could not escape even if you dared press your fingers over your ears.

Enthralled Dawn listened. She was squeezed in close between Anita and Noah and gripped the hands of each tightly for she knew that they were very frightened and that their mother seemed often to be forgetting them in this confused time. She would afterward not recall much of what Reverend Dennis said but she would never forget the elation of the man's voice and how badly she had wanted, during the sermon, which careened and lurched like a drunken boat, the minister's eyes to fix upon *her*.

"'After these things I looked, and behold a door was opened in heaven, and the first voice which I heard was of a trumpet speaking with me saying, "Come up hither, and I will show you these things which must be done hereafter"'—my brothers and sisters in Christ, could any words be more timely than these words of St. John the Divine—of the Book of Revelation? This 'terrorist attack' is God's warning to us, we cannot ignore as we have ignored such warnings as rising tides, rising temperatures, the tides of hell—abortions, birth control—the rise of homosexuality and such abominations and anathema to the Lord—" In a quavering voice Reverend Dennis spoke for more than an hour, raging, and weeping; his fingers plucked at the collar of his shirt, that was dark now with perspiration, so that you could see the shadow of his chest hair beneath, that made Dawn's breath quicken, as if she'd had a glimpse of something forbidden—her father part-unclothed, in the shadows of her parents' bedroom at the old house; her brother Luke shoving a bare foot into the leg of his jeans, his face fixed in concentration so that he had not noticed her staring at his supple body, the small bulge of his tight-fitting white shorts between his legs, the taut muscles of his thighs.

After the sermon, Reverend Dennis appeared to be exhausted. All who heard him were exhausted. Dawn had been waiting for him to speak of her father as sometimes he spoke of Luther Dunphy in the pulpit, to ask the congregation to "send prayers" his way; but today in his excitement over the terrorist attack Reverend Dennis seemed to have forgotten Luther Dunphy.

Edna Mae tried to speak to the minister but could not get through to him past others who were crowded about him.

It was unfair! She was the wife of Luther Dunphy, and they would not let her through to speak with Reverend Dennis.

Luke had driven the family to church, and now

drove them home. In the passenger's seat Edna Mae was fretting and weeping as a baffled child might weep.

"They're forgetting Luther! They're forgetting who he is, what he did—the sacrifices he made."

Dawn said, "Don't cry, Mawmaw. They won't forget him."

Luke said: "God won't forget. That's all that matters, Mawmaw."

In the backseat of the vehicle Dawn sat between the shivering children who were strangely quiet. On either side of their big sister they sat without fidgeting as if, so early in the day, they were already tired and ready for bed. Dawn sought out her brother's evasive eyes in the rearview mirror but he avoided looking at her.

Luke persisted, as if in mockery: "God is all that matters, see? The rest is bullshit."

Help me, Jesus! *My husband needs me with him in his hour of need.*

And yet, in the morning, again Edna Mae could not lift her head from her pillow. A terrible weariness had sunk into her bones in the night turning their marrow to lead.

Each morning before she left for school Dawn came to plead with her—"Mawmaw! Wake up."

Edna Mae wanted to protest, she was awake. Her brain was awake. Yet, she could not open her eyes.

Barely she could move her limbs. If her limbs were not leaden-heavy they were light as air and detached from her, incapable of being moved.

Her mouth so dry from the pills, she could not speak.

And so it was, morning following morning through the remainder of that terrible month September 2001. And each morning a (seeming) surprise to Edna Mae who'd been resolved the night before that the next day would be different.

Yet she would attend the trial. She vowed.

It was the last days, she believed. The Great Tribulation had begun. Cataclysms, firestorms, floods. Earthquakes, plagues. The terrorist attacks were only the first strike of the wrathful God. Yet so strange to her, as to others in Mad River Junction, that, after the devastation at Ground Zero, nothing further had happened—really, nothing at all had happened to the inhabitants of Mad River Junction.

"Edna? Edna!"—a face so close to Edna Mae's face she could scarcely recognize it as her aunt's. Mary Kay Mack was all but snapping her fingers to wake Edna Mae who *was not asleep* at the kitchen table where she'd poured cereal into a bowl but had not gotten around to pouring milk onto the cereal or taking up a spoon to eat.

"Edna Mae. We just had a call. The jury is 'deliberating.' Maybe you should be with Luther?"

Confused, Edna Mae saw that it was twenty-five after twelve. The last she recalled, she'd come downstairs to have breakfast at about nine-thirty.

"Luther's lawyer called. They are 'hoping for the best.' We can drive over now, if you're up to it."

"Yes."

But she was so tired suddenly! She hid her face in her hands.

Verdict

Have you reached a verdict?
   We have, Your Honor.

The judge was handed a slip of paper which he opened, read, handed back to the bailiff.

We find the defendant guilty as charged.

On two counts of homicide in the first degree—guilty as charged.

It was a surprise to him! By the kick of his heart he had to realize he'd been expecting another verdict.

But I am not guilty. God will spare me.

It was a surprise to him and something of a shock, he had to concede it was something of a shock though he'd

believed himself immune, invulnerable to earthly vicis-
situdes but then he realized—God was testing him.

And so Luther smiled, a radiant smile creasing his
face.

In all his limbs, that were hard-muscled now, with
not an ounce of fat encasing them after months of rigor-
ous exercise in his cell, a shudder of newfound strength,
resilience.

Returned to his cell in the detention facility. *His* cell,
it had come to be.

The younger guard was not so friendly now. Since
the exchange in the van when the guard had assured
Luther Dunphy that he would one day walk out of the
courthouse a "free man" there had been virtually no
words between them. And the older guard, who had
not liked Luther Dunphy, who had called him a profane name, was blatant in his dislike now.

Muttering with satisfaction what sounded like
Fucker. Got what you deserve.

Luther's lawyer too had been surprised. Stunned.

Or rather, not so surprised, probably. But stunned.

He would appeal the verdict, he assured Luther.

And whatever sentencing was to come, he would
appeal. Though the young public defender was not so

optimistic now. He spoke slowly, distractedly. His eyes were worried. Something of his former, almost giddy energy had dissipated and Luther felt a stab of sympathy, that he'd let the young man down.

Yet, he was sure that God had not abandoned him.

Sentence

Five days later in the Broome County Courthouse he heard himself sentenced to death.

Those were the actual words he heard, yet could not quite comprehend—*Luther Dunphy you are sentenced to death.*

This morning, the judge spoke at greater length. In his clipped precise voice of disdain, dislike, disapproval that was yet the voice of a son of Ohio very likely born not far from Muskegee Falls, as Luther Dunphy had been born within twenty miles of Muskegee Falls and had lived his entire life in the region, he spoke of how Luther had killed two men "in cold blood." These were "premeditated" killings he had "systematically planned"—he had driven from his home, a distance of more than three miles, with the twelve-gauge shotgun that was the murder weapon in his vehicle; he had remained in his vehicle until his victims arrived, at which time he had "stalked" them in plain view of numerous witnesses; these were not "impulsive, spontaneous" acts of passion or emotion but had grown out of a "carefully calculated scheme" of something like vengeance—"cloaked in a distortion and perversion of Christian religious conviction."

Both Augustus Voorhees and Timothy Barron, as witnesses attested, had "begged for their lives"—yet he had killed them.

Witnesses had remarked upon his lack of emotion. And, in the courtroom, over the course of his trial it was clear that he felt no remorse for his heinous crimes but rather a kind of pride.

"This sentence will send a clear signal to any individuals who believe that they might flout, defy, or violate the laws of the State of Ohio and of the United States of America for reasons of faith or ideology. The court will not tolerate such and will punish to the limit of the law such infractions. Luther Dunphy, you are hereby sentenced to incarceration in the Chillicothe State Correctional Institution for Men where you will be put to death by lethal injection at a time to be determined."

Luther's lawyer gripped his hand to steady not Luther but himself.

No jurors were present in the courtroom this morning. Very few individuals were present. Court officers, staff. There was a brisk air to the proceedings. Luther was waiting for the judge to say more but already the judge was exiting the room. How swiftly everything was happening, that had happened so slowly for months—this did not seem right.

Already Luther was being gripped by guards, to be led away. Startled, he saw that his brothers Norman and Jonathan were in the courtroom, staring at him aghast. He had not noticed them before—had he? Wanly he lifted a hand to them, a brotherly gesture both abashed and reassuring—*Don't worry! It will never happen. This is a test of God. Have faith.*

Afterward he would realize that the second trial had been shorter than the first trial. Fewer "character" witnesses had spoken on his behalf. The ex-priest Stockard had not been present and had not testified. Luther's friend.

Bad News

News came to them in Mad River Junction.

At first Edna Mae didn't recognize the name. The raw-sounding voice.

Luther's public-defender lawyer was calling. The eager anxious young man with whom she'd exchanged awkward remarks a year before whose face and name she had entirely forgotten.

He was saying it was not good news. He was calling her *Mrs. Dunphy.*

He was telling her that the judge had not seemed to find "mitigating" factors in the case. That the judge had sentenced her husband to death.

Death? Edna Mae did not understand.

So still was Edna Mae, standing with the receiver

in her hand, so blank her expression, Mary Kay Mack quickly took the receiver from her.

She asked: "Can he—can you—*appeal?*"

The lawyer told her yes. In death penalty cases, an appeal is axiomatic.

And so yes, he could appeal on Luther's behalf, and he would. Except—

"Yes? What?"

Except they should be prepared for the sentence to remain, he said. For the judge had been careful in his handling of the trial, highly professional, scrupulous. He'd been well aware of the controversial nature of the case and that an appeal was likely . . .

"Oh. My God."

Mary Kay made a sound like sobbing—a harsh hacking sound, surprising in one so usually jocose and breezy.

Still Edna Mae stood close by, unmoving, as if she'd wandered into the kitchen for no particular reason, or had forgotten the reason.

As Mary Kay continued to speak on the phone at some length in a lowered voice, a voice of incredulity, astonishment, dread, the younger children came into the kitchen as if they'd been called—(of course they had not been called)—and Dawn ran into the kitchen breathless and terrified as if she'd managed to hear, from a distant corner of the house, crucial words.

"What is it? Who're you talking to? Is it—"

Mary Kay gestured for Dawn to keep back, and to be quiet.

"Is it about Dad? The verdict?"

At this point Edna Mae suddenly lost her composure, and her balance; intending to push past her brusque, annoying older daughter, as if to seek peace in another part of the house, she lost her footing, swayed, and fell heavily onto the floor with a faint little wail; Dawn tried ineffectually to prevent her from falling, and then knelt over her as she lay moaning—"Mawmaw! Mawmaw!"

Both the young children were crying now. Mary Kay told the lawyer she had to hang up and would call him back within the hour. On the floor Edna Mae lay on her side insensible, white-faced, with tight-shut eyes. Dawn continued to kneel over her crying "Mawmaw"—as Mary Kay would report to the family, as if her heart was broken.

Mud Time

That the one—Dunphy?
    Her father's the one killed those men—
—on Death Row now—
Oh man she is homely! *Face like a bulldog.*

Behind the smelly dumpster she hid. She waited.

For it was a mistake to enter the 7-Eleven store on Sixteenth Street at certain times.

Too soon after school. (But Dawn would never make such a mistake.)

At other times if there were loud-voiced boys inside, or girls who knew Dawn Dunphy from school, or knew of her.

Whatever the loud voices said, she never heard.

She did not mind waiting. She was accustomed to waiting. She was accustomed to the Dumpster smells.

"What will become of us?"—no one wished to ask.

With Edna Mae you took particular care. It had become so extreme that you could not even say "Daddy"—or "Chillicothe" (where Luther was incarcerated)—without upsetting her: Edna Mae pressing the palm of her thin blue-veined hand against her heart and her eyes swimming with pain.

Death Row.

Sentenced to death.

Lethal injection.

They avoided speaking of these matters. Even Luke.

To allude to the situation at all you might say *the Trouble.*

As in, *before the Trouble.* Or, *after the Trouble.*

Though it was not clear if *the Trouble* meant their father shooting the men at the Women's Center, or only just their father being arrested and incarcerated; or whether *the Trouble* meant specifically the second trial, the verdict and the terrible sentence.

Two counts of homicide, first degree.

Condemned to death.

Appeal pending.

Definitely, there was hope in this appeal! A team of lawyers experienced in death penalty law were now involved in the case as well as Luther's original public defender.

They were arguing *not guilty by reason of (temporary) insanity.*

Or were they arguing *not guilty by reason of insanity.*

(Luther Dunphy angrily refused to accept this defense strategy. But by a technicality some variant of the defense could be argued in a presentation to the Ohio State Court of Appeals with which the defendant was not required to concur.)

Among the Dunphys no one believed that the execution would ever really take place for the Republican governor of Ohio could commute Luther Dunphy's sentence to life imprisonment if he wished and it was known that petitions were being sent to the governor by politicians supportive of the Right-to-Life cause as well as by Christian congregations in Ohio and the Midwest. It was believed too that a wealthy Ohio manufacturer was exerting pressure on the governor whose campaign he'd helped finance—the man's name was "Bear" or "Beard"—Dawn had heard . . . Edna Mae did not like to speak of such matters because it made her anxious to be "hopeful" but Dawn wanted to know as much as she could for she wanted to have hope.

In fact there had been good news. Luther's lawyer had called one day with good news.

The execution scheduled for April 16, 2002, had been rescheduled for October 29, 2002.

And there was a "strong probability" that the execution would be rescheduled again, to give the appeals team the opportunity to argue their case to the Court.

Each night Dawn X'd out another day on the calendar she kept hidden in a bureau drawer in her bedroom. Each morning noting how many days to October 29 . . .

It will not really happen, Jesus will intervene.

We know this. We have faith.

Edna Mae would have been upset if she'd seen Dawn's calendar in which October 29 was marked with an ink-black cross. Even Mary Kay might have been upset.

So long as Luther Dunphy was alive, there was hope.

Luther was incarcerated in the Chillicothe State Correctional Institution in Chillicothe, Ohio. It was in Death Row he was incarcerated—the actual name of the unit was *Death Row.*

It was not so easy to visit Luther now, for Chillicothe was a three-hour drive from Mad River Junction. The detention facility at Muskegee Falls had been less than twenty miles away.

Visits had become difficult for other reasons as well. Edna Mae was so often unwell—and Luke was not always available to drive. And once, when they'd made the trip, Luke driving Mary Kay's car that rattled and jolted on the interstate, Edna Mae in the front seat and Dawn and the younger children crammed into the rear, it was to discover that Luther Dunphy was himself unwell, suffering from some kind of "flu" that prevented him from seeing visitors. Another time, it was to discover that all of Chillicothe was in lockdown after the attempted stabbing of a prison guard.

"Your father knows that we are thinking of him and praying for him. Maybe that is enough for now"—so Edna Mae told them, with a brave smile.

Late March 2002. "Mud time"—so called in Mad River Junction, Ohio.

Melting snow, ice. Dripping roofs. Tall snowbanks slow-melting draining into gutters, ditches. Glistening pavement, puddles. Swaths of mud in fields and beside walkways. Everywhere the debris of winter—shattered tree limbs, rotted leaves, skeletons of Christmas trees abandoned in vacant lots, shredded papers, plastic. The sun shone brightly and fiercely at midday then began to fade by afternoon. The air turned cold and smelled of something metallic that made Dawn's nostrils pinch.

She was fifteen years old. She was repeating ninth grade.

For a few weeks that winter she'd played basketball on the girls' high school team. It had happened like a miracle, so suddenly. There'd been a vogue of Dawn Dunphy—*She's not so bad. She's kind of shy actually. Too bad she smells when she gets excited.* Dawn Dunphy had not been the fastest player on the girls' basketball team nor had she been the most skilled player but she'd been the most reliable player, the strongest and one of the tallest at five feet eight inches, 147 pounds; she'd been the most indefatigable player capable of playing a full game without a break, panting, frankly sweating, in a glow of perspiration in her dark green uniform and always willing to pass the ball to those girls who could sink baskets far better than she could—*A fantastic team player, Dawn Dunphy. If she didn't run you down like a horse.*

Just once, Dawn Dunphy had been so conspicuously tripped to the floor by a player on the opposing team that the referee had declared a foul; Dawn was given two foul shots—both of which she'd missed.

But applause in the gym had been deafening along with cheers, cries, foot-stamping. *Dun-phy! Dun-phy!*

Enthusiasm for ruddy-faced Dawn Dunphy with her thick, muscled, dark-haired legs solid as a man's legs was laced with laughter but it was good-natured laughter, Dawn was sure. It was *not mean.*

("This is the happiest day of my life. Thank you, Jesus"—for Dawn had known that Jesus had allowed this to happen; but He had not assisted her in sinking the basket for that was something other, a matter of what was called "free will.")

But then, there'd been complaints. Girls who hadn't been chosen for the team complained to the principal that the girls' gym teacher had favored Dawn Dunphy who wasn't, strictly speaking, eligible for the team since her grades were low, barely passing, second time in ninth grade yet barely passing, also Dawn Dunphy was only in ninth grade and so (in theory) there was plenty of time for her to be on the high school team in subsequent years. (As if Dawn Dunphy was likely to remain in school past the age of sixteen.) And so Dawn had had to be dropped from the team and had never quite recovered from the shock, as she'd never quite adjusted from having been invited to join the team initially, and from having been singled out for such attention for a magical three weeks.

Dawn I'm truly sorry. But next year, I promise. OK?
The girls' gym teacher who also refereed the games

had genuinely liked Dawn Dunphy. Possibly she'd felt sorry for the girl (knowing of the notorious Luther Dunphy on Ohio's Death Row) but that wasn't why she'd invited Dawn to join the team. She'd invited Dawn to join because Dawn was a good enough player, and her size was intimidating to players on opposing teams, and the other girls on the team had not objected, or at least not strenuously. For the vogue of Dawn Dunphy at Mad River Junction High involved students feeling good about themselves for behaving magnanimously and not meanly. But it had ended abruptly as it had begun.

Often there were such surprises in her life. She had grown immured. Or wished to think so.

"'Dun-phy'—*ug-ly!*"

"'Dun-phy'—*done-for!*"

She'd been so distracted thinking about the basketball team, and the foul shots she'd missed, or rather had almost made—(on the second throw the ball had circled the rim teasingly, as the audience erupted)—that she'd taken no notice of her surroundings, and had not heard the boys approaching her from behind as she descended into the dripping underpass at Fort Street. Suddenly then their voices came loud and gleeful and echoing in the concrete underpass and she walked quickly, half-ran, to escape them. Their chanting words were scarcely intelligible to her, for the hard-pounding of her heart—"'Dun-phy'—*done-for!*"

It was her father they mocked. Dully she realized this, with an ache of fury and shame.

There were five boys, or six or seven. They were older than she but in their behavior they were younger, like middle school children. She knew the names of some of these boys, she knew their faces. She did not think that they disliked her. She did not think that they hated her. But there was something about her that made them angry, jeering—something to do with her body that was a female body yet carried like a man's, with a rolling gait, a way of bringing her feet down hard on her heels, pushing herself forward as her arms swung free. Her eyebrows grew heavy above her deep-set eyes. Her forehead was low, and often furrowed. Her shoulders and upper arms were strong. She wore clothing that might've been a man's clothing, dark, or khaki-hued, without color—corduroy trousers, flannel shirt, dark cotton T-shirt beneath, polyester jacket and frayed running shoes. She observed them sidelong, with narrowed eyes.

"'Dun-phy.' Your father is *done for.*"

Their laughter was idiot laughter like pebbles shaken inside a metal container. There was not even cruelty in it, rather a vacuousness, an emptiness, repulsive to her, loathsome. Without looking back at her tormentors she began to run as they cupped their hands to their mouths calling after her—"*Dun-phy! Ug-ly! Where're y'going, cunt!*"

She emerged from the underpass, panting. Desperate to escape the jeering boys she ascended crude stone steps into a vacant lot strewn with the rubble of a ruined building, cut through the lot and into a no-man's-land of scrub trees that opened out into a muddy field, and ran blindly through the field—she thought that they would probably not follow her for it would mean running in mud, and mud sucking at their shoes as it was sucking at her sneakers, and splattering up onto her trousers.

Their cries behind her faded. She made her way to the dead end of Fort Street where she scraped some of the mud off her shoes against a curb. Her heartbeat was subsiding, the danger was past. Still she felt debased, shamed. They had dared to mock Luther Dunphy!

She felt a thrill of murderous rage. A double-barreled shotgun in her hands, she would blast them with buckshot.

At the Fort Street bridge over the Mad River she waited until traffic passed. A thunderous tractor-trailer passed with Illinois license plates. High in the cab the driver cocked his head to observe her on the pedestrian walkway, staring and dismissing in virtually the same instant the lone female figure in shapeless clothing. In that instant she felt a thrill of relief—*No one will see me! I am safe.*

Making a decision then to take the shorter way home to Depot Street, and not the longer, on public streets.

She crossed the bridge ducking her head against the wind. Below was the narrow turbulent river that so fascinated her, in the March thaw a confusion of boulder-sized ice chunks amid dark rushing water. The sound of the river was cascading sound, a waterfall of sound, as of numerous voices murmuring together nearly out of earshot.

Safe. If invisible to the enemy, safe.

On the other side of the river she ascended a hill of tangled trees and underbrush, emerging at the far end of the Baltimore & Ohio railroad yard where freight cars and other railroad equipment no longer in use were kept; the property was posted against trespassing but no one would see her, for no one ever seemed to be around this part of the yard. Dawn was within a quarter mile of Depot Street when she heard an excited mutter of voices somewhere close by; still, she was slow to realize *They are in front of me now. They have crossed in front of me.* Then ahead to her horror she saw several of the boys who'd chased her out of the underpass now approaching her through the railroad yard with broad sniggering smiles—*Dun-phy! Hiya!*—and when she turned she saw the others behind her, quickly approaching and calling *Dun-phy! Hey!*

Of course, they knew where Dawn was headed: Depot Street. They knew, and had outsmarted her, and now it was too late for her to run from them for they were upon her, the big fat-faced boy called Billy Beams, the long-limbed boy called Jay-Jay, another who wore a Cleveland Browns cap reversed on his head, whose jaws were stubbled. Someone shoved Dawn from behind at Billy Beams who laughed and shoved her back again; and suddenly they were upon her, too many to fight; she was pulled down, desperately scrambling to escape even as they grabbed her ankles, her legs, her arms and wrists, turning her over roughly onto her back so that she lay helpless, trying to kick free, thrashing. How quickly it had happened—she was *down*. They were calling her *cunt—dirty cunt.* They were calling her *dyke.* Her cries were hoarse sobs. She could not draw breath to shout or to scream. One of the boys squatted behind her gripping her wrists. Another gripped her ankles. Whooping and laughing they managed to unzip and pull down her corduroys—took time to unlace and pull off her sneakers—and to tear off her white cotton underwear, that fitted her tightly and left red marks on her upper thighs and at her waist. The sight of the thick springy pubic hair, that grew up onto her white-skinned lower belly, roused them to ecstatic whoops and yodels—*Jesus! Look at that! What a pig!* They were made to think of their mothers' bodies perhaps, those bodies out of which they'd emerged as infants, and for this they must punish her.

Their clumsy hands snatched up twigs, rotted leaves, mud to rub into her face, into her hair, and between her legs. With special vehemence, between her legs. They had not taken time to remove her shirt and had now to content themselves with squeezing her breasts hard, and rubbing mud onto them—her breasts that were not large, and not soft, but hard and resilient like sponge rubber. Something about her body maddened them, she saw their faces, flushed and furious, murderous. The tall long-limbed boy wearing the reversed cap seized a broken tree limb of about twelve inches long, to shove up inside her, between her legs; the limb was soft-rotted, and began almost at once to break, though Dawn felt an excruciating pain and managed now to draw breath to scream.

"Dirty cunt! You like this. You know *you like this.*"

Billy Beams grunted seizing a concrete block in both hands, to hold above her, taunting her. Dawn stared up in terror knowing that if the concrete block slipped from his hands her skull would be crushed. Barely Dawn managed to beg—"No please, please don't . . ."

Billy Beams let the concrete block fall—not onto Dawn's head but onto the muddy ground beside her. His expression was one of disgust, rage.

"If you tell anybody you're dead. Dirty cunt, you'd better not tell anybody, got it?—or you're *dead*."

Soon after the boys retreated. She heard them running away, and she heard their low guttural cries of laughter fading. And then there was silence and she was alone.

For a long time she lay unmoving on the ground. She saw that the sky far overhead was silver-cast, as if the sun had withdrawn and had become a pallid thin light. Her eyes flooded with moisture. The ground beneath her was damp, cold. She realized that she was shivering convulsively for her lower body was naked, and a terrible weakness suffused her limbs.

"Jesus. Help me . . ."

Where had Jesus gone? Had He retreated in disgust, like the boys?

She managed to sit up. Her head rang with pain, both her wrists ached and her right shoulder throbbed with pain as if it had been jerked out of its socket. Between her legs was a throbbing pain and a thin cold trickle of blood and so cautiously she moved,

very cautiously pulling up her mud-streaked corduroys, wincing yet determined to regain some measure
of composure in case she was seen, for of course she
would be seen, only a hundred yards or so from Depot
Street (where sparse traffic moved, visible through
a stand of trees; yet no one on Depot Street would
have seen Dawn, and the boys squatting above Dawn
during the several minutes of the assault). She would
abandon the torn underpants but she located her running shoes tossed a few feet away, and managed to put
them on, and to tie the ties securely. Thinking *I am
all right. I am not bleeding hard. I will be all right. It
is up to me.*

Shakily she stood. She felt a rush of blood between her legs—but it was not the dark humid near-
hemorrhage of menstrual blood, that so frightened and
disgusted her every few weeks, but rather a thin chill
trickle, a different sort of bleeding that was not so serious (she believed) and would stop soon. The sharp tree
limb had scratched her—the soft inside of her *vagina*.
But it was only superficial scratches, that would cease
bleeding soon. She told herself this.

With wetted leaves she wiped at herself, down
inside the corduroys, between her legs, awkwardly.
She had been so anxious to pull on the trousers, that
no one might see her part-naked. With wetted leaves

she wiped at her face. Picked clumps of mud out of her hair. Assessing the situation with a measure of calm— *Really I am all right. No one will know.*

"Thank you, Jesus. For sparing me."

It had been her own fault, she knew: taking the shortcut home.

She would make her way limping home through the railroad yard, to Depot Street. She would enter very cautiously at the rear of the house. If Edna Mae was in the kitchen, she could avoid the kitchen. That would be easy—Edna Mae might call out, "Who's that?"— and Dawn would need to say only, "Who'd you think, Ma? Me"—and walk past the door and go upstairs. (Dawn no longer called her mother *Maw-maw.* Even the younger children no longer called Edna Mae this name.) If Anita or Noah were close by they would take little note of their sister. Mary Kay would not be home yet. Quickly Dawn would ascend to the second-floor bathroom and no one would be a witness to her shame—for Jesus would grant this small mercy, she believed.

Yeh we fucked her. *Dun-phy. Some of us did. She liked it fine.*

Dirty cunt. Dyke. Told her we'd kill her if she told anyone but she wouldn't tell anyone 'cause she liked it.

———

She did not return to school. Not the next day, or the next.

Not because she was sick or injured for (she was sure) she was not sick or injured.

Behind the 7-Eleven store she waited in the late afternoon. Beside the Dumpster.

Near the Fort Street underpass she waited.

And then the following week, late afternoon of a Tuesday she sighted several of the boys, the Beams boy, Jay-Jay, the one with the Cleveland Browns cap, one or two others descending the steps at the Fort Street underpass. Quickly she crossed the street, and approached them. In her pocket was a claw hammer she'd found in her aunt's garage, the handle of which she'd wrapped carefully with black tape so that the grip would be more secure.

The boys saw her. A single expression of startled surprise ran across their faces like a headlight flashing. And then they were grinning, and one of them made a mocking gesture like a salute—*Hi there Daw-en Dun-phy.*

They saw the look in her face before they saw the claw hammer in her hand and they ceased grinning.

She rushed at Billy Beams, the slowest and clumsiest of the boys as he was the biggest. Wildly the hammer struck at Billy Beams—swinging in Dawn's hand of its own volition, seemingly—his face, his head—the nape of his neck that was exposed as he tried to duck away. Wanting to break his neck but the flesh at the nape of his neck was too thick. But she felt a gratifying *crack!*—she was sure, she'd cracked Billy Beams's skull, and brains would ooze out onto the filthy pavement to which he fell, jerking convulsively, crying and whimpering like a young child. She moved on then to another boy, swinging the hammer at him, blunt side, claw side, blunt side, claw side, blunt side swinging and striking and drawing blood from wounds in the boy's forehead like skid marks. And then he was down, and Dawn ran after the boy wearing the reversed cap, at the steps at the far side of the underpass she overtook him striking the back of his head with the hammer, gripping the black-taped handle now hard in both hands and swinging it as the boy lost his footing and fell, screaming in pain; one of the others tried to wrest the hammer from her but Dawn was too strong, and too quick, turning the hammer onto this boy, Jay-Jay, striking him on the crown of the head so hard he fell to the dirty pavement like a sack of feed.

Turning back then to the boy who'd fallen on the steps. Dropped the hammer and struck at his face with her fists. She struck the astonished eyes, the nose. She struck the mouth that began at once to leak blood.

The nose was broken. Blood gushed from the nostrils.

The eyes she pounded with her fists as if to blind them. She would burst the capillaries, she would blacken the hateful eyes that had seen the lower part of her body naked. She had never struck anyone with her fists, like this. She had fought with Luke—but never like this. For Luke was too strong for her, she could not prevail against Luke. But these boys had been taken by surprise. Though her fists were aching, the knuckles scraped and thinly bleeding yet she was excited, exhilarated. "Fuckers! Now you know." They had thought she was a good Christian girl, that they might demean her without consequence. But Dawn Dunphy was not to be demeaned. Jesus had not always turned the other cheek to be slapped another time. Jesus had driven the moneylenders out of the temple. In a loud jubilant voice Jesus had said, I bring not peace but a sword. Her fists swung, her booted feet kicked, for Jesus, for Jesus and for her father Luther Dunphy who was a soldier of Jesus and would die for Jesus's sake.

She followed the others out of the underpass but did not pursue them along Fort Street. The bloodied claw hammer she secured in her pocket. She did not want to be seen, she did not want to be seen by witnesses, for she knew from her father's trial how "witnesses" will damn you though you are scarcely aware of them at the time. And she might be seen by witnesses if she pursued the boys on Fort Street.

And so they ran from her, she allowed them to escape calling after them in a jeering voice, "Fuckers! Go to hell." And Jesus observed and saw that it was good.

You are my servant Dawn Dunphy in whom I am well pleased.

It was in ninth grade *it happened, she was expelled.*

The Dunphy girl—the one whose father killed those men at the women's center and was sentenced to death . . .

We persuaded the principal to expel her. Everybody was talking about how she'd attacked some boys from the high school (who'd been teasing her, allegedly) with a hammer or a knife or some deadly weapon which the boys hadn't reported because they were embarrassed or didn't want to get into trouble themselves so we went to the principal and persuaded him she was dangerous and that was that—the Dunphy girl was gone.

You could see in her face she'd be trouble. Though she had not actually caused any trouble at school yet, that we knew of. Probably she was dyslexic. You see that pretty often in these poor-white families where almost nobody graduates from high school or even sometimes middle school and there's high absentee-ism and not a surprise, a father or some other family member is incarcerated.

The surprising thing was, the Dunphy girl—"Dawn"—(later she called herself "D.D." but not when she was at our school)—had a younger sister named Anita, and a younger brother Noah—except for being almost mute in their classes they were not bad students, the girl especially—what you'd call bright-average, and mostly clean and well-mannered. Totally different from the older sister and everybody else in the family, probably.

After being expelled from school Dawn worked somewhere local like Home Depot. Then news came from Cleveland she was some sort of girls' boxing champion—"D.D. Dunphy"—"The Hammer"—this was a surprise! Interviewed on some Cleveland cable TV station after a fight and when they asked her where she was from in Ohio she said Muskegee Falls. Like she'd never lived in Mad River Junction at all.

The Stay

E*dna Mae! Come.* Jesus extended His hand to hers. She felt the fingers grip hers. Jesus's strong fingers. Jesus's patient fingers. If she'd wanted to withdraw her own hand she could not have done so.

She was awake, her brain ached but it was alert and alive. Yet she could not move. The night before she'd taken a new pill, a hexagonal green pill that melted under her tongue. Now her tongue was numb in her mouth like something that had died there.

Edna Mae! Hurry. The cross lay on the barren ground. They were forcing a man down, on his back, and his arms outspread, upon the cross that must have measured seven feet at its height. They would nail the man's hands and feet to the cross.

She was wetting a cloth in cold water. She would

press the wetted cloth against the man's bleeding forehead. She would press the wetted cloth against his bleeding hands, his bleeding feet where the terrible three-inch spikes had been driven in.

He had been a carpenter. That had been his life, before God had singled him out for a special destiny.

It was a melancholy irony, that he who'd once wielded hammers, had once driven three-inch spikes into wood, should suffer in such a way.

Edna Mae! Come now.

Hurriedly she wetted the washcloth to lift to her heated face. Water in the cloth cupped to her eyes so that she sighed in pleasure for her eyes were parched from all she'd seen in the night. She was so exhausted! But she'd been wakened from sleep by the sound of His voice.

Tried to take care, shaking out one of the green hexagonal pills into her hand. A new doctor now in Mad River Junction was prescribing a new medication for her for (he'd said) she had become over-dependent upon the old.

But she had a small quantity of the old. Shrewdly she'd hoarded these precious (white) pills for a time when the new pills would not be strong enough.

On the stairs, running footsteps. Someone rapped on the bathroom door and called her name excitedly

and in that instant the pill slipped from her hand—
"Oh!" She was on her knees groping for the pill that
had rolled beneath the sink on the grimy floor.

"Edna Mae! Edna Mae! Open the door!"

It was the morning of October 29, 2002.

Jesus have mercy *on his soul. Lord have mercy.*

*Beloved husband Luther Dunphy who gave his life
that others might live.*

"This day you shall be with me in paradise."

Except, the astonishing news was: the governor had
granted a stay of execution.

Another time, pending the appeal on his behalf that
was winding its slow way through the Ohio State Court
of Appeals, Luther Dunphy's life had been saved.

She could not comprehend at first. Staring at their
glowing faces.

A stay of execution!

By the grace of God, Luther has been spared.

She had given him up for dead. Her beloved husband. She had prayed for his soul and she had com-
mended him to God and now it seemed to be that God
had granted them a reprieve.

One of Luther's lawyers had called at 9:40 A.M. of
October 29.

Fewer than ten hours before preparations for the execution were to begin at the Chillicothe State Correctional Institution near Lucasville.

"Mrs. Dunphy? Good news! We just heard from the Governor . . ."

She listened. Her hand holding the receiver shook. There came a roaring in her ears as of ice and snow sliding down a steep roof.

This lawyer whose name she could not have recalled was saying now that he and his team would petition the governor to commute Luther's sentence to life in prison without possibility of parole—"We have a very good chance, I think. Mrs. Dunphy? Hello? Are you there?"

Someone took the receiver from her fingers before it fell to the floor.

In the Dunphy family there was rejoicing. Dawn was summoned home from work at Home Depot and Luke arrived soon after. It had been planned that Luke would drive them to the Chillicothe Correctional Institution that afternoon—Edna Mae, Mary Kay, Dawn, and himself—so that they could say good-bye to Luther during the final visitation between three and four o'clock.

Preparations for the execution were scheduled to begin at six o'clock. And the execution was to begin promptly at eight. But the call had disrupted all plans for this special day.

Since they'd begun to visit Luther at Chillicothe, Edna Mae had been in contact with the friendly prison chaplain, who called himself Reverend Davey. Or rather, Reverend Davey had been in contact with Edna Mae, for it was his custom to befriend the wives and close relatives of condemned men, to whom he offered sympathy and commiseration. He'd told Edna Mae that her husband was a "very special Christian" and in a "state of grace"; that of the prisoners on Death Row, that numbered a dozen, it was Luther Dunphy who was "most admired" by COs and by his fellow prisoners. Reverend Davey had said that he would "miss Luther like a brother."

He had also told Edna Mae that it would be a "relief to Luther's soul" if he expressed remorse for having shot and killed Timothy Barron but Edna Mae had not seemed to hear this.

As the execution date had approached, Edna Mae's sister Noreen had been in touch with her to offer sympathy and commiseration as well. The sisters had not been close for years and now Edna Mae had not the energy to telephone Noreen with the good news of the reprieve, as she had not the energy to call anyone in her family.

Mary Kay who was in a very festive mood as if she'd just won the state lottery made these calls. She relayed to the older children the lawyer's intention to appeal again to the governor for a "commutation" of sentence to life in prison and somehow in the relaying it seemed (almost) to be a certainty that Luther's sentence would be commuted. And also, in the relaying, it began to seem that there might be a possibility of parole—"But not for a long time, I'm afraid. Not for a looong time, kids."

Luke was helping himself to beer from Mary Kay's refrigerator. And Mary Kay was drinking too, splashing beer into a glass. "Edna Mae? Dawn? C'mon join us! Celebrate the good news, Luther has been *reprieved.*"

Dawn had been blinking and dazed-looking since she'd come in the door. At Home Depot where (she said) the stockroom area where she worked wasn't heated she wore heavy corduroys, two shirts, a pullover sweater and a hoodie, and on her feet woolen socks and work-boots. Since quitting school—(it was said of Dawn that she had "quit" and not that she'd been "expelled")—she no longer groomed herself quite so carefully as she'd once done and her hair hung in sullen greasy coils around her face. Her forehead was blemished and her fingernails were broken and edged with dirt. When her great-aunt offered her a beer Dawn laughed as if suspecting a joke but Mary Kay was not laughing, and urged her to take the beer. "Lighten up, D.D. 'Today is the first day of the rest of your life.'"

D.D. was some fond-funny name Mary Kay had made up to call Dawn. But *D.D.* had not caught on with anyone else, and so Mary Kay was the only one who called Dawn by this name out of a kind of foolish stubbornness.

Hesitantly Dawn accepted the can of beer, which was very cold. In a mumble she said that sixteen was too young to drink.

"Hell it is. This is a private party, you can drink any G-damn drink you want." Mary Kay laughed pronouncing *G-damn* with a flair.

The phone was ringing. Luther's relatives were calling. Edna Mae's relatives were calling. Word had gotten out, Luther Dunphy had been granted another stay of execution.

And had the execution been rescheduled? No one seemed to know.

In her confused state Edna Mae did not wish to speak to anyone on the phone. She did not want to speak to Noreen, or to her own mother. She did not want to speak to Reverend Davey—or was it Reverend Dennis who'd called? She did not want to speak to a reporter from the *Mad River Junction Weekly.* Some of those who called were neighbors and friends of Mary Kay Mack with whom Mary Kay spoke in a loud celebratory voice and to Edna Mae's horror she heard her aunt invite some of these strangers over to the house.

Edna Mae was sitting in a kitchen chair. Staring at the head of foam on the beer freshly poured into Mary Kay's glass steeling herself to see the foam overflow and run down the side of the glass onto the kitchen table or worse yet onto the linoleum floor where it would be sticky underfoot and no one would notice except Edna Mae.

Lethal

S he wished she hadn't. It was a mistake.
Discovering what *lethal injection* meant.

Without telling anyone they'd gone together to look up *lethal injection* online at the public library.

Soon after the verdict and the sentencing of their father to *death by lethal injection* they'd gone—together—(a rarity in recent years for Luke had little time for his sister)—to the Mad River Junction library where there were computers available to the public; and Luke typed in the terrible words *lethal injection* that acquired a kind of matter-of-fact calm by being so typed into the library computer in a brightly lit space patronized by numerous others.

Dawn had difficulty reading the entry for her eyes filled with moisture. She had to read leaning over her brother's shoulder which was awkward.

Luke read slowly, squinting and grimacing. He brought his eyes near the computer screen as if he had trouble seeing the letters. Luke had never been a good reader in school and was challenged to keep his gaze moving along a line of print and not careening off in other directions as you might do with a picture, a video game, something seen out a window.

Lethal injection was a lengthy entry in Wikipedia. They skimmed the names of the drugs of which only one—"barbiturate"—was familiar to them. Others were "potassium chloride"—"sodium thiopental"—"pancuronium bromide"—which they could not have pronounced. Dawn began to tremble reading that the *execution protocol* "ideally" resulted in the death of the condemned prisoner within seven to eleven minutes after the procedure was started; but sometimes there was considerable difficulty finding a vein into which to inject the chemicals and sometimes there were mistakes in the dosage since it was a set dosage for all subjects no matter their size, age, or physical condition. No doctor or medical worker would participate in an execution for "humanitarian" and "professional" reasons and so the individuals who administered the lethal drugs were prison personnel with no training.

With mounting horror Dawn read that only anesthesiologists –with an MD—were trained to administer anesthesia. It was not like *putting somebody to sleep* which everybody supposed.

One of the drugs injected into the bloodstream was a "paralytic" which rendered speech impossible but did not counteract pain. The anesthesia could not be guaranteed not to wear off before the heart ceased beating.

Sometimes the condemned prisoner suffered a good deal since he did not lose consciousness as planned, or regained consciousness in the midst of the protocol, which was very painful.

The longest recorded "botched" lethal injection took place over several hours during which time the condemned prisoner was frequently conscious and screaming in agony. Afterward it was revealed that the lethal drugs had been injected not into a vein but into soft tissue surrounding the vein.

The scientist who'd developed lethal injection as a "more merciful" means of execution than gas, hanging, or electrocution was quoted: "It never occurred to me that we'd have complete idiots administering the drugs."

There was more to read but Luke deleted the web-site abruptly.

In an undertone he said, "Fuck."

Dawn protested faintly, "But— the governor will commute Daddy's sentence. Everybody thinks so."

Luke shoved back the chair he was sitting in. His face was covered in an oily sweat.

"What 'everybody thinks'? Bullshit."

"What do you mean?"

"What I said, 'D.D.'—bullshit."

Luke uttered the name "D.D." as if he didn't think much of it. He was heading for the rear exit door of the library as Dawn followed after him staring at his back in disbelief.

"But—the execution was just 'stayed.' The lawyers have an 'appeal.' The governor—"

"Fuck the governor. And—just—*shut up.*"

Breathless and dazed Dawn followed after her brother. Before they reached the exit he turned to her glaring with wet furious eyes and shoved her, hard.

Dawn cried in surprise and hurt. "What—what's wrong? Why—"

"I said—*shut up.*"

Dawn slapped at Luke's arm, which was a mistake

for Luke did more than slap her in return, punching her hard on the shoulder.

When Dawn tried to pummel him about the head with flailing fists Luke shoved her with the palms of both hands so hard she was thrown against a library table, and onto the floor.

Everyone was staring. In an instant Dawn was on the floor spread-legged, wincing at pain at the base of her spine.

One of the librarians approached them —"S-Stop! What are you doing! That isn't allowed here . . ."

A second librarian approached. Both women were clearly frightened.

"Are you all right? Did he hurt you?"—the younger librarian asked Dawn,

Luke had already pushed out the exit door. Dawn muttered she was all right and managed to get to her feet before either of the librarians could help her.

Whatever they were saying to her, Dawn didn't hear. She ran limping outside to discover that her angry brother wasn't waiting for her—he'd started the car engine and was driving out of the parking lot as she pursued him crying—"Wait! Luke! God damn you—wait . . ."

It was two miles back to the house on Depot Street.

By this time she'd begun to cry but her tears were

tears of anger and not sorrow or despair and long before she reached her aunt's house her eyes would be tearless and her face dry.

Soon after, news came that their father's execution had been rescheduled for August 9, 2003—eight months away.

Unclean

The first fly, so small it appeared to be a mere speck of dirt, appeared on the refrigerator door as Edna Mae was about to leave the kitchen. With a rolled-up newspaper she managed to kill it but then she noticed a second, very small fly on a windowpane above the sink, and then a third, also very small fly buzzing on the windowsill . . . Clumsily Edna Mae flailed with the rolled-up newspaper and managed to kill both flies though with some difficulty for (it seemed) her hand-eye coordination had deteriorated in recent months, or years; and there was something wrong with her vision, that flooded with moisture when she stared intently at something that was crucial to see.

Edna Mae was about to throw away the befouled and torn *Mad River Junction Weekly* when she saw, as in a bad dream, yet another fly on the ceiling above the stove—too high for her to reach unless she stood on a chair.

Was it a fly? Or a speck of dirt? As she stared her eyes filled with tears so that her vision was occluded.

In fact, there were two flies buzzing against the ceiling—no, three. Unmistakably flies and not specks of dirt.

"Dawn! Where are you! Come help . . ."

Dawn was uttered in a thin impatient whine. Rare for Edna Mae to utter the name of her older daughter in a voice that wasn't whining or reproachful.

But Edna Mae recalled: Dawn was working at Home Depot and would not return for hours. And Mary Kay was working as well, and the children were in school— there was no one to help her.

It was disgusting, and made her very nervous—the sight of so many flies in the kitchen. Edna Mae recalled infestations of tiny ants in the old house in Muskegee Falls, in the spring; and infestations of field mice after the first frost. These infestations had nothing to do— (she was sure)—with the cleanliness of her household, yet she'd been very upset at the time. Luther had gone out to buy aerosol spray cans and mousetraps, and helped her rid the household of pests.

She could not stand on a chair to swat the flies on the

kitchen ceiling. She did not dare—she would become light-headed and faint. Already she was feeling faint seeing more flies—three, four—five, six—ten—so many hateful flies in the kitchen and buzzing against the windows, ceiling and walls! Where were they coming from?

Had something died somewhere in the house, and flies were hatching out of maggots in the corpse? It was a terrible thought.

"Please God *no.*"

Nothing so shameful and frightening as an unclean house in which Edna Mae had no choice but to live.

In fact there was a faint, or not-so-faint smell in the kitchen, sour, unpleasant, which Edna Mae had noticed, as perhaps others had noticed, but had not wished to investigate. For there were other smells in the kitchen, and in Mary Kay's house, that not even opening the windows could quite eradicate.

Her mother's younger sister Mary Kay Mack had invited her and the children to live with her out of Christian charity—initially. This was what Edna Mae had been led to believe. But once they'd come to live in the house on Depot Street it had fallen to them—(mostly to the older children Luke and Dawn, at the time)—to keep the somewhat run-down house reasonably clean, and the small scrubby yard, and to haul trash and garbage to the curb for the weekly pickup. Anita and Noah were assigned chores as well. And Edna Mae had done what she could despite her health problems and the constant strain of Luther's incarceration. In Muskegee Falls Edna Mae had kept a very clean house though the children had been young at the time—all of the relatives, both hers and Luther's, had complimented her on her housekeeping, and on her cooking. Reverend Dennis had praised her for her "Christian optimism" and "Christian spirit" in volunteering at church as much as or more than women who hadn't half Edna Mae's responsibilities. Reverend Dennis had particularly praised Edna Mae for her full-time loving care of her youngest child Daphne. He had understood the terrible grief she'd felt when Daphne had been taken from them.

Nothing will ever be the same again, Reverend Dennis. That is what I fear.

But you have your other children, Edna Mae. You have your husband.

No. I don't, Reverend.

What a strange thing to utter! Reverend Dennis had stared at her speechless.

She did not confide in Reverend Dennis further. There was no one she dared tell: her knowledge that Luther had let their little girl Daphne die in the car crash. Or rather, Luther had not protected their little girl as she'd needed to be protected. For Luther had not loved Daphne, really. He'd been embarrassed and ashamed of their youngest child because she was not "right"—as other children her age were "right"—she had seen it in his face. A man cannot disguise his emotions looking upon his own child.

As Luther was to be embarrassed and ashamed of Edna Mae after Daphne's death. Because her grief made her sick, and less of a woman than she'd been. Less of a mother, and less of a wife. Sometimes it seemed to her—(though she told no one this, not even Reverend Dennis)—that Luther had killed two men in cold blood as a way of ending his marriage and changing his life utterly.

Now it had happened, God was punishing him for such a terrible act. But in punishing Luther Dunphy, God was punishing them all.

(Oh but that was not true—was it? Edna Mae reminded herself how at any time, at any hour, the governor of Ohio could "commute" Luther's sentence. He could grant "clemency." There were legal hearings, appeals. There was much work to keep lawyers busy on both sides: the side of the State of Ohio and the side of the defendant. She'd more or less forgotten exactly what commute meant—what exactly it might mean in terms of Luther's situation—but she'd so often heard this possibility stated, by Luther's legal team and by relatives, she had to believe it was true. Her new friend Reverend Trucross and his wife Merri consoled her: *The will of the Lord at any time can alter lives. There are tempests, plagues, floods, but also harvests. Barren wombs have yielded great fruit. The Lord taketh away but the Lord also giveth.)*

The problem had been, for Edna Mae and the children, how to live without Luther. Which meant where to live, and with whom. For Edna Mae could not support the family even if she'd been a nurse, and not merely a nurse's aide. Even a registered nurse's salary would not have been sufficient in the crisis and even if Luke had been able to help them more than he was willing to help them, once he'd begun working for the county—there was just not enough money. Edna Mae had not worked as a nurse's aide in almost eighteen years. (She had loved the work—she had hoped someday to train as a nurse! But life had intervened.) She would have to be retrained, and be relicensed. It had not occurred to her to apply for a job at Walmart or Home Depot like Mary Kay and Dawn for she (secretly) believed such work to be beneath her. She could not return to her parents' home though they had halfheartedly offered to take her and the children in, and she could not live with any of the Dunphys because they did not want her any more than she wanted them.

And so, Luther's family had gone to live with Mary Kay. But soon it became clear to Edna Mae that her mother's younger sister was a shockingly careless and indifferent housekeeper. Everywhere were dust balls, sticky floors, loose planks, stains. The asphalt-siding exterior of the house badly needed repair. The scrubby grass was always going to seed, and riddled with weeds. Trash accumulated everywhere. Even Luke commented derisively on his great-aunt's house and had never invited any of his friends to come inside while he'd lived there.

Mary Kay was a generous person but a careless and often rude and profane person. She was in her mid-fifties, at least thirty pounds overweight but shapely rather than fat, and brimming with "personality" like a TV weather woman. She favored cheaply glamorous clothes—purple suede, black leather, colorful blouses and shoes with straps. Her hair was dyed red-brown. She spoke chidingly of Edna Mae for "letting herself go" and for being "skinny as a broomstick" as if to be thin was a moral failing.

Worse, Mary Kay was likely to be sharp-tongued if you suggested the slightest criticism of her lifestyle. Her choice in clothes, her choice in friends. Her casual attitude toward religion. If you remarked that a carpet needed to be cleaned, or replaced, or that stairs needed repair; if you dared to remark that the single bathroom (that was used by six people) needed a thorough cleaning, Mary Kay was likely to say, "Really! Well, you know what to do, Edna. You're not crippled."

Edna Mae was not *crippled*. That was so.

But she was not strong. It was unfair and unjust of her solidly-built aunt to suggest that she was shirking her responsibilities in the household.

Often, Edna Mae could barely breathe as if a steel band were tightening around her chest. She could not sleep without medication—if she tried, her brain buzzed like a hornets' nest. Her pulse raced, her eyes flooded with tears, a dull ache throbbed in her head. Always she was hearing the terrible word *Guilty*. She was hearing the words *Sentenced to death by legal injection*.

(Though in fact, Edna Mae had not heard these words uttered aloud by the trial judge in the Broome County Courthouse. They had been repeated to her. But she seemed to recall them as if she'd been there, and had heard, and could not now forget.)

She'd had to find another doctor in Mad River Junction. Dr. Hills had refused to continue to prescribe the medication she required so she'd gone to another, elderly doctor whose hearing was so poor she had to repeat her symptoms several times but who was willing at least to prescribe medication for her—"nerve pills"—"sleeping pills." It was a relief that Luther had ceased asking after her *pill dependency* as he'd called it, as if he'd forgotten, when she visited him at Chillicothe.

At first Edna Mae had tried gamely to keep the house reasonably clean despite her health problems, but Mary Kay's old-fashioned vacuum cleaner was not only inefficient but very heavy, and dragged at Edna Mae's arms. She'd tried to keep the kitchen clean, and the bathroom—the most disgusting, relentless of chores. The children were supposed to help but were not reliable. Dawn could be depended upon only to a point— then, rudely, she rebelled and said terrible things to her mother. For always there was the strain of their father in prison. Always the anxiety that weighed upon them all like a heavy overcast sky.

Edna Mae knew that the children were teased, taunted, tormented on account of their father Luther Dunphy. She knew, and was heartstricken for them, but she did not know what to do about it, and so she tried not to think about it.

Waking each morning in the unfamiliar house on Depot Street startled and confused not knowing for a moment where she was, and why. And then the thought would rush at her—*Your husband is in prison. Your husband is on Death Row.*

No longer did Edna Mae attend Reverend Dennis's church in Muskegee Falls. All that was over—her old life that seemed now to have existed for her on the far side of a rushing river. In this new place she'd joined a new church, the Mad River Junction Pentecostal Church of Christ. Reverend Trucross and his wife Merri had sought Edna Mae out to offer commiseration and sympathy—"Our prayers are with you and your family and with your courageous husband Luther in your hour of need, Mrs. Dunphy." When Merri Trucross embraced her with a sob of sisterly emotion Edna Mae had stiffened in surprise though afterward she'd been deeply moved. No one in her family including her sister Noreen had embraced her in such a way after Luther had been transferred to Death Row. Soon it happened that Reverend Trucross arranged for one of the congregation to pick up Edna Mae and the children to bring them to Sunday services, since Edna Mae no longer drove a car.

She hadn't been able to visit Luther at Chillicothe in months. Illnesses—(flu, pneumonia, shingles)—swept through the prison facility and visitation hours were canceled. On Death Row the prisoners were relatively protected from the general population yet seemingly susceptible to contagions spread by guards and other prison personnel.

Edna Mae continued to hear from the Chillicothe chaplain Reverend Davey who told her how "bravely" and "steadfastly" Luther bore up under the stress of Death Row.

There were eleven men on Death Row awaiting execution. All, including Luther Dunphy, had been granted temporary "stays" pending appeals and clemency hearings. So far as Edna Mae knew, and she did not really want to know such information, just two men had been executed since Luther had been sentenced to death, after delays and postponements of many years; but these were murderers, who had deserved to die, and nothing like Luther Dunphy.

"This gives us hope, Edna Mae. We must always have hope!"—so Reverend Davey consoled her.

At last, she found an old, badly stained flyswatter in a closet. With this, she would hunt down flies.

Yet, more flies appeared. The more Edna Mae swatted, the more appeared as if out of nowhere. Not only in the kitchen but in the hallway, and on the living room walls.

She had never seen so many flies since childhood on her grandparents' farm! Every kind of fly including gigantic horseflies, buzzing about manure heaps. The farmhouse doors were always being left open, the screens were ill-fitted to the windows, or torn; flies crawled over kitchen counters and table, stovetop, anything left out and uncovered. And if covered, flies crawled over the covers. As a fastidiously clean girl Edna Mae had been dismayed by the flies and their insolent buzzing that roused in her now a sensation of shame and nausea.

"Damn you! *Damn.*"

She was becoming adept wielding the flyswatter which was more lethal than a rolled-up newspaper though its surface was smaller.

Yet it was a delicate matter not to stain a wall by smashing a fly against it and leaving a smear, and Edna Mae did not always succeed. She was becoming reckless, impatient. It angered her that the flies struggled so for their lives—escaping her frantic wild swings as if with their microscopic eyes they could envision beforehand the imprecise trajectory of her blows, and were mocking her. Much of the morning she'd been groggy after a poor night's sleep but by quick degrees she was wakened by the exertion and challenge of fly-swatting. Yet, no matter how many flies she swatted, more flies were appearing.

Jesus was sending a sign. Jesus was not pleased with

Edna Mae Dunphy this morning. *Your place of refuge is unclean.*

It had to be, the flies were hatching. Disgusting as this was to contemplate, it had to be true. Edna Mae squatted to determine the source of the flies, somewhere near the baseboard of the kitchen. Then, she saw that a fly was emerging from a corner of the kitchen nearest the hall—near a hall closet. And when she timorously opened the closet door several flies flew at her face. She gave a cry, swung wildly and nearly dropped the swatter.

The closet was crammed with her aunt's things. Old clothing, old boots and shoes, dirt-stiffened mittens. Badly rusted steel wool cleaning pads. An old, filthy wooden-handled mop, plastic buckets, rags needing laundering. Carelessly folded paper bags from the grocery store. An ancient box of dog biscuits from a time, years before, when Mary Kay had owned a dog—out of this box of dog biscuits small moths emerged, fluttering at Edna Mae's face.

The stench here was sickening. By poking and prying with a broom handle Edna Mae discovered to her disgust something soft and furry wedged into a corner on the floor, at the shadowy rear: what appeared to be the desiccated corpse of a small rodent.

"Oh, God . . ."

She felt faint. She felt that she might vomit. She would have slammed the closet door except there was no one else in the house to deal with the emergency situation.

The flies had to be hatching out of the corpse. Or perhaps there was more than one corpse.

How shameful this was! If Luther knew how they were living now . . .

How could you have done this to us!

I will never forgive you.

In the closet, she found an aerosol can of insect spray. She sprayed the corner thoroughly. A few flies fluttered toward her dazed, lurching. On the walls and ceiling of the closet was a small platoon of flies now beating their tiny wings, stricken. She felt a thrill of satisfaction—*Now you know what it is like!*

Creatures had often crawled beneath farmhouses to die, in her childhood. The older farmhouses like her grandparents' had not had basements but only crawl spaces. Mice, rats, gophers, even raccoons, larger animals. Dogs. Cats. The stench would be overpowering for days, it would linger for weeks. The smell of poverty, helplessness. And flies—of course. Everywhere flies and other insects. Just one of any number of signals that God has abandoned you.

Each time she'd visited with Luther he had asked her how she and the children were managing in his absence and each time Edna Mae had said with a brave smile—"Well! We are *managing*."

Thinking—*He does not want to know. He must be shielded.*

Luther had never relented about the "defense fund" on his behalf posted on the Army of God website. In prison, Luther could not access the website; inmates were not allowed computers, as they were not allowed private phones. So Luther had no idea that the defense fund was still posted, though (as Edna Mae had been informed by the Army of God organizers) contributions had dropped to almost nothing, since other Right-to-Life activists had more recently captured followers' attention with women's center protests, vandalism, arson, and attempted shootings of abortion providers.

The new Right-to-Life martyr was James Kopp. Kopp had shot an abortion doctor in Buffalo, New York, in 1998 but had only recently been tried and convicted and sentenced to life imprisonment with no possibility of parole. Much of Kopp's online glamour was, he'd been on the FBI's list of Ten Most Wanted Fugitives. No other Right-to-Life soldier had been elevated to this list, since most were captured or surrendered to police at once. Kopp was affiliated with a militant Roman Catholic anti-abortion organization called The Lambs of Christ but had many admirers in the Army of God and Operation Rescue which were primarily Protestant.

At their last visit, as if reading her thoughts Luther had said quietly, "Don't despair, Edna Mae. God will not take me from you."

"I know. I know that."

"If you despair, our enemies will exult."

"Our enemies . . . Yes. I know."

"You know. But you must have faith, and communicate your faith to our children. You must not allow them to sink into despair."

"Our children are doing well. Luke is working for the county, and Dawn is working at Home Depot. Anita and Noah are still in school—their grades are good . . ."

"Isn't Dawn in school?"

Here was a blunder. Edna Mae hadn't told Luther about Dawn being asked to leave school and she did not feel that she could lie to him now. For a long moment she could not speak at all, feeling her husband stare at her through the scuffed Plexiglas barrier.

She was perspiring now, recalling. Before Luther could repeat his question a bell sounded, loudly signaling that only five minutes remained of the visitation hour.

During a visit Edna Mae rarely spoke to Luther about his "case"—about which she knew relatively little for it seemed always to be changing, very slowly and then with startling abruptness. There was an *appeal* that was still pending. And there was the possibility of *clemency,* and of *commutation . . .*

Elsewhere in the country states were outlawing capital punishment. Illinois had recently outlawed the death penalty. It was possible that Ohio would be among these states sometime soon and Luther Dunphy's sentence would be automatically converted to life in prison like James Kopp's.

It was hurtful to Edna Mae, as to others in the family, that so many of their fellow Christians in Ohio opposed any "weakening" of the criminal code. The very state senators who evinced sympathy for the right-to-life cause were rigorously opposed to changing the death penalty statute though such a change would have saved Luther Dunphy's life.

Edna Mae never spoke of such issues with Luther. It was her wifely duty to be upbeat, "optimistic."

Their visits invariably ended with prayer. What relief Edna Mae felt, when it was time for prayer!

Our Father who art in Heaven. Hallowed be Thy name.

They kingdom come, thy will be done . . .

Edna Mae had peeked through her fingers to see Luther stiffly upright, shoulders back, hiding his face in his big hands. She had grown accustomed to seeing her husband in the shapeless prison uniform—a "jump-suit" in Chillicothe prison colors, navy blue and white. On Death Row he'd concentrated on two things, he'd said: reading the Bible and making of himself a physically strong person. Luther had always been muscular but somewhat heavy, and now in middle age in prison he'd become lean, hard, like something chiseled from stone. His eyebrows had grown craggy, there were grayish hairs in his nostrils and in his ears. He was taking on some of the facial features of his elderly father, who did not approve (Edna Mae knew) of Luther's wife—a stern impassive look, with a tendency to frown rather than smile. His skin had bleached out, and was very pale. He was allowed only one hour outside a day—but some days, for some reason, not at all. His eyes had become ashen eyes, that looked burnt-out as if from staring too long into the sun.

Windex! Edna Mae had always loved the strong astringent smell of the cleaning liquid.

She was wielding a half-filled bottle of Windex she'd found beneath the kitchen sink. Paper towels and rags. A fit of housecleaning was upon her in the wake of the fly crisis which seemed now to have abated. She had not sprayed Windex so lavishly, wiped and polished so energetically, scrubbed, swept, dusted with such zeal since she'd been a frantic young mother in their house in Muskegee Falls. Soon she'd used up the paper towels. She then used toilet paper to wipe up dirt on the floor. She took the filthy mop out of the closet, ran hot water into a red plastic bucket, poured in soap, and began to mop the kitchen floor. Softly she sang:

This little light of mine
I'm going to let it shine!
This little light of mine
I'm going to let it shine!
Let it shine, shine, shine.
Let it shine.

She cleaned the kitchen windows, the windowsills. She wiped the walls where the flies had died. Little piles of fly corpses collected in the dustpan. With steel wool she cleaned the sink that was dull with grease, that had not been seriously cleaned in years. She cleaned the kitchen counters. She cleaned the kitchen table. She cleaned the vinyl chairs that were sticky with the droppings of months and years. A strong bracing smell of disinfectant filled the kitchen. With some effort she pushed open windows. She was tired but she was feeling exhilarated. She had not felt like this in a very long time.

The rotted mouse corpse in the closet corner she swept into the dustpan and with eyes averted she carried it outside and dropped it into the trash barrel on the porch. Once a week Dawn or Noah hauled the barrel out to the curb for pickup.

Next, she would clean the downstairs hallway. She would take on the bathroom.

When her aunt Mary Kay returned in the late afternoon she was astonished by the smell of soap and disinfectant and the gleaming surfaces of her kitchen. "Edna Mae, what on earth has happened? What did you do?"

With a little smile of satisfaction Edna Mae said: "Only just what I should have done long ago. Clean house."

Holy Innocents

*M*omma *please don't make me.*
Momma this is crazy.
And I will lose my damn job! We need my job.

Edna Mae was stung. Edna Mae did not appreciate her daughter speaking so insolently—such profane words as *damn.*

Edna Mae did not appreciate Dawn defying her even if—shortly—within an hour or two—Dawn gave in with an angry sob—*OK, Momma. All right.*

It was unfair! She'd been "promoted" at Home Depot—(this was the term used)—though her hourly salary had not (yet) been increased her weekly hours had been increased and this though she was still considered one of the new employees. She would have two consecutive days off each month and so resented it, that her September days must be used up in the prayer vigil in Cleveland.

For Edna Mae insisted. Dawn had not been able to say *no.*

It was September 13. National Day of Remembrance for Preborn Infants Murdered by Abortion.

Twenty-three volunteers from the Mad River Junction Pentecostal Church of Christ would travel by bus to Cleveland for the vigil, and for the burials in consecrated soil. A number of chartered buses were to bring volunteers from right-to-life congregations through Ohio and West Virginia.

The Trucrosses did not advise bringing children to the vigil and burial in Cleveland. Edna Mae insisted that her circumstances were special and that her children must participate.

The scales will fall from their eyes and their eyes will be opened.

Edna Mae Dunphy had become a vehement woman! In this new season of her life she was suffused with energy like sunlight streaming through a rent in a thundercloud. Like moisture sucked into a living stalk that explodes into riotous bloom. She'd had her tangled hair that was the color of broom sage cut so that it fitted her head like a cap of waves and wan curls. She'd gone to the dentist—a trip dreaded and feared for years—and had several cavities filled. The last time she'd felt a yearning to take pills Jesus had struck them from her hand and they'd scattered onto a damp bathroom floor and she'd knelt whimpering and begging *No no no please* but the pills had been so wetted they had dissolved between her fingers and she could only lick her fingers in desperation like a dog despite bits of grit and hairs in the wetted pill-substance and during these minutes of degradation Jesus had stood at a little distance observing her coldly and Edna Mae had known herself broken in utter shame lifting her eyes to His and vowing *Never again, Jesus. You have shown me the way, the truth and the light.*

And so it was. She did not return to any doctor to beg for pills. Instead in times of weakness she stumbled outside into the harsh cold air and cast her eyes skyward seeking help that never failed to come to her.

Thank you Jesus!

On dark mornings Jesus roused her from bed.

A fierce power raged through her veins that was the very blood of Jesus. Many in the Pentecostal church remarked upon this change in Luther Dunphy's formerly meek and sickly wife with awe and admiration.

Reverend Ben Trucross could attest to the transformation in Edna Mae Dunphy. At first progress had been slow—not so sure. Then suddenly, Edna Mae had *seen the light*. And *the light* had shone out of her eyes. Merri Trucross had encouraged Edna Mae to come swimming with her and several other Pentecostal women at the YWCA and these sessions had worked out so well that Edna Mae sometimes went swimming there by herself—walked into town, a distance of more than a mile, in slacks, sweatshirt, sneakers and carrying a nylon gym bag. (Luke had seen his mother striding along South Street one morning and had almost not recognized her. Was that Edna Mae? With her hair cut, and walking with such purpose? Carrying a *gym bag?* So surprised, Luke had almost run the county road-repair truck he was driving into another vehicle.) At the YWCA she'd seen on a wall a list of courses offered at Farloe Community College and next day enrolled in a nurse's aide program with the intention of updating her certificate.

She'd been such an eager student, nearly twenty years before! Now, she could summon back only a residue of that eagerness yet (Jesus assured her) it would be enough to carry her through.

For Edna Mae would have to start supporting her family, she knew. Anita and Noah at least.

On the morning of September 13 the young children

were groggy being awakened before dawn. It had been particularly difficult to rouse Noah, who flailed at Edna Mae in his sleep. Had they forgotten that today was the day of the "pilgrimage" to Cleveland? Edna Mae had told them only that many from their new church were going and that it would be a day they would remember for the rest of their lives.

"We are living the shallow life of the world. We are like people with our eyes shut, sleepwalking. But the scales will fall from our eyes and we shall see."

The children touched their eyes. Scales?

Immortality suffused her veins. Jesus had taught Edna Mae Dunphy to raise the dead—the dead that was *her*.

It was the taste of her new life. It was not the ashes taste with which she had endured for so long.

Dawn was alarmed that their mother now spoke with such emotion, and something like a schoolteacher's certainty, you could not comprehend what she might mean. She hoped that something terrible would not happen in Cleveland which was sixty-five miles from Mad River Junction for Edna Mae had been saying for days that they would remember what happened there for the rest of their lives.

There was something ominous in this. Edna Mae had even been on the telephone making plans—Edna

Mae, who had not willingly spoken on the phone in years . . .

Dawn had only a vague idea what was planned. Prayer vigil? Burials? *Holy innocents?*

Badly Dawn wanted to stay in Mad River Junction. Her two days off from Home Depot she'd planned to use for a private purpose. Yet, she could not let Anita and Noah go alone with their mother on this mysterious trip that required staying away overnight—being "put up" in the homes of strangers.

And how unlike Edna Mae this was, to wish to spend time with strangers. Even Christian Pentecostal strangers.

Dawn had promised her father that she would help take care of the younger children. Luther had extracted such a promise from both Dawn and Luke at the time of his arrest but Luke had broken the promise and left his sister behind.

Fuck you then, I am strong enough. I can do it by myself.

"it is only a rumor. Unverified."

Volunteers first heard on the bus that the vigil and burials might be televised on a "Christian-friendly" national news channel. Reverend Trucross was excited that such publicity would surely bring more volunteers to Cleveland and donations to the Holy Innocents Right-to-Life Action League.

In Cleveland there were many more of them arriving in buses, minivans, cars. They knew one another at once, by sight—a wild joyousness spread among them like wildfire. In public places, in parks and on sidewalks they knelt and boldly prayed. Loudly they prayed. They chanted. They surrounded the Cleveland County Planned Parenthood Women's Surgical Clinic and (some of them) would have to be dragged away by law enforcement loudly praying, chanting. Some of them said the rosary in loud voices. It was boasted that their prayers were loud enough to be heard in Hell.

In public places they held aloft posters proclaiming SEPTEMBER 13 NATIONAL DAY OF REMEMBRANCE FOR PREBORN HOLY INNOCENTS MURDERED BY ABORTION. Eagerly they offered pamphlets to anyone who came near—*Respect for Life: Your Baby Is Waiting to Be Born*. Of a dozen pamphlets pressed upon strangers though ten might be found discarded on the ground yet two might be kept and (possibly) passed on to others. They marched with picket signs depicting the badly mutilated bodies of infants above such captions as NO BABY CHOOSES TO DIE and I DIED FOR MY MOTHER'S SIN.

The lurid magnified pictures of infant corpses were

not well received by the majority of strangers who saw them. In parks and on sidewalks people walked hurriedly past with averted eyes, or spoke harshly or pleadingly to the volunteers, but in the roadway motorists had no choice but to slow their vehicles as picket-bearing volunteers inched out into traffic. They had been cautioned by their leaders not to interfere with traffic and not to be "aggressive" but the most fervent disobeyed precipitating a barrage of horns and shouts—"Get out of the way!"—"Go to hell!"—"You are terrible, sick people." Police arrived, to drag them out of traffic and onto the sidewalk. Though they were threatened with arrest, no one was (yet) arrested.

Such reactions the volunteers took in stride for they'd been prepared. Many of them had participated in prayer vigils in the past and encouraged the newer volunteers not to be frightened or discouraged. Jesus had not despaired in worse circumstances. Everyone knew they were doing God's bidding. Even their enemies knew—atheists, Socialists, abortionists knew. At the Planned Parenthood clinic, everyone on the staff knew. In such places there were friends and allies who could not speak out for fear of reprisals as there were friends and allies among law enforcement. And often it happened, so wonderfully, an individual would stop to stare, to be moved, to be drawn into conversation, to take away a pamphlet, even to press money into a volunteer's hands.

Bless you. You are doing the work of the Lord.

The most daring knelt on the walkway in front of the clinic. By law they were forbidden to trespass on the property itself. Unflagging in their zeal they continued to pray, and to chant. There were priests among them. There were nuns. There were teenagers, and there were children. There were the elderly, the infirm. Some were in wheelchairs pushed by adult children. Proudly they held picket signs aloft. Their banners—SEPTEMBER 13 NATIONAL DAY OF REMEMBRANCE FOR PREBORN HOLY INNOCENTS MURDERED BY ABORTION. Few women and girls would dare to enter the abortion clinic on this day for no one wished to run such a gauntlet past the shouting volunteers.

Yet, the abortion clinic was not shut for the day. Through the windows the enemy watched them covertly and at the door security guards stood.

Did they fear fire? Firebombs? Gunfire? A deserved conflagration as of hellfire, did the murderers fear?

In the street were TV camera crews, adding to the congestion and confusion.

Edna Mae had been brought to the abortion clinic (somewhere in inner-city Cleveland) with others from the Mad River Junction church. This was her first prayer vigil and she would not tire easily. With Dawn, Anita, and Noah she knelt, prayed, chanted. All around them was an army of the faithful who would not tire easily. But soon the younger Dunphy children were dazed with exhaustion and Edna Mae had no choice but to allow them to nap on the walkway. Sulky-faced Dawn knelt beside Edna Mae with her picket sign over her shoulder at an insolent angle.

In a whiny voice Dawn said they needed to go home. Anita and Noah needed to go home.

Edna Mae said snappishly that they were not going home until the Day of Remembrance was over. Of the volunteers from Reverend Trucross's church, she was not going to weaken and withdraw.

"Momma, for God's sake!"

"Don't you 'for God's sake.' Watch your mouth."

"Maybe you don't care but Anita and Noah are tired . . ."

"The murdered babies are *more than tired*. The rest of us should be ashamed."

From time to time there were shouts, screams. It wasn't clear what was happening but you might catch a glimpse of Cleveland police officers dragging volunteers away. Had they dared to approach the front entrance of the clinic? Had they tried to prevent a pregnant woman or girl from entering? So often had Dawn been told that police favored right-to-life picketers, it was disconcerting to see how roughly the officers treated them, how angrily they shouted at them—"Keep back! Keep the way clear!"

At last, at dusk, the clinic was darkened.

"Momma? Why aren't we leaving?"

"Why? Because we *are not*."

Dawn was baffled why Edna Mae, and some others, were not leaving the Cleveland County Planned Parenthood Women's Surgical Clinic. The last of the clinic staff had quickly departed, to a chorus of cries— *Murderers! Cowards!*

Edna Mae plucked at the children's arms. Hurry! Reverend Trucross was leading them.

Dawn was very tired. Dawn could not comprehend. Where were they going? The clinic was shut for the night. There was no one to pray over, or to harass or threaten. One TV camera crew remained in the street.

Only a few volunteers remained—fewer than twenty. But these appeared to be members of Reverend Trucross's church.

They were led to the rear of the clinic. In the alley behind the clinic where there were trash cans and Dumpsters. It was dark here. Flashlights were lighted. Dawn could not see well. The younger children stumbled and whimpered. Edna Mae spoke in a voice trembling with excitement. One of the TV crew was speaking to Reverend Trucross. A pair of headlights flared in the alley and Dawn saw the sharply shadowed faces of volunteers. Mostly they were strangers but there was Edna Mae Dunphy among them. They had the look of persons who did not know their surroundings, where they were or why. Dawn did recognize Jacqueline, a heavyset girl with asthma, from Mad River Junction, of whom it was said that Jesus had "saved" her when her throat had closed up as a younger girl and she'd been unable to breathe. At the Pentecostal church it had happened, dozens of witnesses would testify that Jesus had "breathed" life into Jacqueline and restored her to the world.

Edna Mae had acquired a flashlight. There was a smell in the alley of rotted fruit, rotted meat. Something sour and rancid. Dawn swallowed hard not wanting to be sick to her stomach. Edna Mae was reaching for her, gripping her hand with surprising strength. "Dawn! Come with me."

She would not come with her mother! She dug her heels into the ground.

Yet still, somehow her mother pulled her. Who would have thought that Edna Mae Dunphy was so *strong.*

In the alley behind the clinic amid the sickening stench they had overturned trash cans to poke in the debris. Boldly they had thrown open Dumpster lids to poke inside and to peer with flashlights.

A cry went up—they had discovered a cache of cardboard boxes in one of the Dumpsters. The first was removed and seen to be secured tight by duct tape neatly wrapped. With a knife they cut the duct tape, and opened the box. Inside were five or six Ziploc bags and in each bag a small star-shaped thing . . . More cries went up, of anguish and jubilation.

Edna Mae said fiercely, "You see? Babies—that didn't get born as you did."

Though Edna Mae was very frightened too, Dawn could see. Her face was drawn and ashen and her mouth was set in a fixed half-smile like the smile of a mannequin. Her fingers were very cold.

In the quivering flashlight beam the first of the babies was examined. For (as Reverend Trucross said) you had to determine if indeed the baby was *truly dead*.

Though it was clear, the poor thing had never lived. A tiny kitten-sized creature with a disproportionately large head. Its limbs were stunted, and one of its arms was missing.

Dawn tried to pull away from Edna Mae's grip. Her heart was beating very fast. She was close to hyperventilating. Yet she could not look away from the tiny, dead baby being removed from the stained Ziploc bag.

In a quavering voice Dawn said to Edna Mae, "The babies are dead. They don't know what you're doing for them."

(Where were Anita and Noah? Dawn hoped they were not near, and that someone was watching over them, for Edna Mae seemed to have forgotten them.)

Edna Mae looked at Dawn with disgust. "You are so ignorant! It's pathetic how ignorant you are. Why do we bury the dead?—because they are *dead.* But their souls are *not dead.* We are honoring the babies' souls, not their poor, broken bodies. For shame, *you.*"

"But—they never lived . . ."

"Of course they lived! They were all alive, in their mothers' wombs. As you were alive, before you were born." Edna Mae spoke to Dawn with a savage sarcasm Dawn had never heard before in her mother though (it seemed to Dawn) Edna Mae was trembling too, with fear and dread.

The volunteers exclaimed in shock, pity, horror. Dawn steeled herself against what she might see. Reverend Trucross was praying loudly.

"Merciful God help us. God who taketh away the sins of the world help us in our rescue of these holy innocents . . ."

In the beam of the flashlight another tiny creature was exposed. This one had been shaken out of the Ziploc bag, in which it had been stuck. It was larger than the first baby, fleshy, meat-colored, damp with blood. You could see the tiny curved legs, the tiny fingers and toes, the misshapen head. You could see the eyes that appeared large and were tight-shut. You could see the miniature pouting mouth, that had never cried.

Other babies appeared to have been dismembered. Their overlarge heads were intact but their bodies had been broken into pieces.

All lay very still on the ground. It seemed wrong to Dawn, that even a dead baby should lie *on the ground.*

Though the eyes of the dead babies were shut tight, tight as slits, and the faces shriveled into grimaces, yet you did expect the eyes to open suddenly. You could not look away from those eyes.

Dawn begged Edna Mae to let her go.

"Let you go *where?* You will wait for me. We are all going home together in the morning."

In horror Dawn stood as Edna Mae and the others lifted boxes out of the Dumpsters with their bare hands. (At Home Depot, Dawn and her co-workers, unloading merchandise, all wore gloves. And if you did not wear gloves, your supervisor would hand a pair of gloves to you!) Some of the boxes were upside down, all were toppled as if they'd been dumped hastily.

Carefully the boxes were placed in the rear of a minivan in the alley. The plan was to bury the aborted infants in a consecrated cemetery a few miles away with a proper Christian burial, Christian prayers.

As Edna Mae insisted, Dawn helped stack the boxes. She could not breathe for the stench, and was feeling light-headed.

(Where was Jesus? Had it been His plan all along, for Dawn to help bury the babies?)

(He had not warned her beforehand. It had been a terrible shock!)

(Since the hammer with the black-taped grip, that had struck the fleeing screaming boys with such power, Dawn had come to respect Jesus in another, unexpected way. Jesus was an ally but you could not take Jesus for granted as an ally, it was that simple.)

In all, there were fourteen boxes secured with duct tape, retrieved from the Dumpsters. In each box, five or six Ziploc bags with aborted babies inside.

Thrown away like garbage! God have mercy on the murderers.

When it was time to drive to the cemetery for the burial Dawn begged Edna Mae again to let her go home and Edna Mae said sharply that she could not go home, how on earth would she get home, she had no idea how to get home from this unfamiliar city and it would be dangerous for a girl of her age to be alone on the streets here—"You are coming with us. You can take care of your sister and brother."

Dawn saw how the others were watching her. In her nylon jacket with dull-silver threads, dungaree-style jeans both badly stained from the Dumpster. She was the youngest person in the alley helping with the boxes.

"Dawn, *come*. Get in here with us."

Edna Mae was pulling at her, urging her toward the minivan in which Anita and Noah were already huddled. But Dawn jerked her arm away.

Suddenly, she was free of her mother's grip. She was taller than Edna Mae, and stronger.

As Edna Mae called after her Dawn fled past the glaring lights of the minivan. She saw the shining eyes of strangers on her and she saw Reverend Trucross and his wife Merri gaping at her—"Dawn? Where are you going, Dawn?" She'd come to hate it, the Trucrosses called her *Dawn* as if she was their daughter too. If there was one truth Jesus had been drumming into her it was—*She was not anyone's daughter.*

At the end of the alley was a TV minivan and camera crew whose lights blinded her as she ran toward them and past them shielding her face with her hands paying them no heed hearing Edna Mae calling after her in an angry pleading voice—"Dawn! Dawn! Come back here at once!"

But Dawn swayed, stumbled, ran. And ran.

It was the greatest shock *of my life I think! More even than the call telling us that my brother-in-law Luther Dunphy had shot two men in cold blood back in November 1999.*

Well, this was a call, too—our neighbor! Noreen, quick turn on your TV, June Gallagher said. Channel forty-nine.

And there was this "prayer vigil" in a cemetery in Cleveland, at night, and people kneeling at a large grave site clasping their hands at their hearts and praying with bowed heads and one of them was Edna Mae— my sister!

I just stared and stared. What was Edna Mae doing there, in a cemetery in Cleveland? And why was she being televised?

It was explained that this was a particular area of a Baptist cemetery reserved for "aborted fetuses"— "preborn children of God"—as they were called. The fetuses had been discarded as medical waste from abortion clinics and had been "rescued" by members of a right-to-life organization for Christian burial in con-

secrated soil and my sister Edna Mae was one of these evidently. We had known that Edna Mae belonged to a new church in Mad River Junction where the family had had to move after the trial but none of us had heard anything about this—National Day of Remembrance for Preborn Infants Murdered by Abortion.

Almost, I would not have recognized Edna Mae. She'd cut her hair, and she looked different than I remembered—a high-strung kind of person that you'd get a little shock from if you touched her. She wasn't aware of the TV camera, or didn't give any sign. With the others she was kneeling and praying and then they were setting some small objects into the grave while a minister said a blessing over them—looked like Ziploc bags, with something in them—the remains of fetuses!—but where the bags were, the screen was blurred like something underwater or in a dream—too raw to show on TV, I guess.

There were close-ups of a few faces. But the camera didn't linger on Edna Mae.

The TV announcer was a blond woman sympathetic with the ceremony but also horrified, you could see. With her microphone in her hand she didn't get too close to the grave site and she was keeping her eyes averted from what was inside it. In a breathless voice she spoke of the faithful coming hundreds of miles from churches "all over Ohio" to rescue the aborted fetuses from being "thrown away like trash." The minister she interviewed was from a Pentecostal church in Mad River Junction—had to be Edna Mae's church—a putty-faced man of about fifty with a strange sad smile and teary eyes squinting into the TV lights saying, "Ma'am, these are holy innocents of God like you and me except they were not allowed to be born as we were. That is the only difference between us!—we were born, and they were not. And they were not even granted Christian burials. And so some of us are stepping in where the mainstream Christian churches have failed in their ministry to protect the least of us."

The blond TV woman tried to think what to say to these words, that were uttered in a low, urgent voice like the voice of someone who has gripped your elbow to make you stop and hear. But all she could reply was—"Ohhh! Yes"—"Thank you, Reverend!"

Already there were 103 aborted infants buried in this cemetery, the minister said. After tonight the number would near 150.

The camera moved onto the gaping grave site again, though still you could not see clearly what was inside the Ziploc bags, only just pale-shadowy outlines. And there was my sister Edna Mae kneeling at the edge with her head bowed and her face shining tears.

These were the strangest minutes in my life. Seeing my sister there on TV, as distant to me as if we'd never known each other. And I had to realize, Edna Mae and I had been out of contact for most of our adult lives. Since the death sentence of my brother-in-law, it had been hard to speak to any Dunphy. What do you say? What can you say? I had tried to keep in contact with Edna Mae but Edna Mae never answered the phone and never returned my calls. And when I called and got Dawn on the phone, Dawn would say she'd tell Edna Mae that I called, but Edna Mae never called back. And if I asked how they were Dawn would say, How'd you think we are?—in this sarcastic voice.

Oh yes. We gave Edna Mae money. What we could afford.

Later we heard how many thousands of dollars had come to Luther Dunphy's defense fund, that was posted online. People would send money, cash, in envelopes, and only God knows how much of this money actually made its way to Luther Dunphy's family.

The scene in the cemetery ended with a close-up, of dirt being shoveled onto the grave. The somber words of the minister—"May God have mercy on our souls." I felt an almost unbearable sadness. I thought—they are mad, to give themselves up to such futility. And I thought—they all know that it is futile, to provide a

Christian burial for infants who have never lived. To pray to God for mercy, when it is God who has shown no mercy, for if God had shown mercy the infants would not have been murdered in their mothers' wombs.

They know that it is futile—but they act as they are bid to do by conscience. Like Luther Dunphy, too. Their faith has made monsters of them—and this too, they accept.

By this point I could no longer make out Edna Mae, among the others. I had lost Edna Mae.

Later on *that TV channel there was a feature on right-to-life "martyrs" and these included Shaun Harris, Michael Griffin, Terence Mitchell, James Kopp and now Luther Dunphy—my brother-in-law!*

All of these men had shot and killed abortion providers at abortion clinics in the United States. Their brooding faces filled the TV screen if but fleetingly. A (male) voice-over spoke of them in reverent summary terms.

At the time, all of the men had been convicted of murder and were incarcerated, three of them on Death Row. And at the time, all were still alive and their cases under appeal.

Death Warrant

Do not sign a petition for me. Do not even pray for me. I do not protest my death any more than my life, it is in the hands of God.

These were Luther Dunphy's own words released to the media in the week of February 21, 2006, in reference to his execution, now scheduled for March 4, 2006.

These words painstakingly he had composed. He had *written these words* syllable by syllable. On yellow lined paper given to him by his lawyer he had written these precisely chosen words gripping a pencil awkwardly in his fingers.

He was not accustomed to writing. He had written virtually nothing in the years since he'd left school. He had not read a book in those years except (of course) the Holy Bible which he read every day of his life and always with a sense of breathless urgency to know *what will happen next* as a child is breathless to know how a story will end even if the end of a story is but the prelude to another story, and the end of that story the prelude to yet another; and even if everything is known beforehand, nothing is truly *known*. Luther could read again and again the first several books of the New Testament that filled him with wonder, hope, terror and joy and each time be surprised, that Jesus would be nailed to the cross as He was, having made no effort to escape His captors; that Jesus would say to the thief crucified beside Him— *Truly I tell thee, today you will be with me in paradise*; that Jesus would despair on the cross, and suffer and die as an ordinary man might suffer and die, and be laid in the tomb, and yet revive, and ascend to Heaven.

A lightness passed through Luther's brain, like heat lightning. He was struck blind, and found himself on the floor of his cell, having fallen without realizing, and yet there was joy in his heart.

Truly I tell thee, today you will be with me in paradise.

"Luther, are you sure?"—his lawyer was not happy with the statement Luther had written.

"Yes. I am sure."

Stubbornly he spoke. But quietly, not defiantly. His voice had become hoarse as if his throat were coated with dust.

His lawyer was a young lawyer from the law school at Columbus. His lawyer was one of a team of young lawyers whose specialty was *death penalty law* and whose subject was Luther Dunphy; before Luther Dunphy their subject had been another Death Row inmate at Chillicothe, who'd been executed the previous November.

"There are petitions being circulated in Ohio protesting the execution. By releasing your statement you will undercut the efforts of those who oppose the death sentence on principle and you will surprise and upset those who oppose the death sentence on your behalf."

"No."

"No—what?"

"I don't want that."

"You don't want—?"

"People to protest. Sign petitions. Interfere."

"But, Luther—"

"I said *no.*"

"But our appeal has been denied. Our final appeal. You know that."

This was what Luther knew: he could not oppose the

execution, on principle. *His* principle was that a man should not defy the will of God in a matter so crucial.

Not quite allowing himself to think—*It will not happen. God will not allow it to happen. It has been postponed many times and will be postponed again.*

At Chillicothe there were happy times. In fact, many happy times.

Daily workouts gave him much pleasure. Heart pumping hard and sweat oozing down his face and sides so with a kind of boyish glee it came to him—*I am alive.*

The man he had killed, the abortion-doctor Voorhees: *he was not alive.*

Perhaps there was not pleasure in this knowledge, exactly. But there was justice.

Prison-issue clothes he wore: jumpsuit, T-shirt, long-sleeved shirt, boxers, socks, cheap coarse fabrics manufactured by American Corrections, Inc. Muchlaundered clothes he'd come to inhabit comfortably.

Each day in his cell that measured six feet by nine feet with a height of nine feet six inches he did his squats—slow, never hurried, with concentration, counting in groups of ten.

He did his sits-ups, push-ups, leg raises counting in groups of ten.

He did his handstands, even headstands. These were particularly slow, and required intense concentration.

His exercises. Particular to *him*.

Like those special prayers, particular to *him*.

Because he was on Death Row and not in the general population at Chillicothe he did not have yard privileges. He did not have exercise room privileges. He was not allowed dumbbells or weights in his cell. He had learned to compensate by exerting pressure on muscles in his upper body in vigorous exercises worked out over a period of time with much care and calculation.

Pressing the palms of his hands against the wall and pushing forward, for instance. Counting (slowly) to ten before releasing pressure so extreme his arms and shoulders trembled and the tendons in his neck stiffened as if about to snap.

Each of these routines, ten times a day spaced through the day at precise intervals.

One hour a day he was brought from his cell and led outside into a penned-off area of the yard like the kind in which quarantined cattle might be kept. This area he estimated to be approximately fifteen feet by twenty feet. The sky was a patch of usually faint light high, high above the dull-gray concrete walls and often if it was raining, the rain did not seem to reach Luther Dunphy lifting his face to it.

In this space, he could "run"—as he could not in his cell.

An entire set of exercises he could do outdoors, once a day, with more pleasure than those he did in his cell.

More often now, there was pain. In cold damp weather, pain.

Considerable pain in knee-joints, thighs and tendons. The squats brought tears to his eyes.

On his back, knees bent, legs rapidly "running"— jolts of pain to his hips that caused tears to leak from his eyes down the sides of his cheeks.

No longer *young*. He had to concede that.

In this place, in the solitary confinement of Death Row, he had become *middle-aged*.

(Though he wasn't always sure of his age. When it had begun, the inexorable sequence of events that led to this cell at Chillicothe, he had been thirty-nine, he knew.)

(Now, six years later? seven years? Had to be forty-five or -six.)

(His children's ages he had forgotten. When he thought of them they were fixed at younger ages. And Daphne among them, the youngest. And though he'd seen Edna Mae recently, in his mind's eye he saw her as a younger woman, a baby in her arms. Always a woman is happy, a baby in her arms.)

At the crown of his head it felt as if some of his hair had fallen out. So slowly, over months and years, he'd hardly noticed. Except touching his head and feeling the hard bumpy skull with patches of fuzz he had not noticed before.

On Death Row there were no mirrors. You do not need to see the person you inhabit. You do not need to examine your own face, stare into your own eyes.

He'd forgotten his face. Except for the birthmark on his cheek.

Very slightly rough, it was. The texture of the birthmark when he drew his fingertips across it.

If he tried to remember his face—(which rarely he did, for why?)—he was likely to recall his brother Jonathan's face, not his own.

His brothers at the kitchen table. Shared moods between the boys that excluded Luther.

He had always liked Jonathan who was two years older than he. He had always feared and disliked their older brother Norman.

In Norman's face in the courtroom at Muskegee Falls he'd seen incredulity, shock—hurt and dismay—at the verdict *guilty*.

The deep shame of *guilty*.

His brothers rarely visited him at Chillicothe. His parents were said to be too ill to make the journey.

Heartsick was a word told to him, by someone.

Five times the execution of Luther Dunphy had been scheduled and four times it had been "stayed" by a judiciary order sent to the Ohio Department of Corrections. The first execution date had been in August 2000 and it was now February 2006 and it was not uncommon (Luther's lawyer had told him) that an inmate might wait on Death Row for ten, twelve, even fifteen and (in a rare case) twenty years before being executed; and in this lengthy period of time there was always the possibility of an appeal being granted, or clemency, or commutation of sentence. *We will not give up, Luther!*—the young lawyer had promised.

In some states there had been no executions since the mid-1970s—though condemned inmates waited on Death Row.

Waited, grew old. Eventually died. On Death Row.

Soon after Luther Dunphy's arrest, even before the trials in the Muskegee Falls courthouse, several right-to-life organizations had expressed support for him even as they took care—publicly—to oppose violence. After the death sentence it was "outrage" these organizations expressed to the media, that Luther Dunphy had been sentenced to death. Churches allied with the St. Paul Missionary Church of Jesus expressed "solidarity" with Luther. There were several Ohio congressmen sympathetic with the pro-life movement in the state who had condemned the "harsh sentence" and had called for "clemency." It was Luther's assumption that such protests had resulted in the stays of execution though (as Edna Mae had inadvertently allowed him to know) the protests had abated over a period of time, and other right-to-life martyrs had taken Luther Dunphy's place. Yet, Luther saw no reason to anticipate that this time would be different though it was the first he'd heard that strangers were organizing to protest his execution *as an execution.*

Who were these people?—Luther asked his lawyer; and was told that they were opponents of the death penalty generally, who demonstrated against impending executions at various prisons.

Some had religious objections. Some demanded a reform of the penal code. Many were lawyers, law students, social workers, teachers who objected to capital punishment as barbaric and discriminatory as most individuals executed in the United States were either black or very poor or both black and very poor.

Luther was not convinced about this. For it seemed clear in the Bible, and Jesus had never repudiated it in any of his teachings—"'An eye for an eye, a tooth for a tooth.'"

"Yes, but Luther—'Let he who is without sin cast the first stone.'"

Luther's lawyer smiled like one of the bright show-offy seminary students Luther had wanted to murder at the Toledo Bible school.

As the date of the execution approached, the young man continued, there would be demonstrators outside the prison. Very likely, some of these would be right-to-life protesters bearing picket signs showing Luther Dunphy's face and some of these would be opponents of the death penalty on principle.

"Individuals who don't ordinarily find themselves on the same side. But in Luther Dunphy, they will find a common cause."

Luther didn't want to think about this—*common cause.* He wasn't sure what it meant but he didn't like the sound of it.

He had never known anyone who opposed legitimate executions. He had never known anyone who opposed war. Vaguely he thought of these persons as foreign, "Socialist" and atheist. He did not want *common cause* with such persons.

Sometimes in the presence of lawyers while Luther

appeared to be attentively listening to the cascade of words that flowed from their mouths like water out of a faucet Luther was in fact flexing certain of his muscles (in secret) and counting to one hundred in groups of tens calmly and steadily and with one part of his brain only as his soul floated free and soared like a cloud skimming the surface of a sea in reflection.

"Are you listening, Luther? Do you understand?"

"Yes."

"The execution will become an issue in the media. There's a strong anti-death penalty movement gathering in the state, as there has been in Illinois since the Innocence Project reversed the verdicts of several men on Death Row. That is why it isn't a good idea—I mean, it isn't a helpful idea—for you to release your statement asking people not to protest for your sake. You see, if—"

Luther's eyelids had shut. Luther was awake but elsewhere. He knew himself safe, serene. His soul was secure within him like the liquid bubble in a carpenter's level and his soul was impervious to earthly harm.

"Luther, thank you! Bless you."

The Death Row chaplain Reverend Davey was a large man: three hundred pounds at least. His face was a heavy moon-shaped face with bulbous cheeks, lips. His small eyes were deep-set in the fatty ridges of his face yet alert, shrewd as the eyes of a bird. He was too heavy now to kneel in prayer with the inmates whose cells he visited never less than weekly though Luther could recall when, years before, Reverend Davey had knelt beside him on the floor of his cell. The two had prayed earnestly side by side like equals.

With the warden's permission Reverend Davey was bringing copies of the New Testament for Luther Dunphy to sign. On an inside, tissue-thin page, in bright blue ink, Luther signed his name—

Luther Amos Dunphy

Each signature was fastidiously wrought. Reverend Davey supplied the fountain pen, about which he was particular. Warmly Reverend Davey said:

"It will mean so much to the Christian Youth League, Luther! It will mean so much to the young people who receive these beautiful books to cherish through life . . ."

Luther was deeply moved to learn that the New Testaments in their soft black covers meant to imitate leather covers were to be passed out among young Christian boys and girls by their pastors. Signed by

Luther Amos Dunphy, copies would be given out at the annual meeting of the Midwestern Coalition of Pro-Life Activists in Indianapolis in June 2006.

Ordinarily, Death Row inmates at Chillicothe were forbidden to receive such quantities of reading material in their cells. Pens of any kind with their sharp points were considered contraband. But these rules had been waived for this special occasion. It was explained to Luther that his signature would confer a blessing on the individual New Testaments.

"In the eyes of many, Luther, you are a 'hero'—you are a 'martyr.' People who do not condone violence nonetheless honor *you*. We are praying for your soul."

Luther took pleasure in signing his name on the front, inside page of the New Testament. Never in his life had he signed his name in such a way—as if his name mattered, and was of value. *Luther Amos Dunphy* seemed to him a significant name, a name of dignity and worth, to which by some accident he was himself attached.

Signing copies of the New Testament through the day, slowly and with care, imagining the young Christian boys and girls to whom the books would be given, and how they would see his name as they opened the books, and began to read, Luther felt as if he were climbing a ladder—with each rung higher, ever higher.

A ladder beyond any ladder to the highest peak of any house.

Reverend Davey took away signed copies of the New Testament with its soft black covers, and brought new copies for Luther to sign.

"Take your time, Luther! You need not hurry."

Luther noted this remark of the chaplain's. Was it calculated to signal to him that, though the execution might be imminent the following week, or rather in five days, Luther could expect another reprieve—another "stay"?

It was possible that Reverend Davey already knew that the execution would be stayed another time, but was not allowed to tell Luther.

The third stay, in August 2004, had been just forty-eight hours before the execution was scheduled. Luther recalled how Edna Mae and the children had come to see him at Chillicothe *for the last time*—looking so scared—but that had turned out to be mistaken.

Luther had not been so very concerned, at the time. Almost, his heart had felt light.

There would be a "stay"—or there would not be a "stay."

How simple that was! God would spare Luther

Dunphy another time, or God would not spare Luther
Dunphy another time. From a great height, like climbing a very high roof, standing at the edge and staring
over—the difference between the two was not significant.

Oh but he wished he'd braked earlier, on the highway. Skidding into the pickup helpless in the light-
falling wet snow it had been too late.

Da-da! the child had screamed behind him. *Da-DA!*

Lately he'd been thinking of the crash. As in a TV
sequence in which a brief scene is played, replayed and
replayed he saw repeatedly in his head the pickup truck
edge out onto the highway; but now he was hearing the
child in the backseat, that he had not heard (he was
certain) at the time of the crash.

Luther had requested of his dear wife Edna Mae that
she not come to see him *for the last time*. It had been
six or eight weeks since Luke had last driven Edna
Mae and Dawn to see him at Chillicothe, a visit that
had been very awkward, and that was recent enough.

For Luther had confidence (he'd told Edna Mae)
that the execution would not take place when it was
scheduled in early March. He requested of her that she
share this confidence with him and express it to the
children.

But what if we never see you again?—oh, Luther!

We will see one another in paradise, then. You know that.

One of the guards on Death Row was also named "Luther"—"Luther Crowe." He was a light-skinned black man with a thin mustache on his upper lip, about Luther Dunphy's age.

From a certain manner in Luther Crowe, a way of smiling, a look of kindness, it was communicated to Luther Dunphy that this was a fellow Christian. Between them was the bond of Jesus, that Jesus had entered the hearts of both men and there was no necessity to speak of it, in a way that would draw the attention of other COs.

Also, Luther Crowe expressed a particular interest in Luther Dunphy signing copies of the New Testament.

He'd showed Luther Dunphy photos of his family. Luther Dunphy stared at these with eyes that so flooded with tears he could not see clearly.

Workout. Meals. Bible reading. New Testament signing.

Workout. Meals. Bible reading. New Testament signing.

There were not enough hours in the day allotted to Death Row prisoners, to accomplish all that was expected of Luther Dunphy.

———————

None of us *wanted to be the one. The warden said, draw lots.*

Sure there's a bonus—three hundred dollars. But still.

Nobody had any training. You would need a medical worker to inject a needle into a vein and to do it correctly but none of us knew shit. Because we had no practice, only just the condemned man. And by then, it's too late.

God damn I did not want to be the one. Because Luther Dunphy was a kind of a friend of mine. That's why it's forbidden—fraternizing.

You can get in all kinds of shit—fraternizing.

But it came to me this time, and it was like my turn because I had not administered the drugs in almost four years because last time I was sick pretty bad and had to cancel just three hours before the execution and took plenty of shit for that.

Nobody wanted to administer the "lethal injection." Not to Luther Dunphy.

Luther was a special case on Death Row. What he'd done had not been for himself like some other, common criminal—the kind of animal you find on Death Row usually. Luther had been protesting an abortion clinic and had shot two abortion doctors there and had not fled but gave himself up right away. He had not presented any danger to law enforcement and at Chillicothe, he had never presented any danger to the staff.

Poor bastard didn't seem to know there was public sentiment now for changing the laws, putting pressure on politicians, not attacking abortion centers or shooting people. Making abortion illegal—that's the goal.

People said, a man like Luther Dunphy is worth more to the cause dead than alive. Jesus!

Good thing, he hadn't a clue.

Luther did not talk politics. He did not even talk— hardly at all—about his religious beliefs. He did not despair, that you could see. Mostly he did his workouts in his cell, and he read the Bible. You would wonder how many times a man could read the Bible from start to finish but that's what Luther seemed to do. It took up all his mental life. He would forget it was mealtime— like, none of the inmates forget when mealtime is! The CO bringing his meal, slid through the slot in the door, the inmate has to say he wants it, give a sign that he isn't sleeping but awake to eat the meal otherwise the meal isn't delivered and some times Luther would just forget—wouldn't seem to hear. And the CO would feel sorry for him and call to him, Luther? Is that "verbal refusal"?—you don't want to eat?—and Luther would say real quick no, or yes, he wanted to eat, he just hadn't heard.

Of all the inmates in the unit, Luther Dunphy was the one who never complained about the food. He would say grace over the meal no matter what shit it was—and he would eat it.

You had to respect the man. His family must've sent him money credit for the commissary but he never cared to purchase much of anything except a new toothbrush now and then and toothpaste. And he had a few letters he was writing when he first came to Death Row, that he never finished and didn't mail.

None of us had ever seen anybody so serious about workouts. The age he was, mid-forties, Luther Dunphy didn't have an ounce of fat on his body, just muscles, and these were big muscles—he was impressive.

It was said he'd been a minister at one time so I asked him about this and he seemed embarrassed saying he'd taken courses at a seminary in Toledo but it hadn't worked out.

"Jesus didn't call me. I guess that was it."

People would ask us, is Luther Dunphy crazy. Is that the one killed two men because God told him to. Does he say that God talks to him right now. Your average inmate on Death Row, the years they have been in solitary, which is what Death Row is, you'd have to say that they are not normal in their minds. They are maybe not raving insane and banging their heads against the walls but they are not sane. Just to be a CO in the unit, you are in some danger of losing your grip. But Luther Dunphy was not one of these. I would swear to this and so would the chaplain who spent a lot of time with Luther.

Must've been, the chaplain and the warden had some kind of deal, Luther Dunphy would sign copies of the New Testament. Supposedly the books would be distributed to Christian youth—that was what Luther told me—but what happened was they were sold on eBay after his death. Some of the copies with Luther Dunphy's signature, they sold for as much as two hundred seventy dollars. For a cheap-printed book worth a couple of bucks! Who got this money had to be the warden and Reverend Davey if it was anyone.

As a kindness, seeing that I was a Christian like him or anyway tried to be, Luther gave me one of these New Testaments. He told me not to tell the chaplain. He said, I better give it to you now Luther before it's too late.

"Luther. Whatever is 'on your mind'—you must clear it away."

In his voice that was low and soft and cajoling Reverend Davey said it would be a salve to Luther's conscience if he made an official statement regarding that other man he'd shot—Timothy Barron.

"For you know, Luther, you are thinking of him. He is 'on your mind.' You have never acknowledged this innocent man and you have not expressed remorse for your act and it would be a kindness to the Barron family, you know, if you did. And if you did soon."

Luther Dunphy stared at the smudged floor of his cell.

Many times he had tried to remember. He had tried to summon back that vision. But he could not for there was blankness and numbness there. After the shotgun blast propelling Voorhees backward and down onto the driveway there was blankness and numbness and a roaring in Luther's ears.

God had acted through Luther Dunphy just this single time. God had given Luther Dunphy the strength to pull the trigger of the shotgun, as a streak of electricity runs through a living being.

Then, God had withdrawn. There had not been a second shot—Luther Dunphy would swear.

Yet Reverend Davey (who had not been in the driveway at that time, who had not been a witness, who could not know) persisted. Saying how "healing" it would be for Luther's conscience, for his soul, if he gave a statement in writing pertaining to Timothy Barron just to acknowledge what he'd done, if (perhaps) he had not meant to do it, had not meant to shoot Timothy Barron, but if (perhaps) he might express remorse for the death of Timothy Barron, as a gesture of kindness to the Barron family.

"Christian charity, Luther. But also—a healing for *your soul.*"

Luther appeared to be thinking. You could not have guessed how furious Luther was, hearing these words. How his muscles clenched, and the tendons in his neck.

But again, Luther said no, explaining patiently that that was not possible for there'd been just one man he had shot in all of his life—"The abortion doctor Voorhees. And I don't regret that act. That act is why I was born, Reverend. I am seeing that now."

But that night Jesus visited Luther's cell. Wakened from sleep by a presence close by Luther did not sit up in his bed but all of his senses were alert and sharpened.

Softly Jesus said *Think again, Luther.*

Jesus said *You are strong enough now, Luther. Strength is required to utter words that, while untrue, will bring peace to troubled souls.*

In Toledo he'd slept in the woman's bed. Smelling of the woman's body, and hair shampoo, or oil. And the pillowcases smeared with the woman's makeup, that was disgusting to him so that when he believed she would not see, he turned over the pillow.

But the other side of the pillow was unclean, too.

He had not really spoken to them. The women in Toledo.

He had brought his anger to them. Swollen and throbbing with yearning his anger he'd brought to them to discharge his hot infuriated seed into them as they lay beneath him locking their arms around him unknowing of the fury in his soul, the terrible boredom that is beyond fury.

How bored he'd been at the Seminary! Boredom like a gigantic yawn to distend his mouth, his jaws. Boredom colossal enough to annihilate the world.

He'd resented the old men who had blocked the doorway to his ministry. Not giving Luther Dunphy their blessing, that Luther might spread the word of Jesus like a wildfire eating up the hearts of strangers.

I wanted only to be Your servant. I do not understand why that was denied me.

He had not really spoken to the woman but had only

just pretended to speak. He'd told her that he was studying to be a minister, that he was a roofer, and a carpenter, and yes he was married and he had children. But he had not spoken to her of himself as she'd spoken to him telling him of her ex-husband who had beaten her and shamed her and made her crawl until one day she had risen to her feet with a vow of never again to crawl before any man. And she'd told him of a child who had died of some childhood illness—measles. In his male vanity and cruelty he'd shut himself off from her. He had wished to think of her as a fallen woman, a whore, a slut with dyed blond-streaked hair and a negligee of some flimsy material of the hue of naked skin through which he could see the shadowy nipples of her breasts and the shadowy pubic-hair patch at her crotch. She'd been kind to him only just lonely. A man is fearful of *lonely* in a woman. She'd prepared meals for him more than once and he had eaten at her table more than once hungrily and with gratitude as he had lost himself in her body and in her embrace more than once and with gratitude. She'd said, I miss not having anyone to cook for. I miss not having anyone to take care of. Her smile was marred by a crooked front tooth. Her eyes were hazel-colored like Edna Mae's eyes as he remembered them when Edna Mae had been a girl and so much in her had been a surprise to him.

When the woman drew her fingertips across his face he'd stiffened for he did not like such familiarity. When she'd caressed the birthmark he'd slapped away her hand with a curse.

Jesus said *It is the act of a Christian to take on remorse that is not his, that the suffering of the world be lightened.*

He had lost count of the days. His ten-counts he did without thinking for his lungs and his muscles had memorized precisely each ten-count of the vigorous exercise routine but he had lost count of the days for the days fell beyond the narrow confine of his cell.

His cell. So he'd come to consider it.

Yet now, Reverend Davey came to see him in this cell each day. Or was it, twice a day: morning and evening.

Earnestly Reverend Davey told him: "Prayer is like a feather."

Reverend Davey's eyes were the eyes of birds quick-darting in damp sand, long thin sharp beaks poised to jab.

"Think of a beautiful white feather. A large feather— like a hawk feather if a hawk could be white. Think of God's hand and the white feather on the palm of His hand. And each prayer is a feather, that is light, weighing almost nothing. But each feather is precious to God. And the feathers accumulate, in the palm of God's hand. So the prayers accumulate, and one day you will see, Luther—I have faith in this, deep in my heart—"

Luther thought—*The governor will commute your sentence.*

"—you will be with our savior in paradise."

Confused, Luther smiled. He was not sure what Reverend Davey meant, for all along he had known that he would be greeted by Jesus in paradise. He had never doubted.

Yet, the death warrant was served. A frowning young bald-headed prison official from the warden's office whom Luther had never seen before brought the document to Luther Dunphy to deliver by hand one morning after breakfast which was congealing oatmeal, just-slightly-"off" milk, a sprinkling of sugar and a small paper cup of sugary orange juice.

There was no mistake that the death warrant was meant for him for *Luther Amos Dunphy* was prominent on the document that bore a gilt replica of the Seal of the State of Ohio.

"Is that me?"—Luther spoke naively, puzzled.

Dazedly his eyes scanned the printed words. There

appeared to be breaks between words and within words, like wormholes in wood.

. . . her eby ordered that the de fen dant *L uther Amos Du phy* who h as adjud ged GUILTY OF CAPITAL MUR DER as charge d in the indict men t and w ose p nishm ent h as been as sessed by t he verd ict of the jur y and ju dgment of the court a t Death sh all be kep t in cust dy by Aut hority of t he Oh o Depa rtment of C rimin al Justice unt il the 4th day of March 2006 upo n which day at the Oh o Dep artment of Crim ina l Justice at the hour of 7 P M in a chamb r designat Ed for the p urpose of Execu tion, the said Author ity acting by and thr ough the Execu tioner design ated by the Warden, as prov ided by law, s hereby comm anded, ordered nd direc ed to carry out his senten ce of Death by *intr venous inject on* of a subs tance or su stanc es in a lethal qua ntity adju dged suffic ent to cause th Death of the afores aid *Luth er Amos Dunphy* un il the sa id *Lu ther Am os Du phy* is Dead.

Abruptly then the printed words ceased. Quickly Luther turned over the document—there was nothing on the reverse side.

He looked up. The prison official had vanished. Luther's cell was empty except for Luther whose legs he could see, and whose hands and arms he could see before him.

Is that who I am, or someone else? Who?

On the floor beside his bed was a stack of five or six New Testaments waiting to be signed, and Reverend Davey's black plastic fountain pen. Luther set aside the death warrant and eagerly Luther took these up.

The night before *an execution I don't even try to sleep. Lay on my bed in my underwear and socks and the TV is on but I am not hearing it. Or maybe it's on mute. Bottle of scotch and a glass and cigarettes to get me through the night.*

When I was living with my wife I'd lay out on the sofa like this. But she couldn't take it, on edge like I am leading up to it for days—hell, might've been weeks. I said to her what if I was a Vietnam vet? You'd have pity for me then.

She said, OK but you are not a Vietnam vet. Should be ashamed of yourself saying such a damn thing.

She'd known what it was to marry a CO. Half the men in her family are COs, how I met Dolores. So it was shitty for her to hold it against me pretending like drinking was something new to her, half the men in her family are alcoholics. For Christ sake.

The thing is no matter how many times you go through the "lethal injection" procedure, something can go wrong.

Like they say in a prison facility if something can go wrong it will go wrong but you won't know when.

So in the early morning like 4:00 A.M. the first wave of the real excitement will come to me. When we were together Dolores would say Hey! I can feel your actual heart. I think this amazed her. It amazed her but also scared her. Because of the drinking, I am not like I usually am but (she has said) some different person. It is easy to drop things and break things and collide with things in this state. It is easy to fall asleep with my eyes open. And there was a clamminess coming off me— Dolores said—like I was sweating-hot but cold too like somebody standing in front of an opened refrigerator.

This feeling of something you can't almost bear, it is so strong.

Some guys will bullshit how they have the "best sex of their lives" at such a time the night before an execution but only somebody who doesn't know shit would believe them.

Because a doctor or a nurse, or even an EMT, for

some "ethical"—"humanitarian"— reason they will not do the procedure. They will not participate in an execution.

There is a prison doctor at the infirmary, some days. But he will not assist in an execution. He has been asked many times but the asshole always refuses.

He will show up to declare the dead man dead, to sign the death certificate and collect his time-and-a-half. That the doctor will do.

(And his breath smelling of whiskey too. Fucking hypocrite.)

You'd think if these medical people were "ethical" they would set up the line at least—that's the hard part, where a non-professional is likely to fuck up. If they got the line going in the man's veins so somebody else could release the drugs into it at intervals that'd be "ethical."

First comes the anesthetic. Then, the paralytic. Then, the actual poison.

The idea being, by the time the poison comes into the man's veins he is deep asleep and will not wake up.

The paralytic is to make sure that, if he does wake up, he will not scream and struggle and you will not know if he is awake.

These matters I do not think about much if I can help it. In nine years I will be eligible for early retirement and I am counting the days.

I think that my marriage is so fucked-up, I am not sure if I want the woman back. The kids from her previous marriage helped fuck all that up.

Doing the kind of work that I do, any kind of prison work but especially Death Row, makes you special—like a leper. Why being a CO runs in families. Like law enforcement. Like Death Row assignment. Nobody else understands, and nobody else is comfortable with it. People will avoid you even at the prison. Even your supervisor. Like they are afraid to look you in the face—like it might be contagious or something. I have seen sons of bitches turn a corner to avoid me. See me at security going through and they hold back. Hypocrite fuckers.

We are like soldiers with a special status. We are paid to kill a human being—but it is not murder.

In some Western states it is by firing squad. You would be one of five or six men. Whoever thought of that!—one of five or six men and you would not know if you were firing blanks. That would be a mercy.

But if you had to fire a rifle at a man, in his heart, just you alone—that would not be possible.

With Luther Dunphy I knew it would be bad. Because Luther was a Christian like myself except a better Christian than I could ever be. Because he was one of those few in my life I believed truly did not see the color of my skin or if he did, that it made any impression on him.

Because he gave me a copy of the New Testament, that I will never sell or give away. It is precious to me.

He had declined a final meal. Instead he would fast.

Except for liquids he would fast for the final forty-eight hours.

Yet: God would not forsake him. He knew.

His brain was so sharply awake it hurt, like broken glass would hurt inside a human brain.

A smell of urine wakened him that morning. A smell of breakfast food, and something sour like vomit. He had not ever seen his fellow inmates on Death Row but often he smelled them, and often he heard their voices raw and yearning and ranting and he heard angry laughter that wakened him from sleep.

Jesus lay His forefinger against His lips—*You must console the family of the man you did not kill. You dare not join me in paradise if you fail to do this in my name, Luther.*

He was awake and alert and prepared but he was not able to fully enter wakefulness as you are not sometimes able to enter a doorway—the size of the doorway is too small, or the threshold is crooked, you see your foot groping for balance. Or, the doorway is actually a window, you need to crawl through. And the roof outside the window (because the window is set in a wall overlooking the slope of a lower roof) is a steep roof and you are not wearing work-boots but shoes with a foolish smooth sole like an ordinary man.

His eyes lifted to the sky. How happy he was even without proper work-boots, on this roof.

"Luther Dunphy"—his name was spoken harshly.

Was it the death warrant? But the death warrant had already been served to him.

It was the *commutation* from the governor!

In the past Luther Dunphy had been informed by his lawyer that the execution had been stayed. But this time, there seemed to be no call.

"Luther."

The wheel of the car, he had not turned sharply enough. If he had turned it more sharply, and more quickly, he might have avoided the pickup truck. But already his vehicle was skidding on the pavement damp from falling snow and in the backseat Daphne was screaming *Da-da! Da-DA!*

There had not (yet) come the call from the governor. Some men would not walk to the execution chamber, or could not walk. Of course, Luther Dunphy could walk for he was remarkably fit and strong and agile for a man of his age.

There came Reverend Davey to walk beside him. The chaplain was breathing hoarsely as if he had hurried. His parchment-colored face lightly oozed perspiration. His large hand fitted into Luther Dunphy's hand as in a warm handshake that became a handclasp to bring solace to Luther, and comfort.

In a lowered voice that startled Luther, for it was so close to his ear, Reverend Davey said, "They are here, Luther. Two of Timothy Barron's adult children."

To this, Luther had no reply. A strange numbness had settled upon him like a thin mist.

Reverend Davey said: "I've spoken with them. They are still—both—aggrieved about the loss of their father."

"But none of my family is here?"—Luther was concerned to know.

"No, Luther. They are not."

His heart lightened. This was a relief to hear. He could not bear to disappoint them further.

"Will my body be sent to them, then? For—burial?"

"Yes."

Still it was not too late for his sentence to be *commuted*. And there was the possibility of—what was the word?—*clemency*. Well before this time in the past the call had come to stay the execution but still it was not too late.

A test from God. As God had tested and tormented His only begotten son. *My God, my God, why hast thou forsaken me?*—Jesus had cried on the cross.

"There are many protesters outside the prison, Luther. Some are carrying picket signs with your name and picture on them, and some are carrying picket signs protesting capital punishment—'A Civilized Nation Does Not Execute.'"

Luther felt a twinge of guilt. Who were these people, and why did they exert themselves on behalf of *him?* It was only God's intervention that mattered and if there was not God's intervention, the exertions of these others were in vain.

"It is very touching, Luther. To see so many protesters."

But Luther was not listening closely. He was being led along a windowless corridor. And then, along another windowless corridor. His pride was somewhat wounded, the COs who urged him along did not allow him to walk at a quickened pace—as Luther would have done, voluntarily—but pushed him forward as one might push forward a recalcitrant man or one who is unsteady on his feet.

Some men had to be carried to the execution chamber, it was said. Refusing to walk, or paralyzed and unable to walk—carried in chairs, or pushed in wheelchairs, or carried on stretchers.

Recalling then he had not finished signing the copies of the New Testament left for him by Reverend Davey in his cell. Half-consciously he'd been thinking he would finish the signing later that night, or in the morning, but when he tried to explain to Reverend Davey, Reverend Davey interrupted as if unhearing.

"It isn't much farther, Luther. Jesus is with us now."

His footsteps slowed—what was this room? The ceiling was low and the lights were very bright inside as in an operating room. Luther hesitated and was gripped by both arms rudely and walked through the low-ceilinged doorway.

"There is no need for that!"—Reverend Davey spoke reprovingly to the COs.

Luther was beginning to feel light-headed. Barely could he see for the brightness of the lights in this cramped space that smelled of disinfectant and something sweetly chemical. Barely could he hear Reverend Davey ask if he had any final words as he handed Luther a small microphone.

Final words!—the thought was so strange to him, his lips lifted in a smile.

Final words. He had never been one to make others laugh (like certain of his friends at school) yet a wild impulse came over him, to pat at his pockets as if searching for *final words.* But there were no pockets in his clothing.

Luther could not speak for it seemed to him that he had used up all of the words of his life.

And how strange, Reverend Davey had handed him a microphone. It came to Luther, the first time he would hold a microphone in his hand, and the last time he would hold a microphone in his hand, were one and the same time.

Shyness came over him. His throat had shut up tight.

A microphone! Like someone on TV.

The execution chamber was much smaller than he had expected—and the ceiling strangely low. He worried that it might be soundproof—(he had heard that it was soundproof)—in which case, if a call came to stay the execution, the ringing might not be heard inside the room.

Nor could he see through the Plexiglas window, that was a horizontal window of about eight inches in height and seven feet in length, with pushed-open black curtains at both ends. But he knew that there were witnesses beyond the barrier—the prison

warden and other authorities, law enforcement officers, relatives of the deceased. Strangers assembled to
witness a death.

Not *his death* but *a death*. A large clumsy bird flap-
ping its wings, *a death* could happen to anyone in this
vicinity.

There, the gurney to which the condemned man
would be strapped. It was surprisingly narrow, spare.
It did not seem long enough for Luther Dunphy's body,
or substantial enough.

A metal rod with straps extended perpendicularly
from the gurney, about twelve inches from the top.
Luther stared at this trying to think what its purpose
might be

"Luther? Have you anything to say?"—Reverend
Davey repeated.

All this while Luther's heart was beating hard and
steady. His heart did not believe that this would happen
to him. At last he began to speak slowly into the microphone as if each word were being pulled out of the air
with difficulty.

"In Jesus's name—I repent my sins. The act that
I did—that brought death to Mr. Barron—I did not
intend. It may have been—the shotgun went off by
itself . . ." Luther paused, breathing audibly. His forehead shone with perspiration.

Gently Reverend Davey urged: "Yes, Luther?"

"—yet it is my fault I know. Because the shotgun was in my hands. I—I beg forgiveness from the family of Mr. Barron who—whose life—was taken from him wrongly . . . And if you cannot forgive me I understand . . . It is only Jesus's forgiveness that matters." Again Luther paused. He was swallowing compulsively and his eyes had filled with moisture.

"Yes, Luther? And—?"

"May God have mercy on my soul, that I have done such an act. And all other—other—mistakes of my life, that are my fault alone and no one else's."

Abruptly Luther ceased as if he had run out of words.

Reverend Davey was deeply moved. Bright tears streaked his ruddy cheeks.

"Luther, thank you! God bless you, my son. Now let us pray."

His instinct was to kneel but they would not let Luther kneel. Their hands gripped his upper arms tight. He would pray standing as Reverend Davey stood awkward on his feet in the presence of the Lord until at last his knees began to shake.

Made to feel like shit *coming to the prison.*

Protesters with picket signs in the roadway. Waving signs and shouting at me.

Their eyes on me like they knew it was me—the executioner.

And the shock in Luther's eyes when he saw who was waiting for him.

Feeling like shit. Like Judas.

In Luther's eyes there was that thought too—like Judas.

But there was forgiveness in his eyes too. For Luther Dunphy knew that I was his friend.

Asked him to lay on the gurney and he did. When he had to lean on me, to lift himself up onto it, I felt how strong he was, the hard-quivering muscles of his arm. It is always strange to stand so close to a white man. You expect them to shudder away from you. I thought if he tried to fight us we'd need at least four men— two to hold the ankles and two to hold the wrists. But Luther Dunphy didn't fight us.

Then, we strapped him down. Fumbled with the damn straps. You could hear him breathing like through his mouth and not his nose—like an animal panting.

On the other side of the Plexiglas the sons of bitches watching. Fuckers sitting in seats like in a little theater and the closest seats maybe two feet from the window. Their knees had to be pressing against the window. The way the lights are you can't see the "witnesses" too clear because of reflections but you know that the sons of bitches are there.

The warden and the assistant warden and officials from the prosecutor's office. Law enforcement, journalists.

A son and a daughter of one of the victims were there. We had been told.

Now Luther Dunphy was lying on the gurney still-like and strapped down and his left arm stretched out on the rod. And it happened in that way that is what we dread the worst—it was not possible to find a good vein.

Sticking the needle in the man's arm, trying to raise blood into the hypodermic, and feeling the man stiffen with pain (but not saying anything—like Luther wanted to spare me)—this was damn hard.

Soon, I was sweating.

Tried all the veins I could find in his left arm, and not one of them worked. Or maybe I just did not know how to do it—fuck!

You wind a rubber strip tight around the upper arm to make the veins bulge but a vein can "roll"—just rolls away from the fucking needle.

If a man is dehydrated the veins are not firm. Maybe Luther Dunphy had not drunk liquids in a while.

In the right arm I tried with a large ropey blue vein running the length of his arm but I had forgotten to use the rubber strip so I wrapped that tight around his upper arm and tried again—no luck. Damn vein just rolled away from the needle. Sweating bad now and poor Luther was trying not to groan with pain from the fucking needle. And he was bleeding bad from me sticking him.

Finally after eight stabs it looked like the line was in, at the crook of his arm, that soft skin at the elbow, and we could start the first drug—the barbiturate.

This is the sleep drug—the anesthesia.

The containers are clearly labeled. There is number one and there is number two and there is number three.

The instructions are printed clear in steps. From this point onward there would be an estimated ten-eleven minutes at the longest before the man is dead.

But then, the fucking line came out! The needle sunk into the skin at the crook of the elbow just popped out and started bleeding.

(At this point the assistant warden entered the room with a curse yanking the black curtains shut so the witnesses could not see anything further. On his face a special look of disgust for me.)

Had to start again and this time my hands were not too steady. And Luther Dunphy white-faced and trying not to gag. And I tried to keep my hand from shaking, holding my right hand with the needle with the left hand though I had not had a drink in many hours—not since driving to the prison.

In the glove compartment of my car there's a quart bottle of scotch. All I can think of is getting back to my car, opening that glove compartment and drinking from the bottle which I will do as soon as this is over.

I will feel the warm liquor in my mouth, going down my throat and into my chest like the warmth of the sun. I will want to cry, I will be so grateful.

How many stabs it took, I don't want to remember.

Gave up on the right arm and tried the left arm again and both arms bleeding from the damn needle. (Which was maybe blunt and dull now from so much use.) And so, we cut open Luther's trousers, to try for a vein in the inner thigh, there's a vein there (I knew from past experience)—a kind of a big fat vein. But by this time I'm shaking pretty bad. So I'm fucking that up too.

But just keep trying. That's all you can do. How many stabs of the needle until finally I got in a line—must've been an hour, or more. My fingers are numb and my neck is stiff from the tension. And Luther Dunphy squirming on the gurney trying not to groan, or scream. Finally now the anesthetic is dripping into the vein, or should be—(unless we screwed up the

*order of the drugs)—Luther is praying aloud Our
Father who art in Heaven and suddenly he is crying
I'm on fire, I'm on fire—like it's the wrong drug, it's
the poison drug not the anesthetic—but we are certain
that it is the right drug—but still Luther is crying and
groaning and then he is screaming and writhing and
vomit leaks from his mouth and his eyes roll back in his
head but he doesn't lose consciousness—he is not being
put "to sleep"—the line has to be removed because
some mistake has been made and a fresh vein will have
to be found.*

*Sick to death. So sick! Telling myself God damn you
knew you should have told the warden to find somebody else and fuck that three hundred dollars.*

Two hours, eighteen minutes were required for Luther Dunphy to die from the time he was strapped to
the gurney to the time he was declared dead by the attending physician Dr. E——.

His brain was extinguished by degrees. His soul was
extinguished by degrees like a panicked bird fluttering
in a small space being struck by a broom again, again,
again.

Into a vein in his left ankle the hot poison entered and
once it began to stream inside it could not be stopped.

It was astonishing to him—he could feel the hot poison entering. Yet still he could not believe that it was *his death* that was entering him.

As the poison flooded his bloodstream his organs shut down one by one. Liver, kidneys, heart. His blood turned to liquid scalding lava. He was resolved not to scream but—he heard himself scream. A young raw boy's voice. *Oh God oh God help me. Oh God.* He had been sweating and shivering and his teeth chattering wildly and now his temperature spiked. His heart was racing to keep ahead of the poison. He began to die in quicker degrees. His clenched fingers had turned white and were becoming cold, and his toes and feet were becoming cold. As his fingers became cold and numb they ceased clenching yet spread stiffly like claws. An icy mist crept up his body like a devil's embrace. He had not given sufficient thought to devils and demons in God's creation—that had been a failure of his. He had not truly believed in Hell. He had believed in Heaven but not so much in Hell. He was astonished at himself, to think—*Am I still alive?* And then, he was not alive.

Neurons in his brain were extinguished like lights going out one by one—a string of Christmas tree lights. His most painful memories were extinguished. His birthmark was extinguished as if it had never clung to his cheek like a rabid bat. His happiest memories were extinguished. A very young child laughed into his face and closed its arms around his neck and was gone in that instant. Another cried—*Da-DA!*—and was gone in that instant. He was being lifted, with care—a woman's hand gentle at the small of his back, and a woman's gentle hand at the nape of his neck. A sweet smell of milk overwhelmed him. He was bathed in liquid heat and in blinding light opening his eyes wide, wider to take in such a wonder. Dr. E—— who'd been waiting outside the execution chamber in a private place as was his wont as a thirty-year veteran of Chillicothe not witnessing the horrific execution thus obliged to wait an unconscionable two hours eighteen minutes having to exit the premises to use a lavatory not once but two times though a few shots of whiskey usually slowed urine production, so Dr. E—— was humbled, humiliated and infuriated and totally disgusted, returning then to a further vigil trying not to hear the dying man's screams of agony through the purportedly soundproof wall and the inane accusations of the asshole COs responsible for the lethal injection blaming one another for the fiasco arguably worse, more heinous and outrageous than the previous execution fiasco several years before; now grimly charging forward into the reeking room to examine the deceased man's livid body stinking of bowels, blood, chemicals, horror with rubber-gloved hands checking the pulse of the deceased, heartbeat, no pulse and no heartbeat, shining a pencil-flashlight into the unresponsive eye of the deceased to declare time of death 9:18 P.M. and date March 4, 2006, and sign the death certificate in his scornful illegible hand.

If they'd said *thank you doctor* he would say *sure. And fuck you* but no one thanked him. He exited.

Shortly then the body that had ceased writhing and was now very still was covered in a white bloodstained cloth of the size of a tablecloth. The red-mottled contorted face with opened eyes and mouth agape as in childlike terror and wonder was mercifully covered.

The gurney bearing the body was wheeled to the prison morgue by the COs who'd administered the drugs. Shame-faced and sullen and swaying on their feet with exhaustion. And their uniforms covered in blood from their myriad mishandlings of the needle. And in the morgue the fevered body began at once to cool. In this place of sudden calm, quiet. A drop in body temperature from 102°F to 99°F and then in inexorable and irreversible decline to 90°F, within an hour 82°F, eventually 60°F, and at last 36°F. which was the temperature of the aluminum gurney beneath the corpse and the temperature of the very still air of the morgue.

Total darkness in this place and not a single reflection of even muted light. Even the faintest eclipse of light, there was none. The darkness on the face of the deep before the creation of light before the first day of creation and total silence, not a breath neither inhalation nor exhalation.

The Embrace

March 2006–March 2010

Autoimmune

N ot yet."

Waiting for the news. Waiting to learn that Luther Dunphy had at last been *put to death*.

In this borrowed room in Ann Arbor she'd forgotten where she was. And Darren two thousand miles away in Newhalem, Washington.

Hours they'd been waiting together. Since 5:55 P.M. and now it was 9:18 P.M. and no news had come from Chillicothe and the strain of the vigil was exhausting.

On an arm of the vinyl sofa where Naomi sat stiffly was a mobile receiver set to speakerphone. At the other end of the line was her brother Darren two thousand miles away in a place she could not imagine (for she had never seen it) with a similar phone similarly positioned.

It was Darren who had two phones primed for use.

One of them, a landline, was connected to Naomi in Ann Arbor and the other was a cell phone poised to receive a call from Chillicothe, Ohio.

In Chillicothe a journalist named Elliot Roberts who'd known the Voorhees family when they'd lived in Detroit was witnessing the execution of Luther Dunphy in order to write about it for the Associated Press. Roberts had contacted Darren, to arrange for a private call to notify Darren when the execution was completed; but Roberts had to leave his cell phone in his vehicle parked outside the prison facility, for electronic equipment was not allowed inside the facility. Not until Roberts was released from the facility, presumably with other civilian witnesses after the execution, could he call Darren with the news.

Roberts had had to arrive at Chillicothe, to be admitted through security into the Death Row unit, by 6:00 P.M. The execution had been scheduled to begin at 7:00 P.M. But now it was much later—more than two hours later.

Naomi had called her brother in Washington State more than an hour before she'd needed to have called. For Darren could not possibly hear from Roberts until after 7:00 P.M.

Darren had answered at once, irritably.

Yes, what? What do you want?

Just to talk. Before . . .

It's too early! Christ.

But—please . . .

He'd relented. He'd heard the fear in her voice.

In this phase of his life which (Naomi thought accusingly) might be described as *post-family*, as it was determinedly *post-modernist*, Darren had taken a leave of absence from college, and had then dropped out of college, in order to devote his time to his "art"—graphic novels in a mordant vein, obsessively detailed, dark-comic-grotesque fantasies of contemporary American suburban life in conflict with what Darren called the "other side."

D. Voorhees's graphic novels were not easy of access. At least, Naomi did not find them easy. The first was titled *Welcome to the Other Side*—a Midwestern suburban family of maddening normalcy and complacency beset by demons like flying ants, mostly invisible; the second was titled *Do You Want Me to Tell You When, Where, Why?*—sexual ambiguity among young adults in an Ann Arbor, Michigan, setting; the third, most ambitious and most acclaimed, was titled *Lethal Injection: A Romance*—lurid scenes of executions by lethal injection in American prisons, drawn in excruciating detail. (For each of the executions was botched in a unique and lurid way.) Naomi had tried several times to read *Lethal Injection: A Romance* but had never been able to finish it.

She was fascinated and repelled by Darren's work, and impressed by his obvious talent. But mostly she was envious of the use to which her brother had put two of his obsessions: narrative comics and lethal injection.

He is myself. My surviving self.

Since dropping out of U-M in his junior year, and moving to the west coast, initially Seattle, then Puget Sound, and now the Skagit River Valley Darren had become associated with a small press in Seattle, which had published all three of his graphic novels; he'd illustrated other books for the press which Naomi had not seen; he'd acquired an online presence—a much-visited website called *Do You Want Me to Tell You When, Where, Why?* She wondered how Darren supported himself, with whom he might be living, what his life was like now—she had but a vague idea.

Her own obsession had led mostly to failure. The loss of her father was the only significant event of her life but she could not give a shape to the experience, she could only inhabit it, helplessly, as a child inhabits a place of confinement, or handed-down bulky clothes.

She had tried! God knew, she had tried to assemble *The Life and Death of Gus Voorhees: An Archive*—but she'd been defeated by the enormity of her subject that fell into pieces like something that has been broken and inexpertly mended, that shatters again at the slightest pressure.

In her zeal she'd amassed a dozen folders. Hundreds of pages of notes. Newspaper and magazine clippings, taped interviews with people who'd known and worked with her father (most of which she had yet to transcribe and edit—indeed, some of these she had never returned to). Photocopies of letters written by her father, which recipients had provided; and letters to her father, which Jenna had allowed her to take. (Of course, Jenna had selected an undisclosed number of letters to keep for herself, or perhaps even to destroy, that were "too private" for Naomi to see.) Documents, timelines, sketches. Photographs—every kind of photograph including baby pictures. Much of the material Naomi had typed carefully online but it existed in scattered files of which several had been lost inside malfunctioning computers . . .

Most awkwardly she'd tried to "interview" relatives. What might have seemed like the most obvious course, as well as the easiest, turned out to be extremely difficult. Her mother refused to speak with her at all on this painful subject and her absentee grandmother Madelena Kein had rebuffed her in a terse email—"Maybe someday. But now is too soon. Please do not ask me again."

Even Darren had discouraged her. He'd have liked to assemble an archive of Gus Voorhees of his own, Naomi supposed.

It had seemed to her also that the complete history of *The Life and Death of Gus Voorhees* could not be written so long as her father's murderer remained alive.

Worse, the archive would have to contain material about the assassin, and the highly charged "political environment" out of which he had sprung.

This was the most bitter irony: to wish to honor her father was inexorably bound up with a fixation upon his murderer which filled her with despair, rage, shame.

She did not want to *care* about Luther Dunphy— whether the man lived or died. She did not want to be consumed by hatred for him, and for the many (hundreds? thousands?) of individuals who'd applauded the "assassination" (as it was called) among the right-to-life movement.

Yet, *Voorhees* and *Dunphy* were bound together, unavoidably.

Through history the assassin has attached himself, like a blood-gorged tic, to the individual he has killed. Of the many indignities provided by death, this is the most insulting.

Each time Dunphy had been scheduled to die, Naomi had begun an involuntary count. She had no need to mark the date on the calendar, for it was imprinted in her memory.

Like Darren, she'd become something of an amateur expert in lethal injection. She knew how increasingly difficult it was for penal authorities in the United States to purchase the lethal drugs, from European manufacturers; often it was the case that executions had to be postponed for this reason.

It was possible that Chillicothe had failed to secure the proper drugs in time for Dunphy's execution. Or, something had gone wrong with the administration of the drugs. Or, the Ohio Judiciary had granted another reprieve.

For Naomi knew, if the drugs had been properly administered to the condemned man at the prescribed time that evening, the execution would have been over by 7:30 P.M.

That it was now 9:20 P.M. and Roberts had not called meant that something had gone terribly wrong.

Pointless to speculate. Yet Naomi was too restless to remain silent.

"The worst news is that it's been stayed—again."

"I don't think so."

"Don't think—what?"

"I don't think it has been stayed this time."

"But—how do you know?"

"Because their final appeal was turned down."

"But Dunphy's lawyers will file other claims, or whatever they are called—they file these automatically, even if it's the final appeal."

"Well—I don't think so."

"But—how do you know?"

"I told you, Christ! *I don't know.*"

"But you said—*no.*"

Quick as a match flaring up, their old childhood animosity. Naomi's heart beat in opposition to her brother whose authority she must always undermine even as she wanted (badly) for Darren to like her.

Love was not an issue, as *love* was not a possibility. Naomi knew that Darren did not love her as (probably) Darren did not love anyone in the family except their father who had died.

Very likely, Darren didn't *love* anyone at all. In a way, Naomi hoped this was so.

Desperately she had to keep him on the line. She dreaded his hanging up before the news came to him.

"Darren? What time is it there?"

"What *time*? You know it's three hours earlier than you."

"So you've been waiting since three P.M."

It was an inane remark. It was a child's remark, which Darren barely acknowledged.

Tell me of your life, then! Tell me something that is secret, that no one else knows like our hatred for Luther Dunphy and our wish for him to die.

But Darren was sounding distracted. (Was he speaking to someone there with him? Was someone speaking to him? She could imagine Darren pressing the palm of his hand over the receiver.)

More likely, Darren was online. As well as speaking with her on the phone he was cruising the Internet, searching out *Luther Dunphy, execution, Chillicothe Ohio.*

Naomi could not have dared this. She could not have typed the hateful name into her computer to bring hundreds, thousands of bright blue titles up like sewage.

Could not bear to read of *Luther Dunphy* online and could not bear to think what Darren might be seeing.

He will never die. *It will go on forever. This is our Hell.*

Each time it had been a shock to Naomi, a knife blade turning in her heart, when Dunphy's execution had been postponed and rescheduled.

Their father had died on November 2, 1999. It was now March 4, 2006. These years, months, Gus Voorhees had been dead. It did not seem possible that a man once so vital, so energetic, so kind, loving—a man so valued—had been dead for so long. Yet, it was so. And these years and months his murderer Luther Dunphy had been alive.

It was not *closure* (which was an offensive term) they awaited but *an end*.

Her life could not begin. Not until *an end* was reached.

She could not love anyone. Always there was a kind of scrim through which she perceived another person. She was preoccupied, deceitful. What mattered most to her could not be shared with another, like a shameful medical condition or illness of which she dared not speak.

Though she had learned to go through the motions of "love"—"friendship"—to a degree. Shrewdly she'd created a personality inside which she could live as she might have stitched together a quilt of colorful mismatched cloth-squares, dazzling to the eye.

Or was it a kind of mask atop a puppet. *She* was somewhere inside, in hiding.

She could not be an intimate friend with anyone—female or male. She could scarcely bear to be touched and she felt something like panic to find herself in close quarters with another person.

She could not speak of it—the loss, and the anger at the loss. Not to anyone except Darren.

Twins conjoined by hate.

Twins yearning to be free!

At eighteen she felt both old for her age and immature, a stunted adult. She carried herself with a kind of caution like one venturing near the edge of a steep precipice. She was not so obviously angry as she'd been as a younger adolescent. Her blemished skin had cleared, her fingernails no longer picked at her face. Her fury had become more subtle as her spite was mostly turned upon herself.

"It's like an autoimmune disease"—Darren first diagnosed their condition.

Grief that is not pure but mixed with fury. Murderous grief, that no amount of tears can placate.

"No. It is an autoimmune disease"—Naomi had to correct him.

In the first weeks and months after their father's death Naomi had been too stunned to fully comprehend that their father was not going to return. She knew that he was *dead*, but she could not accept that he was *gone*.

She had hated being a freak among her high school classmates in the Birmingham school. The girl whose father had been publicly murdered. The girl whose father had been an "abortion provider."

There was further humiliation and shame, that their mother had left them to live with their grandparents. This could be explained in terms of Jenna's *breakdown* as it came to be called.

What Naomi most dreaded was intrusive sympathy, commiseration. Steeling herself to endure—*I can't imagine what it must be like for you* . . . Worse yet, *I can imagine what it must be like for you.*

"No. You can't. You can't ever."

Very coldly Naomi rehearsed these words. She had yet to utter them except in private.

Trembling with rage, and in dread of crying.

Though Naomi rarely cried. As *crying* might be understood.

Tears sprang into her eyes, but she did not *cry.*

Her first year at the University of Michigan she'd been particularly alert to incursions into her privacy. The name *Voorhees* was not so well known among undergraduates as she had feared it might be but it was certainly a name known to older residents of Ann Arbor, as Gus Voorhees himself had been known; it was difficult for Naomi to avoid these people, though they were exemplary persons, wonderfully generous, "good"—often inviting Naomi to dinner, eager to ask after Jenna, and to reminisce.

Did I ever tell you, Jenna, how I'd first met your father . . .

Excuse me. I am not Jenna, I am Naomi.

She'd fled well-intentioned "family" dinners. A seder, a Christmas Day dinner, Thanksgiving dinner at the McMahans.

Apologizing—*So sorry! I don't know what is wrong with me.*

Thinking—*Just leave me alone for Christ's sake.*

She'd transferred out of university courses when it seemed to her that the instructor knew who she was, whose daughter she was, and would have liked to speak with her privately. A (woman) professor of linguistics, a (male) professor of social psychology—with no explanation Naomi dropped their courses in the second week of the semester, and never saw them again.

Was she imagining it? Darren thought so. She did not.

(She shared such follies with Darren, of course. Her brother was the only person to whom she could confess how childish she was, how insecure, immature, how ungenerous, suspicious, venal. He was the only person who knew—without being told, in fact—that Naomi Voorhees volunteered to be a literacy tutor in Ann Arbor, working with black children and illegal immigrants, not because she was a *good person* but because it was in the tradition of her *good, liberal parents* to volunteer in such ways and she was still trying to impress them long after it had become impossible.)

She'd become hypersensitive to a certain expression in a stranger's face, that look of startled recognition, and pity, and a kind of covert excitement, that "Naomi Voorhees" was surely the daughter of "Gus Voorhees" who'd acquired, since his death, a mythic-heroic reputation in leftist political circles in the Midwest, and was revered by activists involved in the reform of legislation involving women's reproductive rights.

She'd become particularly alert to the (literal) approach of such individuals. Invariably they were middle-aged, or older; female more often than male.

Naomi—is it? I didn't know your father personally, but—I admired Gus Voorhees very much.

How could you reply to such a statement except with a pained

Thank you.

Dreading the next remark—*What a tragedy! That terrible man! What became of him—he's in prison, I hope?*

Wanting only to flee. But too polite to turn her back and walk away.

Resenting having to speak of Luther Dunphy.

Even indirectly, obliquely. Having to concede that yes, Dunphy was in prison in Ohio, and alive.

Resentment she felt too, having to be as Gus Voorhees's daughter so damned *good*.

No doubt this was why Jenna had retreated from public life, and so abruptly. Canceling engagements, resigning positions, shocking and disappointing comrades who'd seen in Gus Voorhees's widow a means of extending Gus Voorhees's work.

Emails sent without apology. No more able to fulfill obligations, you must look elsewhere.

That did not explain why Jenna had also retreated from her own children. From family life.

Naomi had never told Darren what their mother had said to her when she'd left the house in Birmingham that morning. *I can't be your "Mommy" any longer. No more.*

And worse. *Gus has ceased to exist and Gus is not coming back.*

He'd hated Jenna already. (Unfairly?) She did not want him to hate her more.

Soon after she'd left her children with their grandparents in Birmingham Jenna had been hospitalized (in Chicago) with severe anemia, exhaustion, malnutrition. She'd been diagnosed with a rare (autoimmune) disorder in which food was not being properly digested in her stomach. There had been a possibility of permanent liver damage.

In the hospital, Jenna had wanted no visitors. It was believed (by her father- and mother-in-law in Birmingham) that her own parents, who lived in nearby Evanston, had visited her regularly; but no one else had been welcome in her hospital room.

Jenna had recovered, to a degree. She'd told them that her health was "shaky" but "stabilized." After she'd been discharged from the hospital she hadn't chosen to return to Birmingham, or to Ann Arbor, but to live elsewhere, initially in New York City, and then in Vermont.

There was a cell phone number for Jenna, and there was an email address. But these did not make her readily accessible to Naomi.

Shortly after the New Year, as the date of Dunphy's execution approached, Naomi began calling Darren more frequently.

Darren did not always answer the phone. He did not always return her calls. But when he did, it (sometimes) seemed to Naomi that there was someone with him in the place in rural Washington State which she could not envision.

Once or twice she'd heard a voice—voices—in the

background. She was certain. But when she'd asked Darren who was with him he'd replied coldly—*Sorry. That's my business.*

She felt a stab of acute jealousy. Could Darren be—*in love?*

That was not possible. She was sure. Darren might (maybe) have a sexual relationship with someone—but even that wasn't likely. Not a sustained relationship. No.

If Darren was a twin of hers he would shrink instinctively from another's touch.

She understood that her brother was not so sympathetic with her any longer. Their only link (she feared) was their parents—Gus's death, Jenna's departure and estrangement.

He'd fled the Midwest, he told her, to put distance between himself and family history.

How could he do *that*!—Naomi had been horrified.

Especially, Darren said, he didn't want to talk about Luther Dunphy if he could avoid it.

But he couldn't avoid it! Not with the execution scheduled.

He felt the way she did, didn't she?—Naomi had to ask.

Waiting for Dunphy to die? Yes.

Darren had laughed harshly. It was a shameful admission, somehow—waiting for another person to die.

She'd asked him if anyone from the Chillicothe prison had contacted him. He was over twenty-one, he could be an observer at the execution if he'd wished.

Darren had been shocked at the suggestion. "Jesus! No."

She'd shocked him further by saying that she could imagine herself attending the execution—maybe.

"Fuck you would, Naomi. That's bullshit."

"It's just that I hate him so much. I hate all of them— 'Dunphys.'"

The very name was repellent to her. A rush of something like nausea overcame her, seeing *Dunphy* in print.

As the widow of the murdered man Jenna must have been contacted by the prison authority. She had not mentioned this to either Naomi nor Darren—but then, they were not often in touch.

Of course, Jenna would never have considered observing an execution for a moment.

She'd explained on several occasions—"Gus opposed the death penalty. I do, too. Executing that man will not bring back Gus."

Often on the phone Jenna sounded like someone making a careful, precise public utterance not like a mother speaking to a daughter who'd called her because she'd been feeling lonely, and anxious.

All that Naomi knew was that her mother was living now in Bennington, Vermont; that she worked with a small law firm, very likely comprised of women, in Bennington, and that she had a visiting appointment at Bennington College.

Whenever it was proposed that Naomi visit Jenna, Jenna quickly said, "Yes of course, soon. We will look forward to that."

Or, "Soon! When this 'bungalow' I'm renting is habitable for a guest."

Naomi's legal address was her grandparents' home in Birmingham, Michigan. De facto, Clem and Adele had been their grandchildren's guardians since Jenna's departure. They were such good people! Gus's death had ravaged Grandfather Clem but he rarely spoke of his loss and neither he nor Adele spoke critically of their wayward daughter-in-law. Naomi tried to keep in frequent contact with them for she was grateful for them—their unstinting support, their affection. Even the smiling step-grandmother, Naomi tried to love.

Well—*love* was an overstatement.

She tried also to keep in touch with Melissa who remained so young—sixteen. Living with their grandparents in the house in Birmingham and attending now the prestigious Cranbrook Schools in Bloomfield Hills where she took a course in Mandarin Chinese, cello lessons, played soccer, and earned uniformly high grades. A life their father would have disdained as suburban, "preppy."

When Naomi spoke to Melissa she never alluded to *the subject*. She could not have brought herself to utter the name *Dunphy*. She supposed that Melissa was aware of the imminent execution in Ohio for there was sure to be coverage in local media, considering Gus Voorhees's renown in that part of Michigan. But she couldn't speak of such an ugly matter to her sensitive young sister.

Melissa was a shy girl who could be urged to speak enthusiastically about her courses and school "activities." She seemed to Naomi to belong to another era, long ago when the Voorhees family had all been different people.

Naomi was telling darren about Melissa when, at 9:34 P.M., Darren interrupted her.

"Jesus! He's calling me. It must be over."

Naomi listened intently. She could hear her brother speaking with Roberts—she assumed it must be Roberts.

"Darren? Hello? Hello? What has happened? Is he—dead?"

She could hear Darren's voice—(he was asking Elliot questions)—but couldn't make out his words. She was beginning to feel light-headed as if the floorboards of this unfamiliar place were shifting beneath her feet.

Then, Darren's voice was loud on the phone. "Yes! He's dead."

Naomi wasn't sure she'd heard correctly. "Dead . . ."

Darren told her grimly that the execution had been "botched." It had gone on for two hours. The observers hadn't seen it—most of it.

"They drew a curtain so that no one could see how terrible it was . . . Jesus!"

Dead! Luther Dunphy was dead.

Naomi tried to stammer a question but Darren wasn't on the phone. She could hear him talking with Elliot Roberts and in the next instant the line went dead.

Tried to call Darren back. But no answer.

After several rings, a recording switched on. Naomi pleaded:

"Darren! Pick up! Talk to me! Please."

For several desperate minutes she tried to call her brother. The landline, the cell phone. "Damn you! Darren. Don't leave me alone now."

She sent him an email. Darren rarely answered her emails.

She called again, and no answer.

It had happened, at last: Luther Dunphy was dead.

It was over. It had *ended*.

She was feeling—well, what was she feeling? As if the top of her skull had been sheared away. Such lightness! Was this—joyousness?

She was outside. On the street. (But which street? She'd forgotten where she was—an apartment borrowed for the evening from an Ann Arbor graduate student friend.)

Here was a surprise—she was weak with hunger. She supposed it was hunger, she'd forgotten to eat since breakfast. She'd forgotten to drink liquids and was feeling faint now, dehydrated.

In the borrowed apartment she'd considered drinking a glass or two of (borrowed) wine out of a bottle she'd found in a cupboard. But she had not dared, for fear that she would lose control and drink much of the bottle.

She'd begun drinking at the age of seventeen, at high school parties in Birmingham. Not serious drinking. Of course, she never drank alone.

What had Darren said—the execution had been

"botched." It had gone on for more than two hours. She'd read of such executions, the suffering of the victim. She felt a twinge of horror, that Luther Dunphy must have suffered in this way.

For the first time, she thought of Dunphy's family—wife, children. What did they know of what had happened to him. How had the execution been for *them*.

At one time, she and Darren had taken note of the Dunphys. They had seen pictures online of Edna Mae, Luke, Dawn, Anita, and Noah. These had not been clear pictures but blurred photos taken without the consent of the Dunphys.

Dawn was the child closest in age to Naomi. Hardly a "child"—a big-boned Eskimo-faced girl with defiant eyes. Luke was the one closest in age to Darren.

What had become of the Dunphy family? Naomi wondered. It was not likely that they lived in Muskegee Falls any longer. Seven years had passed, much had changed in their lives too.

She was walking quickly. But she was not walking steadily. Seen from a distance, she might've been mistaken for an undergraduate girl who had had too much to drink, and was not accustomed to drinking.

(*Had* she poured a glass of red wine, out of Mercedes's bottle? She didn't think so. She wondered if her breath smelled.)

Here was another surprise—it was snowing. Every day this week snowfall. Despite alarms of global warming the Michigan winter had been bitter cold. And something was wrong—like a fool she'd run outside without her fleece-lined jacket. Another pair of gloves she'd lost somewhere. Her head was bare. Her hair was damp and tangled from wind-driven snow. She was running recklessly, slipping on the pavement. She'd been neglecting her classes. She'd been neglecting her literacy tutorials. She was letting everyone down exactly as Jenna had let everyone down.

A smile distorted her face like a clamp. Someone called to her—"Whoa! Watch out, girl."

Snowflakes were blown against her hot face. Veins, capillaries exposed. The heat of blood beating beneath her skin melted the snowflakes at once.

She had thought that she was headed toward the university campus, a shortcut across the snowy stretch in front of the Rackham Building which would take her in the direction of her residence hall but—somehow—she'd taken a wrong turn, or she wasn't on State Street after all. Or, she'd gone in the wrong direction on State Street.

She was panting. She was very tired suddenly. She did not want to be seen—recognized. She was huddled beneath a scaffolding. Across the street was a Chinese restaurant that had once been her parents' favorite Ann Arbor restaurant but it had a new name now and the front window was opaque with steam. A voice echoed with astonished glee in her head—*Dead! Luther Dunphy is dead.*

The smile remained on her mouth, clamped in place. Rivulets of tears were freezing on her cheeks.

She left the shelter of the scaffolding. She needed to be alone. She did not want to answer questions. She did not want to be interviewed. *And now how do you feel, you and your siblings? Now that the assassin of your father Gus Voorhees has been executed?* Hurrying along an alley. An odor of beer and greasy food wafted through a vent and made her feel nauseated. There was an overflowing Dumpster, litter scattered on the ground. It was the most bitter truth, she had not wanted to tell Darren—no undergraduate she'd met seemed to know who Gus Voorhees was, or had been. Her roommates did not know. Her closest friend in the residence hall had clearly never heard the name *Voorhees.*

Someone had asked her with a quizzical smile, isn't *Voorhees* the name of a university building?

These were contemporaries who'd been born, like Naomi, in the late 1980s. They'd scarcely been in middle school when Gus Voorhees had died.

The fact is: none of this matters.

Gus has ceased to exist and Gus is not coming back.

Recklessly she was crossing an icy-slushy street. Headlights blurred as if underwater. Someone sounded a horn sharply—"Get out of the street, bitch!" She was very cold and could not remember where the hell she'd left her fleece-lined jacket with the zipper hood. And the beautiful leather gloves her grandmother Madelena had sent her—out of nowhere—at Christmas. *Thinking of you, Naomi. No need to get back to me but let's keep in touch.*

In front of her were concrete steps leading down— somewhere. She had a vague idea that this was the way to the arboretum—though it was dark, and snowing, and the arboretum was miles away.

They'd been happy there, in the arboretum! She could not recall but she knew because she'd been told.

Little Naomi carried in a backpack, on Daddy's strong back. Why could she not remember? She hated Darren, who'd stolen all her memories.

Not seeing where she placed her foot she slipped, fell heavily on icy stone steps, and lay stunned on freezing pavement six feet below. Her mouth was bleeding but she felt no pain. A wonderful numbness coursed through her. In the distance were festive voices, a sound of traffic. It was not late on State Street in Ann Arbor: the drinking places were open.

We'd been so happy there. Ann Arbor, when we were newlyweds.

Badly she wanted to be with them! Her young parents.

Wanted to remember that exquisite happiness, before she'd been born.

Alone

Next of kin? Whom to notify?

No wallet? No ID? No name?

In the early morning she was found by Ann Arbor sanitation workers, where she'd fallen down a flight of stone steps at Terrace Place which was a dead end of vacated buildings. Blood coagulated at her mouth and in a hard little trickle on her forehead. Snow covered her motionless body like a shroud.

She was not dead: though she was suffering from hypothermia there remained a heartbeat.

Medical workers found a pulse, detected a breath, checked her blood pressure and partly revived her, lifted her onto a stretcher and bore her by ambulance to the emergency room of the University Hospital where once as a young man decades ago Gus Voorhees had been a resident physician.

Her fingers and toes were stiff with cold. Her temperature was 95.2°F.

Mistaken for a homeless person, maybe. A mentally ill person, of about twenty, Caucasian and weighing approximately 108 pounds.

Had she been beaten? Robbed? Sexually assaulted?

Had she been drinking? Fell, and fractured her skull?

Despite the ringing in her head and her bruised mouth trying to explain: she was not a homeless person but a student at the university. She was not ill and not drunk but yes, she must have fallen on the icy steps the night before and struck her head.

Had she been with someone, who had harmed her? And left her lying in the street?

No! No one. She'd been alone.

Wearing no jacket or coat, in such cold weather? No gloves, nothing on her head?

Had she been fleeing someone? Trying to escape someone?

Had she ingested any drugs? Prescription medicine, controlled substance? Recreational drugs?

Her blood tested negative for alcohol or drugs, which

was not a surprise to her. But the bloodwork showed a mild anemia.

The emergency brain scan detected no fracture or concussion. No evident abnormalities.

She smiled to think—*There is no sign, then. Not a trace!*

An IV line was dripping liquid into a vein at the crook of her left arm. She had no memory of a needle being stuck into her. She'd been seriously dehydrated, she was told.

In the ER she lay exhausted in a cubicle, covered in layers of thin white woolen blankets. Her outer clothes had been removed. On her feet were cotton slippers. Curtains had been drawn around the bed, to assure privacy.

How safe it was here. In the University Hospital ER, each patient in a cubicle shrouded by white curtains, anonymous, muted. And no shoes: white cotton slippers.

If Jenna knew. If Jenna saw.

You see what has happened to your daughter. There are consequences.

In fact the consequences were muted: by midday she was speaking coherently. The ringing in her ears had abated. She was able to establish her identity as a bright and (to a degree) socially sophisticated undergraduate enrolled in the College of Arts and Sciences at U-M.

Carefully she spelled her last name—*V-o-o-r-h-e-e-s*. The young Asian woman intern who was taking down this information did not seem to think that *Voorhees* was anything out of the ordinary.

She insisted, she was ready to leave the ER. Whatever had happened to her would not happen again, she was sure.

"There has been a death in the family. I was upset but I am feeling much better now."

I died, but *I was revived.*

So longing to stay in that place, where we'd been happy.

Aftershock

A day, a night. More than twenty-four hours since the execution.

In Ann Arbor no one whom she encountered seemed to know about it. No one to whom she spoke. No one who spoke to her. The name *Luther Dunphy* was not once uttered.

Wasn't news of the execution in the newspaper? On TV, online?

Didn't everyone *know*?

She could not sleep. She did not attend classes. She avoided her friends. She avoided strangers. She could not have explained. No one knew, she'd confided in no one. It was the aftershock of the execution.

She vowed that she would not call her brother again.

But then, she called Darren's number in Washington State.

Darren did not answer.

She had many times vowed that she would not call her mother. But then, she called her mother's number in Bennington, Vermont.

Jenna did not answer.

She was feeling just slightly disappointed. There was joy and relief and gratitude to celebrate—Luther Dunphy was dead at last.

The curvy cut on her forehead resembled an exposed vein, that quivered with life. The cut on the left side of her mouth had turned purple.

When she was asked what had happened to her she said she'd had a small accident, slipping on icy steps.

She went away exulting in secret. The long wait was over!

"My life can now begin."

"Something fantastic happened in my life the other day."

So she announced. But when the query came to her rapid as the return of a Ping-Pong serve *Really? What?*—she could not speak.

That reckless feeling. Giddy-happy.

Drunk, stoned. "High."

But, well—just slightly down.

Had not the new life begun? She was sure the new life had begun.

But where?

Fuck she could not sleep. Missing fucking classes. No wonder Jenna was fed up with her as Gus would be fed up with her (if Gus could but know) beginning a semester with such hope, such energy, such promise, such enthusiasm, high grades—then the inevitable downslide, wreck. It did not give her much solace to note that among her peers at the university this pattern emerged in numerous others—the bright, fresh start of the term, the slow car wreck that followed. Except a daughter of Gus Voorhees understood that she was special, she was specially fated, doomed. She found herself online typing the name *Luther Dunphy* and the word *execution*.

ANTI-ABORTION SHOOTER DUNPHY EXECUTED IN CHILLICOTHE, OHIO

LETHAL INJECTION FOLLOWS YEARS OF POSTPONEMENTS

RIGHT-TO-LIFE MOVEMENT ISSUES STATEMENT "LUTHER DUNPHY DID NOT DIE IN VAIN"

It had happened, then! The death of Luther Dunphy.

Quickly skimming the screen. Forgetting what she read in the very instant of reading it.

Unavoidably linked with *Luther Dunphy—Augustus Voorhees*. A headline of November 1999 she'd was sure she'd never seen before.

OHIO ABORTION DOCTOR VOORHEES, EX-MARINE KILLED IN SHOTGUN ASSAULT

SELF-PROFESSED "SOLDIER OF GOD" DUNPHY SURRENDERS TO POLICE

In the aftershock of the death forced to realize that nothing had changed in her life after all.

Her father was still dead. Luther Dunphy had still killed him. The two names were linked together inextricably and one of these names was her own.

Another time she called her mother in Bennington, Vermont.

Naomi imagined a phone ringing in an empty room.

Was it March, yet? Still winter.

Still white, and still very cold.

She imagined a vast wilderness of white in Bennington, Vermont.

When she was about to give up a woman answered the phone—a woman's voice. But it was not Jenna Matheson's voice.

"May I speak with Jenna?—this is her daughter."

"Her daughter!"—the voice registered a quiet sort of shock.

But then, the voice went away without further inquiry. *Which daughter?* might have been expected.

She had no idea if she had called Jenna's residence, or Jenna's office. Or maybe they were one and the same. She realized that she knew virtually nothing of her mother's life now. So far as she knew, Darren knew nothing.

Such resentment she'd felt for years, that their mother had abandoned them! Almost she'd wished that Jenna had died with Gus. In that way her children could have continued to love her as they loved their father.

Hang up. What do you care for her.

This is your new life now. She is your old life.

But then, her mother was on the phone. "Yes? Hello?"

Jenna sounded uncertain, hesitant. Naomi had been prepared to hate her mother but at the sound of her voice she felt a wave of emotion that left her weak.

"Hello. It's m-me."

"Is it—Naomi?"

"Yes. Naomi."

There was a moment's stunned silence. How long had it been since they'd spoken together? Months, a year?

Naomi tried to speak evenly, without stammering.

"Well. I guess you know why I'm calling, Mom—he's dead."

How awkward, the word *Mom*! It had come naturally, without Naomi's volition.

So long, she had not uttered *Mom*.

Jenna was saying yes—"I know."

Then again, there was an awkward silence.

Was Jenna going to say nothing more? Would Naomi have to speak for both of them?

Recalling the hateful words—*I can't be your "Mommy" any longer.*

Naomi tried to speak. In the bright clear way in which she spoke in her classes, to make a strong impression upon her instructors. Saying, the execution had been postponed so many times, it had sometimes seemed that it might never happen. In some states condemned men remained on Death Row for years . . .

Jenna murmured *yes*. Naomi imagined a look of fastidious distaste in her mother's face.

Naomi asked if anyone from Chillicothe had contacted Jenna about observing the execution?—and again Jenna murmured *yes.*

"And you said—no."

"That's right. I said no."

There was a shudder in Jenna's voice, and something else—mirthless laughter?

"Of course—I said *no.*"

Daringly Naomi said, "I shocked Darren, I think—I told him that I could have witnessed the execution, if I'd been invited. I think he thought I'm barbaric."

"Well. You weren't serious, maybe."

"Maybe."

There'd been a ripple of excitement between them. In Naomi, a ticklish sensation as if her mother had reached out to lightly touch her, as a mother might.

And now she thought—*If she makes some damn priggish statement about opposing capital punishment, her and Gus both, I will hang up.*

In fact, she was fearful of Jenna suddenly hanging up. She had so much to say to her mother!

She said she'd been speaking with Darren at the time of the execution forty-eight hours ago. Their father's old friend Elliot Roberts—"D'you remember him, Mom? From Detroit? Used to write for the *Detroit News?*"—was covering the execution for the AP and he'd volunteered to call Darren from Chillicothe as soon as it was over.

"Because Elliot knew we would want to know. As soon as it was over. Before the news was released . . ."

How eager Naomi was sounding, like a child running to bring good news to a parent who scarcely cares to hear it. She wondered if it had always been like this between them—she'd rushed to bring to her coolly distant, beautiful and elusive mother some shred of information that might bolster her standing with her mother in the humblest of ways.

But why did it matter so much? Naomi wondered. Just the other evening it had seemed, to her and to Darren, crucial that they know as soon as possible if and when Luther Dunphy had died; now, it did not seem like precious knowledge at all but something sordid, sad.

Jenna said, as if she'd just thought of it, "Darren called me too. Darren left a message."

"I thought he might! How did he sound?"

"How did he *sound*?" Jenna considered this.

"I mean—what did he say?"

"He just left a message about Dunphy. That was the way I'd learned that Dunphy had died. That the execution had actually taken place, after so many delays."

"How did you—how did you feel, then?"

"How did I *feel?* Like—nothing."

Jenna spoke with infinite sadness. She did not sound relieved. She did not sound celebratory. She did not sound angry nor did she sound disappointed.

"You didn't speak with Darren, then?"

"No. I didn't speak with Darren."

You mean, you didn't call him back.

"D'you know where Darren is living now? In a place called Newhalem, Washington?"

"I think so, yes. I mean, he told me."

Naomi felt a small mean stab of satisfaction. Darren was no closer to Jenna than she was.

"We've been waiting—so long. And he has been alive so long—I mean, he had been—Luther Dunphy. And now . . ."

Naomi's voice trailed off into an awkward silence. She wasn't sure in which direction these words were leading her.

Haltingly she said, "I guess there's a kind of— 'aftershock.' Like, after an earthquake . . ."

Why was she saying such things? She was fearful that Jenna would hang up the phone. She was fearful that, if Jenna hung up, she would hate Jenna with such passion, it would make her ill.

"I've been feeling kind of—excited, I guess. As soon as—it happened."

She listened closely. Had Jenna replied? A very gentle murmur—*yes. Yes?*

She wondered if someone else was in the room with Jenna. She could not bear it, that Jenna might be glancing at another person, a stranger, even as she, Naomi, the daughter, was speaking so passionately to Jenna.

"I'd been sick for years waiting for that son of a bitch to die—and he *would not die.* I'd been feeling so anxious and so exhausted but as soon as Darren told me the news I've been feeling so *alive.* It's as if this fierce blinding light has flowed into me—it's so powerful, it's almost visible at my fingertips—a kind of phosphorescence, like undersea life."

What was she saying? She stared at her fingertips and indeed it almost seemed to her, she saw there a shimmering *life.*

Now that she'd begun, she could not stop. Remembering that as she'd groped with her foot onto the icy step, and missed the step, and fell, and struck her head, this conviction had swept through her; or maybe the conviction had preceded the fall, and had caused it.

"Usually it's hidden within us—this *life.* We are so frightened of it, and ashamed of it, and people like us who are 'secular'—we don't have the vocabulary to speak of it. But this morning I woke up filled with this happiness and this conviction that it is *life* that courses through us and binds us to one another. It was after the execution I realized this—I slipped and fell on an icy step, and hit my head—I wasn't found until the morning—"

"Naomi, what? What are you saying?"

"I had to get outside—to get fresh air. I had a kind of attack of something like happiness—I was out in the street and running—I slipped, and fell, and hit my head—and was taken to an emergency room . . ." She wondered if she should tell Jenna that it was the University Hospital ER. Jenna would think at once of Gus as a young physician.

"Are you all right, Naomi? Were you unconscious?" For the first time Jenna was sounding concerned.

"It was a minor accident. I wasn't really injured. None of this is why I'm calling you. I am calling to tell you that I feel so certain now—so sure about myself. And about life. Our lives."

"What do you mean, Naomi? I don't understand."

"It came to me—a conviction. But it's almost impossible to explain. That Daddy is dead—and Luther Dunphy is dead—but you are my *mother*—I am your *daughter*—and we are alive. This is a great revelation to me after years of blindness and self-absorption. It's a revelation like a boulder rolled away from the mouth of a cave."

Naomi was speaking rapidly now. She could not have stopped if she had wished to stop.

"There has been this silence between us—it's been so painful. When Daddy died we were wrong to accuse you—Darren and me—it was as if we'd thought you had driven Daddy away, to live in another place, and to leave us, and it was in that other place that Daddy was murdered, and it would not have happened as it had happened *because of you*. We were so angry, and bitter. We were—we felt—we hated you so . . . But now, Luther Dunphy's death has changed everything."

She could not believe she'd said what she'd said—*we hated you so.* The words had sprung from her like toads out of a gaping mouth. And now, they could not be recalled.

At the other end of the line there was silence.

"Mom? Are you still there? Hello?"

A near-inaudible murmur. Might've been *yes.*

Repentant, agitated Naomi heard herself say: "I'm sorry. *You* left *us.* Not once but many times—*all the time*—you left us. And then you left us for good, in Birmingham with Daddy's parents. But I'm not calling to accuse you, Mom—Jenna. Really it's the reverse—I am calling to *not accuse you.* I just wanted to say—I wanted to explain—it came to me like a vision—that we are alive . . . We are both alive even if Daddy is dead, and now Luther Dunphy is dead." Naomi spoke excitedly, her teeth were chattering with sudden cold.

She was crying. It came upon her like a seizure, harsh helpless crying like grief.

"I missed you—in the ER. When they brought me in. They thought that I was *dying*, they said I was *dehydrated, anemic* . . . Why didn't you come to see me there . . ."

Crying so hard, she could no longer speak.

Jenna begged her to stop crying—"You will make yourself sick, Naomi."

But Naomi couldn't stop crying. She could not understand why she was crying when she was not unhappy; when in fact, she was very happy.

The happiest she'd been in years.

Still, she was crying. Hoarse wracking sobs. And Jenna was saying she would have to hang up, if Naomi didn't stop.

"Then hang up! Hang up the fucking phone! You know that's what you want to do anyway! *Hang up!*"— Naomi screamed.

Slammed the receiver down, hard enough so that it clattered onto the floor where she gave it a little kick.

Hatefuge

Hate hate hate hate hate hate hate hate hate hate
hate hate hate hate hate hate hate hate hate hate
hate hate hate hate hate hate hate hate hate hate
hate hate hate hate hate hate hate hate hate hate
hate hate hate hate hate hate

until it is burnt away, until it has lost its meaning,
until you are transformed, until you are not even
you but another

"Emptiness":
January 2007

There is an emptiness you can't see—where the twin towers were. Unfortunately, I can see it."

What a view! Naomi had not ever before stared from a window at such a height in a private residence, a floor-to-ceiling plate-glass window, looking miles into the distance, to the very end of the island.

Clouds in the sky horizontal, shredded and thinning. A crescent sun like a bloodied egg poised to sink into the horizon.

Standing so close to the window she felt a wave of vertigo. She could feel cold emanate from the glass. She was on the thirty-first floor of her grandmother's apartment in the West Village, New York City. Her gaze swung downward to the street below—(what was its name? West Houston?)—then up again swiftly to flat rectangular rooftops seen from above, water towers, church spires, high-rise buildings columnar and dazzling in the late afternoon sun that stretched for miles, to lower Manhattan and beyond.

She was nineteen years old. That was an accomplishment—just still *being*.

It was a hiatus in her life. Still in the aftershock of her father's murderer's death. Still stunned by her fury that had the power of black bile to boil up into her mouth, leak out of the corners of the mask-mouth at unpredictable times.

And then, mid-winter of what would have been her third year at the university she'd been invited to stay with her grandmother Madelena Kein whom she scarcely knew, for a week or more, in Madelena's apartment in the West Village, New York City.

Out of nowhere, the mysterious and elusive Madelena had contacted her—*If you would like to speak of your father, dear Naomi. If you are still interested.*

Of course Naomi was interested! She was consumed with curiosity but also with dread of what her father's mother might tell her.

Within the Voorhees family Madelena Kein was a remote and glamorously forbidding figure. She had left her husband Clement when their only child was young and had lived for decades in New York City. She'd been a graduate student in philosophy, and then a professor of philosophy and linguistics; she had written many essays, reviews, and books, esoteric and demanding and difficult of access for a general reader. She had not remarried but was known to have had a succession of lovers. She was known to be sharp-tongued, sardonic. She did not soften her words. Her wit could be slashing. It was rare for her to return to the Midwest to visit, and rarer still for her to invite anyone among the relatives to visit her.

But Madelena Kein was capable of sudden—unexpected—acts of generosity. Over the years, somewhat randomly, she'd sent gifts to her grandchildren for Christmas, birthdays. She'd endowed a residency at the University of Michigan Medical School, named for Augustus Voorhees. In recent years she'd become more attentive to Naomi in particular as if, nearing the end of her own life, she'd taken a renewed interest in the lives of others.

Or it may have been, the loss of her only son had profoundly shaken her.

There were no photographs of Gus in the apartment, that Naomi had noticed. Of course, she had seen only a few rooms so far; she had not seen Madelena's bedroom.

The room in which Naomi was to stay, one of several bedrooms in the apartment, was not a large room but appeared large and airy, with three white walls and one wall that was a plate-glass window looking out, it seemed at first glance, into blank bright air.

The view outside the window—stretching to the horizon, lifting to the sky, plunging below into the street—was mesmerizing to Naomi. She could stare, and stare. She could lose herself in staring. Her brain that often felt wounded, as if with tiny bits of glass, felt peaceful here, after only a few minutes of such solitude.

A consoling thought came to her—*I am closer to him here. My father.*

Something about the height. The sudden distance her vision was thrown, that was so usually blocked within a few yards. In most urban settings you can see only a short distance and soon you come to forget that your vision is unnaturally foreshortened.

But at this height there was nothing to impede vision. The sensation was, you could see past all earthly things.

That was foolish of course. That was "primitive thinking." She'd been trained not to think in such a way. Her mother would be shocked. Her father would have laughed.

That is why my grandmother has invited me here. To be closer to my father.

On the eggshell-white walls of the small guest bed-room were works of art, framed drawings, woodcuts, paintings in Fauve colors. These were contemporary artists of whom Naomi had possibly heard—Moser, Daub, Kahn. There were bookcases crammed with books including outsized art books with slightly torn covers suggesting how closely they'd been read, stud-ied. Naomi pulled one out—*The Complete Little Nemo.* A massive book of color plates of the classic surreal-ist comic strip of the early twentieth century—Naomi seemed to recall, Madelena had sent an identical copy to Darren for one of his birthdays.

Was it after receiving *Little Nemo* that Darren had become so interested in drawing comics? Or had Mad-elena known of his interest, and had carefully selected the book?

Naomi remembered: for her thirteenth birthday, no card or explanation included, her grandmother had sent her a hardbound copy of Homer's *Odyssey*; for Melissa, barely able to read at the time, an illustrated copy of Lewis Carroll's *Alice's Adventures in Wonderland* and *Through the Looking-Glass* in an edition identical to the one Naomi had cherished as a child—Naomi hadn't known, or had forgotten, that this favorite book of her childhood must have been a gift from Madelena Kein!

Naomi had grown up knowing very little about her

father's mother. Wryly Jenna had spoken of Madelena as her "phantom mother-in-law." In the Voorhees household among countless books, magazines, journals and newspapers stacked on tables, chairs, sofas, floors and stairs there'd been books by Madelena Kein with such titles as *An Inquiry into (Human) Consciousness* (Oxford University Press), *Do We Mean What We Say; or, Do We Say What We Mean?* (Columbia University Press), *Transformational Ethics: A History* (University of Chicago Press). It wasn't clear whether Gus had read these books though he had certainly hoped to read them. Darren and Naomi had tried, without much success. At the University of Michigan graduate library Naomi had made an effort to seek out articles and essays by Madelena Kein in publications not otherwise available—*Philosophical Studies, Philosophical Review, Harvard Review of Philosophy, Journal of Psychology and Linguistics, Ethics, Meme*; she'd had slightly more success reading reviews by Madelena in popular publications like the *New York Review of Books* and the *Times Literary Supplement*.

But what did she know of her grandmother, having read, or having tried to read, these works of Madelena Kein? The pieces were densely argued, opaque with obscure phrases, enigmatic, riddle-like, possibly brilliant, resistant of paraphrase. Was this what philosophy had become? Confounding questions and paradoxes, and no *answers*?

Naomi lay her suitcase on a cedar chest at the foot of the bed. She would stay *here*? In this perfect place? She felt a twinge of excitement and yet uneasiness, apprehension.

A tinge of homesickness like a faint blue shadow falling over her face.

How absurd! Homesickness for—what? Where? She had not had a permanent home for years. She had never felt comfortable in her grandparents' house in Birmingham, Michigan, a girl's room in rosy wallpaper, a girl's bed with a pink satin coverlet, white lattice windows. Her memory of the last house in which she'd lived with her family, before her father had departed, was the rented, fly-infested house on Salt Hill Road in Huron County, Michigan. She had hated that house as much as her poor trapped mother had hated it.

I can live here, with my grandmother—can I?

Is that what she is offering me? A life with her?

In the aftershock of the murderer's death she had not been "freed" after all—not as she'd expected.

She'd been ill for some time. A mud-malaise of the spirit.

She'd returned to the archive—now grandly and bravely retitled *Life/Death/Life of Augustus Voorhees, MD.*

Or maybe less formally—*Life/Death/Life of Gus Voorhees.*

Life/Death/Life of My Father Gus Voorhees.

Life/Death/Life of My Dad Gus Voorhees.

She'd considered (not seriously: desperately) marrying a young biology post-doc at the U-M medical school from Ceylon whose mother was an American epidemiologist and whose father was a Ceylonese pharmaceutical executive—their feeling for each other had been intense, but short-lived.

She'd considered dropping out of college. Or, deferring college.

She'd considered transferring to Bennington. (Was this even possible? Bennington College was a private college, reputedly very expensive. The University of Michigan was a state university, with tuition and costs kept reasonably low for residents of the state.)

She'd considered—well, it was not serious enough, it was not *minutely imagined enough*, to merit the word "consider"—killing herself, from time to time.

(Except: her father would have been devastated if he knew. Worse than devastated, disapproving. *What's my little worrywart done to herself? Sweetie, no!* And so, suicide was out of the question.)

She'd returned again to the archive . . . She'd amassed so much material, she could not give up; yet, so much material amassed, she could not bring herself to assess it, even to catalogue it. At the same time she knew that more was needed for a fuller portrait of Gus Voorhees. Much more.

Out of nowhere, then: the invitation to visit Madelena Kein.

Please understand: I will not be "interviewed." I will speak to you—you will not question me.

There are some things I wish to tell you (that were not secrets from Gus, he knew of them). These are spare, sparse truths—but crucial.

Your visit with me will be more than just this subject, I hope!

It had been seven years—more than seven years—since Naomi had seen Madelena, at her father's funeral. At the time she'd had only a confused glimpse of the woman, stylish black clothes, silver hair obscured by a black hat with a curving brim, skin very white, stern and dry-eyed amid the gathering of mourners of whom many were vocal and emotional.

Naomi recalled the surprise, disapproval—that, soon after the funeral, Madelena had left Ann Arbor. She'd made no arrangements to stay overnight. She'd declined invitations to stay with Jenna or with Gus's friends. She'd been coolly courteous with her ex-husband Clement—of course she'd declined his and Adele's invitation to stay with them for a few days in Birmingham, an hour's drive from Ann Arbor.

She'd spent some time with Jenna. Not in public but in private.

What had they talked about? Naomi wondered.

Jenna would have been very reticent. Confronted with stronger personalities like Madelena, more willful and dominant individuals like her husband, Jenna often lapsed into silence.

Naomi couldn't recall Madelena speaking with her, Darren, or Melissa at the funeral or at the reception afterward. Probably she'd avoided the children of the deceased stunned and stricken like young zombies.

For what is there to say to children whose father has been murdered? Even if they are your grandchildren? Other adults had tried, clumsily. But not Madelena Kein.

But Naomi's grandmother had not ceased to be aware of Naomi altogether.

At Kennedy Airport Naomi had been greeted at the

baggage claim by a uniformed limousine driver bearing a white cardboard sign—NAOMI VOORHEES. Madelena had insisted upon hiring a car for her, as she'd insisted upon paying for Naomi's airline tickets.

Naomi was touched. She was made to feel privileged, cherished. She had never seen her name so conspicuously displayed.

In Ann Arbor she was highly conscious of her name. It seemed to her a beautiful name, and a significant name—*Voorhees*, at least. But there was relief to assume that, in New York City, the name would mean nothing.

It was winter break at the university. She'd told no one where she was going. She had not told her Voorhees grandparents in Birmingham knowing that they would disapprove, or feel hurt, subtly insulted—thinking that after they'd been so generous with Naomi, as with their other grandchildren, had done so much for her, her allegiance should be to them, and not with the selfish "career" woman who'd scorned the role of grandparent.

Her Matheson grandparents, in Evanston, Illinois, were not much in her life any longer. She wondered how often they saw Jenna, or rather how often Jenna chose to see them.

Of course she had not told Jenna. Since the disastrous telephone call of the previous March the two had not spoken.

And she had not told Darren. She was trying to telephone her brother less frequently. Her emails to him were very belatedly answered, if answered at all. She had to accept—*He is moving away from me. I remind him of what he wants to forget, and who can blame him.*

In a state of intense anticipation she'd stared from the rear, tinted windows of the car hired to bring her into the city. She had not been to New York City more than a few times, with her parents—not for a long time. The drive was slow and halting and her view was truncated by lanes of traffic, heavy-duty construction equipment making a deafening racket, elevated railroads, girders. Billboards, fleeting patches of sky. Highway ramps, bridge ramps. More elevated railroads, girders. More traffic, slow and halting. Her head began to ache with the strain of anticipation. She had packed only a few things but she had not forgotten her camcorder. She was wearing her heaviest winter jacket and layers of clothes beneath. It was January, that cheerless month. In Michigan, snow had accumulated in dunes like slag.

In New York there was much less snow. From the rear of the hired car she saw patches of dirty white like soiled Styrofoam.

She tormented herself with a fantasy of arriving at the address on Bleecker Street her grandmother had provided her and finding—nothing.

A barren lot, an abandoned building in a derelict urban setting. And slow-falling snow to obscure her tracks.

It was a malevolent fairy tale. She did not want to think of her life as a malevolent fairy tale.

And then, the car was moving swiftly onto a ramp—across the Williamsburg Bridge—was this the East River below? High-rise buildings loomed above the choppy water. The sky was mottled with cloud, a deep bruised sky of myriad layers as in a painting of El Greco that had been one of her father's favorites—*A View of Toledo.*

Her heart lifted, she began to feel hope.

The driver continued to Houston Street. Her grandmother's apartment building was located near the intersection of West Houston and West Broadway, near Washington Square Park.

At LaGuardia Place were three high-rise buildings, with vertical panels of glass. There were nothing like these in Ann Arbor.

She gave her grandmother's name, and her own name, to a doorman. Again the fleeting thought came to her—*It is a mistake. I am not expected.*

Ascending then to the thirty-first floor in an elevator.

And there, waiting by the elevator, her beautiful silver-haired straight-backed grandmother Madelena Kein—the woman who'd made it clear years ago that she had no interest in being *someone's gram-muddy.*

"Naomi! Welcome."

There was an embrace—slightly stiff, awkward, but eager—for which Naomi wasn't prepared. The older woman's arms were thin but strong.

Madelena was just slightly shorter than Naomi. Her striking silver hair was plaited around her head like a crown. She was dressed in rippling black pleats, trousers with flaring cuffs. The skin of her perfect-petal face was unlined and smooth as the skin of a woman decades younger.

Her eyes were veiled by large tinted glasses with chic black frames. In these glasses Naomi's pale girl's face hovered uncertainly.

"Let me take that, dear."

Before Naomi could protest Madelena took her suitcase from her fingers and bore it to the opened door at the end of the corridor. As if, so much younger than Madelena, Naomi were not capable of carrying the suitcase herself. How embarrassing!

"And how was your flight?—and how are *you?*"

"Fine. I am—fine."

"And is that how you are *really?*"—Madelena was smiling at Naomi with a kind of warm, teasing affection as if they were old acquaintances, or accomplices.

Was this her father's mother, who had to be in her mid-seventies at least? It did not seem possible. Naomi was feeling dazzled by the vigorous straight-backed woman who'd snatched the suitcase from her fingers with the impetuousness of one whose will is rarely challenged.

She remembered her father ruefully joking that in time his youthful and energetic mother would be mistaken for his sister—"A slightly older, bossy sister."

Madelena was saying that she hated plane travel. Hated putting herself in the trust of strangers. "Traveling is so *passive*. It's a toss of the dice whether we survive the simplest flight. I've been checking your flight out of the Detroit airport, it was unsettling to be told that the plane was delayed while the wings were being *de-iced.*"

Naomi was surprised and touched that Madelena had cared so much. She could think to say, haltingly, "Yes. It was very cold and icy there . . ." She was smiling foolishly.

Inside the apartment Madelena insisted that Naomi drink a glass of water—"You're dehydrated from traveling. It can't be avoided. If you aren't careful you will get a very bad headache. And tomorrow is your first full day in New York City—you must not be indisposed."

"Thank you." Naomi drank from the crystal-cut glass she was handed, dutifully. It was so, her head had been aching since before the plane had landed.

Madelena led her into a large, light-filled living room—floor-to-ceiling windows overlooking a remarkable vista of rooftops, spires, streets, small patches of snowy parkland. "That's the Hudson River—that blue haze at the horizon. And over there, just visible from this window, the arch at Washington Square Park." Naomi stared but did not see—wasn't sure what she was seeing.

"It's so beautiful . . ."

"From a height, yes. 'Distance enhances.'"

On the walls of the living room were large canvases that looked waterstained. Pale-pastel abstract paintings in (seeming) mimicry of the sky. Elegant contemporary furnishings, a rough-textured eggshell-colored rug on a polished hardwood floor. On a table, an antique stringed instrument. Sculpted figures, white marble heads. The living room opened into a dining room in which there was a long mahogany table, large enough to seat ten or twelve people; at the farther end were just two place mats set across from each other, with neatly folded colorful cloth napkins.

Naomi was naively touched. Thinking that her grandmother had set the table in readiness for her.

She recalled that, long ago when she'd been a young child, her parents had often had friends for dinner, friends and their children, informally, crowded around a table half the size of this table and with nothing of its formal elegance. These dinners had been boisterous, fun. It was true as people said—Gus Voorhees made you laugh. You would not have guessed how intense and often anxious the man was, for he delighted in making others laugh. The adults had drunk wine, beer—they'd quarreled about politics—they'd traded stories about their jobs, their bosses—they'd told jokes. Gus had not been reticent. But he had not dominated—usually.

Eventually at these protracted dinners the children had drifted away to watch TV or, if they were younger, to be put to bed by their mothers. She could not recall if she'd been one of these young children, or if she'd always been older, and spared the humiliation of being *put to bed.*

She wiped at her eyes. She had not thought of these dinners in some time. In Detroit, in Grand Rapids—of course, in Ann Arbor—but there had been few boisterous dinners in the rented house on Salt Hill Road, in rural Huron County, where (she saw now) things had begun to deteriorate in the life of their family.

On Madelena's dining room table was an elaborately designed wrought iron candelabra bearing a half-dozen slender candles, each of a different height, and color; each candleholder was lavishly encrusted with wax, like something sculpted. Naomi remembered that her parents had had a similar candelabra, slightly smaller, very striking, but impractical; it was usually kept on a sideboard, unused. She wondered now if it had been a gift, an impractical gift, from Madelena Kein.

"It's from Mexico. The candelabra. Does it look familiar?"—Madelena regarded her with bemused eyes.

Naomi wondered where her parents' candelabra was now. What had Jenna done with the household furnishings? Put them in storage, sold or gave them away . . .

"And how has your mother been, Naomi?"

"I think—my mother has been well . . ."

"Jenna isn't in Ann Arbor any longer, I've heard?"

"Yes. I mean—no. She's in Bennington, Vermont."

How halting, Naomi's speech. And why did she think it was necessary to add "Vermont"—as if Madelena would not know where Bennington was.

"She's grieving, Naomi. It doesn't end."

Was Madelena defending Jenna? But why would Madelena suppose that Jenna needed to be defended, to her daughter?

"Are you in touch with her—with Mom?"

"In a way. No and yes. Not obviously."

Naomi would consider this elusive remark, at length.

Madelena told Naomi that she'd planned several outings for them during Naomi's visit—to the Metropolitan Opera, to the Metropolitan Museum of Art, to the Neue Galerie, to Lincoln Center for the New York City Ballet—but she would be away from the apartment for much of the day most days, at the university; she would be away some evenings as well—"You'll be on your own. As much as you wish. Or, if things work out, you can accompany me."

If things work out. What did that mean?

"Life is not inevitably more complicated in New York City than in the Midwest but for those who thrive on complications, this is our city."

Madelena led Naomi along a narrow corridor into a sparely furnished white-walled room flooded with waning afternoon light.

On a sleek white plastic desk in this room Madelena had laid several pages of the *New York Times* listing museum exhibits, concerts, plays, films, lectures and poetry readings for the upcoming week. Beside some of the listings, a red check.

"Feel free to add anything of your own that you'd like to see, and if we have time, we will. This is a 'holiday' for me, too."

The closet door was ajar as if to suggest that Naomi should open it farther, and hang her things inside. At the foot of the bed was a small cedar chest.

"There's a bathroom just across the hall, for you."

"Thank you . . ."

Naomi didn't know how to address her grandmother. "Madelena" did not sound right, but "grandmother" was out of the question.

As if reading her mind Madelena said, "Please just call me 'Lena.' I realize it's awkward, but you will get used to it."

"'Lena.'"

"With more emphasis, dear! '*Le-na.*'"

"'*Le-na.*'"

Madelena laughed happily, and touched Naomi's arm. For a moment Naomi thought her grandmother might embrace her again, swiftly and tightly, but that did not happen.

Next, Naomi was asked by Madelena if she had any questions—she could not think of a single question!—

except questions she dared not ask of the straight-backed silver-haired woman whose eyes were obscured by tinted glasses. *Why am I here, why did you invite me, do you care for me, is it expected that I will care for you?*

When she was alone she lay her suitcase on the cedar chest and began to unpack, slowly. Her gaze was drawn to the floor-to-ceiling window of the outer wall, that opened out into pure shimmering light. She was feeling weak with excitement, and had to sit on the edge of the bed.

The coverlet was made of a stiff white puckered fabric, with rough-textured pillows in bright colors and designs that might have been Native American, Mexican. She smiled happily. She was a child who has crawled through a looking-glass and come into an amazing world—like Alice, her old, lost heroine.

When your father died *I came here to live. I could not breathe in the low place I'd been living, a brownstone in Washington Square Mews.*

For a long time then I slept mostly in this room—though it's meant to be obviously a child's room. I fell asleep to the view outside this window, at night. I woke to this view in the morning. It was months before I got around to unpacking. I hardly went into the other rooms . . . During the day I was a professor at the University.

I have always been hypnotized by my work and essentially my life is this "hypnosis." It has not been a personal life, much.

At the Institute it was suggested that I take a semester's sabbatical but I refused. I took on new responsibilities—a new graduate seminar in the philosophy of linguistics, a new course with a colleague in art history titled "The Art of Estrangement." A university committee on minority hiring, a selection committee for post-docs at the Institute for Independent Study.

I could not bear a protracted time during which I would mourn my son for there was no thought of Gus that was not an infinity into which I could fall, and fall.

I am not by nature a mourner. That is not my personality. What it was that happened to me, I have never understood. But it was in this room and not the other rooms of the apartment that it happened.

Though I was very tired at this time I was also tireless.

You may find yourself in this state someday. I think it is a woman's state of being. Your mother would know.

And then, it was September 2001—the morning of September eleventh.

This window faces south—downtown. Of all the windows in the apartment it is this window, ironically, in this small room, that gives the most direct view of what would be called Ground Zero. I happened to be in this room on the morning of September eleventh. I don't think that I had slept here the night before but sometime in the early morning, at dawn, when I was awake and couldn't get back to sleep, I came into this room, which has such an extraordinary view of the avenues and streets and their lights and the taxis—on West Houston, the taxis cruise at all hours. To watch the sky change its colors—the clouds change—that is very comforting. And then, later, as I was about to leave to go to the University, there was—suddenly—a few miles away—in the area of the World Trade Center—a patch of something fiery-red.

Was it a fire? An explosion? Out of nowhere it had seemed to come. I had just glanced out the window and now, I could not look away.

One of the tall towers of the World Trade Center tower was on fire, billowing smoke—it was instantly recognizable though miles away.

Almost sometimes, years later I can see the fire there, in that emptiness—the terrible smoke, like boiling black air. And then, as I was watching, the second plane struck . . .

I would not look away for a long time.

At the time there was only astonishment. This is what I recall—there were no words for what had happened, or was happening, only just astonishment. It was like trying to wake from a dream—I could not comprehend what I was seeing—for it had no end, it was continuous, it would not end for hours, for days.

And the churning air that came up from the explosions, that looked like a cyclone or whirlwind of something like gravel, and smelled so terrible—for a long time. The spell was over all of us . . .

So it happened that your father's death was somehow part of this. Gus had died approximately one year ten months before the terrorist attack and in all that time I had been grieving for him—in silence mostly. But on that morning there came the catastrophe out of the sky killing thousands of men and women and within a few hours, or a day—a day and a night—my son's terrible death seemed to fall into place like a waterfall emptying into water . . . My sorrow for Gus came to an end lost in the sorrow of others.

When so many die, a single death is one of these deaths. It is not singular.

Is that a good thing? Or is that terrible, unspeakable?

What "terrorism" means—the end of grief.

The wound is just too great. One limb you might mourn, but all of your limbs torn from you—it is just too much.

That's the emptiness there, at Ground Zero, Naomi— that you can't see.

Unfortunately, I can see it.

Each day, the promise that Madelena would reveal something crucial to Naomi about her father.

Each day, the anxious anticipation. Then disappointment, or relief.

She knew: she must not ask. Madelena had warned her months ago in that email. She must not offend Madelena Kein by seeming impatient.

I will speak to you—you will not question me.

There are some things I wish to tell you . . .

She'd been shocked by her grandmother's remark, that her sorrow for Gus had come to an end.

That was not possible, was it?—*an end.*

Two months before in November of the previous year she'd received via parcel post a badly battered, much-duct-taped box addressed to *Naomi Voorhees.* The box was from a former colleague of her father's with whom he'd worked at a women's clinic in Grand Rapids in the 1990s.

Inside was a hand-scrawled note: *Naomi?—remember me? Whit Smith.*

Retiring this month & clearing out my office & files & surprised I had so much of Gus's things here. I did not want to just toss it out, not even sure what there is here & if valuable to you or not.

Tried to contact Jenna a few times but no luck. "No forwarding address"—hope your mom is OK.

Heard about L.D. execution. Still can't think about losing Gus without feeling just sick to heart & not feeling so optimistic about the political future frankly in this recession & the right wing campaigning against everything we've put in place like Sherman marching to the sea.

Hope you & your brother (Darin?) & sister are OK also. Say hi to your mom for me, will you. Can't believe it has been seven years since I've seen you all.

Naomi had unpacked the box with trembling fingers. A smell of mold lifted to her nostrils. Inside were letters both professional and personal, addressed to Gus Voorhees; documents of all kinds—medical, legal, financial, IRS; printouts, clippings, pocket-sized appointment books, desk calendars, wall calendars . . . An eight-by-twelve frayed manila envelope containing greeting cards—*Dear Dr. Voorhees, Thank you for saving my life.*

Dear Doctor Voorhees, Thank you. Thank you. God bless you.

Dear Doctor Voorhees, Thank you from the bottom of my heart for all you did for me in my hour of need both before & after. I will never forget you Doctor. I will pray for you all the days of my life. You gave my life back to me. God bless you & keep you.

Inside one of the cards, with a multifoliate rose cover, was a snapshot of an attractive woman with shoulder-length curly hair, smiling earnestly into the camera. *Dear Dr. Voorhees THANK YOU!*

Your friend Irene.

Were these women who'd had abortions at the Grand Rapids clinic? Naomi supposed so, until she discovered a card embossed with gilt letters *THANK YOU!* and inside a snapshot of a smiling young woman with an infant in her arms. *Thank you Dr. Voorhees for our beautiful blessed little girl we are naming Augusta. Dwight & I will hope to drop by & see you SOON.*

Here and there in the box were other snapshots of babies. Some had names and dates on the reverse, others were unmarked, anonymous.

And then there were cards, hand-scrawled private messages—

Gus—Tonight is no good, sorry. E. decided not to drive to the conference after all, he's taking a plane in the morning. OK? Call?

> *Love etcetera*
> *Kat*

And—Gus darling, I have to drive Carrie to basketball practice & can swing by the office at about 4:00 P.M.—hoping you will be there. Will enter at rear—make sure door unlocked OK? Also hoping J. is all right. That was SCARY.

> *Your Kitty-Kat*

Naomi's heart beat hard in childish fury, resentment. *Your Kitty-Kat.* She hoped that Jenna had never known.

(And what did it mean—*Hoping J. is all right.* Obviously "J" was Jenna. Had Jenna been ill, had Jenna found out that her husband was having an affair with a mutual friend, had Jenna been upset, angry, humiliated? Resigned?)

Abruptly then the messages from Kat ceased. There were other suggestive and enigmatic notes from Val, Roslyn, Stuart (judging by the context this had to be a female: *Gus, we have to talk. I wasn't altogether truthful on the phone, I think each of us owes the other an expla-nation).* These Naomi read in disbelief and disdain, hur-riedly, crumpled in her hand, but did not set aside . . .

Had Jenna known? Had Jenna been hurt?

It was not clear that these were full-fledged affairs. (Naomi told herself.) Just as likely flirtations that had come to nothing.

Yet: those years when Jenna was pointedly quiet, or distracted, or (intermittently) depressed; even at meal-times when Gus was home with his family, exuding the warm genial always-entertaining *personality* that so captivated his children.

They'd sensed their mother's unhappiness—she and Darren. But like the shrewdly selfish children they were, they had not wanted to inquire.

And if they'd inquired Jenna would have said she had a "migraine," or—"Too much damned work to do, for which I'm paid less than the minimum wage."

Laughing then, to show them that she wasn't com-plaining *really.*

Wasn't depressed or furious *really.*

You could not help but love Daddy best—of course.

You could not help but forgive Daddy for being himself—of course.

Naomi was sure (sure!) that she couldn't recall a single exchange between her parents in which Jenna had even obliquely accused Gus of being unfaithful to her—unless it was Jenna's silence that was the accusation.

It was rare that their parents quarreled. If a voice was raised it was Gus's voice, penetrating the bedroom walls. Often Daddy was exasperated, not angry. Daddy was never *mean*.

Nor had they heard Jenna crying. Naomi was sure.

She would call Darren! He might know who "Kitty-Kat" was, in Grand Rapids.

Possibly, the mother of a friend or classmate. (Who was "Carrie"?)

Naomi was sitting on the floor unpacking the box, that had been haphazardly packed. Telling herself that she was grateful to have received it. Telling herself that she was not beginning to panic.

Gamely she was sorting out material, dividing it into piles. Whit Smith had included much that was impersonal, and of no interest—as if he'd dumped drawers into the box without glancing at them.

She didn't remember Whit Smith, of course—her father's colleague in Grand Rapids. She'd been too young.

A succession of Daddy's colleagues, co-workers, young assistants. At mealtimes, sometimes staying overnight on a pull-out sofa. Gus thought nothing of arriving home at 6:00 P.M. with a guest, or two guests, in tow—

Jenna! Hope it isn't too late for dinner . . . I'll open some wine.

And Jenna would say *Of course! Come right in.*

One of these visitors had surely been Whit Smith. Another might have been "Kat."

Naomi's head was beginning to ache. She'd become overwhelmed by the material that had initially excited her. Trying to draw conclusions about her father's (personal, professional) life from random items that overlapped, to a degree, with similarly random material she'd acquired from other sources . . . Looking through the pocket-sized appointments books she felt a sensation of vertigo. These well-worn and frayed little books had lived inside her father's clothing. Near his heart.

There had to be a number of individuals who knew or could shrewdly guess what these entries meant, as they would know who "Kat" and the other women were. But if initials were identified, to what purpose?

The more she knew of the dailiness, the minutiae, of her father's life, the more that life was eluding her. From a distance she could see the contours of an intriguing landscape while up close she could see virtually nothing.

By this time numerous others had written about Gus Voorhees in a range of publications—*The Nation, Mother Jones, Atlantic.* Most had written with impressive knowledge of the Planned Parenthood/pro-choice community in the United States in the latter decades of the twentieth century, in which Gus Voorhees had been a prominent figure: he'd been "fearless"—he'd been "controversial." These were observers who'd known Gus personally and professionally, who'd been friends of his, or friendly acquaintances; individuals who weren't afraid to be critical of him even when admiring of him.

Also by this time several other abortion providers had been murdered by right-to-life activists and many others injured or threatened. Abortion clinics had been vandalized, firebombed. All these had been covered in the media. The most concerted anti-abortion efforts were now political, waged in state legislatures and in state elections, and not confrontational.

Risky to open one of her father's little notebooks and to see his familiar slanted handwriting. Even if she had no idea what the words meant. *9/6/91 Ob mtg C.H.T. office 4:30 PM. 6/23/93 10:30 AM Rackham 313-447-1766.* (This was a Detroit-area number, she might call. But so many years had passed!) There were pages of lists, dates, initials and abbreviations in which even K was lost—an indecipherable code she could never crack.

Naomi had to turn away, feeling suddenly ill.

None of this will bring me back, honey. Maybe you should let this go.

Trying to explain. Trying to choose her words with care but there was something wrong with her speech, her very tongue.

It is not a memorial for Daddy alone—for "Gus Voorhees." It is a commemoration of the world that surrounded him and that died with him.

She felt it so keenly!—all that she could not utter in words.

She wanted to explain to the woman who was her father's mother. Who had given birth to a child and then seemingly abandoned him, as a boy of eight or nine. Naomi wanted to ask how such an act had been possible.

And so, for the ten days of her stay with her grandmother in the high-rise apartment at 110 Bleecker Street she had to be alert to the most casual of remarks made by Madelena. She could not ask explicitly. Nor would Madelena reply explicitly.

In their seats at Lincoln Center, at the Balanchine ballet. On an escalator at the Museum of Modern Art, ascending into an exhibit of Picasso drawings and paintings. At the Polish film festival at the NYU Film Institute. At Carnegie Hall, at a Kronos Quartet concert. At the International Center of Photography on Sixth Avenue, at the Whitney Museum, at the Guggenheim and at the Neue Galerie, at a performance of Offenbach's *Tales of Hoffmann* at the Metropolitan Opera. In a taxi, or on the subway—(it was a revelation to Naomi, her beautifully dressed and not-young grandmother took the subway frequently, and seemed oblivious to its noisy distractions). At a lecture titled "The Rise of Consciousness and the Development of the Emotions" sponsored by the Psychology Department at NYU and at a lecture titled "The Birth of Ethics" sponsored by the NYU Institute for Independent Study, where Madelena Kein introduced the speaker.

Offhandedly Madelena might say, "You know, Naomi—we were very close. Your father and me. Not geographically close. But we spoke often on the phone."

Naomi was surprised to hear this. Almost, she would wonder if it was true.

"Gus understood that by leaving him and his father I didn't cease to love him—only that I couldn't continue to be his mother because I was not that person. I was another person."

There was a kind of spell upon them. If this were a ballet an entranced music would signal it. So long as Naomi did not interrupt with an inane remark or a question Madelena would speak as if she were thinking aloud, choosing her words precisely; but only in the interstices of an "outing"—an "activity"—in which she and Naomi were in a public place in which the occasion for such remarks was limited.

"Gus didn't judge me as others in the family did. He'd always respected the autonomy of individuals. That was why he'd believed that women must never be under the control of men—or even other women. A woman's body is no one's property but her own. Gus seemed naturally to understand." Madelena paused, touching her fingertips to her eyes. "*You* understand, Naomi, I hope?"

"Yes."

"Though I hope you will never need to have—or have not needed to have—an abortion . . ."

Naomi felt her face grow warm. Was her grandmother asking her in this awkwardly oblique way if she'd had an abortion?

Stiffly she said she hoped not, too.

Fortunately the opportunity for further conversation abruptly ended as a bell chimed, signaling the end of an intermission.

So distracted was Naomi, she'd forgotten for a moment where she was.

_____

She is remarkable! *She will never admit that she did anything wrong—even for a moment.*

Abandoning her son and his father, leaving to establish a "career" for herself—she is not apologetic, she feels no guilt.

But is this so?—Madelena Kein feels no guilt?

I adore her. I want to be her.

I hate her. She is a monster!

At the window flooded with late-morning sunlight. With a ruler Naomi had drawn lines on a sheet of white paper.

Wanting to take notes by hand. As in an old-fashioned diary or logbook.

As Gus had done in the notebooks she'd discovered. But not in code as Gus had done.

Ten days, that passed both rapidly and with dream-like slowness.

Amid the busyness of the city that seemed at times almost frantic Naomi yet managed to keep some time for herself, in the solitude of the white-walled room floating in air.

She took notes on lined paper. She stared out the window. She paged through books from her grandmother's crammed shelves searching for—what, she wasn't sure.

She tried to see the "emptiness" of which Madelena had spoken with such feeling, miles away at Ground Zero; but since she had not ever seen the twin towers there originally, she could not fathom their absence.

"Naomi, dear?"—there might come a light rap at the door.

Madelena was slipping away for a few hours, or for most of the day. But they would be going out in the evening—of course.

So many people! Names and faces soon began to blur.

Madelena's colleagues in philosophy, linguistics, theater; musicians and composers; painters and sculptors, journalists, writers and poets . . . There was a tall courtly white-haired and -bearded Hungarian-born semioticist named Laslov whose heavily accented English was difficult to decipher, who seemed very fond of Madelena, as Madelena was of him; during Naomi's visit she would meet Laslov several times, at restaurant dinners in the West Village arranged by Madelena. (Naomi wondered: were Laslov and Madelena lovers, or had they been lovers? She was struck by a playful ease between them that she hadn't observed between her grandmother and other men, and a particular gentleness in the way Laslov pronounced "Lena.") There was the *New Yorker* writer Janet Malcolm whom Madelena much admired as "fearless" and "intransigent" in her non-fiction essays, and who seemed to admire Madelena as a "kindred spirit"; there was the controversial gay writer Edmund White, who hosted a dinner party for Madelena and her visiting granddaughter in his elegant Chelsea apartment, and quite charmed Naomi with his wit, warmth, and erudition. An Israeli filmmaker named Yael Ravel, a visiting fellow at the Institute known for her documentaries about communities of Israeli and Palestinian women, made a strong impression upon Naomi by saying, to the audience, following a showing of one of her films: "What is most required for the documentary filmmaker is patience. When you encounter your true subject, you will know it."

And then there was Karl Kinch, the most memorable of all the New Yorkers.

"We won't stay long. Kinch rarely has visitors. He expressed some interest in meeting you."

Naomi noted the qualification—*some interest.*

Yet more improbably—*meeting you.*

Doubtfully she asked why would this friend of Madelena's want to meet her?

"Why? Why d'you think?"—Madelena smiled, though with rather an edge.

"I—I don't know . . ."

"Of course you don't 'know.' But you might infer, Naomi, that I've spoken of you to him."

Naomi could not think of a reply. Wondering what on earth her grandmother could have said about her to arouse the interest and curiosity of this stranger?

Madelena added, "And Kinch is not a 'friend' of mine, exactly. We are too close, we know each other too intimately, to be for each other what the bland word friend implies."

Kinch had been variously a poet—("A prodigy, who published his first book of poems at the age of twenty-one")—a composer—("Atonal music, exquisite and subtle if grating to the ordinary ear")—a memoirist—("*Memento Mori* is the title of Kinch's precocious first memoir, told from a posthumous perspective")—a translator—("Working with a native speaker and 'translating' texts into his own, idiosyncratic English prose")—a critic—("Fiercely original, with terribly high standards, and feared by many"). He'd made himself into something of an amateur-expert Biblical scholar, with a particular interest in the poetry of

Psalms; he'd taught himself Hebrew, Sanskrit, and Aramaic. He had no advanced degrees—he'd begun Ph.D. programs at Harvard, Yale, and Columbia but dropped out after realizing that the individuals entrusted with assessing his work were "inferior" to him intellectually and imaginatively; he did teach from time to time, graduate seminars in esoteric special topics, at Hunter College, Columbia College, New York University, and Princeton, as a "distinguished" visitor.

"Of course, Kinch is 'not well.' That is the first thing that is said about him though when you are with him, it is the last thing, or nearly, that you are struck by."

Naomi asked in what way Kinch was "not well"?— but Madelena seemed reluctant to explain.

"Kinch has written beautifully and persuasively of the tyranny of 'wellness'—'normality'—'sanity.' You will see for yourself."

The first time Madelena took Naomi to visit the mysterious Kinch, who lived on the sixteenth floor of a grimly featureless high-rise building several blocks north of Washington Square Park, they were rebuffed in the foyer by an embarrassed doorman who informed Madelena—(whom he called "Professor Wein")—that "Professor Kinch" could not have visitors that day, and "deeply regretted" that their visit would have to be rescheduled.

"Really!" Madelena laughed, though visibly annoyed. "May I speak with Professor Kinch? Will you call him?"

But the doorman regretted no, he could not call Professor Kinch for Professor Kinch had expressly forbidden any calls that afternoon.

"Is he unwell? I mean—has he been unwell? Unusually unwell? Has there been an emergency?"

"No, ma'am. Not that I know."

"His 'assistant' is with him? He isn't alone?"

"Yes, ma'am. She's there. He isn't alone."

Outside on Fifteenth Street Naomi dared to ask Madelena again what was wrong with Karl Kinch?— and Madelena said airily, "Oh, Kinch has numerous ailments. His genius has effloresced in unexpected ways and not all of them aesthetic. The most obvious is MS—multiple sclerosis—that was diagnosed when he was in his late twenties. (But it isn't clear what MS *is*—not a single ailment or condition but a syndrome.) Reputedly, Kinch was a young lover of the philosopher Michel Foucault who died of AIDS in the mid-1980s—it is believed by some, including Kinch himself, that he contracted an HIV infection from Foucault, if not AIDS itself. And the poor man is very visually impaired— 'legally blind.'" Madelena paused, considering Naomi's alarmed expression. "But that's enough for now, dear.

We never speak of such matters with Kinch but if he wants to tell you more about himself, he will."

They returned two days later, also in the late afternoon. This time they were not rebuffed but directed to an elevator by the doorman who continued to call Madelena "Professor Wein" and was not corrected by her.

In the elevator Naomi asked her grandmother why she didn't trouble to correct the doorman and Madelena explained: "I always feel that it's impolite to correct a civilian. I am paid to 'correct' students of mine, who have enrolled in my courses, and so it's expected in that context; but it is not expected that I should go around 'correcting' others. And why should I care what I am called by a stranger?—as long as the mis-'calling' is consistent, and Kinch knows who is coming to see him."

Madelena smiled as she spoke. Naomi felt a rush of affection for her grandmother who was in an unusually friendly and accessible mood.

"Has the doorman always called you 'Wein'?"

"Yes! But I think I didn't notice at first."

"How long have you been coming to visit Mr. Kinch?"

"How long *here*? As long as he's been living here— he'd used to live in Washington Mews, in one of those charming brownstones owned by the university. But when he became seriously ill, about fifteen years ago, he decided to move away from Washington Square Park—he thinks the city is too intense there, it grates against his nerves. So I've been visiting Kinch in this building for approximately fifteen years. In fact, I'd helped him find his 'bourgeois'—that is, 'deeply boring'—apartment, which he finds protective as a kind of 'quarantine.' And I must say, I never—really— know how Kinch will greet me."

Madelena was feeling so exhilarated, having been not-rebuffed in the foyer, she didn't object to her grand-daughter asking so many questions.

For the visit Madelena wasn't wearing her usual styl-ish black clothes but a dark magenta suede coat with a matching hat, that hid much of her silver hair. She'd stopped at an expensive food shop on University Place to buy a bag of mangoes for Kinch—"His favorite fruit, he claims." Her usual cool, slightly ironic composure seemed to have vanished leaving her both excited and apprehensive, as Naomi had rarely seen her.

As they waited for the doorbell to be answered Mad-elena cautioned Naomi: "Don't be surprised when you see Kinch. And don't feel sorry for him, please! He's very sensitive to what he calls 'gratuitous pity.' He is quite happy with his life, which has been very creative. He has won many awards which he won't mention. He has few friends—but those he has are special to him, and love him. What you will see is just the outer man, the surface. Our true lives are interior and inaccessible to the eye."

The door was opened by a middle-aged woman with a severe expression who let them in without a word, and took their coats to hang in a closet.

Was this person a nurse? Caretaker? She wore a shapeless cardigan sweater over white nylon slacks and white crepe-soled shoes. Stiffly she smiled at Madelena, who called her "Sonia." She took no notice of Naomi at all.

Blindly Naomi followed her grandmother into the apartment—through a small dim-lighted foyer in which books were stacked on the floor like stalagmites and into an equally dim-lighted living room in which books were similarly stacked on tables and on the floor, as well as crammed into floor-to-ceiling bookshelves. The single window in this room was obscured by heavy velvet drapes. Madelena moved briskly without waiting for Sonia to escort her as if there were some old, familiar friction between them, which Madelena blithely ignored.

Naomi was dismayed by the smell of the apartment— airless, gingery-medicinal, faintly rancid. Worse yet, there was an underlying odor of tobacco smoke. How strange that Madelena who was fastidious about the air in her own apartment seemed oblivious of the stale air here.

"Professor Kein! *Bonjour.*"

A young-old man in a motorized wheelchair rolled in their direction, to greet them with a wide smile.

"*Bonjour,* Professor Kinch. Thank you for seeing us!"—gaily Madelena stooped to brush her lips against the young-old man's cheek, even as he stiffened just perceptibly as if fearing being touched, yet not wanting to offend. "And here she is, the granddaughter from the wilds of the Midwest, Naomi."

"Ah yes—'Na-o-mi Voor-hees.'"

So Kinch knew her name. Her full name. Well, that was not so surprising perhaps. Madelena must have told him.

Naomi wondered if *Voorhees* meant anything to Kinch? Surely he would know that Madelena had been married to a man with that name, though she'd never taken on the name; and possibly, he knew of Gus Voorhees.

(Except: Madelena was so elusive, and so exulted in secrecy, it was possible that even her longtime New York City friends didn't know of her former marriage or that she'd had a doctor-son who had been assassinated.)

"Naomi, this is Karl Kinch—you need not call him 'Professor'—but he does not like to be called 'Karl.'"

Naomi had no idea what this might mean. Surely she could not call him *Kinch?*

Now came the motorized chair in Naomi's direction. Kinch's manner was playful as an adolescent with an oversized dangerous toy. *Do you dare step aside, try to escape me?*—Kinch's wide smile, filled with discolored teeth, seemed to be taunting her. Naomi guessed that, wheelchair-bound, a man would resent having always to look upward, crane his neck, at persons of normal height. Kinch lifted a long slender soft-boned hand to be shaken by Naomi even as she tried to sidestep the motorized chair.

"*Bonjour*, Naomi! Welcome to the *mausoleum*." The word was given an exuberant French pronunciation.

In an aside Madelena murmured to Kinch, "*Elle est belle, est-elle?*" and Kinch murmured, "*Pas si belle que tu, ma chère.*"

Madelena smiled with a look of irritated pain to signal that she did not approve of this remark. Naomi pretended not to have heard.

Kinch had a large head that looked sculpted out of some fragile material like eggshell. Sparse graying hair fell in ringlets to his bowed shoulders. He wore formal clothes—white dress shirt buttoned to his thin throat, dark trousers with a crease. He might have been any age between thirty and fifty—his skin was papery-smooth and white, presumably from lack of sunshine. Yet his manner was youthful, even boyish. A sort of bad-boyish. He fidgeted constantly, his legs and long white toes in (open) sandals twitched on the footrest of the wheelchair. Except for a subtle deformation of his face and the exceptional size of his head he would have been an attractive man. His features were fine-chiseled. His voice was subtly modulated like an actor's or a singer's voice. He was not wearing glasses though one of his eyes was milky and the other appeared severely myopic. His mouth was strangely wide, his lips wetly sensuous. From the way he blinked, smiled, squinted at Naomi she supposed he was seeing her as a blur.

"Please sit, 'Naomi Voorhees'! Wherever you wish. Just push those books aside." Kinch's tone was both mocking and tender.

They were slender books of poetry with stiff, slightly warped hardbound covers that gave off an odor of mold. Not in a language Naomi recognized.

She sat. The sofa was of well-worn leather though seemingly of high quality like other furnishings in the room. How strange it was in this airless place! Very little light was allowed here. All was dim as if undersea. The very reverse of Madelena's high-rise apartment with floor-to-ceiling windows rarely shaded from the sun. Madelena had said that Kinch's eyes were sensitive to light. He could not watch television, he could not go outdoors—during the day the sun's rays were too bright, even if the sky was overcast; at night, streetlights and neon lighting gave him migraine headaches. He could not work with the shimmering screen of a computer that affected his sensitive brain but had to write by hand, or type manuscripts on an old-fashioned manual typewriter, though such typing required muscular coordination of a kind he could no longer depend upon. So Madelena had reported, with a curious sort of detachment.

Naomi felt something beneath her foot on the carpet—a cigarette butt? She was noticing ashtrays on tables, with a look of having been hastily cleaned with a paper towel; and on each table, a book of matches formally displayed.

Madelena didn't smoke, of course; she would never have allowed anyone to smoke in her apartment. Most of her friends whom Naomi had met did not smoke nor was smoking allowed in any restaurant in the city. How bizarre, that the invalid Kinch should smoke . . .

"Naomi, don't worry! No one will force you to smoke in this den of iniquity."

With a wheezing sound Kinch laughed as if he'd said something very witty, intended to annoy his dignified silver-haired visitor.

"I realize it isn't very 'fresh' in here—I can't open any window, unfortunately. The noise—the drafty cold—would annihilate me. And I have to keep the damn drapes closed most of the time. In my quarantine life it's always a kind of pre-dusk—as in a painting of Hopper—that wan, fading light, the mannequin-people who seem scarcely to be breathing, the melancholy *clumsiness* of the world from which there is no escape since that is the world."

Kinch spoke eloquently, sadly. Yet his sensuous, damp-looking lips quivered as if he were about to burst into an irreverent smile.

To spare Naomi the awkwardness of a reply Madelena deftly intervened. "Hopper is 'clumsy'—set beside painters like Whistler and Homer who can replicate the world so precisely. Yet when you're looking at Hopper's paintings you are utterly persuaded, you don't feel that 'clumsiness' at all."

Kinch made a derisive snorting sound. "*You* may not, Professor Kein. More discerning others do."

With a vague naive hope of aligning herself with her grandmother who was looking vexed, and making some statement of her own, for surely it was time for her to speak, Naomi remarked that Madelena had taken her to the Whitney Museum the other day where they'd seen paintings by Hopper she had never seen before in reproductions and these she'd thought very "beautiful," "haunting" . . .

"Of course you did, Naomi. 'Beautiful'—'haunting.'"

Was Kinch speaking ironically? Was he laughing at her? Yet he seemed kindly, and not at all malicious.

Dour-faced Sonia approached asking if their guests would like something to drink? Tea, sparkling water, wine . . . With some fuss she set down a tray containing several cheeses, a scattering of pale crackers, shriveled-looking olives.

Tea for Madelena, sparkling water for Naomi. "Nothing for me just now"—Kinch said primly.

"Ah, before I forget—here. Your favorites."

Madelena handed the little bag of mangoes to Kinch who accepted it with a childish sort of delight, all but smacking his lips.

"Take these away, Sonia, will you?—and prepare a little dish for us."

Dour-faced Sonia took away the mangoes without a word.

Madelena inquired after a new medication Kinch

had begun taking, and what progress he was making on a composition commissioned by the Juilliard String Quartet; Kinch inquired after "your old Laslov."

A gruff sort of intimacy existed between the two. Each appeared to be just slightly critical of the other, or bemused; yet affectionate, even proud. Especially, Madelena glanced at Naomi to see how she was taking Kinch's provocative manner, that was always on the edge of rudeness. Madelena was the more gracious of the two, speaking of "we"—"Naomi and me"— who'd been seeing such interesting exhibits in the city, and such an excellent performance of *Les Contes d'Hoffmann*.

"Really! The review in the *Times* wasn't so enthusiastic, I think."

"I thought it was very enthusiastic."

"Not if you know how to decode that critic's 'enthusiasm.' If you read between the lines . . ."

"The Picasso exhibit is really quite extraordinary . . ."

"No. Not possible. Nothing in Picasso is *extraordinary* any longer. An artist with just two modes— naive-primitive, and prurient. Both are outworn in the twenty-first century."

As they spoke together in their quasi-flirtatious banter Naomi glanced about the room. She was becoming accustomed to the acrid smell, and her eyes were adjusting to the diminished light. Through a doorway she saw, in an adjoining room, that had formerly been a dining room she supposed, an article of furniture that must have been a mobile desk, with sliding parts; on the desk-top were an old-fashioned manual typewriter, neatly stacked sheets of paper, journals, books. The desk was somewhat lower to the floor than an ordinary desk, ideal for one in a wheelchair. Against a wall was a "baby grand" piano outfitted with crane-necked lights.

In the living room were mismatched furnishings. Leather sofa, upholstered chairs, glass-topped coffee table. Against a farther wall was a display of what appeared to be antique musical instruments, predominately strings; on the hardwood floor a large, faded but still beautiful rug of the kind Naomi knew to be "Persian"—quite a dazzling rug, in fact, that reminded Naomi of a smaller rug in Madelena's living room. The walls were solid-packed with mostly hardcover books. Naomi wondered if, like the books in Madelena's apartment, these were carefully alphabetized.

"And how d'you find New York, chère Naomi? A 'blooming, buzzing confusion'—n'est-ce pas?"

Now Kinch turned his full attention upon his younger visitor. You could see, in the way in which he addressed Naomi, and in his manner of seeming to care about her remarks, that he had cultivated a courteous teacherly self; he had had experience with young people. Though he might consider Naomi's replies no more than schoolgirl banality he would not turn upon the nineteen-year-old the satirical manner he turned upon the silver-haired Madelena with whom he seemed to share a complex history.

Naomi thought, with horror—*Could they be lovers?*

The way in which Madelena observed Kinch, that was clearly affectionate, yet exasperated; her unease in his presence, that shaded into a kind of dread, or into emotional anticipation, a kind of gaiety—this did suggest a history even more complex, Naomi thought, than with the courtly white-haired Laslov.

And the more closely you considered Kinch's young-old face, the more likely it seemed that Kinch was older than he appeared at first glance. There were fine, near-invisible lines at the corners of his ruined eyes, and his hair was graying and receding from his forehead. Naomi noted that the fingers on both Kinch's hands were nicotine-stained. His wide, sensuous mouth was not a young mouth. If the sexes were reversed it would not be at all bizarre to suspect that a vigorous and attractive man in his seventies might be having an affair, or some sort of emotional entanglement, with a woman in her mid-fifties.

Of course, they'd met years before. When both had been younger, and Kinch had not been so incapacitated. Naomi supposed.

In his kindly-teacher mode Kinch inquired of Naomi how old she was, and where was her home in Michigan; were her university courses exciting and challenging to her; what were her plans for after graduation, and— "What is your life's passion? Have you stumbled upon it yet, or are you still searching?"

"I—I don't know yet," Naomi said. *Life's passion* was a daunting term.

She tried to deflect Kinch's interrogation by speaking with enthusiasm of the New York City Ballet, exhibits at the Metropolitan Museum, the documentary by the Israeli filmmaker. Walking with Madelena in Central Park in a light-falling snow . . . (Or was this a blunder? Thoughtless? For Kinch could not walk with anyone in Central Park in a light-falling snow.) She was feeling slightly panicked trying even to recall her life back in the Midwest.

She told Kinch that yes, she'd been "searching"— she guessed. She was nineteen years old and felt sometimes as if she were twice that age, or half that age—"I haven't been very happy for a while which makes time pass slowly, yet at the same time I haven't exactly 'lived'—which makes me immature, stunted. I don't know what to do with my life that will make any difference to anyone else. I don't even feel sometimes that it is my 'life'—it could be anyone's life, I could be anyone, except that my father died prematurely which makes me different from most people—but Daddy's death didn't happen to me, it happened to him."

But why had she said *Daddy?*—a child's word. Better for her to have said *my father.*

She did not want to say *My father was killed—"assassinated."* This was claiming too much for herself—a way of raising her voice, to capture attention. Though she supposed that Madelena must have told Kinch such a crucial fact in both their lives.

With his left, sighted eye Kinch was staring intently at her. He seemed actually to be listening to her. And Madelena too was listening intently though with a kind of apprehension as if dreading what Naomi might utter next.

"Well, Naomi! You are being very honest. But it isn't just at age nineteen that one feels as you do—at least, your remark about feeling immature, stunted. And some of us are in fact, as you say—'immature and stunted' no matter our age." Kinch laughed, and began coughing wheezily.

Madelena asked, in an undertone, if Kinch needed

his inhaler and Kinch shrugged irritably, and did not reply.

"Madelena tells me you are interested in documentary filmmaking? Though 'film' is not the correct term any longer, is it?—everything is 'digital' today. The beautiful old *films* of the past will never be replicated . . ."

At this point Sonia returned with a plate of quartered mangoes to set beside the cheese tray. Kinch looked at her, and at the mangoes, with an expression of disdain.

"Why on earth are you bringing us these? Take them away, please."

This was startling. Had Kinch forgotten he'd sent Sonia away to prepare the mangoes? Seeing that Madelena did not seem about to intervene, maintaining a discreet neutral expression, Naomi surmised that she must say nothing either.

Without a flicker of expression dour-faced Sonia retreated.

"As Baudelaire observed—'Parfois, *j'adore* les mangues. Et parfois mangues sicken moi.'"

He had forgotten, evidently. No one wished to remind him.

"I know a little of your father's 'premature' death, Naomi. Madelena has told me."

Naomi was feeling self-conscious beneath the scrutiny of the left, singular eye. She wished that Kinch would turn his attention back to Madelena; she wished the awkward visit would end, and she could breathe fresher air. She had tried to drink the sparkling water brought to her by Sonia but the water was tepid, and flat; and the glass was scummy.

Still Kinch was in his kindly mode. You were meant to know that this was a generous, even altruistic mode.

"'Pro-choice'—yes! We must honor free will, even if we don't altogether believe in it. A woman—a girl—must be free to terminate a pregnancy if she wishes. It is abominable and outrageous that the state might curtail this right, like the right to suicide—that is equally precious! In fact, abortion does not seem to me anything but a good, heroic deed. Life is the horror, abortion or miscarriage is the redemption. As Sophocles said so beautifully, 'Never to have been born is best, but once you've entered this world, return as quickly as possible to the place you came from.'"

Naomi winced, hearing these words so bluntly uttered. This was hardly Gus Voorhees's belief at all . . .

"Abortion, miscarriage—these should be more common. Pregnancy is the aberration. Our lives—lives endured in consciousness—are the evolutionary blunder. Considering our absurd 'central nervous systems' the wonder is that anyone is ever *born*."

Kinch was speaking vehemently. So worked up, so suddenly, he fumbled for a pack of cigarettes squeezed beside his thin haunch and the side of the motorized chair; he extracted a long parchment-colored cigarette and made a snapping gesture with his fingers, that Madelena should hand him some matches from a nearby table.

Madelena pleaded: "Please don't smoke, Kinch. You know how bad it is for your lungs. And I detest the filthy habit."

"Many filthy habits are detested, that are nonetheless indulged. Will you hand me the matches, please?"

"No!"

"*Chère* Naomi, will you? This is not your *grand-mère*'s territory, you know. It is mine."

Naomi hesitated. She did not want to offend Madelena.

"Will you make me call in poor oppressed Sonia, who escaped from a lesser Chekhov play to work at a minimum wage in this country, to perform an act you might perform very easily, by passing me those fucking matches?"

Naomi wondered why on earth Kinch could not get

his matches for himself, since it was no great effort in his motorized chair.

A signal of disgusted resignation from Madelena freed Naomi to obey Kinch, though she had no wish to obey him.

With a sigh of sensuous relief Kinch lit his cigarette, exhaling smoke from both nostrils. His milky eye gleamed at Naomi.

"Your father—'Augustus Voorhees' is the rather distinguished-sounding name—was not personally known to me. We might have met—that was entirely possible. Your grandmother might have introduced us. But it did not happen. My loss, I am sure. Among many losses in 'this disease, my life'—to paraphrase Alexander Pope." Kinch smiled, and smoked his cigarette. He glanced at Madelena with an expression of solicitude.

"Of course—Voorhees's death was indeed 'premature'—a tragedy. In America, such tragedies are not uncommon. The death of an idealist, a selfless individual. That is the price the individual must pay, pitting himself against the black tide of ignorance and superstition. There is a war in the United States—there has always been this war. Those of us who are rationalists can never win for there is a stronger, more primordial and more *spiteful* will to American irrationality. What is it—'my country right or wrong'—that sick, servile patriotism. And that patriotism is a God-ism, for they are all Christians. All we can hope for is to prevent a total defeat. Pockets of relative enlightenment across the country—the larger cities, where people of education and intelligence have clustered. The rest is a vast wasteland—'religious' and 'patriotic.' You venture into it at your own peril—so many of them are armed! And they carry their weapons concealed! Even if I were physically strong I would never be an activist like Gus Voorhees. The activist must be willing to die for his cause, and no 'cause' is worth dying for— this is what rationalism tells us. My refuge is another, more oblique sort of activism—a quest for truth . . . Madelena, why are you glaring at me like that? I am not going to blurt out any uncomfortable truth at this moment, I assure you."

Madelena said coldly, "You're frightening my granddaughter, speaking so harshly. And it isn't good for your blood pressure to become over-excited, you must know."

Kinch laughed. But it was clear that Kinch was angry.

"*Your* blood pressure is low, is it, Professor! Very low, I'm sure—appropriate for one who is barely alive."

"Kinch, enough. That is not even true, as well as being insulting."

"So? Some untruths are more interesting than truths. And many untruths become truths, in time."

"You will drive your visitors away, Kinch. If you are not more hospitable."

"I am hospitable! For God's sake, it is virtually a *hospital* here—a *hospice.* You should see my bedroom—my IV line—poor Sonia is entrusted to keep clean. Among other indignities—mine as well as hers." Kinch fluttered his hands, meaning to be funny. Ashes flew from the parchment-colored cigarette and settled on his clothing and wheelchair.

"To return to the subject of 'Voorhees'—as I think we must do.

"The only demurral I would make regarding the heroic abortion doctor is the absurd sanctification that has followed his death. The man is not a saint, a martyr—he was a fool. Utterly foolish to act as he did, blindly, heedlessly, provoking the enemies of rationality to 'assassinate' him—which such assassins are delighted to do. They are desperate people—fundamentalist Christians. You can't come between a desperate people and their God—they will tear you limb from limb. By definition, a martyr is a fool—the perpetrator of *une folie.*"

Madelena was white-faced, furious. Hurriedly she'd set aside her cup of tea and was on her feet.

"I told you, I won't have you upsetting my grand-daughter, Kinch. You are behaving unconscionably, and I won't forgive you."

"'Granddaughter'—since when? One might be suspicious, you are playing the loving *grand-mère* now—so belatedly."

"Kinch, enough. You are not amusing."

"Oh hell—what's wrong with what I've said? You've said as much yourself, to me. Is there a single syllable I've uttered, that isn't glaringly true?"

"Naomi, come. We're leaving."

But Naomi was already on her feet and eager to leave.

She'd scarcely been able to breathe since Kinch had begun smoking. She felt sick to her stomach, wanting only to run out of the suffocating apartment.

This sick, selfish man had said terrible things about her father. In her confusion and distress she would not remember much of what he'd said.

"Wait, wait! Professor Kein . . ."

In his motorized chair Kinch followed Madelena and Naomi to the foyer, protesting and muttering to himself. The damned chair drew aggressively close to Naomi's heels. By this time Sonia reappeared, to remove their coats from the closet without a word.

Kinch did not follow his departing visitors over the

threshold of the doorway but called after them as they hurried to the elevator.

"*Au revoir!* A brief and not very satisfying visit, but I hope you will return, *ma chère* Naomi. Now that you know the way, you might come next time *non accompagnée.*"

"Forgive me, Naomi! I had no idea."

In the cramped rear of a taxi returning to 110 Bleecker Street Madelena gripped Naomi's hand tight. It was surprising to Naomi that the sky was still light—the sun had not yet set—for it had seemed to her that they'd been in Kinch's airless apartment for a very long time, and it must be nighttime by now. But it was not even dusk.

"He had promised—he would not behave so badly . . ."

Madelena was very upset, wiping at her face with a tissue.

"He is unwell, you see. He has had small strokes. He has threatened suicide, if his health continues to deteriorate. I worry so for him, but I am disgusted with him. *He had promised.*" Madelena paused, breathing rapidly.

Saying then, with a heedless air, since Naomi remained so silent, "Well, you see—no one knows—not even my oldest friends—Karl Kinch is my son."

Naomi wasn't sure she'd heard correctly. Son?

"My second son. Younger than your father by eleven years."

Naomi was speechless. She stared at Madelena open-mouthed. Was this known within her family? Why was this not known?

"No, I haven't told anyone in the family. You are the first to know.

"My former husband doesn't know. Gus may have suspected—from remarks I'd made to him, from time to time . . . I mean, he may have suspected that he had a half-brother. I'd considered introducing them, more than once. Gus would have been thrilled to learn that he had a half-brother and Karl—well, he knew about Gus; fortunately there was such a gap in their ages, Karl couldn't possibly have felt jealous. Or, if he'd felt jealous, he couldn't have acted upon it—much."

Naomi wasn't making sense of most of this. She was trying to comprehend: Karl Kinch was Madelena's son? Which meant: Karl Kinch was her uncle, or half-uncle?

"Well, I never told anyone. Some friends may suspect—something. But no one knows with certainty.

'Kinch' is a name randomly chosen by the father and by me—'Kinch' is no one's surname. The baby—the child—lived with the father's older sister who was eager to take care of him, in her vast, near-empty apartment on Central Park West. I visited often, but I did not live there. It was rare that I would stay overnight. I have always cherished privacy, solitude—it is the great luxury for a woman! Karl learned young to be utterly independent, indeed rebellious, and to resist authority. Until his health began to deteriorate he was remarkably independent. Of course Karl was brilliant from the start, before he could even read. It has been a kind of fate, his brilliance. Because he is also scattered in his interests, and he is easily bored. You saw how fidgety he is—he has always been that way. He was that way in the womb! He can keep a secret at least, or has kept our secret all these years—I don't know what will become of him when his health worsens, how he will behave. Those psychotropic medications he takes are very powerful, and can corrode the personality. You might not believe it from today, but Karl is a good, kind, moral person—he is not vindictive or malicious. But when he loses control . . ."

Madelena was speaking rapidly, gripping Naomi's hand. Lights from the street rippled across her face like fitful emotions. Naomi was astonished, she had never heard her usually poised and evasive grandmother speak so openly, heedlessly.

"My life is no one's concern but my own. I don't defend myself. Karl has nothing to do with the Voorhees family. It is none of Clement's business. Karl is mine, exclusively—he has no one else. His father is no longer living but if he were, he wouldn't be concerned about the state of his offspring. Though he did leave a reasonable amount of money for Karl, in trust."

Naomi was still rather dazed thinking: *uncle? Half-uncle?*

She was eager to share the news with Darren.

"I am hoping that you will keep this secret, Naomi. Will you?"

Naomi murmured *yes.*

Reluctantly, *yes.*

"You see, Naomi: I am so worried about Karl. He takes medications for MS, and medications for HIV. He has a very fluctuating white blood cell count. His eyesight is worsening. Sometimes he has such tremors, he can't hold a pen. He can't play piano, which he needs badly to do, when he composes. After your father was killed I became vulnerable to—many things . . . And after the terrorist attack on the World Trade Center, from which some of us have yet to recover . . . I had once been fearless, or so I'd thought. People still say that about me—'Oh, Madelena is fearless.' But I know better. I am not fearless at all. I am filled with fear. I loathe myself, that I didn't try to reason with Gus more—I might have pleaded with him to quit the line of medical work he was in, to channel his idealism and energy elsewhere—anywhere . . . God knows there are plenty of poor people, including children, he might have cared for. I did try a little to reason with him, but not enough. I have been such a great believer in the freedom of others, to choose their own lives. I regret that now. Maybe I could have saved him . . . I can imagine how anxious your poor mother was, all those years. For of course something was going to happen to Gus, eventually. It was terrible, terrible! Those years, and so much fear. Abortion centers were being firebombed, abortion providers were being threatened. And killed. In my dreams even now sometimes I am arguing with Gus. And Gus laughs and tells me to relax, nothing will happen, he will be fine, it's all exaggerated—remember, Gus would so often say *It's all exaggerated* . . . Do you remember? Yes? At the funeral I thought someone might say, as a joke, or rather not as a joke, in Gus's voice—*Hell, it's all exaggerated.* Or, I was thinking, that might be carved on his gravestone—*It's all exag-*

gerated. Naomi, I'm sorry—I don't know what I am saying. Where are we? Are we almost home?"

Naomi assured the agitated woman yes, they were almost home.

The neighborhood had become familiar to her now. She could speak of *home.* A taxi circling Washington Square Park, making its way to LaGuardia Place and the tall silver towers just beginning to be illuminated from within.

"You see, Naomi. I wanted you to meet. I wanted to bring you here, to meet your 'half-uncle.' I am so worried what will become of Karl if—when—something happens to me . . . There is enough money for him in the trust, not much but enough, and I provide for him too of course, and there is my medical insurance from the university, and my life insurance, and my social security . . . I wire the money to his bank account, for his medical expenses . . . and his other expenses. Fortunately his rent in the 'mausoleum' is stabilized. But Karl needs a friend. A friend who will care for him, not merely admire him from a distance. A 'blood relative'—so to speak. And so, I have brought you together. I am so sorry it turned out as it did, dear Naomi, I am hoping—you will not judge Karl too harshly? He is your father's half-brother, and I know that Gus would have been concerned for him, and kind to him—that was how Gus was, he couldn't help himself. The more impaired, maimed, 'kooky'—(remember how often Gus used that word?—it was a favorite word of his, that used to annoy me)—the more sympathetic he was. And Karl was very taken with you, however he behaved today. In fact I think he behaved badly because of you—wanting to impress you. He'd said to me beforehand, 'But I've never had a niece before. How does one behave with a *niece*?' And so, Naomi—I hope you will forgive me for this afternoon, which has been so upsetting. But I hope—can you promise me?—you will see Karl again? You will not—abandon him?"

The taxi had pulled up to the curb. It was time to ascend to the thirty-first floor.

Quickly Naomi said, to placate the distressed woman, "Yes."

Afterward in the solitude of the white-walled room overlooking the nighttime city calmly thinking *Not ever again. Not ever again, Karl Kinch.*

"Unwanted"—"Wanted"

This is hard to speak of. And it was a long time ago. But now that I have begun to confide in you, dear Naomi—I think that I should tell you this.

In essence—your father was not a "wanted" child. He was certainly not an "intended" child. You might say he was, very emphatically, a "not-wanted" child.

When I became pregnant—more or less by chance— with my younger son, I was well into my thirties and established in my work. Out of a kind of excess of well-being, I decided to have that child—(though "have" is a strange term; I have always disliked the "having"— "possessing"—nature of the parent-child relationship, that is so fraught with a wrongful appropriation of the younger by the elder and more powerful)—though there was never the slightest intention of establishing a family with the man who was the father, or even with the child . . .

But the first pregnancy was a very different case. In 1956 I was just slightly older than you are now, I was a graduate student at the University of Chicago, and I did not want a baby. Very passionately, I did not want a baby. I didn't even like babies. I preferred baby animals. I did not want the father to know because I did not want to be dependent upon him. I believed that he would want us to marry, in fact he was a medical student and might have helped me but I could not involve him. So I tried to find a doctor who would help me terminate this pregnancy. I consulted friends, I made calls, I was referred by "friends-of-friends"—I was trying not to become desperate. I would call someone, and be given another number to call, and I would call that number, and I would be told it was a wrong number, but I was told to leave my number, and maybe someone would call me. Finally I had to pay seventy dollars to get a number to call, and after several calls I managed to make an appointment, and it was an actual doctor's office, or maybe they were just renting the office from an actual doctor. There was a man, the "doctor," and there was a woman who was his "nurse." I had to pay them three hundred seventy dollars ahead of time, in cash. This was so much money in 1956—

you can't imagine! But I managed to get hold of three hundred seventy dollars which I handed over to them and by this time I was so anxious, so exhausted . . . In a state of terror I lay down on the examination table. The woman—the "nurse"—was giving me pills in a little cup to sedate me when there was a phone call, in the next room. I could hear the man—the "doctor"— talking in an excited voice, clearly something had gone wrong—I was starting to become sleepy but made an effort to stay awake. A panic came over me that the police were on their way to arrest us all—or they were going to kill me—or that I would bleed to death afterward. I saw the worried look in the woman's face—I thought, I don't want to be killed by these people. So—I told them to stop the procedure. I could not allow myself to fall asleep. I did not believe in God but the wild thought came to me—"God is sparing you and your baby. Run away!" And so—that's what I did.

The father had wanted to marry me. He had no idea that I was pregnant. He'd said he was in love with me. Your grandfather Clement.

I didn't love him but I respected him. I liked him. Our parents knew one another. Our wedding present from his parents was ten place settings of heirloom silver—Oneida, 1905.

So we were married, and Gus was born—he had not been wanted (by me) but he was born.

I'd thought that I would be bitter. I'd worried about post-partum depression. But I had no expectations about being a mother and so I wasn't disappointed. I kind of liked the little guy. As an infant Gus was filled with life, curiosity, heat—his little body gave off a powerful heat. I devised little games for him to accelerate, as I thought, the baby's mental growth. Clement was enthusiastic about this, too. I read to him long before he could understand words, I spelled out words for him on cards, I arranged a game in which he could pull a cord, and change pictures on a slide projector—things you learn about in developmental psychology. I'd insisted upon naming him Augustus, to suggest his great worth.

None of this was anything I'd expected. Everything that had to do with my pregnancy and with the childbirth and the baby was unexpected, unpredictable. I wasn't religious of course, I was certainly not Catholic but reading Augustine's The City of God had made an impression on me.

All the classics have had their effect upon me, I realize now. Secular, religious. Ancient, modern.

Through Gus's life I came to love him and to admire

and respect him though I did not live with him. Though
I was not his "mother"—he was not my "son"—in the
old way of the family.

Everyone called him Gus but I thought of him as
Augustus—truly he was a special person. I never
stopped believing that.

But when Gus was two or three I knew that I would
have to leave him eventually. I would have to leave
Clement. I stayed for years—eight years. I would have
to leave my life as Mrs. Clement Voorhees. I would
have to leave a house in Birmingham, Michigan. A
doctor-husband, a child of eight. The Oneida set was
tarnished in the sideboard—I don't think I'd ever
touched it. Being that kind of woman wasn't my personality. "Motherhood" did not make my heart beat
faster. Family life was like being trapped in a shell—a
kind of turtle shell that doesn't grow with the turtle
but confines it, and squeezes it to death.

Yet, I loved the child. I loved Gus, that he was the
person he was. I just did not want to be "his" mother
and I did not think that it was necessary for his development and his happiness, that I pretend to be this
person.

When I told this story to Gus—(he was an adult by
this time with children of his own)—he was wincing

and uneasy as you can imagine. He asked me what was the point of the story, and I told him the point is that abortion is what I'd thought I had wanted—absolutely. I had not the slightest doubt about this.

And yet, I'd been mistaken to want to be rid of the baby-to-be. Because the baby-to-be was him.

Bullshit, Gus said.

Somehow, in my telling, Gus had not seen where it was leading until this moment. And now—he could not think how to respond. What I had told him was like a blow to him that went so deep he could not absorb it.

It is not bullshit, I said. It is not any kind of shit.

I told him if I'd had access to abortion, to a sane, sensible, safe abortion on demand (which was his ideal as a medical reformer) he would not have been born. And don't you think it's a good idea, that Gus Voorhees managed to be born?

Gus brooded. Gus had no ready answer to this.

Did you not ever suspect that your mother didn't "want" you—dear Gus? Wasn't it obvious? And if she'd been able to "abort" you . . .

Jesus, Lena! You are certainly blunt.

I have not been blunt at all. I have been circuitous. I have told you a lengthy story in the hope that you might see a perspective not naturally your own.

By now Gus had managed to smile. A kind of a smile—abashed, somewhat dazed.

I hoped that he would not hate me now. I thought it was a risk I must take in the interests of honesty.

Finally he conceded, OK. I see the irony. The paradox. But still—women must make their own decisions.

I could see how your father was building his argument now. Arranging his words. For he'd been dealt a blow, and it had been a physical blow—now, he must elude the consequences of the physical blow by employing familiar words.

What is unfamiliar, rendered less profound by familiar words.

Saying, You should have had the freedom to make your own decision no matter the outcome at a later time. That is the fact.

Is it? There would have been no later time to contemplate you—you'd never have been born. Just— nothing. An emptiness.

You might have had other children, Lena. To take the place of the one you'd aborted.

But none of these children would have been you. And you are precious to me, you have acquired responsibility and stature in the world and have done inestimable good for many others.

Yet stubbornly Gus insisted, Women must make their own decisions. Their bodies are theirs, not ours. It is obscene for a man—any man—to tell a woman what to do with her body. To prescribe childbirth if she isn't ready. Or will never be ready.

So—you think it would have been better if I'd aborted you?

(It was harsh to say such words. But how otherwise to make my point.)

Lena, there is no "better"—"worse." It's ridiculous to be speaking in these terms. If I hadn't been born, you would not have known of me—I would not have existed. But others might have existed in my place, superior to me. We will never know.

If Gus Voorhees had never been born no one would miss him, right?

Well, I would miss you. If I'd known, I would miss you like hell, Madelena. No mother quite like you.

You can be sarcastic, Gus, but the fact is: you are wrong to think that because you have been born you are in a position to prevent others from being born.

"Wrong" in what way—logically?

Morally.

Abortion is morally neutral. What matters is that a woman must have the freedom to control her own body which means the freedom to make mistakes. At least,

these are her own mistakes. And even if for some abortion might be a mistake it is not an irrevocable mistake,
for most women can become pregnant again.

I agree with you, Gus. I don't disagree. I believe that
women must have their freedom as you do. Abortion is
inevitable—there will always be abortion. It must be
freely available, I believe this. And yet—there was just
one Gus Voorhees.

Jesus, Lena! You're being perverse. And you're being
too literal. We are concerned for all women, not just for
you—or me.

It is not possible to be too literal, Gus. There was
only just one Gus Voorhees.

"Hammer of Jesus":
March 2008–February 2009

First he'd seen her he hadn't thought much of her. Hadn't even taken in the fact (if it was a fact) she was *female*.

She'd just appeared one day in the Dayton gym. Late afternoon near 6:00 P.M.

Gray sweatpants, gray sweatshirt, hoodie. Hair cropped short like a guy's. Not tall and body solid as a young heifer's. Narrowed stony-gray eyes that looked damp. And a runny nose she'd kept swiping with the flat of her hand.

She was shy like somebody you'd discover to be mute—deaf-mute. Kind of clumsy on her feet. Self-conscious like she was worried people were watching her. (They were not. Not yet.) Asking if she could arrange for "lessons." How much each "lesson" would cost.

He'd said that depended.

"Well—I want to be a *boxer.*"

Seeing him regard her frank and near-to-sneering quickly she added, "I mean—I want to learn to box."

Seeing he still hadn't replied, adding—"Then, I want to be a boxer."

"'Want to be a boxer.' What kind?"

"The kind that fights fights like on TV."

"A pro?"

"Yeh. 'Pro.'"

He wasn't smiling. He was a long way from laughing.

Thinking it was rare they'd be white, like this one. If female, they'd be black or Hispanic. Or what some of them called themselves—*Latina.*

There were "Latinas" at the gym. Came in after work, to *work-out.* Fleshy bodies, not muscled. Sexy-fleshy-female bodies displaying themselves at the machines, pummeling the heavy bag with sixteen-ounce boxing gloves until within a scant minute or two they were breathing through their mouths, panting. Red mouths, mascara, makeup beginning to run with sweat. A man's nostrils picked up their special smell—perfumy sweat. Their fingernails were glossy, perfect. Nothing mattered more than the perfection of their fingernails. In the gym the guys could not not look and it was a relief, when they departed. No interest in actual boxing, even amateur, but sometimes they paid for "lessons"—not many. In the ring, sparring with an instructor, getting slapped in the face, in the midriff, on the upper arms not hard but yes, *slapped*—that wasn't what these girls wanted.

Well, once in a while one of the Latinas would say sucking in her rib cage and smiling at him sidelong *Hey Ernie, think I could be a boxer? Like M'lissa Hernandez?* and he'd say with an indulgent smile like you'd smile at a young child *Sure.*

Soon then, she'd disappear. Got engaged, got married, moved away. It was rare that any female had a true interest in the body's *fitness.* Their care was for how they looked, in the eyes of men.

This girl, he could see was different. Her face was plain like something scrubbed with a rag. Her eyebrows were heavy but her eyes appeared to be lashless. Stone-colored damp eyes and skin the hue of a tarnished winter sky or a porcelain sink covered by a thin film of grime. Could be eighteen, or twenty-eight. The kind of female that matures at a young age. Thickwaisted, wide-shouldered. Probably her thighs were large as shanks of beef and tight with muscle. Beefy at the knee. Broken fingernails and dirt ridged beneath. Couldn't expect makeup to improve this girl's looks in the ring and especially on TV where every blemish is exposed yet you could see (almost, he could see) that she might be attractive to a certain set of boxing fans who'd get off seeing a female of this type homely and stolid like somebody's bitch-sister pummeled, knocked down, humiliated and bloodied by one of the rising stars in female boxing—that'd be some kind of sexual charge. Maybe.

Did he want to make money off that? He did not.

Still: someone else would. He could think of plenty.

Up to the WBA, the promoters. Don King.

You had to respect the clueless ones. Desperate ones. Male, female. Most were male. Most were black, from Dayton. This girl wasn't local but had to be from Ohio, possibly West Virginia. The damp yearning eyes fixed on his face. Mouth reminded him of some kind of mollusk. Not-great teeth.

"You done any boxing? Ever?"

Shook her head *no*. Like the question was just a vexation like a buzzing fly.

"Karate?"

Shook her head *no*.

"Any kind of athletics? Basketball?"

Shook her head *yes*. Frowning to signal that hadn't turned out too well which he'd already know seeing she was short in the legs and arms.

"Like, high school?"

"Yeh."

"How recently?"

"Few years."

"What's that mean?"

"Two-three years."

Her reply was tentative, uncertain. She wasn't one to remember dates precisely. But if this was accurate, it meant she was still young—not yet twenty.

"Why d'you think you want to box?"

"'Cause I think—I'd be good at it."

"What's the evidence?"

Staring at him with her damp stone-colored eyes. *Evidence?*

The very word seemed to baffle her. He could see her brain shifting, thinking like the old computer in his office where the miniature whirling rainbow icon was what you'd get when the computer was baffled.

"I—I'm strong. Pretty strong. I can lift heavy things—boxes, weights . . . I know how to protect myself. Nobody gives me any shit. I don't back down from nothing."

Seeing he wasn't laughing at her but appeared to be listening she continued saying she'd seen plenty of boxing on TV. Her and her brother, that was mostly what they'd watched when they were kids. Their favorite boxers were Mayweather, Gatti, de la Hoya,

Roy Jones, Mike Tyson—"Not how he is now but how he was then." She spoke earnestly, frowning. As if he might not understand the distinction of Mike Tyson *now* and Mike Tyson *then*.

Also, she said, she'd seen some female boxers on TV—impressing him by knowing their names: Hernandez, Gogarty, Crowe, Johnette Taylor—she was sure she could learn to box as good as they did.

Now he had to smile. Not a mean smile but the girl picked up on it.

"They had to start out like me, didn't they? How'm I so different from them?" Her voice had a sudden edge of belligerence to it, that surprised him.

"Depends if you're that hungry. That desperate."

She laughed, uncertain. Not sure if this was a joke.

Many things were jokes, she knew. Didn't matter if you found them funny.

"Y'know, Johnette Taylor was trained here?"

Had not known. Mortified by not-knowing.

Not exactly true that Johnette had "trained" for her pro fights in this gym but he'd seen the promise in the girl at age sixteen for (maybe) women's Olympic boxing which was being talked about then—but had not (yet) been approved. Soon as Johnette turned at age nineteen pro she left Dayton: new trainer, new manager, Cleveland-based. He had not followed her career after she'd lost the WBA women's welterweight title a year ago and there were rumors of injuries.

"Y'think you could learn to box like Taylor? Eh?"

Shyly the girl nodded her head *yes*.

Her face was mottled with embarrassment. She smiled inanely. He wondered if she was just slightly retarded—speaking at a pitch that was audible seemed to require an effort from her, a measure of audacity. As if she had been made to believe that no words uttered by her, no expression possible from her, could be of the slightest interest to another person; yet, she had the audacity to imagine that she could become a professional boxer . . .

And how much effort had it required for her to enter the gym, step inside this place almost entirely male, and smelling of bodies, funky sweat-smell, and everybody in sight male, at the machines, at the heavy bags, speed bags, in the badly stained ring (two lanky-limbed young guys in their twenties, black-Hispanic, eight-ounce gloves, headgear, sparring with quick sharp fists), loud voices entirely male, and on the walls posters and photos of male boxers. She had nerve, at least.

Feeling impatient with the stolid plain-faced girl but protective too thinking *Keep your money. I don't want your money. Just turn around and get out of here if you know what's good for you.*

"So—is it OK?"

"'OK'—what?"

"You can give me lessons? Like to be a b-boxer?"

Her voice was so pleading, and the way she was breathing through her mouth like her life depended upon the next words a stranger might utter quick and glib like dealing out cards in a game in which he had nothing at stake and she had everything, how in hell could he say anything except—"Tell you what: come back tomorrow. There's nobody got time for you tonight."

Relief in her face, and a sudden smile that made her appear even younger, childlike with hope.

Muttering *Thanks!* and turning quick to leave before the stranger changed his mind.

"Wait. What's your name?"

Mumbled what sounded like *D.D. Dun-fie.*

"'D.D.'—? That's a name?"

She laughed, blushing but pleased. "Yah. It is."

Hammer of Jesus. That *was her.*

With Jesus's help, that *would be her.*

She knew she was crude, clumsy. She knew she had

much to learn. Her legs didn't move her fast enough (yet) and her arms were short for a boxer so she'd be at a disadvantage with a longer-armed opponent. She would have to learn to take punches if she wanted to throw punches. (Which she was willing to do.) There are fights won when the stronger boxer has punched himself out on the body of his opponent like young George Foreman on the body of not-young Muhammad Ali (she'd seen on ESPN TV) and if that is a way of winning, D.D. Dunphy was eager for it.

Though she was strong she became winded quickly in the gym which was surprising to her—at work, at the Target unloading dock, D.D. Dunphy had the most stamina of anyone including the young guys.

D.D. was the one who didn't bellyache. Didn't complain even on freezing-cold days. Did her job and kept her mouth shut. Thinking her private thoughts while her co-workers kept up a steady stream of stupid chatter and nasty jokes of which some (she knew) were addressed to her— *Just means I have to work hard at the gym. I will work hard.*

She would make the name proud: *Dunphy.*

She would not call attention to herself for that reason, that she wished to honor her father *Luther Amos Dunphy.*

But, if she was questioned, if she was interviewed, on TV for instance, then she would say quietly—*I am dedicating my boxing to my father Luther Amos Dunphy and to Jesus who is my Savior.*

Many of the boxers she and Luke had seen on TV thanked Jesus for their victories. Many knelt in the ring to bow their heads in a quick prayer or to cross themselves if they were Catholic. The great heavyweight Evander Holyfield (who'd beat Mike Tyson in two fights for the heavyweight title) wore a baseball cap with the stitching JESUS IS LORD. George Foreman became a Christian minister. The female boxer D.D. admired most was the junior lightweight WBA champion Tanya Koznick ("The Wildcat") who could not have been taller than five feet two inches and who fought like a wildcat in fact in defiance of safety and caution, overwhelming and intimidating her opponents with fierce flurries of blows. On the biceps of both arms Tanya Koznick brandished tattoos of the cross and she wore a small gold cross on a thin gold chain around her neck even in the boxing ring. She began TV interviews saying in a throaty broken voice she owed everything to Jesus and most of all she owed her life—*Before Jesus my life was trash. Jesus lifted me up out of that trash.*

Hearing these words D.D. Dunphy shuddered and felt faint as if Jesus had touched her on the forehead—lightly, with just His fingertips.

It was strange then, in the gym with D.D. Dunphy Jesus kept His distance. He did not (yet) approve. There were strong feelings against female boxers. She dreaded the day her Target co-workers found out how she was training at the downtown gym (which was mostly a black and Hispanic gym) and what her hopes were. She confided in no one of course. Not even the female supervisor who'd seemed to perceive (how?—D.D. had not told her) that here was a girl whose mother did not wish to lay eyes on her.

Edna Mae had evinced disgust saying it had to be the influence of Satan that young women would wish to box like men displaying their bodies to the most ignorant crowds and hitting one another in the face like savages for money. D.D. had not known how to refute her mother or any others at her mother's church for some part of her did not disagree with these harsh words. But it was not true, as Edna Mae accused—she was not *Satan's daughter.* She was hurt but she was angry also. She was often hurt, and she was often angry. She felt a kind of disgust and rage herself seeing on TV female boxers heavily made-up and in sexy tight clothes more like swimsuits than proper ring attire like the male boxers wore. For her fights D.D. Dunphy would wear black (like Mike Tyson had done)—black T-shirt over a sturdy sports bra, black shorts to just above the knee which was the length for men.

Soon it would be her time. The time of D.D. Dunphy—"The Hammer of Jesus."

At work, at Target she was mesmerized by such thoughts. At the heavy bag, at the speed bag, doing her squats, lifting weights and doing push-ups, sit-ups, jumping rope she was mesmerized. Her lips parted, her breath came quickly. The voices of others were remote to her. The voices of others were like radio stations fading. Derisive and jeering male eyes she did not see. Crude remarks she did not hear. *Ugly bitch, homely cunt somebody put a bag over her head willya?*—she did not hear. What fascinated was *The Hammer of Jesus* in the ring in TV lights. The female boxer who was not herself but "D.D. Dunphy" in black T-shirt, black trunks. Tight-laced black shoes. Muscled shoulders and arms, muscled thighs, legs. Vaseline rubbed into her face. Mingling with the sweat-glisten. Her hair trimmed short and neatly shaved at the nape of her neck. Her hands tight-bound inside the handsome eight-ounce red gloves. Climbing into the ring and the TV lights blinding in a delirium of anticipation. Cheers and whistles of the crowd and there was the referee lifting her gloved hand in triumph declaring *Winner by a knockout and new WBA Women's Welterweight Champion of the World— D.D. Dunphy the Hammer of Jesus.*

"Jesus, help me. 'Jesus is Lord.'"

She would wear a black cord cap stitched with these words. One day (if it was God's will) she would have sponsors to pay her expenses and support her—Adidas, Nike, Reebok.

Or maybe, a local car dealership. Dayton Sports Supplies.

Johnette Taylor had had a local sponsor when she'd lived in Dayton. She'd had sponsors through her career until she'd begun to lose, then the sponsors dropped away.

D.D. wanted to ask about sponsors for she knew how crucial it was to have a sponsor, you could not afford to be a boxer otherwise for the money was too little especially for female boxers and even those female boxers who were ranked and had won titles. From Ernie she'd learned that the current WBA women's welterweight champion had to work part-time at a Walgreen's in Omaha, Nebraska—this was surprising to her, and disappointing.

"Just to inform you, D.D. Just so you know."

"Know *what?*—that that is how things are right now but won't be always, maybe."

A wildness came into her voice. She understood that this man was trying to discourage her and she could not bear it.

"I don't want to fight for money, anyway."

"What, then?"

"For—a reason."

"What reason?"

She considered. She could not tell him all that was in her heart—the memory of her father who had sacrificed his life, and who was being forgotten.

She could not tell him—*To make of myself something worthy. To make of myself something proud in Jesus's name.*

She heard herself laugh, instead. The way she laughed when she caught her feet in the damn jump rope, or punched herself out on the heavy bag and had to grab it to keep from fainting.

Things that upset her and angered and frustrated her she'd learned to laugh at. The wildness came into her like flame, you had to laugh or scream like a crazy person.

It was a surprise to others, who expected you not to laugh but hide your face in shame. But Jesus counseled her—*Laugh to show you are not not-laughing. Laugh to show that you can laugh.*

"Might be, no reason is worth it. Just sayin, D.D."

He was what you'd call a light-skinned black man or (she thought) some kind of Hispanic mixed with black. Seeing him with others in the gym who were dark-black Ernie Beecher did not look "black" especially but seeing him with so-called "whites" (like herself she supposed) he did look "black"—what they called "African-American."

Later on she'd hear that Ernie Beecher had every kind of "mixed" blood—black, Jamaican, Hispanic, Native American, Asian (Cambodian). How accurate this was she could not know. Or that he was fifty years old, or more!—this was a surprise to her, she'd thought he was much younger given how he sparred in the ring with some of the guys and how tireless he was with her trying to drum into her head *defense strategy*. He had a wife it was said. He had children by several women it was said. He'd been a light-heavyweight a long time ago—you could see his name in small letters on a frayed poster headlined TOMMY HEARNS VS. PIPINO CUEVAS. That had been August 1980, Detroit.

So long ago!—1980. D.D. tried to imagine what Ernie Beecher had looked like then.

He was not a normal-looking man. There was something intense and alert about him, in his eyes like the eyes of a hawk. His face had a twisted look like tree roots that have grown together. Eventually, she would perceive that his face was badly scarred.

She'd have liked to ask this man about his boxing career. Liked to have seen some photos.

But she knew better. She would never ask. She feared losing his goodwill. His patience with her.

It was amazing to her, he'd been so kind. He had not allowed her to pay the full amount for gym hours but a "discount."

He did not ask questions. If the name *Dunphy* meant anything to him—(she had no reason to suspect that it did: no one remembered)—he gave no sign. He was gentlemanly. He did not tolerate bullshit, rowdy behavior, any kind of disruptive or disrespectful behavior in the gym. He would kick you out, you merited it. She had witnessed this with her own eyes. She had heard him speak critically to a young gym instructor, one of his own relatives. He did not forget but he might forgive.

His eyes were soft liquidy-black. His voice was so soft for a man's voice sometimes she could not really hear him but could only murmur *Yes. Yes Ernie.*

The smell of him was such, so defined, *his smell.* Alone in the place she rented on Post Street a few blocks away in the bed that was her bed where often, so tired, she slept in most of her clothes and on cold nights her woolen socks she would wake suddenly in the night smelling *his smell* and in her confusion not know where she was.

She loved him so much! She wanted to tell him of her father who had given his life for the lives of innocent babies who could not protect themselves. She wanted to tell him how badly she missed her father and also she missed her mother and her family in Mad River Junction where she could not return for she was not welcome.

And he would ask *Why are you not welcome, D.D.*

And she would say *Because my mother believes that I am a daughter of Satan.*

But she was shy. And when she was in any proximity to him she was likely to be winded—panting to catch her breath, and her heart beating crazily in her chest. The worry was constant—*Am I strong enough? Maybe I am not strong enough.*

She recalled how Luke had laughed at her. Dawn Dunphy, thinking she could *box.*

She had to smile. It was—well, it was *weird.* Anybody would laugh at her. She would laugh at herself if she hadn't been herself. But Jesus had faith in her, she was sure. As Jesus had had faith in her rising against the high school boys who had hoped to shame her but had only shamed themselves.

The hammer of Jesus she'd wielded in her hand! When she'd finished with her enemies the hammer-head had been slick with their blood.

"One-sixty-one."

He'd weighed her, like a steer. By the expression in his face she saw that he was not happy.

"What'm I s'posed to be?"—her question was piteous.

"One-forty-seven. Welterweight."

Welterweight! It was the first he'd named what she would be.

Her heart flooded with what felt like warm blood. Her eyes flooded with tears. She could not bring herself to look at him, at his face, for fear of betraying what was in her heart.

"Yah. OK. I c'n do that. I guess."

She was a heavy girl. "Stout"—her aunt Mary Kay said of her, and of herself.

Much of it was muscle. But not all.

Had to stop eating any kind of junk food in her hand, food out of Styrofoam boxes, sugary sodas, fries. Her weakness was French fries so greasy-salty her fingers stung as she ate ravenously. The appeal of those fries in the strip mall Wendy's you could douse as much catsup on them you wanted, nobody to stop you or even notice.

The sharp taste of catsup, mustard, diced onions she liked. A lot.

Also she loved doughnuts. Dipped in fat, fat-saturated. Plain doughnuts, white-powder sugar doughnuts, cinnamon doughnuts, cream doughnuts, doughnuts sprinkled with gritty brown sugar—D.D.'s mouth filled with saliva at just the thought.

At Target in the food department with your employee discount you could buy doughnuts marked down for quick sale, that were no longer fresh or were broken into pieces . . .

He was talking to her about *diet*. He'd given her a printout listing foods to eat and foods to avoid. She would try but she could not afford most of the foods to eat (*fresh greens, lean meats*) as he might've known.

But already she was beginning to lose weight even as she was adding muscle, and feeling better, stronger even as she was (often) feeling allover aches and pain and numbness and a ringing in her head like church bells at a distance. And her heart filled with jubilation of all that was to come.

Welterweight was one-four-seven or under. That was the ideal weight for D.D. Dunphy at five feet eight inches in gym shoes.

Her dream was within the year having her first fight and soon then—(she was vague about how this would come about: her trainer would know)—making enough money to quit Target or work part-time. If things went well—(if she won her fights)—she would be matched with contenders Angel Diaz, Pryde Elka ("The Squaw"), Yolinda Crowe. If she won these fights she would be matched with the WBA women's welterweight champion Ilse Kinder if Ilse Kinder was still the champion.

In Mad River Junction they'd see her. On the TV. Maybe not Edna Mae who never watched TV but her great-aunt Mary Kay, her brother Luke, Anita, Noah, neighbors, kids from school, and teachers.

Miss Schine would see her! Miss Schine would be happy for her.

And in Muskegee Falls, they'd see her. People who'd known them in that place where her father Luther Amos Dunphy had lived and worked and where in the courthouse he'd been found guilty and sentenced to death.

She would speak quietly. She would give thanks to

Jesus in a voice of pride. She would reveal to the interviewer that her career as a boxer was in memory of her father Luther Amos Dunphy.

"And I want to thank my teacher Miss Schine . . . She had faith in me, too."

She would overhear him. His voice.

She didn't eavesdrop. She did not ever eavesdrop.

She had not eavesdropped as a girl though knowing (guessing) that her parents were speaking of her little sister Daphne in their lowered worried voices. For it was being said (by certain of the relatives) that the little girl was *not right in the head.*

Badly she wished to hear. But she did not hear.

For she was worried about Daphne too. She and Luke would exchange a look, when Daphne could not seem to stand without being held upright but tumbled onto the floor as if her spine had broken.

Dropped objects onto the floor as if her fingers would not function.

And there were other times, she'd wanted to hear what adults were saying. When her father's brothers came to the house to speak of *what Luther has done. And what must be done now.*

So too in the Dayton gym, she wanted to overhear what Ernie Beecher might be saying. The hope was so keen it was a dread that he might be speaking of *her.*

For Ernie was on the phone often. It was a mobile phone, he carried it with him out of his office. He spoke, and he listened, frowning at the floor. Sometimes his mouth twitched and he was laughing. Sometimes he scarcely spoke at all. The mystery of another's life, inaccessible to her, yet riveting to her, filled her with an anxious sort of wonder.

She liked to hear him giving boxing instructions. There was a comfort in the familiar words spoken in a familiar voice, in familiar rhythms. She did not feel jealousy—much.

Put your weight into it. Lean in.

OK. Again.

Not bad. But not great.

Again.

On the squat old tv in his office she saw videos.

She would sit on a sagging, stained sofa. She would watch the videos entranced. By the end of a fight she was sitting far forward, her back strained and her eyes dry and unblinking.

Great Fights of the Century. Jack Johnson, Jack Dempsey, Gene Tunney, Joe Louis, Jersey Joe Walcott, Rocky Marciano, Floyd Patterson, Cassius Clay/ Muhammad Ali, Mike Tyson. Henry Armstrong, Sugar Ray Robinson, Jake LaMotta, Rocky Graziano, Tony Zale. Carmen Basilio, Marvin Hagler, Thomas Hearns,

Roberto Durán, Sugar Ray Leonard, Oscar de la Hoya, Bernard Hopkins, Floyd Mayweather . . . Not a woman among these and never would be.

And she saw too how over the decades from the early 1900s boxing had largely shifted from white-skinned to dark-skinned, Hispanic.

She wondered if it was too late for her. The best women boxers were black, Hispanic, Native American.

What had Ernie said—*Depends if you're that hungry. That desperate.*

He had not told her *no*. Not yet.

Eight hours at Target, three hours at the gym.

Day following day, week following week, month following month.

She was losing weight—"soft" weight. Her muscles were hardening, her body was an astonishment to her, a promise.

Her breasts she flattened to her chest as well as she could. She wore a sturdy sports bra and over this a T-shirt that did not fit too loosely or too tightly. She did not like to glance at herself in any mirror and especially if she stood naked after a shower. Even the word *naked* was shameful—Edna Mae could not ever have uttered such a word.

But if there was steam on a mirror she might lean

to the mirror to see a ghost-reflection combing wet hair quickly, impatiently, and then brushing it back from her forehead, flat against her scalp. The bristles of the blue plastic brush Miss Schine had given her were no longer possible to get clean and the handle was cracked but she did not want to replace it with another.

She did not tell her trainer that she had relapses when she ate ravenously those foods she should not eat—French fries, doughnuts, pizzas swimming with pepperoni grease. Still, her weight dropped slowly, steadily. It would stabilize between one-forty-two and one-forty-five which Ernie said was ideal.

"OK. Next step. See what you can do."

She was allowed to begin sparring. Very cautiously at first, with one of the gym instructors. Then, with whoever Ernie could talk into climbing into the ring with D.D. Dunphy.

Neighborhood kids looking to be boxers. Young guys in their twenties. Older guys who'd begun careers as boxers but had lost their first fights or suffered injuries and dropped out and were hoping to try again. It was not uncommon at the gym that a male boxer might spar with a female—there were only three instructors, and all were male.

These males were reluctant to spar with D.D.

Dunphy. They meant to pull their punches—at first. But there came Dunphy in a crouch, graceless, grim-determined, with furrowed forehead and lashless eyes, so hard-hitting, when her wildly flung punches hit, the sparring partners were stunned.

"Hey! Shit, man."

They backed away, laughing. They kept her off with flurries of blows.

Ernie followed outside the ring. Ernie commanded: "Move in, Dun-phy. Press in. Don't hold back. Go."

She obeyed. She tried. Very soon she was panting through her mouth.

"Move in. Use your right. *Go.*"

Blindly she pressed forward. On her short legs she threw herself forward. Blows struck her exposed face but she did not shrink away.

These early sessions passed in a blur. Adrenaline flooded her, an exhilarating rush. She had no clear idea what she was doing except she must push forward, and she must fight.

For her life, she would fight. She could not turn back.

Of the historic boxers, she identified with Jack Dempsey who could only push forward and who was thwarted by Gene Tunney capable of moving backward even as he fought.

Word in the gym came to be—*That girl boxer Beecher is training? She a pitbull.*

That Dun-phy some kind of killing machine.

Ernie was amused, she'd wrung from her sparring partners a grudging acknowledgment. He listened to them claiming *Had to hold back, could've broke her face and sent her into the ropes and onto her ass—you saw it. But that girl one hell of a puncher.*

Then, she sparred with her first female. The experience was devastating to her.

Never had she struck any female face before. Never the face of a girl. Only just boy-faces leering at her, deserving to be hit.

Can't do it. Just can't.

It was a shock to her. She would not have anticipated such a surprise. The new sparring partner was a young neighborhood woman hoping also to be a boxer, five or six years older than D.D. Dunphy, taller by at least two inches, somewhat lean, flat-bodied, with a wan-pretty face like something smudged and straw-colored hair showing dark at the roots. Flaming-heart tattoos were displayed on her bare biceps and on her wrists were bracelet-tattoos. She was lighter than D.D. Dunphy by at least fifteen pounds, just fast enough on her feet to keep out of Dunphy's flailing punches.

D.D. sank into her crouch, hiding behind upraised gloves. Hairs stirred on the nape of her neck. To see a female face confronting her beneath the safety headgear! It did not seem right. In her fantasies of winning fights, winning titles, she had not envisioned her opponent except as a blur. It would be like hitting Miss Schine! It would be like hitting her sister . . . The males she had no difficulty wishing to hurt for she hated them but she did not hate this young woman and did not want to hurt her.

What she knew of the female sparring partner was that her name was Mickey Burd and she'd been in training with Ernie Beecher intermittently over the past several years. She had a job in the Dayton General Hospital cafeteria. She'd had to take time off from training to support her family—(her mother had died a few months ago). Maybe she was married, or separated. Maybe she had children. Her only evident skill in the ring was a rapid nervous jab. Her punches were weak, tentative. Her hardest punch was a left hook to the upper chest D.D. Dunphy scarcely felt. But she had a devious way of backing up, laterally, unpredictably, like one skidding on ice, so that D.D. could not catch her.

And when she did, her punches flew wild, or struck glancingly as Burd jerked away.

They fell into clinches, panting. Burd's arms grasped

at D.D.'s broad shoulders like the arms of a drowning woman. She knew, if D.D. broke loose to hit her, she could not protect herself.

"Break. Move."

Ernie was losing patience. "*Break*. I said."

Yet D.D. could not bring herself to shove Burd away. She was much stronger, she was much the superior boxer—that was clear. Yet she was overwhelmed, helpless. She had had no experience with clinching. The closeness of the other girl was annihilating to her. The embrace of the other, the hot slick wetness of the other's skin, the smell of the straw-hair, the breath in her face—she stood paralyzed.

"C'mon, girl! Use that right."

She tried but she could not. Her right arm was so heavy. She could not bear to see the other's face, smudged-white skin like her own.

In disgust Ernie halted the session after three rounds—nine arduous minutes. D.D. Dunphy was swaying on her feet. Her black T-shirt and shorts clung to her body soaked with sweat. Her very scalp tingled with sweat. Her breath came in gasps. Her face stung from the other boxer's quick nervous jabs, mottled red, a trickle of red leaking from her nostrils. Her brain was dazed as Ernie spoke sharply to her.

Had to escape. Climbing out of the ring stumbling.

Dripping blood. Trail of blood from the ring to the rear of the gym, to the women's cramped dank locker room, lavatory and single shower with concrete walls, narrow grimy horizontal window like a cellar window at a height of six feet. The other hurried after her— "Hey. D.D."—sweat-faced and out of breath too but splashing cold water into the sink, to soak paper towels to wipe D.D.'s smarting face.

"Hey. Don't feel bad. You did OK. It's like I always do, or try to—can't hit worth shit so I stay away or clinch. Ernie pushes too hard sometimes. OK?"

Stayed away from the gym for two days. Three days.

(Would he call her? No.)

(She knew he would not, and he did not.)

When she returned he made no comment. It was as if she had not been away or if she'd been away, if she had crawled away to die, it had not mattered to anyone.

And so she was resolved to please him, even if she hated him. She would throw herself harder into the training routine that had come to be a comfort to her even as it was an agony to her. Fast bag, heavy bag, squats, weight-lift, mat exercises, fifteen minutes jump rope. Practicing punches: jab, cross, hook, uppercut. Left jab, right cross, left hook, right uppercut. She would impress him though he would give no sign. The harsh words he'd spoken to her were fraught between

them like a faint, sickening odor that would fade but
slowly.

She was less shy now. Months had passed, she was beginning to be known in the gym. She wished to think—
They are beginning to see how I belong here, too.

She avoided the other females who came into the
gym after work for an hour or less at the machines
openly eyeing themselves in the wall mirror preening
in Spandex tops and tights, run-walking on the tread-
mill in expensive pink ladies' running shoes, bright
made-up faces and glossy fingernails like claws. She
saw how their mascara eyes cut at her, cold and bemused, or pitying—dismissing her in a glance.

Go to hell. Fuck you. Fuck you I'd want to be you.

It was not D.D. Dunphy who uttered such harsh
words, but another. Hoping that Jesus did not hear.

She was waiting for Mickey Burd to return. The
straw-color hair with brunette roots, the quick tease
of a smile—"Hey. You OK?"—but Mickey did not
return. She would not inquire after Mickey.

She might have gone to the young woman's house
to knock at the door. She knew that Mickey Burd
lived close by on a street called Barrister. But she
would not inquire after Mickey, her pride would not
allow this.

Nor did Ernie speak of Mickey Burd to her. The humiliating session in the ring, both were determined to forget.

Lingered in the gym to watch boxers sparring in the ring. Remarkable young black boxers in their twenties, lightweights. She despaired, she could never be so fast on her feet, or so skillful. Their punches were not hard enough to inflict serious damage though hard enough to open cuts on an unprotected face.

She became fascinated by a light heavyweight named Rodriguez, the gym's star boxer. He had once been Ernie Beecher's boxer but now he worked with another, younger trainer who was a protégé of Ernie's, under his guidance.

If he was in the prime of his career, or just past his prime, it did not matter to her. In the gym, sparring with other, younger boxers Hector Rodriguez was capable of flurries of powerful boxing. He reminded her of certain of the old-style boxers she'd been seeing on Ernie's videos—Graziano, LaMotta. His ring style was a minimum of wariness and caution alternating with sheer aggression. He had a strong short left hook that was impressive. He seemed angry when unleashing his most powerful blows as if the sparring partner were an opponent who stood between him and a sizable purse. And the hurt and fury in his eyes, D.D. Dunphy perceived with a thrill of excitement.

She'd said to Ernie, she wanted to box like Rodriguez. She wanted to be that good.

And another time she said, she wanted to spar with
Rodriguez. Just once.

Ernie frowned at such a notion. Ernie shook his head
no. Not a good idea.

Why not? She could learn from Rodriguez better
than anyone else in the gym.

"Why not? He's a light-heavy. He'll hurt you."

"I need that. I need to *know*."

But Ernie was resolute. Not a good idea. *No*.

For weeks she was fixated on Rodriguez who was
training for a fight in Cincinnati. The idea of Rodriguez filled her head like a balloon inflating. She began
to neglect some of her own routines, observing his. And
he'd begun to notice her. In the gym, D.D. Dunphy
was beginning to be known as a female boxer Ernie
was training, and Rodriguez knew of her, and (she
could tell) did not approve of her. He did not approve
of female boxers, and he did not approve of *her*.

She saw him glancing at her. Not-friendly, but cold.
Disdainful. Hispanic male, in disdain of a serious female
athlete. He was hawk-faced, with small scars in his eyebrows, sleek black hair tied tight in a little pigtail at the
back of his head. Despite blemished skin on his face and
neck he was good-looking, vain. His light-heavyweight

body was muscled and fit and the flesh at his waist had not yet become flaccid. On his back, biceps and forearms were cobwebs of tattoos like florid wounds.

Rodriguez sparred with a succession of partners. D.D. Dunphy yearned to be one of these.

She pleaded with Ernie. "I c'n learn."

"Learn what? Getting your jaw broke?"

He was indignant. His praise of her, precious as water to a creature avid with thirst, had become sparing, grudging.

(Was Ernie jealous of Hector Rodriguez? She smiled to think so.)

At Target, those long hours. Dreaming of the gym, its pungent smells, male-sweat, windows opaque with grime. As at her exercises when Rodriguez was not in the gym she dreamt of him. Her eyelids were so heavy! Suddenly they were sparring together as equals. Or almost.

They were sparring together as equals until suddenly Rodriguez released a fury of blows aimed at D.D.'s head, body, head—for the first time, D.D. Dunphy was *knocked down*.

He relented, and crouched over her. He spoke her name—"D.D."

It was Graziano and LaMotta. On their feet, embracing. At the conclusion of a long fight in which one man was the winner and the other the loser yet the face of each was battered, bloody.

She dared to greet Hector Rodriguez when he arrived at the gym one evening with two friends. He was wearing a dove-gray suede jacket, not new, slightly soiled. On his feet, tooled leather boots. His manner with Ernie Beecher's new-girl-in-training was curt, indifferent. There was some tension between Rodriguez and Beecher, as between a son and a father who have disappointed each other and will not forget. But D.D. had timed the encounter with such care, she was in motion, moving past the men, not a moment of indecision, not a backward glance it was so casual to her.

She was observed shadowboxing, in the style of Rodriguez. The inclination of the head, the flurries of sharp quick precise blows to head, body, head of the (imagined) opponent. That short left hook, in an arc of six inches.

In a hoodie drawn over her head, in a chilly corner of the gym. So that, from a little distance, you could not see who it was—female, male.

"'physical.'"

The sound of the word was fascinating to her: "phys-i-cal."

She had never said this word aloud. But now Ernie

Beecher had made an appointment with a Dayton doctor for her *physical*.

The doctor-visit was not a pleasant experience. It had been explained to her that in order to box she had to be "licensed"—in order to be licensed she had to pass a physical examination. She had never had such an examination in her life, she was sure.

Dr. Danks was a heavyset (white) man in his sixties with thin white-feathery hair, blood-veined eyes and nose, a mild tremor in his hands. His stomach was round and prominent, he could not easily move from the chair in which he sat beside his girl patient. His eyes behind bifocal glasses moved along her body to her prim-tucked feet and up again to her stiffened wax-face.

"No problems, eh? Though you are training hard for your first fight?"

Training hard. First fight.

She had not heard it so phrased, that she was *training hard for her first fight*.

Had Ernie Beecher told the doctor this? She felt a flood of great happiness, and could not speak.

"Your trainer has requested a prescription for you. When a female is boxing there's concern for—well, the 'menstral cycle' it is called. A female athlete should take precautions so she is always at her peak. I'd hoped to examine you a little more thoroughly but, well—you are obviously in excellent condition. Ernie Beecher has a reputation for working with only the best athletes he can find. So now, miss, if you can cooperate just a little—we can complete these formalities and you can be on your merry way."

She hadn't heard much of this. She had not quite heard the shameful words *menstral cycle*. And *merry way*—what did that mean?

She could think only *first fight. Training hard.*

Wheezing Dr. Danks was not going to touch her further, that was all that mattered.

He conferred with the nurse-receptionist, and shuffled out of the room. In a bright cajoling voice of the kind one might employ with a recalcitrant child the woman told D.D. that she could "provide a swab" from between her legs herself, with a cotton Q-stick—"That should be enough, then. Like a 'Pap smear.'" D.D. was very much embarrassed, but took the little stick from her, and cautiously touched herself with it, between the legs where (she supposed) there was some sticky dampness. Blushing deeply she handed the befouled stick to the nurse-receptionist who took it with gloved fingers. "Thank you!"

Alone in the examination room she lay on the table for a moment unable to move. She had been spared the outrage of a *pelvic exam*.

Edna Mae would be relieved, and not so disgusted with her.

Never would she forget those words—*Training hard. For your first fight.* Waves of relief, gratitude, hope swept over her.

"Thank you, Jesus!"

He had not abandoned her after all. But she knew that.

In the wake of the doctor-visit she was given by her trainer a small plastic container of white pills. One-a-day, each morning.

"What's this for?"—D.D. was doubtful about taking pills recalling how pills had affected Edna Mae.

These were smaller pills, but also white.

Ernie told her it was to "prevent problems"—"like, once a month"—since she was a "female athlete, who has to take precautions."

He seemed embarrassed, irritated. As if D.D. should have known what he was talking about.

For a long slow moment D.D. did not comprehend, then a kind of comprehension came over her, like murky water rising.

Near-inaudibly, shamefaced she murmured *OK*.

The first fight was scheduled that very day.

Now there was a date, a goal. Now she could measure the days on the calendar until February 11, 2009.

Not wishing to recall the previous times she'd marked calendar dates.

Now she was officially in training, now everyone knew. There was respect for her. In the eyes of the others, except maybe the young women who came to the gym only to "exercise"—there was a new interest, maybe a kind of awe.

That her?—Dunphy?

Christ! That's a female Tyson.

One day sparring with Eduardo, a lapsed welter-weight, formerly one of Ernie's promising young boxers, D.D. was stunned by a blow to the right temple that seemed to fly out from Eduardo's right glove. She was dazed, and slipped to one knee; she felt how the ring floor pulled at her, like a magnet; but there came Ernie's terse command—*Get up. Get on him*—and she managed to get her balance, and to rush at her opponent with a flurry of blows to his midriff and lower belly, groin—in her desperation, and with a murderous intent, driving him back into the ropes.

"Hey! Fucking Christ! What're you doing!—" Eduardo was gasping for breath, bent double. Tears shone on his cheeks.

Adrenaline rushed through her veins. So fierce she felt that flames might be oozing through her pores.

Ernie halted the match. Dunphy had hit low, with a vicious intent. He had not seen that in the girl, until this hour. There was something about her pebble-colored eyes and small mean mouth that was frightening to him, but exhilarating.

So then I knew. Dunphy could do it.

You got to be hungry, and to want to kill the opponent.

That's all. That's everything.

"My first fight."

Spoken aloud these words had almost the resonance of an echo.

"Six weeks from now, *my first fight.*"

She was beginning to tell people. Co-workers at Target. The supervisor Evelyn who seemed to like her. (But was very surprised to hear her good news.) A neighbor in the apartment building in which she rented a single, ground-floor room overlooking a front yard of mostly concrete.

Shyly, yet boastfully—*My first fight. Cleveland. I have a trainer and a manager—yes.*

It was a wonder to her, to say so matter-of-factly—*I have a trainer. Ernie Beecher is my trainer.*

Stranger to say—*I have a manager. Mr. Cassidy . . .*

Cass Cassidy was a partner in the Dayton gym. It wasn't clear (to D.D.) if he was a business partner of Ernie Beecher or if he was Ernie's employer. He was very friendly with Ernie often laying his hand on Ernie's shoulder and calling him *old buddy.* He was a middle-aged (white) man who "managed" boxers and who appeared at the gym from time to time. If you heard a loud voice, laughter—it was likely to be Cass Cassidy trading wisecracks with the young (brown-skinned) boxers.

Cassidy had been Hector Rodriguez's manager at some previous time. But Rodriguez no longer won fights and so he had another manager. (D.D. had been crushed to learn that Rodriguez had lost his fight in Cincinnati by a "split" decision. This was his third straight loss. It was said of Rodriguez that "his luck had turned against him" which was alarming to D.D. Dunphy to hear for it suggested something like a tidal wave, a shudder of the earth and a flooding that could not be prevented—an Act of God.)

Hector Rodriguez had not reappeared in the gym in weeks and D.D. was so immersed in her own training, she had given up looking for him.

"H'lo, 'D.D.' How's it going."

The voice was flat yet coercive. D.D. heard herself murmur, "OK."

Often, D.D.'s voice sounded sullen, grudging when she was asked any question. She did not mean this. She had a fear of stammering, or saying the wrong thing and being laughed-at.

They were in Ernie's office. D.D. had been summoned here. She had had a vigorous workout that afternoon and had showered and her hair was wet and lank, brushed back from her forehead. Every part of her body ached and yet—she was very happy! Ernie had told her she was "making progress." A dozen times a day she whispered *Thank you, Jesus.*

Ernie introduced her to Cass Cassidy who was to be her "manager."

Cassidy's hand snaked out, and D.D. was shaking the hand. The fingers felt somewhat cold. For a scant moment she feared the fingers would not release her hand.

Cassidy addressed her in a drawling voice that seemed too expansive for Ernie Beecher's small office. He told her he'd been hearing "damn good things" about her from Ernie Beecher and all that he'd seen with his own eyes had confirmed this.

D.D. wasn't sure if she was meant to reply to this.

She was finding it hard to smile but she managed to say—"Thank you."

The man was eyeing her with a look of wary good cheer. His face was a youngish-old face of creases and dents and yet on his upper lip was a mustache of the bright hue of fox fur. He was not a tall man though he wore tooled-leather cowboy boots with a heel, a shirt of some shiny material, deep purple. His hair, a duller hue than his mustache, was slicked back thinly from his forehead. His eyes were bemused, somewhat cold. Cold dead eyes like a reptile. D.D. swallowed hard, and forced herself to smile, for Ernie was watching, and Ernie wished this. Her trainer was looking at her with that particular crease between his eyes she saw in his face sometimes when she was working out. There came Edna Mae's hissing voice in her ear—*He is Satan. They are all Satan. You are surrounded by Satan.*

Some decision had been made in the trainer's office. D.D. smiled for she did not want to appear ignorant. She understood that the men had been discussing her before she'd entered the office and she felt a small thrill of pride, that two men, two adults, should confer about her.

She thought that her father might be proud of her, if he knew. Luke would be jealous but proud, too.

The decision seemed to be, D.D. would go on half-time at Target. A schedule had been worked out leading to the fight which was February 11, 2009, in the Cleveland Armory. Cassidy—"Cass"— would provide money for D.D. as needed. A kind of allowance.

"Did you ever have an allowance, D.D.? When you were a kid?"

D.D. was overwhelmed by this news. She did not know how to reply. She did not even comprehend the question.

"Yah. I guess so."

"Well, this will be a lot more. I guarantee."

There was a sheet of stiff white paper—a "contract"—for her to sign. In a haze of excitement, gratitude, wonderment she signed it—*Dawn D. Dunphy.* Her schoolgirl signature beside a large slanted scrawl she could not decipher but had to suppose that it was Mr. Cassidy's signature above the words which were new to her—*Dayton Fights, Inc.*

To her astonishment she was given eight crisp new-smelling one-hundred-dollar bills. These were counted out in her hand by Cass Cassidy—"*Vy-la,* D.D.!—as they say in France. The rest is boxing history."

Clumsily then, with no warning, Cass Cassidy brought his hand down on D.D.'s head, rubbing her damp hair, in a gesture of rough affection, as one might pat the head of a favored dog. He then dared to hug her, not hard, but in the way some of the Dunphy women would hug Dawn, loose-armed, somewhat wary of the stocky girl's stiff spine and uplifted elbows, no sooner embracing her than releasing her.

So startled by this sudden gesture from a man she feared, as by the contract and the money, the wonderful-smelling crisp new bills, Dawn Dunphy stood staring, flat-footed and speechless, arms at her sides and her hands feeling bare, without gloves.

In an envelope carefully printed EDNA MAE DUN-PHY c/o MARY KAY MACK on Depot Street, Mad River Junction, she mailed five of these crisp new-smelling one-hundred-dollar bills to her mother whose work (as a nurse's aide in a nursing home) paid her something like seven dollars an hour.

Dear Momma, this is for you. Sorry I am out of touch for a wile. Hope you & Anita & Noah are doing OK.

I am doing well. I am in Dayton now.
Look for me on TV in February 2009!

Love
Your Daughter Dawn
"D.D. Dunphy"—"Hammer of Jesus"

"Jesus Is Lord"

The *first fight* would pass in a blur.

Abruptly terminated at two minutes forty-two seconds of the first round.

There was but a small crowd scattered through the Cleveland Armory. Of five hundred seats in the shabby old arena less than one hundred were occupied. *Lorina "The Cougar" Starr vs. D.D. Dunphy—"The Hammer of Jesus."*

The match between two (unranked) female welterweights scheduled for five rounds was number four on the undercard, and was scheduled to begin early—7:00 P.M. The main bout of the evening was a twelve-round match between heavyweight contenders (Deontay Wilder, Tony Thompson) ranked by the World Boxing

Association at numbers four and six respectively, and would begin at approximately 9:00 P.M.

The undercard consisted of matches of ascending interest. Only the last two matches were to be televised on a cable channel.

"Lorina Starr"—(D.D. would never forget this name)—was the opponent they'd found for her, for the *first fight.* A woman of some age beyond thirty who lived and trained in Gary, Indiana. Lorina Starr had once been ranked at number seven (WBA women's welterweight) but after several losses had dropped off the charts. She was said to be of Chickasaw Indian extraction.

(D.D. had learned: there were no Indian reservations in either Ohio or Illinois only just the scattered descendants of the original Indians who'd been removed to a desolate area of Oklahoma by the Indian Removal Act of the U.S. government in some long-ago time. Lorina Starr was one of these—the descendant of Chickasaws who'd managed to escape the mass evacuation to Oklahoma.)

In her publicity photos Lorina "The Cougar" Starr appeared to be a sexy-glamorous young woman despite a scarred face. It was a surprise to D.D. to see her in person (at the weigh-in) for she was considerably older than her photos. Her features were Caucasian except for very dark eyes and very black straight hair which had been cut short and streaked with platinum-blond highlights. Her skin was coarsely made up with a red-tinted beige powder. She wore sexy boxing attire—a sequin-spangled red sports bra, Spandex-tight blue trunks that fitted her shapely buttocks tightly. Above her left breast was a tattoo of a red boxing glove and on her right shoulder, a snarling cougar with a curving tail. It was boasted that the Cougar "never gave up a fight" and "never disappointed a crowd."

At the weigh-in D.D.'s opponent was giddy and edgy with a grating laugh like a cough. She could not seem to bring herself to look at her much-younger opponent still less shake hands with her. "Hey shit, I'm not your friend, girl"—Lorina Starr recoiled from D.D.'s approach when the boxers were urged to shake hands.

D.D. had to restrain herself from saying *Sorry!* This was a word that came too readily to her.

It was revealed that D.D. Dunphy was heavier than Lorina Starr by six pounds and shorter by two inches. Her reach was fifty-nine inches, Lorina Starr's reach was sixty-one inches.

(D.D. did not want to think that these two inches might be crucial. Ernie said with a shrug, *You got to get inside.*)

Lorina Starr's ring record was three wins, seven losses, one draw.

D.D. Dunphy's ring record was zero wins, zero losses.

There came scattered applause in the arena as the female boxers, the first bout of the evening, were introduced by the big-voiced male announcer. A few wan whistles stimulated by Lorina's spangled red sports bra and Spandex trunks and a few spirited handclaps when D.D. Dunphy's ring record was announced and it was revealed that this was Dunphy's first fight.

In the front rows only a few spectators were sitting, all male. These were loud-voiced, very possibly drunk. Some were eating hot dogs and drinking from paper cups. (Beer? Officially, not allowed in the Armory.)

In a trance of exhilaration and dread D.D. had entered the Armory. Her ears were ringing. Her mouth was so dry she could not have swallowed except a plastic water bottle was lifted to her mouth by one of her handlers.

She'd been exercising vigorously, somewhat desperately, in the locker room. She was covered in sweat which was consoling to her as a fine-mesh blanket.

Here was a disappointment—just slightly. Her manager Cass Cassidy had not allowed her to wear black in imitation of Mike Tyson. He had not allowed her to wear a cap with the words JESUS IS LORD stitched on it.

Maybe later, he'd said ambiguously. When the Hammer of Jesus had some followers.

D.D. Dunphy had been issued dark-red trunks, dark-red T-shirt trimmed in white. Her shoes were not black shoes but a girl's shoes, dark red with tassels. There had been some reason for this, she'd had to accept.

She was a soldier now. She was a robot-soldier. Her trainer had instructed her: fix your gaze on your opponent and never look away. "Rivet" your opponent with your gaze "like a viper" and never, never look away.

Did she understand? Yes. She did.

For weeks she'd been told that the fight was hers to win. She could not lose. She believed this.

In the seconds before the bell rang for the first round Ernie spoke matter-of-factly in her ear giving instructions. She was a *killing machine*. She was a *deadly viper*. She was a *pitbull*. She had only to fight as she'd been taught and as she'd been practicing. So many times her trainer had led her through the sequence of punches which she executed flawlessly, tirelessly. She must *get inside*, for her arms were short. She must *move forward*, never back. Executing her practice-routines in the gym D.D. Dunphy was near-flawless but with a sparring partner she was less predictable and in this unfamiliar setting, in a vast arena of hundreds of seats, very bright lights, isolated shouts and cries and whistles, and facing an opponent with whom she'd never sparred, she was feeling like one who has opened a door and is about to step inside, trusting that there is a floor on the other side and not—nothing.

The bell rang at last. The boxers emerged from their corners staring at each other like sleepwalkers who have been rudely awakened.

As a cougar might approach a viper Lorina Starr approached her younger opponent with caution. Lorina Starr paid no heed to catcalls from the audience. She was skilled in prevarication, evasion. She had no wish to be hit for she had (many times) been hit and knew what *being hit* could mean. She was poking at Dunphy with her left jab, looking for an opening to hit the big-shouldered chunky white girl square in the face with her poised right hand and send the girl staggering back into the ropes but this did not happen for Dunphy crouched low, shielding her face with her raised gloves, and managed to slip Lorina Starr's blows. This was the *peek-a-boo* style Ernie Beecher had drilled into her, which had been Mike Tyson's defensive strategy drilled into him by his great trainer Cus d'Amato.

You're short, short-armed. You need to go shorter.

The welterweights circled each other as isolated calls and whistles came from the arena. D.D. was surprised that the rapid left jab of her opponent scarcely registered against her arms and shoulders, awkwardly thrown, with no evident force behind it.

Strange, unnerving, to see the other's face and eyes so close to her! The small white scars in the eyebrows that had been darkened with eyebrow pencil, glittering piercings in the ears that were not a good idea (D.D. was sure) to wear into the ring. The skin was damply flushed like her own, somewhat pale, coarse, without the red-tinged beige powder that was meant (D.D. supposed) to suggest "red skin."

Sensing herself the stronger of the two D.D. pressed forward, hitting with her jab, harder than the opponent could hit, forcing the opponent backward, off balance. Always she was pressing forward, trying to *get inside* the reach of the taller boxer. As she positioned herself to throw a right cross the opponent jerked away like a frightened rabbit. Yet D.D. managed to hit her, a rapid right, a rapid and hard left hook, striking the opponent on the right temple, and sending her down onto one knee.

Immediately, a flurry of excitement in the arena.

The referee began his count. Five, six, seven . . . Dazed and blinking Lorina Starr rose to her feet at seven. She might have taken a count of nine to give herself a little more recovery time but she seemed defiant, brash. She was bleeding from a cut lip. Already she was badly out of breath. The referee peered frowningly at her but allowed the fight to continue as Lorina Starr backed away raising her gloves to prepare for an assault which she knew was coming, and which she could not prevent.

The younger and stronger boxer pushed forward aggressively, swarming over her, striking with both fists, a powerful volley of blows as cries lifted from the arena in approval.

The sight of blood on the opponent's face was exciting to D.D. like the sight of something forbidden. She had not expected to wound the opponent so quickly. She had expected a more experienced opponent, and a more dangerous opponent.

Go forward! Get inside! Hit her!—there came her trainer's urgent voice, or the memory of his voice.

A kind of madness came over her. A red mist. She was exultant, pushing forward. It was as if she and the opponent were drowning together in some terrible bright-lit place and D.D. had to fight the other woman off, defeat her utterly, to save herself.

Cries of the crowd like the shrieks of rapacious birds.

In this first fight D.D. understands: that is how

a boxer knows that she is doing well. She is not just scoring points—she is arousing the crowd. She is intimidating her opponent who hears these cries and understands them utterly. She has no need to wait for a trainer's terse praise.

An astonishment, the response of strangers. The reaction of the crowd that was so immediate. *The crowd was on her side and wanted her to hurt the other, and to win.*

D.D. Dunphy's powerful left hook, her sharp right cross. She had practiced these for months, and could now "unpack" them. Inside the other's feeble defense raining frenzied blows on the opponent as the opponent stumbled back into the ropes, trying desperately to clinch with her stronger opponent, being shoved away, failing, falling.

Lorina Starr fell heavily, her legs could no longer support her. With an audible thud her head struck the canvas. Panting with excitement D.D. crouched over the opponent not knowing what to do—she had not (yet) had the experience of knocking down, knocking out, an opponent; the situation did not seem real to her, and so she wondered—was this a trick? Was the opponent going to leap up, and attack her? Her heart was beating wildly, flooded with adrenaline. When someone touched her arm—(the referee: urging her to cross the ring into a neutral corner)—her instinct was to punch this person, hard.

But she did not. She understood. Her handlers had been yelling at her, and she understood.

In the neutral corner staring with wide blinking sweat-stinging eyes as (at the count of five) the referee stopped the fight, with a swift gesture of crossed forearms, for Lorina Starr was unresponsive.

In the arena, cries and applause. The first fight of D.D. Dunphy, welterweight, from Dayton, Ohio, had ended in a knockout, a rarity in women's boxing.

And in the first round: two minutes forty-two seconds of the first round.

Was this possible? She had stumbled out of the neutral corner, summoned by the referee. She did not want to look too closely at the fallen Lorina Starr—"The Cougar."

Her arm was being raised. Her name was being uttered, amplified—*D.D. Dunphy, "Hammer of Jesus"—two minutes forty-two seconds, first round.*

Her trainer was beside her. Her mouthpiece was removed. Her smile was the smile of a blind person confused by waves of sound. Her face looked as if it had been slapped, reddened by the jabs of her opponent, but not bloodied. Her skin was intact. Her lips had not been split. Flat-footed now she stood bathed in sweat, glittering in the bright lights. With a stab of something like guilt she was staring at the fallen opponent, slowly coming to consciousness, helped to her feet by her handlers as the small crowd continued to clap, cheer, whistle. There was approval of D.D. Dunphy's performance and now there was some (fleeting) acknowledgment of the losing boxer Lorina Starr whose last fight this would be.

In the ring, in the bright lights, D.D. stood with her gloves lowered at her sides uncertain what to do. She seemed not to know where to go next.

Then—there was someone—a man—grabbing her, embracing her.

Her trainer! Ernie Beecher virtually never touched D.D. Dunphy except to tie on and remove her boxing gloves. Now, Ernie was embracing her.

"Good work, D.D.! Perfect uppercut. Viper-fast."

But she'd missed many punches. She'd made mistakes. All that had happened was that her opponent had made more.

He would tell her that later, in the gym. But not now.

Lorina Starr was able now to stand without her corner men steadying her, though they were close beside her. Her sallow, scarred face was bleeding from numerous cuts. She was looking so tired now—much older than thirty—possibly by ten years. Trying to speak, even to smile jauntily—but she could not. In a rush of emotion D.D. pushed away from her trainer to run to Lorina, to embrace her with girlish enthusiasm, as she'd seen winning boxers embrace their defeated opponents. She was feeling almost weak now with gratitude, relief that the fight was over, that *she had won.*

Their skins that were both hot and clammy-feeling skidded together, slick with sweat. From a great distance the cries from the arena echoed around their heads like thunder.

The opponent's mouth was swollen, Lorina could not speak. D.D. heard herself cry in a wild wail of a voice—"God bless you—Jesus loves you, too—*thank you.*"

Hurriedly then they were made by their handlers to leave the ring. The next boxers, (male) middleweights, buoyed by fresh waves of applause, were already at ringside.

"D.D. Dunphy's *first fight.*"

Blurred photos were posted on the front wall at the gym. A newspaper clipping of the fight night in Cleveland on which, in the final, brief paragraph, crucial lines were highlighted in yellow.

In the gym, spontaneous applause when D.D. appeared the following week.

Now the eyes were on her, just slightly differently. Not derisive—(not so that she could see)—but subtly envious, admiring.

For the *first fight* she was given, in an envelope, $900 in crisp new-smelling bills.

She had not known how much money she would receive—she'd been reluctant to ask. For she had signed a contract and would be expected to know such details; and yet, she'd had difficulty reading the contract which contained words she had not ever seen before in print. And so she'd put her copy of the contract carefully away for safekeeping in a manila folder in a small cardboard box kept beneath the bed of her rented room. She did not want to be embarrassed in front of her trainer. She did not want to be embarrassed before Mr. Cassidy who seemed both mildly amused by D.D. Dunphy and somewhat perplexed by her, if not disdainful of her as a *female boxer.* (She'd overheard Cassidy speaking of her as *our girl-ox*—which was meant to be affectionate, she thought; recalling how for a brief while, at the high school, when she'd been a player on the girls' basketball team, such remarks were made of Dawn Dunphy, and not meanly.)

She was thrilled by the sight of so much money. Hundred-dollar bills—nine of them! Her first impulse was to call Luke, to tell him. For some reason she was thinking of her brother. *See? What did I tell you? Ass-hole.*

But no: she felt generous, magnanimous. She loved her brother—*she loved them all.*

Though she had not heard from Edna Mae since sending her five hundred dollars some months ago she would send Edna Mae, again in cash, in an envelope addressed to EDNA MAE DUNPHY c/o MARY KAY MACK on Depot Street, Mad River Junction, five hundred of the nine hundred dollars contained inside a plain sheet of paper folded neatly.

Dear Momma, this is for you.

Hope you & Anita & Noah are doing OK.

Please say Hello to Luke & to Mary Kay for me.

I "won" my first fight in Cleveland. They are saying that I am "on my way." I did not get on TV this time but maybe next time.

Hope that your nurse-work is going real well.

Love
Your Daughter Dawn
"D.D. Dunphy"—"Hammer of Jesus"

———————

"**When you** win, lots of people want to be your friend. When you lose, your own damn family don't want to see you."

But Mickey Burd was joking, mostly. Mickey had a high nervous laugh that felt to D.D. like somebody tickling her ribs.

Somehow it had happened, after the triumph of the *first fight*, Mickey Burd was her friend. Mickey showed up at the gym one afternoon to watch D.D. Dunphy train, and that was the beginning—she'd rushed at D.D. to embrace her in a tight hug, congratulating her on her win over her first opponent, daring to brush her lips against D.D.'s sweaty cheek. "Damn girl, you are on your way!"

D.D. had been so taken by surprise she'd let her gloves fall to her sides. Ernie frowned seeing his ex-girl-boxer hugging his new girl-boxer but did not speak harshly to her.

Between Mickey and D.D. it was Mickey who did 90 percent of the talking which was a relief to D.D. also because Mickey had such a wild sense of humor, D.D. would laugh until her stomach hurt.

Most of the time, and always when she was alone, D.D. never laughed. What was so funny? Her mind just naturally lapsed into sadness when she was alone. Or when she was shelving merchandise at Target which was almost the same as being alone. She would try to think of how she'd won her first boxing match and how she was already signed up for a second boxing match and how proud her father would be of her, except her father was not living to know, and anyway when she thought honestly about it, she was not so sure that Luther Dunphy would approve of a *girl boxer*. She would put it to Jesus for an opinion but He stood a way off if the issue was something trivial for He did not like D.D. to be "brooding" and "sad." The admonition is to *make a joyful noise unto the Lord* as she'd been told as a child in the St. Paul Missionary Church. And so she could never think of a single thing funny but Mickey Burd always could.

Mickey took D.D. Dunphy to her favorite pizzeria, to celebrate her victory over Lorina Starr. "Some 'cougar'! That bitch is lucky you didn't break her jaw and it'd have to be *wired*."

On her fingers Mickey counted off things that D.D. should do for herself now that she had a little money.

"Number one, you can do something with your hair. Right now it's like you don't do anything with it, except wash it once in a while, but if you're in the public eye which is what boxing is, especially women's boxing, you should stand out, like, in some way special to you. Like, I used to bleach my hair all kinds of colors until it got dried out and brittle like shit so now I'm letting it go back to just brown. But I'll have blond streaks in it. What you should do, and I can help you, is have streaks put in your hair—like blond, or red—even purple, orange, green—and have the hair cut like a Mohawk, y'know what that is? So you look real butch, but in a fun way."

D.D. blushed to hear these words. She knew what a Mohawk was—a haircut that some guys wore.

"Well, maybe not *fun*. Because you are a serious athlete—of course. But some connection with, like, Indians—your manager Cassidy can say you have 'Indian blood'—like Lorina Starr except that poor bitch really is from some damn Indian tribe that gets special tax breaks." Mickey laughed scornfully. "Lot of good it did her!"

D.D. wondered why Mickey was so derisive speaking of Lorina Starr. Hadn't it been enough for the woman to have been knocked out in the ring by a first-time boxer, and to have lost the fight? D.D. had begun to see how in boxing there was ridicule and a kind of fury associated with losers as if putting distance between yourself and them was a way of protecting yourself from them.

"Did you ever box her?"—D.D. asked impulsively.

"Fuck her. Never mind her."

Mickey seemed annoyed. Probably yes, she'd fought Lorina Starr, and probably she had lost. D.D. wasn't going to pursue the subject.

"It's you we're talking about, girl. 'The Hammer of Jesus'—that calls for something special."

D.D. was mesmerized by this new friend whom she scarcely knew speaking so matter-of-factly and familiarly about her. Since she'd been Dawn Dunphy living at home she'd never considered that she was a person about whom others might have opinions, let alone strong opinions. Streaks in her hair? *Mohawk?*

Only the most asshole guys she knew, working at the mall at Safeway, Walmart, Walgreen's, Target, wore their hair in Mohawks and these were short, abbreviated Mohawks you could almost mistake for just ordinary spike-haircuts.

"Let me take you to the beauty salon where my cousin works, and see what they can do for you. Maybe not a Mohawk but something sharp and cool. Ernie says you win your next fight you'll be on TV probably. You know Ernie never exaggerates. Some color-streaks in your hair will be terrific. Plus tats."

"'Tats'?"

"Tattoos. You need some great tattoos, to go with your great body."

D.D. laughed, shaking her head. She would never consent to a tattoo. It would be the final break between her and Edna Mae and all of Edna Mae's church-friends, if she did. There was nothing more savage and heathen than tattoos, her parents had believed.

"I don't think so, Mickey. That would not be good."

"Why'n hell *not?*"

"Because—it's like a heathen thing. It isn't Christian."

"Christ spoke against tats? Like hell He did."

D.D. laughed, shocked. She could not recall that Jesus had ever spoken of tattooing the body but it was not like Jesus to restrain or scold.

"I just think—my church—my kind of church—where my family goes—would not approve . . ."

But she spoke tentatively. Mickey scowled and laughed at her.

"There's all kind of Christian tats. Some of the best tats. There's Christian rock music, did you know? There's Christian heavy metal bands. It's way cool. Fuck, it's *hot.* Have some of my beer. You're not in training every damn minute."

"Ernie wouldn't like it . . ."

"Fuck Ernie. What're you, engaged to him? Shit."

D.D. was stunned to hear these words. She could

not believe that her friend had said such things about
Ernie Beecher.

"See, girl—Ernie doesn't have to know."

Mickey poured water out of D.D.'s water glass and
into her own water glass, and poured the remainder of
her beer into D.D.'s glass.

"Go ahead, drink it. It won't kill you."

D.D. lifted the glass reluctantly. The smell of beer
had always been intriguing to her. Edna Mae had been
upset when Luther drank beer, when she could smell
beer on his breath; but others in the Dunphy family
drank beer, she knew. Luther's brothers.

D.D. took a small taste. Her nose crinkled. The
taste was so strong, something flamey ran up her
nose. Seeing her friend regarding her so closely D.D.
laughed, and hiccupped.

Mickey's eyes were mascara-smudged. Often she
looked sleepy, as if she'd just wakened from a deep
sleep. The dark roots of her hair had grown so that
the straw-colored hairs seemed to float an inch or two
above her head like a halo. Mickey had a way of lick-
ing her lower lip that made D.D. feel shivery as she felt
when a cat licked her hand.

"So, we'll get your hair cut and streaked, just a little.
And a beautiful cool tat. You can pick it out yourself."

Blushing D.D. shook her head *no*. That could never happen.

Mickey took her to the Golden Arrow Tattoo Parlor on Division Avenue.

This was downtown Dayton where D.D. had not yet been. At the edge of downtown in a neighborhood of taverns, nail salons, pawnshops, tattoo parlors. Division Avenue was a wide windswept littered street, they had to run to cross before the light changed like two high school girls—laughing and shrieking as traffic advanced upon them.

"Marco, h'lo! Here's my friend D.D. Dunphy— 'The Hammer of Jesus.' Next God-damn women's welterweight champion of the *world*."

Mickey swaggered into the fluorescent-lit tattoo parlor in which the girls were mirrored on the walls in distorted, distended versions of themselves. D.D. saw herself and quickly looked away. Her face was so coarse and plain, her eyebrows so heavy, she felt a pang of loathing.

"Here. Look here"—Mickey was pointing at tattoo designs displayed on the wall.

On D.D. Dunphy's right bicep there came to be tattooed a cross made of crimson roses, four inches in length. On her left bicep, a matching cross of white lilies.

On her back, close beneath her neck, in an ornamental black font, were tattooed the words JESUS IS LORD.

It was an enormous undertaking! Hours were required.

Mickey had gone away, and returned with Cokes and cheeseburgers. D.D. was determined not to wince with pain as the needle pricked, poked, jabbed into her skin, like something alive that was eating her.

"Oh God, D.D. Those are fucking *beautiful.*"

In the mirror D.D. stared at herself. On each of her bare upper arms, a cross. On her back, below her neck, JESUS IS LORD. She'd expected to feel a rush of shame but it was another kind of rush she was feeling.

Crude and clumsy *but she had heart. That, D.D. Dunphy had.*

In a boxer the heart is the last thing to go. Just before his life.

First, they lose heart. Then, they lose their lives.

"Thank you, Jesus."

Within the year she was rising within the women's welterweight division. *D.D. Dunphy* ranked at number thirteen, then number ten, then number eight . . . The second match was with a Canadian girl, a former super lightweight boxer from Nova Scotia, moving up now to welterweight, beautifully precise, poised, very fast on her feet, yet like Lorina Starr confounded by Dunphy's aggressive ring style—*Push forward. Get inside. Use your strength. Keep in focus. Hurt her.*

The Canadian girl was named Cameron Krist. She had an American trainer now, an American manager and promoter. She'd had six professional bouts in the States and had won each by a decision. She wore white satin trunks with red trim, a white top with a red maple leaf embossed on front and back. Her pale hair was tight-braided. Her skin was unlined, smooth. She had the poise of an athlete who is confident that she cannot be hit, she is too fast on her feet, and too smart.

A tall graceful bird confronted by a short graceless shrike-bird on the attack.

The Hammer was not cautious. The Hammer rushed forward as if blindly.

The Hammer wore silky black trunks, black T-shirt. Black shoes. On the Hammer's biceps, vivid tattoos: a cross festooned with white lilies, and a cross festooned with red roses. On her back just beneath her neck the words JESUS IS LORD.

It had been obvious as soon as the girl-boxers climbed into the ring: the one in the white trunks trimmed with red was the sexually attractive female, the one in the black trunks was the unattractive female. Yet, the excited interest of the (mostly male) spectators leapt to the boxer in the black trunks as she began to batter her opponent and render her hapless, helpless as a girl.

Because you become a man, battering the other. That is what "man" is—battering the other into submission.

Krist's unblemished unlined face was bloodied. Both her eyes would be blackened. A flash of slick red appeared in her nostrils. An inch-long cut in her eyebrow leaked blood. The referee peered at her frowning but did not stop the fight. When Krist tried again to clinch he roughly separated the boxers.

"Break! Step back."

There came isolated cries as the Hammer rushed in for the kill with powerful blows like the sweep of a scythe.

Remembering Mike Tyson—*I like to hit the nose, shove the nose-bone back into the brain.*

Krist was down, tangled in her own feet. Krist lay facedown, and would not get up for some minutes.

This time, D.D. Dunphy was not so confused. On her steady strong unhurried legs she went to a neutral corner and awaited the count.

Suffused with adrenaline, her heart pumped in joy, exhilaration. The fight was stopped. Her trainer was in the ring stepping toward her rapidly.

His embrace, and a jubilant murmur in her ear— *Great work. Even better than the first.*

The referee was congratulating her. She had not fully looked at him until now—a middle-aged black man, sharp-eyed. The way this man was looking at *her.*

Her mouthpiece soaked with saliva was removed. Her arm that had not yet begun to ache was being lifted aloft. The boxing glove smeared with her opponent's blood was lifted aloft. Though D.D. Dunphy understood that she had won the fight the enormity of the victory had not yet fully sunk into her consciousness like cotton batting absorbing moisture and so she glanced about the arena blinking and moist-eyed as if seeking amid the faces contorted with cheering a face that was familiar to her.

Winner by knockout—one minute fifty-five seconds of the first round—D.D. Dunphy—"Hammer of Jesus."

"She's a killer. Christ, she scares me!"

But it was a delicious sort of scare. The Hammer felt it like a cat shivering as it is being stroked.

She was in the gym every day. She loved the gym. On the front wall by the counter was a clipping from the *Dayton News* with a photograph of "D.D. Dunphy— 'Hammer of Jesus'"—above a single-paragraph article with the headline *Ohio Woman Welterweight, 21, Scores Upset Win Over Canadian Star.*

Had it been an "upset win"?—D.D. had not realized.

She was reasonably certain that Cameron Krist had not been a "star."

She still worked part-time at Target. She had received $1,200 for her second fight but there were considerable expenses now and so she had not been able to send more than five hundred dollars to Edna Mae.

(She knew that Edna Mae had received the money she'd sent because she had heard from Luke after her second fight. Her brother had started off congratulating her for winning her fights but his tone turned mean midway in their conversation and he'd ended up telling her that Edna Mae "wouldn't touch a penny of the money you sent, she called 'money from Satan'"— though she'd passed it on to Mary Kay Mack who "didn't give a shit whose money it was as long as she could spend it on herself.")

(Yes, Edna Mae, Anita, and Noah were still living with Mary Kay in that "run-down old house" on Depot Street. Edna Mae worked night shifts at the nursing home and attended church twice a week where she was, as Luke said, "somebody special"—not because of Luther but because of her devotion to the church and the right-to-life cause. Anita and Noah were in high school. Mary Kay had had to take disability retirement from work, she was near-crippled from arthritis. And he, Luke, was "probably going to be married"—he'd been living with a woman with two young children for a year—"Feels like it's time." Luke had laughed as if this was a joke or perhaps a somber reflection presented as a joke. After Luke hung up D.D. realized that her brother hadn't asked a thing about *her*—only just a question about how much she'd be making from boxing if she "ever got on TV.")

There was a third match, in Gary, Indiana, which D.D. Dunphy won in five rounds by a TKO but which was not televised on ESPN. There was a fourth match, in Wheeling, West Virginia, against a local female boxer with a 6–2 record which D.D. Dunphy won by a split decision after five grueling rounds.

It was said in her hearing *That ain't a she. That's a he.*

In the few newspaper accounts of D.D. Dunphy's

boxing performance it was said *Here is a female boxer who lives up to her hype—"Hammer of Jesus." Dunphy is a hammer!*

In Dayton which was her "hometown" she began to be known. A radio talk show host, male, interviewed her on *Good Morning, Dayton!*—"Here is a female athlete who takes her sport as seriously as any male. 'D.D. Dunphy' does not boast, and 'D.D. Dunphy' does not waste her breath. How'd you get into this dangerous sport, D.D.? Can you elaborate?"

Her brain was blank. She could not remember—how had she become a boxer? Had it something to do with her father?

"Seeing boxing on TV. I guess."

"Who are your influences?"

This she could answer. Gatti, de la Hoya, Roy Jones, Mike Tyson—"Not the way he is now but the way he was." The words seemed to roll off her tongue, and seemed to be the correct words since the interviewer smiled.

"Did you ever meet Mike Tyson?"

"N-No . . ."

"Do you think that women's boxing will ever approach the achievement of men's boxing?"

Was this a trick question? She knew that the answer

was *no*. But it would be a mistake to say this and so she said, hesitantly, "Maybe someday—not for a while."

"And why is that, D.D.?"

"Because there are not many women boxers. Yet."

"There is prejudice against women boxers, D.D., you probably know. People don't want to see girls and women covered in blood, beating each other up. Comment?"

She wasn't sure what to say. She sat biting at a cuticle of her thumbnail, waiting for the words.

"People think that women are 'nurturers'—not 'warriors.' But of course, a woman should be allowed to participate in any sport that men participate in, that's the current thinking. Agreed?"

D.D. nodded her head *yes*.

But this was radio! The interviewer gestured for her to speak.

"Y-yes . . ."

"You are on board, I'd guess, for females boxing in the Olympics?"

D.D. nodded *yes*.

"I mean—y-yes . . ."

"Though you didn't have any amateur career at all, it seems. Would you have been better served, better trained, more prepared for professional boxing if you'd been able to box as an amateur? For instance, on a women's Olympic team?"

D.D. tried to comprehend this. She did not want to say—she did not want to *hint*—that there was anything lacking in her training, or anything lacking in her career. What had the interviewer asked her, exactly? Her left ear rang just slightly from the fight. A dull throbbing pain at the base of her neck.

"Well, D.D.! Tell our radio audience: are you a dyed-in-the-wool feminist? Seems like a female boxer would be a feminist."

Dyed-in-the-wool. She did not comprehend this nor could she interpret the interviewer's broad smile.

"Yes. I guess so."

"And are you pro-choice?"

"'Pro-choice'—how?"

"Pro-abortion. Y'know, women 'taking control of their bodies.'"

"I—don't know. I guess not."

"*Not*? You are not in favor of abortion?"

Shook her head *no*. The subject was distasteful to her, the interviewer took note and backed off.

"Well. It's been great to have you on WOHI-radio this morning, D.D. Dunphy! Tell our radio audience when they can see you boxing next, will you?"

She knew the answer to this question. She recited a date, the name of an opponent, the location—Indianapolis, Indiana.

"Have you ever been to Indianapolis, D.D.? Ever seen where you'll be fighting there?"

Shook her head *no.*

First time she was hit—that is, *hit.*

Out of nowhere the blow had come stunning her. Left side of her face she had not seen—anything— must've lowered her left glove without realizing (as her trainer had tried to drill into her countless times) but in the adrenaline-flood of the fight she'd forgotten, and her opponent (sleek-black super-welterweight from Chicago she'd gained six pounds to fight, another former kickbox champion, ranked number two in her division in the Midwest Women's Boxing League, aged twenty-eight, 148 pounds and reach sixty-two inches: dynamite) was on her.

"Move your ass and fight, white-girl!"

Jamala's gloves were beside her face that was savage and beautiful. D.D. felt her soul swerve seeing such beauty as she'd once gone weak in the knees seeing Penelope Schine.

And so she was hit as she'd never (before) been hit. She had not seen the blow coming, flying at her left eye-socket, a crunching blow to the cheekbone sleek with Vaseline—(but the Vaseline had not spared the cheekbone)—and the ridge of bone above the eye in which an inch-long gash appeared instantaneously, filling with blood before even D.D. Dunphy could register how she'd been hit. It was necessary to counter-punch—but she could not, she had not the strength. For several confused seconds not knowing what had happened or even that she was *down* (which was radically new to her, and new to her and shocking the delirium of the crowd screaming for the local, hometown "Princess" Jamala Prentis with gold-flashing dagger tattoos on her biceps and a gold incisor to match, beautifully shaped Nefertiti head razor-shaved and gleaming with sweat like jewels) but she was determined to rise to her feet, climb up, like steps climbing up, up—now shakily standing, as the referee stepped aside to allow Jamala Prentis to rush at her, a hard stinging blow to her (unprotected) midriff, and she was down again, or almost down—on one knee, shaking her head to clear it as Jamala jeered—"White bitch!" And blood collecting in her mouth. And blood choking her, causing her to cough heedlessly. (The crowd was shrieking—was this a warning to her? Or in encouragement to Jamala Prentis, to destroy her?) But then she was up, it would seem like a miracle—Dunphy is *up*.

Trying to salvage the wreck of the fight. She could not clear her head to recall—was it round four? Three? (And how many rounds lay ahead?) She would need time to recover—she would need time to make amends for her mistake—yet, was she strong enough to remain on her feet for two more rounds?—she did not think so.) Like a wounded creature she knew to retreat to her strategic defense-posture: knees bent, head lowered, gloves raised to protect her bleeding and bruised face as the taller Jamala Prentis stood before her striking her freely, punches which Dunphy could not block, and could not return—her arms were so weak . . . *Jesus, help me!* She had not ever called upon Him before, in her new life.

In the elevated ring, in the hot lights, miniature rainbows of wet. Sweat shaken in droplets from a head backlit by lights, and the eyes darkened like the eye-sockets of a skull, and she understood that the triumphant Princess was exhausted too, suddenly—having punched herself out on her unresponsive and stoic-stubborn white-girl opponent whose very crouching-low forced her, at her taller height, to bend her knees, her back, to crouch in a posture unnatural to her, against instinct.

It was not uncommon, such exhaustion mid-fight—D.D. Dunphy felt a stab of hope, the fight was not yet over. She had not yet been defeated. Her face was bloodied, her ribs and upper arms throbbed with pain, but it was a numbed sort of pain, at a little distance.

She could recognize the sensation as pain, but not *her pain*. Her opponent too was breathing through her mouth.

They lapsed into a clinch. They grasped at one another. Drowning together yet each did not dare to release the other until the referee slapped them apart—"Break!"

A bell rang close beside their heads. D.D. Dunphy blinked to get her vision clear, that was blood-blurred with hematomas in both eyes. She could not comprehend where she was—which corner was hers, she must stagger to in terror of falling to the canvas.

Someone was shouting at her—"Here!"

Blindly she made her way to this person. She was staggering stiff-legged, her opponent had pounded her lower back in the clinch.

Such disgust the man felt for her, he did not utter her name; nor could she have said his name. She sank, slumped onto the stool. She shut her eyes in order not to see him. The dark-scarred face, the furious eyes. She was letting him down! She was not giving him *her best*.

Rapidly, desperately someone was working on Dunphy's ruined face with a styptic pencil to staunch the bleeding. Inch-long slash in her right eyelid the referee would come to inspect, stooping over her with an expression of carefully controlled disdain.

The *boxing world*, as it was called, did not like *female boxers*.

And how foolish, how pathetic, contemptible—the *female boxer* with streaks in her coarse, short-cut hair and crosses (white, crimson) on her biceps.

Had Jesus abandoned her? She was desperate to protest to Him, she was not a daughter of Satan.

Something like a pleat in her brain. She was staring at a coarse-textured wall. A fly on the wall, its wings quivering. She stood hesitant, not clear if this was herself?—the pathos of quivering wings?

"Wake up! One more round."

Her eyes sprang open. One more round! Three minutes.

Her head was strangely heavy on her shoulders, she could barely hold her head up. Something had happened to her neck, the cervical spine . . . And her lower back, throbbing with pain.

The bell rang. The new round began. She was pushed from her stool. She had to look for her opponent—where was her opponent?—the other boxer was slow to rise from her stool as if reluctant to approach D.D. Dunphy in the center of the ring.

Sleekly-beautiful Princess Jamala with gold-flashing dagger tattoos, shaved head, skin-tight Spandex—not so arrogant and self-assured now but slack-armed and dazed with fatigue. That was the black kickbox-champion's secret—she had never boxed beyond a few rounds. She had always won fights early. She was all dazzle, display and a few very hard, sharp and precise punches. But her stamina had never been tested.

Hammer of Jesus had not been tested either. Now she would reveal herself.

She was wondering if Jamala could see her clearly—if (maybe) the opponent's eyesight was blurred as hers was blurred. And if adrenaline had over-stimulated Jamala's heart that was now racing, dangerously fast . . . D.D. knew that she must go on the attack but her legs were like lead. Her feet were leaden hooves. Could scarcely move her upper body to slip punches, could not have stepped out of the way of a serious blow but fortunately the Princess could not hit her—not squarely, not hard.

The effort of her wild right swing sent droplets of sweat flying off her contorted face.

There was a scuffle. Hot breaths, sharp pungent smell of the other's body. The effort of each was to avoid being thrown down by the other.

Jamala muttered what sounded like *Damn you girl, fuck white bitch let go of me* even as D.D. pushed her away with both gloves.

(Was it the last round? D.D. could not remember.)

Exhausted and bloodied D.D. nonetheless managed

to outbox her opponent and to push her away each time she tried to protect herself by clinching. Almost she wanted to murmur in Jamala's ear—*Forgive me.*

She would win the fight on points—she would not try to knock out her opponent. Her strength was diminished, she was not sure that she could throw a crucial punch, and trying to throw would open her up to being punched by her opponent. And there would be no triumph for her in knocking down and humiliating Princess Jamala Prentis—even if she was capable of this.

The last round ended. Panting and staggering Jamala Prentis had not returned a single punch in this round.

D.D. Dunphy had won!—she was sure. Her trainer did not embrace her as he usually did at such a time but touched her shoulder in acknowledgment—"Good. You ended strong."

The announcer called the boxers to the center of the ring to stand side by side drenched in perspiration, bruised and bloodied, abashed. Wanly the black girl lifted her gloves, to draw a chorus of cheers from her supporters, and so D.D. lifted her gloves as well, to faint applause. Or perhaps it was mocking applause, for the female boxers had not performed well. Dunphy had scored the most punches by the end of the fight but had failed to knock out her opponent.

"The judges' decision is—a draw."

A draw! There was a moment's quiet, as the crowd absorbed the decision—the white girl, who should have won the fight, had not won; the black girl, who should have lost, had not lost.

Among three judges a draw is a rare decision. There was a scattering of applause, catcalls and boos.

With a shriek of relief Jamala threw her arms around D.D. Dunphy—"They sayin both of us *won.*"

D.D. laughed wildly. That was not what a "draw" meant—she knew; a draw meant that neither had won.

Jamala turned away to lift her gloves in triumph, and D.D. tried to hug her again, for she hadn't hugged her properly the first time; the gesture was clumsy, embarrassing—Jamala laughed at her, a shriek of a laugh, and went limping to her corner to leave the ring. D.D. stood at the edge of the spotlight as ringside spectators cheered for Jamala as if she'd defeated her opponent.

A towel was draped over her shoulders. Her skin was scalding-hot, yet beginning to be clammy. Her teeth were chattering with something like panic. Her lower back ached, she could hardly move her legs. Yet hastily then, for the next bout was being announced and the next boxers approaching, D.D. Dunphy left the ring. Her trainer was cursing the decision—she had never heard Ernie Beecher so disgusted.

"Fuck. Fuck. *Fuck.* This stinks."

D.D. was eager to push from him. She did not like to see his face so distorted.

"And you—the two of you—stank up the place. Hanging on like you did, the both of you—fucking *clinching.* Fucking *draw.* That's 'stinking up the place'—now you know."

She knew: she had heard this expression. She had not thought that it would apply to *her.*

She was feeling sick, dazed. She had to push away from the furious man.

Hurrying after the tall shaved-head black girl who was moving up the aisle toward the locker room resplendent in a gold-embossed robe, surrounded by admirers.

"Jamala! Wait . . ."

The girl turned to D.D., frowning and blinking as if she couldn't see well.

"Yah? What you want?"

D.D. had no idea what she wanted. What came from her battered mouth was unexpected—"You are the greatest!"

"Ima—what?"

"The greatest. Jamala. You are."

"Bullshit, girl. You just sayin that—'cause I *am.*"

Jamala's eyes were swollen, beginning to blacken.

Her face that had been a savage-beautiful face scarcely a half hour before was now battered and raw-looking. The gold tooth might be loose in her jaw, she might be spitting blood. She might urinate blood that night. But she was ecstatic, euphoric. A kind of boundless love leapt from her to D.D. Dunphy like an explosion of music too loud to be heard but only felt as sheer throbbing vibrations for the swollen-faced white girl standing in the aisle gazing at her in adoration—except there came friends screaming "Jamala! J'mala!"—swarming at her, screaming their love for her and grabbing at her. And in the arena supporters were on their feet wildly applauding Princess Jamala Prentis as if she'd won the fight.

In the aisle flatfooted D.D. Dunphy stood forgotten, watching, trying with her hurt mouth to smile too.

Until the next fight which would eradicate the shame of the draw-fight it would be said to her *You won. Should have won. God damn bastards stole it from you.*

Training without complaint though often her head felt like the interior of a bell. A thin high ringing in her ears. The bruised ribs ached and at last it was discovered in an X-ray that the rib had been fractured.

Scars in the area of the eye which would heal but not fade. In the eyebrow, a tiny sickle-shaped white scar.

Slowly returning to her full strength. Not immediately beginning to spar again but, in time.

Drilled into her *Do not lower your left when you throw a cross. Do not ever lower your left. And do not look away from your opponent.*

She was being groomed for the WBA women's welterweight championship. But first, she must win the Midwest Women's Boxing Association title.

In the MWBA, D.D. Dunphy was ranked at number nine.

In the WBA, D.D. Dunphy was ranked at number twelve.

Smiling nervously to think how the next fight would be televised—"Almost probably" as Cass Cassidy said.

ESPN boxing night, Pittsburgh Armory on undercard of a fight between (male) heavyweights Kevin Johnson, Homer Cruze. This was a possibility!

Smiled thinking of this as slowly she was plaiting the hair.

Jamala had entrusted her. Rich oily-black hair plaited into cornrows. It was a loving process—it was very slow, exacting. Her fingers were (just slightly) clumsy. Large fingers, small plaits of hair.

Seemed that she was standing before a mirror bent over the girl, the head, an attentively lowered head, no longer shaved but springy with hair, thick with hair, that had to be arranged in fastidious cornrows. But she could not see the face of the (brown-skinned) girl. Still she knew that the girl was Jamala with long hair now, that had to be tight-plaited. Oily fragrance of the hair, slightly coarse in her fingers as her own was coarse, wiry-tough. She loved this smell, wanting to press her face against the hair. Those parts of the scalp that were exposed.

Love you like Jesus loves you. Wish you loved me.

The next fight, she won by a TKO. And the next, by a third-round knockout.

But no TV. (Not yet.)

Showered her body running her hands briskly up and down her sides. Water as hot as she could bear. The pleasure of hot water against her aching muscles, the torn-feeling ligament in her neck, throb of her lower back where (impossible to avoid!) her kidneys had been pounded. Lifting her face to the spray. Shut her eyes, opened her mouth, with the soap poking shyly about her body, between legs, between breasts. That sensation of hot water streaming over her, a sensation like caressing.

Rough embraces of the other boxer, after the

fight. Grabbing at each other. Dazed and exhilarated, stunned, drunk with adrenaline, like carbonation in the blood—feeling no pain, or anyway not yet.

Sharp pains in her neck, dull throb at the base of her skull. Dr. Danks prescribed pills, Ernie gave her. And the other, smaller white pills Ernie gave her, one each morning, never forget for it was essential that she *not bleed.*

Still she was working at Target. Part-time, not half-time. There were no workers' benefits for either half- or part-time but if (for instance) D.D. Dunphy needed prescription meds, needing to make an appointment with Dr. Danks, needed X-rays—all covered by Dayton Fights, Inc.

Plus dentistry. Plus new boots, new gloves, new fleece-lined nylon jacket of a higher quality than the Target merchandise she could get with her worker's discount.

Plus, each Sunday at the Zion Missionary Church she left a (folded, inconspicuous) ten-dollar bill in the collection basket.

She was proud—*That girl can take a punch.*

Not so fast on her feet as certain of her rivals. But harder-hitting, with the (alleged) punch of a man. She was trained to defend herself but boxing is not about defense but offense. Two defensive boxers, you stink up the arena. Fans will boo, catcall. Female boxers too often fell into clinches. Dunphy did not like clinches— you could count on her to shove the other female away. Often she was not fast enough to slip a punch and so it was drilled into her, how to *take a punch.*

That was how the (aging, slower) Ali won his famous fight against (very young, very hard-hitting) George Foreman. *Rope-a-dope. Foreman punched himself out on Ali, lost all his strength and could no more punch than a girl or a child by the end of the fight. Fantastic!*

Her eyes were becoming more sensitive. She wore dark glasses outdoors. Her eyes swelled easily. Hematomas developed more quickly than in the past. She could "see"—all she needed to see, to fight.

Rainbows, shimmering blurs. The strongest fighting is by instinct not by craft or calculation.

She did not tell her trainer, corner men, Mr. Cassidy or even her friend Mickey Burd how blurred her vision was sometimes. During the fight if she told them, the fight would be stopped. If the referee knew, or the ringside physician, the fight would be stopped.

Or, Ernie would not stop the fight and she would understand that they didn't give a damn for D.D. Dunphy only for the crowd applauding her. For the *Hammer of Jesus* had fans, followers. These were men. Bringing the crowd to its feet, or almost. Some of the crowd. The kind of fans willing to pay money for serious boxing.

In the car where they'd told her to wait D.D. Dunphy sat eating a hero sandwich with shaky fingers. They'd taken her to Dr. Danks for vitamin shots. She was so hungry: sausage, tomato, onion, drenched in mustard, running down her hands.

She wasn't sending Edna Mae much money lately. Seemed like, Edna Mae could have written to her, to thank her. But her great-aunt Mary Kay wrote. Mary Kay was promising to see her fight "real soon" if it wasn't too far away like Cleveland, Cincinnati.

Saying she was a "good brave girl." Saying that Edna Mae loved her but "found it hard to say what is in her heart."

After the sixth fight when D.D. Dunphy was raised to number three MWBA welterweight contender and number seven WBA contender a televised fight was almost certain sometime in the New Year (2010).

In an envelope carefully printed EDNA MAE DUNPHY she mailed five hundred-dollar bills as she'd mailed in the past. Of this Jesus approved for it was turning the other cheek, returning love where there was not love, or did not seem to be love.

Momma, this is for you. Hope everybody there is
OK.

If you want to call me my number is ———.

I am a "ranked" fighter now. I am a "contender."
I am doing pretty well. Look for me on TV in
(maybe) January next year.

Love
Your Daughter Dawn
"D.D. Dunphy"—"Hammer of Jesus"

Another time she'd been pounded in the lower back.
In the kidneys.

In the lavatory before she flushed the toilet she saw,
and looked quickly away. Oh, why had she looked!

That languid curl of red in her urine.

Have to say, *I was surprised Dunphy turned out so*
terrific.

First sight of her (in the gym) was not impressive.
Looked to me like some homely girl stumbling over her
own feet, that clumsy. And her legs short, and her arms—
you could see her reach was shit. But Ernie Beecher kept
saying, Dunphy has promise. Give her a chance.

Turned out Ernie was correct. Just took a little time.

A girl boxer is not much different from a male in training. They can be just as serious. But they can get discouraged faster. Dunphy was not like that—Dunphy did not get discouraged.

Right away you could see how strong she could punch. It's said—you are born with a punch, or you are not. If you are born with a punch you can be trained to use it. If not, not.

Dunphy was real promising with that left hook and a cross-over right and a left uppercut she could sometimes land exactly on the tip of the chin like you are supposed to—despite her short reach. She was a terrific counter-puncher once she got excited—nothing could stop her.

Everyone commented how Dunphy had heart. She would not be stopped. You'd have to kill her to stop her. That is the warrior-type—you would have to kill them to stop them. People were saying, Cass you got a girl-Tyson there.

But there's no comparison, see. Girls don't hit hard—not like Tyson. Any injury that happens it's a weakness in the opponent, or she falls sideways and hits her head on the ring post. Or in sparring, they clinch and hit each other's kidneys. The actual punch, even

Dunphy's—is not that great no matter how it looks. A man could take it.

Well—they can get concussed in a fight. That is true. There's female boxers pretty punch-drunk, I guess. That is so.

It's a weakness in the female skull. You can't hit it without the brain kind of swishing inside like something in water—like if there's a sac or something, and you shake it. But Dunphy had a hard punch, male or female notwithstanding, and could protect herself.

Problem was, the public don't like to look at females who look like athletes or like men. That's what the promoters say, and the TV producers, and advertisers. What they say is correct because they say it. They are buying goods and nobody blames them.

We got this neighborhood girl Mickey Burd who'd been one of Ernie's girl-boxers to help us out. She sweet-talked Dunphy into having her hair streaked, getting showy tattoos, ear studs. Even thinned Dunphy's eyebrows a little so she didn't look like some kind of female orangutan.

Dunphy had a high threshold for pain. The fans can mistake that for courage. If she was hit, she'd laugh. If she'd lost a tooth she'd have spat it out on the canvas and just laughed, and kept on with the fight. Like Arturo

Gatti or what's-his-name—"Boom Boom" Mancini—
she'd give all she had for the crowd, wouldn't hold
nothing back. A boxer like that will risk everything
trying for a knockout, make the fans cheer.

If she was lonely, that had to feel good to her. Hearing people she didn't know cheering for her.

Her breasts were kind of heavy for a female boxer
but we taped them as close to flat as we could without injury. Or maybe there was injury. Dunphy would
never let on. The pills she took we arranged for her,
she never had a period. She didn't bleed like a normal
girl or woman will bleed. You'd think the black blood
would be backed up inside them like sewage, wouldn't
you?

Maybe that is so. You hear all kinds of things.

The Consolation of Grief

September 2011–February 2012

"True Subject"

When you encounter your true subject, you will know it.

She had faith. She had not ceased waiting.

Muskegee Falls, Ohio:
September 2011

S un-splotched Muskegee River, dazzling the eye.

The hue of the river was tarnished pewter. Patches of reflected sun like fire in the choppy waves.

A strange beauty in the sound: "Mus-kee-gee."

She'd been driving through Ohio farmland for hours. Rolling hills like those sculpted hills in the paintings of Thomas Hart Benton. Acres of cornfields dun-colored, and the cornstalks dried and broken, fields of harvested wheat, stubble.

Early autumn. Beauty of slanted light, desiccated things.

Beside the highway the river's current was quickened, there had been a heavy rain the previous day.

Slow-circling hawks high overhead. She'd been noticing, glancing skyward. Did hawks hunt together?

There were several wide-winged birds soaring, dip-
ping, gliding on wings that scarcely moved. Like those
drifting thoughts of which you are not altogether aware.

He'd have driven this route, she thought. When he'd
driven south and east from Michigan.

Exiting the interstate at Bowling Green, or Findlay.
South through Upper Sandusky to Broome County south
of Wyandotte. On two-lane state highways through rural
Ohio (hilly, farmland, dense-wooded) to Muskegee Falls
where he'd begun his new life.

She'd learned that Gus Voorhees's life had been
threatened many times. She had not known, and didn't
believe that Darren had ever known, that their father
had been verbally attacked numerous times in public
places, and physically attacked several times; when
they'd lived in Grand Rapids he'd been accosted in the
parking lot of the women's center, beaten so badly he'd
had to be taken to the ER. (Yet, when Naomi tried to
remember anything like this, her father visibly injured,
hospitalized, she could not remember a thing. Possibly, there'd been a pretense that Daddy was out of town
for a while.) Fires had been started at virtually all of
the women's centers in which he had worked—there'd
been vandalism to the buildings, and to vehicles parked
outside. Not just doctors but nurses and other staffers
had been threatened. It was shocking to learn belatedly

that they'd all been threatened—Gus Voorhees's wife, children.

All this had been kept secret from the children. Perhaps some of it had been kept secret from the wife.

Madelena had said *But that's why he moved away, Naomi. And Jenna had refused to go with him. To protect you. The children.*

She hadn't wanted to think that this might be true. That her father had known he might be killed, and had continued with his medical work nonetheless.

Gus Voorhees had not given into his enemies, as he'd insisted. But his enemies had had their revenge nonetheless.

How lonely the countryside was, in this part of rural Ohio! Farmhouses were far apart, and set far back from the road; the communities through which she drove were just a few scattered houses, a gas station and a few stores, churches.

(Did this part of Ohio remind her of Huron County, Michigan? Any of these country roads might have been the Salt Hill Road.)

Thinking such thoughts she almost missed her turn to Muskegee Falls. Turning left, to the east, to cross the Muskegee River.

And this route too, her father had taken. Carefully she'd mapped out the routes he must have driven.

The bridge to Muskegee Falls (population 26,000) was an old, dignified, single-span bridge of another era. It was narrow: barely two lanes. Speed limit fifteen miles an hour.

If she hadn't known she (probably) could not have guessed: the choppy pewter-colored river was flowing north to south, perpendicular to the bridge she crossed in her small rented vehicle. The falls for which the town was named was a quarter mile upstream shrouded in mist.

A rapid succession of shadows cast by the bridge's rusted girders fell onto the vehicle. Across the hood, fleetingly onto the windshield (insect- and seed-flecked, that needed washing—she must stop for gas soon), invisibly then onto the roof, and gone.

Splotched sunlight, the moving shadows of the girders, the gleam of the car hood—Naomi recalled how strobe lighting can trigger epileptic fits. Rapid patterned flashes of light can have a narcotic effect upon the brain. Her (half-)uncle Karl Kinch, her grandmother's invalid son, could not tolerate ordinary daylight still less electric or fluorescent lighting. If Kinch ventured outside he wore dark glasses to protect his brain from further poisoning but mostly he did not venture outside. He'd had to hide himself from the world in order to save himself.

But she did not want to think of Kinch, not now. Not in Muskegee Falls, Ohio, where (at last) she'd traveled, alone.

Clearly visible now were the falls, that spanned the width of the river, approximately thirty feet high, whitely churning, sending up spray and froth. There is a fascination in cascading water, Naomi had to wrench her eyes away for fear of becoming entranced behind the wheel of her car. She'd affixed the video recorder to the window beside her to record the view her father would have seen in the last months of his life.

She was determined to make a video of the place in which Gus Voorhees had briefly lived, bravely worked, died. The circumstances of his life in Muskegee Falls. So many years had passed, she believed that she must be strong enough now.

Madelena had said *Just go, dear. Take as long as you need. It will take courage. Do what you need to do. Call me.*

She had come to love her grandmother. This love had happened without her wishing it to have happened and now that Madelena was not well, she felt her love for the woman with a particular sort of desperation. She felt like one who has had a vast quantity of time and so has squandered much of that time, feeling now the horror of time rapidly passing like water through her fingers.

But please call me. We will miss you!

At first Madelena had not thought that Naomi's intention of creating an archive of her father's life was a good, or even a workable idea. How long would such a project be? How could she bring it to a reasonable end? And what would she do if and when she uncovered damaging things about her father?

She didn't expect to discover "damaging" things about her father—Naomi said.

Amending then, of course she understood: all lives are imperfect. Even Gus Voorhees was *imperfect.*

She was twenty-four years old—which seemed to her no longer young. She must *hurry.*

For the past two years she'd been working as an assistant to a documentary filmmaker attached to the New York Institute—her first real job. The project was tracking the lives of a family of Somalis living in New York City and in Minnesota. The work had been exacting, and exciting; she had learned a great deal. She believed that she was ready to prepare a documentary of her own.

She parked her car, a rented Nissan she'd acquired at the Detroit airport, on a service road just off the bridge. On a pedestrian walkway she walked about one-third of the way back across the bridge, to position her camera atop the railing, and record the small city of Muskegee Falls from this perspective. Later, she would add a voice—commentary.

This is the Muskegee River in central Ohio. There, Muskegee Falls.

The Muskegee Bridge was originally built in 1939.

My father Gus Voorhees moved here to live and to work—temporarily he believed—in the late summer of 1999.

On the phone often he'd been guilty-sounding. He'd laughed a good deal. He'd called her *sweetheart.* He'd extracted from her a vague promise to *Come visit Daddy, OK? Some weekend?*

That weekend had never come. But now, she was here.

But she'd been angry at Daddy! They all were.

They were not angry at Daddy, that was silly. If they'd been angry at anyone it was at Mommy—(with the cruel acuity of children they knew this)—for her failure to be sufficiently loved, to keep a man like Gus Voorhees at home.

For a long time she had not liked to speak the name aloud—"Muskegee Falls." The very sound "Ohio"—the mocking drawl of the vowels—was repugnant to her.

She'd composed a detailed timeline of that year 1999. The last year. Her files had grown voluminous and had become difficult to peruse at a single sitting.

That her father had come here, to this place out of all the places of the world—he had *died here.*

No answer to the plaintive query—*Why?*

She'd done research. She'd become adept at using the Internet in pursuit of (at least) a statistical and computational notion of the environment in which her father had lived for those brief months before he'd died.

So she'd known, before seeing the shuttered mills and factories along the riverfront, and the shabbiness of the riverfront, that Muskegee Falls had not recovered from an economic crisis dating back to the mid-1990s. A branch of General Motors had shut down, a women's-wear manufacturer had shut down, homes had been foreclosed in a wave of bankruptcies. The small city had lost approximately one-fifth of its population.

On a pot-holed roadway along the river recording with her camera stretches of abandoned riverfront buildings, docks, warehouses and trucking companies, vacant lots piled with rubble, open grassy lots that had become fields in which (she saw through the magnified camera eye) dust-colored rats scavenged energetically amid dumped trash. She felt her skin crawl. The rats were visually exciting, in the camera eye.

Baltimore & Ohio railway yard, railroad tracks, freight cars that looked old, battered, abandoned. A sharp smell of creosote.

And the Muskegee River beyond, splotched with sunlight like small flaring fires startling and beautiful to the eye.

Her father had seen these sights, she was sure. Especially the river—beautiful despite the ugliness on shore.

He had so loved Katechay Island!—the morning mist over Lake Huron. Loons on the lake, a high whistling wind. Hiking along the shore, prints of Daddy's bare feet deep-impressed in the hard-packed sand, and his young daughter trotting along behind earnestly trying to fit her small feet into those prints . . .

On Main Street, slow afternoon traffic. Slow traffic lights. Turn onto Center Street, to First Avenue, to Capitol Square—the Broome County Courthouse that was a dour-faced sandstone municipal building with a brighter, beige-brick wing at the rear.

It was something of a mild shock to encounter this building, so abruptly.

Jenna had attended the first trial of Luther Amos Dunphy here—the "mistrial."

Their poor distraught mother, alone in this place! She had not wanted Naomi or Darren to accompany her.

Jenna had hidden from her children her terrible despair, her grief that was a kind of bone-marrow cancer draining her soul. She had hoped to spare them.

They had not realized at the time. Like children they'd thought mostly of themselves. Yet they'd never quite forgiven her. Almost, it was getting to be too late.

Naomi turned her camera onto the Broome County Courthouse, a building of little distinction. Through the camera lens the sandstone building looked a little more interesting—but only a little. Along with the criminal and civil judiciary for the county it also contained the Office of Public Records and a branch of the Ohio Motor Vehicle Agency and these accounted for most of the business in the courthouse that she could see.

Had her father ever stepped inside this building? (She had no reason to suppose that he had.) Yet it was here, at the second trial, that his murderer Luther Dunphy had been found guilty and sentenced to death.

She had to record the courthouse for that reason. She had to see for herself the interior to which her mother had been subjected pitilessly in the tedium and anxiety of the first Dunphy trial.

In the front foyer, after she'd gone through a desultory security check, Naomi asked permission of a county sheriff's deputy to film the interior of the courtroom. (There was only a single, large courtroom in the building, which happened not to be in use at the time.) "Why?"—the deputy squinted at her suspiciously.

"For a school project. I'm in film school."

"'Film school' where?"

Naomi considered. If she said New York City, that might be a less judicious answer than Ann Arbor, Michigan.

In fact, she had taken courses in what was called *film studies* at both the University of Michigan and at New York University.

She told the deputy Michigan. This appeared to be a good answer.

Still, he asked to see ID. She gave him her Michigan driver's license which he examined closely.

"'Voorhees.'"

(What did this mean? Why had the deputy spoken the name aloud? Did he recall the name, somehow?)

The deputy was about forty years old. It was quite possible that he'd been on duty at the time of the trials. Possibly, he'd even been on duty guarding the Women's Center on the morning that Luther Dunphy had shown up with a shotgun and killed two people before anyone could stop him.

Naomi waited uneasily, smiling. Always in such circumstances you smile.

Good that she was white-skinned, an attractive girl with a friendly and forthright manner, obviously no threat to Broome County Courthouse security or to the Broome County sheriff's deputy.

"OK, miss—'Naomi.'"

With a smile the deputy handed the little laminated card back to her. The name *Voorhees* had meant nothing to him.

He'd smiled, but not with his eyes. He was a thickset man with narrow suspicious eyes, heavy jaw. His dull-blue uniform fitted him tightly; you could see the holstered firearm prominent at his hip. Yet Naomi was grateful to him for a few minutes inside the courtroom with her video camera.

Here is the courtroom where Luther Dunphy was tried. Twice.

First trial declared a "mistrial."

Second trial resulting in guilty verdict. Sentenced to death for the murders of Gus Voorhees and Timothy Barron.

In March 2006, executed.

The camera eye is neutral, unjudging. Her own eye saw the futility of the effort: (empty) judge's bench, (empty) jurors' box, (empty) rows of seats. On the wall at the front of the room the heraldic coppery Seal of the State of Ohio. Near the judge's bench, a U.S. flag.

Tall windows ablaze with sunshine, swirling motes of dust-molecules.

Nothing here. Nothing will come of nothing.

A remark of Gus Voorhees usually uttered with a smile.

A sweetly ironic smile. Not a mean or sardonic smile.

The trials were long over. Nothing of those days could be evoked now.

"Stay as long as you want to, miss. There's no trials scheduled for today."

The voice was intrusive, jarring. Noami had known that the deputy was watching her but she did not want to encourage a conversation.

"Thank you. I'm almost finished."

"What kind of film course is it?"

"Our assignment is to make a visual record of municipal buildings, historic buildings, in Ohio."

An answer so dull, even the deputy intrigued by a young woman who has wandered into his vicinity could not think of a reply.

For her visit to Muskegee Falls Naomi had dressed inconspicuously: loose-fitting khaki pants, shirt, sweater. On her head a baseball cap whose rim she could pull low over her forehead to shield her eyes from the sun while driving, and from the scrutiny of strangers. Her hair that was shoulder-length, wavy, a warm-mahogany brown, was pulled back pragmatically into a ponytail. There were no rings on her fingers except a single small milky opal in a white gold setting which her grandmother Madelena had given her as a "keepsake"—a ring that had belonged to Madelena.

She was a filmmaker—a documentarian. She had no wish to be seen, but to see. Everything in her appearance and in her manner was a signal to observers— *Don't take note of me please. I am nothing, nobody. I am invisible.*

"Says you're from Michigan, on your license? Why'd you come so far, here?"

Naomi saw that the deputy was watching her intently, with a kind of mild masculine belligerence that could be easily placated by a smile, an exchange of banter, a (female) air of coquettish deference. Any law enforcement officer of any age with a shiny badge, a gun on his hip, in uniform has been conditioned to expect such placating: it should not have cost Naomi Voorhees much to perform. Yet, she spoke matter-of-factly, just slightly coolly and not quite looking at the man.

"Because there was a trial here, in 2000. A man named Luther Dunphy was tried for murder. Two murders. Do you remember that?" Naomi heard herself speak less matter-of-factly than she'd intended.

"'Luther Dunphy.' Yes . . ."

The deputy spoke uncertainly, frowning. Naomi had to wonder what *Dunphy* might mean to him, who had no recollection of *Voorhees*.

She told him that there had been two trials. The first had been a mistrial.

"What was the name again?"

"'Luther Dunphy.' He lived in Muskegee Falls . . .'"

"'Dunphy'—the name is kind of familiar. But I wasn't here then. I didn't move to Broome County until 2002."

The murders had occurred in November 1999, Naomi said. A man named Luther Dunphy had killed two people, with a shotgun, at the Women's Center here. "At the second trial Dunphy was sentenced to death and he died—he was executed—in 2006."

So strangely, her voice faltered. The deputy stared at her. She wondered if he was thinking that she might be related to Luther Dunphy.

Returning to the courthouse where he'd been sentenced to death—and with what intention? To do damage? Set off a bomb?

But she'd been allowed through the metal detector. Her camera bag had been examined. She had to be harmless.

Feeling sorry for me, that Luther Dunphy was my father!

"What's wrong, miss? What's going on?"

"Nothing is 'going on.' Excuse me."

He was distrustful of her. He didn't like her so much now.

Clutching her camera, forcing herself to smile, Naomi made an attempt to walk away; but the deputy blocked her passage.

"Miss? Let me see that camera, please."

"But why? It's just a camera . . ."

"I said, miss—let me see that camera."

Naomi handed it over. Adrenaline flooded her body, she felt almost that she might faint. How she hated this person!—this uniformed bully with a gun on his hip, a shiny badge. His initial interest in her had been casually sexual, not exactly intimidating but not altogether benign, either; yet she could have made no complaint about him. And now she said nothing further, she did not want to antagonize him. Self-importantly he examined the camera, turned it over in his hands, roughly; asked to see the camera bag as well, and examined the interior of the bag. Examined lenses, shaking the cases. What did he expect to find? What did he hope to find? It was a craven thought—how fortunate for her, she was white-skinned. A person of color, a person whose skin tone might suggest foreignness, "terrorism"—how would the Broome County, Ohio, deputy have treated him, or her? A skirmish might be made to occur; as the law enforcement officer laid hands on her, and instinctively she resisted, he might respond with force; even if she did not resist, she might not have been able to comply quickly enough to spare herself rough treatment. And how quickly this might happen! In the corner of her eye Naomi saw passersby in the foyer glancing at her and at the deputy who'd detained her. At least, there were witnesses.

When the deputy was finished with his examination, grudgingly satisfied that there was nothing suspicious inside the camera or in the bag, and he had no choice but to release her, Naomi did not say a word, not a murmur of displeasure, not a murmur of gratitude, but only took her things from the deputy and walked quickly away.

Of this encounter, she had no video recording. No memory, and no proof. As if it had never been.

Invisibly afoot in the "city center" of the old Ohio river town.

Camera eye restless in continuous motion.

Broome County Family Services. Broome County Senior Center. Broome County Board of Education.

How she'd come to hate the very words—*Broome County!*

Years she'd hated these words. Feared these words.

Fountain Square bounded by sparsely leafed young trees. Open paved area, salmon-colored flagstones. Park benches newly painted bright green. Pedestrian mall—but few pedestrians. Bus stops with new-looking plastic awnings where elderly persons, some of them dark-skinned, sat patiently awaiting buses or shuttles.

Unless these were homeless persons simply sitting amid shopping bags, boxes, laundry baskets heaped with possessions.

Solitary figures in the "city center" motionless as statues in a tableau of blight. Though this part of Muskegee Falls had undergone an ambitious urban renewal (evidently) it did not appear renewed but rather enervated, eviscerated. The camera eye dwelled upon open, near-empty "plazas" with fountains sparkling giddily in the sun, and no one to see, as in a painting of de Chirico. Patches of burnt-out grass. Spindling trees seemingly abandoned to die in the dry sunny heat of autumn.

At the edge of the sandstone square a smart, new-looking building where there was a flurry of activity—Broome County Public Library.

Her hands were less shaky now, gripping the camera. She was feeling a delayed rush of fear, anger, dismay— how helpless she'd have been, if the deputy had confiscated her camera, or smashed it . . . Was it an exaggeration, to imagine this happening? Had she misread the man's hostility to her, that had seemed to come on so swiftly? She didn't want to think that, if he'd known her identity, not *Dunphy* but *Voorhees* the daughter of the murdered abortion provider, he might have been even more hostile to her.

With her camera she drifted like a ghost. Strangers glanced at her, some of them with quizzical smiles. Do I know you, miss? Do you know *me*?

She did not know these strangers. She did not know any of them. She could not bring herself to ask if anyone had known, or had even heard of, her father Gus Voorhees.

And why here, why these scattered and random sights recorded in her camera, she could not have said. Except that he had been here in 1999, or in the vicinity. And she was recording what she could of Muskegee Falls in the (desperate, quixotic) hope that out of these scattered and random sights at some future time she could extract a meaning that eluded her now.

The Israeli filmmaker Yael Ravel whom she'd so admired had said you must accumulate hours, days, weeks of video material to extract from it just a few precious minutes to preserve—if you are lucky.

She wanted to believe this. She had no option.

In the lobby of the Muskegee Falls Inn, est. 1894. Handsome old "historic" hotel, faded Tudor facade. Lobby very quiet at this hour of mid-afternoon. Dimly lighted, wood-paneled walls, staid leather couches, chairs. Fireplace piled with (unlit) birch logs. Ornate chandelier with tall slender white faux candles.

Through a doorway a large room, banquet room, with myriad round tables, empty.

Through another doorway, an entrance to the dim-lit Sign of the Ram Pub.

He'd stayed in this hotel sometimes, she had reason to think. Before he'd rented a place of his own in town.

Or had he stayed with friends, initially? Newly acquired friends here in Muskegee Falls. Colleagues in public health work. Planned Parenthood, abortion providers.

The comaraderie of the beleaguered. The threatened, despised.

Baby killers. Your souls will burn in Hell.

She knew that Jenna had stayed in the Muskegee Falls Inn for the duration of the first trial.

Alone, as Jenna had preferred.

Newly widowed, and in dread of sympathy. The swarm of sympathy-bearers with their plaintive cries—*Oh Jenna I feel so sad about Gus, just terrible about Gus . . . Terrible, terrible!*

They'd laughed wildly together. Jenna, Darren, Naomi. A kind of drunken revelry. The stress of so much (well-intentioned) sympathy. For a long time fearful of going outside (Jenna had said) without wearing a veil or a mask or a paper bag over your head, so that no one could recognize you and clamp you in an embrace.

"Miss? May I be of assistance?"

The big-haired woman behind the check-in counter cast her voice across the lobby at Naomi, with a thin slice of a smile.

Skilled in assessing strangers, seeing that the young woman who'd entered the lobby in rumpled khakis, sneakers, baseball cap pulled low over her forehead was carrying just a shoulder bag and a camera and did not have a suitcase with her.

Politely Naomi asked if there was a room available for the night.

The thin-sliced smile turned to a frown. "A single room?"

"Yes. A single room."

It was perceived to be just slightly strange, was it—

that Naomi was alone? Obviously a traveler, a stranger to Muskegee Falls, wanting a single room.

"For how many nights, miss?"

"I'm not sure. Maybe two, or three."

The big-haired woman smiled at Naomi with an expression of frank curiosity. "D'you have family here?"

"No. I don't."

"Here on business?"

"No."

"Friends?"

"No."

"Just traveling then? Passing through?"

"Not really."

Confounded, the desk clerk could think of no further inquiry. With a deeper frown she checked her computer, yes there was a room. Non-smoking, double bed, river view, fourth floor.

There was an air of reluctance in this disclosure. Naomi wondered if there were, in fact, many rooms available in the stolid old Muskegee Falls Inn. Many vacancies mid-week.

At the interstate exit some miles away there'd been a cluster of motor hotels, motels, fast-food restaurants, gas stations. These facilities seemed to have been laid upon bare, scoured earth as one might set similar facilities upon the most barren landscape, the moon for instance, or Mars, with no attempt at fixing them in place. They were generic, interchangeable. Yet she'd thought it might be better for her (emotionally) to drive back to the exit, to stay the night in such a place and to return to Muskegee Falls in the morning, than to stay in a hotel in Muskegee Falls.

Naomi asked the price of the room. It was not so high as she'd expected.

The desk clerk seemed to misunderstand her silence: "There's a room on the second floor, without a river view, if you'd prefer a room at a lower price . . ."

Politely Naomi said that she would prefer a room with a window view. "But I would like to see the room first, please."

"Of course! I can show you."

In the elevator the big-haired woman asked Naomi if she'd ever visited Muskegee Falls before. Naomi told her *no*.

"But my mother visited here. About ten years ago."

"Did she!" The woman seemed stymied by Naomi, uncertain how to interpret her tone. The affable exchange of banal pleasantries to which she was accustomed as a hotel employee was thwarted here and the result was awkward. "She had relatives here, did she?— your mother?"

"No."

The room was high-ceilinged but not large: at once, Naomi felt a shiver of claustrophobia.

Quickly she went to the window—the room had but a single window—to draw back dark purple velvet drapes and let in sunshine.

She stared out, leaning her face close to the glass, at the river a quarter-mile away, over a scattering of rooftops and water towers.

"There's a nice sunset, on the river. You can see it from this floor."

Adding then, when Naomi seemed not to have heard:

"There's new TVs in all the fourth-floor rooms. Flat screen."

But Naomi paid no heed to the flat-screen TV. Nor the minibar. She was far more interested in the view from the window though she wasn't sure what she was seeing.

"Excuse me, is that the courthouse? Over there?"

"Yes. I think so."

"Where is Howard Avenue? Can you see it from here?"

"I'm not sure . . ."

The address she had for the Broome County Women's Center was 1183 Howard Avenue.

"Can you see Shawnee Street from here?"

"'Shawnee'? I don't think so . . ."

"Front Street?"

But the woman had not heard of Front Street.

Naomi heard herself say, as if she were thinking aloud, "My mother once attended a trial here in Muskegee Falls, in the courthouse."

"Did she!"—the woman smiled uncertainly.

"It was in 2000. The trial of Luther Dunphy. Do you remember?"

"'Luther Dunphy.' Oh yes. Everyone remembers that trial."

"What do you remember about it?"

"It—was a sad case."

"Why was it sad?"

"Because Luther Dunphy killed two people—just shot them down on the street. Two doctors."

Two doctors. Naomi considered this.

"Did you know either of the men who were killed?"

"*I* didn't. But my husband's sister lived next-door to one of them. He was a nice guy, a Vietnam vet."

"Do you remember his name?"

"'Barron'—I think. Tom, or Tim."

"And the other man's name?"

"N-No . . . He wasn't from Muskegee Falls, I think."

"Did you know Luther Dunphy?"

"Oh no. Of course not. Nobody in my family knew *him*."

Naomi turned her attention away from the big-haired woman who'd begun to frown, so interrogated. Since working as a documentary filmmaker Naomi had become far more aggressive with strangers than was natural for her; it was not a personality trait she admired in others, or in herself.

She noted: a scent of air freshener in the room. A cushioned chair with curved legs, covered in dark purple velvet. A small writing desk with a top that quaintly opened and shut, not very practical for one with a laptop. Queen-sized bed with brass headboard and eggshell-white coverlet upon which a half-dozen pillows had been artfully arranged.

Above a bureau a large mirror framed in eggshell-white in which Naomi Voorhees and the big-haired woman appeared. The younger with a baseball cap shielding half her face, the other a woman in her early or mid-forties, with bright-dyed russet hair.

Naomi asked: "Do you remember much about the trial?"

"Well—no. Not really. I never got to it, I had to work. Some of my friends went, and relatives. But you had a hard time getting in—getting a seat. The court-room isn't large. The trial drew a lot of attention. It was

in the papers and on TV. And all these people picketing outside the courthouse . . ."

"Picketing? Why?"

"I think they were anti-abortion people. Some
of them were Catholics. I mean, Catholic priests and
nuns. But there were others too—all kinds. They came
in buses. There was an abortion clinic here, where the
doctors were shot."

The woman was speaking carefully now, aware of
Naomi's interest.

Naomi asked if she remembered how the trial had
turned out.

"He was found guilty—I think. He was sentenced to
death."

Adding, "There was a lot of upset over that. It was
thought to be a harsh sentence. People who knew
Luther Dunphy and his family, worked with him or
belonged to the same church. In the paper there were
interviews with people who knew him and all of them
saying what a good man he was, a good husband and
father, how he'd done carpentry work for his church.
One neighbor said how after a windstorm, when some
shingles on her roof were blown off, Luther Dunphy
replaced them for nothing—no charge . . ." Pausing as
if unsure what this might mean.

Good man. Husband, father. Carpentry. No charge.

There was a ringing in her ears. She was not hearing this.

"Does the Dunphy family still live here?"

"I don't *know*."

The woman spoke sharply. A faint flush came into her face.

"Miss, are you a—reporter?"

"No."

"Not a reporter? You ask questions like they did. There were lots of them here during the trial. TV people, with cameras, in the street . . ."

"I am not a reporter."

Naomi noted: on three walls of the room were framed daguerreotypes depicting scenes on the Muskegee River, of another century. On the floor was a deep plush rug, that had been recently vacuumed. The small bathroom appeared to have been remodeled with shining fixtures and a bathtub that looked as if it were made out of white plastic.

A fleeting face in the bathroom mirror. Naomi felt a touch of panic—her mother had stayed here, in this room. She was certain of this.

In a conciliatory tone the desk clerk was describing features of the "historic" Muskegee Falls Inn of which she seemed to be proud. Its restaurant, its pub, its room service. When the breakfast room opened in the morning, how late the restaurant served. Naomi listened politely, while returning to the window. She saw that the afternoon was waning. The river was luminous as shaken foil and at this distance it appeared to be without motion.

"Well, miss! It's a nice room, isn't it?"

"It is."

"Do you think you will be taking it?"—the question was awkwardly phrased.

"No."

Naomi heard the other draw in her breath, sharply. But she had not meant to say *no*, she'd meant to say *yes*.

"Excuse me, I'm sorry. I meant to say yes."

In the elevator descending to the lobby neither woman could think of a thing to say.

Downstairs at the front desk Naomi provided the clerk with her name and with a credit card. It was a relief to her, though also a disappointment, that the name *Naomi Voorhees* seemed to make no impression.

She was given her room card. She was given a key for the minibar. She was about to leave, to bring her car around to park at the rear of the hotel, when the big-haired woman said suddenly, as if she'd just thought of exciting news, "You know—there's some relative of Luther Dunphy we've been hearing about. A female boxer—'D.D. Dunphy.'"

Naomi was intrigued. Female boxer?

"One of the Dunphys. Luther's daughter. I think she just won some championship. Not sure but think it was in Cleveland. We saw an interview with her by accident on TV. My niece says she went to school with her."

"Do you mean Dawn Dunphy? She's a boxer?"

"Well, one of them is. One of the daughters."

Naomi was mildly incredulous. Dawn Dunphy, a boxer! And on TV.

Yet, it should not have surprised her. From photographs she recalled the graceless smirking Dawn Dunphy, the murderer's daughter whom she'd particularly hated.

In Muskegee Falls, her compass needles spun.

She was *here*, at the site. *Here*, where the death had occurred.

Therefore, she did not want to call anyone from Muskegee Falls. She did not want to acknowledge Muskegee Falls.

She did not want to utter the words—"Muskegee Falls."

She no longer called Darren except if it was an absolutely necessary call, and there were fewer and fewer of these. For she was a fully adult woman now. She could not be burdening her brother with his younger ghost-sister.

She did call her mother Jenna, from time to time. And (unpredictably) Jenna called her. But she did not want Jenna to know that she'd resumed working on the archive, for the archive had seemed a very bad idea to Jenna.

Please do not put me in this "documentary." Please do not quote me.

I can't forbid you and I don't want to censor you. But I beg you.

Of course, Jenna did want to censor her. She had no clear idea why.

"Isn't my grief as legitimate as yours? Why is it not as legitimate?"—she could not demand of her mother.

Instead, she would call Madelena Kein. Though she was apprehensive of what she might hear in her grandmother's voice that might be faint, weak. Not the warm and assured voice of Madelena Kein that had long been the woman's public voice but the voice of a woman who has been made to feel her mortality.

Hello! It's me—Naomi.

I am in—well, that place. I am recording with my camera.

I will call you again, Lena.

I hope—I hope you are well.

Not able to bring herself to say, even in a rushed murmur—*I love you.*

At 1183 Howard Avenue, painted a cheery canary-yellow and decorated with colorful cutouts of cartoon animals, was the PEONY CHRISTIAN DAYCARE CENTER.

Naomi sat for a moment in the rented Nissan. Her brain felt as if a black wing had brushed over it.

"A daycare center . . ."

She thought—*But he died here. In the driveway, here.*

She would have to record what she found. The camera eye is neutral and unjudging.

The driveway beside the Peony Christian Daycare Center was cracked, and in cracks grew small hardy weeds like lace. There was no sign of blood in this ordinary setting, no sign of death. Too many days, years, weather had intervened.

In the camera eye, the very ordinariness of the scene would comprise a mystery. Why are we looking at *this*?

The neighborhood itself was hard to describe. Part-commercial, part-residential. A sprawling lumberyard on one side of Howard Avenue, a block of bungalows in tiny grassless lots on the other. A single large clapboard house with turrets and bay windows partitioned into apartments calling itself *Howard Manor: Apt's For Rent.*

Peony Christian Daycare Center had a slapdash homemade look. Bright red letters painted by hand on the yellow background. The cartoon animals were clearly hand-crafted, and had large friendly brown eyes. There were no signs to indicate that the day care center was Christian. The atmosphere was lively, noisy. If you lived in the neighborhood you might smile seeing the bright primary colors every day or you might be discomforted, annoyed by such resolute and unwavering cheeriness.

Vehicles were parked at the rear of the single-story canary-yellow building. Mothers were arriving with very young children. It was a warm September morning: a number of the children and child-care staff were outside, in a small playground.

Cries of young children, laughter and excitement.

Seeing the children in the makeshift playground Naomi found herself smiling.

Nobody's baby wants to die.

It was life always that would prevail. That was the singular lesson beside which all others are diminished.

"Hello!"—Naomi introduced herself to a harried-looking but friendly woman named Diana in jeans and knitted smock who told her yes, they were aware that the previous tenant of the building had been a women's center but no, they had not actually seen the center because the building had been vacant for several years before they'd acquired it. And they didn't know anyone who'd been associated with the Women's Center.

"'The Broome County Women's Center'—has it moved to another location?"

"No. I think it was just shut down. Let me ask—" Diana turned to an older co-worker who provided the information that so far as she knew the women's center had been absorbed into the hospital on East Avenue.

"There's radiology there—mammograms. There's doctors, physical therapy, classes in yoga, Pilates. Do you need directions?"

Naomi thanked her, *no.*

Naomi asked if they knew why the Women's Center had been shut down and the women exchanged glances and said vaguely that they'd heard there had been "trouble"—"picketers."

"You'd never heard that there were murders at the center? Because it was an abortion clinic?"

She'd spoken too bluntly. Belatedly she realized.

It was not the way of Muskegee Falls, Ohio, to speak so bluntly of ugly matters. Ugly local matters. Seeing the camera in her hands, the slant of the baseball cap on her head, the Peony Christian Daycare women looked uneasy. Vaguely they shook their heads, *no.*

Naomi wondered: *no,* they knew nothing of what had happened; or *no,* they did not want to talk about it.

She told them that the Center had provided other services beside abortions for women and girls but it had been under attack from pro-life protesters in the late 1990s and in November 1999 two men had been shot down in the driveway . . .

Diana said, pained: "Excuse me, are you a journalist?"

They were staring at her camera. They were staring at her, and they were not smiling now.

Naomi said: "No. I'm not a journalist."

A young child came to pluck at Diana's arm. "In a minute, Billy! Be right there."

Naomi relented. She did not want to detain them further.

She did not want to upset these women, or annoy them, or harass them. She did not want to inflict upon them what they did not wish to hear on this mild dry September morning in 2011.

She said: "Your day care center looks wonderful. It must be great fun, and very rewarding . . ."

"Yes. It is."

". . . hard work, but . . ."

". . . very rewarding."

She walked away, with a wave of her hand. She could see the relief in their faces. Several other women, who appeared to be mothers, were staring after Naomi too; she knew that they would excitedly discuss her as soon as she departed.

Journalist? Some newspaper? Taking pictures? Looking for the abortion clinic? Out-of-state? Pro-choice?

At 56 Front Street the Dunphys had lived in 1999. She had learned this fact.

Two-story clapboard house in a neighborhood of near-identical small houses and all of them dating back to—mid-twentieth century? The paint on the house was faded, weatherworn like something left out too long in the rain.

The windows were partly covered by blinds. Almost, you could imagine someone peering out one of the up-stairs windows.

She saw: narrow driveway, single-car garage too crammed with things to accommodate any vehicle. Small front concrete stoop, small yard of burnt-out grass and dirt and at the curb a badly dented and stained metal trash can, empty.

Tricycle overturned in the yard. Dog's red plastic water bowl, no water. Scattering of much-gnawed-at bones.

The neighborhood was quiet except for a barking dog. Children on bicycles calling to one another.

This is the house in which Luther Dunphy lived with his family in November 1999.

About four miles from the Broome County Women's Center.

A middle-aged woman appeared in the driveway, in loose-fitting clothing. Flip-flops on her long-toed white feet. She was smiling in Naomi's direction, unless she was scowling.

This was not a neighborhood in which strangers wandered into yards or stood at the end of driveways cameras in hand, staring.

Strangers live here now—of course.

Almost twelve years have passed.

"Excuse me? Are you looking for someone?"—the woman shaded her eyes, squinting at Naomi. Still she might have been perceived as friendly, curious.

"Oh, I'm sorry"—the intruder was trying for disarming frankness—"I don't think they live here any longer. The Dunphys? I used to know their daughter . . ."

The woman had ceased smiling. Naomi saw her jaw tighten.

Naomi was holding the camera casually in her left hand. Unobtrusively recording what the camera saw but in such a way that the middle-aged woman staring at Naomi suspiciously could not have known.

"Yes, well. Nobody with that name lives here anymore."

"The Dunphys? Do you know the name?"

Big-shouldered, hostile, the woman shrugged.

"Do you know—when did they move away?"

Again the woman shrugged. Her gesture signaled not *I don't know when they moved away* but *Why should I tell you if I know when they moved away.*

"Do you happen to know where they moved?"

The woman shook her head, *no.*

"Are there any other Dunphys in Muskegee Falls? Anyone I could speak with?"

The woman shook her head, *no.*

A large ungainly straggly-haired dog came limping out to join the truculent woman. A Labrador-terrier mixture, with a stump of a tail. Sensing the woman's unease the dog bared its yellow teeth and began to bark at the girl in the baseball cap as if knowing very well the significance of the small black object in her left hand.

Obviously it was fraudulent on Naomi's part. No one would be seeking one of the Dunphy children without knowing about Luther Dunphy. To pretend otherwise was deceit. Yet Naomi felt she had no choice but to maintain the awkward deception even as the woman stared at her unsmiling and the straggly-haired dog beside her growled.

"I wasn't a friend of Dawn Dunphy—I mean, we weren't close. But I heard she's become an athlete—a boxer . . ."

How strange, the name *Dawn Dunphy* on her lips! Naomi was sure she'd never spoken this name aloud in her life.

"Nobody living here with that name—'Dunphy.' Not for years."

The woman spoke in a loud voice. Clearly, Naomi was dismissed.

Yet she was staring at the house. She could not tear her eyes from the house. For it was *so ordinary* a house. And she had known that beforehand. A house in which the murderer of her father had plotted her father's murder, and in which he'd kept his weapons. In the cellar perhaps.

Had she been allowed access to the house by the scowling woman, had she been allowed to film the interior, even the cellar where (she speculated) the weapons might have been kept—to what purpose?

"I said, miss—there's nobody living here, or anywhere around here, with that name. OK?"

"Yes! I'm sorry." Naomi smiled, inanely. The camera felt unwieldy in her hand, redundant. "Very sorry . . ."

Awkwardly turning to walk to her car parked at the curb beside the badly dented trash can. Glancing back she saw the woman unmoving in the driveway, standing her ground with the snarling dog beside her, staring at Naomi as if she'd sighted the enemy.

She is living in the murderer's house. There is some shame to this. Of course she does not want to be reminded.

In the compact rented car south on Front Street to Mason Street and so to Woodbind. Left on Summit. Another left on Howard Avenue. The route the murderer had almost certainly taken on his way to 1183 Howard on that morning.

She'd devised a timeline. It is always helpful to devise outlines, structures. From all that she'd learned over a period of years arranging the (probable) sequence of events, imagining parallel trajectories: Luther Dunphy leaving the two-story clapboard house on Front Street, approximately four miles from the Women's Center, sometime in the early morning of November 2, 1999, in his pickup; Timothy Barron, Women's Center volunteer, leaving his home in his minivan and arriving at Gus Voorhees's residence on Shawnee Street, three miles from the Center, at approximately 7:10 A.M., to pick up Gus and to drive together to the Center . . .

She drove to Shawnee Street in another part of Muskegee Falls. This was a residential neighborhood of single-family houses, larger and set in larger lots than those on Front Street; at 88 Shawnee, which was the address of her father's rented apartment, was a graceless foursquare beige stucco building with a sign advertising *prestige condos 1-, 2-, 3-bedroom.*

She wondered if the building had changed much in the past eleven years. She wondered if her mother had ever seen the inside of the apartment.

She recalled Gus saying that the rental was "temporary." He intended to move to another apartment, in a building nearer downtown. Or had he said (Naomi had been a young girl then, and it was before the murder, she would not have remembered each precious word her father uttered) that he was "waiting to hear" if Jenna might change her mind about moving to Ohio— "In which case we'll rent a really nice house. You kids can help pick it out."

Shortly after 7:00 A.M. of the morning of November 2, 1999, with no knowledge that within a half hour he would be dead, Dr. Voorhees had emerged from this building to get into a Dodge minivan driven by Timothy Barron. Together the men drove to the Women's Center.

By 7:30 A.M., both Gus Voorhees and Timothy Barron would be dead.

No one was ever to know what the men had talked about, en route to the Center.

Naomi hoped it had been a friendly exchange. She hoped the men had liked each other. She hoped they had not ever been in fear of their lives as they approached the Women's Center where hostile demonstrators were beginning to gather.

Driving the route to Howard Avenue Naomi felt a mounting sense of unreality. For all that had happened years ago could so very easily have not happened.

There was nothing intrinsic in the geography of the place. There was no *fatedness*. Gus Voorhees might so easily have been elsewhere, including Huron County, Michigan. Luther Dunphy might so easily have been distracted by other matters in his life—a child's illness, or his own. A change of heart. A change of mind. You had to conclude that it was purely chance, without meaning.

He killed them. They died. That is all there was.

Soon, before she was quite prepared, she found herself back at 1183 Howard Avenue. But the Broome County Women's Center was gone and in its place the canary-yellow Peony Christian Daycare Center. *That is all there is.*

———

Yet, she would persevere.

Calling Madelena to leave a message—*I am discouraged but I will not give up.*

In a hoarse voice adding—*I love you.*

At last, Thelma Barron consented to see her. But only for less than an hour, and only for a recording and not a video.

"No one needs to see my face in your video. It's enough, you will use my father's face."

Thelma Barron spoke flatly, resentfully. The word *use* was inflected, scornful.

A middle-aged woman, with ironic eyes. An intelligent woman, doing her best to be courteous with a stranger.

Badly Naomi missed the solace of the camera. For a camera lens is turned away from us allowing us to hide behind it. There is the illusion of invisibility, innocence.

Instead, she would record the interview—the other daughter's words. The two would sit across from each other at a weatherworn picnic table behind the Barrons's handsome old Victorian house on Mercy Street, in a backyard in need of mowing and raking. Naomi's

cheeks burned to hear the other's words that were al-
ternately faltering and angry, wounded and incensed.

*For a long time we could not speak of it. Your fa-
ther's name was bitter to us.*

*This grief we felt, that our father we loved so much
had been killed because he had volunteered at the
Center, and he had died beside Dr. Voorhees—and no
one knew or cared except his family and a few others.*

*In the news stories always the headline was VOOR-
HEES. Always the focus was VOORHEES. The name
is terrible to us to this day, we cannot speak it aloud.*

*After they died, it was VOORHEES who was hon-
ored. It was VOORHEES'S picture you would see. It
was VOORHEES that was the martyr. On the anti-
abortion websites it was stated that Timothy Barron's
death was COLLATERAL DAMAGE and in a war
COLLATERAL DAMAGE is to be regretted but not
to be avoided.*

*I am sorry to speak like this to you—Naomi. I know
that there is a terrible wound in your heart too. But I
am not a "sister" to you. That will not be.*

*Dr. Voorhees was not our father's friend though our
father wished that Dr. Voorhees would be his friend.
He had invited your father to our house for supper
more than once, and always your father had an excuse.*

Dad would speak of Gus Voorhees as his friend, proudly. But it was not to be.

Our loss is a more bitter thing than yours and unjust because your father is acclaimed and honored and will not be forgotten while our father Timothy Barron is forgotten by all but a few.

Let me tell you—our father was a truly good man. He was retired from the U.S. Army where he had had the rank of major. He had served in the Vietnam War from 1966 to 1971. In his private life he had dedicated himself to helping others, he would say that was why he had been allowed to live while other men in his platoon had died. He had returned he said from Hell.

Because Dad was a big man people misunderstood him for Dad was a quiet man and in his heart he was gentle. He would say, he had made himself into a "warrior" to protect his country. But he did not have the soul of a "warrior"—he said. He would compare himself to one of our dogs who was a sheepdog-collie mix. We would joke how Andy could scare off a burglar if the burglar just saw him but if Andy saw the burglar, he would run in the other direction—Andy never even barked, if he could help it. His bark was like somebody coughing. Andy weighed one hundred fifteen pounds at his heaviest . . .

Nobody grieved for Dad more than Andy. Poor

sweet dog would whine and whimper and could not stay still. The first week or so Dad was gone, Andy was beside himself. His tail would thump, he'd try to convince himself that Dad was on his way into the house, he'd get excited, but then it came to nothing and you could see the life die out in his eyes. Andy is an old dog now and sometimes still he will go out into the driveway and lie stretched down waiting for Dad to turn into the driveway.

It breaks your heart. You can't tell an animal what has happened to change his entire life and take away his happiness.

Our father had always been supportive of women and girls. It wasn't just that he had four daughters and one son. That was how Dad felt.

Some people in the family were surprised and maybe did not approve—Dad said "women's rights" are the wave of the future.

All us girls, his daughters, Dad made sure we were educated—so we could do better than him, he said. (Dad did pretty well in his life! He owned Barron's Auto Supplies here in town with one of his brothers.)

Our grandmother, Dad's mother, had done volunteer work too. Church, school, hospital, hospice. Grandma was a volunteer at the Muskegee Falls Animal Shelter until a week before she died at age eighty-seven and the day she died was just a day after the anniversary of Dad's death last year.

We are not angry toward the Voorhees family—of course. We are over that now. I'm sorry if I spoke harshly and without thinking. I did not think that I could speak with you at all which is why I did not answer your first letter. There is no interest on our part in a "documentary" on Dr. Voorhees. It is very painful for any of us even now to recall what happened to our father. And justice was just so slow, the trial kept getting postponed . . .

For three years our father Tim Barron was an escort at the Broome County Women's Center and in those years he did not encounter any opposition out of the ordinary. Being a big man, he was not naturally fearful of anyone who hoped to push him around or intimidate him. Of course, the protesters at the Center were mostly peaceful. The most they did was shout at the women entering the Center, sometimes—they did not physically threaten them. The majority participated in prayer vigils and tried to provide counseling to the pregnant women if any would listen—of course, they never did. But when Gus Voorhees came to head the Center, that was changed. There was a lot of publicity and much of it was bad. The protesters were angrier and more confrontational, and there were more of them. Dad noticed the change almost overnight. He would say somebody was going to be hurt. Stronger security was needed from the police. Right away too, nasty things appeared on anti-abortion websites. Broome County was singled out. Dr. Voorhees was singled out. Army of God is strong in Ohio especially rural Ohio. Operation Rescue is still strong. (We all know people who are involved in these organizations. Some of us went to school with them. But we did not ever think any one of them would murder any one of us.)

Now I am not intending to upset you, Naomi. But it was widely believed around here that your father behaved provocatively in giving interviews as he did to the local newspaper and on local TV. I know, Dr. Voorhees believed that if people understood the mission of the Women's Center, which is to give medical care and advice to "any and all" women regardless of their ability to pay, they would not be angry; but Dr. Voorhees seemed not to understand that just his presence, his words, whatever he was saying, was inflammatory in some quarters, and only made things worse. He was brash and outspoken and believed himself "in the right." I think that Dad tried to tell him this but if he did, Dr. Voorhees did not listen.

Dad understood the risk he was taking every day he

went to the Center. He was a brave man but he was not an abortion doctor himself, he should not have been shot down as he was.

It was claimed by the pro-life people that Luther Dunphy did not shoot my father, that someone else did. Because Luther Dunphy refused to acknowledge that he pulled the trigger.

It is still being claimed that one of the law enforcement officers shot Dad, not Luther Dunphy. Which is ridiculous since law enforcement had only hand guns, not shotguns. And witnesses saw Luther Dunphy turn fast after he'd shot your father—and aim his shotgun at our father—then he pulled the trigger again. They said there was a "glazed" look in Dunphy's face and no emotion.

He was a cold-blooded murderer with a heart of stone. He did not deserve to live and breathe in the same air shared by decent people.

Those weeks before his death Dad was getting up early to drive the doctor to the Center. He had particularly volunteered to drive Dr. Voorhees in case there was an attack on the van. The plan was, the doctor would duck down, and Dad would drive the van as fast as possible to escape. Dad did not sleep well the last eight years of his life, so getting up early was not difficult for him. He had undergone chemotherapy for cancer—colon cancer. It had been just stage two when the doctor caught it, but Dad had a hard time with chemo that wiped him out, he'd say—"Like something rubbed off a blackboard." All of Dad's curly hair fell out—when we first saw him, with no hair, we burst into tears, it was such a shock. But Dad laughed at us— "Hey kids, I wasn't going to win any beauty contest anyway, was I?" That was Dad's kind of humor. Everybody loved him.

By the time Dad met your father he was finished with the chemo and his hair had grown back, but not like it was, not curly, and very thin and dry. He did not tell your father about his medical history because he was not the type to speak of private things. He was not the type to cause others to worry about him. So, almost, we never quite trusted Dad, after the cancer— we'd ask him how he was, and he'd say "Fine" but we never knew what that meant; so we'd ask Mom and she would say, "Why do you think he'd tell me?" The opposite of self-pity was what our father was but that left us feeling anxious. Once, he said, your father happened to mention to him that he—that is, your father—was going to have to postpone some of his surgical appointments because he had bronchitis and "couldn't stop his damn coughing"—and Dad thought that was such a confidential thing to say, to share, like he and Dr. Voor-

hees were old friends or even closer, like brothers—
Dad was very touched . . .

He was a good man, murdered like a dog.

We are not sorry that the Broome County Women's
Center has closed. In all the stories of the Center, the
staff did not speak of Timothy Barron except slight-
ingly. Of course they will say—"Tim was a wonderful man"—"Everybody loved Tim"—"We miss Tim."
But that was it. All serious focus was on Dr. Voorhees.
All the media gave a damn for was Dr. Voorhees. We
understand the reason for this but it did not make it any
easier to bear. When people talk of Gus Voorhees as a
martyr even today we want to say yes and our father
Tim Barron was a martyr too.

———————

Excuse me, I am feeling very upset. It has been a
while since I have spoken like this to anyone. In our
family we never speak of it now and the young children know nothing of it, and we don't want to upset
them and make them bitter. But I think—I am not
able to speak with you any longer now.

What is your name?—Naomi?

I am sorry, Naomi. Please turn off that damned machine and go away now.

The next interview was friendly, even chatty. Far
from being kept outside at a rickety picnic table
Naomi was invited inside to sit at a Formica-topped
table in a kitchen, and to share a sixteen-ounce just-
slightly-flat bottle of Diet-Coke with the daughter of
a Muskegee Falls police office who had "passed away"
several years before.

*Oh well—my dad did not actually witness the shoot-
ings. That was a misconception.*

*Him and the other officer were just en route to the
scene. They were scheduled to arrive at 7:30 A.M. and
the shootings were just before that and the call came
to them in the cruiser to get to the scene at once. They
hardly had time to put on the siren, they said.*

*Dad would think—almost—that he'd heard the
gunfire. He heard the screams as soon as they pulled
up. He dealt with the panicked people. He was the
one who "arrested" Luther Dunphy. He put cuffs on
the man.*

Shingled roof. Small country church shaped like a
box. And of the hue of cardboard. Box-shaped country church. Small country church, brown-aluminum-

shingled, new-looking roof, set in an uncultivated field, dun-colored grasses, gravel driveway, hand-painted sign—*ST. PAUL MISSIONARY CHURCH OF JESUS SUNDAY SERVICE 9:00 A.M., WEDNESDAY PRAYER MEETING 7:00 P.M.*

This was on the Schylerville Road. Approximately six miles from downtown Muskegee Falls in a rural area of farms, ramshackle country houses, trailer homes.

She had made telephone calls. She had hoped to meet with the minister of the church but she'd been told that that was not possible for Reverend Dennis was "away" and "would not be back" for twelve days.

She asked if she might have a telephone number for Reverend Dennis, or an email address, and was told these were "private."

(How did they know who she was? she wondered. Had word spread in Muskegee Falls, another "journalist" from out of town had arrived?)

Several times it had been assured her: *no one with the name of Dunphy lives here now.*

Circling the church, camera in hand. Grasses rustled dryly beneath her feet.

Behind the church was a small graveyard. Grave markers amid tufts of spiky grass, wooden crosses and stone slabs and artificial flowers in clay pots. It came over her in a rush, Luther Dunphy must be buried here! But when she investigated the more recent graves she did not see the name *Dunphy.*

She had learned that Luther Dunphy's immediate family, wife and children, had moved to a small town not far away called Mad River Junction. But she had no plans to pursue them there. She had no wish to interfere with their lives. Even Dawn Dunphy, whom she particularly disliked, was of no interest to her any longer.

Once, she and Darren had fantasized "revenge" upon the Dunphys. But that was long ago, when they'd been young adolescents, deranged by grief.

"Hello? Hello? Hel-*lo?* No one here?"—her voice lifted lightly, sadly.

No one was here. No one saw. No one turned into the gravel drive in a vehicle, incensed at her trespassing and demanding to know who she was.

No sound but autumnal insects and the random cries of birds. Bat-like birds she supposed must be cliff swallows or swifts, swooping and diving near the river. On her way to the St. Paul Missionary Church of Jesus driving beside the river she'd seen the falls where a shimmering vapor arose, evaporating as it lifted.

At the peak of the church roof was an aluminum cross not prominent or showy, about five feet in height.

Daddy help me. I am failing, I am drowning. I don't know what to do, to reach you.

She turned off the camera. She had recorded all there was to record.

That night in her room in the Muskegee Falls Inn she dreamt of her father as she had not seen him in a long time. With urgency he'd been speaking to her, half-angrily as one might speak to a stubborn child who is in danger.

"Honey, look: let me go."

And a voice meant to be her voice, yet not issued from her exactly: "Let you go, Daddy—where?"

And he says, "Where the dead go, honey. Let me go there."

"But—I can't do that. How can I do that?"

And he says, "I wasn't so special, honey. Except that I was your dad, I wasn't so special."

Her heart begins to pound violently. She wakes, sick with horror, and she will not sleep for the rest of the night.

Katechay Island:

October 2011

At the motel on Katechay Island they waited.

"She'd said she was definitely coming."

"'Definitely'? I don't think so. She'd said she hoped to come."

"*Hoped to come.* Not to me, she didn't say that."

Naomi spoke with more certainty than she felt. Almost, a kind of defiance.

Darren had brought the urn containing their father's ashes. On a table it stood like a primitive artifact generating its own dark shadow.

In the confusion of her life at the time (in the early months of 2000) Jenna had not buried the urn in an Ann Arbor cemetery but had entrusted it to one of Gus's oldest friends in Ann Arbor who'd kept it on a shelf in his book-lined study for years.

There'd been some bitterness between them—between the brother and sister, and their mother.

Naomi and Darren had wanted to scatter the ashes on Katechay Island, but Jenna had resisted. Why?—had not ever been clear.

Much in those months after their father's death had not been clear and even to recall that time now, or to attempt to recall it, made Naomi uneasy as if the earth were shifting beneath her.

Naomi had assumed that the ashes had been buried in Ann Arbor. Darren had assumed that the ashes had been buried in Ann Arbor. It had been something of a shock to learn only just recently from Jenna that their father's ashes had been with someone outside the family for more than a decade—"For safekeeping."

Safekeeping. What did this mean?

They'd decided that it was not a good idea to look too closely into their mother's motives. Still, this was a startling revelation. And it was a happy revelation, for now, at last, their father's ashes could be scattered on Katechay Island as he'd wished.

"You'd think if Mom was going to leave the urn with anyone, she'd have left it with Grandpa Voorhees . . ."

"Or just given it to us, and we could have scattered the ashes . . ."

A pang in the heart. Conjoined twins. Each felt the

fleet tremor, the shiver of a fierce shared emotion, they might have imagined they'd outgrown by now.

Our mother doesn't love us. Our mother has abandoned us.

But it was ridiculous, at their ages! To feel that old hurt, bewilderment. As Darren was lately saying they should have been more protective of *her.*

There was a new maturity in Darren. The older brother who had his own life now, totally separate from hers.

She missed him! She missed her young, furious self, that had long abided in her brother.

It was something of a shock to realize that Darren was almost thirty years old. He'd given up comic strips and graphic novels (for the time being at least) and was in his second year of medical school at the University of Washington, in Seattle; he intended to specialize in public health, as Gus had done. He was living with a woman named Rachel, a speech therapist, whom Naomi had not (yet) met but with whom she'd spoken on the phone—"Naomi? Hello! I almost feel that I know you, Darren has told me so much about you." Naomi had been struck dumb with wonder what this could possibly be, that her brother had told a stranger.

Hey we were just your ordinary older brother, kid

sister plotting mayhem against the enemy like freaks joined at the hip. Did we actually hurt anyone?—no. Just ourselves.

And what a surprise, her first glimpse of Darren! Her brother had been awaiting her that noon at the Katechay Inn, where he'd arrived the previous evening; when Naomi turned her rented car into the parking lot there came at a run a tall smiling young man in khaki shorts, T-shirt, dark glasses and hiking shoes. A wide smile as if he'd been watching from a window.

"Hey! Hiya."

Her first impression was—*He is not wary, guarded. He has changed.*

He'd hugged her so hard she winced. The change in her brother was obvious—*He is happy.*

Of course she'd recognized Darren at once. The changes in his appearance were superficial. His thick dark hair was threaded with premature gray like their father's at a young age and was not so long and straggly as it had been. Nor was he quite so lanky-lean as he'd been, his face was fuller, on his jaws a short-trimmed beard that reminded Naomi of their father's beard in one of its incarnations, in some long-ago time.

Why does a man wear a beard? Naomi had once asked their father. Gus had laughed and said it was a more appropriate question why a man might shave off his beard. *D'you think "clean-shaven" is natural, sweetie? Why would you think such a thing?*

She'd have liked to search through old family photos, to see if she could locate precisely the beard of their father's that Darren's beard emulated . . . It would have been gratifying to see Darren's face, when he realized it.

But she didn't have the cache of photographs with her. Some were at the grandparents' house in Birmingham, Michigan. Some were with her things in New York City, in the room that was "hers" in Madelena Kein's apartment.

(If Naomi was living anywhere, it was with her grandmother Madelena Kein. She'd lived with Madelena while attending film school at NYU and she'd returned to live with her after Madelena was diagnosed with cancer in the spring of 2010, in order to see Madelena through the ordeal of surgery and chemotherapy.)

Behind the Katechay Inn, a wooden deck overlooking a shallow marshy shore of Wild Fowl Bay at the southernmost tip of Saginaw Bay/Lake Huron. A sound of red-winged blackbirds, bullfrogs. In sunlit autumnal mud flats, remnants of monarch butterflies and dragonflies. So vividly Naomi remembered hiking in this area with her father, her eyes were constantly filling up with tears.

(Did Darren notice? If he did, he was tactful and said nothing.)

"If she's late, she would call . . ."

"Would she!"

Brother, sister laughed together. Pleasure in this shared exasperation over their (eccentric, difficult) mother.

Certainly there was a new ease between them, that they didn't have to depend upon Jenna for what they'd come here to do: scatter their father's ashes. This they could do without her as they'd been living their lives without her for more than a decade.

Yet, they waited. As Darren said another fifteen minutes would not hurt.

And when fifteen minutes passed, and no vehicle appeared on the roadway as far as they could see into the distance, Naomi said, "Well. Another five minutes won't hurt." She paused. (Should she make a joke of this? Was humor appropriate?) "Ten."

It was quite possible, Jenna's airplane had arrived late at the Detroit airport. Or, Jenna had had trouble with the car rental. Though neither of these could explain why Jenna wasn't calling them, unless—"Her phone might be dead. You know how distracted she can be."

They smiled remembering the house on Salt Hill

Road. They'd hear the teakettle whistling manically in the kitchen—and there was their mother (whom they would not have dreamt of calling Jenna in those years) upstairs in the drafty room she called her office, typing on the keyboard of an outsized computer, oblivious to the shrieking below.

So cold upstairs, sometimes she'd worn a jacket and gloves.

"Fingerless gloves. Remember?"

"'Fingerless.' That was weird."

"It was. It was weird."

"Where'd she get them?"

"Don't know."

"D'you think—children can't grasp the concept of *fingerless gloves* . . ."

"I remember us like ghost children . . ."

"D'you think the house is haunted—by *us?*"

Each was thinking—*We can drive to see the house. Salt Hill Road. Huron Township. After scattering the ashes, we can drive there.*

But neither spoke. The prospect of revisiting the house in which their father had not died but in which news of his death had come was too awful.

The smell of death had permeated the house. Some living thing had (literally) died in the basement of the house and the smell had never faded . . .

"D'you remember, the flies in that terrible place?"

"Flies? I'm not sure . . ."

"Upstairs. Inside the walls. You must remember . . ."

"I remember a *smell*."

They were silent, shuddering.

In bright autumnal sunshine they were sitting on the wood-plank deck behind their (adjacent) rented rooms in the motel. (Adjacent rooms had been deliberate. Jenna had rented a room in another wing.) They were staring toward the road that curved through marshy mudflats in the direction of the bridge to the mainland on which Jenna would be sighted in her rented car, if Jenna were coming to join them.

A few vehicles had appeared on the bridge, and driven past the motel. Minivans, recreational vehicles. No car with just a single passenger.

Jenna was just slightly more than an hour late. Considering how far she'd had to come from Bennington, Vermont, this was not really *late*.

And what of Melissa?—it was painful to speak of Melissa.

Very regretful their young sister had been. In terse emails explaining *I am so sorry. I am not able to take time from school so far away from Michigan. I will be thinking of you.*

It was like Melissa not to sign *love, Melissa* but only just *Melissa*.

For a while it had seemed that Melissa would join them, to scatter their father's ashes on Katechay Island. She had not exactly said yes, but she had not exactly said no.

But it was a long distance to come, from California. This was so. She'd only just flown out the previous month to start the fall term at UC-Berkeley. And it may have been that the prospect of scattering their father's ashes in this beautiful desolate place didn't mean so much to Melissa as to the others.

Initially it had seemed that Melissa would go to Bennington College for a liberal arts degree, and live with Jenna in the small town of Bennington, in a house now owned by Jenna and a companion. (Who was this companion? A man? The name was ambiguous—it sounded like *Noy.*) But then, suddenly it came about that Melissa had been accepted at the University of California at Berkeley with the intention of studying molecular biology.

No one in the family had known that Melissa had even applied to Berkeley. Nor that she had an interest in molecular biology.

As soon as she'd arrived at Berkeley (Naomi had

learned) Melissa had joined the Asian Christian Students Association and was living in a residence comprised largely of Asian Christian students. Naomi had not known that such residences existed at Berkeley. She had not known that her sister was so emphatically religious. She had been surprised to learn that Melissa had told their grandparents that she'd been in touch, through the Internet, with her birth mother in Shanghai, and hoped to visit this woman, a stranger to all of the Voorhees, within a few years.

Melissa had been studying Mandarin Chinese in high school. She'd been going to a Baptist church with a school friend, in a suburb of Detroit called Oak Park. She told her grandparents that she felt "most comfortable" with other Christians and "not so comfortable" with non-Christians. In an email to all of the family Melissa had written *We accept Jesus as our savior. Jesus is not always pushing, He does not judge us except by our intentions.*

Naomi was thinking of how, that day, the last time they'd gone hiking with their father on Katechay Island, she and Melissa had fallen behind. They had not been able to keep up with Daddy and Darren hiking along the coarse pebbly shore where cold soapy-looking waves broke.

Oh Daddy!—wait.

Wait for us. Daddy!

Melissa had clutched at Naomi's hand. Naomi had held the little hand tight.

But it hadn't been enough, somehow. Their love for Melissa had not been enough and they had not ever understood why.

Because she was adopted? Because she was *of another ethnic background*? These were such obvious reasons, you rejected them irritably.

It wasn't known what Jenna thought about this. Naomi had felt a small twinge of jealousy, that, for a while, Melissa was planning to live with their mother in Bennington; which meant that Jenna had invited her, and had made a place for her in her (new) life. But that had not happened.

That day they'd had lunch at the Light House Restaurant on the island, that was of particular interest to children. You could climb an outdoor stairway, and see a long distance over Lake Huron—(though you could not ever see the Canadian shore only just the Michigan shore on both sides). Daddy and Mommy had spoken sharply to each other as sometimes they did but Daddy and Mommy had laughed and whispered together, and had linked fingers in a playful manner. But Mommy had decided not to accompany them on the hike along the shore.

It was not easy walking in the coarse sand. The dunes were hard-packed and cold even in the sun. The beach had been littered with kelp, rotted pieces of wood, long-rotted little fish and bodies of birds you did not want to step on with your bare feet, that were scary to see, and emitted a sour smell. A blinding-bright day to be near the water, a cold day, and a windy day, so that the water was like something shaken, sharp as tinfoil.

He'd said it, then. Words they had not compre-hended.

Promise me you will scatter my ashes here after I die.

They'd had no idea what he meant. Even Darren who was the oldest had no idea. And it was some-thing of a joke—wasn't it? Daddy had been smiling, his eyes wet with tears. But if you'd ask him why, why were his eyes wet, Daddy would say *Because I am so happy. Because I love you kids, and I love your mother. That's why.*

It was foolish to wait. Yet, in a kind of torpor they waited, drinking scalding-hot black and tasteless cof-fee from a vending machine in the motel lobby.

Neither wanted to think what was obvious—of course, their mother wasn't coming. How naive, how foolish, to imagine that Jenna would join them in this task she had not wished to confront for eleven years.

Darren said: "Five more minutes. No more."

So long they'd been waiting for Jenna, God-damned self-centered unreliable Jenna, Naomi had to use the bathroom in her motel room another time, and while she was in the room she made a call on her cell phone, and left a message; and when she returned to the deck she heard voices—and her heart leapt.

There stood a woman with feathery gray-white hair, embracing Darren. At first Naomi didn't recognize her—"Jenna?"

"Naomi! Honey."

No one, not even Madelena, called Naomi *honey.* Only her parents whom (almost) she'd come to think were both deceased.

"Oh honey! Hel-*lo.*"

They embraced. Jenna's grasp was hard, fierce. Naomi was dazed with surprise, happiness and surprise, a kind of profound relief—*Now I don't have to hate my mother. Now, all that is over.* She was feeling the thinness of her mother's back, the lightness of her mother's bones, through Jenna's clothing. It seemed strange to her, Jenna was as tall as she, and not shorter, shrunken as Naomi had been imagining.

And her arms were strong, in this first, breathless embrace.

Jenna was swiping at her eyes with both hands. Her face was pale as alabaster that has been worn smooth. She did not look *old*, Naomi thought. This was a relief.

But her hair had faded and seemed dry, brittle. A curious sort of silvery-white, not distinctive and glamorous as Madelena's hair, though attractive in its way, very light, feathery, brushed back behind her ears in no discernible style.

Clutching at Naomi's hand, and at Darren's hand, Jenna was murmuring how sorry she was to be late— "I've made you wait. I've made Gus wait."

With an awkward sort of adolescent humor Darren said that Gus wouldn't mind. Gus had been waiting long enough, a few minutes more wouldn't matter.

Naomi laughed though she was feeling disoriented, giddy. How strange this was, and how wonderful— their mother had not abandoned them after all. And here—this handsome young man with the broad, warm smile—was her brother Darren, as well.

Another time she embraced them both. Her family!

In a hoarse voice Jenna was saying that she'd been afraid to call them, to explain why she was late. She'd thought that, if she'd said that she was lost somewhere between the airport and the lake, they would tell her not to bother to come—"You would tell me that you didn't need me, you could do this alone."

Her voice trembled. Her hands clutched at them to hold them fast.

"Mom, for Christ's sake! What a silly thing to say."

"Yes, Mom. Silly."

Though exactly what they'd been thinking, just before Jenna had arrived.

Delightful, delicious and thrilling, to lightly scold their mother who smiled shyly at them, not certain how to respond.

"In any case, I think my cell phone is dead. I'd forgotten to turn it off for the plane flight, and the battery has run out."

Together in Darren's car they drove two miles to Wild Fowl State Park, and to the trailhead (which Naomi recalled as soon as she saw the green-painted paired outhouses). Jenna had not wanted to take time to check into the motel, unpack and hang up her clothing, she'd already made them wait—"There's plenty of time for that afterward."

Pausing then, for the word *afterward* had sounded strange to their ears for no reason they could have named.

On the trail, Darren led the way and carried the

urn. He'd said that Gus's ashes were "ashy-light"—
"weightless"—but the pewter urn was somewhat heavy.

"As Dad would say, 'death with dignity.' You would
not want an urn made of Styrofoam or plastic."

Naomi laughed. Why was this funny?

Jenna said, "Oh Darren. You sound so like—*him*."

"I guess I do. Sometimes I hear it, myself. A kind of
echo."

They hiked along the trail, single file. Darren in the
lead but turning back to Naomi and Jenna, to speak
over his shoulder. Darren in an ebullient mood, expansive, like one who is very relieved. Like one who is in
charge.

On any trail they'd taken Gus had always been in
charge—of course. In any vehicle in which he'd ridden,
Gus had always driven. But now in his place Darren
would do as well, it seemed.

It was a bright, chill autumn day. At the height of
the day the sun was warm but as soon as the sun declined, the temperature would drop into the low fifties.

Naomi saw that Jenna was wearing sensible hiking
clothing: lightweight mosquito-repellent trousers, a
khaki jacket, a cap with a visor to protect her eyes,
hiking shoes. Gus had insisted that his wife and his children wear proper hiking shoes for such hikes, as they

had to wear proper hiking boots for rockier trails. It did not surprise Naomi that their mother who seemed to have drifted so far from their old life was observing Gus's requirements.

Darren had brought walking sticks for them all. A hiking stick would have been Gus's *recommendation* for such a hike along the pebbly lakeshore, with the possibility of encountering rocks, boulders, fallen logs and other impediments on the trail, it was a good idea to be prepared.

Gripping her stick, Naomi was beginning to feel just slightly panicked. She had vowed, *she would not break down.*

Many times she'd heard the *click-click-click* of her father's hiking stick against rock, in front of her. She had not heard that sound for a long time.

Yet: so many years had passed, she wasn't the grieving child any longer. She did not think of Gus Voorhees every hour of every day—hardly. Nor did she think so often of Jenna, ironically now that, at last, Jenna seemed to be moving back into their lives.

The fact is, Naomi had been thinking since Muskegee Falls: we are all growing older.

Though she looked younger, waif-like, wan, Jenna was in her mid-fifties. Poor Madelena was nearly eighty—(and looked her age, or nearly). Their Voorhees grandfather was eighty-five at least. If Gus were still alive, he would be fifty-seven years old.

Many times Naomi had thought, she would not ever see her father *old*. She would not see him *aged, ailing*. She had seen him only in the prime of his life, in the prime of his robust manhood. She had never heard his voice except as a strong voice, even a commanding voice.

The first part of the trail led through a wooded area of birch trees, cedars, pines. There were outcroppings of rock, you had to take care hiking. Then the trail opened onto a grassy marshy area, and then onto a rock-strewn area, and then they were at the lakeshore where the sky opened above them, somewhat abruptly, before they were altogether ready. The horizon was distant, there came a chill wind from the north with a faint familiar smell of rotted things—fish, kelp, driftwood.

Jenna was hiking well, considering. Of course, Jenna could not have kept up with Darren and Naomi if they'd chosen to hike ahead. But Naomi had positioned herself at the rear. Wanting to be last, to watch the others. Her tall confident brother, her silvery-white-haired mother. *Hers.*

She would tell Madelena—*My mother and I are reconciled, I think.*

And Madelena would say—*I'm happy for you. That is a good thing.*

It had happened, without Naomi quite realizing, she was closer to her grandmother now than to her mother. She'd come to love her grandmother more than she loved her mother.

Was that unnatural? It seemed to have happened without her awareness.

But she loved Jenna, too. Her love for Jenna was wary, guarded. She did not quite trust Jenna, as she had grown to trust Madelena. The one had kept her at arm's length, hinting at an invitation to come, that Naomi might stay with Jenna in Bennington for a while; the other had made it clear that Naomi was welcome to stay with her, to live with her, at any time and for as long as she wished.

Madelena loved her, but Madelena also needed her. It was not clear that Jenna needed any of her children.

On the hike Darren was telling Jenna about his medical school life. His courses, his professors. The climate in Washington, the cabin he and Rachel had built on the Skagit River, which they tried to get to whenever they could. Naomi was half-listening. She had heard some of this before from Darren, and could take pleasure in her brother's voice. And Jenna's murmurous—*Oh yes? Really? Really!* Naomi was staring at her mother's back, her mother's head. Wanting to touch her mother's hair, or her shoulder, or an arm. Just the lightest touch.

They were to have dinner together, at the Light House. Exactly the restaurant Gus would have chosen. And Gus would have insisted upon calling to "book" a table, though it wasn't likely that a reservation would be needed midweek at this time of year, on Katechay Island.

In his place, Darren had called to "book" a table. Naomi had smiled to hear her brother speaking earnestly on the phone, and had heard Gus's voice in his. That echo.

Mid-October, a pearlescent cast to the choppy lake. At a distance, a lake freighter passed with the stately aplomb of a prehistoric sea creature. Since they had lived in Michigan, near the Great Lakes, freighter traffic had diminished significantly. (Naomi had learned.) Gus had always pointed out the "lakers," as they were called; as an undergraduate at U-M he'd worked on one of them in summer months, with the odd name *Outlander Integrity*, moving cargo from Sault Ste. Marie to Chicago to Buffalo and the Port of Montreal and back.

After a forty-minute hike along the shore, at a beautiful rocky point, Darren called a halt. It was a small cove, amid large sunbaked boulders. There were clouds of iridescent dragonflies here. A faint smell of desiccated life, not unpleasant. Naomi thought that she vaguely recognized this place and Darren was declaring it the "perfect" place.

Darren set the urn down on a rock and labored to open the tight-fitting lid. Both urn and lid were made of some dark earthen-looking material that was probably synthetic, an ingenious kind of plastic meant to mimic the organic.

Naomi shut her eyes, at first not wanting to see.

A spasm of hilarity threatened. What if, after all these years, the lid would not open . . .

In her hoarse, wondering voice Jenna said, "Gus would laugh at us, if he could see. He hated any kind of fuss and formality . . ."

The lid was off. Darren turned, tilted the urn in such a way that ashes began to fall out. (She did not want to see if Darren's hands were trembling.) (Should she be recording this scene on her camera? She had left her camera behind, she had totally forgotten her camera.) Larger chunks of what had to be bone, at which Noami stared now, not seeming to know what she saw.

"Mom? Y'want to take hold of this? Naomi?"— numbly they came to stand beside him, to assist.

"I feel as if we should 'pray'—but—"

"No! Daddy would be furious."

"He might not have minded . . . I saw Daddy once pretending to pray, at some ceremony."

"At one of your commencements Gus said the pledge of allegiance to the flag, like everyone else."

"He'd love the attention . . ."

"He'd know we loved him. That's what matters."

Almost too quickly the "scattering" was over: ashes and bone-chunks in the choppy water already dissipated, disappearing.

Had it happened so swiftly? And now, now what? For a moment Naomi's brain was struck blank.

"In the end it's just—silence. The world without us."

Why had she said such a thing? She licked her dry lips, that felt scaly. Her eyes now were dry and burnt from the sun and wind.

She did not want to look at her mother's dead-white ravaged face. The parted lips like her own, parched and numbed.

Is this all there is?—this?

It was not to be believed. What they had done.

Instead of a proper burial in a grassy cemetery where you might kneel, mourn.

Instead of a grave marker, the shore of Lake Huron.

Joking. They'd been trying to joke. Trying to laugh.

Trying to breathe.

Trying not to stumble, fall on the sharp-angled rocks. (Oh but where were the frothy ashes going? Where had the pale bone-chunks gone? Naomi was in terror of falling to her knees, reaching into the cold slapping water after a trail of ashes to retrieve a handful . . .)

"I—I wish—"

What was she saying? She could not speak, her breath was sucked from her.

The others did not seem to hear her. They could not face one another. Darren was shaking the last of the ashes out of the urn, tight-faced, frowning.

Why was it so important, so crucial, to shake the last of the ashes out of the urn? It was Darren's plan to leave the urn behind too, in the inlet.

Except Jenna said suddenly, she would take it. The urn.

The sun was slanted in the western sky like an eye that is beginning to squint. The wind had come up. They were shivering. They turned to hike back the way they'd come, to the trailhead where Darren's rented car was parked, and this hike was accomplished in less than a half hour, as if their burden had been lightened, and they were in a hurry to escape the beautiful desolate Wild Fowl Bay.

Exhausted, they returned to the Katechay Inn.

It was just five-twenty. They had not been gone long. Though it felt as if they'd been gone for a very long time, an entire day hiking an arduous trail.

"The reservation is for seven. We should leave for the restaurant at about a quarter to seven, OK? I'll drive."

They were reeling with tiredness. Naomi, Jenna. Even Darren.

Naomi saw her mother stagger a little as if the earthen-colored urn were heavy and not light as Styrofoam, and slipped her arm around Jenna's waist to steady her. Now Jenna did not seem quite so tall, and her body felt frail, insubstantial. She had removed her cap and her feathery hair was matted and flat, and her skin seemed bloodless, dead white with fatigue.

"We should all rest. Try to take a nap, Mom."

"Yes. I will. And you too, Naomi. Promise!"

As if she were a young child, who had to promise her mother to *nap.*

How deeply Naomi slept! Fell onto the bed in her room only just kicking off her muddy-soled hiking shoes, too tired to unbutton or unzip clothing. She had time to sleep—enough time. They would all take naps and be rejuvenated for the evening.

But when at six-fifty Darren and Naomi went to knock on the door of B18, their mother's room, no one answered.

"H'lo? Mom? It's us."

"Mom? Hello . . ."

Knowing to their chagrin that it was an empty room. No one inside.

At the front desk the clerk said yes, a woman named "Jenna Matheson" had paid for the room, for one night, with a credit card; but so far as anyone knew Ms. Matheson had not actually moved any of her belongings into the room—"I think she just used the room, used the bathroom, a towel or two. That was all."

"But—what did she say to you?"

"She said she was 'checking out'—she'd changed her plans and wasn't going to stay the night. She didn't give any reason. She drove away around an hour ago."

"Which direction did she drive in?"

"I think—toward the bridge."

"Did she leave a note?"

The desk clerk checked the mail slot for Darren's room, and for Naomi's. In Naomi's was a folded sheet of paper with a handwritten message—*Forgive me, very sorry. Jenna.*

They read the terse little message several times.

Darren was muttering, "But—this isn't possible . . ."
Naomi was too shocked to speak at all.

Seeing their faces the clerk asked sympathetically, "Was Ms. Matheson some relative of yours? Are you all related?"

Fight Night, Cincinnati:

November 2011

**MIDWESTERN BOXING LEAGUE WOMEN'S 8-ROUND
WELTERWEIGHT BOUT**

**PRYDE ELKA ("THE SQUAW") VS. D.D. DUNPHY
("THE HAMMER OF JESUS")**

**EAST CINCINNATI WAR MEMORIAL ARMORY
—NOVEMBER 18, 2011**

**TICKETS AVAILABLE BOX OFFICE, MAIL
ORDER & ONLINE**

S he bought a ticket to the fight online. Ninety-four dollars plus tax for an aisle seat, eleventh row. She had no idea what she was doing only just that she would do it.

With the same air of impulse and deliberation she bought plane tickets. Round-trip New York City–Cincinnati.

Two nights she would stay in Cincinnati. Maybe that was a mistake, one night in Cincinnati might be all she could bear.

Nonetheless, two nights she booked at an airport motel.

Naomi where are you going? Again? What on earth is there in—Cincinnati?

She had no answer to give to her grandmother Madelena. She had no explanation. It was like that first grief, she'd felt the interior of her mouth stitched together with coarse black thread.

Don't know. Or maybe I will know, when I get there.

In the collapse of her life she wasn't unhappy. In the ruins in which she stumbled she would salvage something valuable, she was sure.

Why she seemed to be returning to the Midwest every month and always clutching her camera.

Why she'd given up the archive of her father's life (and death) yet had not destroyed the archive.

(Not a single notebook once belonging to Gus Voorhees had she destroyed. Not a single letter, postcard, Post-It, newspaper clipping, torn and creased snapshot. Not a single taped interview. All remained neatly labeled in files, folders, boxes in her room in Madelena Kein's apartment in New York City.)

Why (in secret) she'd been tracking the career of "The Hammer of Jesus"—D.D. Dunphy.

It had been all new to her, a total surprise—that Luther Dunphy's daughter had become a professional boxer. At first she'd been jeering, skeptical. For she disliked Dawn Dunphy, intensely.

She recalled the young girl's sullen face in newspaper photos.

It had roused her, and Darren, to a kind of rage, that the children of Luther Dunphy *existed*.

After she'd returned from Muskegee Falls she'd researched "D.D. Dunphy" online and learned to her surprise (and something like chagrin) that Luther Dunphy's daughter had acquired a solid reputation as a boxer since she'd begun fighting professionally in early 2009; Dunphy had won all of her fights except for a single draw, in venues in Cleveland, Dayton, East Chicago, Indianapolis, Gary, Scranton, Pittsburgh. She seemed to be fighting often. She was not yet a top contender for a title but on several lists "D.D. Dunphy" was ranked in the top ten in her weight division.

In some online sites she was called *the female Tyson*.

Naomi recalled how the desk clerk at the Muskegee

Falls Inn had spoken of Luther Dunphy's daughter as a boxer—the first time Naomi had heard of such a thing.

It had seemed bizarre to her then, repugnant. For she hated boxing—what she knew of boxing. She hated violent sports.

In this she was echoing Jenna, who had written about the exploitation of women in such violent entertainments as boxing, wrestling, mixed-martial arts. A kind of prostitution, Jenna Matheson had claimed. And as always, men were the ones who profited from this exploitation of women.

Jenna Matheson had written such feminist polemics long ago, in the 1990s. She was continuing to write, and to publish, but less frequently, so far as Naomi knew.

A coincidence: the following night, in the Muskegee Falls hotel, in the pub attached to the hotel called the Sign of the Ram, a TV had been on above the bar; and on the TV, a clip of a women's boxing match. It was pure chance that Naomi had come into the pub for a late supper—the hotel dining room had closed. Though she hadn't done more than glance at the TV screen she happened to overhear the bartender and several other men discussing the fight—*That there is Luther Dunphy's daughter. Jesus!*

Luther Dunphy's daughter! In an instant, Naomi's attention was riveted.

It was not a broadcast of a live boxing match but rather a sports news program. The boxing clip had been brief. And there followed excerpts from a post-fight interview with the winning boxer who was still panting, smiling with childish excitement, covered in sweat, with heavy eyebrows and a coarse-skinned face mottled from her opponent's stinging jabs—"D.D. Dunphy."

Naomi stared. She would not have recognized this young woman.

How strange, how incongruous—there were streaks of crimson and green in Dunphy's spiky dark hair. On the biceps of both her arms were lurid tattoos.

Naomi felt a sharp visceral dislike of Dunphy. What she most hated was the *happiness* of the female boxer, what she perceived as Dunphy's childish gloating in victory.

Dunphy spoke excitedly but uncertainly. She faltered, stammered.

Clearly she was not accustomed to speaking with a microphone extended to her mouth—she was not accustomed to speaking at all. And she was being asked questions by an aggressive (male) interviewer that seemed to intimidate her and so repeatedly she glanced to the side, seeking help from someone off-camera.

"What're my 'plans for the future'?—I guess—training real hard—for—maybe—a title fight . . ."

"And when will that be, 'D.D.'?"

"When? I—I don't know—it's up to . . ."

"Which title are you looking to, 'D.D.'? Midwest Boxing League? World Boxing Association?"

"I d-don't know . . ."

"Ready for the big time, eh? Atlantic City? Vegas?"

". . . d-don't know . . ."

Naomi observed the TV screen covertly. How pathetic, this interview with "D.D. Dunphy"! She hoped that no one in the pub would notice her interest. Especially she didn't want the bartender or the men drinking at the bar to note her interest and to draw her into their conversation.

The men murmured together, laughed. In their voices a grudging admiration.

That's her—Dunphy. Wouldn't recognize her.

They lived over on Front Street. Luther was a roofer like my dad.

Shit yes. Wouldn't forget that poor bastard Luther Dunphy.

My brother hung out with her brother—what's-his-name . . .

Jesus she is homely! But she can hit.

A female boxer, some kind of joke. Make you feel

like puking. But there's some that're OK—like Mu-hammad Ali's daughter.

"'**Scuse me,** ma'am—"

"Sorry ma'am—"

"Shit! Sorry ma'am—"

Squeezing past her one of them spilled a dark frothy liquid and ice cubes onto her knees out of a giant Styrofoam cup.

"That's all right"—quickly Naomi dabbed at the corduroy trousers with a tissue, smiling to show that she wasn't upset or annoyed.

Loud-laughing the gangling young men took their seats. They were not laughing at the lone white girl in a seat on the aisle in the Armory, in an instant they'd forgotten her.

But others had noticed her, with curiosity. Not exactly unfriendly but not smiling.

Naomi Voorhees in her wanly "white" skin! Like exposed bone from which marrow is leaking. And she was alone.

It was a fact: no one else in sight in the cavernous space appeared to be alone. Groups of a dozen or more boxing fans, taking up entire rows.

These were mostly dark-skinned and Hispanic and male. A predominance of males in their twenties, thirties, forties, who'd come to see the major fights of the evening and for whom the female boxers were of very little interest.

The bout in which D.D. Dunphy was fighting Pryde Elka was but number three on a bill of five boxing matches culminating in a heavyweight "contest" (as it was called) between two top-ranked (male) boxers (African-American, Jamaican) who were the stars of the evening.

Not knowing how to dress for the East Cincinnati Armory fight night Naomi had worn dark corduroy trousers, dark pullover sweater, nondescript jacket, boots. Her hair was brushed back from her face. On her head, a khaki-colored rain hat. Her face was pale, plain as if scrubbed: she rarely wore makeup, thus disappointing (she presumed: Madelena had not actually told her this) her stylish and still-beautiful grandmother for whom artfully applied cosmetics were as crucial as the exquisite silver human-hair wig she now wore.

Naomi had hoped to look like the most ordinary of boxing fans but a quick glance informed her that in this festive gathering there was no *ordinary*.

Everyone in sight was conspicuously well dressed: money had been spent on clothes, shoes, hair, jewelry. Dark-skinned and Hispanic women and girls were lavishly attired, glamorously made up. They might have been models, actresses. They might have been figures in romantic films. Their fingernails were polished and remarkably long. Their hair was spectacular, defying gravity. Their jewelry winked and dazzled even in the gloom of the arena and piercings made their faces glitter. And the men with them were as elaborately dressed, many with gold chains around their necks, stylish shirts open at the throat.

Naomi was grateful to be ignored and grateful that young black men squeezing past her to their seats were not rude or disrespectful but rather lighthearted, gleeful.

"Sorry ma'am—God *damn*."

"Sor-ry—"

The eight-hundred-seat arena was scarcely half-filled by the time of the Elka-Dunphy fight at 8:10 P.M. There came virtually no applause for dark-robed D.D. Dunphy hurrying as if abashed down the aisle on the farther side of the ring, and an outburst of enthusiastic applause for Pryde Elka that faded by the time both boxers were in the ring.

Naomi was shocked by the vulgarity of the match— "The Squaw" vs. "The Hammer of Jesus."

Pryde Elka wore quasi-Indian attire into the ring, an aqua-feathered robe, feathery aqua tassels on her ankle-high shoes. Her hair was very black, as if dyed,

in stiff six-inch plaits. Her cheeks appeared to be tattooed in emulation of the savage-painted cheeks of
Apache warriors. She was a tight-faced sinewy woman
in her early thirties with a deep-tanned skin, close-set
eyes, a grim expression about the mouth. She wore
dark Spandex shorts to the knee with some sort of
advertising logo on them, unless these were Shawnee
word-symbols. Her tight-fitting T-shirt was similarly
inscribed. Her shoulder and arm muscles were ropy,
her dark-tanned legs hard-muscled but desiccated-
seeming, like something organic, living wood that has
been dehydrated and distilled. Dunphy was wearing
plainer attire, black shorts and T-shirt with a sturdy
sports bra beneath that did not flatter her body that
was thick-set as a heifer's.

Naomi stared in alarmed sympathy. She did not
want to be patronizing or condescending. Her parents
had taught her: do not measure others by yourself for
(often) you have had advantages that others have not.
Yet how pathetic it seemed to her, that Pryde Elka, said
to be a Native American descendant of the Shawnee
tribe of Ohio, was billed as "The Squaw"—in combat
with D.D. Dunphy, a decade younger, heavier, taller,
stronger-looking, billed as "The Hammer of Jesus."

Squaw. Hammer of Jesus. Pagan vs. Christian? It
was appalling to Naomi Voorhees, child of a culture

in which the mere enunciation of "squaw" was an obscenity, and feminist principles of equality and dignity inviolable as scientific facts, that women should be so debased and exploited, presumably willingly.

In the ring the aqua-feathered robe was removed from Pryde Elka's shoulders and she strutted about lifting her gleaming red gloves to a splattering of applause. Someone at ringside made a war-whooping sound. As D.D. Dunphy disrobed in her corner, no one responded.

"Ladies and gentlemen, eight rounds of women's welterweight boxing courtesy of Midwestern Boxing League . . ."

There came isolated cries, catcalls and whistles as a bell rang loudly signaling the beginning of the fight. The women boxers rushed at each other meeting in the center of the ring with red-gloved fists pummeling.

Naomi shrank in her seat. She felt a stab of panic—that one of the women boxers would be *hurt*, and she would be a witness.

In a trance of apprehension she sat very still in the hard wooden seat. Wanting to shut her eyes, press her hands against her ears. Blurred and nightmarish the boxers' flying gloves, swift-thrown punches, grim-set faces. She could hear the women grunting—she could hear their shoes making dry skidding sounds on the canvas.

God help me why am I here. Why did I think I should come here to discover—what?

Apart from isolated cries, shouts of encouragement, mocking boos the fight was silent—no broadcasters' voices, no TV. Naomi was not a sports fan but she recognized the absence of sports commentary. Without the continuous chatter of broadcasters boxing is mute and the observer is disoriented with no idea what is happening.

A crude sound of blows against flesh. She saw that D.D. Dunphy was hitting, and had been hit. She'd been knocked back onto her heels for a moment stunned. Naomi felt a thrill of something like satisfaction—that Dunphy was *being hit.*

Relief then, when the fighting abruptly ceased. The boxers were clutching at each other—clinching.

Or possibly, one of them was trying to throw the other off balance and knock her onto the canvas. Several times the (white, male) referee commanded curtly: "Break!"

How long the first round was!— by the time the bell rang signaling its end Naomi could scarcely breathe. Immediately both boxers dropped their gloved hands like puppets whose strings have been cut and turned away, to hurry to their corners.

Naomi was feeling hyper-alert, vigilant. She

wondered—which of the boxers had won the round? Had one of the women outfought the other? She saw that a fine line of red gleamed at Dunphy's hairline even as it was swiftly wiped away by one of the corner men.

It seemed to Naomi that the elder boxer had been just discernibly more agile on her feet than the younger, backing away from her, moving from side to side to elude blows, while Dunphy had pushed forward aggressively, flatfooted, head lowered like a cobra poised to strike.

Strange that inside the bright-lit ring there was such concentration, tension! But outside the ring, in the partially filled rows of the Armory, in the aisles where vendors loitered with soft drinks, hot dogs, snacks, the spectators were talking and laughing as if the fight so hard-fought between the two women was of little significance to them, if not something to sneer at. Through the action of the first round a steady stream of spectators entered the Armory, loud-talking and jocular.

"Man, who's this? Females? Jesus!"

The second round began like the first: bell ringing, boxers rushing at each other. But this time (it seemed to Naomi) the younger boxer, the "white" boxer with streaks of color in her spiky hair, was driving her Native American opponent back, skidding-back, cringing-back, toward the ropes where (so suddenly this happened) she appeared to be trapped, and could not protect herself against the other's wild swinging blows.

Yet—(and this too, suddenly)—there was an ugly red gash on Dunphy's forehead, just above her right eye. How had that happened?

Bleeding badly, wiping blood from her eye with her glove, Dunphy stumbled and staggered. At once Elka was on her with a barrage of blows, some of them wild, some striking their target as spectators began to shout and call out encouragement—*Hit her! Hit her! Elka! El-KA!*

Naomi was seized with a sensation of dread. What was happening? A kind of wildness whipped through the Armory. She had an impulse to leap to her feet to join the cry—*Hit her! El-KA!*

On her knees the camera was forgotten. The braying of voices close about her was frightening and exciting to her.

She felt a low, mean thrill of satisfaction, that Luther Dunphy's daughter had been hit, and hurt. Blood streaking her face and giving her a ghastly blind look. *Now you know. You know what it is to be hurt. You are hateful, you deserve to be punished.*

Was the referee about to stop the fight? Naomi didn't

know if she wanted this to happen, for then Dunphy's punishment would end.

Fortunately then, the bell rang signaling the end of round two.

Her heartbeat was quickened. Her breath was quickened. From comments in the seats behind her Naomi gathered that D.D. Dunphy had been "head-butted." The wily Shawnee warrior had lowered her head and struck Dunphy hard against the ridge of bone above her right eye, seemingly by accident; yet, the referee was deducting points from her for a *foul*.

There was a scattering of boos from the audience. Against the referee's ruling? Against Pryde Elka? Or—-D.D. Dunphy?

"Who is ahead?"—Naomi was anxious to know.

"Nah, nobody ahead. Not yet."

Naomi was hoping that Pryde Elka would win, soon. Hoping that the cut above D.D. Dunphy's eye would begin bleeding again. And the ugly fight would be halted. For she did not like the feelings it was arousing in her, that were new to her, crude and barbaric and shameful.

Admit it: you want Dunphy hurt. You want Dunphy badly hurt.

Like her father the murderer: destroyed.

But at the start of the third round there came D.D.

Dunphy rushing at her opponent with renewed energy, with a kind of pit bull ferocity, flatfooted but relentless, pressing blindly forward. Dunphy resembled both a stocky-bodied adolescent girl and a mature woman, so driven. Her strategy appeared to be sheer pressure: using her weight, her height, her indifference to being hit, to her advantage. Naomi had heard of "counterpunching"—she could see that Dunphy, the less skilled boxer, took a kind of energy from being hit, receiving sharp-stinging jabs to her face, that inflamed her lower face, and bloodied her nose. Each blow seemed to rejuvenate her, inspire her. Elka could punch, and Elka could connect, yet no blow of hers was strong enough to stop Dunphy's assault; and when the bell rang to end the round, there was applause from the audience and even a cry—*Dun-PHY!*

How fickle they are, Naomi thought in disdain. You could not place any faith in *them.*

In the next round, and in the next, Dunphy continued to push Elka backward. Many jabs struck Dunphy's reddened face, many blows struck her shoulder, her midriff, even her breasts, but Dunphy was not deterred. The effect was of a blind creature like a mollusk pressing forward, always forward. In her seat Naomi felt paralyzed. Her mouth had gone dry, she could not stop swallowing, or trying to swallow.

Each time she opened her eyes it was to see D.D. Dunphy lowering her head, coming forward, swinging. And another time, the cut above Dunphy's eye began to bleed. Surely the fight would be stopped now? Surely—soon? But Dunphy hardly paused, peering through a mask of blood, blinking and fixing her opponent in her vision, grunting as she struck at Elka with both fists, a left, a right, a blow to the underside of Elka's chin, unprotected for a fleet second. And Elka was staggered but held on to her opponent as a drowning person would clutch at a rescuer, gasping for breath. Until at last the bell rang again.

"Now, who is winning?"

"White girl winning."

"*White girl?*"—Naomi's voice trailed off in dismay.

The row of black boys laughed at her. Wasn't she a *white girl*, herself?

Another time, it occurred to Naomi that she could leave. Very quickly, unobtrusively, get to her feet and hurry up the aisle and disappear out of the Armory, find a taxi to take her back to her hotel . . .

She would call Darren, just to hear his voice. She would laugh with Darren, reminiscing about Katechay Island. Their impossible mother! *Was Ms. Matheson some relative of yours? Are you all related?*

No one but Darren with whom she might laugh,

laugh until she was exhausted. Both of them sobbing with laughter. *Are you all related?*

Fifth round, the boxers got tangled in each other's legs. Amid a clinch Elka struck furiously at Dunphy's lower back (was this a foul? kidney-punching?), grabbed at Dunphy's muscled shoulders, and Dunphy wrenched herself back to get leverage to strike at Elka's (lowered) head, and suddenly, comically—the two women had fallen to the canvas, and the crowd erupted into laughter as the annoyed referee commanded them: "On your feet. *On your feet.*"

Almost, Naomi thought she'd heard the referee say *ladies.*

On your feet ladies. Mocking, muttered.

Or—had she imagined this?

Badly she wished that Luther Dunphy's daughter would be knocked down, humiliated—lose this terrible fight. Yet, she did not really want either of the boxers to be seriously *hurt.*

Especially she did not want Pryde Elka—(could that really be her name? *Pryde Elka?*)—to be hurt, and to lose. She had read that Elka was the divorced mother of two young children, one of whom was "severely autistic"; she was a factory worker in Electra, Illinois; she'd begun boxing intermittently at the age of seventeen and had had two title fights (which she'd lost); the previous year she'd acquired a new manager and new trainer and was embarked now upon a "comeback campaign."

(Some online sources challenged Pryde Elka's affiliation with the Shawnee Nation. But these were vigorously denied by Elka's handlers.)

Information about D.D. Dunphy was sparse. You would not have known that Dunphy was the daughter of a notorious murderer executed in Ohio in 2006. Apart from her boxing record all that was claimed for "The Hammer of Jesus" was that she was *active in the Zion Missionary Church in her hometown Dayton, Ohio.*

Eight rounds! The strain was near-unbearable.

At last the fight was ending. Both boxers appeared exhausted. In the closing seconds Dunphy continued to hammer at Elka who tried to clutch and clinch and (another time) head-butt—but Dunphy was shrewd enough now to avoid being struck in the face by the other's head.

Through the fight Elka had moved about the ring far more agilely than Dunphy who'd remained flat-footed, relentless as a landslide. Of the two boxers it was Dunphy whose face was the more battered; her nose was bloody, her right eye swollen shut. How grotesque the quasi-glamorous swaths of color in her hair, the lurid gleaming tattoos on her upper arms! (Naomi had only just noticed a tattoo on Dunphy's back, just below the nape of her neck—looking like *Jesus Is Lord*.) She was feeling a hostility for D.D. Dunphy that was near-overwhelming, visceral as nausea.

Bell rang! Naomi could breathe. The terrible ordeal was over, she would never subject herself to anything like this again.

Lifting her camera, taking pictures. No one objected, no one noticed. She would record "The Squaw" Pryde Elka barely able to lift her gloved hands in a simulation of boastful victory—"Hammer of Jesus" D.D. Dunphy stunned-seeming (not comprehending that the fight was over?) wiping blood out of her eyes as her handlers hurried to her.

From the audience came isolated calls, cries, bursts of applause. Pryde Elka had her supporters and so did (evidently) D.D. Dunphy. But many patrons had entered the arena during the final round without any interest in the frenzied action between the women boxers in the ring. There was a collective impatience for this fight to end, and the next fight to begin.

Naomi believed that Elka had won. Enthusiasm for Elka had been more evident in the Armory. She'd been the more skilled boxer, if the more devious with her attempts at head-butting and kidney punches. As a Native American, Elka was more sympathetic. All you could say of Dunphy was that she was tough, resilient. She was *clumsy*.

Naomi would return to New York City happily, if Pryde Elka had won. She would take a few photographs in the Armory and return to New York City and to the care of her grandmother and (how this had happened, she couldn't quite comprehend) her "half-uncle" Kinch. They were her family now. They needed her, and she was happy to be needed. She was accumulating photo-portraits, and portraits of "The Squaw" and "The Hammer of Jesus" would be appropriate. She would not ever think of Luther Dunphy's daughter again.

But to her surprise all three judges gave the fight to Dunphy. Naomi had not been aware of the "judges" until now—two middle-aged white men and a middle-aged black man, seated at ringside. The first judge had "awarded" seven rounds to Dunphy, one round to Elka; the second, six rounds to Dunphy and two rounds to Elka; the third, all eight rounds to Dunphy.

How was this possible? Naomi was astonished.

The ring announcer's amplified voice exuded an air of zest, exhilaration: "'D.D. Dunphy'—'The Hammer of Jesus'—unanimous win increasing this young fighter's record to eight wins, one draw, zero losses!"

Now came a final outburst of applause. Spectators

who'd just trailed into the Armory, who'd seen nothing of the fight, clapped loudly, catcalled and whistled. The mood in the arena was festive, elevated. The mood was impatient. *Get the bitches out of the ring!*—there came braying cries laced with laughter.

In the ring, in the blinding light, without her gleaming red boxing gloves uplifted to protect her, D.D. Dunphy was very ill at ease. She smiled inanely as a nervous child might smile. She'd been invited by the ring announcer to "say a few words to our audience"— but before she could speak there was a change of plans, and Dunphy's handlers were instructed to escort her from the ring. Equipment had to be set up for the next fight, which was to be televised within a few minutes.

Naomi asked of the young boxing fans beside her how Dunphy could have won the fight when she was so clumsy it seemed like she couldn't "box" at all; and they retorted, "She win, man. That white girl can *hit*."

This was a rebuke. Naomi felt her face burn as if she'd betrayed someone to whom she was expected to have been loyal.

With her camera Naomi hurried after D.D. Dunphy and her several handlers up the aisle, taking flash pictures. She saw now what she hadn't seen before the fight: Dunphy's black robe, that fell to just her knees, bore gilt letters on the back—D.D. DUNPHY HAMMER OF JESUS. And on Dunphy's head was a black cap with the inscription, also in gilt letters, JESUS IS LORD.

In the giddy aftermath of her victory there were several other photographers taking pictures of D.D. Dunphy. A barrage of flash photos. Naomi was grateful for the anonymity. She had to suppose that a boxer is a kind of public property and that Dunphy's handlers were happy for her to be photographed if it meant publicity.

Naomi heard herself ask one of the corner men if their boxer was available for an interview and was told—"Maybe. Depends."

Another told her, over his shoulder, "Contact *Dayton Fights, Inc.*"

Dunphy and her retinue disappeared into the interior of the Armory where no one unauthorized was allowed to follow. Naomi saw that one of the photographers, whom they seemed to know, probably with a local newspaper, had been allowed to accompany them to Dunphy's dressing room.

Ridiculous, Naomi thought. Why would I want to interview *her?*

She was feeling just slightly dazed, light-headed.

Her heart pounded with excitement and also a kind of chagrin, or shame. She had never witnessed anything quite like the "eight rounds of boxing" between Pryde Elka and D.D. Dunphy.

Quickly then, for she was feeling as if she might faint, Naomi left the Armory, and stood for some minutes out on the avenue, breathing deeply, fresh air, or rather a fresher air than inside the Armory, though tinged with something metallic and yeasty—a smell of the Ohio River not far away. In her confusion and disorientation she scarcely knew where she was. She could not stop thinking about the fight—she could not stop seeing the fight—she had only to shut her eyes and immediately images of the female boxers and their swinging gloves, their stricken faces, assailed her like dream images loosed from some primitive nightmare.

"D.D. Dunphy"—that was the disguise.

Wondering: did Dawn Dunphy know *her*, as intimately as she knew Dawn Dunphy?

Forty minutes were allotted for the interview, the next morning. In a drafty utilitarian space described as a conference banquet room at the Cincinnati Marriot near the airport.

"Hello. My name is—"

Glibly the name rolled off her tongue: *Naomi Matheson.*

(And what a beautiful name it was! Never had Naomi uttered this name aloud before.)

"—and I am preparing a documentary film on women boxers."

Pausing then to add with a friendly sort of frankness, smiling at both the abashed-looking D.D. Dunphy and at a dyed-blond woman of about thirty-five who'd introduced herself as "Marika"—*chief of public relations at Dayton Fights, Inc.*: "Only the preeminent women boxers who are champions, or leading contenders for titles. The film is financed by"—glibly too the name rolled off her tongue: *The New York Film Institute*—"which is a private institute that has prepared documentaries shown on PBS and other TV channels as well as at film festivals like Sundance, Telluride, and Lincoln Center."

The dyed-blond woman seemed impressed. D.D. Dunphy blinked and stared at the floor with her bruised eyes, that were nearly swollen shut. The wound above her right eyebrow seemed to have been stitched tight and one side of her mouth was swollen and bruised.

She wore a dark gray sweatshirt and sweatpants

that fitted her stocky body loosely, and these were un-
adorned. Naomi looked about for the black hat with
gilt letters *Jesus Is Lord* but did not see it. She said:

"My partner and I have made a number of films
focusing on women pioneering in fields tradition-
ally belonging to men. There has been much interest
in women boxers and there is a possibility that ESPN
would help finance the film . . ."

Nothing uttered by "Naomi Matheson" was in the
slightest implausible. Nor was it impossible that, one
day soon, a documentary might be made of women
boxers in the United States, including D.D. Dunphy, to
be aired on PBS, or indeed ESPN.

It was clear that D.D. Dunphy and Marika would
believe anything that was flattering to them. Or rather,
Dunphy would cooperate with anything Marika approved that might advance her career for *Dayton
Fights, Inc.*

"You will make a video available to us of the interview with D.D., Ms. Matheson?—for our own use,
also?"—the dyed-blond Marika spoke shrewdly; and
Naomi said, with the warmest sort of sisterly sincerity,
"Certainly, yes."

To Dunphy the woman said, as one might speak to a
child, "Just forty minutes, D.D. I'll come back to make
sure it doesn't go longer. Are you OK with this? You've

been interviewed before for video. Or do you need me to stay with you?"

Gravely, bravely D.D. Dunphy shook her head *no*. A plaintive expression in the young woman's face, in her somber bruised downlooking eyes, would have suggested to a more perceptive protector that *no* really meant *yes*; but the dyed-blond woman, already on her feet, an unlighted cigarette in her fingers, chose not to perceive this.

Though Marika did linger in the doorway for a minute or two listening to the interviewer's initial questions, long enough to ascertain that the interview would be an altogether conventional one following a familiar journalistic form: *what made you decide to be a boxer, what are your hopes for your career, is it exciting to be a part of the "revolution" in women's boxing?*

These questions Dunphy answered slowly, with care, like one making her way across a plank above an abyss. At times she ceased speaking completely, though she was easily prodded to continue by a few words from the interviewer. Her shyness, or her reticence, or perhaps it was her bovine stubbornness, did not allow her to lift her eyes to meet the interviewer's frank friendly gaze. Not so easy to establish a sisterly *rapport* here.

Astonishing to Naomi and not altogether real, that she was being allowed such access to "D.D. Dunphy"—

virtually no questions asked about her credentials, and not a moment of doubt or skepticism on the part of the PR woman. Since arriving in Cincinnati the day before she'd been feeling not altogether real; she'd felt both conspicuous in her white skin at the Armory, and invisible. It was like crawling through a mirror into a looking-glass world in which, if she was perceived at all, it was as someone other than herself.

Naomi had positioned her camera on the table between them. She'd explained that it was a "recording" camera but Dunphy did not seem to hear. Answering her questions Dunphy spoke so softly, Naomi had to ask her politely to repeat what she'd said.

Dunphy looked startled, perplexed. Repeat what she'd said?

Naomi thought—*Has she forgotten? So quickly?*

She wondered if the young boxer had suffered a concussion. Or rather, concussions. So many blows to the head, just the previous night . . .

Gently saying, "You might look into the camera lens also, 'D.D.' This is a visual medium, not just audio."

Nervously Dunphy swiped at her nose with the edge of her hand and murmured what sounded like *OK*.

"You've been interviewed before? For TV? For video?"

Vaguely Dunphy nodded *yes*. She was having difficulty lifting her bruised eyes to the interviewer, or to the camera lens. Naomi thought—*Is she ashamed? But why?*

Naomi had approached the interview with a feeling of strong repugnance for the task. A faint nausea of dislike stirred in her bowels, that Luther Dunphy's daughter *existed*, and was sitting, slightly hunched, her wounded mouth working silently, just a few feet away from her across a table.

The tabletop was very plain, and looked to be made of some cheap material like cork. Presumably, white linen tablecloths would be draped over such a table on the occasion of a banquet.

"Well, 'D.D.'! That was a terrific fight last night—an excellent performance. All three judges . . ."

Dunphy appeared to be listening. But she did not smile.

"Are you—not happy with the fight? You *won*."

Dunphy shrugged. A look of faint embarrassment crossed her face, as if she were enduring gas pains.

"Nah. It was OK. Ernie says, I got work to do."

"'Ernie'—your trainer?"

But Dunphy had fallen silent. Marika had left for her a bottle of spring water, from which she now drank, thirstily, somewhat clumsily with her swollen mouth. Naomi saw that the young woman's nose was mottled with fine, broken capillaries. Her teeth were uneven, the color of weak tea. It was unsettling when she lifted her eyes, for a moment, and Naomi saw how bloodshot the whites of the eyes were, nearly hidden by the swollen and discolored eyelids.

The coarse hair, cut short and razor-cut at the sides and at the nape of the neck, had been matted flat, in need of washing. The streaks of color were the more incongruous, clownish, in the bleak light of day.

"You have been examined by a doctor, I hope?"

Dunphy murmured what sounded like *Yah*.

"Is it more than a cursory exam? Does a—an actual—doctor examine you? X-rays, a brain scan?"

Dunphy murmured again, this time irritably. Roughly she wiped her running nose with the edge of her hand.

Naomi was recalling the intense, exacting physical examinations of her childhood. Bloodwork was essential: you could not avoid the needle drawing blood out of a delicate vein. A badly bruised and aching rib would have to be X-rayed—of course. Insect-bite infections and infections caused by childhood accidents were to be treated with antibiotics immediately. There was no taking a chance with Lyme disease. To grow up in the household of a doctor is to become aware of the slovenly-wide range of what is called "medical care" by the world. Gus Voorhees was egalitarian in every respect except medically: either a doctor was good, or a doctor was not-good.

You avoided the not-good. Unfortunately, the not-good were everywhere except at principal medical centers and medical schools.

"Well, 'D.D.'! Or—is your name 'Dawn'? Someone said . . ."

Dunphy shifted in her chair. The sound of her name was unexpected and startling to her but she did not deny it. Rather, she smiled just slightly, glancing up abashed at her interviewer.

Naomi thought—*She has been found out. There is nowhere for her to hide.*

"Just tell me, Dawn. In your own words. What gave you the idea of—becoming a boxer . . ."

Naomi smiled encouragingly at Dunphy. She did not hate Dunphy—really. It was Dunphy's *existence* that maddened her as, for years, it had been the *existence* of Luther Dunphy after her father had died, that had maddened her.

Still, Naomi would impersonate a sincere interviewer. In a way, so far as anyone could know, she was that sincere interviewer. Through the night she'd been sleepless with excitement at the possibility of making a documentary film about women boxers, including both D.D. Dunphy and Pryde Elka. Yael Ravel's words came to her—*When you encounter your true subject you will know it.*

Was this Naomi's *true subject*? She had waited so long.

Dunphy continued to speak in her slow groping way of caution and dread. She was a poor interview subject—surely Pryde Elka would be more interesting.

"The average person has a fear of being hit—a dread of being hit. But you have no fear, it seems."

Was this a question? Dunphy gnawed at her lower lip, and made no reply.

"You're not afraid of being hurt?—I mean, seriously hurt?"

Vigorously Dunphy shook her head *no.*

"And why is that?"

"'Why?'—" Dunphy looked at the interviewer as if the interviewer had asked a very stupid question, or had to be joking. "'Cause I'm too good."

"You are—'too good'?"

"My training is to avoid being hurt. Even if I am hit, it doesn't hurt like it would somebody else." A slight sneer to *somebody else.*

Naomi perceived that Dunphy was repeating words told to her. *I'm too good. Even if I am hit . . .*

"You've never been defeated in any fight. That's very impressive."

Dunphy shrugged. Very slightly, the swollen lips smiled.

"I did some checking and it's surprising—some of the champion boxers have lost fights. But you have not." Naomi paused, waiting for Dunphy to murmur *yet.*

How expected it was, in such a situation, that the young athlete would murmur *yet.*

After a moment Naomi continued, in her friendly, frank way:

"Do you make a good living as a boxer? Could you tell us—for instance—how much you'd made on last night's fight?"—Naomi smiled to soften the rudeness of such a question; but Dunphy did not seem to register an effrontery. Rapidly her swollen eyes were blinking as if she were trying to recall a figure, a sum.

"I guess—I don't know . . . There's 'expenses'. . ."

"Expenses come out of the boxer's earnings? I guess that's the tradition . . . I suppose there are considerable expenses?"

Dunphy nodded grimly. "There's hotel rooms,

and meals, and all kinds of—'supplies.' There's a 'medical kit.'"

"But you don't receive a fixed sum? You don't remember what this fixed sum is?"

Dunphy shook her head *no*.

"You've signed a contract? Yes?"

Warily Dunphy shook her head *yes*.

"Did you have a lawyer look over the contract before you signed it?"

"L-Lawyer? No . . ." Dunphy frowned, trying to think. "Maybe yah. Maybe I did."

"A lawyer in Dayton? *Your* lawyer?"

Dunphy made a vague grunting noise of discomfort. Naomi relented.

"Do you send money home to your family?"

More emphatically, Dunphy nodded *yes*.

"That's very generous of you. You are a good daughter."

(Was this going too far? Would Dunphy register the flattery here, just barely masking contempt? She did not seem to.)

Naomi continued, with convincing concern: "I was reading online that most women boxers are helping to support their families. Some of them have young children . . . Pryde Elka, for instance. Do you know much about her background?"

Dunphy shrugged irritably. As if to say *Why the hell would I care about Pryde Elka!*

"I think you are still working? At a Target store in Dayton? That must be difficult . . . working at the same time that you're training as a boxer, and traveling to fights . . ."

Dunphy said, with the air of recalling something both pleasurable and painful, "There was going to be a 'community sponsor'—sports store—in Dayton—but that fell through. Though—it might happen yet . . . There's champions that have to work. Can't live off their boxing." She paused ruefully. "Women boxers, I mean. Not men."

"The men make more money?"

Dunphy sneered as if the interviewer had said something meant to be funny. "Yah. The men make more."

"It seems surprising that a 'champion' has to work . . . whether male or female. That would be surprising to many boxing fans."

The line of questioning was making Dunphy uneasy and irritable. Naomi had never interviewed anyone in her life and was coming to comprehend the subtle but unmistakable adversarial challenge, a kind of bull-fighting, with very sharp blades. Whoever wielded the questions wielded the blades.

"How many hours a week do you work, Dawn?"

Dawn. The name came naturally. Dunphy did not react.

"How many hours? I don't know . . . At Target if you're not full-time they call you when they need you. It could be different every week. Especially if you work in the stockroom or unloading. Mr. Cassidy worked out a schedule for me at Target where he knows the store manager. There's a special arrangement for when I need to train before a fight and when I'm away for a fight."

"That's 'Cass Cassidy'—your manager?"

Dunphy nodded *yes.* Clearly it gave her a measure of pride, that it could be said of her that she had a *manager.*

"And Ernie Beecher is your trainer? Mr. Beecher has an excellent reputation, I've learned."

Dunphy smiled, hesitantly. Clearly she was proud of Ernie Beecher her *trainer.*

"Is it strange to work with a man? To be so close, physically close, to a man like Ernie Beecher?"

Dunphy considered this. She did not feel comfortable with the words *physically close,* Naomi could see.

"And also, Mr. Beecher is a black man. That must be—just a little—given your background—strange . . ."

Dunphy shrugged as if embarrassed. It was clear that she had not given the strangeness much thought until now.

"What does your family think?"

"What does my family *think*?"

"About your boxing career. Working so closely with Ernie Beecher, for instance."

Dunphy rubbed her swollen eyelids. Her skin was sallow and doughy. Naomi could see small white scars at her hairline, like miniature gems. It was a revelation that a winning boxer, a young woman who had never lost a fight, could yet wear the signs of rough usage on her face. Half-consciously too, as she labored to answer Naomi's questions, Dunphy was rubbing the nape of her neck and upper spine as if she were in pain.

Naomi said, sympathetically: "But of course there are no women trainers. Especially no white women trainers. If you want to train to box you have to train with someone like Ernie Beecher. In fact you are very lucky to be working with Ernie Beecher."

"Yah. I am lucky."

"I guess—from what I've read— boxing has become a mostly black sport? Black and Hispanic? 'Persons of color' dominate—like Angel Hernandez, who's in your weight class? Will you fight her—Angel Hernandez?"

Dunphy shivered, shuddered. A look in her doughy face of sudden excitement, yet dread.

"Yah. Guess so."

"The only boxer you haven't beaten conclusively has been a black girl—'Jamala'. . ."

Naomi had researched D.D. Dunphy on the Internet. She'd made a list of the boxers Dunphy had fought. She saw how the name "Jamala" was startling to Dunphy who stared at her now with an inscrutable expression.

"'Jamala' . . . yah. She the best."

Strange, Dunphy had lapsed into black vernacular. Her voice had become throaty, musical. She'd murmured these words with a look of pained adoration.

"'Jamala Prentis'—'The Princess'? No, she lost her last fight. She's lost three or four fights and she's ranked below 'D.D. Dunphy.' I've done my homework. Midwestern Boxing League, World Boxing Association. On both lists you're ahead of Jamala. *You're* the best."

Naomi spoke with a wild sort of extravagance as if daring Dunphy to believe her.

But Dunphy stared at Naomi uncomprehending. Possibly, she had not known that Jamala Prentis had lost recent fights.

"Nah, Jamala is the best. 'The Princess'—she got style."

Though the banquet room was chilly Dunphy seemed to be overwarm. With a little grunt she removed her sweatshirt, tugging it roughly over her head;

Naomi had an impulse to help her, but did not. Below the sweatshirt Dunphy wore a T-shirt of some thin synthetic material, tight across her hard, heavy breasts, and cut high on the shoulder, so that the bright lurid tattoos on both her arms were revealed.

On one muscled bicep a cross of what appeared to be crimson flames, and on the other bicep a cross of white lilies. On Dunphy's left forearm, a purple hammer— *Hammer of Jesus.*

What a sight! Doesn't she know what she looks like . . .

She is so naive! So pathetic.

Wanting to believe that she is important.

Wanting to believe that anyone would want to interview her. That anything in her pitiful life matters.

"What striking tattoos!"—Naomi spoke with convincing admiration.

"Yah. I guess." Dunphy smiled shyly. Tucking in her chin to look at the tattoos in a way that suggested she often looked at them. Naomi thought—*She looks at the tattoos instead of looking into a mirror. The tattoos are her mirror.*

Badly Naomi wanted to end the interview. She believed that her parents would disapprove of what she was doing, if they could know. Yet she was transfixed, and could not seem to stop.

"Please tell me a little more about your background, Dawn. Your hometown is said to be Dayton but—that isn't where you were born, is it?"

Dunphy shrugged ambiguously as if to say *Guess not. Maybe.*

"I read on the Internet that you're from Muskegee Falls, a small city in central Ohio."

Was this a question? Dunphy frowned, warily.

"What was it like, growing up in Muskegee Falls?"

"What was it like?"—Dunphy seemed perplexed by the question.

"Did you have a happy childhood?"

Happy childhood seemed to confound Dunphy, who did not reply for a long time.

"Well—did anyone in your family encourage you?"

"N-No . . . They did not want me to be a boxer, I think."

Dunphy spoke haltingly, with a look of yearning.

"No one? At all? Where did you get the idea, then?"

"I guess—watching TV. With my brother Luke." Dunphy laughed suddenly. "*He* never thought I could make it!"

"What attracted you to boxing, when you were watching TV? Assuming that there were other things to watch—including other violent sports . . ." Dar-

ingly Naomi spoke, but Dunphy did not register any
irony.

"I guess—hitting. If somebody hits you you hit
them. I guess—maybe—that was it."

"'Boxing is about hitting'—is that it?"

"Nah. Boxing about hitting and not being hit back."
Dunphy laughed, surprising herself. These witty words
in a quasi-black idiom were not her own but had been
memorized and recited now and this pleased her.

"Can you tell us—(just speak to the camera naturally, as if you are in a conversation)—(my voice will be
edited out)—in a fight, what are you *thinking?* What
goes through your mind?"

Dunphy frowned, trying to think. Almost Naomi
thought you could see bulky-sized thoughts moving
through the young woman's brain, just slightly too large
for the space, as through narrow arteries, making her
wince.

"In a fight, it's like drowning. I mean—you feel that
you are drowning and the only thing is to save yourself.
The only way you save yourself is by hitting the other
boxer, hurting her, knocking her down so she can't
grab you and pull you down. It's her, or you. My trainer's voice is in my head. *Jab jab jab. Get inside. Go for
the right cross. Get inside. Left hook. Counter punch.*

Get inside. Keep your gloves up. Keep your left glove up. Get inside. LEFT GLOVE UP." She laughed, and wiped her perspiring face on the sweatshirt. "'Cause my arms are short, that's why he says—*Get inside.*"

"Isn't it dangerous? I noticed—the other boxer continuously retreated, and you advanced. But you must get hit a lot."

This was a sly understatement. But Dunphy did not register slyness.

"Like I said, if you're good you don't get hurt. 'Hammer of Jesus' can take a punch. That is well known."

This too was spoken with the air of a memorized remark. And spoken with pride.

"Really, you aren't afraid that you will be hurt? The head, the skull, the brain seem so vulnerable in boxing . . ." Naomi's voice trailed off, with a pleading sound.

But Dunphy shook her head, stubbornly. For someone had assured her *Hammer of Jesus can take a punch.*

"Do you have medical insurance? Hospital insurance? In case you are ever injured—seriously . . ."

"All that kind of thing is taken care of. My manager . . ."

"Does your contract include medical coverage? What would happen if . . ."

Dunphy lifted the water bottle to drink from it, thirstily. There was impatience and rudeness in the gesture and her doughy face had tightened.

Meanly Naomi thought—*I dislike you, too. I want you to be hurt. I want you to fail. I am not your friend!*

She should end the interview, she knew. What had she been thinking! A documentary film on women boxers—too awful, too filled with pain, exposure. No one would care to see such a film. There was some interest in women's champion boxers—to a degree. But D.D. Dunphy would never be a charismatic champion. And no one would wish to see the diminished private lives, that are never shown on TV. No one would wish to know about the losers.

"Just a few more questions, Dawn. Do your parents still live in Muskegee Falls, and do you have family there?" Naomi spoke easily, encouragingly.

Dunphy murmured what sounded like *Nah. Not now.*

"They have moved away? Where?"

"Mad River Junction—it's called. Where they live."

"All of your family?"

"My mother is a nurse, she works at a 'home' there. My brother has a job with the county."

"Your mother is a nurse?"—Naomi had not known this, and wondered if it could be true.

But Dunphy insisted *yes.* Her mother was a nurse.

"That's some kind of work you can respect—a nurse. But it is hard work." Dunphy paused, considering what she'd said. The words had seemed to surprise her.

"Would you like to be a nurse, too? I mean—if you weren't a boxer?"

"Nah."

Then, relenting: "Well maybe. It's some kind of work people respect and it is helping people. And— people respect you."

"And what of your father, Dawn?"

"My father—my father is not living."

Dunphy had been preparing for this question and answered it bravely. But then, she came to a full stop as if a bell had rung sounding the end of a round.

"I'm sorry to hear of that . . . He would have been proud of you, as a successful boxer, don't you think?"

Successful boxer caught Dunphy's attention. She was staring into a dim corner of the banquet room with a faint smile and seemed for a moment to have forgotten the interview.

"Especially if you become a champion, as it looks you will, soon . . ."

Dunphy looked at Naomi, blankly.

"I mean—your father would be proud of you. Especially if you become a champion."

Dunphy nodded, vaguely. She had been rubbing at the nape of her neck as if to alleviate pain.

"What did your father do, Dawn?"

"He was a roofer and a carpenter. He was a *master* roofer and carpenter, people said."

"How did your father die?"

"My father died in a bad car crash."

Dunphy spoke rapidly now, to get the words out. Her bloodshot eyes were welling with tears and shifting in their sockets like loosened marbles. She was a very poor liar.

Cruelly Naomi continued:

"How old were you when your father died, Dawn?"

For a long moment Dunphy did not reply. With the lack of self-consciousness of a child she lifted her T-shirt and wiped her eyes. Naomi had an impression of a black sports bra solid and tight as a brace.

"I don't remember too well. Maybe ten, eleven . . ."

"What do you remember of your father?"

Dunphy sat very still. Her face quivered, as if she were about to burst into tears. Her injured eyes continued to well with tears that did not spill over onto her face.

After a long moment Dunphy's lips moved. Naomi strained to hear her murmur— . . . *loved my Daddy.*

Naomi waited, but Dunphy said nothing more. In

her brightly friendly disingenuous interviewer voice she continued as if nothing were wrong:

"Do you try to get back home as often as you can? It must be lonely—on the road as you are, so often."

"Yah." Dunphy spoke tonelessly, without conviction.

"You visit your father's grave, I guess? When you go home?"

Dunphy nodded *yes*. A veiled, vague look had come into her face.

"Is your father buried in—'Mad River Junction'—?"

Dunphy stiffened, and made no reply. Her swollen eyes blinked rapidly.

Naomi wondered at the young woman boxer, that she didn't rise from her chair, lean across the table and strike the nervy and intrusive interviewer in the face with her rock-hard fist.

"Your mother is a nurse! That's a very crucial profession. Are you close with your mother?"

Dunphy nodded *yes*. But she was a very poor liar.

"Any of your siblings?"

Naomi thought—*What a foolish word, siblings!* She felt a wave of revulsion for herself, and wondered how she could proceed. It was a hateful exercise. Yet, she could not seem to stop.

If your opponent is on the ropes, you continue to

punch. Evidently. If you are a professional. That much, Naomi had gathered from the previous night in the Armory.

"'Siblings'—I mean, your sister—or your brothers. Are you close?"

Belatedly she worried that Dunphy would be suspicious, the interviewer seemed to know a good deal about her family. But Dunphy only shrugged, pained. Her forehead, that was creased with faint lines, creased more visibly now. She muttered she was OK with them.

"Are they proud of having a professional boxer in the family? With an undefeated record?"

Dunphy shook her head yes. But without conviction.

"Do they come to see your fights?"

Dunphy considered. A look came into her face, almost of cunning.

"Yah sometimes. They do. My aunt came. To Cleveland. She was scared for me real bad but she was proud of me when I won, she said."

Dunphy fell silent. It did not seem likely that she had told the complete truth here, but the interviewer would not pursue it.

"Is there any discrepancy, d'you think, between being a Christian and hitting other people? Hurting other women, in the ring?"

Dunphy frowned. Roughly she wiped her nose with

the edge of her hand. For a long time it seemed that she might answer this question but finally she said nothing, staring at the floor.

"Well. I guess it is a *sport*. And that is the point of the *sport*."

Dunphy nodded *yes*, vaguely.

"Are you friendly with other women boxers?"

"Not too much . . ."

"You don't know any? Or—you are just not friendly with the ones you know?"

Grimly Dunphy explained: "You don't be friends much with somebody you're gonna fight. You don't be friends with any of them."

"Is it a lonely life, then?"

"No. If you have Jesus you are not ever lonely."

These words had a brassy sound of having been memorized and many times recited. And now a look of defiance came into Dunphy's face.

"And what is your religion?"

"I am a Christian with the Zion Missionary Church in Dayton."

"Is that—Baptist?"

"Christian Zion Missionary Church."

"That is a Protestant church?"

"Y-Yes . . . I guess so."

"Is your religion helpful to you, as a boxer?"

"'Helpful' . . . ?"

"Does your religion inspire you?"

"Jesus is my religion. Yes, Jesus inspires me."

"In what way?"

"Jesus is my friend. I dedicate all my fights to Jesus, and Jesus helps me."

Dunphy spoke proudly, passionately. This was the one thing that seemed certain to her.

"Jesus helps you. But Jesus does not help the other boxers, your opponents?"

Dunphy frowned. She had not considered this.

"Maybe. Maybe Jesus helps them. Or maybe He helps us both to do the best we can do."

What a good answer this was! Naomi had to concede.

"So what Jesus helps you is to realize your own talent and potential. He does not sway the fight."

"I guess not." Dunphy seemed wary of agreeing.

"Jesus is fair-minded, he does not play favorites."

Naomi spoke clearly and simply as if to a small child. Truly she was not being ironic now but wanting badly to know what Dawn Dunphy would say.

Dunphy surprised her by saying sharply: "Why don't you ask Him, you want to know?"

A quick hard jab. Naomi felt the sting of the jab. Yet

with a cool smile she said: "I'm afraid I am not on close speaking terms with your Jesus."

Thinking—*Take care! If you mock her god you will be mocking her.*

You will not want Dunphy to know you are the enemy.

In a sudden angry voice Dunphy said: "My fights are for the glory of Jesus. So the heathen will know His name."

Her jaw was trembling. Her fists clenched as if she'd have liked to punch someone in the face.

Saying, as if someone were defying her, or laughing at her, in a quavering voice like one in pain: "My fights are *for Jesus*. That is all they are for—*for Jesus*. If they are not *for Jesus* but only *for me* then—God will punish me, and send me to Hell."

Why was Dunphy so upset?—why was she crying? Naomi was astonished.

It had happened so swiftly. One moment Dunphy had been proudly defiant, the other agitated, her face shining with tears.

"Is something wrong, Dawn? What is wrong? I'm sorry . . ."

Impulsively Naomi reached out as if to take Dunphy's hand but the young woman was too quick for her and drew both hands back as one might shrink from a snake.

"I guess—I don't want to talk anymore. I'm going now."

Dunphy rose to her feet unsteadily. She was breathing audibly, panting. Her savage bloodshot eyes were wet with tears, not of sorrow but of rage. Naomi steeled herself—*She could kill me with her fists. She could pound me to death. I would not be able to lift a finger to defend myself.*

"Of course—the interview is almost over anyway. Thank you so much for—"

"Yah. G'bye."

Agitated, Dunphy strode away. Without a backward glance pushing through a set of double doors that led into the hotel.

Naomi switched off the camera. She was shaken. Excited. Still it seemed unreal to her, that she had contrived to "interview" Luther Dunphy's daughter. Her first impulse was to call Darren, to gloat and jeer.

You will never guess . . .

Oh but I am so—ashamed . . .

Her hands were so shaky, she nearly dropped her camera onto the floor inserting it in its snug black leather bag.

Outside in the parking lot the dyed-blond Marika, chief of public relations for *Dayton Fights, Inc.,* was smoking a cigarette and speaking on a cell phone.

"Oh. The interview's over? How'd it go? D.D. Dunphy's not a great talker, is she? We can send you pictures if you need more. Like, 'The Hammer of Jesus at the heavy bag—in the boxing ring. There's maybe going to be a local Dayton sponsor for her, a sports store—we could have some pictures there. Ernie says, she takes after Joe Louis. Meaning—I guess—they don't talk much but they hit hard."

Marika gave Naomi her card, and did not seem to notice that Naomi had no card to give her.

"Send me the video—Natalie, is it? Please. Next time D.D. fights, could be a title match. She could be the next women's welterweight champion of the world. You won't want to miss that."

"Family"

It was true. A prediction.

You won't want to miss that.

She'd gone away, back to New York City. She wasn't going to recall anything about Cincinnati. She wasn't going to recall D.D. Dunphy for in so doing she would be forced to recall how cruelly, how crudely, even viciously she'd behaved in contriving to interview the naive young woman boxer. How *unethical* Naomi Voorhees's behavior.

Fortunately, no one knew. She had not called Darren to gloat over her audacity—hardly.

Neither Gus nor Jenna could know. That was the great relief, that they be spared such knowledge. *Your daughter is disfigured, warped in some way. Your daughter lacks humanity, charity, decency. Mercy.*

She had not told her grandmother much about the trip, and she had not told Kinch.

(Always, there was the temptation to share a secret with Kinch. The more deliciously shameful the secret, the more the temptation to share with her father's half-brother who inhabited his dwelling place like a spider emaciated from lack of food and thus ravenous, grateful for any morsel you could give him. But Naomi resisted.)

Yet she wasn't readily forgetting D.D. Dunphy. How recklessly close she'd come to taking the girl's hand, to comfort her. And what would have followed from that?—would Dunphy have shoved her violently away, with a curse? *Don't touch me! You are a heathen, you are not to touch me.*

It was perhaps the most extraordinary memory of her life: how close she'd come to taking the hand of Luther Dunphy's daughter.

In the white-walled room thirty floors above the clamorous city streets of the West Village she'd learned to sleep with part-opened eyes, unable or unwilling to sleep fully, trustingly. For fear that something terrible would happen if she relaxed. *Keep your left up.*

Get inside. Inside! Opening her eyes when a bell rang sharply ending a round. And there were the veiled bloodshot swollen and accusing eyes confronting her and a voice that seemed to be in the room with her, close in her ear: "My fights are for the glory of Jesus so the heathen will know His name."

Naomi understood that she'd been issued a challenge. What were *her fights* for? She had not a clue.

"Naomi, dear. We have to talk."

Reluctantly she came to sit near her grandmother. Icy fingers seeking hers, that were not so very warm, either.

"Oh why—now? Some other time."

"Ah but now is precisely the 'some other time' of last time, *chérie*."

Madelena laughed. It gave her pleasure to be witty, droll. To be witty and droll you require at least one other person to listen, to be amused or to shudder.

Fortunately at that moment a phone rang, to interrupt.

Like a coltish child the granddaughter ran to snatch up the mobile phone to bring to her grandmother seated by one of the floor-to-ceiling windows overlooking the abyss.

"Lena, for *you*."

These fragile times. *Thin-ice* fragile. Phone calls from Sloan Kettering. Radiology lab, oncology. She'd learned to recognize the caller IDs that most exuded dread. By her estimate there was not one that guaranteed safety.

At the start of the first series of chemotherapy treatments Madelena had made a dramatic decision: rather than wait for her hair to come out in handfuls she'd had it totally buzz-cut from her scalp so that she could be fitted with a wig of a near-identical hue, but tougher and more resilient than her own hair had been.

Naomi had accompanied her grandmother to the glamorous wig emporium in a high-rise building in midtown. She and a saleswoman had helped Madelena Kein try on wigs, trying not to see how Madelena's eyes shone with tears—of embarrassment, repugnance, self-pity or disdain you could not have said.

"No one needs to know. Even if they suspect, they don't know. And if they don't know, they can't commiserate with me."

Surgery, chemo, hair loss, wig. Madelena's pride had been astonishing to Naomi for it had seemed to her the most obvious sort of desperation on her (rational, reasonable) grandmother's part, meant to deflect a terror of mortality.

Over eight months Naomi had become familiar with
the attractive, light-filled, just perceptibly malodorous
waiting rooms at Sloan Kettering, in midtown Manhattan. She'd brought work with her, schoolwork, a
laptop, waiting for the several hours of chemotherapy
to run its course in an interior room to which she had
no access. (For chemotherapy meant chemicals, chemicals meant hazardous medical materials. Clinical protocol surrounding chemotherapy and radiation was
high-security and only specially trained nurses came
anywhere near such patients.)

Waiting by one of the tall windows in the waiting
room for her grandmother to be pushed out in a wheelchair by one of the infusion nurses. "Naomi? Here
is your grandmother"—glancing up, and feeling her
heart clutch.

Seeing poor Madelena so white-faced, so tired.
Not wearing the beautiful silver human-hair wig at
this time, and her poor head bare, fragile-seeming as
eggshell. Yet in one of her dressy-casual sweater-and-
trouser sets. And wearing earrings.

Bravely Madelena managed to smile: "Hi there!
Sorry to make you wait so long."

Madelena was only pushed in the wheelchair out to
the waiting room, where she stood shakily, and took
Naomi's arm, and walked with her to the elevator. The

wheelchair was part of the protocol. Perhaps it had to do with insurance. But it was invariably a shock to Naomi, to see her grandmother in a wheelchair.

Always, or nearly always, Madelena had been stoic, uncomplaining. Pride would not allow her to complain. Chemo days were fraught with stress, the drama of not knowing if (in the hired car descending to the Village, in the elevator at 110 Bleecker, in the clammy sheets of her bed that night) Madelena might have a sudden reaction to the poison that had been pumping through her heart—a temperature spike, or a temperature drop; sudden nausea and vomiting, or diarrhea; a piercing headache, a ghoulish bloodshot eye.

(Why was it only one bloodshot eye, and not two? And unpredictably the right eye, or the left? No one seemed to know.)

At least there was no fussing over dinner that evening, Madelena liked to say. Naomi would prepare her a small bowl of chicken broth, a small bowl of white rice, a small bowl of applesauce.

On these evenings Madelena would go to bed early. Or rather, she would shut the door to her bedroom, and Naomi might hear her speaking on the phone—(to her friend Laslov?—they spoke each day at least once, so far as Naomi knew); a murmur of words, even laughter, not quite audible.

In those months neither Madelena nor Naomi had seriously considered that Madelena might die. If Naomi had examined her naive assumptions she might have thought—*My father died. My mother is dead to me. It is not possible that my grandmother will die, too.*

In this way Naomi had come to love Madelena. By unmeasured degree she'd come to love her grandmother. Between them had grown a bond like a soft, clotted, delicate cobweb that has appeared in the night, unobserved. Such a bond might be easily broken but— why would you break anything so beautiful?

On the street, in the subway, Naomi exuded an air of female strength; she'd made herself into a New Yorker, sub-species young-woman-professional. With those with whom she interacted she was brisk, competent, un-complaining; she was never (seemingly) distracted.

Her single most vulnerable time wasn't in public but returning to the apartment building at 110 Bleecker, en-tering her grandmother's apartment when no one else was there. Especially when Madelena was scheduled to be in the hospital overnight. During the second course of treatment there were six sieges of several days each of intensive twenty-four-hour chemotherapy not in the quasi-social infusion room at Sloan Kettering but in a private hospital bed on another floor.

Switching on a light in the apartment in which the

large plate-glass windows floated in the night sky and in the nighttime city below winking with lights. As shadows leapt back in a mimicry of human movement she could not stop from saying, in a hopeful voice "Hello?"—but of course, there was no one.

She was not unhappy really. She could not quite recall what *happy* was, but she was not *unhappy*.

Reasoning: the chemo treatments seemed to be helping her grandmother. Despite the hair-loss, the weight-loss. Initially there had been treatments every two weeks over eight months. There had been a brief three-month period of remission. But now, a new period of relapse. And more extreme therapy. For oncologists at Sloan Kettering were inspired by the rarest of cancers, metastases (for instance) from the kidney to the colon, or from the colon to the kidney. There was less interest in "ordinary" cancers—colon, kidney, breast, bone, blood. There was revealed an intense and jealous scholarly narrowness to cancer that Naomi had not ever guessed. She had to think that her father could not have guessed, for his medical specialization was of a very different sort. How intrigued Gus would have been by the oncologists who were treating his mother! He would have liked to discuss her condition with them, and the treatment they were prescribing. Not for

the first time Naomi felt all that her father was missing, being dead.

At any rate, the terrible twenty-four-hour five-day
chemotherapy did appear to be working. In the last lab
report from the oncologist, Madelena Kein's bloodwork
indicated that the patient was *holding her own*.

"'Holding my own.' This is a touching metaphor. It
seems to mean that something, some force, is trying to
wrest something, some possession of mine, from me—
from out of my arms, for instance. But I am not allowing it to be wrested away—I am not passive in the face
of my destiny but I am *holding my own*. Thank you for
this good news."

Once, these words would have been ironic, out of
Madelena's mouth. But now, Naomi knew they were
sincere. And she thought how conscientious her grandmother was being, in resisting irony at such a time.

For good news, even if it may be temporary and precarious, is good news. Though a fact may be reversed
with the next PET scan, or the next bloodwork, it is
not less a fact because it is temporary and precarious.

"If the dead could return to life, they would rejoice
in 'life'—whatever it was. They would not be picky
and quarrelsome. They would not be *ironic*. And so we
who are alive had better rejoice in their place."

"Yes, Lena."

"Good! You've learned to call me 'Lena.' What next?"—Madelena laughed, delighted.

"I will learn to call Kinch 'Kinch.'"

In fact, Naomi could not call Kinch anything except, if she could not avoid it, "you."

When she'd returned to New York City from the first of her Midwestern trips, to Muskegee Falls, it was to discover that Madelena had become cheerfully "resigned." Prematurely "resigned." There was a new airiness, lightness in her grandmother's bones. It wasn't the ravages of chemotherapy—rather a ravage of the soul. A rarefying of the soul. To her surprise Naomi discovered, and would have liked to toss out into the incinerator chute in the corridor, a copy of *The Tibetan Book of the Dead* on Madelena's nightside table.

She'd leafed through the book dreading what she might read. She knew how derisive Gus had been of "wisdom" literature—the sacred texts of the great religions, apologias for oppression, ignorance, superstition, pacifism in the face of political tyranny. Not to mention enslavement and mistreatment of women. No "wisdom" is worth such ignorance, Gus had said. And it was laced with anti-science as with anthrax.

Naomi supposed that *The Tibetan Book of the Dead* was not to be taken literally but rather symbolically.

The subtitle was *Liberation Through Hearing During the Intermediate State.*

For you did not die instantaneously, it was claimed. By degrees you died, as your consciousness waned. Many days and many nights were required for complete extinction. Possibly this was once true, or true in some way, before modern medical technology. Now, consciousness in the dying individual waned, and was extinguished, while the body continued to live a zombie-life in its reduced state. This was *living*—but only physically.

Naomi put the book down, and did not confront her grandmother with it. For she knew that, if she did, Madelena would make a joke of it in some way painful to Naomi.

She missed Madelena's former contentiousness. Madelena's contrarian spirit. Since the onset of the cancer Madelena scarcely seemed to care if someone disagreed with her—she rarely troubled to disagree with others. She had lost her strong opinions as you might lose bulky household objects and never miss them. She did not refute colleagues, she did not take sides in disputes. When Kinch said something preposterous, or provocative, Madelena simply smiled.

Clasped her hands tightly together, as if in restraint. Smiled.

When Naomi told Madelena that she thought she might have at last found her "subject"—("A film documentary about women boxers")—Madelena had said, "Good!"—and had not raised the obvious objections Naomi had expected.

"Will you apply for a grant? From the Institute? Or—are you looking for private investors? If so, maybe I can help."

Quickly Naomi told her grandmother that she wasn't looking for money—yet. It was mortifying to her that Madelena would offer to support her documentary filmmaking, along with allowing her to live in her apartment for no rent.

Madelena said, "But I want to help you, in any way I can. Why would I not want to help you, Naomi? You're my granddaughter: I love you."

She'd seen this clearly: Madelena had intended to maneuver her into a relationship of some intimacy with the *half-uncle* Kinch. She'd known almost at once. Oh, she *had known*.

Yet, it had happened nonetheless. Not that she'd been powerless to stop it but that she had not stopped it, as if powerless.

As she'd come to love Madelena over a period of time so she'd come to love Karl Kinch. (To a degree.)

My family. Mine!

She didn't know whether to smile over this, or to cry. Often she had a fleeting vision of something—ashes, bone—swirling sucked away into a stream.

Until Madelena's illness Naomi had never visited Kinch without her—of course. It had seemed very strange, awkward—visiting the *half-uncle* without her grandmother present.

When she came alone to see Kinch he was bright, cheerful, garrulous and inquisitive as usual. He'd made an effort to groom himself: fresh-laundered white shirt, shaving cologne. With playful rudeness he sent the dour Sonia away to "molder" in a back room and not bother them. Yet: he didn't ask in detail about Madelena.

He didn't tease Naomi nearly so much as he had at the start of their acquaintance. She'd become for him a familiar presence, a "relative"—almost, a relative he'd known for a long time, about whom there was no need to ask probing questions.

Kinch liked to surprise Naomi by giving her presents at unpredictable times. A pristine first edition of *Selected Poems of Marianne Moore*. A paperback copy of Julian Jaynes's *The Origins of Consciousness in the Breakdown of the Bicameral Mind* with Kinch's own annotations in the margins. A copy of Kinch's own, early book of poems *Tristes* published when he'd been

Naomi's age, and out of print (as Kinch said) for three decades, with a lavishly obscure inscription—*To my dear niece Naomi with hope for the happiness of her life to come. Yrs with Love, "Uncle Karl."*

She took away the books, and tried to read them. Grateful that Kinch never asked her about them.

In return for these gifts Kinch sometimes asked Naomi to read to him. Anything, everything—passages from that morning's *New York Times* or from a new book on epistemology from Cambridge, captions beneath *New Yorker* cartoons in a font too small and thin for his single good eye.

Sighing with happiness Kinch said: "Very nice, to have a 'niece.' For one who'd never had the slightest interest in children of his own a 'niece' is the perfect solution."

"Solution to what?"

"To the problem of aloneness. Sometimes overlapping with 'loneliness.'"

Naomi had cultivated a mildly skeptical response to Kinch's remarks—a bright-schoolgirl manner appropriate to a young niece.

There was nowhere else that Naomi Voorhees spoke in such a way, that was both younger than she felt, yet older, "sophisticated" like a young girl in a romantic film by Jean Renoir.

(Madelena had taken her to a Renoir festival at the local Film Forum. Naomi had fallen under the spell of the visually beautiful cinematic Renoir world slow-moving and insular as a dream.)

Kinch spoke of his medical problems in a similar tone: casual, conversational, bemused. He liked to tell anecdotes of his hospital misadventures, nightmare tests and "procedures," things that might have gone disastrously wrong but somehow did not. He did not want pity for his condition but he did want attention—an audience. When he had genuinely good news, a new medication that was working well, a new test that turned out negative, the slowing of the "progression" of his MS, Kinch had more difficulty speaking of it. What he most feared was hope, Naomi thought.

Yet there was hope in Kinch's life, of a kind. A new intravenous medication was now available for the treatment of the kind of MS he had, and it was possible that in fact Kinch didn't have HIV after all but a rare blood disorder—his condition might have been misdiagnosed.

Speaking of such matters Kinch maintained a light, bantering tone. Naomi understood—he did not want her to express hope of any kind. Better to fall in with Kinch's pose of cynicism: "'The treatment was a great success, the patient died.'"

And: "Life is what spills over from a *New Yorker* cartoon caption."

She resisted Kinch. A middle-aged man who remained perennially young, unnaturally "boyish"— "childish." To be in the presence of Karl Kinch was to seem to be conspiring, making mischief—though you did not quite know what kind of mischief you were making. She did not really want to *like* Kinch. She suspected that, if Gus were alive, Gus would not approve of Kinch—there was a kind of zestful morbidity in the man, much at odds with Gus Voorhees's forthright and unironic nature.

Yet, Naomi found herself confiding in Kinch. One afternoon when she was visiting him alone in his austere dwelling at Fifteenth Street just east of Fifth Avenue. She'd recently returned from Muskegee Falls and had fallen into a fugue of inertia. Or maybe it was a fugue of self-doubt and despair which she strove to hide from her grandmother. She'd decided—finally—to stop work on the archive; yet, she had no other project of her own. Her work for the documentary filmmaker was part-time, erratic; she enjoyed it, and had learned a great deal, but the career of a documentary filmmaker was episodic, and if you could not choose your own subjects it could be sheer drudgery, unrewarding.

Yael Ravel had warned her: There is no romance of *film*. Except in the eye of the beholder.

Kinch had observed his young niece's quietness. He'd observed, with his sharp, singular eye, the sadness in her manner, that had not only to do with her grandmother's medical condition (of which he knew but obliquely) but with something more personal to her, more private. He'd asked her what was wrong, and she had told him—she'd journeyed to Muskegee Falls, she'd taken pictures, made videos.

"But it's all exterior. No one from the Dunphy family was even there. And he's been dead for six years."

Kinch said, "Your father has been dead for even longer."

Naomi winced, she had no idea what this meant. But she'd deserved it being said for she had made herself vulnerable to her father's (rivalrous) half-brother.

Unexpectedly then Kinch began to speak of "Luther Dunphy." She had not known that he'd had the slightest interest in Dunphy, even that he'd known the assassin's name; still less that he'd researched the case. She could not have guessed that Kinch in his pretense of indifference to domestic relations had had much interest in Gus Voorhees. But now he lighted a cigarette and exhaled luxuriously like a man in a movie, assured of being the center of attention. It was transfixing to Naomi, that anyone should approach the obsession of her young life, which she had shared with few others.

"Dunphy. Luther Amos. As I see it the man consecrated himself as a 'Soldier of God'—or a 'Soldier of Christ'—if there's any distinction. The essential thing is, Dunphy was a martyr. He didn't expect to survive what he'd done. He precipitated his own execution. He was a suicide."

Kinch paused. He was leaning forward in his wheelchair, smiling a ghastly wet excited smile, exhaling smoke, clearly enjoying himself. He would never have expounded on this subject if Madelena had been present, Naomi thought.

Naomi asked, "Was Jesus's crucifixion a kind of suicide?"

"Not if Jesus was resurrected. That's the happy ending."

"But—we don't believe that Jesus was resurrected. Do we?"

"*We* don't, but others do. Very likely, Jesus thought he would be resurrected, at least before the crucifixion."

Kinch continued: "Remember, on the cross Jesus calls out in a loud voice—'My God, my God, why has thou forsaken me?'—'*Eli, Eli, lema sabachthani?*'—the saddest words in the New Testament. (But the words are an echo of the Old Testament *Psalms.* Jesus was a Biblical scholar!) The rest of the story, the death, the burial in the tomb, the resurrection and the rising to heaven—is obviously of another, later era. This is the fairy-tale ending—the prescribed ending. It's the verses leading to the crucifixion that depict a stark sort of reality. The betrayal of Judas—the denial of Peter—the anointing of Jesus's feet by Mary, as if he were already a corpse—the matter-of-fact words of Jesus presaging his death: 'Yet a little while is the light with you. Walk while you have the light, lest darkness come upon you: for he that walks in darkness knows not whither he goes.'"

Kinch ceased speaking as if struck dumb by words he'd only comprehended as he uttered them. Naomi was sitting straight-backed on the sofa facing him in the wheelchair, cast into a state of mind not unlike the confusion of a dream, the waking-from-a-dream, when what you have lost is yet with you, though you can't say its name.

It had enveloped Gus—this darkness. Stealthily it continued to advance. No human effort could forestall it.

In his stricken state Kinch sucked at his ridiculous parchment-cigarette, that Naomi hated. She'd have liked to hate *him.*

Kinch recovered something of his jaunty composure and continued:

"What is 'suicide'? What do we mean by 'martyrdom'? In the Gospels Jesus clearly accepts his own death—that is, the death that precedes resurrection. 'The poor you shall always have with you, but me you shall not.' This is a poignant remark, matter-of-fact, not self-pitying. Jesus accepts his death but he is 'deluded' you might say—he believes that his Father in Heaven can save him at any moment. But he knows that he must die, to wash away the sins of humankind. It's a tragic story if you don't believe—if you can't believe—that Jesus was actually a demigod, and Jesus was resurrected and ascended to the throne of the Father in Heaven. Jesus is not a 'suicide' because Jesus believes that he is the savior of humankind—he can be killed, but he can't be destroyed. The man who murdered your father, and another person, is the truer suicide. He never tried to save himself, it's said. He never lost faith and he died in the service of faith—a delusion. Yet he wasn't entirely deluded—he knew that God would forsake him, and he would die *dead.* You have to admire someone like that, eh?"

Particularly, the *eh?* was outrageous. Naomi shrank from Kinch as if he'd uttered something obscene. She could not reply.

Kinch persisted: "Very few people would die for any ideal. Even a delusion. Such courage is rare."

"It wasn't 'courage.' It was—cruelty, stupidity . . ."

"He wasn't insane. No one tried seriously to suggest that Luther Dunphy was insane. But what of your father Gus Voorhees? *He* was not insane, of course."

Mutely Naomi stared at Karl Kinch. What was the man saying?

"But Gus Voorhees was a kind of 'suicide' too—*de facto.* In his defiance of his enemies, in the risks he took, your father was courageous, but also—as he must have known—'suicidal.' He weighed the likelihood of his own death against the value of his services to women who needed him and decided it was worth it, whatever happened. The perfect martyr is a suicide."

In distress Naomi stood. She would run out and leave Kinch in his motorized wheelchair, with a forlorn, faint smell of cologne about his wasted body, and a scattering of ashes on his bony knees.

"I hate you. I don't have to listen to this."

"But I don't hate *you.* I *adore you.* And your father Gus Voorhees—I admire him immensely. The more I've learned about him, the more I admire him; and Luther Dunphy too, in his sad deluded way . . .

"But I would worry, Gus Voorhees wouldn't admire *me.*"

Kinch began to cough. The parchment cigarette in his hand trembled, and ashes fell. Naomi wanted to snatch the cigarette from him and throw it at his face.

"Excuse me, Naomi—"

Kinch's cough worsened. Within seconds it became a wracking spasm of a cough. Naomi hoped that Sonia would come running to give aid to her invalid-employer but Sonia was feigning deafness perhaps, hiding in a remote room watching TV.

Naomi came to Kinch, hunched now in his wheelchair, white-faced, shaken, the size and heft of a pre-pubescent boy. With a paper napkin she wiped at his damp face. The hateful cigarette she detached from his fingers and briskly stubbed out in a tray.

Soon then, Kinch recovered. Irritably he said, "Just something I swallowed wrong. It's nothing, much."

The Consolation of Grief:

February 2012

Another time, she flew to the Midwest.
The last time. She promised herself.

At Kennedy her flight was delayed so that the plane's wide wings could be "de-iced"—fascinating if harrowing to watch from her window seat at the rear of the plane. At the airport outside Cleveland, runways were bordered by six-foot banks of plowed-up snow and passengers already exhausted from a turbulent flight and a bumpy landing were made to sit on the plane for forty minutes awaiting an "arrival gate"—telling herself *It is your choice that you are here. It is no one else's but your own.*

That evening, at the Cleveland Sports Arena, on a card with a much-promoted middleweight boxing match between two top-ranked (male) contenders, was the title fight for the Midwest Boxing League Women's Welterweight championship—(title-holder) Siri Aya "Icewoman" vs. D.D. Dunphy "Hammer of Jesus."

This time Naomi had a better seat: third row, center. A complimentary ticket courtesy of *Dayton Fights, Inc.*

Since the Cincinnati visit she'd kept in contact with Marika who was under the impression (to a degree, this was not unfounded) that Naomi Matheson was preparing a documentary film on women boxers in which D.D. Dunphy would be prominent.

Each woman believing herself shrewd in "keeping in contact" with the other.

Marika had no doubt that D.D. Dunphy would win the MBL title in February, in Cleveland. The "really big" title fight would be with a boxer named Ilse Kinder who was the WBA champion and a box-office draw—"They can't ignore us then. They will have to make a TV deal."

Adding, "This will be a major fight, probably in the summer. Atlantic City at least. Vegas is a long shot but a possibility."

And, "You might end up making your film all about D.D. Dunphy, Naomi. 'The First Great Woman Boxer'—'The First Great American Woman Boxer'—some title like that."

Difficult not to be caught up in such enthusiasm, such optimism for what's-to-come, even in one who had grown cautious, if not apprehensive, of peering blithely into the future—as if one could peer into any future and not rather into a kind of distorting reflective surface mirroring one's own anxious face.

Naomi heard herself say carefully: "That would be a possibility. Yes."

Vehement and righteous Marika continued: "Jesus! The situation is, sportswriters are all men. You'd think that would be changed by now but essentially it isn't. Sports photographers are all men. TV sports producers. They don't give a shit for women boxers, and they don't give a shit for our boxer because she isn't 'photogenic.' Know what they say? ESPN has said? 'Dunphy looks too much like an athlete—viewers won't like that.' Like, Mike Tyson doesn't look like an 'athlete'? What's Dunphy supposed to look like, a ballet dancer? Ice-skater? Our boxer looks like *who she is*."

This time, Naomi knew to come to the fights late. To avoid the grueling earlier fights, between inexperienced or lesser boxers, that aroused such scorn among the spectators scattered through the arena.

In the clamorous arena Naomi sat alone. Already her nerves were on edge amid such noise.

This time she didn't feel so self-conscious. It had not been her aloneness after all in Cincinnati that had made her conspicuous but the color of her skin and here in the more attractive Cleveland Sports Arena, at least within the first dozen or so rows, the majority of spectators were white.

White-skinned, and a number of them women. Women in groups, in rows. Rowdy and funny. From comments Naomi had been overhearing these fight fans had come some distance to see "Icewoman" fight.

Siri Aya had defended her title two years before in Cleveland, in this venue, and was a three-to-one favorite tonight.

No one seemed to know much about D.D. Dunphy, or to care.

Naomi did not want to see Dunphy win this fight, and become a "champion." Yet, she did not want to see Dunphy lose badly, or be injured. Online she'd watched several fights in which the elegantly poised, seemingly invincible "Icewoman" Aya had outboxed, outmaneuvered, outlasted her opponents. Aya's ring record was eighteen wins, two losses. Dunphy's record was nine wins, no losses, one draw.

Aya was twenty-nine years old and had been boxing for eleven years. She'd famously said in an interview that she would "never retire"—she'd have to be "carried out of the ring feet first." In her hometown of Milwaukee, Wisconsin, she'd been trained in martial arts and kickboxing and had been an amateur champion in these sports as a young teenager. Her older brother had been a WBA heavyweight contender until he'd been convicted of domestic assault and incarcerated. Her only losses had come at the start of her career. She'd defended her MBL title several times. When she entered the Cleveland arena in a silky ivory-white robe, with an ebullient greeting to the crowd, cheers went up, and sustained applause. When D.D. Dunphy had entered a few minutes before there'd been sporadic applause that had quickly faded.

In the ring, the two women boxers could not have been more unlike. Aya's ivory-white robe was embossed with icicle-lightning bolts and her boxing trunks and Spandex top were of the same showy fabric; her chic buzz-cut hair was bleached platinum-blond; on her slender muscled arms was a tattoo-lacework of ivory and gold. Aya was sleek, long-legged as an antelope, her arms seemed to glitter like scimitars. Her skin was a pale cocoa-color but her features were "Caucasian." Everything about Dunphy was cruder—matt-black ring attire, spiky streaked hair, lurid tattoos on her biceps. Her skin was sallow. Her body was thick, muscled, graceless. On the back of her T-shirt was colorful advertising for a Dayton sports store, Naomi was embarrassed to see.

Siri Aya wore ivory-white shoes with gold tassels. D.D. Dunphy wore ungainly black shoes on feet large as hooves.

"Ladies and gentlemen, ten rounds of women's welterweight boxing for the Midwest Boxing League title . . ."

In the first several seconds of the first round it seemed evident: Aya was the quicker, Dunphy the more forceful. Very likely, Dunphy was outmatched by her taller, leaner, more mature and more devious opponent who stymied her with a rapid jab, a succession of blows, a way of moving to the side as if in retreat yet not in retreat but aggressively, unexpectedly pushing forward—so that the stocky-bodied, stronger boxer was led to throw punches wildly, that missed their mark, or, striking her opponent, were but glancing blows.

Aya wasn't letting Dunphy *get inside.* So long as she could not *get inside* the shorter-armed boxer was helpless.

Naomi saw too, Dunphy wasn't consistently keeping up her left glove. She was distracted, off-stride. A kind of panic must have set in as soon as Dunphy realized that her ring style would not be effective against an opponent who could so easily slip her hard-thrown punches, and was so much lighter on her feet.

When the bell rang, Naomi realized that her back teeth ached; she'd been clenching her jaws tight.

Truly she did not want D.D. Dunphy to win this fight, she did not want the name *Dunphy* to triumph. Yet she could not help it, she dreaded seeing Dunphy hurt. She had scarcely been able to breathe during the three-minute round.

If Dunphy could lose the fight without being *hurt, knocked out.*

She tried to see the fight as an event. A spectacle. Why did it matter to her who won?—neither boxer meant anything to her. Her own life was not affected in any way.

So far as Marika knew, Naomi Matheson was a documentary filmmaker with the intention of interviewing women boxers. It could not matter to her which boxer won this fight for her subject was *women boxers* and this would include those who lost as rightfully as those who won.

The second round was more intense and more hard-fought than the first. Aya was pressing Dunphy, forcing her to step back, misstep. Strange that the antelope was fierce in aggression, quick and deft and pitiless; the steer plodding, stoic, blindly pressing forward, determined not to betray weakness. In the corner between rounds Dunphy's trainer Ernie Beecher must have been giving her urgent instructions which she could not follow.

By mid-fight Dunphy was panting, red-faced, cuts opening above both eyes from her opponent's blows. Yet she prevailed, shoulders hunched, trying to protect her face and head with her raised gloves. She could not *get inside*, she could only punch frantically at her opponent's arms and gloves.

"Who is winning?"—Naomi asked fight fans behind her after the fifth round.

"You kidding? 'Icewoman.'"

She felt a low mean thrill of satisfaction, hearing this. Of course, it had to be true. She was feeling Dunphy's humiliation in her own gut.

And that ridiculous and demeaning advertising on the back of Dunphy's T-shirt—*Give up! Give up! You don't have a chance.*

Yet, a few seconds into the sixth round Dunphy managed to strike her elusive opponent on the side of the head with one of her blindly-thrown blows. At once the dazzling Aya staggered, thrown back on her heels.

There came cries of disappointment and dismay from the crowd. Dunphy continued to swarm forward, throwing punches. Her broad doughy face was bleeding, contorted. She was breathing through her mouth. Though Dunphy was plodding and graceless the mercurial will of the crowd was shifting to her, to the flailing white girl-boxer, that she might overcome the other, more beautiful figure, out of a kind of perversity.

Dun-phy!

But Aya was too smart, and too experienced. Even in distress Aya knew to clinch, to punch at her opponent's kidneys, to get through the round without collapsing.

And then in the next round, as if her corner men had injected her with a magical potion Aya seemed to have completely recovered. Or almost completely. She even danced about the slower-footed Dunphy, like a bullfighter taunting and tormenting a bull. And Dunphy was slow, leaden-legged. You could feel the effort required for her to lift her dense arms, to protect herself with her gloves.

And again, the will of the crowd had shifted from Dunphy. Aya was the favorite after all. Of course— "Icewoman" was the favorite: look how beautiful she is, how easily she moves, with what contempt she eludes the fierce-thrown blows of her opponent. When one of Dunphy's feet slipped and she almost fell, and Aya took advantage to strike Dunphy hard on the side of the head with a lightning-quick blow, the crowd erupted in cheers and whistles.

Ay-a! A-ya!

Naomi saw, or believed she could see, small white scars in Dunphy's eyebrows like bits of exposed bone amid streaks and smears of blood.

The round ended with flurries of blows from both women. Siri Aya too was breathing through her mouth. Not very steadily she "strode" back to her corner when the bell rang.

"Who won that round?"—Naomi asked, with dread.

"Can't tell. Pretty close."

"But is Aya ahead?"

"Yah. Aya 'way ahead."

Yet in the following round Aya behaved unpredictably. She tried to clinch with Dunphy whenever she could—as if, for her, the fight was over: she had won on points. Barring an upset she could not not win the fight, she had only to prevail against her opponent. The crowd sensed this, and became restless. In frustration Dunphy threw off the other's binding arms, and lunged forward blindly. For a moment the boxers teetered together, and might have fallen except Aya pushed away. Aya was back on her toes. Aya was smiling and taunting her opponent, mocking the other's clumsiness.

Always the elegant devious Aya was moving back from her stymied opponent, moving away, moving laterally, out of the range of Dunphy's wayward blows. When it was necessary she defended herself with raised arms, elbows. Her tight-curled platinum-blond head bobbed and weaved like a snake's head. She seemed to be taking pleasure in the very strain of the struggle though her beautiful cocoa-skinned face too was flushed, wet with perspiration. Still Dunphy pushed forward, trying to *get inside*. It was habitual, Dunphy's dropping of her left glove, unconscious, lethal—in a moment of vulnerability Aya struck Dunphy with a precisely executed right cross to her chin.

Naomi understood from the eruption of the crowd that Dunphy was hurt. Staggering on her feet she was stunned, she appeared blinded. She could not defend herself. Her gloves sank as if the weight of them were too much for her.

Naomi cried: "No! No . . ."

Another blow to Dunphy's head, blows to her torso, midriff, as the crowd erupted. Naomi felt a tremendous hatred for the crowd, like a pack of animals they were, savage, stupid.

Yet, Dunphy did not fall even to her knees. Dunphy remained standing, dazed, as the referee began to count: for the referee would not allow Dunphy to continue, in this state; the other boxer would destroy her.

At the count of six, the bell rang.

Naomi realized that she was on her feet, horrified. Others in the audience were standing.

Dunphy stood bleeding and confused in the center of the ring, not knowing what to do. Her corner men came hurriedly to get her.

Voices were heard—*Stop the fight!*

The ring physician was examining Dunphy in her corner. Naomi stood in the aisle, staring. She wanted to cup her hands to her mouth and call—*Stop the fight!*

Her throat was hoarse. She hadn't been aware that she must have been screaming.

Unbelievably then, the examining physician must have determined that Dunphy was able to continue the fight. Dunphy's corner men were adamant that Dunphy continue. Dunphy herself was looking less confused, more clear-eyed. Her bloodied face had been washed, styptic deftly applied to her wounds.

When the bell rang, and the fight continued, Naomi found herself hurriedly descending the steps, approaching the bright-lit ring. There was a roaring in her ears as of a distant waterfall—the noise of the crowd, or the sound of her quick-beating blood in her ears. She was just below the struggling boxers. She could see Dunphy's grim-set battered face, and she could see the face of the other, not a young face, a drawn and taut face, and she could hear the women grunting, and the scuffing sound of their feet. She had never been so close, so terrifically close to anyone so locked in struggle, in combat. She could smell the struggling bodies. She could smell her own fear. At ringside she tried to make her way to the farther side of the ring where Dunphy's corner men were seated, for she intended to appeal to them, to plead with them to stop the fight; but her way was blocked by legs and feet, and furious ringside patrons were shouting at her—"Get away! Get the fuck out of here! Crazy bitch."

A security guard stopped her—"Whoa there, girl!"

Her face pounded with heat. Her voice came pleading.

"The fight—the fight should be stopped. She's badly hurt. She might have a concussion. Isn't there anything that can be done?"—even in her distress Naomi made an effort to be reasonable.

How her parents would smile, she thought. *Don't raise your voice. If you raise your voice you have already lost the argument.*

The guard, tall, youthful middle-age, dark-skinned, regarded her with incredulity. "Ma'am this's a fight—y'know?"

"But—Dunphy is being hurt . . ."

"They taken care of her all right, ma'am. She c'n quit anytime she wants to quit. Best go back to your seat, ma'am. You need help?"

Naomi drew away, offended. Of course she didn't need help returning to her seat.

In her seat, however, she felt very strange. The shouts and cries of the arena came to her as an undersea vertigo. Her eyes had narrowed as in a mimicry of tunnel vision and so she was spared the spectacle in the boxing ring at which she dared not look.

One of the boxers had slipped, or had been struck, and had fallen to one knee. Astonishingly it was not Dunphy but the other, the opponent with the tight-curled platinum-blond hair and smooth cocoa skin: the cries of the crowd made it difficult for Naomi to concentrate on identifying who had been hurt.

Was this a "knockdown"?—the referee had begun his count. Dunphy had crossed to a neutral corner.

By a count of nine Aya was on her feet. Shrewdly the veteran boxer knew to take nearly the full count, to recover her strength.

But she was shaky, out of breath. Dunphy ran at her like a maddened steer and struck at her as her gloves flailed helplessly. At last Dunphy was *inside*. Dunphy struck Aya several blows yet Aya did not fall but clutched at her, desperate to stay on her feet. The boxers swayed, nearly fell into the ropes. Curtly the referee said: "Break!" Dunphy wrenched away preparing to fight but Aya lowered her head, seemed to be ducking, and falling against Dunphy—

Sudden bright blood on Dunphy's forehead, over her right eye. A terrible gash of several inches in thin scar tissue that had scarcely healed since the last fight.

It had been a head-butt. Not a legitimate blow but a foul. Dunphy sank to her knees, and fell to her hands and knees, and what looked like part of her mouth fell out onto the canvas—broken teeth?—Naomi was horrified until she realized that it must be a mouthpiece . . .

Shouts and screams in the arena. Protests. The referee was waving his arms briskly over his head, stopping the fight.

At once Dunphy's corner men climbed into the ring, to loudly protest. And there was the forlorn, badly bleeding boxer now on her feet, trying to protest.

So abruptly, the fight was ended. Dunphy was led to her corner where she sat heavily, dazed as the wound in her forehead was examined.

Naomi could not see what was happening in the ring. Too many individuals climbed through the ropes and all of them men—except for Siri Aya strutting about lifting her gloves in triumph.

The crowd was not happy. The ring announcer was asking for attention.

". . . winner and still champion Midwest Boxing League Women's Welterweight Siri "Icewoman" Aya . . ."

A hefty belt studded with *faux* gems, absurdly ornamental, was buckled about Aya's waist.

Defiantly Aya raised her gloves, circling the ring like royalty. Her long shapely arms glittered with tattoos. Her face was drawn with fatigue and yet she was smiling, she would not cease smiling so long as she was in the ring and cameras were flashing. Applause erupted, but many protests. The ring announcer raised his voice to be heard over the commotion.

". . . and let's have a round of applause for contender D.D. 'Hammer of Jesus' Dunphy for a fine, spectacular performance this evening . . ."

Dunphy was not to be seen. Boos and catcalls continued. Naomi found herself standing in the aisle beside her third-row seat which (it seemed) she'd abandoned. She was clutching her camera which she'd forgotten to use. She was exhausted, emotionally drained as if she'd been locked in a pitiless struggle herself, and had been defeated.

There was jostling in the aisle. Security guards were preventing anyone from approaching the ring.

"Ma'am, move along. Everybody clear the aisle."

Clearing the aisle was not so easy. Slowly she made

her way up the steps, to the exit. This involved a good deal of jostling and many minutes. But the exit was also an entrance. Many patrons were streaming in.

In her bag she'd found Marika's card—*Dayson Fights, Inc.* She tried to show this to a security guard insisting that she was a friend of D.D. Dunphy and was expected in Dunphy's dressing room but the guard scarcely glanced at it.

"Ma'am, this area off-limits. You need special ID here."

She would learn: the fight had had to be stopped because D.D. Dunphy had been too badly injured to continue. The gash above her eye could not be remedied by mere styptic medication but required stitching.

Though the gash had been caused by a foul that appeared to have been intentionally committed, and though Dunphy had been unexpectedly "winning" at the time, and points would be deducted from Aya, still Aya was the winner of the fight because she'd been ahead on the judges' scorecards. There was no way to prove that the head-butt had been deliberate. Dunphy's corner protested vehemently but the decision of the referee and the judges was final.

From Marika, she would learn this. Embittered Marika explaining to Naomi why the fight had been stopped and the championship lost—"That should have gone to D.D.! Everybody knows."

It seemed then, the interview with D.D. Dunphy scheduled for the next morning had been canceled.

Except, a call came to Naomi on her cell phone. She'd been about to call the airline to see if she could move up her return ticket to New York City but there was a harried-sounding Marika on the phone.

She could see Dunphy for a few minutes if she wished—"To tell our side of the story."

Waiting then for Dunphy to arrive. In another windowless drafty utilitarian "banquet room" in a hotel.

Marika was vehement, on her cell phone. In a corner of the room and ignoring Naomi.

Naomi could overhear only a few sibilant words, curses. Dyed-blond Marika was not so attractive as she'd appeared initially and she was not so friendly to Naomi as Naomi had recalled.

There was fury at *Dayton Fights, Inc.* There was genuine indignation as if the championship belt had been buckled about their boxer's waist and had then been taken away, by force, by another.

Naomi was not listening to this. Naomi was a neutral party, a documentary filmmaker. She was scrolling news on her cell phone seeking *Dunphy, D.D.* Then she realized—of course—she should be seeking *Aya, Siri.*

The news items were terse, merely factual. *Siri Aya, 29, Milwaukee, Wisconsin, retained Midwest Boxing League women's welterweight title in Cleveland fight last night defeating D.D. Dunphy, 24, Dayton, Ohio.*

She was wondering how badly injured Dawn Dunphy had been. The worst of a boxer's injuries (she had to suppose) are not visible to the eye.

Not exterior bleeding but interior bleeding. That would be fatal.

Marika was standing over her. "H'lo? She's on her way. She's coming."

She. Naomi had to think for a moment who *she* was.

Marika added, hotly, "You need to say in the interview that D.D. was cheated of the championship. Make that clear. A head-butt, that's a foul. That's like an assault. Twenty-two stitches! That's why Tyson bit Holyfield's ears, twice—Holyfield head-butted him. Those shits, it was a conspiracy. Cass is consulting a lawyer, if he can sue. Except if you sue, you're fucked. No one will touch you. TV, ESPN, Vegas—forget it. Cass is demanding a rematch. Aya's manager made a deal with the referee. You'd have to be blind to miss that. Aya's a crack-head. They clean her up for training. They feed her steroids. Half her fights, they're fixed. Deals are made. You can't say any of that in the film—(though everybody knows it)—but you can make it clear how Dunphy was cheated of the championship. Twenty-two stitches! Next time, she'll bite the bitch's ears off. She'll fucking destroy her. You better believe, there will be a next time—a rematch. Understand?"

Mutely Naomi nodded *yes*, she understood.

Following the debacle of the fight Naomi had had the night to compose herself. Back at her hotel she'd had two, possibly three, glasses of wine before falling into bed.

A very long night like all nights on the road. She'd slept poorly. She'd felt her head being hit. Whiplash. The strain in the neck. Broken capillaries in the eyes. Poor Madelena, capillaries bursting after chemo. She'd worn dark glasses. No one could see. Naomi helped adjust the beautiful silver-haired wig. It was so lonely to be away. She could only sleep well now when she was in her bed on the thirty-first floor of her grandmother's building in New York City because there she'd decided was *home*.

She wondered if she would tell Madelena about Dawn Dunphy. Of course Madelena knew about Luther Dunphy—she knew of Naomi's fruitless journey to Muskegee Falls. At least, she knew what Naomi had told her.

But Madelena knew nothing about Dawn Dunphy. Naomi was not sure what there was to be known.

She'd decided yes, she would attempt a documentary on women boxers. She would interview D.D. Dunphy at greater length, and she would interview Siri Aya if she could. She foresaw a project whose merit she would have to argue for. Not boxers who happened to be women but women who happened to be boxers.

"Naomi, dear. We have to talk."

Madelena had clasped her hand, at last. Naomi hadn't been able to slip away.

It appeared that she was in remission now, Madelena conceded. The last bloodwork she'd had, her meticulous Chinese-American oncologist at Sloan Kettering had declared her blood "robust."

But—"Remission does not last forever."

And—"Please face it, Naomi: you will outlive me by decades."

Naomi winced at her grandmother's remarks. It was like adults to embarrass you, under the pretext of being kind to you.

That such remarks were made matter-of-factly, as her grandmother might happen to mention that a friend of hers was coming for dinner, or that she had tickets for Naomi and herself for a Philip Glass concert that evening, made them all the more upsetting.

Naomi said, "You could outlive me, Lena."

"Want to bet?"

Madelena laughed, heartily. There is a particular sort of gut-wrenching laughter in an older woman, Naomi thought.

Madelena was saying that she intended to leave a "considerable amount of money" to Naomi in her will. In fact, she had named Naomi her executrix—"It will be an educational experience."

But she preferred to leave some of the money, perhaps most of it, to Naomi while she, Madelena, was still alive. That was so much a better idea. "That way we can both enjoy it."

Madelena had inherited money from her parents, and this money had grown through investments. She'd accumulated some money in the course of her life, teaching, writing, living an essentially frugal life. In speaking of her estate she brightened, visibly. There was a girlishness in her manner, not often evident since the cancer diagnosis.

Naomi wanted to press her hands over her ears. *Please. I don't want to talk about this.*

She'd tried to explain to Madelena that she did not want or need money—really. Her parents had both believed that inherited money was deleterious to the well-being of the young. Gus had always wanted to work.

Jenna had always wanted to work. Neither had been happy in the slightest, without work. Of course, work had to be meaningful. Work had to be, in some way, *creative*.

Madelena laughed at her, not unkindly. "But I want to leave my money to you, Naomi. I have charitable organizations of course. I will establish a scholarship or two. And there is always Karl—the insatiable. But I want to leave money expressly to *you*."

Naomi had been deeply embarrassed.

"Well—I—I could use some funding, I suppose. For the documentary. If—"

Madelena said, "Exactly. You are correct."

Forty minutes after the hour, when Naomi was about to pack up her equipment and leave, Dunphy arrived.

"H'lo."

Her voice was flat, toneless and unapologetic. Her cracked and swollen mouth drooped downward in a sullen mockery of a smile.

"Hi. Thanks for coming."

"Yah."

"My name is Naomi, if you've forgotten . . ."

In careful primer sentences she addressed Dawn Dunphy. It was like speaking to a wild creature: feral cat, bird. The slightest misstep, the creature will flee.

The slightest misspeaking, you are left alone and abashed.

"We can continue the interview—if it's agreeable. Marika said . . ."

"Yah. Fuck Marika."

Naomi wondered if she'd heard correctly. Dunphy's battered face was inscrutable. Her eyelids quivered as if with rage.

(Marika was in a corner of the room, talking excitedly on her cell phone. Smoking.)

Apologetically Naomi murmured, "She said it was all right, for a half hour maybe. I realize this isn't a good time." Pausing then, and wondering if she'd said something tactless. "Well. I have just a few more questions . . ."

Dunphy waited impassively as Naomi fumbled with her camera. Her fingers were unusually clumsy, stiff with cold.

It was cold, drafty in this inhospitable space. And outside it was very cold, Naomi's fingers had been chilled inside her leather gloves making her way to the hotel.

Naomi saw that Dawn Dunphy's nails were blunt, just perceptibly dirt-edged, cut close to the flesh and not filed. Her fingers were larger than Naomi's, her hand large enough (Naomi thought) to swallow up Naomi's hand in her own if she wished.

And if Dawn Dunphy squeezed hard and would not let go, the bones in Naomi's hand would be shattered.

Dunphy laughed mirthlessly. "Like last time. But I guess—I look worse . . ."

"Oh no . . . Well maybe."

Naomi wondered if Dawn Dunphy knew what *déjà vu* meant.

The drafty utilitarian setting in a hotel. Bleak-fluorescent light of a windowless space. Facing each other across a tabletop of some cheap cork material that would crumble into bits if hit the right way.

"I guess the eye-cut is worse. How many stitches?"

Dunphy shrugged. Dunphy wiped her nose with the edge of her hand.

"I'd guess—twenty? Twenty-five?"

"Yah." Dunphy's lips twitched in a bitter smile.

"Does it hurt?"

"What d'you think? Shit!"

"Well. I'm sorry."

"It's OK. They give me what's-it, Ty-len-all."

"You should put ice on the wound. That will help with the swelling."

"Yah I did. Last night."

"Could you sleep?"

"Yah. So tired, you sleep."

The damage to Dunphy's face was marginally worse than the damage had been in Cincinnati. Both her eyes were bruised and bloodshot and there were small cuts across her forehead. The black cross-stitches above her right eye were ferocious-looking, ugly. Almost there was a comic-grotesque look to her. But Naomi wasn't about to smile.

It seemed possible that Dawn Dunphy was wearing slept-in clothes. A stale, not unpleasant odor wafted from her. Dull-gray sweatpants and a pullover with a hood and the front of the pullover stained.

"If it's any consolation people are saying that you won the fight—or would have won it. In that last round—"

Naomi spoke encouragingly. But Dunphy stared brooding at the tabletop.

"If the fight hadn't been stopped, if your opponent hadn't 'head-butted' you . . ."

Naomi heard herself speaking as if knowledgeably and wondered if she sounded as naive to Dawn Dunphy as she did to herself.

For this interview Marika had neglected to provide a bottle of Evian water for Dawn. Awaiting her Naomi had been drinking coffee out of a Styrofoam cup, from a vending machine in the hall, and this cup was prominently on the table. Naomi had a sudden sensation of vertigo, that Dawn Dunphy might take up the Styrofoam cup impulsively and drink from it, and her regret was, the coffee was both very poor and no longer hot.

"Would you like me to get you some coffee? There's a vending machine in the hall . . ."

"Nah. Thanks."

"It's no trouble, Dawn. It's just in the hall."

Dawn. So naturally Naomi uttered the name, Dawn Dunphy seemed scarcely to notice.

When Dawn didn't insist *no*, Naomi went out into the hall. At the vending machine she pushed quarters into the slot. She was feeling disoriented, almost giddy.

She returned with the (hot) Styrofoam cup in both hands. She'd brought tiny packets of sugar, "cream."

Set the cup down in front of Dawn Dunphy who seemed not to see it at first.

"Thanks."

"I was saying—everybody knows you won the fight. You should be the WBL champion . . ."

"MBL."

"I mean—'MBL.' You should be the welterweight champion."

"Yah. OK."

"They will give you a rematch. People say."

"Yah."

"Next time, you will beat 'Siri Aya.' Everybody says so."

Dawn Dunphy shifted her shoulders. She lifted the Styrofoam cup in both hands and peered into it but didn't drink.

"If there's a 'next time.' I guess."

"Everybody is saying . . ."

"Yah. I know."

"You shouldn't be discouraged. Until last night you were undefeated . . ."

What was she saying? She didn't mean this at all.

Of course you should be discouraged. You should quit this terrible sport before . . .

Dunphy was saying that her trainer Ernie had told her to take the week off—"Just rest."

"You're not still working—are you? At Target?"

"Not full-time. Just when they need me."

Dunphy sipped at the hot black coffee into which she'd put neither sugar nor cream. The taste had to be bitter in her mouth.

"You know, we could find a Starbucks. I could buy you some really good coffee."

"'Star-bucks'?"—Dawn Dunphy seemed not to have heard this name.

"Maybe not in this neighborhood. I don't know

where we are, exactly. But—somewhere . . . Is there a downtown in Cleveland?"

"How'd I know?"

"Anyway. There's all kinds of coffee flavors at Starbucks, and it's real coffee not instant like this."

Naomi returned to the interview. Dawn Dunphy had not shown much enthusiasm for Starbucks.

"Marika was saying—your manager Mr. Cassidy will negotiate a 'rematch'?"

Dawn Dunphy shrugged. "Yah. Maybe."

"D'you think this will happen? Any idea when?"

"Prob'ly won't happen."

"But why not?"

"They know I will beat Aya next time. And it won't be as much money with me as with someone else."

"But—don't title-holders have to fight contenders? Won't Aya's manager have to negotiate with you?"

"*Have to?*—no."

"There are other 'champions,' I think? In 'WBL'—"

"'WBA.'"

"—maybe they would negotiate? With your record . . ."

"They know I'm too good. I can win, and I can hurt people. It's too risky for them." Dunphy paused, frowning. "If they make me quit I could go to nursing school like my mother did."

"Oh—why'd they make you quit?"

"If I lose the next fight. If I can't keep going."

"But—until last night you were undefeated . . . Everyone says you are a wonderful boxer, Dawn."

You are crude, and you are clumsy. But you can take a punch.

"Yah. Bullshit."

"Last time you told me, you were fighting for Jesus. Is that still the way it is?"

"Jesus has had enough of me, maybe. Sometimes I think so."

"But—why?"

Dawn Dunphy's eyes moved restlessly about as if seeking the ghost-figure of Jesus in this very room.

"Don't know. Just a feeling."

"Would your mother like you to quit boxing?"

"Yah. I guess."

"She worries about you getting hurt . . ."

"Nah. She doesn't. I don't think so."

"Did they take you to a hospital last night?"

"Some kind of clinic. They put in the stitches."

"Did they take X-rays?"

"I don't know."

"But—how do you feel? Does your head hurt?"

"After a fight you hurt all over. No matter if you win or lose."

"Dawn, I don't like to tell you what to do, but—you should see a neurologist. You might have been concussed last night. When you fell to your hands and knees . . ."

"When was that? I didn't *fall*."

Dawn Dunphy spoke contemptuously. Naomi realized with a thrill of horror that she'd forgotten.

". . . wasn't never *out*, and didn't *fall*. Ernie would've told me if I had."

"I think you should have a brain scan. In case of a hairline fracture. You should insist."

Naomi was speaking rapidly, in a lowered voice. In a corner of the room Marika continued to talk on her cell phone, aggrieved and angry, oblivious to the interview.

"There's a doctor in Dayton. They take me to him."

"Oh but—what kind of doctor? Is he—actually—a *doctor*?"

"There's some diploma-like, on his wall. He gives me medications."

"What kind of medications?"

"I don't know."

"D'you think—steroids?"

"Don't know."

"Maybe you could show me the medications, sometime. I could see what they are."

"How'd you know?"

"I'm a doctor's daughter. What I don't know, I can look up."

Dawn Dunphy considered this. For a moment she seemed about to speak, but did not.

Naomi said, "You should see a more reliable doctor. I could take you."

"How'd you do that?"—Dawn smiled, disbelieving.

"How? Why not?"

"Who's gonna pay for that?"

"I will."

"You will!"

Dawn laughed, almost jeering.

Naomi persisted: "I can. I could pay for it."

"Why'd you do that?"

"Because I would want to."

"Why'd you want to?"

"Because—you need better medical treatment than you're getting. That's my feeling."

"But why'd you do that for *me*? You don't know me."

"I would do it for anyone who needed it . . ."

This was untrue. Naomi spoke quickly, feeling blood rush into her face.

"Your father? Your father is a doctor? Is that who I would see?"

"No. Not my father."

"This doctor they take me to, he's OK. I'll be OK. Even if you win a fight you hurt like hell for a long time."

"Do you pass blood?"

"Nah."

So quickly Dawn answered, with an embarrassed frown, Naomi knew that there must be blood in her urine.

"That's a kidney injury. That needs attention."

"Nah it's OK. Never mind."

"Look, please. I will pay for it. Are you driving back to Dayton today? I can check, and see who is available in Dayton. There's a network of doctors, they know one another and recommend one another and I can—I can check for you. I could call, and make an appointment. I could do that, in Dayton. I wouldn't even need to be there—though I could be there. If that was necessary."

"I'm OK. I *said*."

Dawn was becoming irritable. Naomi knew she must not press the issue. But she was feeling excited. Reckless.

The night before, she'd written a message to Dawn Dunphy. She'd been unable to sleep in the unfamiliar hotel bed, and writing a message to Dawn Dunphy had been soothing to her. She had not believed that she would actually give this message to Dawn Dunphy—of course.

But she'd brought it with her this morning, neatly folded inside her bag.

Stubbornly Naomi said, "I'll look into it, Dawn. I'll find a doctor. And I'll take you."

"Jesus! Why'd you do *that*."

"Why? Because I can. Excuse me."

Naomi stood. Her hands were trembling badly. She had the message, the folded sheet of hotel stationery, to present to Dawn Dunphy.

She said, "This is for you. I'll be right back. I need to use a restroom."

She went away, pushing through double doors into the corridor. Her ears were ringing. She felt as if both sides of her head had been smacked with boxing gloves.

In a restroom in a panel of mirrors was a pale excited face, she did not recognize at first.

Dear Dawn—

   I did not tell you the truth the first time I met you.

   The truth of why I have come to see you.

   I am the daughter of Gus Voorhees. I am Naomi Voorhees.

I am sorry to deceive you. I did not know how otherwise it would be possible to meet you.

I will return in 10 minutes. I hope you will still be here.

If you are not, I will understand.

We are the only two who will understand. But maybe that is not possible.

If you would like to see me some other time but not right now, I will leave my phone number here. My email address.

If you do not wish to see me again I will understand & I will not make any attempt to see you.

It is true, I am a documentary filmmaker. I am just beginning this project of women boxers. I would like you to be a part of it but I don't know how it will go.

My life has been like that—I have started projects, and I have started courses in college, and not finished them.

I used to think it was because my father was killed when I was a young girl. But now I am wondering if that is just an excuse for my life that is broken in pieces and some of these pieces lost.

Or maybe that is just everyone's life. & I am no one special.

I hope that I will see you again. But if not, I understand.

Sincerely,
Naomi Voorhees

Her head was aching as if she'd been punched repeatedly. Her mouth kept twisting into a foolish smile.

She could run outside, she didn't have to return to the banquet room.

Except she'd left her expensive camera there. She had no choice, she would have to return.

But she could snatch up the camera, whether Dawn Dunphy was still there, or had left.

Her camera she would grip in her fingers. Anxiously she would check the lens. She would check what the camera had just recorded. Someday, it might be stitched into a documentary film. It might be screened in a darkened room. Strangers would stare at the battered faces of women boxers. Strangers would strain to hear their halting voices.

Strangers might cry—*You have told my story! You have touched my heart. Thank you.*

Boldly Naomi pushed through the double door, and there was Dawn Dunphy on her feet, in her gray hoodie and sweatpants looking shocked, irresolute.

The expression in Dunphy's face! Beneath the bruises, cuts and swellings you could see astonishment and wonder breaking.

Naomi would wonder: had Dawn Dunphy been about to slam out of the room or had she been about to come look for Naomi in the corridor?

"Hi . . ."

Naomi's heart was pounding tremendously. She could not believe that Dawn Dunphy was still standing before her and had not walked away without a backward glance.

So quickly it happened. The decision had been made for them.

In the consolation of grief they held each other tight and wanted never to let go.